THE YEAR'S BEST SCIENCE FICTION & FANTASY NOVELLAS

2016 Edition

THE YEAR'S BEST SCIENCE FICTION & FANTASY NOVELLAS

2016 Edition

EDITED BY PAULA GURAN

○

PRIME BOOKS

THE YEAR'S BEST SCIENCE FICTION & FANTASY NOVELLAS: 2016

Cover design by Sherin Nicole.
Cover art by Julie Dillon.

Prime Books
Germantown, MD, USA
www.prime-books.com

For more information, contact Prime Books:
prime@prime-books.com

Print ISBN: 978-1-60701-472-0
Ebook ISBN: 978-1-60701-480-5

CONTENTS

INTRODUCTION

Paula Guran

The novella is not destined to be stuck inelegantly between a short story and a novel, with none of the strengths of either. Indeed, the opposite is true: an expert novella combines the best of a short story with the best of a novel, the dynamic thighs of a sprinter with the long-distance lungs of a mountaineer.
—William Giraldi, "The Novella's Long Life"

Here we are at the beginning of the second volume of *The Year's Best Science Fiction and Fantasy Novellas*. In the introduction to the first volume we tackled the definition of "novella" beyond "a work of fiction longer than a short story but shorter than a novel." Ultimately, for that edition and this, the definition boiled down to "fiction between 17,500 words and 40,000 words." And we've stuck with that this year. The shortest novella herein is about 19,000 words in length; the longest is a smidgen over 34,000.

Not long after our 2015 edition was released, Tor.com began publishing what they called "stories at their right length"—mostly novellas. When the imprint was first announced earlier last year, associate publisher Irene Gallo stated, "The novella is a foundational format for the speculative fiction genre. Novellas provide the perfect blend between the stylistic concision of the short story and the engagement of the novel." She noted that although such longer stories/short novels were common during an earlier era, the market for such works contracted, without necessarily reducing demand for them.

(Gallo is probably correct, but as far as I know no one has been keeping count. The print periodical market has certainly dwindled, but online, digital, limited edition, and anthology publishing provide new novella markets.)

Carl Engle-Laird, a Tor.com editor, said at the time, that " . . . novellas aren't just the future of genre, they're also our past. Science fiction and fantasy were born in penny dreadfuls, came of age in magazines, and novellas have been essential to their development, from *The War of the Worlds* [H. G. Wells] to *The Shadow Over Innsmouth* [H. P. Lovecraft] to *Empire Star* [Samuel R. Delany]."

[Just how foundational, essential, and/or influential have novellas been? Glad you asked! An appendix of such from 1883-1980, an admittedly arbitrary time period, is included on page 527.]

Tor.com is not the only publishing entity to be touting a bright future—assisted in one way or another by digital publication—for the novella. Much of the optimism is found in genre publishing, but there have been ventures to make the form commercially viable elsewhere as well.

This cheery outlook is based, at least in part, on the assumption that modern readers have less time to read, and what time they do have is temporally fragmented. (Thanks for that phrase, Carl.) Novellas are supposed to be particularly attractive to those who read on mobile devices.

The "comeback" of the novella has been being proclaimed by literati since at least 2010. Not coincidentally, that is about the same time ebooks became firmly established as a reading and publishing reality rather than a passing phenomenon.

However, short novels are evidently not appealing on all screens. Despite the fact that the pioneering *Omni Online* (1995-1998) and *Sci Fiction* (2000-2005)—both edited by Ellen Datlow—published excellent novellas, of the more current established online magazines, only *Subterranean* regularly published novellas, and it is now (sadly) dead. (*Beneath Ceaseless Skies* occasionally publishes novellas as two-part serials.)

Some web-based periodicals will consider up to 10,000 words—*Clarkesworld* upped its guidelines to 16,000 in June 2015—but, overall, they tend to prefer stories of 5,000 or less.

Convenient length is not the only reason the novella supposedly appeals. In a *New Yorker* essay a few years back, Ian McEwan pointed out another attraction for the modern reader:

> To sit with a novella is analogous to watching a play or a longish movie. In fact, there's a strong resemblance between the screenplay (twenty odd thousand words) and the novella, both operating within the same useful constraints of economy—space for a subplot (two at a stretch), characters to be established with quick strokes but allowed enough room to live and breathe, and the central idea, even if it is just below the horizon, always exerting its gravitational pull. The analogy with film or theatre is a reminder that there is an element of performance in the novella. We are more strongly aware of the curtain and the stage,

of the author as illusionist. The smoke and mirrors, rabbits and hats are more self-consciously applied than in the full-length novel.

Although McEwan's analogy includes live theatre—an experience that is probably not as influential—that twenty-first century concepts of story and entertainment are shaped by film can go without saying.

So, does this add up to a renaissance of the form that can be financially successful enough to support itself?

One can view the world as divided into those who read, those who don't, and those who will occasionally read a cultural phenomena. Within the two groups of readers, at least as far as we are concerned, you are still dealing with a subset of sf/f readers who have so many new titles available that no one can keep up with them all. They also have a wealth of classics—more than ever, thanks to ebooks and print-on-demand—at their digital or paper page-turning fingertips. Does length really matter to them?

What may matter is quality and availability. Tor.com's classy entrance to the field provides both. A program like Tor.com's—and digital books as a whole—may truly make a difference.

The use of the novella as a form of promotion—again, aided by digital publication—may also make a difference. Novellas set in the same universe as a series or offering a sample of the author's work in general allow easy and relatively inexpensive access to readers who would like to dip a toe into the fiction before committing to a full plunge.

And, of course, novellas can also be used to expand on an established fictional universe or fill in details for loyal fans who already can't get enough of it.

As thick as this tome is, it cannot contain *all* of "the best" novellas published in 2015. Realize, too, that although novellas may not be all that "commercially viable," they often have enough viability for authors and/or publishers keep exclusive digital and/or print rights. This means they are not available for republication in an anthology like this.

One problem with arbitrary word counts is that it limits what one otherwise might term "novella." I don't even try to keep count of stories in the ten thousand-to-seventeen thousand four hundred and ninety-nine word range that might be considered in the category.

From 2015, two that exceeded (not by much) 40,000 words must be noted: *The Sorcerer of the Wildeeps*, Kai Ashante Wilson's inimitable take on sword and sorcery (that may actually be sf), and Elizabeth Hand's *Wylding Hall*, a haunting evocation of a certain era and vanished dreams. Neither is to be missed no matter what you want to call them.

Here are some other recommended works from last year:

• *The Harlequin* by Nina Allan (Sandstone Press): Physically unharmed but mentally altered by what he has witnessed in WWI, a young man hopes to re-establish a normal life—but his world only grows darker. Cross-genre, metafictional, and brilliant.

• *Invisible Filth* by Nathan Ballingrud (This Is Horror): Unsettling photos and video on a lost cell phone lead to unimaginable horrors. Strong characterization, great atmosphere, and not for the faint of heart.

• *X's for Eyes* by Laird Barron (JournalStone): You can seldom go wrong reading anything by Barron. Ross Lockhart's description of this novella—a "cosmic horror Hardy Boys adventure"—is apt.

• *Penric's Demon* by Lois McMaster Bujold (Spectrum Literary Agency): A pleasant visit to Bujold's beloved Chalion/World of the Five Gods.

• *The Two Paupers* by C. S. E. Cooney (Fairchild Books): The second installment of her Dark Breakers series and another look at her fascinating world of Seafall. Reprinted in our sister anthology *The Year's Best Science Fiction & Fantasy: 2016*.

• *The Vital Abyss* by James S.A. Corey (Hachette): Another entertaining novella set in the Expanse universe. May not stand alone quite as well as previous novella *The Churn* that we included in last year's edition, but still recommended.

• *Witches of Lychford* by Paul Cornell (Tor.com): Modern civilization threatens the magical borders of Lychford; borders which, if breached, will become gateways to Very Bad Things. Charming, creepy, and masterfully crafted.

• "The Four Thousand, the Eight Hundred" by Greg Egan (*Asimov's*): Solid characterization in hard sf mixed with the sociopolitical.

• "The New Mother" by Eugene Fischer (*Asimov's*): How would society react if women suddenly began reproducing asexually?

• "In Negative Space" by Brian Hodge (*Dark City: A Novella Collection*, Necro Publications): Post-apocalypse mystery; a plot that flows like a river—a very dark river with many twists, turns, and churning rapids.

• *The Box Jumper* by Lisa Mannetti (Smart Rhino): Layers of intrigue, madness, mystery, and Houdini. What more could you want?

• *Slow Bullets* by Alastair Reynolds (Tachyon). Superlative space opera and a compelling read. Would have been here if we'd been able to reprint.

• *Waters of Versailles* by Kelly Robson (Tor.com): Delightful story of court intrigue set in Louis XV's Versailles involving water, toilets, and magic.

• *All That Outer Space Allows* by Ian Sales (Whippleshield Books): The wife of an astronaut is a science fiction author in an alternate reality in which sf is a "women's genre" offering escape for the far-from-liberated housewives of the 1960s. The last of the alternate-history Apollo Quartet.

• *Perfect State* by Brandon Sanderson (Dragonsteel Entertainment): Solid science fiction with a splash of fantasy; little more can be said without being a spoiler.

• "Ripper" by Angela Slatter (*Horrorology,* ed. Stephen Jones): Set in the Whitechapel of Jack the Ripper, the novella features a most unusual constable and a touch of the supernatural. Included in *The Year's Best Dark Fantassy & Horror: 2016.*

• *Of Sorrow and Such* by Angela Slatter (Tor.com): A witchy journey into Slatter's Bitterwood/Sourdough world that can be enjoyed even if you have no idea of what the Bitterwood/Sourdough world is.

• *Speak Easy* by Catherynne M. Valente (Subterranean Press): Ostensibly a re-telling of "The Twelve Dancing Princesses" set in an alternate Jazz Age, it is really much, much more.

New Golden Age of the Novella or not, these works—and the nine included here—are proof of high quality sf and fantasy longer than a short story but not as long as a novel to enjoy!

Paula Guran
20 April 2016
[One hundred seventy-five years ago on this date, Edgar Allan Poe's
"The Murders in the Rue Morgue" (about 14,000 words in length)
first appeared in *Graham's Lady's and Gentleman's Magazine.*]

BINTI

=◆=

Nnedi Okorafor

I powered up the transporter and said a silent prayer. I had no idea what I was going to do if it didn't work. My transporter was cheap, so even a droplet of moisture, or more likely, a grain of sand, would cause it to short. It was faulty and most of the time I had to restart it over and over before it worked. *Please not now, please not now, I thought.*

The transporter shivered in the sand and I held my breath. Tiny, flat, and black as a prayer stone, it buzzed softly and then slowly rose from the sand. Finally, it produced the baggage-lifting force. I grinned. Now I could make it to the shuttle. I swiped *otjize* from my forehead with my index finger and knelt down. Then I touched the finger to the sand, grounding the sweet smelling red clay into it. "Thank you," I whispered. It was a half-mile walk along the dark desert road. With the transporter working, I would make it there on time.

Straightening up, I paused and shut my eyes. Now the weight of my entire life was pressing on my shoulders. I was defying the most traditional part of myself for the first time in my entire life. I was leaving in the dead of night and they had no clue. My nine siblings, all older than me except for my younger sister and brother, would never see this coming. My parents would never imagine I'd do such a thing in a million years. By the time they all realized what I'd done and where I was going, I'd have left the planet. In my absence, my parents would growl to each other that I was to never set foot in their home again. My four aunties and two uncles who lived down the road would shout and gossip among themselves about how I'd scandalized our entire bloodline. I was going to be a pariah.

"Go," I softly whispered to the transporter, stamping my foot. The thin metal rings I wore around each ankle jingled noisily, but I stamped my foot again. Once on, the transporter worked best when I didn't touch it. "Go," I said again, sweat forming on my brow. When nothing moved, I chanced giving the two large suitcases sitting atop the force field a shove.

They moved smoothly and I breathed another sigh of relief. At least some luck was on my side.

Fifteen minutes later I purchased a ticket and boarded the shuttle. The sun was barely beginning to peak over the horizon. As I moved past seated passengers far too aware of the bushy ends of my plaited hair softly slapping people in the face, I cast my eyes to the floor. Our hair is thick and mine has always been *very* thick. My old auntie liked to call it "ododo" because it grew wild and dense like ododo grass. Just before leaving, I'd rolled my plaited hair with fresh sweet-smelling *otjize* I'd made specifically for this trip. Who knew what I looked like to these people who didn't know my people so well.

A woman leaned away from me as I passed, her face pinched as if she smelled something foul. "Sorry," I whispered, watching my feet and trying to ignore the stares of almost everyone in the shuttle. Still, I couldn't help glancing around. Two girls who might have been a few years older than me, covered their mouths with hands so pale that they looked untouched by the sun. Everyone looked as if the sun was his or her enemy. I was the only Himba on the shuttle. I quickly found and moved to a seat.

The shuttle was one of the new sleek models that looked like the bullets my teachers used to calculate ballistic coefficients during my A-levels when I was growing up. These ones glided fast over land using a combination of air current, magnetic fields, and exponential energy—an easy craft to build if you had the equipment and the time. It was also a nice vehicle for hot desert terrain where the roads leading out of town were terribly maintained. My people didn't like to leave the homeland. I sat in the back so I could look out the large window.

I could see the lights from my father's astrolabe shop and the sand storm analyzer my brother had built at the top of the Root—that's what we called my parents' big, big house. Six generations of my family had lived there. It was the oldest house in my village, maybe the oldest in the city. It was made of stone and concrete, cool in the night, hot in the day. And it was patched with solar planes and covered with bioluminescent plants that liked to stop glowing just before sunrise. My bedroom was at the top of the house. The shuttle began to move and I stared until I couldn't see it anymore. "What am I doing?" I whispered.

An hour and a half later, the shuttle arrived at the launch port. I was the last off, which was good because the sight of the launch port overwhelmed me so much that all I could do for several moments was stand there. I was wearing a long red skirt, one that was silky like water, a light orange wind-top that was stiff and durable, thin leather sandals, and my anklets.

No one around me wore such an outfit. All I saw were light flowing garments and veils; not one woman's ankles were exposed, let alone jingling with steel anklets. I breathed through my mouth and felt my face grow hot.

"Stupid stupid stupid," I whispered. We Himba don't travel. We stay put. Our ancestral land is life; move away from it and you diminish. We even cover our bodies with it. *Otjize* is red land. Here in the launch port, most were Khoush and a few other non-Himba. Here, I was an outsider; I was outside. "What was I thinking?" I whispered.

I was sixteen years old and had never been beyond my city, let alone near a launch station. I was by myself and I had just left my family. My prospects of marriage had been one hundred percent and now they would be zero. No man wanted a woman who'd run away. However, beyond my prospects of normal life being ruined, I had scored so high on the planetary exams in mathematics that the Oomza University had not only admitted me, but promised to pay for whatever I needed in order to attend. No matter what choice I made, I was never going to have a normal life, really.

I looked around and immediately knew what to do next. I walked to the help desk.

The travel security officer scanned my astrolabe, a full *deep* scan. Dizzy with shock, I shut my eyes and breathed through my mouth to steady myself. Just to leave the planet, I had to give them access to my *entire* life—me, my family, and all forecasts of my future. I stood there, frozen, hearing my mother's voice in my head. "There is a reason why our people do not go to that university. Oomza Uni wants you for its own gain, Binti. You go to that school and you become its slave." I couldn't help but contemplate the possible truth in her words. I hadn't even gotten there yet and already I'd given them my life. I wanted to ask the officer if he did this for everyone, but I was afraid now that he'd done it. They could do anything to me, at this point. Best not to make trouble.

When the officer handed me my astrolabe, I resisted the urge to snatch it back. He was an old Khoush man, so old that he was privileged to wear the blackest turban and face veil. His shaky hands were so gnarled and arthritic that he nearly dropped my astrolabe. He was bent like a dying palm tree and when he'd said, "You have never traveled; I must do a full scan. Remain where you are," his voice was drier than the red desert outside my city. But he read my astrolabe as fast as my father, which both impressed and scared me. He'd coaxed it open by whispering a few choice equations and his suddenly steady hands worked the dials as if they were his own.

When he finished, he looked up at me with his light green piercing eyes that seemed to see deeper into me than his scan of my astrolabe. There were people behind me and I was aware of their whispers, soft laughter and a young child murmuring. It was cool in the terminal, but I felt the heat of social pressure. My temples ached and my feet tingled.

"Congratulations," he said to me in his parched voice, holding out my astrolabe.

I frowned at him, confused. "What for?"

"You are the pride of your people, child," he said, looking me in the eye. Then he smiled broadly and patted my shoulder. He'd just seen my entire life. He knew of my admission into Oomza Uni.

"Oh." My eyes pricked with tears. "Thank you, sir," I said, hoarsely, as I took my astrolabe.

I quickly made my way through the many people in the terminal, too aware of their closeness. I considered finding a lavatory and applying more *otjize* to my skin and tying my hair back, but instead I kept moving. Most of the people in the busy terminal wore the black and white garments of the Khoush people—the women draped in white with multicolored belts and veils and the men draped in black like powerful spirits. I had seen plenty of them on television and here and there in my city, but never had I been in a sea of Khoush. This was the rest of the world and I was finally in it.

As I stood in line for boarding security, I felt a tug at my hair. I turned around and met the eyes of a group of Khoush women. They were all staring at me; everyone behind me was staring at me.

The woman who'd tugged my plait was looking at her fingers and rubbing them together, frowning. Her fingertips were orange red with my *otjize*. She sniffed them. "It smells like jasmine flowers," she said to the woman on her left, surprised.

"Not shit?" one woman said. "I hear it smells like shit because it is shit."

"No, definitely jasmine flowers. It is thick like shit, though."

"Is her hair even real?" another woman asked the woman rubbing her fingers.

"I don't know."

"These 'dirt bathers' are a filthy people," the first woman muttered.

I just turned back around, my shoulders hunched. My mother had counseled me to be quiet around Khoush. My father told me that when he was around Khoush merchants when they came to our city to buy astrolabes, he tried to make himself as small as possible. "It is either that or I will start a war with them that I will finish," he said. My father didn't believe in war. He said war was evil, but if it came he would revel in it like sand in a storm. Then he'd say a little prayer to the Seven to keep war away and then another prayer to seal his words.

I pulled my plaits to my front and touched the *edan* in my pocket. I let my mind focus on it, its strange language, its strange metal, its strange feel. I'd found the *edan* eight years ago while exploring the sands of the hinter deserts one late afternoon. *"Edan"* was a general name for a device too old for anyone to know it functions, so old that they were now just art.

My *edan* was more interesting than any book, than any new astrolabe design I made in my father's shop that these women would probably kill each other to buy. And it was mine, in my pocket, and these nosy women behind me could never know. Those women talked about me, the men probably did too. But none of them knew what I had, where I was going, who I was. Let them gossip and judge. Thankfully, they knew not to touch my hair again. I don't like war either.

The security guard scowled when I stepped forward. Behind him I could see three entrances, the one in the middle led into the ship called "Third Fish," the ship I was to take to Oomza Uni. Its open door was large and round leading into a long corridor illuminated by soft blue lights.

"Step forward," the guard said. He wore the uniform of all launch site lower-level personnel—a long white gown and grey gloves. I'd only seen this uniform in streaming stories and books and I wanted to giggle, despite myself. He looked ridiculous. I stepped forward and everything went red and warm.

When the body scan beeped its completion, the security guard reached right into my left pocket and brought out my *edan*. He held it to his face with a deep scowl.

I waited. What would he know?

He was inspecting its stellated cube shape, pressing its many points with his finger and eyeing the strange symbols on it that I had spent two years unsuccessfully trying to decode. He held it to his face to better see the intricate loops and swirls of blue and black and white, so much like the lace placed on the heads of young girls when they turn eleven and go through their eleventh-year rite.

"What is this made of?" the guard asked, holding it over a scanner. "It's not reading as any known metal."

I shrugged, too aware of the people behind me waiting in line and staring at me. To them, I was probably like one of the people who lived in caves deep in the hinter desert who were so blackened by the sun that they looked like walking shadows. I'm not proud to say that I have some Desert People blood in me from my father's side of the family, that's where my dark skin and extra-bushy hair come from.

"Your identity reads that you're a harmonizer, a masterful one who builds some of the finest astrolabes," he said. "But this object isn't an astrolabe. Did you build it? And how can you build something and not know what it's made of?"

"I didn't build it," I said.

"Who did?"

"It's . . . it's just an old, old thing," I said. "It has no math or current. It's just an inert computative apparatus that I carry for good luck." This was partially a lie. But even I didn't know exactly what it could and couldn't do.

The man looked as if he would ask more, but didn't. Inside, I smiled. Government security guards were only educated up to age ten, yet because of their jobs, they were used to ordering people around. And they especially looked down on people like me. Apparently, they were the same everywhere, no matter the tribe. He had no idea what a "computative apparatus" was, but he didn't want to show that I, a poor Himba girl, was more educated than he. Not in front of all these people. So he quickly moved me along and, finally, there I stood at my ship's entrance.

I couldn't see the end of the corridor, so I stared at the entrance. The ship was a magnificent piece of living technology. *Third Fish* was a Miri 12, a type of ship closely related to a shrimp. Miri 12s were stable calm creatures with natural exoskeletons that could withstand the harshness of space. They were genetically enhanced to grow three breathing chambers within their bodies.

Scientists planted rapidly growing plants within these three enormous rooms that not only produced oxygen from the CO_2 directed in from other parts of the ship, but also absorbed benzene, formaldehyde, and trichloroethylene. This was some of the most amazing technology I'd ever read about. Once settled on the ship, I was determined to convince someone to let me see one of these amazing rooms. But at the moment, I wasn't thinking about the technology of the ship. I was on the threshold now, between home and my future.

I stepped into the blue corridor.

So that is how it all began. I found my room. I found my group—twelve other new students, all human, all Khoush, between the ages of fifteen and eighteen. An hour later, my group and I located a ship technician to show us one of the breathing chambers. I wasn't the only new Oomza Uni student who desperately wanted to see the technology at work. The air in there smelled like the jungles and forests I'd only read about. The plants had tough leaves and they grew everywhere, from ceiling to walls to floor. They were wild with flowers, and I could have stood there breathing that soft, fragrant air for days.

We met our group leader hours later. He was a stern old Khoush man who looked the twelve of us over and paused at me and asked, "Why are you covered in red greasy clay and weighed down by all those steel anklets?"

When I told him that I was Himba, he coolly said, "I know, but that doesn't answer my question." I explained to him the tradition of my people's skin care and how we wore the steel rings on our ankles to protect us from snakebites. He looked at me for a long time, the others in my group staring at me like a rare bizarre butterfly.

"Wear your *otjize*," he said. "But not so much that you stain up this ship. And if those anklets are to protect you from snakebites, you no longer need them."

I took my anklets off, except for two on each ankle. Enough to jingle with each step.

I was the only Himba on the ship, out of nearly five hundred passengers. My tribe is obsessed with innovation and technology, but it is small, private, and, as I said, we don't like to leave Earth. We prefer to explore the universe by traveling inward, as opposed to outward. No Himba has ever gone to Oomza Uni. So me being the only one on the ship was not that surprising. However, just because something isn't surprising doesn't mean it's easy to deal with.

The ship was packed with outward-looking people who loved mathematics, experimenting, learning, reading, inventing, studying, obsessing, revealing. The people on the ship weren't Himba, but I soon understood that they were still my people. I stood out as a Himba, but the commonalities shined brighter. I made friends quickly. And by the second week in space, they were *good* friends.

Olo, Remi, Kwuga, Nur, Anajama, Rhoden. Only Olo and Remi were in my group. Everyone else I met in the dining area or the learning room where various lectures were held by professors onboard the ship. They were all girls who grew up in sprawling houses, who'd never walked through the desert, who'd never stepped on a snake in the dry grass. They were girls who could not stand the rays of Earth's sun unless it was shining through a tinted window.

Yet they were girls who knew what I meant when I spoke of "treeing." We sat in my room (because, having so few travel items, mine was the emptiest) and challenged each other to look out at the stars and imagine the most complex equation and then split it in half and then in half again and again. When you do math fractals long enough, you kick yourself into treeing just enough to get lost in the shallows of the mathematical sea. None of us would have made it into the university if we couldn't tree, but it's not easy. We were the best and we pushed each other to get closer to "God."

Then there was Heru. I had never spoken to him, but we smiled across the table at each other during mealtimes. He was from one of those cities so far from mine that they seemed like a figment of my imagination, where there was snow and where men rode those enormous grey birds and the women could speak with those birds without moving their mouths.

Once Heru was standing behind me in the dinner line with one of his friends. I felt someone pick up one of my plaits and I whirled around, ready to be angry. I met his eyes and he'd quickly let go of my hair, smiled, and raised his hands up defensively. "I couldn't help it," he said, his fingertips reddish with my *otjize*.

"You can't control yourself?" I snapped.

"You have exactly twenty-one," he said. "And they're braided in tessellating triangles. Is it some sort of code?"

I wanted to tell him that there *was* a code, that the pattern spoke my family's bloodline, culture, and history. That my father had designed the code and my mother and aunties had shown me how to braid it into my hair. However, looking at Heru made my heart beat too fast and my words escaped me, so I merely shrugged and turned back around to pick up a bowl of soup. Heru was tall and had the whitest teeth I'd ever seen. And he was very good in mathematics; few would have noticed the code in my hair.

But I never got the chance to tell him that my hair was braided into the history of my people. Because what happened, happened. It occurred on the eighteenth day of the journey. The five days before we arrived on the planet Oomza Uni, the most powerful and innovative sprawling university in the Milky Way. I was the happiest I'd ever been in my life and I was farther from my beloved family than I'd ever been in my life.

I was at the table savoring a mouthful of a gelatinous milk-based dessert with slivers of coconut in it; I was gazing at Heru, who wasn't gazing at me. I'd put my fork down and had my *edan* in my hands. I fiddled with it as I watched Heru talk to the boy beside him. The delicious creamy dessert was melting coolly on my tongue. Beside me, Olo and Remi were singing a traditional song from their city because they missed home, a song that had to be sung with a wavery voice like a water spirit.

Then someone screamed and Heru's chest burst open, spattering me with his warm blood. There was a Meduse right behind him.

In my culture, it is blasphemy to pray to inanimate objects, but I did anyway. I prayed to a metal even my father had been unable to identify. I held it to my chest, shut my eyes, and prayed to it, *I am in your protection. Please protect me. I am in your protection. Please protect me.*

My body was shuddering so hard that I could imagine what it would be like to die from terror. I held my breath, the stench of *them* still in my nasal cavity and mouth. Heru's blood was on my face, wet and thick. I prayed to the mystery metal my *edan* was made of because that had to be the only thing keeping me alive at this moment.

Breathing hard from my mouth, I peeked from one eye. I shut it again. The Meduse were hovering less than a foot away. One had launched itself at me but then froze an inch from my flesh; it had reached a tentacle toward my *edan* and then suddenly collapsed, the tentacle turning ash grey as it quickly dried up like a dead leaf.

I could hear the others, their near-substantial bodies softly rustling as their transparent domes filled with and released the gas they breathed back in. They were tall as grown men, their domes' flesh thin as fine silk, their long tentacles spilling down to the floor like a series of gigantic ghostly noodles. I grasped my *edan* closer to me. *I am in your protection. Please protect me.*

Everyone in the dining hall was dead. At least one hundred people. I had a feeling everyone on the ship was dead. The Meduse had burst into the hall and begun committing *moojh-ha ki-bira* before anyone knew what was happening. That's what the Khoush call it. We'd all been taught this Meduse form of killing in history class. The Khoush built the lessons into history, literature, and culture classes across several regions. Even my people were required to learn about it, despite the fact that it wasn't our fight. The Khoush expected everyone to remember their greatest enemy and injustice. They even worked Meduse anatomy and rudimentary technology into mathematics and science classes.

Moojh-ha ki-bira means the "great wave." The Meduse move like water when at war. There is no water on their planet, but they worship water as a god. Their ancestors came from water long ago. The Khoush were settled on the most water-soaked lands on Earth, a planet made mostly of water, and they saw the Meduse as inferior.

The trouble between the Meduse and the Khoush was an old fight and an older disagreement. Somehow, they had agreed to a treaty not to attack each other's ships. Yet here the Meduse were performing *moojh-ha ki-bira*.

I'd been talking to my friends.

My *friends.*

Olo, Remi, Kwuga, Nur, Anajama, Rhoden, and Dullaz. We had spent so many late nights laughing over our fears about how difficult and strange Oomza Uni would be. All of us had twisted ideas that were probably wrong . . . maybe partially right. We had so much in common. I wasn't thinking about home or how I'd *had* to leave it or the horrible messages my family had sent to my astrolabe hours after I'd left. I was looking ahead toward my future and I was laughing because it was so bright.

Then the Meduse came through the dining hall entrance. I was looking right at Heru when the red circle appeared in the upper left side of his shirt.

The thing that tore through was like a sword, but thin as paper . . . and flexible and easily stained by blood. The tip wiggled and grasped like a finger. I saw it pinch and hook to the flesh near his collarbone.

Moojh-ha ki-bira.

I don't remember what I did or said. My eyes were open, taking it all in, but the rest of my brain was screaming. For no reason at all, I focused on the number five. Over and over, I thought, *5–5–5–5–5–5–5–5–5*, as Heru's eyes went from shocked to blank. His open mouth let out a gagging sound, then a spurt of thick red blood, then blood frothed with saliva as he began to fall forward. His head hit the table with a flat thud. His neck was turned and I could see that his eyes were open. His left hand flexed spasmodically, until it stopped. But his eyes were still open. He wasn't blinking.

Heru was dead. Olo, Remi, Kwuga, Nur, Anajama, Rhoden, and Dullaz were dead. Everyone was dead.The dinner hall stank of blood.

None of my family had wanted me to go to Oomza Uni. Even my best friend Dele hadn't wanted me to go. Still, not long after I received the news of my university acceptance and my whole family was saying no, Dele had joked that if I went, I at least wouldn't have to worry about the Meduse, because I would be the only Himba on the ship.

"So even if they kill everyone else, they won't even *see* you!" he'd said. Then he'd laughed and laughed, sure that I wasn't going anyway.

Now his words came back to me. Dele. I'd pushed thoughts of him deep into my mind and read none of his messages. Ignoring the people I loved was the only way I could keep going. When I'd received the scholarship to study at Oomza Uni, I'd gone into the desert and cried for hours. With joy.

I'd wanted this since I knew what a university was. Oomza Uni was the top of the top, its population was only 5 percent human. Imagine what it meant to go there as one of that 5 percent; to be with others obsessed with knowledge, creation, and discovery. Then I went home and told my family and wept with shock.

"You can't go," my oldest sister said. "You're a master harmonizer. Who else is good enough to take over father's shop?"

"Don't be selfish," my sister Suum spat. She was only a year older than me, but she still felt she could run my life. "Stop chasing fame and be rational. You can't just leave and fly across the *galaxy*."

My brothers had all just laughed and dismissed the idea. My parents said nothing, not even congratulations. Their silence was answer enough. Even my best friend Dele. He congratulated and told me that I was smarter than everyone at Oomza Uni, but then he'd laughed, too. "You cannot go," he simply said. "We're Himba. God has already chosen our paths."

I was the first Himba in history to be bestowed with the honor of acceptance into Oomza Uni. The hate messages, threats to my life, laughter and ridicule that came from the Khoush in my city made me want to hide more. But deep down inside me, I wanted . . . I *needed* it. I couldn't help but act on it. The urge was so strong that it was mathematical. When I'd sit in the desert, alone, listening to the wind, I would see and feel the numbers the way I did when I was deep in my work in my father's shop. And those numbers added up to the sum of my destiny.

So in secret, I filled out and uploaded the acceptance forms. The desert was the perfect place for privacy when they contacted my astrolabe for university interviews. When everything was set, I packed my things and got on that shuttle. I come from a family of *Bitolus*; my father is a master harmonizer and I was to be his successor. We *Bitolus* know true deep mathematics and we can control their current, we know systems. We are few and we are happy and uninterested in weapons and war, but we can protect ourselves. And as my father says, "God favors us."

I clutched my *edan* to my chest now as I opened my eyes. The Meduse in front of me was blue and translucent, except for one of its tentacles, which was tinted pink like the waters of the salty lake beside my village and curled up like the branch of a confined tree. I held up my *edan* and the Meduse jerked back, pluming out its gas and loudly inhaling. Fear, I thought. *That was fear.*

I stood up, realizing that my time of death was not here yet. I took a quick look around the giant hall. I could smell dinner over the stink of blood and Meduse gases. Roasted and marinated meats, brown long-grained rice, spicy red stews, flat breads, and that rich gelatinous dessert I loved so much. They were all still laid out on the grand table, the hot foods cooling as the bodies cooled and the dessert melting as the dead Meduse melted.

"Back!" I hissed, thrusting the *edan* at the Meduse. My garments rustled and my anklets jingled as I got up. I pressed my backside against the table. The Meduse were behind me and on my sides, but I focused on the one before me. "This will kill you!" I said as forcibly as I could. I cleared my throat and raised my voice. "You saw what it did to your brother."

I motioned to the shriveled dead one two feet away; its mushy flesh had dried and begun to turn brown and opaque. It had tried to take me and then something made it die. Bits of it had crumbled to dust as I spoke, the mere vibration of my voice enough to destabilize the remains. I grabbed my satchel as I slid away from the table and moved toward the grand table of food. My mind was moving fast now. I was seeing numbers and then blurs.

Good. I was my father's daughter. He'd taught me in the tradition of my ancestors and I was the best in the family.

"I am Binti Ekeopara Zuzu Dambu Kaipka of Namib," I whispered. This is what my father always reminded me when he saw my face go blank and I started to tree. He would then loudly speak his lessons to me about astrolabes, including how they worked, the art of them, the true negotiation of them, the lineage. While I was in this state, my father passed me three hundred years of oral knowledge about circuits, wire, metals, oils, heat, electricity, math current, sand bar.

And so I had become a master harmonizer by the age of twelve. I could communicate with spirit flow and convince them to become one current. I was born with my mother's gift of mathematical sight. My mother only used it to protect the family, and now I was going to grow that skill at the best university in the galaxy . . . if I survived. "Binti Ekeopara Zuzu Dambu Kaipka of Namib, that is my name," I said again.

My mind cleared as the equations flew through it, opening it wider, growing progressively more complex and satisfying. $V-E + F=2$, $a^2 + b^2 = c^2$, I thought. I knew what to do now. I moved to the table of food and grabbed a tray. I heaped chicken wings, a turkey leg, and three steaks of beef onto it. Then several rolls; bread would stay fresh longer. I dumped three oranges on my tray, because they carried juice and vitamin C. I grabbed two whole bladders of water and shoved them into my satchel as well. Then I slid a slice of white milky dessert on my tray. I did not know its name, but it was easily the most wonderful thing I'd ever tasted. Each bite would fuel my mental well-being. And if I were going to survive, I'd need that, especially.

I moved quickly, holding up the *edan*, my back straining with the weight of my loaded satchel as I held the large food-heavy tray with my left hand. The Meduse followed me, their tentacles caressing the floor as they floated. They had no eyes, but from what I knew of the Meduse, they had scent receptors on the tips of their tentacles. They saw me through smell.

The hallway leading to the rooms was wide and all the doors were plated with sheets of gold metal. My father would have spat at this wastefulness. Gold was an information conductor and its mathematical signals were stronger than anything. Yet here it was wasted on gaudy extravagance.

When I arrived at my room, the trance lifted from me without warning and I suddenly had no idea what to do next. I stopped treeing and the clarity of mind retreated like a loss of confidence. All I could think to do was let the door scan my eye. It opened, I slipped in and it shut behind me with a sucking sound, sealing the room, a mechanism probably triggered by the ship's emergency programming.

I managed to put the tray and satchel on my bed just before my legs gave. Then I sunk to the cool floor beside the black landing chair on the fair side of the room. My face was sweaty and I rested my cheek on the floor for a moment and sighed. Images of my friends Olo, Remi, Kwuga, Nur, Anajama, Rhoden crowded my mind. I thought I heard Heru's soft laughter above me . . . then the sound of his chest bursting open, then the heat of his blood on my face. I whimpered, biting my lip. "I'm here, I'm here, I'm here," I whispered. Because I was and there was no way out. I shut my eyes tightly as the tears came. I curled my body and stayed like that for several minutes.

I brought my astrolabe to my face. I'd made the casing with golden sand bar that I'd molded, sculpted, and polished myself. It was the size of a child's hand and far better than any astrolabe one could buy from the finest seller. I'd taken care to fashion its weight to suit my hands, the dials to respond to only my fingers, and its currents were so true that they'd probably outlast my own future children. I'd made this astrolabe two months ago specifically for my journey, replacing the one my father had made for me when I was three years old.

I started to speak my family name to my astrolabe, but then I whispered, "No," and rested it on my belly. My family was planets away by now; what more could they do than weep? I rubbed the on button and spoke, "Emergency." The astrolabe warmed in my hands and emitted the calming scent of roses as it vibrated. Then it went cool. "Emergency," I said again. This time it didn't even warm up.

"Map," I said. I held my breath, waiting. I glanced at the door. I'd read that Meduse could not move through walls, but even I knew that just because information was in a book didn't make it true. Especially when the information concerned the Meduse. My door was secure, but I was Himba and I doubted the Khoush had given me one of the rooms with full security locks. The Meduse would come in when they wanted or when they were willing to risk death to do away with me. I may not have been Khoush . . . but I was a human on a Khoush ship.

My astrolabe suddenly warmed and vibrated. "Your location is 121 hours from your destination of Oomza Uni," it said in its whispery voice. So the Meduse felt it okay for me to know where the ship was. The virtual constellation lit up my room with white, light blue, red, yellow, and orange dots, slowly rotating globes from the size of a large fly to the size of my fist. Suns, planets, bloom territories all sectioned in the mathematical net that I'd always found easy to read. The ship had long since left my solar system. We'd slowed down right in the middle of what was known as "the Jungle."

The pilots of the ship should have been more vigilant. "And maybe less arrogant," I said, feeling ill.

The ship was still heading for Oomza Uni, though, and that was mildly encouraging. I shut my eyes and prayed to the Seven. I wanted to ask, "Why did you let this happen?" but that was blasphemy. You never ask why. It was not a question for you to ask.

"I'm going to die here."

Seventy-two hours later, I was still alive. But I'd run out of food and had very little water left. Me and my thoughts in that small room, no escape outside. I had to stop crying; I couldn't afford to lose water. The toilet facilities were just outside my room so I'd been forced to use the case that carried my beaded jewelry collection. All I had was my jar of *otjize*, some of which I used to clean my body as much as possible. I paced, recited equations, and was sure that if I didn't die of thirst or starvation I'd die by fire from the currents I'd nervously created and discharged to keep myself busy.

I looked at the map yet again and saw what I knew I'd see; we were still heading to Oomza Uni. "But why?" I whispered. "Security will . . . "

I shut my eyes, trying to stop myself from completing the thought yet again. But I could never stop myself and this time was no different. In my mind's eye, I saw a bright yellow beam zip from Oomza Uni and the ship scattering in a radiating mass of silent light and flame. I got up and shuffled to the far side of my room and back as I talked. "But suicidal Meduse? It just doesn't make sense. Maybe they don't know how to . . . "

There was a slow knock at the door and I nearly jumped to the ceiling. Then I froze, listening with every part of my body. Other than the sound of my voice, I hadn't heard a thing from them since that first twenty-four hours. The knock came again. The last knock was hard, more like a kick, but not near the bottom of the door.

"L . . . leave me alone!" I screamed, grabbing my *edan*. My words were met with a hard bang at the door and an angry, harsh hiss. I screeched and moved as far from the door as my room would permit, nearly falling over my largest suitcase. *Think think think*. No weapons, except the *edan* . . . and I didn't know what made it a weapon.

Everyone was dead. I was still about forty-eight hours from safety or being blown up. They say that when faced with a fight you cannot win, you can never predict what you will do next. But I'd always known I'd fight until I was killed. It was an abomination to commit suicide or to give up your life. I was sure that I was ready. The Meduse were very intelligent; they'd find a way to kill me, despite my *edan*.

Nevertheless, I didn't pick up the nearest weapon. I didn't prepare for my last violent rabid stand. Instead, I looked my death square in the face and then . . . then I surrendered to it. I sat on my bed and waited for my death. Already, my body felt as if it were no longer mine; I'd let it go. And in that moment, deep in my submission, I laid my eyes on my *edan* and stared at its branching splitting dividing blue fractals.

And I saw it.

I *really* saw it.

And all I could do was smile and think, *How did I not know?*

I sat in the landing chair beside my window, hand-rolling *otjize* into my plaits. I looked at my reddened hands, brought them to my nose and sniffed. Oily clay that sang of sweet flowers, desert wind, and soil. Home, I thought, tears stinging my eyes. I should not have left. I picked up the *edan*, looking for what I'd seen. I turned the *edan* over and over before my eyes. The blue object whose many points I'd rubbed, pressed, stared at, and pondered for so many years.

More thumping came from the door. "Leave me alone," I muttered weakly.

I smeared *otjize* onto the point of the *edan* with the spiral that always reminded me of a fingerprint. I rubbed it in a slow circular motion. My shoulders relaxed as I calmed. Then my starved and thirsty brain dropped into a mathematical trance like a stone dropped into deep water. And I felt the water envelop me as down down down I went.

My clouded mind cleared and everything went silent and motionless, my finger still polishing the *edan*. I smelled home, heard the desert wind blowing grains of sand over each other. My stomach fluttered as I dropped deeper in and my entire body felt sweet and pure and empty and light. The *edan* was heavy in my hands; so heavy that it would fall right through my flesh.

"Oh," I breathed, realizing that there was now a tiny button in the center of the spiral. This was what I'd seen. It had always been there, but now it was as if it were in focus. I pushed it with my index finger. It depressed with a soft "click" and then the stone felt like warm wax and my world wavered. There was another loud knock at the door. Then through the clearest silence I'd ever experienced, so clear that the slightest sound would tear its fabric, I heard a solid oily low voice say, "Girl."

I was catapulted out of my trance, my eyes wide, my mouth yawning in a silent scream.

"Girl," I heard again. I hadn't heard a human voice since the final screams of those killed by the Meduse, over seventy-two hours ago.

I looked around my room. I was alone. Slowly, I turned and looked out the window beside me. There was nothing out there for me but the blackness of space.

"Girl. You will die," the voice said slowly. "Soon." I heard more voices, but they were too low to understand. "Suffering is against the Way. Let us end you."

I jumped up and the rush of blood made me nearly collapse and crash to the floor. Instead I fell painfully to my knees, still clutching the *edan*. There was another knock at the door. "Open this door," the voice demanded.

My hands began to shake, but I didn't drop my *edan*. It was warm and a brilliant blue light was glowing from within it now. A current was running through it so steadily that it made the muscles of my hand constrict. I couldn't let go of it if I tried.

"I will not," I said, through clenched teeth. "Rather die in here, on *my* terms."

The knocking stopped. Then I heard several things at once. Scuffling at the door, not toward it, but *away*. Terrified moaning and wailing. More voices. Several of them.

"This is evil!"

"It carries shame," another voice said. This was the first voice I heard that sounded high-pitched, almost female. "The shame she carries allows her to mimic speech."

"No. It has to have sense for that," another voice said.

"Evil! Let me deactivate the door and kill it."

"Okwu, you will die if you . . ."

"I will kill it!" the one called Okwu growled. "Death will be my honor! We're too close now, we can't have . . ."

"Me!" I shouted suddenly. "O . . . Okwu!" Calling its name, addressing it so directly sounded strange on my lips. I pushed on. "Okwu, why don't you talk to me?"

I looked at my cramped hands. From within it, from my *edan*, possibly the strongest current I'd ever produced streamed in jagged connected bright blue branches. It slowly etched and lurched through the closed door, a line of connected bright blue treelike branches that shifted in shape but never broke their connection. The current was touching the Meduse. Connecting them to me. And though I'd created it, I couldn't control it now. I wanted to scream, revolted. But I had to save my life first. "I am speaking to you!" I said. "Me!"

Silence.

I slowly stood up, my heart pounding. I stumbled to the shut door on aching trembling legs. The door's organic steel was so thin, but one of the strongest substances on my planet. Where the current touched it, tiny green leaves unfurled. I touched them, focusing on the leaves and not the fact that the door was covered with a sheet of gold, a super communication conductor. Nor the fact of the Meduse just beyond my door.

I heard a rustle and I used all my strength not to scuttle back. I flared my nostrils as I grasped the *edan*. The weight of my hair on my shoulders was assuring, my hair was heavy with *otjize*, and this was good luck and the strength of my people, even if my people were far far away.

The loud bang of something hard and powerful hitting the door made me yelp. I stayed where I was. "Evil thing," I heard the one called Okwu say. Of all the voices, that one I could recognize. It was the angriest and scariest. The voice sounded spoken, not transmitted in my mind. I could hear the vibration of the "v" in "evil" and the hard breathy "th" in "thing." Did they have mouths?

"I'm not evil," I said.

I heard whispering and rustling behind the door. Then the more female voice said, "Open this door."

"No!"

They muttered among themselves. Minutes passed. I sunk to the floor, leaning against the door. The blue current sunk with me, streaming through the door at my shoulder; more green leaves bloomed there, some fell down my shoulder onto my lap. I leaned my head against the door and stared down at them. Green tiny leaves of green tiny life when I was so close to death. I giggled and my empty belly rumbled and my sore abdominal muscles ached.

Then, quietly, calmly, "You are understanding us?" this was the growling voice that had been calling me evil. Okwu.

"Yes," I said.

"Humans only understand violence."

I closed my eyes and felt my weak body relax. I sighed and said, "The only thing I have killed are small animals for food, and only with swift grace and after prayer and thanking the beast for its sacrifice." I was exhausted.

"I do not believe you."

"Just as I do not believe you will not kill me if I open the door. All you do is kill." I opened my eyes. Energy that I didn't know I still had rippled through me and I was so angry that I couldn't catch my breath. "Like . . . like you . . . killed my friends!" I coughed and slumped down, weakly. "My friends," I whispered, tears welling in my eyes. "Oooh, my friends!"

"Humans must be killed before they kill us," the voice said.

"You're all stupid," I spat, wiping my tears as they kept coming. I sobbed hard and then took a deep breath, trying to pull it together. I exhaled loudly, snot flying from my nose. As I wiped my face with my arm, there were more whispers. Then the higher pitched voice spoke.

"What is this blue ghost you have sent to help us communicate?"

"I don't know," I said, sniffing. I got up and walked to my bed. Moving away from the door instantly made me feel better. The blue current extended with me.

"Why do we understand you?" Okwu asked. I could still hear its voice perfectly from where I was.

"I . . . I don't know," I said, sitting on my bed and then lying back.

"No Meduse has ever spoken to a human . . . except long ago."

"I don't care," I grunted.

"Open the door. We won't harm you."

"No."

There was a long pause. So long that I must have fallen asleep. I was awakened by a sucking sound. At first I paid no mind to it, taking the moment to wipe off the caked snot on my face with my arm. The ship made all sorts of sounds, even before the Meduse attacked. It was a living thing and like any beast, its bowels gurgled and quaked every so often. Then I sat up straight as the sucking sound grew louder. The door trembled. It buckled a bit and then completely crumpled, the gold plating on the outside now visible. The stale air of my room whooshed out into the hallway and suddenly the air cooled and smelled fresher.

There stood the Meduse. I could not tell how many of them, for they were transparent and when they stood together, all I could see were a tangle of translucent tentacles and undulating domes. I clutched the *edan* to my chest as I pressed myself on the other side of the room, against the window.

It happened fast like the desert wolves who attack travelers at night back home. One of the Meduse shot toward me. I watched it come. I saw my parents, sisters, brothers, aunts, and uncles, all gathered at a remembrance for me—full of pain and loss. I saw my spirit break from my body and return to my planet, to the desert, where I would tell stories to the sand people.

Time must have slowed down because the Meduse was motionless, yet suddenly it was hovering over me, its tentacles hanging an inch from my head. I gasped, bracing myself for pain and then death. Its pink withered tentacle brushed my arm firmly enough to rub off some of the *otjize* there. Soft, I thought. Smooth.

There it was. So close now. White like the ice I'd only seen in pictures and entertainment streams, its stinger was longer than my leg. I stared at it, jutting from its bundle of tentacles. It crackled and dried, wisps of white mist wafting from it. Inches from my chest. Now it went from white to a dull light-grey. I looked down at my cramped hands, the *edan* between them. The current flowing from it washed over the Meduse and extended beyond it. Then I looked up at the Meduse and grinned. "I hope it hurts," I whispered.

The Meduse's tentacles shuddered and it began to back away. I could see its pink deformed tentacle, part of it smeared red with my *otjize*.

"You are the foundation of evil," it said. It was the one called Okwu. I nearly laughed. Why did this one hate me so strongly?

"She still holds the shame," I heard one say from near the door.

Okwu began to recover as it moved away from me. Quickly, it left with the others.

Ten hours passed.

I had no food left. No water. I packed and repacked my things. Keeping busy staved off the dehydration and hunger a bit, though my constant need to urinate kept reminding me of my predicament. And movement was tricky because the *edan*'s current still wouldn't release my hands' muscles, but I managed. I tried not to indulge in my fear of the Meduse finding a way to get the ship to stop producing and circulating air and maintaining its internal pressure, or just coming back and killing me.

When I wasn't packing and repacking, I was staring at my *edan*, studying it; the patterns on it now glowed with the current. I needed to know how it was allowing me to communicate. I tried different soft equations on it and received no response. After a while, when not even hard equations affected it, I lay back on my bed and let myself tree. This was my state of mind when the Meduse came in.

"What is that?"

I screamed. I'd been gazing out the window, so I heard the Meduse before I saw it.

"What?" I shrieked, breathless. "I . . . what is what?"

Okwu, the one who'd tried to kill me. Contrary to how it had looked when it left, it was very much alive, though I could not see its stinger.

"What is the substance on your skin?" it asked firmly. "None of the other humans have it."

"Of course they don't," I snapped. "It is *otjize*, only my people wear it and I am the only one of my people on the ship. I'm not Khoush."

"What is it?" it asked, remaining in the doorway.

"Why?"

It moved into my room and I held up the *edan* and quickly said, "Mostly . . . mostly clay and oil from my homeland. Our land is desert, but we live in the region where there is sacred red clay."

"Why do you spread it on your skins?"

"Because my people are sons and daughters of the soil," I said. "And . . . and it's beautiful."

It paused for a long moment and I just stared at it. Really looking at the thing. It moved as if it had a front and a back. And though it seemed to be fully transparent, I could not see its solid white stinger within the drapes of hanging tentacles. Whether it was thinking about what I'd said or considering how best to kill me, I didn't know. But moments later, it turned and left. And it was only after several minutes, when my heart rate slowed, that I realized something odd. Its withered tentacle didn't look as withered. Where it had been curled up tightly into itself, now it was merely bent.

It came back fifteen minutes later. And immediately, I looked to make sure I'd seen what I knew I'd seen. And there it was, pink and not so curled up. That tentacle had been different when Okwu had accidently touched me and rubbed off my _otjize_.

"Give me some of it," it said, gliding into my room.

"I don't have any more!" I said, panicking. I only had one large jar of _otjize_, the most I'd ever made in one batch. It was enough to last me until I could find red clay on Oomza Uni and make more. And even then, I wasn't sure if I'd find the right kind of clay. It was another planet. Maybe it wouldn't have clay at all.

In all my preparation, the one thing I didn't take enough time to do was research the Oomza Uni planet itself, so focused I was on just _getting_ there. All I knew was that though it was much smaller than earth, it had a similar atmosphere and I wouldn't have to wear a special suit or adaptive lungs or anything like that. But its surface could easily be made of something my skin couldn't tolerate. I couldn't give all my _otjize_ to this Meduse; this was my _culture_.

"The chief knows of your people, you have much with you."

"If your chief knows my people, then he will have told you that taking it from me is like taking my soul," I said, my voice cracking. My jar was under my bed. I held up my _edan_.

But Okwu didn't leave or approach. Its curled pink tentacle twitched.

I decided to take a chance. "It helped you, didn't it? Your tentacle."

It blew out a great puff of its gas, sucked it in and left.

It returned five minutes later with five others.

"What is that object made of?" Okwu asked, the others standing silently behind it.

I was still on my bed and I pushed my legs under the covers. "I don't know. But a desert woman once said it was made from something called 'god stone.' My father said there is no such . . . "

"It is shame," it insisted.

None of them moved to enter my room. Three of them made loud puffing sounds as they let out the reeking gasses they inhaled in order to breathe.

"There is nothing shameful about an object that keeps me alive," I said.

"It poisons Meduse," one of the others said.

"Only if you get too close to me," I said, looking straight at it. "Only if you try and *kill* me."

Pause.

"How are you communicating with us?"

"I don't know, Okwu." I spoke its name as if I owned it.

"What are you called?"

I sat up straight, ignoring the fatigue trying to pull my bones to the bed. "I am Binti Ekeopara Zuzu Dambu Kaipka of Namib." I considered speaking its single name to reflect its cultural simplicity compared to mine, but my strength and bravado were already waning.

Okwu moved forward and I held up the *edan*. "Stay back! You know what it'll do!" I said. However, it did not try to attack me again, though it didn't start to shrivel up as it approached, either. It stopped feet away, beside the metal table jutting from the wall carrying my open suitcase and one of the containers of water.

"What do you need?" it flatly asked.

I stared, weighing my options. I didn't have any. "Water, food," I said.

Before I could say more, it left. I leaned against the window and tried not to look outside into the blackness. Feet away from me, the door was crushed to the side, the path of my fate was no longer mine. I lay back and fell into the deepest sleep I'd had since the ship left Earth.

The faint smell of smoke woke me up. There was a plate on my bed, right before my nose. On it was a small slab of smoked fish. Beside it was a bowl of water.

I sat up, still tightly grasping the *edan*. I leaned forward, and sucked up as much water from the bowl as I could. Then, still holding the *edan*, I pressed my forearms together and worked the food onto them. I brought the fish up, bent forward and took a bite of it. Smoky salty goodness burst across my taste buds. The chefs on the ship fed these fish well and allowed them to grow strong and mate copiously. Then they lulled the fish into a sleep that the fish never woke from and slow cooked their flesh long enough for flavor and short enough to maintain texture. I'd asked the chefs about their process as any good Himba would before eating it. The chefs were all Khoush, and Khoush did not normally perform what they called "superstitious ritual." But these chefs were Oomza Uni students and they said they did, even lulling the fish to sleep in a similar way. Again, I'd been assured that I was heading in the right direction.

The fish was delicious, but it was full of bones. And it was as I was using my tongue to work a long, flexible, but tough bone from my teeth that I looked up and noticed the Meduse hovering in the doorway. I didn't have to see the withered tentacle to know it was Okwu. Inhaling with surprise, I nearly choked on the bone. I dropped what was left, spat out the bone and opened my mouth to speak. Then I closed it.

I was still alive.

Okwu didn't move or speak, though the blue current still connected us. Moments passed, Okwu hovering and emitting the foul-smelling gasp as it breathed and me sucking bits of fish from my mouth wondering if this was my last meal. After a while, I grasped the remaining hunk of fish with my forearms and continued eating.

"You know," I finally said, to fill the silence. "There are a people in my village who have lived for generations at the edge of the lake." I looked at the Meduse. Nothing. "They know all the fish in it," I continued. "There is a fish that grows plenty in that lake and they catch and smoke them like this. The only difference is that my people can prepare it in such a way where there are no bones. They remove them all." I pulled a bone from between my teeth. "They have studied this fish. They have worked it out mathematically. They know where every bone will be, no matter the age, size, sex of the fish. They go in and remove every bone without disturbing the body. It is delicious!" I put down the remaining bones. "This was delicious, too." I hesitated and then said, "Thank you."

Okwu didn't move, continuing to hover and puff out gas. I got up and walked to the counter where a tray had been set. I leaned down and sucked up the water from this bowl as well. Already, I felt much stronger and more alert. I jumped when it spoke.

"I wish I could just kill you."

I paused. "Like my mother always says, 'we all wish for many things,'" I said, touching a last bit of fish in my back tooth.

"You don't look like a human Oomza Uni student," it said. "Your color is darker and you . . . " It blasted out a large plume of gas and I fought not to wrinkle my nose. "You have *okuoko*."

I frowned at the unfamiliar word. "What is *okuoko*?"

And that's when it moved for the first time since I'd awakened. It's long tentacles jiggled playfully and a laugh escaped my mouth before I could stop it. It plumed out more gas in rapid succession and made a deep thrumming sound. This made me laugh even harder. "You mean my hair?" I asked, shaking my thick plaits.

"*Okuoko*, yes," it said.

"*Okuoko*," I said. I had to admit, I liked the sound of it. "How come the word is different?"

"I don't know," it said. "I hear you in my language as well. When you said okuoko it is *okuoko*." It paused. "The Khoush are the color of the flesh of the fish you ate and they have no *okuoko*. You are red brown like the fish's outer skin and you have *okuoko* like Meduse, though small."

"There are different kinds of humans," I said. "My people don't normally leave my planet." Several Meduse came to the door and crowded in. Okwu moved closer, pluming out more gas and inhaling it. This time I did cough at the stench of it.

"Why have you?" it asked. "You are probably the most evil of your people."

I frowned at it. Realizing something. It spoke like one of my brothers, Bena. I was born only three years after him yet we'd never been very close. He was angry and always speaking out about the way my people were maltreated by the Khoush majority despite the fact that they needed us and our astrolabes to survive. He was always calling them evil, though he'd never traveled to a Khoush country or known a Khoush. His anger was rightful, but all that he said was from what he didn't truly know.

Even I could tell that Okwu was not an elder among these Meduse; it was too hotheaded and . . . there was something about it that reminded me of me. Maybe its curiosity; I think I'd have been one of the first to come see, if I were it, too. My father said that my curiosity was the last obstacle I had to overcome to be a true master harmonizer. If there was one thing my father and I disagreed on, it was that; I believed I could only be great if I were curious enough to seek greatness. Okwu was young, like me. And maybe that's why it was so eager to die and prove itself to the others and that's why the others were fine with it.

"You know nothing of me," I said. I felt myself grow hot. "This is not a military ship, this is a ship full of professors! Students! All dead! You killed everyone!"

It seemed to chuckle. "Not your pilot. We did not sting that one."

And just like that, I understood. They would get through the university's security if the security people thought the ship was still full of living breathing unmurdered professors and students. Then the Meduse would be able to invade Oomza Uni.

"We don't need *you*. But that one is useful."

"That's why we are still on course," I said.

"No. We can fly this creature ship," it said. "But your pilot can speak to the people on Oomza Uni in the way they expect." It paused, then moved closer. "See? We never *needed* you."

I felt the force of its threat physically. The sharp tingle came in white bursts in my toes and traveled up my body to the top of my head. I opened my mouth, suddenly short of breath. *This* was what fearing death truly felt like, not my initial submission to it. I leaned away, holding up my *edan*. I was sitting on my bed, its red covers making me think of blood. There was nowhere to go.

"That shame is the only reason you are alive," it said.

"Your *okuoko* is better," I whispered, pointing at the tentacle. "Won't you spare me for curing that?" I could barely breathe. When it didn't respond, I asked, "Why? Or maybe there is no reason."

"You think we are like you humans?" it asked, angrily. "We don't kill for sport or even for gain. Only for purpose."

I frowned. They sounded like the same thing to me, gain and purpose.

"In your university, in one of its museums, placed on display like a piece of rare meat is the stinger of our chief," it said. I wrinkled my face, but said nothing. "Our chief is . . . " It paused. "We know of the attack and mutilation of our chief, but we do not know how it got there. We do not care. We will land on Oomza Uni and take it back. So you see? We have purpose."

It billowed out gas and left the room. I lay back in my bed, exhausted.

But they brought me more food and water. Okwu brought it. And it sat with me while I ate and drank. More fish and some dried-up dates and a flask of water. This time, I barely tasted it as I ate.

"It's suicide," I said.

"What is . . . suicide," it asked.

"What you are doing!" I said. "On Oomza Uni, there's a city where all the students and professors do is study, test, create *weapons*. Weapons for taking every form of life. Your own weapons were probably made there!"

"Our weapons are made within our bodies," it said.

"What of the current-killer you used against the Khoush in the Meduse-Khoush War?" I asked.

It said nothing.

"Suicide is death on purpose!"

"Meduse aren't afraid of death," it said. "And this would be honorable. We will show them never to dishonor Meduse again. Our people will remember our sacrifice and celebrat . . . "

"I . . . I have an idea!" I shouted. My voice cracked. I pushed forward. "Let me talk to your chief!" I shrieked. I don't know if it was the delicious fish I'd eaten, shock, hopelessness, or exhaustion. I stood up and stepped to it, my legs shaky and my eyes wild. "Let me . . . I'm a master harmonizer.

That's why I'm going to Oomza Uni. I am the best of the best, Okwu. I can create harmony *anywhere*." I was so out of breath that I was wheezing. I inhaled deeply, seeing stars explode before my eyes. "Let me be . . . let me speak for the Meduse. The people in Oomza Uni are academics, so they'll understand honor and history and symbolism and matters of the body." I didn't know any of this for sure. These were only my dreams . . . and my experience of those on the ship.

"Now you speak of 'suicide' for the both of us," it said.

"Please," I said. "I can make your chief listen."

"Our chief hates humans," Okwu said. "Humans took his stinger. Do you know what . . . "

"I'll give you my jar of *otjize*," I blurted. "You can put it all over your . . . on every *okuoko*, your dome, who knows, it might make you glow like a star or give you super-powers or sting harder and faster or . . . "

"We don't like stinging."

"Please," I begged. "Imagine what you will be. Imagine if my plan works. You'll get the stinger back and none of you will have died. You'll be a hero." *And I get to live*, I thought.

"We don't care about being heroes." But its pink tentacle twitched when it said this.

The Meduse ship was docked beside the *Third Fish*. I'd walked across the large chitinous corridor linking them, ignoring the fact that the chances of my returning were very low.

Their ship stank. I was sure of it, even if I couldn't smell it through my breather. Everything about the Meduse stank. I could barely concentrate on the spongy blue surface beneath my bare feet. Or the cool gasses Okwu promised would not harm my flesh even though I could not breathe it. Or the Meduse, some green, some blue, some pink, moving on every surface, floor, high ceiling, wall, or stopping and probably staring at me with whatever they stared with. Or the current-connected *edan* I still grasped in my hands. I was doing equations in my head. I needed everything I had to do what I was about to do.

The room was so enormous that it almost felt as if we were outside. Almost. I'm a child of the desert; nothing indoors can feel like the outdoors to me. But this room was huge. The chief was no bigger than the others, no more colorful. It had no more tentacles than the others. It was surrounded by other Meduse. It looked so much like those around it that Okwu had to stand beside it to let me know who it was.

The current from the *edan* was going crazy—branching out in every direction bringing me their words. I should have been terrified. Okwu had told me that requesting a meeting like this with the chief was risking not only my life, but Okwu's life as well. For the chief hated human beings and Okwu had just begged to bring one into their "great ship."

Spongy. As if it were full of the firm jelly beads in the milky pudding my mother liked to make. I could sense current all around me. These people had deep active technology built into the walls and many of them had it running within their very bodies. Some of them were walking astrolabes, it was part of their biology.

I adjusted my face mask. The air that it pumped in smelled like desert flowers. The makers of the mask had to have been Khoush women. They liked everything to smell like flowers, even their privates. But at the moment, I could have kissed those women, for as I gazed at the chief, the smell of flowers burst into my nose and mouth and suddenly I was imagining the chief hovering in the desert surrounded by the dry sweet-smelling flowers that only bloomed at night. I felt calm. I didn't feel at home, because in the part of the desert that I knew, only tiny scentless flowers grew. But I sensed Earth.

I slowly stopped treeing, my mind clean and clear, but much stupider. I needed to speak, not act. So I had no choice. I held my chin up and then did as Okwu instructed me. I sunk to the spongy floor. Then right there, within the ship that brought the death of my friends, the boy I was coming to love, my fellow Oomza Uni human citizens from Earth, before the one who had instructed its people to perform *moojh-ha ki-bira*, also called the "great wave" of death, on my people—still grasping the *edan*, I prostrated. I pressed my face to the floor. Then I waited.

"This is Binti Ekeopara Zuzu Dambu Kaipka of Namib, the one . . . the one who survives," Okwu said.

"You may just call me Binti," I whispered, keeping my head down. My first name was singular and two syllabled like Okwu's name and I thought maybe it would please the chief.

"Tell the girl to sit up," the chief said. "If there is the slightest damage to the ship's flesh because of this one, I will have you executed first, Okwu. Then this creature."

"Binti," Okwu said, his voice was hard, flat. "Get up."

I shut my eyes. I could feel the *edan*'s current working through me, touching everything. Including the floor beneath me. And I could *hear* it. The floor. It was singing. But not words. Just humming. Happy and aloof. It wasn't paying attention. I pushed myself up, and leaned back on my knees. Then I looked at where my chest had been. Still a deep blue. I looked up at the chief.

"My people are the creators and builders of astrolabes," I said. "We use math to create the currents within them. The best of us have the gift to bring harmony so delicious that we can make atoms caress each other like lovers. That's what my sister said." I blinked as it came to me. "I think that's why this *edan* works for me! I found it. In the desert. A wild woman there once told me that it is a piece of old old technology; she called it a 'god stone.' I didn't believe her then, but I do now. I've had it for five years, but it only worked for *me* now." I pounded my chest. "For *me*! On that ship full of you after you'd all done . . . done that. Let me speak for you, let me speak to them. So no more have to die."

I lowered my head, pressing my *edan* to my belly. Just as Okwu told me. I could hear others behind me. They could have stung me a thousand times.

"You know what they have taken from me," the chief asked.

"Yes," I said, keeping my head down.

"My stinger is my people's power," it said. "They took it from us. That's an act of war."

"My way will get your stinger back," I quickly said. Then I braced myself for the rough stab in the back. I felt the sharpness press against the nape of my neck. I bit my lower lip to keep from screaming.

"Tell your plan," Okwu said.

I spoke fast. "The pilot gets us cleared to land, then I leave the ship with one of you to negotiate with Oomza Uni to get the stinger back . . . peacefully."

"That will take our element of surprise," the chief said. "You know nothing about strategy."

"If you attack, you will kill many, but then they will kill you. All of you," I said. "Ahh," I hissed as the stinger pointed at my neck was pressed harder against my flesh. "Please, I'm just . . . "

"Chief, Binti doesn't know how to speak," Okwu said. "Binti is uncivilized. Forgive it. It is young, a girl."

"How can we trust it?" the Meduse beside the chief asked Okwu.

"What would I do?" I asked, my face squeezed with pain. "Run?" I wiped tears from my face. I wiped and wiped, but they kept coming. The nightmare kept happening.

"You people are good at hiding," another Meduse sneered. "especially the females like you." Several of the Meduse, including the chief, shook their tentacles and vibrated their domes in a clear display of laughter.

"Let Binti put down the *edan*," Okwu said.

I stared at Okwu, astonished. "What?"

"Put it *down*," it said. "You will be completely vulnerable. How can you be our ambassador, if you need that to stay safe from us."

"It's what allows me to hear you!" I shrieked. And it was all I had.

The chief whipped up one of its tentacles and every single Meduse in that enormous room stopped moving. They stopped as if the very currents of time stopped. Everything stopped as it does when things get so cold that they become ice. I looked around and when none of them moved, slowly, carefully I dragged myself inches forward and turned to see the Meduse behind me. Its stinger was up, at the height of where my neck had been. I looked at Okwu, who said nothing. Then at the chief. I lowered my eyes. Then I ventured another look, keeping my head low.

"Choose," the chief said.

My shield. My translator. I tried to flex the muscles in my hands. I was greeted with sharp intense pain. It had been over three days. We were five hours from Oomza Uni. I tried again. I screamed. The *edan* pulsed a bright blue deep within its black and grey crevices, lighting up its loops and swirls. Like one of the bioluminescent snails that invaded the edges of my home's lake.

When my left index finger pulled away from the *edan*, I couldn't hold the tears back. The *edan*'s blue-white glow blurred before my eyes. My joints popped and the muscles spasmed. Then my middle finger and pinky pulled away. I bit my lip so hard that I tasted blood. I took several quick breaths and then flexed every single one of my fingers at the same time. All of my joints went CRACK! I heard a thousand wasps in my head. My body went numb. The *edan* fell from my hands. Right before my eyes, I saw it and I wanted to laugh. The blue current I'd conjured danced before me, the definition of harmony made from chaos.

There was a soft *pap* as the *edan* hit the floor, rolled twice, then stopped. I had just killed myself. My head grew heavy . . . and all went black.

The Meduse were right. I could not have represented them if I was holding the *edan*. This was Oomza Uni. Someone there would know everything there was to know about the *edan* and thus its toxicity to the Meduse. No one at Oomza Uni would have really believed I was their ambassador unless I let go.

Death. When I left my home, I died. I had not prayed to the Seven before I left. I didn't think it was time. I had not gone on my pilgrimage like a proper woman. I was sure I'd return to my village as a full woman to do that. I had left my family. I thought I could return to them when I'd done what I needed to do.

Now I could never go back. The Meduse. The Meduse are not what we humans think. They are truth. They are clarity. They are decisive. There are sharp lines and edges. They understand honor and dishonor. I had to earn their honor and the only way to do that was by dying a second time.

I felt the stinger plunge into my spine just before I blacked out and just after I'd conjured up the wild line of current that I guided to the *edan*. It was a terrible pain. Then I left. I left them, I left that ship. I could hear the ship singing its half-word song and I knew it was singing to me. My last thought was to my family, and I hoped it reached them.

Home. I smelled the earth at the border of the desert just before it rained, during Fertile Season. The place right behind the Root, where I dug up the clay I used for my *otjize* and chased the geckos who were too fragile to survive a mile away in the desert. I opened my eyes; I was on my bed in my room, naked except for my wrapped skirt. The rest of my body was smooth with a thick layer of *otjize*. I flared my nostrils and inhaled the smell of me. Home . . .

I sat up and something rolled off my chest. It landed in my crotch and I grabbed it. The *edan*. It was cool in my hand and all dull blue as it had been for years before. I reached behind and felt my back. The spot where the stinger had stabbed me was sore and I could feel something rough and scabby there. It too was covered with *otjize*. My astrolabe sat on the curve of the window and I checked my map and stared outside for a very long time. I grunted, slowly standing up. My foot hit something on the floor. My jar. I put the *edan* down and picked it up, grasping it with both hands. The jar was more than half-empty. I laughed, dressed and stared out the window again. We were landing on Oomza Uni in an hour and the view was spectacular.

They did not come. Not to tell me what to do or when to do it. So I strapped myself in the black landing chair beside the window and stared at the incredible sight expanding before my eyes. There were two suns, one that was very small and one that was large but comfortably far away. Hours of sunshine on all parts of the planet were far more than hours of dark, but there were few deserts on Oomza Uni.

I used my astrolabe in binocular vision to see things up close. Oomza Uni, such a small planet compared to Earth. Only one-third water, its lands were every shade of the rainbow—some parts blue, green, white, purple, red, white, black, orange. And some areas were smooth, others jagged with peaks that touched the clouds. And the area we were hurtling toward was orange, but interrupted by patches of the dense green of large forests of trees, small lakes, and the hard grey-blue forests of tall skyscrapers.

My ears popped as we entered the atmosphere. The sky started to turn a light pinkish color, then red orange. I was looking out from within a fireball. We were inside the air that was being ripped apart as we entered the atmosphere. There wasn't much shaking or vibrating, but I could see the heat generated by the ship. The ship would shed its skin the day after we arrived as it readjusted to gravity.

We descended from the sky and zoomed between monstrously beautiful structures that made the skyscrapers of Earth look miniscule. I laughed wildly as we descended lower and lower. Down, down we fell. No military ships came to shoot us out of the sky. We landed and, moments after smiling with excitement, I wondered if they would kill the pilot now that he was useless? I had not negotiated that with the Meduse. I ripped off my safety belt and jumped up and then fell to the floor. My legs felt like weights.

"What is . . . "

I heard a horrible noise, a low rumble that boiled to an angry-sounding growl. I looked around, sure there was a monster about to enter my room. But then I realized two things. Okwu was standing in my doorway and I understood what it was saying.

I did as it said and pushed myself into a sitting position, bringing my legs to my chest. I grasped the side of my bed and dragged myself up to sit on it.

"Take your time," Okwu said. "Your kind do not adjust quickly to *jadevia*."

"You mean gravity?" I asked.

"Yes."

I slowly stood up. I took a step and looked at Okwu, then past it at the empty doorway. "Where are the others?"

"Waiting in the dining room."

"The pilot?" I asked

"In the dining room as well."

"Alive?"

"Yes."

I sighed, relieved, and then paused. The sound of its speech vibrating against my skin. This was its true voice. I could not only hear at its frequency, but I saw its tentacles quiver as it spoke. And I could understand it. Before, it had just looked like their tentacles were quivering for no reason.

"Was it the sting?" I asked.

"No," it said. "That is something else. You understand, because you truly are what you say you are—a harmonizer."

I didn't care to understand. Not at the moment.

"Your tentacle," I said. "Your *okuoko*." It hung straight, still pink but now translucent like the others.

"The rest was used to help several of our sick," it said. "Your people will be remembered by my people."

The more it spoke, the less monstrous its voice sounded. I took another step.

"Are you ready?" Okwu asked.

I was. I left the *edan* behind with my other things.

• • •

I was still weak from the landing, but this had to happen fast. I don't know how they broke the news of their presence to Oomza Uni authorities, but they must have. Otherwise, how would we be able to leave the ship during the brightest part of the day?

I understood the plan as soon as Okwu and the chief came to my room. I followed them down the hallway. We did not pass through the dining room where so many had been brutally killed, and I was glad. But as we passed the entrance, I saw all the Meduse in there. The bodies were all gone. The chairs and tables were all stacked on one side of the large room as if a windstorm had swept through it. Between the transparent folds and tentacles, I thought I glimpsed someone in the red flowing uniform of the pilot, but I wasn't sure.

"You know what you will say," the chief said. Not a question, but a statement. And within the statement, a threat.

I wore my best red shirt and wrapper, made from the threads of well-fed silkworms. I'd bought it for my first day of class at Oomza Uni, but this was a more important occasion. And I'd used fresh *otjize* on my skin and to thicken my plaited hair even more. As I'd palm rolled my plaits smooth like the bodies of snakes, I noticed that my hair had grown about an inch since I'd left home. This was odd. I looked at the thick wiry new growth, admiring its dark brown color before pressing the *otjize* onto it, making it red. There was a tingling sensation on my scalp as I worked the *otjize* in and my head ached. I was exhausted. I held my *otjize*-covered hands to my nose and inhaled the scent of home.

Years ago, I had snuck out to the lake one night with some other girls and we'd all washed and scrubbed off all our *otjize* using the lake's salty water. It took us half the night. Then we'd stared at each other horrified by what we'd done. If any man saw us, we'd be ruined for life. If our parents saw us, we'd all be beaten and that would only be a fraction of the punishment. Our families and people we knew would think us mentally unstable when they heard, and that too would ruin our chances of marriage.

But above all this, outside of the horror of what we'd done, we all felt an awesome glorious . . . shock. Our hair hung in thick clumps, black in the moonlight. Our skin glistened, dark brown. Glistened. And there had been a breeze that night and it felt amazing on our exposed skin. I thought of this as I applied the *otjize* to my new growth, covering up the dark brown color of my hair. What if I washed it all off now? I was the first of my people to come to Oomza Uni, would the people here even know the difference? But Okwu and the chief came minutes later and there was no time. Plus, really, this was

Oomza Uni, someone would have researched and known of my people. And that person would know I was naked if I washed all my *otjize* off . . . and crazy.

I didn't want to do it anyway, I thought as I walked behind Okwu and the chief. There were soldiers waiting at the doorway; both were human and I wondered what point they were trying to make by doing that. Just like the photos in the books I read, they wore all-blue kaftans and no shoes.

"You first," the chief growled, moving behind me. I felt one of its tentacles, heavy and smooth, shove me softly in the back right where I'd been stung. The soreness there caused me to stand up taller. And then more softly in a voice that only tickled my ear with its strange vibration. "Look strong, girl."

Following the soldiers and followed by two Meduse, I stepped onto the surface of another planet for the first time in my life. My scalp was still tingling, and this added to the magical sensation of being so far from home. The first thing I noticed was the smell and weight of the air when I walked off the ship. It smelled jungly, green, heavy with leaves. The air was full of *water*. It was just like the air in the ship's plant-filled breathing chambers!

I parted my lips and inhaled it as I followed the soldiers down the open black walkway. Behind me, I heard the Meduse, pluming out and sucking in gas. Softly, though, unlike on the ship. We were walking toward a great building, the ship port.

"We will take you to the Oomza Uni Presidential Building," one of the soldiers said in to me in perfect Khoush. He looked up at the Meduse and I saw a crease of worry wrinkle his brow. "I don't know . . . their language. Can you . . . "

I nodded.

He looked about twenty-five and was dark brown skinned like me, but unlike the men of my people, his skin was naked, his hair shaven low, and he was quite short, standing a head shorter than me. "Do you mind swift transport?"

I turned and translated for Okwu and the chief.

"These people are primitive," the chief responded. But it and Okwu agreed to board the shuttle.

The room's wall and floor were a light blue, the large open windows letting in sunshine and a warm breeze. There were ten professors, one from each of the ten university departments. They sat, stood, hovered, and crouched behind a long table of glass. Against every wall were soldiers wearing blue uniforms of cloth, color, and light. There were so many different types of people in the room that I found it hard to concentrate. But I had to or there would be more death.

The one who spoke for all the professors looked like one of the sand people's gods and I almost laughed. It was like a spider made of wind, grey and undulating, here and not quite there. When it spoke, it was in a whisper that I could clearly hear despite the fact that I was several feet away. And it spoke in the language of the Meduse.

It introduced itself as something that sounded like "Haras" and said, "Tell me what you need to tell me."

And then all attention was suddenly on me.

"None of you have ever seen anyone like me," I said. "I come from a people who live near a small salty lake on the edge of a desert. On my people's land, fresh water, water humans can drink, is so little that we do not use it to bathe as so many others do. We wash with *otjize*, a mix of red clay from our land and oils from our local flowers."

Several of the human professors looked at each other and chuckled. One of the large insectile people clicked its mandibles. I frowned, flaring my nostrils. It was the first time I'd received treatment similar to the way my people were treated on Earth by the Khoush. In a way, this set me at ease. People were people, everywhere. These professors were just like anyone else.

"This was my first time leaving the home of my parents. I had never even left my own city, let alone my planet Earth. Days later, in the blackness of space, everyone on my ship but the pilot was killed, many right before my eyes, by a people at war with those who view my own people as near slaves." I waited for this to sink in, then continued. "You've never seen the Meduse, either. Only studied them . . . from afar. I know. I have read about them too." I stepped forward. "Or maybe some of you or your students have studied the stinger you have in the weapons museum up close."

I saw several of them look at each other. Some murmured to one another. Others, I did not know well enough to tell what they were doing. As I spoke, I fell into a rhythm, a meditative state very much like my math-induced ones. Except I was fully present, and before long tears were falling from my eyes. I told them in detail about watching Heru's chest burst open, desperately grabbing food, staying in that room waiting to die, the *edan* saving me and not knowing how or why or what.

I spoke of Okwu and how my *otjize* had really been what saved me. I spoke of the Meduse's cold exactness, focus, violence, sense of honor, and willingness to listen. I said things that I didn't know I'd thought about or comprehended. I found words I didn't even know I knew. And eventually, I told them how they could satisfy the Meduse and prevent a bloodbath in which everyone would lose.

I was sure they would agree. These professors were educated beyond anything I could imagine. Thoughtful. Insightful. United. Individual. The Meduse chief came forward and spoke its piece, as well. It was angry, but thorough, eloquent with a sterile logic. "If you do not give it to us willingly, we have the right to take back what was brutally stolen from us without provocation," the chief said.

After the chief spoke, the professors discussed among themselves for over an hour. They did not retreat to a separate room to do this. They did it right before the chief, Okwu, and me. They moved from the glass table and stood in a group.

Okwu, the chief, and I just stood there. Back in my home, the elders were always stoic and quiet and they always discussed everything in private. It must have been the same for the Meduse, because Okwu's tentacles shuddered and it said, "What kind of people are these?"

"Let them do the right thing," the chief said.

Feet away from us, beyond the glass table, these professors were shouting with anger, sometimes guffawing with glee, flicking antennae in each other's faces, making ear-popping clicks to get the attention of colleagues. One professor, about the size of my head, flew from one part of the group to the other, producing webs of grey light that slowly descended on the group. This chaotic method of madness would decide whether I would live or die.

I caught bits and pieces of the discussion about Meduse history and methods, the mechanics of the *Third Fish*, the scholars who'd brought the stinger. Okwu and the chief didn't seem to mind hovering there waiting. However, my legs soon grew tired and I sat down right there on the blue floor.

Finally, the professors quieted and took their places at the glass table again. I stood up, my heart seeming to pound in my mouth, my palms sweaty. I glanced at the chief and felt even more nervous; its *okuoko* were vibrating and its blue color was deeper, almost glowing. When I looked at Okwu, where its *okuoko* hung, I caught a glimpse of the white of its stinger, ready to strike.

The spiderlike Haras raised two front legs and spoke in the language of the Meduse and said, "On behalf of all the people of Oomza Uni and on behalf of Oomza University, I apologize for the actions of a group of our own in taking the stinger from you, Chief Meduse. The scholars who did this will be found, expelled, and exiled. Museum specimens of such prestige are highly prized at our university, however such things must only be acquired with permission from the people to whom they belong. Oomza protocol is based on honor, respect, wisdom, and knowledge. We will return it to you immediately."

My legs grew weak and before I knew it, I was sitting back on the floor. My head felt heavy and tingly, my thoughts scattered. "I'm sorry," I said, in the language I'd spoken all my life. I felt something press my back, steadying me. Okwu.

"I am all right," I said, pushing my hands to the floor and standing back up. But Okwu kept a tentacle to my back.

The one named Haras continued. "Binti, you have made your people proud and I'd personally like to welcome you to Oomza Uni." It motioned one of its limbs toward the human woman beside it. She looked Khoush and wore tight-fitting green garments that clasped every part of her body, from neck to toe. "This is Okpala. She is in our mathematics department. When you are settled, aside from taking classes with her, you will study your *edan* with her. According to Okpala, what you did is impossible."

I opened my mouth to speak, but Okpala put up a hand and I shut my mouth.

"We have one request," Haras said. "We of Oomza Uni wish Okwu to stay behind as the first Meduse student to attend the university and as a showing of allegiance between Oomza Uni governments and the Meduse and a renewal of the pact between human and Meduse."

I heard Okwu rumble behind me, then the chief was speaking up. "For the first time in my own lifetime, I am learning something completely outside of core beliefs," the chief said. "Who'd have thought that a place harboring human beings could carry such honor and foresight." It paused and then said, "I will confer with my advisors before I make my decision."

The chief was pleased. I could hear it in its voice. I looked around me. No one from my tribe. At once, I felt both part of something historic and very alone. Would my family even comprehend it all when I explained it to them? Or would they just fixate on the fact that I'd almost died, was now too far to return home and had left them in order to make the "biggest mistake of my life"?

I swayed on my feet, a smile on my face.

"Binti," the one named Okpala said. "What will you do now?"

"What do you mean?" I asked. "I want to study mathematics and currents. Maybe create a new type of astrolabe. The *edan*, I want to study that and . . ."

"Yes," she said. "That is true, but what about your home? Will you ever return?"

"Of course," I said. "Eventually, I will visit and . . ."

"I have studied your people," she said. "They don't like outsiders."

"I'm not an outsider," I said, with a twinge of irritation. "I am . . ." And that's when it caught my eye. My hair was rested against my back, weighed down by the *otjize*, but as I'd gotten up, one lock had come to rest on my shoulder. I felt it rub against the front of my shoulder and I saw it now.

I frowned, not wanting to move. Before the realization hit me, I knew to drop into meditation, treeing out of desperation. I held myself in there for a moment, equations flying through my mind, like wind and sand. Around me, I heard movement and, still treeing, I saw that the soldiers were leaving the room. The professors were getting up, talking among themselves in their various ways. All except Okpala. She was looking right at me.

I slowly lifted up one of my locks and brought it forward I rubbed off the ojtize. It glowed a strong deep blue like the sky back on earth on a clear day, like Okwu and so many of the other Meduse, like the uniforms of the Oomza Uni soldiers. And it was translucent. Soft, but tough. I touched the top of my head and pressed. They felt the same and . . . I felt my hand touching them. The tingling sensation was gone. My hair was no longer hair. There was a ringing in my ear as I began to breathe heavily, still in meditation. I wanted to tear off my clothes and inspect every part of my body. To see what else that sting had changed. It had not been a sting. A sting would have torn out my insides, as it did for Heru.

"Only those," Okwu said. "Nothing else."

"This is why I understand you?" I flatly asked. Talking while in meditation was like softly whispering from a hole deep in the ground. I was looking up from a cool dark place.

"Yes."

"Why?"

"Because you had to understand us and it was the only way," Okwu said.

"And you needed to prove to them that you were truly our ambassador, not prisoner," the chief said. It paused. "I will return to the ship; we will make our decision about Okwu." It turned to leave and then turned back. "Binti, you will forever hold the highest honor among the Meduse. My destiny is stronger for leading me to you." Then it left.

I stood there, in my strange body. If I hadn't been deep in meditation I would have screamed and screamed. I was so far from home.

I'm told that news of what had happened spread across all Oomza Uni within minutes. It was said that a human tribal female from a distant blue planet saved the university from Meduse terrorists by sacrificing her blood and using her unique gift of mathematical harmony and ancestral magic. "Tribal": that's what they called humans from ethnic groups too remote and "uncivilized" to regularly send students to attend Oomza Uni.

Over the next two days, I learned that people viewed my reddened dark skin and strange hair with wonder. And when they saw me with Okwu, they grew tense and quiet, moving away. Where they saw me as a fascinating exotic human, they saw Okwu as a dangerous threat. Okwu was of a warlike people who, up until now, had only been viewed with fear among people from all over. Okwu enjoyed its infamy, whereas I just wanted to find a quiet desert to walk into so I could study in peace.

"All people fear decisive, proud honor," Okwu proclaimed.

We were in one of the Weapons City libraries, staring at the empty chamber where the chief's stinger had been kept. A three-hour transport from Math City, Weapons City was packed with activity on every street and crowded with sprawling flat grey buildings made of stone. Beneath each of these structures were inverted buildings that extended at least a half-mile underground where only those students, researchers, and professors involved knew what was being invented, tested, or destroyed. After the meeting, this was where they'd taken me, the chief, and Okwu for the retrieval of the stinger.

We'd been escorted by a person who looked like a small green child with roots for a head, who I later learned was the head professor of Weapons City. He was the one who went into the five-by-five-foot case made of thick clear crystal and opened it. The stinger was placed atop a slab of crystal and looked like a sharp tusk of ice.

The chief slowly approached the case, extended an *okuoko*, and then let out a large bluish plume of gas the moment its *okuoko* touched the stinger. I'll never forget the way the chief's body went from blue to clear the moment the stinger became a part of it again. Only a blue line remained at the point of demarcation where it had reattached—a scar that would always remind it of what human beings of Oomza Uni had done to it for the sake of research and academics.

Afterward, just before the chief and the others boarded the *Third Fish* that would take them back to their own ship just outside the atmosphere, upon Okwu's request, I knelt before the chief and placed its stinger on my lap. It was heavy and it felt like a slab of solid water and the edge at its tip looked like it could slice into another universe. I smeared a dollop of my *otjize* on the blue scar where it had reattached. After a minute, I wiped some of it away. The blue scar was gone. Their chief was returned to its full royal translucence, they had the half jar of *otjize* Okwu had taken from me, which healed their flesh like magic, and they were leaving one of their own as the first Meduse to study at the great Oomza University. The Meduse left Oomza Uni happier and better off than when they'd arrived.

My *otjize*. Yes, there is a story there. Weeks later, after I'd started classes and people had finally started to leave me be, opting to simply stare and gossip in silence instead, I ran out of *otjize*. For days, I'd known it would happen. I'd found a sweet-smelling oil of the same chemical makeup in the market. A black flower that grew in a series of nearby caverns produced the oil. But a similar clay was much harder to find. There was a forest not far from my dorm, across the busy streets, just beyond one of the classroom buildings. I'd never seen anyone go into it, but there was a path opening.

That evening, before dark, I walked in there. I walked fast, ignoring all the stares and grateful when the presence of people tapered off the closer I got to the path entrance. I carried my satchel with my astrolabe, a bag of nuts, my *edan* in my hands, cool and small. I squeezed my *edan* as I left the road and stepped onto the path. The forest seemed to swallow me within a few steps and I could no longer see the purpling sky. My skin felt near naked, the layer of *otjize* I wore was so thin.

I frowned, hesitating for a moment. We didn't have such places where I came from and the denseness of the trees, all the leaves, the small buzzing creatures, made me feel like the forest was choking me. But then I looked at the ground. I looked right there, at my sandaled feet and found precisely what I needed.

I made the *otjize* that night. I mixed it and then let it sit in the strong sunshine for the next day. I didn't go to class, nor did I eat that day. In the evening, I went to the dorm and showered and did that which my people rarely do: I washed with water. As I let the water run through my hair and down my face, I wept. This was all I had left of my homeland and it was being washed into the runnels that would feed the trees outside my dorm.

When I finished, I stood there, away from the running stream of water that flowed from the ceiling. Slowly, I reached up. I touched my "hair." The *okuoko* were soft but firm and slippery with wetness. They touched my back, soft and slick. I shook them, feeling them *otjize*-free for the first time.

I shut my eyes and prayed to the Seven; I hadn't done this since arriving on the planet. I prayed to my living parents and ancestors. I opened my eyes. It was time to call home. Soon.

I peeked out of the washing space. I shared the space with five other human students. One of them just happened to be leaving as I peeked out. As soon as he was gone, I grabbed my wrapper and came out. I wrapped it around my waist and I looked at myself in the large mirror. I looked for a very very long time. Not at my dark brown skin, but where my hair had been. The *okuoko* were a soft transparent blue with darker blue dots at their tips. They grew out of my head as if they'd been doing that all my life, so natural looking that I couldn't say they were ugly. They were just a little longer than my hair had been, hanging just past my backside, and they were thick as sizable snakes.

There were ten of them and I could no longer braid them into my family's code pattern as I had done with my own hair. I pinched one and felt the pressure. Would they grow like hair? Were they hair? I could ask Okwu, but I wasn't ready to ask it anything. Not yet. I quickly ran to my room and sat in the sun and let them dry.

Ten hours later, when dark finally fell, it was time. I'd bought the container at the market; it was made from the shed exoskeleton of students who sold them for spending money. It was clear like one of Okwu's tentacles and dyed red. I'd packed it with the fresh *otjize*, which now looked thick and ready.

I pressed my right index and middle finger together and was about to dig out the first dollop when I hesitated, suddenly incredibly unsure. What if my fingers passed right through it like liquid soap? What if what I'd harvested from the forest wasn't clay at all? What if it was hard like stone?

I pulled my hand away and took a deep breath. If I couldn't make *otjize* here, then I'd have to . . . change. I touched one of my tentacle-like locks and felt a painful pressure in my chest as my mind tried to take me to a place I wasn't ready to go to. I plunged my two fingers into my new concoction . . . and scooped it up. I spread it on my flesh. Then I wept.

I went to see Okwu in its dorm. I was still unsure what to call those who lived in this large gas-filled spherical complex. When you entered, it was just one great space where plants grew on the walls and hung from the ceiling. There were no individual rooms, and people who looked like Okwu in some ways but different in others walked across the expansive floor, up the walls, on the ceiling. Somehow, when I came to the front entrance, Okwu would always come within the next few minutes. It would always emit a large plume of gas as it readjusted to the air outside.

"You look well," it said, as we walked down the walkway. We both loved the walkway because of the winds the warm clear seawater created as it rushed by below.

I smiled. "I *feel* well."

"When did you make it?"

"Over the last two suns," I said.

"I'm glad," it said. "You were beginning to fade."

It held up a*n okuoko*. "I was working with a yellow current to use in one of my classmate's body tech," it said.

"Oh," I said, looking at its burned flesh.

We paused, looking down at the rushing waters. The relief I'd felt at the naturalness, the trueness of the *otjize* immediately started waning. This was the real test. I rubbed some *otjize* from my arm and them took Okwu's *okuoko* in my hand. I applied the *otjize* and then let the *okuoko* drop as I held my breath. We walked back to my dorm. My *otjize* from Earth had healed Okwu and then the chief. It would heal many others. The *otjize* created by my people, mixed with my homeland. This was the foundation of the Meduse's respect for me. Now all of it was gone. I was someone else. Not even fully Himba anymore. What would Okwu think of me now?

When we got to my dorm, we stopped.

"I know what you are thinking," Okwu said.

"I know you Meduse," I said. "You're people of honor, but you're firm and rigid. And traditional." I felt sorrow wash over and I sobbed, covering my face with my hand. Feeling my *otjize* smear beneath it. "But you've become my friend," I said. When I brought my hand away, my palm was red with *otjize*. "You are all I have here. I don't know how it happened, but you are . . ."

"You will call your family and have them," Okwu said.

I frowned and stepped away from Okwu. "So callous," I whispered.

"Binti," Okwu said. It plumed out gas, in what I knew was a laugh. "Whether you carry the substance that can heal and bring life back to my people or not, I am your friend. I am honored to know you." It shook its *okuoko*, making one of them vibrate. I yelped when I felt the vibration in one of mine.

"What is that?" I shouted, holding up my hands.

"It means we are family through battle," it said. "You are the first to join our family in this way in a long time. We do not like humans."

I smiled.

He held up an *okuoko*. "Show it to me tomorrow," I said, doubtfully.

"Tomorrow will be the same," it said.

When I rubbed off the *otjize* the burn was gone.

I sat in the silence of my room looking at my *edan* as I sent out a signal to my family with my astrolabe. Outside was dark and I looked into the sky, at the stars, knowing the pink one was home. The first to answer was my mother.

⇐◆⇒

THE CITADEL OF WEEPING PEARLS

Aliette de Bodard

The Officer

There was a sound on the edge of sleep: Suu Nuoc wasn't sure if it was a bell and a drum calling for enlightenment, or the tactics-master sounding the call to arms in that breathless instant—hanging like a bead of blood from a sword's blade—that marked the boundary between the stylized life of the court and the confused, lawless fury of the battlefield.

"Book of Heaven, Book of Heaven."

The soft, reedy voice echoed under the dome of the ceiling, but the room itself had changed—receding, taking on the shape of the mindship—curved metal corridors with scrolling columns of memorial excerpts, the oily sheen of the Mind's presence spread over the watercolors of starscapes and the carved longevity character at the head of the bed. For a confused, terrible moment as Suu Nuoc woke up, he wasn't sure if he was still in his bedroom in the Purple Forbidden City on the First Planet or hanging, weightless, in the void of space.

It wasn't a dream. It was the mindship: *The Turtle's Golden Claw*, the only one addressing Suu Nuoc with that peculiar form of his title, the one that the empress had conferred on him half out of awe, half out of jest.

The Turtle's Golden Claw wasn't there in his bedroom, of course: she was a Mind, an artificial intelligence encased in the heartroom of a ship, and she was too heavy to leave orbit. But she was good at things; and one of those was hacking his comms and using the communal network to project new surroundings over his bedroom.

"Ship," he whispered, the words tasting like grit on his tongue. His eyes felt glued together; his brain still fogged by sleep. "It's the Bi-Hour of the Tiger." People plotted or made love or slept the sleep of the just; they didn't wake up and find themselves dragged into an impossible conversation.

But then, of course, *The Turtle's Golden Claw* was technically part of the Imperial family: before her implantation in the ship that would become her body, the Mind had been borne by Thousand-Heart Ngoc Ha, the empress's youngest daughter. *The Turtle's Golden Claw* was mostly sweet, but sometimes she could act with the same casual arrogance as the empress.

"What is it this time?" Suu Nuoc asked.

The Turtle's Golden Claw's voice was thin and quivering; nothing like her usual, effortless arrogance. "She's not answering. I called her again and again, but she's not answering."

Ten thousand words bloomed into Suu Nuoc's mind; were sorted out as ruthlessly as he'd once sorted out battalions. "Who?" he said.

"Grandmother."

There were two people whom the mindship thought of as Grandmother; but if the Keeper of the Peace Empress had been dead, Suu Nuoc's quarters would have been in effervescence, the night servants barely containing their impatience at their master's lack of knowledge. "The Grand Master of Design Harmony?"

The lights flickered around him; the characters oozed like squeezed wounds. "She's not answering," the ship said again, sounding more and more like the child she was with every passing moment. "She was here; and then she . . . faded away on the comms."

Suu Nuoc put out a command for the system to get in touch with Grand Master of Design Harmony Bach Cuc—wondering if that would work, with the shipmind hacked into his comms. But no; the progress of the call appeared overlaid on the bottom half of his field of vision, same as normal; except, of course, that no one picked up. Bach Cuc's last known location, according to the communal network, was in her laboratory near the Spire of Literary Eminence—where the radio comms toward *The Turtle's Golden Claw* would be clearest and most economical.

"Did you hack the rest of my comms?" he asked—even as he got up, pulling up clothes from his autumn chest, unfolding and discarding uniforms that seemed too formal until he found his python tunic.

"You know I didn't." *The Turtle's Golden Claw*'s voice was stiff.

"Had to ask," Suu Nuoc said. He pulled the tunic over his shoulders and stared at himself in the mirror by the four seasons chests: pale and disheveled, his hair hastily pulled back into a topknot—but the tunic was embroidered with pythons, a mark of the empress's special favor, bestowed on him after the battle at Four Stations: a clear message, for those who affected not to know who he was, that this jumped-up, uncouth soldier wielded authority by special dispensation.

The call was still ringing in the emptiness; he cut it with a wave of his hands. There was a clear, present problem, and in such situations he knew exactly what to do.

"Let's go," he said.

Grand Master Bach Cuc's laboratory was spread around a courtyard: at this late hour, only the ambient lights were on, throwing shadows on the pavement—bringing to mind the old colonist superstitions of fox shapeshifters and blood-sucking demons.

It was the dry season in the Forbidden Purple City, and Bach Cuc had set up installations on trestle tables in the courtyard—Suu Nuoc didn't remember what half the assemblages of wires and metal were and didn't much care.

"Where was she when you saw her last?" he asked *The Turtle's Golden Claw.*

The ship couldn't descend from orbit around the First Planet, of course; she'd simply animated an avatar of herself. Most mindships chose something the size of a child or a Mind; *The Turtle's Golden Claw*'s avatar was as small as a clenched fist, but perfect, rendering in exquisite detail the contours of her hull, the protrusions of her thrusters—if Suu Nuoc had been inclined to squint, he was sure he'd have caught a glimpse of the orchids painted near the prow.

"Inside," *The Turtle's Golden Claw* said. "Tinkering with things." She sounded like she'd recovered; her voice was cool again, effortlessly taking on the accents and vocabulary of the court. She made Suu Nuoc feel like a fish out of water, but at least he wouldn't have to deal with a panicked, bewildered mindship—he was no mother, no master of wind and water, and would have had no idea what to do in such a situation.

He followed the ship into one of the largest pavilions: the outside was lacquered wood, painstakingly recreated identical to Old Earth design, with thin metal tiles embossed with longevity symbols. The inside, however, was more modern, a mess of tables with instruments: the communal network a knot of virtual messages with cryptic reminders like PUT MORE KHI AT G4 and REDO THE CONNECTIONS, PLEASE, notes left by researchers to themselves and to each other.

He kept a wary eye on the room—two tables, loaded with instruments; a terminal, blinking forlornly in a corner; a faint smell he couldn't quite identify on the air: charred wood, with a tinge of a sharper, sweeter flavor, as if someone had burnt lime or longan fruit. No threat that he could see; but equally, a slow, spreading silence characteristic of a hastily emptied room.

"Is anyone here?" Suu Nuoc asked—superfluous, really. The network would have told him if there were, but he was too used to battlefields, where one could not afford to rely on its presence or its integrity.

"She's not here," *The Turtle's Golden Claw* said, slowly, patiently; an adult to a child. As if he needed another patronizing highborn of the court . . . But she was his charge; and so, technically, was Grand Master Bach Cuc, the Citadel project being under the watchful eye of the military. Even if he understood next to nothing about the science.

"I can see that." Suu Nuoc's eye was caught by the door at the furthest end of the room: the access to the shielded chamber, gaping wide open, the harmonization arch showing up as deactivated on his network access. No one inside, then.

Except . . . he walked up to it and peered beyond the arch, careful to remain on the right side of the threshold. Harmonization arches decontaminated, making sure the environment on the other side was sterile, and the cleansing of extraneous particles from every pore of his skin was an unpleasant process he would avoid if he needed to. There was nothing and no one, no virtual notes or messages, just helpful prompts from the communal network offering to tell him what the various machines in the chamber did—pointing him to Grand Master Bach Cuc's progress reports.

Not what he was interested in, currently.

He had another look around the room. *The Turtle's Golden Claw* had said Grand Master Bach Cuc had vanished mid-call. But there was nothing here that suggested anything beyond a normal night, the laboratory deserted because the researchers had gone to bed.

Except . . .

His gaze caught on the table by the harmonization arch. There was an object there, but he couldn't tell what it was because Grand Master Bach Cuc had laid her seal on it, hiding it from the view of anyone who didn't have the proper access privileges—a private seal, one that wouldn't vanish even if the communal network was muted. Suu Nuoc walked toward it, hesitating. So far, he had done Bach Cuc the courtesy of not using his accesses as an Official of the First Rank; hadn't broken into her private notes or correspondences, as he would have been entitled to. Long Quan would have called him weak—behind his back when he wasn't listening, of course, his aide wasn't that foolish—but he knew better than to use his accesses unwisely. There were those at the court that hadn't forgiven him for rising so high, so quickly; without years of learning the classics to pass the examinations, years of toiling in some less prestigious job in the College of Brushes until the court recognized his merit. They called him the empress's folly—never mind his successes as a general, the battle of Four Stations, the crushing of the rebel army at He Huong, the successful invasion of the Smoke People's territory: all they remembered was that he had once slept with the empress and been elevated to a rank far exceeding what was proper for a former (or current) favorite.

But *The Turtle's Golden Claw* wasn't flighty, or likely to panic over nothing. Suu Nuoc reached out, invoking his privileged access—the seal wavered and disappeared. Beneath it was . . .

He sucked in a deep breath—clarity filling his mind like a pane of ice, everything in the room sharpened to unbearable focus; the harmonization arch limned with cold, crystalline light as cutting as the edges of a scalpel.

The seal had hidden five pellets of metal; dropped casually into a porcelain bowl like discarded food, and still smelling, faintly, of anesthetic and disinfectant.

Mem-Implants. Ancestor implants. The link between the living and the memories of their ancestors: the repository of ghost-personalities who would dispense advice and knowledge on everything from navigating court intrigues to providing suitable responses in discussions replete with literary allusions. Five of them; no wonder Grand Master Bach Cuc had always been so graceful, so effortless at showing the proper levels of address and languages whatever the situation.

To so casually discard such precious allies—no, you didn't voluntarily leave those behind, not for any reason. But why would an abductor leave them behind?

"She wouldn't remove—" *The Turtle's Golden Claw* said. Suu Nuoc lifted a hand to interrupt the obvious.

"I need to know where the Grand Master's research stood. Concisely." There wasn't much time, and evidence was vanishing as they spoke. The ship would know that, too.

The Turtle's Golden Claw didn't make the mocking comment he'd expected—about Suu Nuoc being Supervisor of Military Research and with barely enough mathematics to operate an abacus. "You can access the logs of my last journeys into deep spaces," she said, slowly. "I brought back samples for her."

Travel logs. Suu Nuoc asked his own, ordinary implants to compile every note in the room by owner and chronological order.

"Did Grand Master Bach Cuc know where the Citadel was?" he asked. That was, after all, what those travels were meant to achieve: *The Turtle's Golden Claw*, Bach Cuc's masterpiece, diving into the furthest deep spaces, seeking traces of something that had vanished many years ago, in a time when Suu Nuoc was still a dream in his parents' minds.

The Citadel of Weeping Pearls—and, with it, its founder and ruler, the empress's eldest and favorite daughter, Bright Princess Ngoc Minh.

The Citadel had been Ngoc Minh's refuge, her domain away from the court after her last, disastrous quarrel with her mother, and her flight from the First Planet. Until the empress, weary of her daughter's defiance, had sent the Imperial Armies to destroy it—and the Citadel vanished in a single night with all souls onboard, never to reappear.

"There were . . . trace elements from orbitals and ships," *The Turtle's Golden Claw* said, slowly, cautiously; he had the feeling she was translating into a language he could understand—was it mindship stuff, or merely scientific language? "Images and memories of dresses; and porcelain dishes. . . . " The ship paused, hovering before the harmonization arch. "Everything as fresh as if they'd been made yesterday."

"I understood that much," Suu Nuoc said, wryly. He didn't know what arguments Grand Master Bach Cuc had used to sway the empress, but Bach Cuc's theory about deep spaces was well known. Perhaps at the furthest corners, where time flowed at a different rate and folded back onto itself, the past was but a handspan away. If so, then the Citadel, which had vanished without a trace thirty years ago, might be found in the vastness of space.

If you were a mindship, of course; humans couldn't go in that deep and hope to survive.

"Then you'll understand why she was excited," *The Turtle's Golden Claw* said.

"Yes." He could imagine it—Grand Master Bach Cuc would have been cautious, the ship ecstatic. "She thought you were close."

"No," *The Turtle's Golden Claw* said. "You don't understand, Book of Heaven. There were a few analyses to run before she could pinpoint a—a location I could latch onto. But she thought she had the trail. That I could plunge back into deep spaces, and follow it to wherever the Citadel was hiding itself. She thought she could find Bright Princess Ngoc Minh and her people."

Suu Nuoc was silent, then, staring at the harmonization arch.

He wasn't privy to the thoughts of the empress anymore; he didn't know why she wanted Bright Princess Ngoc Minh back.

Some said she was getting soft and regretted quarrelling with her daughter. Some said she wanted the weapons that Bright Princess Ngoc Minh had designed, the technologies that had enabled the Citadel to effortlessly evade every Outsider or Dai Viet battalion sent to apprehend the princess. And still others thought that the empress's long life was finally running to an end, and that she wanted Ngoc Minh to be her heir, over the dozen daughters and sons within the Purple Forbidden City.

Suu Nuoc had heard all of those rumors. In truth, he didn't much care: the empress's will was absolute, and it wasn't his place to question it. But he had listened in enough shuttles and pavilions, and his spies had reported enough gossip from poetry club competitions and celebratory banquets to know that not everyone welcomed the prospect of the princess's return.

Bright Princess Ngoc Minh had been blunt, and unpleasant; and many had not forgiven her for disregarding her mother's orders and marrying a minor station-born; and still others didn't much care about her but thought she would disrupt court life—and thus threaten the privileges they'd gained from attending one or another of the princes and princesses. One was not meant, of course, to gainsay the empress's orders; but there were other ways to disobey. . . .

"Book of Heaven?"

Suu Nuoc swallowed past the bile in his throat. "We must report this to the empress. Now."

The Engineer

Diem Huong had been six when the Citadel of Weeping Pearls had vanished. Her last and most vivid memory of it was of standing on the decks of one of the ships—*Attained Serenity*, or perhaps *Pine Ermitage*—gazing out at the stars. Mother held her hand; around them, various inhabitants flickered in and out of existence, teleporting from one to another of the ships that made up the city. Everything was bathed in the same cold, crisp air of the Citadel—a feeling that invigorated the bones and sharpened the breath in one's lungs until it could have cut through diamonds.

"It still stands," Mother said, to her neighbor: a tall, corpulent man dressed in robes of indigo, embroidered with cranes in flight. "The Bright Princess will protect us, to the end. I have faith. . . . "

Diem Huong was trying to see the stars better—standing on tiptoe with her arms leaning on the bay window, twisting so that the ships of the Citadel moved out of her way. Thuy had told her that, if you could line things up right, you had a view all the way to the black hole near the Thirtieth Planet. A real black hole—she kind of hoped she'd see ships sucked into it, though Thuy had always been a liar.

The man said something Diem Huong didn't remember; Mother answered something equally unintelligible, though she sounded worried. Then she caught sight of what Diem Huong was doing. "Child, no! Don't shame me by behaving like a little savage."

It had been thirty years, and she didn't know—not anymore—which parts of it were true, and which parts she had embellished. Had she only imagined the worry in Mother's voice? Certainly there had been no worry when she and Father had boarded the ship back to the Scattered Pearls orbitals—enjoy your holiday, Mother had said, smiling and hugging them as if nothing were wrong. I will join you soon.

But she never had.

On the following morning, as they docked into the central orbital of the Scattered Pearls, the news came via mindship: that the Citadel had vanished in a single night with all its citizens, and was nowhere to be found. The Empire's invading army—the soldiers tasked by the empress to burn the Citadel to cinders—had reached the designated coordinates, and found nothing but the void between the stars.

Not a trace of anyone aboard—not Mother, not the Bright Princess, not the hermits—everyone gone as though they had never existed.

As time went on, and the hopes of finding the Citadel dwindled, the memory wavered and faded; but in Diem Huong's dreams, the scene went on. In her confused, fearful dreams, she knew every word of the conversation Mother had had; and every single conversation she had ever listened to—playing with her doll Em Be Be on the floor while Mother cooked in her compartment, with the smell of garlic and fish sauce rising all around them, an anchor to the childhood she had lost. In her dreams, she knew why Mother had chosen to abandon them.

But then she would wake up, her heart in her throat, and remember that she was still alone. That Father was never there; drowning his sorrows in his work aboard a merchant ship, coming home from months-long missions stupefied on fatigue, sorghum liquor, and Heaven knew what illegal drugs. That she had no brother or sister; and that even her aunts would not understand how crushingly alone and frightened she was, in the darkness of her cradle bed, with no kind words to banish the nightmares.

After a while, she started adding her own offerings to the ancestral altar, below the hologram of Mother, that treacherous image that would never change, never age; her tacit admission that Mother might not be dead, but that she was as lost to them as if she had been.

But that didn't matter, because Diem Huong had another way to find the answers she needed.

Thirty years after the Citadel disappeared, Diem Huong woke up with the absolute knowledge that today was the day—and that, whatever she did, the trajectory of her life would be irrevocably altered. This time, it would work: after Heaven knew how many setbacks and broken parts. She wasn't sure where that certainty came from—assuredly not from her trust in a prototype made by a handful of half-baked engineers and a disorganized genius scientist in their spare time—but it was within her, cold and unshakeable. Perhaps it was merely her conviction that she would succeed: that the machine would work, sending her where she needed to be. *When* she needed to be.

She did her morning exercises, flowing from one Piece of Brocade to the next, effortlessly—focusing on her breath, inhaling, exhaling as her body moved through Separating Heaven and Earth to Wise Owl Gazing Backward; and finally settling on her toes after the last exercises with the familiar, energized feeling of sweat on her body.

They didn't have a lab, of course. They were just private citizens with a hobby, and all they'd managed to get hold of on the overcrowded orbital was a deserted teahouse, cluttered with unused tables and decorative scrolls. Lam, always practical, had used some of the celadon drinking cups to hold samples; and the porcelain dishes with painted figures had turned out to withstand heat and acid quite nicely.

The teahouse was deserted: not a surprise, as most of the others were late risers. In the oven—repurposed from the kitchen—she found the last of the machine's pieces with the ceramic completely hardened. The bots scuttling over the surface to check on the piece withdrew as she reached for it. The etching of circuits was perfect, a silvery network as intricate as woven silk.

Diem Huong turned, for a moment, to look at the machine.

It wasn't much to look at: a rectangular, man-sized frame propped with four protruding metal struts, reminiscent of a high-caste palanquin with its all-but-obsolete bearers. They had used tables and chairs to get the materials, and some of the carvings could still be seen around the frame.

It had a roof, but no walls; mostly for structural reasons: all that mattered was the frame—the rods, cooled below freezing temperature, served as anchors for the generated fields. A lot of it was beyond her: she was a bots-handler, a maker and engraver of circuits on metal and ceramic, but she wasn't the one to design or master the machine. That was Lam—the only scientist among them, the holder of an Imperial degree from the prestigious College of Brushes, equally at ease with the Classics of Mathematics as she was with the Classics of Literature. Lam had been set for a grand career, before she gave it all up and came home to take care of her sick father—to a small, insignificant station on the edge of nowhere where science was just another way to fix failing appliances.

The machine, naturally, had been a welcome challenge to her. Lam had pored over articles from everywhere in the Empire; used her old networks of scientists in posts in various branches of the Imperial Administration, from those designing war mindships to the ones on far-flung planets, tinkering with bots to help the local magistrate with the rice harvest. And, somehow, between all their late-night sessions with too much rice wine and fried soft crabs, between all their early-morning rushes with noodle soup heavy and warm in their bellies, they had built this.

Diem Huong's fingers closed on the part. Like the previous one, it was smooth: the etchings barely perceptible, the surface cold. Would it be unlike the other one, and hold the charge?

She knelt by the machine's side, finding by memory and touch the empty slot, and gently slid the piece into its rack. She could have relied on the bots to do it—and they would have been more accurate than her, to a fraction of measure—but some things shouldn't be left to bots.

Then she withdrew, connected to the room's network, and switched the machine on.

A warm red light like the lanterns of New Year's Eve filled the room as the machine started its warm-up cycle. She should have waited, she knew—for Lam and the others, so they could see what they had labored for—it wasn't fair to them, to start things without their knowledge. But she needed to check whether the piece worked—after all, no point in making a ceremony of it if the piece snapped like the previous one, or if something else went wrong, as it had done, countless times before.

Put like that, it almost sounded reasonable. But, in her heart of hearts, Diem Huong knew this wasn't about tests, or being sure. It was simply that she had to see the machine work; to be sure that her vision would come to fruition.

The others wouldn't have understood: to them, the Citadel of Weeping Pearls was an object of curiosity, the machine a technical challenge that relieved the crushing boredom of mining the asteroid fields. To Diem Huong, it was her only path to salvation.

Mother had gone on ahead, Ancestors only knew where. So there was no way forward. But, somewhere in the starlit hours of the past—somewhere in the days when the Citadel still existed, and Bright Princess Ngoc Minh's quarrel with the empress was still fresh and raw—Mother was still alive.

There was a way *back*.

The temperature in the room plummeted. Ice formed on the rods, became slick and iridescent, covered with a sheen like oil—and a feel like that of deep spaces permeated the room, a growing feeling of wrongness, of pressures in odd places the body wasn't meant to experience. The air within the box seemed to change—nothing obvious, but it shimmered and danced as if in a heat wave, and the harmonization arch slowly revved up to full capacity, its edges becoming a hard blue.

"Up early?"

Lam. Here? Startled, Diem Huong turned around and saw her friend leaning against the door, with a sarcastic smile.

"I was—" she said.

Lam shook her head. Her smile faded; became something else—sadness and understanding, mingled in a way that made Diem Huong want to curl up in a ball. "You don't need to explain."

But she did. "I have to—"

"Of course you do." Lam's voice was soft. She walked into the laboratory, stopped, and looked at the machine with a critical frown. "Mmm."

"It's not working?" Diem Huong asked, her heart in her throat.

"I don't know," Lam said. "Let me remind you no one's tried this before."

"I thought that was the point. You said everyone was wrong."

"Not in so many words, no." Lam knelt by the rods, started to reach out a hand, and changed her mind. "I merely said some approaches had no chance of working. It has to do with the nature of deep spaces."

"The mindships' deep spaces?"

"They don't belong to the mindships," Lam said, absent-mindedly—the role of teacher came to her naturally, and after all, who was Diem Huong to blame her? Lam had built all of this; she deserved a little showing off. "The ships merely . . . cross them to get elsewhere? Space gets weird within deep spaces, that's why you get to places earlier than you should be allowed to. And where space gets weird, time gets weird, too."

She called up a control screen: out of deference to Diem Huong, she displayed it rather than merely keeping it on her implants. Her hand moved in an ever-quickening dance, sliding one cursor after the other, moving one dial after the next—a ballet of shifting colors and displays that she seemed to navigate as fast as she breathed, as utterly focused and at ease as Diem Huong was with her morning exercises.

Then she paused—and left the screen hanging in the air, filled with the red of New Year's lanterns. "Heaven help me. I think it's working."

Working. Emperor in Heaven, it was working. Lam's words—she knew what she was talking about—made it all real. "You think—" Diem Huong hardly dared to imagine. She would see the Citadel of Weeping Pearls again—would talk to Mother again, know why she and Father had been abandoned. . . .

Lam walked closer to the harmonization arch, frowning. Without warning, she uncoiled, as fluid as a fighter, and threw something she held in her hand. It passed through the door—a small, elongated shape like a pebble—arched on its descent downward, and faded as it did so, until a translucent shadow settled on the floor and dwindled away to nothing.

On the display screen, a cursor slid all the way to the left. Diem Huong looked at Lam, questioningly. "It's gone back? In time?"

Lam peered at the display and frowned again. "Looks like it. I entered the time you gave me, about ten days before the Citadel vanished." She didn't sound convinced. Diem Huong didn't blame her. It was a mad, unrealistic adventure—but then, the Citadel had been a mad adventure in the first place, in so many ways, a rebellion of Bright Princess Ngoc Minh and her followers against the staidness of court life.

A mad, unrealistic adventure—until it had vanished.

Lam walked back to the display. Slowly, gently, she slid the cursor back to the right. At first, Diem Huong thought nothing had happened. But then, gradually, she saw a shadow; and then a translucent mass; and then the inkstone that Lam had thrown became visible again on the floor of the machine, as sharp and as clearly defined as though it had never left. "At least it's come back," Lam said. She sounded relieved. "But . . ."

Back. So there was a chance she would survive this. And if she didn't— then she'd be there, where it mattered. She'd have her answers. Or would, once and for all, stop feeling the shadow of unsaid words hanging over her.

Diem Huong moved—as though through thick tar—and made the gestures she had been steeling herself to make since this morning.

"L'il sis?" Lam asked, behind her. "You can't—"

Diem Huong knew what Lam would say: that they weren't sure. That the machine was half-built, barely tested, barely run through its paces. For all she knew, that door opened into a black hole; or in the right time, but into a vacuum where she couldn't breathe, or on the edge of a lava field so hot her lungs would burst into cinders. That they could find someone, or pay someone—or even use animals, though that would be as bad as humans, really, to use other living souls. "You know how it is," Diem Huong said. The door before her shimmered blue, and there was a wind on her face, a touch of cold like the bristles of a brush made of ice.

Answers. An end to her nightmares and the fears of her confused dreams.

"I've known, yes," Lam said, slowly. Her hands moved; her arms encircled Diem Huong's chest. "But that's no reason. Come back, l'il sis. We'll make sure it's safe, before you go haring off into Heaven knows what."

There was still a chance. Diem Huong could still turn back. If she did turn back, she would see Lam's eyes brimming with tears—would read the folly of what she was about to do.

"I know it's not safe," Diem Huong said, and, gently disengaging herself from Lam's arms, stepped forward—into a cold deeper than the void of space.

The Empress

Mi Hiep had been up since the Bi-Hour of the Ox—as old age settled into her bones, she found that she needed less and less sleep.

In these days of strife in the empire, sleep was a luxury she couldn't afford to have.

She would receive the envoys of the Nam Federation at the Bi-Hour of the Horse, which left her plenty of time to discuss the current situation with her advisors.

Lady Linh pulled a map of the nearby star system, and carefully highlighted a patch at the edge of Dai Viet space. "The Nam Federation is gathering fleets," she said.

"How long until they can reach us?" Mi Hiep asked.

Lady Linh shook her head. "I don't know. The Ministry of War wasn't able to ascertain the range of their engines."

Mi Hiep looked at the fleet. If they'd been normal outsider ships, it would have taken them months or years to make their way inward—past the first defenses and straight to the heart of the empire. If they'd been normal outsider ships, she would have deployed a mindship in their midst, moving with the deadly grace of primed weapons; a single pinpoint strike that would have crippled any of them in a heartbeat. But these were new ships, with the La Hoa drive, and her spies' reports suggested they could equal or surpass any mindships she might field.

"What do you think?" Mi Hiep asked, to her ancestors.

Around her, holograms flickered to life: emperors and empresses in old-fashioned court dresses, from the five-panels after the Exodus to the more elaborate, baroque style of clothing made possible by the accuracy of bots.

The first ancestor, the Righteously Martial Emperor—hoary, wizened without the benefit of rejuv treatments—was the one who spoke. "This much is clear, child: they're not here to be friends with you."

The twenty-third ancestor, the Friend of Reform Emperor—named after an Old Earth emperor who had died in exile—frowned as he studied the map. "Assuming they can move through deep spaces"—he frowned at the map—"I suspect their target is the Imperial shipyards."

"It makes sense," Lady Linh said, slowly, carefully. She looked older than any of the emperors around her, and the twenty-second emperor, who stood by her side, had once imprisoned her for treason. Mi Hiep knew well that none of them made her comfortable. "It would enable them to capture mindships—"

"Who wouldn't serve them," Mi Hiep said, more sharply than she'd intended. "They would still remember their families."

"Yes," Lady Linh said, weighing every word. She looked at Mi Hiep, a little uncertainly: an expression Mi Hiep recognized as reluctance. It had to be something serious, then; Lady Linh had never been shy about her opinions—indeed, a misplaced memorial had been the cause of her thirty-year imprisonment.

"Go on," Mi Hiep said, inclining her head. She braced herself for the worst.

Lady Linh reached out to the screen. There was a brief lag while her implants synchronized with it—a brief flowering of color, the red seal of an agent of the Embroidered Guard clearly visible—and then something else appeared on the screen.

It was a mindship—looking almost ordinary, innocuous at first sight. There was an odd protuberance on the hull, near the head, and a few more scattered here and there, like pustules. Then the ship started moving, and it became clear something was very, very wrong with it. No deadly grace, no ageless elegance, but the zigzagging, tottering course of a drunkard; curves that turned into unexpectedly sharp lines, movements that started closing back on themselves.

What had they done? Oh Ancestors, what had they done?

"It's a hijack," Lady Linh said, curtly. "Plug in a few modules at key points, and you can influence what the ship sees and thinks. Then it's just a matter of . . . fine manipulation."

There was silence, for a while. Then a snort from the first emperor, who had taken the reign name Righteously Martial after ascending to the throne over the ruins of his rivals. "That doesn't look like fine movements to me. If that's all they have against us . . . "

"That," Lady Linh said, gently, almost apologetically, "is almost a full year old. We've had reports that the technology has evolved, but no pictures or vids. It has been harder and harder to get Embroidered Guard undercover. The Nam Federation are suspicious."

Suspicious. Mi Hiep massaged her forehead. Vast movements of troops. A technology to turn their own mindships against them. The Imperial shipyards. It didn't take a Master of Wind and Water to know which way things lay.

"I see," she said. The envoys of the Nam Federation were not due for another two hours, but she already knew what they would say. They would make pretty excuses and tell her about military maneuvers and the necessity to maintain the peace on their fractious borders. And she would smile and nod, and not believe a word of it.

The twenty-second emperor turned, a ghostly shape against the metal paneling. "Someone is coming," he said.

The sixteenth empress raised her head, like a hound sniffing the wind. "Suu Nuoc. The child is in a hurry. He is arguing with the guards at the entrance. You had left orders not to be disturbed?"

"Yes," Mi Hiep said, disguising a sigh. None of the ancestors liked Suu Nuoc—it wasn't clear if they thought he had been an inappropriate lover for an empress, or if they resented his lower-class origins. Mi Hiep was no fool: she had not promoted her former lover to the Board of Military Affairs. She had promoted a smart, resourceful man with utter loyalty to her, and that was what mattered. The ancestors could talk and talk and disapprove, but she was long since inured to being shamed by a mere look or stern talking-to.

Sometimes, she wondered what it would be like to be truly alone—not to be the last descendent of a line of twenty-four emperors and empresses, her ancestors embodied into simulations so detailed they needed an entire wing of the palace to run. Sacrilege, of course; and the ancestors were useful, but still . . .

Of course, in truth, she was lonely all the time.

"Let him in," she sent to her bodyguards.

Suu Nuoc entered, out of breath, followed by the small, fist-sized avatar of *The Turtle's Golden Claw*. He took one quick glance around the room, and slowly lowered himself to the floor, his head touching the slats of the parquet.

"Your Highnesses," he said. The emperors and empresses frowned, the temperature in the room lowered by their disapproval. "Empress."

"General." Mi Hiep gestured at him to rise, but he remained where he was, his gaze stubbornly fixed on the floor. "Something bad?" she asked. The disapproval of the ancestors passed to her—her choice of words too familiar for a relationship between empress and general.

Lady Linh used the commotion caused by Suu Nuoc's arrival to slowly and discreetly slide out of the room—correctly judging Mi Hiep's desire to be alone, or as alone as one could be, with twenty-four ancestors in her thoughts.

Suu Nuoc was in the mindset she'd jokingly called "the arrow"—clear and focused, with little time for propriety or respect. "Grand Master Bach Cuc has disappeared," he said. "The ship here says she had found the trail of the Citadel."

Oh.

"Close the door," Mi Hiep said to the guards outside. She waited for them to comply, and then turned her vision back into the room. She, too, was deadly focused, instantly aware of every single implication of his words. "You mean she found my daughter. And her Citadel."

Suu Nuoc was still staring at the floor—all she could see of him was an impeccably manicured topknot, with not a grey hair in sight. How young he was; thirty-five full years younger than her at least—even younger than Ngoc Minh. A lover to remind her of life and youth, which she'd lost such a long time ago; a caprice, to sleep with someone who was not one of her concubines—one of the few impulses she could allow herself.

"Did she leave of her own volition?" Mi Hiep asked.

Suu Nuoc said nothing for a while. "I—don't think so. The timing is convenient. Too convenient."

"Then you think someone abducted her. Who?" Mi Hiep asked.

"I don't know," Suu Nuoc said. "I judged it pertinent to inform you ahead of every other consideration." She probably didn't imagine the faint sarcasm in his voice—he had never been one for common courtesies. Without her support, he would not have risen far at court.

"I see." There were many reasons people disapproved of Grand Master Bach Cuc and *The Turtle's Golden Claw*—thinking it unnatural that Bach Cuc should create a mindship who was part of the Imperial Family; fearing the return of Bright Princess Ngoc Minh and what it would mean to court life; even disapproving of her policy of war against the Nam Federation. Some advocated passionately for peace as the only way to survival.

She didn't begrudge them their opinion; the court would think as it desired, in a multiplicity of cliques and alliances that kept the scholars busy at each other's throats. But acting against Grand Master Bach Cuc . . .

"You will find her," she said to Suu Nuoc. "Her, or her corpse. And punish whoever has done this."

Suu Nuoc bowed, and left the room. *The Turtle's Golden Claw* didn't; it hovered closer and said, in a calm and dispassionate voice, "Grandmother."

Mi Hiep nodded, noting with a sharp pang of perverse pleasure the discomfort of the gathered Ancestors at this acknowledgement of their relationship. "You are sure of what you told the General Who Read the Book of Heaven?"

The ship bobbed from side to side, thoughtfully. "Bach Cuc sounded confident enough. And she usually—"

Never sounded confident until it actually worked. Grand Master Bach Cuc had been cautious, unlikely to give in to fancies or announce results ahead of time solely to please an empress or the Board of Military Affairs. Everything Mi Hiep valued in a research scientist. "I see," she said. And, more softly, "How are you?"

Bach Cuc had been her Grand Master of Design Harmony, after all, the other grandmother *The Turtle's Golden Claw* could count on—the only family that would accept her and trust her. Mi Hiep's other children had not been so welcoming. Even Thousand-Heart Princess Ngoc Ha, who had carried *The Turtle's Golden Claw* in her womb, was not affectionate.

"I will be fine," *The Turtle's Golden Claw* said, slowly, carefully. "She is alive, isn't she?"

Mi Hiep could have lied. She could have nodded with the same conviction she'd bring into her interview with the envoys of the Nam Federation; but it wouldn't have been fair, or kind, to her granddaughter. "I hope she is."

"I see," *The Turtle's Golden Claw* said, stiffly. "I will help Book of Heaven in his investigations, then."

"It will be fine," Mi Hiep said—she only had an avatar, nothing she could hold or kiss for reassurance. Mindships were machines and blood and flesh, and they felt things as keenly as humans. "We will find her."

"Thank you, Grandmother."

Mi Hiep watched the ship go—she moved as smoothly as ever, but of course with an avatar it was difficult to determine what she truly felt, wasn't it? How hurt or screaming the ship could be, inside?

She thought again of the picture Lady Linh had presented; the crippled ship tricked into believing lies: hijacked, Lady Linh had said. Blinded until their only purpose was to serve their new masters—and she felt a fresh stab of anger at this. This wasn't the way to treat anyone, whether human or mindship.

But, if she couldn't halt the progress of the Nam Federation, this would happen. They would take ships and twist them into emotionless tools with forced loyalties.

Her people needed weapons: not merely war mindships, but something more potent, more advanced; something to strike fear into their enemies' hearts and dissuade them from ever entering Dai Viet space.

They needed Ngoc Minh's weapons—and Grand Master Bach Cuc and *The Turtle's Golden Claw* had been meant to find them for her.

The Citadel of Weeping Pearls had gone down in history as a refuge of peace; as a place that taught its denizens the serenity that came from not fearing anything—not bandits, or corrupt officials, or apathetic scholars. But such things—the serenity, the lack of fear—did not happen unless one had powerful means of defense.

Mi Hiep remembered visiting Ngoc Minh in her room once—not yet the Bright Princess, but merely a gangly girl on the cusp of adulthood, always in discussion with a group of hermits she'd found on Heaven knew what forsaken planet or station. Her daughter had looked up from her conversation and smiled at her: a smile that she'd always wonder about later, about whether it was loving or forced, fearful or genuinely serene. "You haven't come to your lessons," Mi Hiep had said.

"No," Ngoc Minh had said. "I was learning things here."

Mi Hiep had turned a jaded eye on the horde of hermits—all of them lying prostrate in obedience. As if obedience could make them respectable— their dresses varied from torn robes to rags, and some of them were so withdrawn from public life they were all but invisible on the communal network, with no information beyond their planet of birth showing up on her implants. "You will be Empress of Dai Viet one day, daughter; not an itinerant monk. The Grand Secretary's lessons are on statecraft and the rituals that keep us all safe."

"We are safe, Mother. Look." Ngoc Minh took a vase from a lacquered table: a beautiful piece of celadon with a network of cracks like a fragile eggshell. She pressed something to it—a lump that was no bigger than a grain of rice—and gestured to one of the monks, who bowed and took it out into the adjoining courtyard.

What in Heaven?

"This is pointless," Mi Hiep said. "You will go to your lessons now, child." She used the sternest voice of authority she could think of; the one she'd reserved for her children as toddlers, and for sentencing prisoners to death.

Ngoc Minh's face was serene. "Look, Mother." She was looking at the vase, too, frowning; some Buddhist meditation exercise, focusing her will on it or something similar—not that Mi Hiep had anything against Buddhism, but its philosophy of peace and acceptance was not what an emperor needed. The empire needed to fight every day for its survival, and an emperor needed to choose the hard answers, rather than the most serene ones.

"If you think I have time for your nonsense—"

And then the vase winked out of existence.

There was no other word for it. It seemed to fracture along the seams of the cracks first, even as a soft radiance flowed from within it as if it had held the pure, bottled light of late afternoon—but then the pieces themselves fractured and fractured into ever-smaller pieces, until nothing but a faint, colorless dust filled the courtyard; a dust that a rising wind carried upward, into the empty space between the pagoda spires.

That was . . . Mi Hiep looked again at the courtyard: still empty and desolate, with the dust still rising in a fine, almost invisible whirlwind. "That's impossible," she said, sharply.

Ngoc Minh smiled; serene and utterly frightening. "Everything is possible, if you listen to the right people."

Looking back, that was when she'd started to be scared of her daughter. Scared of what she might do; of what she was thinking, which was clearly so different than what moved Mi Hiep. When Ngoc Minh had married her commoner wife, they'd fallen out; but the root of this last, explosive quarrel lay much earlier, in that tranquil afternoon scene where her small, quiet world bounded by ritual and habit had been utterly shattered.

She'd been a scared fool. Ngoc Minh had been right: anything that could safeguard the empire in its hour of need was a boon. What did it matter where it came from?

It was time for war—and, if anyone had dared to harm her Grand Master of Design Harmony, they would feel the full weight of her fury.

• • •

The Younger Sister

Thousand-Heart Princess Ngoc Ha found Suu Nuoc and her daughter *The Turtle's Golden Claw* in the laboratory, at the tail end of what looked to be a long and grueling series of interviews with everyone who had worked with Grand Master Bach Cuc. By his look, the Supervisor of Military Research was not having a good day.

Suu Nuoc acknowledged her with a brief nod. He was in one of his moods where he would eschew ritual in favor of efficiency, a frequent source of complaints and memorials against him. Normally, Ngoc Ha would have forced him to provide proper respect: she knew the importance of appearances, and the need to remind people of her place, as an Imperial Princess who was not the heir and only had honorary postions. But today she needed to see something else.

The laboratory had been cleanly swept. The only virtual notes attached to objects were the ones with the seal of the army, officially warning people of the penalty attached to tinkering with an ongoing investigation. The shielded chamber with its harmonization arch was swarming with bots, supervised in a bored fashion by an old technician with a withered hand. Ngoc Ha walked closer to the arch, but saw nothing that spoke to her.

"Mother!"

Of course, it was inevitable that *The Turtle's Golden Claw* would see her, and churlish of her, really, to ignore the ship. "Hello, daughter."

Ngoc Ha knew she was being irrational when she saw the ship and didn't feel an ounce of maternal love—merely a faint sense of repulsion, a memory of Mother overwhelming her objections to the implantation of the Mind in her; the scared, sick feeling she'd had during most of the pregnancy; and the sense of exhausted dread when she realized that having delivered the Mind merely meant she was now the mother, stuck in that role until the day she died.

And, if she was honest with herself, it wasn't the pregnancy, or motherhood, or even the Mind that was the issue—it was that, seeing *The Turtle's Golden Claw*, she remembered, once again, that everything in her life had been twisted out of shape for her elder sister's benefit. Thirty years since Ngoc Minh had disappeared, and still she haunted Ngoc Ha's life. Even the name bestowed on Ngoc Ha by the court—the Thousand-Heart—was not entirely hers: she was named that way because she'd been filial and dutiful, unlike Ngoc Minh; because she had set up proper spousal quarters and regularly slept with her concubines—even though none of them brought her much comfort, or alleviated the taste of ashes that had been in her mouth for thirty years.

"I'm sorry about Grand Master Bach Cuc," Ngoc Ha said to *The Turtle's Golden Claw*. "I'm sure General Suu Nuoc will find her. He's good at what he does."

"I'm sure he is," the ship said. Her avatar turned, taking in the laboratory. "Mother . . . "

Ngoc Ha braced herself—surely that sick feeling of panic in her belly wasn't what one was meant to feel when one's child came to them with problems? "Yes, child?"

"I'm scared." *The Turtle's Golden Claw*'s voice was barely audible. "This is too large. How could the Grand Master disappear like that—with no warning, in the heart of the Purple Forbidden City?"

Meaning inside influence. Meaning court intrigues; the same ones Ngoc Ha stepped away from after Ngoc Minh's disappearance. "I don't know," she said. "But not everyone wanted Ngoc Minh to come back." Including herself. She was glad to be rid of her sister the Bright Princess; to never have to be compared to her again; to never look at her and realize they had so little in common—not even Mother's love. But she wasn't the only one. Lady Linh was loyal to Mother; but the rest of the scholars weren't, not so much. Huu Tam, Mother's choice of heir, was dutiful and wise: not wild, not incomprehensibly attractive like Bright Princess Ngoc Minh, but safe. "Not everyone likes their little worlds overturned."

"What about you?" the ship asked, with simple and devastating perspicacity.

"I don't know," Ngoc Ha lied. She didn't know what she'd do, if she saw Ngoc Minh again—embrace her, shout at her, show her how much her life had twisted and stretched in the wake of her elder sister's flight?

"Princess," Suu Nuoc said. He stood by her, at quiet ease. "My apologies. I was busy."

"I can imagine," Ngoc Ha said.

"I'm surprised to see you here," Suu Nuoc said, slowly. "I thought you had no interest in what Grand Master Bach Cuc was doing."

"*The Turtle's Golden Claw* is my daughter," Ngoc Ha said.

"Of course," Suu Nuoc said. He watched her, for a while, with that intent expression on his face that made her feel pierced by a spear. "But that's not why you're here, is it?"

Ngoc Ha said nothing for a while. She watched the harmonization arch, the faint blue light playing on its edges. "I did follow what Bach Cuc was doing," she said, at last. It had taken an effort: Grand Master Bach Cuc was proud, and sometimes unpleasant. "Because it mattered. To me, to my place in court." It wasn't quite that, of course. She'd needed to know whether Ngoc Minh would come back. Whether what had passed had been worth it—the agony of being pregnant with *The Turtle's Golden Claw*; of giving birth in blood and pain and loneliness, all because her mother, the empress, had ordered it.

"How did you think things would change?"

"I don't know," Ngoc Ha said. He was assessing her, wondering what she was worth as a suspect. It would have been amusing, if she hadn't been so nervous already. "I wanted to know what you'd found, but I assume you won't share it while you're still working out if I harmed her."

"Indeed," Suu Nuoc said. He made a small, ironic smile, and turned to embrace the lab. "Or perhaps I simply have nothing to share."

Ngoc Ha steeled herself—better to tell him now than later, or else she'd become a suspect like everyone else. And she knew better than to expect Mother's influence to protect her.

After all, it hadn't worked for Ngoc Minh.

"I know who saw Grand Master Bach Cuc last," she said, slowly, carefully. "Or close to last."

There was silence, in the wake of her words.

"Who?" Suu Nuoc asked, at the same time as *The Turtle's Golden Claw* asked "Why?"

Ngoc Ha smiled, coldly; putting all the weight of the freezing disapproval she sometimes trained on courtiers. "As I said—I was interested. In whether Ngoc Minh would come back. Someone came to me with information on the Citadel of Weeping Pearls."

Suu Nuoc's face had frozen into a harsh cast, as unyielding as cut diamonds. "Go on."

"He was a man named Quoc Quang, part of a small merchant delegation that was doing a run between the Scattered Pearls belt and the First Planet." She'd had her agents check him out: a small, pathetic man addicted to alcohol and a few less savory things: hardly a threat, and hardly worth bringing to her attention, as the chief of her escort had said. Except that he'd said something about Grand Master Bach Cuc.

Ngoc Ha had her work administering the Twenty-Third Planet—trying to bring Lady Linh's home back to the glory it had had before the war, building graceful pagodas and orbitals from a pile of ashes and dust. But it was mostly a sinecure to keep her busy; and so, curious, she had made time to see Quoc Quang.

"He said his daughter was doing something to find the Citadel of Weeping Pearls—her and a woman named Tran Thi Long Lam, a Distinguished Scholar of Mathematics who returned home to mind her sick father. Apparently they thought they could do better than Grand Master Bach Cuc. He said"—she closed her eyes—"he needed to speak to Bach Cuc, to warn her."

"Warn her of what?"

"He wouldn't tell me."

Suu Nuoc's impeccably trimmed eyebrows rose. Ngoc Ha went on as though she'd seen nothing—after all, it was only the truth, and demons take the man if he didn't believe it. "And you believed him?" Suu Nuoc asked.

If Ngoc Ha closed her eyes, she could see Quoc Quang; could still smell the raw despair from him; could still hear his voice. "My wife disappeared with the Citadel. We were away, thirty years ago, when it happened. I apologize for my presumption, but I share your pain." And she hadn't been quite sure what to answer him; had let the emotionless, hardened mask of the imperial princess stare at him and nod, in a way that conveyed acceptance, and a modicum of disapproval. But, in her mind, she'd heard the dark, twisted part of her whisper: *What pain? You were glad Ngoc Minh disappeared.*

"He was very convincing," she said.

"So you sent him to Grand Master Bach Cuc," *The Turtle's Golden Claw* said. "And then . . . Bach Cuc disappeared."

Ngoc Ha shook her head, irritated at the implications. "Credit me with a little thoughtfulness, General. I sent guards with him; and though he had his interview with Bach Cuc without me, they watched him all the while, and escorted him back to his quarters in the Fifth District. The interview ended at the Bi-Hour of the Dog; Grand Master Bach Cuc was still within the Forbidden City long after that."

"It was the Bi-Hour of the Tiger," *The Turtle's Golden Claw* said. "Eight hours after that, at least."

"Right," Suu Nuoc said, in a way that suggested he didn't believe any of her intentions, or her words—he could be so terribly, so inadequately blunt some times. "And where is this—Quoc Quang now?"

She had checked, before coming. "He left this morning, with his ship. The destination he announced was his home on the Scattered Pearls Belt. I have no reason to disbelieve that."

"Except that he left in rather a hurry after Bach Cuc disappeared?"

Ngoc Ha did her best not to bristle, but it was hard. "I checked. There was no extra passenger on board. Apart from him, nothing was taken onboard; not even a live woman or a corpse. The airport bots would have seen it otherwise." She felt more than heard *The Turtle's Golden Claw* tense. "Sorry. I had to consider all eventualities."

"That's all right," *The Turtle's Golden Claw* said. "I'm sure she's alive. She's resourceful."

Suu Nuoc and Ngoc Ha exchanged a long, deep look; he was as skeptical as her, but he wouldn't say anything. For her sake, she mouthed, and Suu Nuoc nodded.

"Fine." Suu Nuoc was silent, for a while. He stared at the harmonization door, his face hard again; his gaze distant, probably considering something on the network via his implants. He had no mem-implants from ancestors—but then, Ngoc Ha, the unfavored daughter of the family, had none either. "I will check, and let you know. "

"I see," Ngoc Ha said. And, to the ship, "Will you come with me to my quarters? We can have tea together."

"Of course!" *The Turtle's Golden Claw* said—happy to spend an afternoon with her mother, a rare occurrence for her. Once again, Ngoc Ha fought a wave of shame. She should be more present in the ship's life; should see her through her tumultuous childhood and into adulthood—surely it wasn't easy for the ship either, to have been born only for the purpose of finding someone else.

"Thank you for your evidence. You will be apprised, one way or another."

And she wasn't sure, as she walked away with the ship in tow, if she ought to be relieved or scared, or both.

The Officer

Suu Nuoc found the entrance to his chamber crowded with officials, and his mailbox overflowing with a variety of memorials from the court—from those chastising him for his carefree behavior to short messages asking for the results of his investigation. They were all so fresh from the Grand Secretarial off ice that he could still see the marks of the rescripts—it was bad, then, if even he could see it: the court had to be in disarray; the Grand Secretariat overwhelmed.

"General, General." A chorus of voices; but the ones that stood out belonged to Vinh and Hanh, two of the heir Huu Tam's supporters. "What happened to Grand Master Bach Cuc?"

"Are we safe?"

"How soon will we know?"

He closed his eyes and wished, again, for the serenity that had come over him on the edge of the battlefield. It wasn't his world. It would never be his world—except that being a general meant sleepless, dirty nights in the field with ten thousand bots hacked into his feeds, sending him contradictory information and expecting a split-second decision—and pay that came too slight and too late to make any difference to his family's life. Whereas, as a court official, he could shower his relatives with clothes and food, and jewelry so beautifully fragile it seemed a mere breath would cut it in half.

And he could see the empress—and hide the twinge of regret that took him whenever he did so; that deep-seated knowledge that no lover he'd had since her had ever filled the void she'd left.

It wouldn't last, of course. It couldn't last. The empress was old, and the heir Huu Tam had no liking for her discards. Suu Nuoc would go home in disgrace one day, if he was lucky, or rot away in a jail somewhere if he was not. He lived with that fear as he'd lived with the fear of losing his battles when he'd been a general. Most days, it didn't affect him. Most days, he could sleep quietly in his bed and reflect on a duty carried to its end.

And sometimes, he would look at these—at the arrogant courtiers before him—and remember they would be among the ones baying for his head after the empress died.

"You have no business infringing on an imperial investigation," Suu Nuoc said. "The empress, may she reign ten thousand years, is the one who will decide who is told what, and when."

Winces, from the front of the mob—Courtier Hanh was clearly sniggering at this upstart who could not even speak proper Viet, and her companion Vinh was working himself up for a peremptory answer. Meanwhile, in the background of Suu Nuoc's own consciousness—in the space where he hung motionless, connected to a thousand bots crawling all over the palace, a churning of activities—a taking apart of messages and private notes, an analysis of witnesses' testimonies, and a forensic report on the state of the laboratory.

Later.

He watched the courtiers Vinh and Hanh; dared them to speak. As he had known, they did not have his patience; and it was the florid, middle-aged man who spoke first. "There are rumors that Grand Master Bach Cuc is dead, and Bright Princess Ngoc Minh forever lost."

"Perhaps," Suu Nuoc said, with a shrug, and watched the ripples of that through the crowd. Neither Vinh nor Hanh seemed much surprised, though they could not have sweated more if it had been monsoon season. "That is none of my business. I will find Grand Master Bach Cuc, and then all will be made clear."

Again, he watched them—there was no further reaction, but the air was charged, as if just before a storm. Ngoc Minh's return was not welcome, then. Not a surprise. "I suggest you disperse. As I said—you will be apprised, one way or another."

Quick, furtive glances at him; he remembered he'd said much the same thing to Ngoc Ha—had he meant it with her as well? She was an odd one, the younger princess—mousy and silent, by all accounts a dull reflection of her elder sister. They might not have liked each other; but then again, would Bright Princess Ngoc Minh's return change anything for the worse in her situation? Ngoc Ha was isolated and in disfavor, and her prospects were unlikely to improve.

"You have heard the general. I would highly suggest you do disperse." A sharp, aged voice: Lady Linh, with a red seal of off ice imprinted into her clothes that made it clear she spoke as the empress's voice; and flanked by two ghost-emperors—the twenty-third and the thirteenth, if Suu Nuoc remembered correctly. The bots scuttling around her held the folds of her robe in a perfect circle.

Lady Linh gestured for him to enter his own room. "We need to talk," she said, gracefully.

Inside, the two dead emperors prowled, staring at the rumpled bed and the half-closed chests of drawers as if they were some kind of personal insult. Suu Nuoc did his best to ignore them as he offered tea to Lady Linh, but from time to time one of the emperors would make a sharp sound in his throat, like a mother disapproving of a child's antics, and the general would freeze, his heart beating like the wings of a caged bird.

Not his world. Did they know about his relatives—his cousins and aunts and uncles, greedily asking for favors from the court and never understanding why he couldn't grant them? Did they know about Mother, the poor bots-handler who held her chopsticks close to the tip and slurped her soup like a laborer?

Of course they did. And of course they would never forgive him that.

"Tell me," Lady Linh said. She shook her clothes; in the communal network, the seal unfolded, spreading until it covered the entire room—a red filigree peeking underneath the painted floor, its edges licking at the base of the walls like flames. Bao Hoa. Keeper of the Peace.

Not so different from the battlefield, after all. Suu Nuoc shut off the bots for a moment, and called to mind all that they'd poured into his brain on the way back from Grand Master Bach Cuc's laboratory.

"She removed the implants herself," he said, finally. "It might have been under duress, all the same—for someone who was skilled with bots, it's a shoddy job—bits of flesh still sticking to the connectors, and a few wires twisted. Nothing irreplaceable, of course. If I were to guess—"

"Yes?"

"I think she was about to do something that needed absolute focus, and that's why the implants were removed. No distractions." No ancestors whispering in her mind; no ghostly manifestations of the past—he could only imagine it, of course; but it would be a bit like removing all his network syncs before leaping into battle.

"Go on," Lady Linh said, sipping her tea.

"Her correspondence is also interesting. The mails taper off: I think she was so busy with her work, so close to a breakthrough, that she wasn't answering as quickly as usual. I asked, but nothing seemed to be going on in her personal life—she had a girlfriend and a baby, but the girlfriend didn't see anything wrong."

"The girlfriend?" Lady Linh asked.

Suu Nuoc knew what she meant. The partner was often the first suspect. "I don't think so," he said. He'd interviewed her—Cam Tu, a technician in a city lab, working so far away from court intrigues she hadn't even had any idea of who he was or what he wanted. "She wasn't in that night, nor was she aware of any of the context behind Grand Master Bach Cuc's research." It was—sad, in a way, to see this hunched woman with the child at her breast and realize that Bach Cuc had deliberately shut her out of her life. But then again, he barely talked about the court when he did go home, so who was he to criticize? "Whatever happened to her, it was linked to the court."

"You talked of a breakthrough. The trail of the Citadel?"

"I think so, yes," Suu Nuoc said, slowly. "But that's not all." Something felt off to him, and he couldn't pinpoint what. "I'm still analyzing the communications." It was the one thing the bots couldn't do for him; and he wasn't too sure he would be able to do it by himself either—where were the mem-implant ancestors when one needed them? A lot of it was abstruse mathematics; communications with other scientists in faraway labs, discussing methods and best practices, and screen after screen of equations until it felt his brain would burst. He was a soldier, a general, a passable courtier, but certainly never a mathematician. "There is . . . something," he said. He hesitated—looking at the two emperors, who had stopped walking around the room, and come to stand, like two bodyguards, by Lady Linh's side. "I'm not sure—"

Lady Linh set her teacup down, and looked at him for a while, her seamed face inexpressive. "I was forty years old when I wrote my memorial," she said, with a nod to the twenty-second emperor. "The one that sent me to trial. I've never regretted speaking up, Suu Nuoc; and you don't strike me as the type that would regret it, either." Her voice had lost the courtly accent, and taken on the earthy tones of the outlying planets—he couldn't quite place it, but of course there were dozens of numbered planets, each of them with a multitude of provinces and magistrate fiefs.

The twenty-second emperor spoke—still in the body of a boy, his youthful face at odds with the measured voice, the reasonable tone. "Speaking up is sometimes unwise," he said, with a pointed look at Lady Linh. "But one should always tell the truth to emperors or their representatives."

"Indeed," Lady Linh's face was, again, expressionless. A truth that had sent her to jail for years, but that wasn't what Suu Nuoc feared.

He looked again at her, at the two emperors. Someone at court might be responsible for Grand Master Bach Cuc's disappearance, and they wouldn't take too kindly to efforts to make her reappear. Who could he trust?

It was a sacrilegious thought, but he wasn't even sure he could trust the dead emperors. Yet, because he would not disobey a direct order, or the intimation of one: "A man came to see Grand Master Bach Cuc. A merchant from the Scattered Pearls Belt named Quoc Quang, who said he needed to warn her."

"Warn her? Why should he need to warn her? A peasant from the outreaches of the empire, to see the best Grand Master of Design Harmony in the empire?" The twenty-second emperor asked.

"I don't know," Suu Nuoc said. "But he did see her; and she disappeared after that. And then he disappeared, too. With your permission, I would like to go to the Scattered Pearls Belt and question him." He'd thought long and hard about this: the Belt was a few days' journey from the First Planet via mindship; and, should he leave now, he wouldn't be far behind Quoc Quang.

"You assume he will return home," Lady Linh said.

"I see no indication he won't," Suu Nuoc said. His intuition—and he'd had time to learn when to trust his intuition—was that Quoc Quang was a witness, not a killer. He'd left well before Grand Master Bach Cuc disappeared, and the analysis of Bach Cuc's mem-implants showed, beyond a shadow of a doubt, that she'd removed them hours after her meeting with him. But whatever he'd said to her—it had struck home, because he had a record of her pacing the laboratory for half an hour after Quoc Quang had left—the only video he could grab from the feeds. After that, Bach Cuc herself had turned everything off.

Absolute focus. What had she been doing—or been forced into doing?

"I see," Lady Linh said. "You could send the Embroidered Guard to arrest him."

"Yes," Suu Nuoc said. "I could. But I'm not sure he would arrive here alive." Fast, and blunt, like a gut punch. He saw the other emperor, the thirteenth, wince, his boy's face twisted and rippling like a visage underwater.

"Court intrigues?" Lady Linh said, with a slight smile—Heaven only knew how many intrigues she'd weathered. On whose side did she stand? Not with the emperors, that was for sure—she was loyal to the empress, perhaps, seeking only the return of Bright Princess Ngoc Minh. And yet, if Ngoc Minh did come back, her small, comfortable world where she was once more esteemed and listened to might vanish. . . .

Lady Linh's eyes unfocused slightly, and the red seal on the floor blinked, slowly, like the eye of some monster. "The empress is informed. She agrees with your assessment. You will take *The Turtle's Golden Claw* to the Scattered Pearls Belt, and interrogate this . . . Quoc Quang." Lady Linh's tone was slightly acerbic and slightly too resonant: clearly she was still in contact with the empress. "You will also take Thousand-Heart Princess Ngoc Ha with you."

What? Suu Nuoc fought the first imprecation that came to his lips. He didn't need a courtier with him; no, worse than a courtier, a princess who might have direct interest in burying her sister for good. You can't possibly—He took a deep, shaking breath. "Respectfully—"

"You disagree." Lady Linh's face was the empress's serene, otherworldly mask, the one she wore when passing judgment; the same one she'd probably worn when exiling Bright Princess Ngoc Minh—though he hadn't been there to see it, of course, and he wouldn't have dared ask it of her. He was—had been—the lover of an empress—pleasant, good in bed—but in no way a close confidante or a friend. He'd smiled and never admitted how much it hurt to do so. "That is not a possibility, I'm afraid, General."

The thirteenth emperor leant over the table, his hand going through the teapot. "You will need someone versed in court intrigues." He'd been eight when he'd died; a boy, crowned by the ruling officials because they needed someone malleable and innocent. But in the implants he sounded older and wiser than both of them.

"I don't know where Ngoc Ha stands," Suu Nuoc said, stiffly.

"The Thousand-Heart Princess stands exactly where I need her, as I need her," Lady Linh said, except it was neither her voice, nor her expression.

Suu Nuoc bowed to the face of his empress. "Of course, Empress. As you desire."

The Engineer

When she'd stepped through the harmonization arch, Diem Huong had expected to die. In spite of what Lam had said—that the door did indeed open into the past—it could have led to so many places; an inhabitable planet, the middle of the vacuum, the deadly pressured heart of a star. . . .

Instead, she'd found herself in a wide, open corridor, with the low, warm light typical of space habitats—and the same sharp, familiar tang of recycled air in her nostrils. She turned and saw the outline of the arch in the wall behind her, half-hidden beneath the scrolling calligraphy of Old Earth characters, spelling out words and poems she could not read.

So there was a way back, at least. Or something that looked like one.

The corridor was deserted and silent. She reached out, cautiously, for the wall, and felt the surface slightly give way to her, the text flowing around her outstretched hand, and then back again once she withdrew her hand. She was here, then, for real. Wherever this was, or whenever—but she remembered the smell, that faint memory of sandalwood and incense that was always home to her, and that sense of something large and ponderous always hovering in the background, that feeling of calm before words of condemnation or praise were uttered.

The Citadel.

At last.

Mother . . .

She was back, standing in what would become the memories of her childhood home, and she didn't know what to feel anymore—if she should weep or shout or leap for joy. She simply stood, breathing it all in, savoring that feeling. For a moment, she was a child again—running down the corridors with Thuy and Hanh, reprogramming the kitchen's bots to manufacture fireworks they could set off in the little park—secure in the knowledge that she'd find Mother in the kitchen, her hands smelling of garlic and lime and fish sauce, and there would be rice on the table and broth boiling away on the stove, clinging to her hands and clothes like perfumed smoke.

A moment only; but in so many ways, she was no longer a child. She had lived six years on the Citadel in blissful ignorance, but ignorance was no longer bliss.

She needed to find Mother.

In the alcove by her side was a little altar to gods with fruit and sticks of burning incense. She reached out and touched it, feeling the stickiness on her hands; the smell clinging to her clothes—whispering a prayer to whoever might be listening. Her touch set the mangos slightly askew, and she did not dare touch them again: superstition, but who knew what might help her, in this strange place that was neither now nor then?

Lam had given her a speech, once, about going back in time; about paradoxes and the fact that she wouldn't be able to affect anything; but Diem Huong hadn't been paying enough attention. She wished she had. She wished she knew what would happen, if she met herself; if she harmed Mother, one way or another.

There was a stack of eight incense sticks by the altar: on impulse, she lit one, and kept one with her, for good luck. As she did so the screen above the altar came alive, asking her what she wanted—as if it had seen her, recognized her as a citizen, even though she didn't have the implants that would have enabled such a thing. She felt a thrill run through her, even as she told the screen to go dark.

The Citadel.

She wanted to leap, to rush to where Mother would be, to talk to her before it all disappeared, before whatever miracle had brought her here vanished, before Lam somehow found a way to bring her back, before she died. She forced herself to stop; to hold herself still, as if Mother were standing with her, one hand steadying her shoul.der, her body tranquil beside her, absorbing all her eagerness to move. She needed . . .

She needed to think.

As she walked out of the corridor and onto a large plaza, she saw people giving her odd looks—she wore the wrong clothes, or walked the wrong way. As long as she didn't stop for long, it wouldn't matter. But, eventually . . .

Diem Huong closed her eyes. Once, thirty years ago, Mother had had her memorize the address and network contact for the house, in case she got lost. She'd had so many addresses and contacts since then; but this was the first and most treasured one she'd learnt.

Compartment 206, Eastern Quadrant, The Jade Pool. And a string of numbers and symbols that, input into any comms system, would call home.

The network implants she'd had as a child had been removed six months after the Citadel vanished, when Father finally decided there was no coming back—when he started the long slow slide into drinking himself to death. She'd been too young to be taught by the hermits, and couldn't teleport or weaponize her thoughts, the way the others did.

She would need to ask someone for help.

The thought was enough to turn her legs to jelly. She wanted to keep her head down—she didn't need to be noticed as a time traveler or a vagrant, or whatever they'd make of her.

To calm herself down, she walked farther. The plaza was flanked by a training center: citizens in black robes went through their exercises—the Eight Pieces of Brocade, the same ones she still did every morning—under the watchful eyes of a yellow-robed Order member. At the furthest end, an old woman was staring at sand; eventually the sand would blow up, as if there had been a small explosion; and then she'd stare at some other patch.

Who to ask? Someone who would take her seriously, but who wouldn't report her. So not the order member, or the trainees. The noodle seller on the side, watching negligently as her bots spun dough into body-length noodles, and dropped them into soup bowls filled with greens and meat? The storyteller, who was using his swarm of bots to project the shadows of a dragon and a princess on the walls?

Something was wrong.

Diem Huong looked around her. Nothing seemed to have changed: the noodle seller was still churning out bowl after bowl; the same crowd of people with multiple body mods was walking by, idly staring at the trainees.

Something—

She opened her hand. The incense stick she'd taken was no longer in it—no, that wasn't quite accurate. It had left a faint trace: a ghost image of itself, that was vanishing even as she stared at it, until nothing was left—as if she'd never taken it from the altar at all.

That was impossible. She ran her fingers on her hand, over and over again. No stick. Not even the smell of it on her skin. And something else, too: her hands had been sticky from touching the ripe mangoes on the altar, but now that, too, was gone.

As if she'd never touched it at all.

No.

That wasn't possible.

She ran, then. Heedless of the disapproving stares that followed her, she pelted back to the deserted corridor she'd arrived in—back to that small altar where she'd lit an incense stick and disturbed the fruit.

All the while, she could hear Lam's lecture in her mind—spacetime projections, presence matrices, a jumble of words bleeding into each other until they were all but incomprehensible. It had been late, and Diem Huong had been on her fiftieth adjustment to a piece's circuits—waiting by the side of the oven for her pattern to set in, absent-mindedly nibbling on a rice cake as a substitute for dinner. She hadn't meant to shut Lam out, but she'd thought she could ask again—that there would be another opportunity to listen to that particular lecture.

The altar was there. But other things weren't: the incense stick she'd lit had disappeared, and the fruit was back to the configuration she'd originally found it in. Her heart madly beating against her chest, she turned to the stack of incense sticks. Eight. Not seven, or even six. Eight, exactly the number she had found.

Bots could have done it, she supposed—could have brought back the missing sticks and straightened out the altar, for some incomprehensible reason—but bots couldn't remove a stick from her hands, or wash the mangoes' sugar from her skin. No, that wasn't it.

Her heart in her throat, she turned toward the space in the wall, to see the imprint of the arch.

But that, too, was gone; vanished as though it had never been.

• • •

You won't affect anything. That's the beauty of it. No paradoxes. Don't worry about killing yourself or your mother. Can't be done.

Later, much later, after Diem Huong had walked the length and breadth of the ship she was on (*The Tiger in the Banyan's Hollow*, one of the smaller, peripheral ones that composed the Citadel), she measured the full import of Lam's words.

She was there, but not there. The things she took went back to where she had taken them; the food she tasted remained in her stomach for a few moments before it, too, faded away. She wasn't starving, though; wasn't growing faint from hunger or thirst—it was as if nothing affected her. In her conversations with people, their eyes would start to glaze after anything simpler than a question—forgetting that she stood there at all, that she had ever been there. She could speak again, and receive only a puzzled look—and then only puzzled words as the conversation started over again, with no memory of what had been said before. If she made no effort to be noticed—if she did not run or scream or make herself stand out from the crowd in any way—people's gazes would pause on her for a split second, and then move on to something else.

You won't affect anything, Lam had said, but that wasn't true. She could affect things—she just couldn't make them stick. It was as if the Universe was wound like some coiled spring, and no matter how hard she pulled, it would always return to its position of equilibrium. The bigger the change she made, the more slowly it would be erased—she broke a vase on one of the altars, and it took two hours for the shards to knit themselves together again—but erasure always happened.

She moved plates and vases, turned on screens and ambient moods, and saw everything moving back into place, everything turning itself off, and people dismissing it as nothing more than a glitch.

At length, she sat down on the steps before the training center and stared at nothing for a while. She was there, and not there—how long would she even be in the Citadel? How long before the Universe righted itself, and she was pulled back—into Lam's laboratory, or into some other nothingness? She stared at her own hands, wondering if they were turning more ghostly, if her whole being was vanishing?

Focus. She needed to. Focus. She looked at the screens: time had passed from morning to later afternoon, and the light of the ship was already dimming to the golden glow before sunset. Ten days before the Citadel vanished—nine and a half, now. And if she was still onboard . . .

If it was all for nothing, she might as well try to get the answers she'd come here for.

She got up and went to one of the monks in the training center: she picked one who was not teaching any students, and simply seemed to be sitting on a bench in the middle of the gardens, though not meditating either: simply relaxing after a hard day's work. "Yes, daughter?" he asked, looking at her. His eyes narrowed, wondering what she was doing there— she stood out in so many painful ways.

She had perhaps a handful of moments before he started forgetting she was there.

"I was wondering if you could help me. I need to get to The Jade Pool." *Compartment 206, Eastern Quadrant.*

"You need to get elsewhere. Like the militia's off ices," the monk said. He was still watching her, eyes narrowed. "You're not a citizen. How did you steal onboard?"

"Please," she said.

His eyes moved away from her, then focused again, with the same shocked suspicion of the first look. "How can I help you, daughter?"

"I need to get to The Jade Pool," Diem Huong said. "Please. I'm lost."

"That's not a matter for me. I need to report this to the Embroidered Guard."

She felt a spike of fear, and then remembered that no one would remember the report minutes after he had made it. "You don't need to do this." But his eyes again had moved away. It was useless. "Thank you," she said.

She walked away from him, feeling his eyes on the back of her head, and then, as time passed, the gaze lessen in intensity, until he looked right past her, not remembering who she was or that he had talked to her.

A ghost. Worse than a ghost—a presence everyone forgot as soon as she left their life. A stranger in her own childhood, fighting against the spring of the Universe snapping back into place. How was she ever going to get to Mother?

Lam. Help me. But it was useless. Her friend couldn't hear her. No one could.

Unless—

She wasn't really here, was she? She walked and took things like anyone else, except nothing stuck. She didn't have the implants everyone had that enabled them to teleport from one end of the Citadel to another. She didn't really have any presence here, and yet she could still move things for a while; could still make screens respond to her.

Mother had talked about teleportation, and so had Father, in his cups or on the long nights when he railed against the unfairness of the world. It had been a matter of state of mind, they'd both said—of being one with the mindships that composed the Citadel—to see the world in their terms until everything seemed to be connected—until the world itself was but a footstep away. And of implants; but perhaps it wasn't about implants after all. Perhaps the rules of the past were different from those of the present.

Compartment 206, Eastern Quadrant. The Jade Pool.

Diem Huong closed her eyes, and concentrated.

The Empress

Mi Hiep prepared for her audience with the envoys of the Nam Federation as if she were preparing for war. Her attendants gave her the dress habitually reserved for receiving foreign envoys: a yellow robe with five-clawed dragons wending their ways across her body; a headdress bedecked with jewels. For the occasion, she had the alchemists alter her body chemistry to grow the fingernails of her two smallest fingers on each hand to three times their usual size, encasing them in long, gold protectors that turned her fingers into claws.

Huu Tam, her heir, waited by her side decked in the robe with the five-clawed dragons that denoted his position. He looked nervous—she'd had him leave his usual mob of supporters at the door, and she knew it would make him feel vulnerable, a small child scolded for wrongdoing. Good, because he needed vulnerability; needed to be off-balance and question himself to negate his tendency to be so sure of himself that he didn't stop to consider what was best for the empire. "Mother," he said, slowly, as Mi Hiep dismissed the attendants. "I'm not sure—"

"We've been over this," Mi Hiep said. "Do you think peace is worth any sacrifice?"

"We can't fight a war," Huu Tam said. He grimaced, looking for a moment much older than he was.

"No," Mi Hiep said. "And I'll do my best to see we don't. But we might have to, nevertheless."

Huu Tam nodded, slowly. He didn't like war; an occupation unworthy of a scholar. But he'd never been faced with decisions like these—wasn't the one who'd looked into Ngoc Minh's face and sent ships toward the Citadel of the Bright Princess with the order to raze it—wasn't the one who'd lain down on his bed afterward, waiting for the sound of his heartbeat to become inaudible again, for the pain against her ribs to vanish into nothingness.

He was her heir. He had to learn; and better early on, while she was still flesh-and-blood and not some disembodied, loveless ancestor on the data banks.

Mi Hiep sat on her throne, and waited—muting the communal network, as it would be a distraction more than anything else. She didn't need to see the banners above her head to know her full name and titles, and neither did she need access to her implants to remember everything Lady Linh and her advisors had told her.

The envoys would deny everything; dance and smile and pretend nothing was wrong. She, in turn, would have to make it clear that she was ready for war; and hint that she was not without resources, in the hopes the Nam Federation would seek easier prey.

Huu Tam moved to stand on her left, and she summoned, with a gesture, all of her ancestors' simulations, from the first emperor to her mother, the twenty-fourth empress: her chain of uninterrupted wisdom, all the way since the beginning of the dynasty, her living link to the past. Her true ancestors might well be dead, spun by the Wheel of Rebirth into other lives, but their words and personalities lived on, preserved with the same care Old Earthers had preserved poems and books.

They stood, on either side of her, as the envoys approached.

It was a small delegation: a florid, rotund woman flanked by a pinch-faced man and another, more relaxed one who reminded Mi Hiep of the hermits that had once attended Bright Princess Ngoc Minh. They both knelt on the floor until Mi Hiep gave them permission to rise: they remained on their knees, facing her—though there was nothing servile or fearful in their attitude. They looked around the lacquered pillars of the hall at the proverbs engraved on the floor, and the exquisite constructs of the communal network—and their eyes were those of tigers among the sheep.

The woman's name was Diem Vy; after the exchanges of pleasantries and of ritual gifts, she spoke without waiting for Mi Hiep to invite her to do so. "We are pleased that you have accepted to receive us, Empress. I understand that you have expressed some . . . concerns about our exercises."

Interesting. Mi Hiep expected dancing around the evidence, but Vy clearly did not care for this. Two could play this game. "Indeed," Mi Hiep said, wryly. "Massive movements of ships entirely too close to my borders tend to have this effect."

Vy's face crinkled in a smile—a pleasant, joyful one. Mi Hiep didn't trust her one measure. "Military exercises happen at borders," she said. "Generally, doing them near the capital tends to make citizens nervous."

"Fair point," Mi Hiep said. "Then this is nothing more than the norm?"

Vy did not answer. It was the other envoy, the serene-faced hermit—a man named Thich An Son—who answered. "A federation such as ours must always be ready to defend itself, Empress; and our neighbors have had . . . troubling activities."

"Not us," Mi Hiep said. If they were determined to be this transparent, she would not obfuscate. "We have no interest, at this time, in cryptic military games." Let them make of that what they willed.

Thich An Son smiled. "Of course not, Empress. We know we can trust you."

As if anyone here believed that, or the reverse. Mi Hiep returned the smile. "Of course. We will honor the treaties. We trust that you will do the same." And then, slowly, carefully, "I have heard . . . rumors, though."

Vy froze. "Rumors?"

Mi Hiep gestured to Lady Linh, who handed her a ghostly image of a folder stamped with the seal of the Embroidered Guard: a gesture merely for show, as she knew the contents of said folder by heart and had no need to materialize it in the communal network. "Troubling things," she said, coldly, as if she already knew it all. "Ships that look like distorted versions of mindships."

"Copying designs is not a crime," Vy said, a touch more heatedly than the occasion warranted.

"Indeed, not," Mi Hiep said. "If that is all there is to it." She opened the folder in network space, making sure that it was as theatrical as possible—letting them see blurred images of ships and planets seen in every wavelength from radio to gamma rays.

"I assure you, Empress, you have no reason to be afraid," Vy said, sounding uncommonly nervous.

"Good," Mi Hiep said. "We are not, as you know, without resources. Or without weapons. We have, indeed, made much progress on that front, recently."

"I see," the hermit delegate Thich An Son said, his serene face almost—but not quite—undisturbed. The interview had not gone quite as planned. Good. "If I may be so bold, Empress?"

"Go ahead," Mi Hiep said.

"On an unrelated matter . . . there are rumors that you might be . . . " He paused, seemingly to pick his words with care—but really more for show than for anything else. " . . . considering changes at court?"

Reconsidering your choice of heir. Locating Bright Princess Ngoc Minh and her errant weapons. Mi Hiep glanced at Huu Tam, knowing everyone would do the same. Her son still stood by her side, with no change in his expression. He believed his sister dead for many years, and the lack of a body, or the recent search, had not changed his mind. At least, Mi Hiep hoped it hadn't; hoped he wasn't the one responsible for Grand Master Bach Cuc's disappearance. Whatever happened, his position at court was secure; and he knew it.

But, nevertheless, she had to make her point. She'd known she might have to do this beforehand, and had prepared both herself and Huu Tam for this moment.

"I believe there will be changes at court," Mi Hiep said, coldly. "Though if you're referring to my choice of heir, I see no reason to alter it."

The envoys looked at each other. "I see," Thich An Son said. "Thank you for the audience, Empress. We will not trouble you any further."

After they had left, Lady Linh approached the throne and bowed. "It's bad, isn't it?" she said, without preamble.

Mi Hiep did not have the heart to chide her for the breach of protocol, though she could see a few of the more hidebound emperors frown and make a visible effort not to speak up to censure either her or Lady Linh. "You said you didn't know how far away their fleet was."

"Yes," Lady Linh said.

"It's close," Mi Hiep said, trying to loosen the fist of ice that seemed to have closed around her stomach. Close enough that they would send these envoys—not the ones that would lie and prevaricate better, not the ones that would buy time. The Nam Federation had seen no reason to do so, and that meant they expected to make an imminent attack.

"You gave them something to think about," the twenty-fourth empress said. Every time she spoke up, Mi Hiep's heart broke a little—it was her mother as a younger woman, but the simulation had preserved none of what had made her alive—simply collated her advice and her drive to preserve the empire into a personality the alchemists had thought would be useful—never thinking that the child who would become empress would need love and affection and all the support that could not be boiled down to appropriate words. It was one thing to know this for the old ones, the ones she'd never known; but for her own mother . . . "They think you have the Bright Princess's weapons, or something close."

"But we don't," Huu Tam said. "Her Citadel and weapons died with her."

Mi Hiep said nothing for a while. "Perhaps."

"Ngoc Minh has been dead thirty years, Mother," Huu Tam's voice was gentle but firm. "If she could, don't you think she would have sent you a message? Even when she was in rebellion against the throne she sent you communications."

She had; and in all of them she was bright and feverish with that inner fire Mi Hiep so desperately wanted to harness for the empire and couldn't.

Ngoc Minh, the Bright Princess, who only had to stare at things to make them detonate—her little tricks with vases and sand had expanded to less savory things: to people who moved through space as though it were water, who would implant trackers and bombs on ship hulls as easily as if they'd been bots; to substances that could eat at anything faster than the strongest acid; and to teleportation, the hallmark of the Citadel's inhabitants. It had given Mi Hiep cold sweats, thirty years ago—the thought of an assassin materializing in her bedchambers, walking through walls and bodyguards as though they'd never been there . . .

But now she desperately needed those weapons; or even a fraction of them. Now the empire was at risk, and she couldn't afford to turn anything down, not even her errant daughter.

"Has there been any word from Suu Nuoc?" she asked.

Lady Linh shook her head. "Some of your supporters are getting quite vocal against him," she said to Huu Tam.

He looked affronted. "I'm not responsible for what they choose to say."

Lady Linh grimaced, but said nothing. Mi Hiep had no such compunction. "They follow your cues," she said to Huu Tam. And Huu Tam didn't like Suu Nuoc—he never had. She didn't know if it was because of Suu Nuoc's bluntness or because he had once been her lover and thus close in a way Huu Tam himself never had been.

"No accusations yet," the first emperor said. "But a couple of strongly worded memorials making their way upward to the Grand Secretariat." He looked at Huu Tam with a frown. "Your mother is right. It is your responsibility to inspire your followers by your behavior"—it was said in a way that very clearly implied said behavior had not been above reproach, and Huu Tam visibly bristled—"or, failing that, rein them in with your authority."

"Fine, fine," Huu Tam said, sullenly. "But it's all nonsense, and you know it, Mother. It's not delusions that will help us. We need to focus on what matters."

"Military research and intelligence?" Mi Hiep asked. "That is also happening, child. Don't underestimate me."

"Never," Huu Tam said; and she didn't like the look in his eyes. He was . . . fragile in a way that none of her other children were; desperate for approval and affection, even from his concubines. But, out of all of them, he was the only one who had the backbone to rule an empire spanning dozens of numbered planets. *The best of a bad choice*, as Suu Nuoc would have said—trust the man to always find the most tactless answer to everything. No wonder Huu Tam didn't like him.

"We'll get through this," Mi Hiep said, with more confidence than she felt. "As you said, we are not without resources."

Huu Tam nodded, slowly and unconvincingly. "As you say, Mother. I will go talk to my supporters."

After he was gone, Lady Linh frowned. "I will ask the Embroidered Guard to keep an eye on him."

He's innocent, Mi Hiep wanted to say. A little weak, a little too easily flattered; but surely not even he would dare to go against her will?

But still . . . one never knew. She hadn't raised him that way, and even he was smart enough to know that being family would not protect him against her wrath. He had seen her send armies against Ngoc Minh when the threat of the Citadel had loomed so large in her mind she'd known she either had to do something, or remain paralyzed in fear that Ngoc Minh herself would act. She would weep if she had to exile or execute him, but she would not flinch. The empire could not afford weakness.

Mi Hiep erased the folder from the communal network, and tried to remember what the next audience was—something about water rights on the Third Planet, wasn't it? She had the file somewhere, with abundant notes on the decision she'd uphold—the district magistrate had been absolutely correct, and the appeal would be closed on those terms. But every time she paused, even for a minute, she would remember her daughter.

Ngoc Minh had said nothing when Mi Hiep had exiled her. She'd merely bowed. But though she'd lowered her eyes, her gaze still burnt through Mi Hiep's soul like a lance of fire, as if she'd laid bare every one of Mi Hiep's fears and petty thoughts.

Officially, the Bright Princess had disobeyed court orders one too many; had refused to set aside her commoner wife as a concubine and set up proper spouses' quarters. It was one thing to take lovers, but fidelity to one particular person was absurd: those days, it wasn't the risk of infertility—alchemists' implantations had all but removed it—but merely the fact that no one could be allowed to own too much of an empress's heart and mind. Favorites were one thing; wives quite another.

Unofficially—Mi Hiep had seen the vase, over and over, the monks teleporting from one end to another of the courtyards, and thought of what this would do the day it was turned against her.

"I will obey," Ngoc Minh had said. Had she known? She must have; must have guessed. And still she had said nothing.

"You're thinking of Ngoc Minh," the twenty-fourth empress said.

"Yes. How do you know?" She wasn't meant to be so perceptive.

"I'm your mother," the twenty-fourth empress said, with the bare hint of a smile; a reminder of the person she had been, once, the parent Mi Hiep had loved.

But she was none of those things. An empress stood alone, and yet not alone—with no compassion or affection; merely the rituals and rebukes handed on by the ghosts of the dead. "I suppose so," Mi Hiep said. And then, because she was still seeing her daughter's gaze, "Was I unfair?"

"Never," the first emperor said.

"You are the empress," the sixteenth empress said.

"Your word is law," the twenty-second emperor said, his boy's face creased in a frown. "The law is your word."

All true, and yet none of it a comfort.

Lady Linh said nothing. Of course she wouldn't. She had been imprisoned once already; she wasn't foolish enough to overstep her boundaries again. What Mi Hiep needed was one of her lovers or former lovers—Suu Nuoc or Ky Vo or Hong Quy—to whisper sweet nothings to her; to hold her and reassure her with words they didn't mean or couldn't understand the import of. But there was a time and place for that, and her audience room wasn't it.

But then, to her surprise, Lady Linh spoke up. "I don't know. You did the best you could, with what you had. An empress should listen to the wisdom of her ancestors, her parents, and her advisors—else how would the empire stand fast? This isn't a tyranny or a dictatorship where one can rule as whim dictates. There are rules, and rituals, and emperors must abide by them. Else we will descend into chaos again, and brother will fight brother, daughter abandon mother, and son defy father. You cannot do as you will. Ngoc Minh . . . didn't listen."

No. She never had.

But that wasn't the reason why Mi Hiep had exiled her. That wasn't the reason why, years later, Mi Hiep sent the army to destroy her and her Citadel.

Perhaps the rumors were right, after all; perhaps Mi Hiep was getting old, and counting the years until the King of Hell's demons came to take her; and wishing she could make amends for all that had happened.

As if amends would ever change anything.

The Younger Sister

Ngoc Ha had always felt ill at ease on *The Turtle's Golden Claw*. It was there that she'd given birth, panting and moaning like some animal, bottling in all the pain of contractions until a primal scream tore its way out of her like a spear point thrust through her lungs—and she'd lain, exhausted, amidst the smell of blood and machine oil, while everyone else clustered around the Mind she'd borne—checking vitals and blood flow, and rushing her to the cradle in the heartroom.

Alone. On *The Turtle's Golden Claw*, Ngoc Ha would always be alone and vulnerable, abandoned by everyone else. It was a foolish, unsubstantiated fear, but she couldn't let go of it.

But Mother had ordered her to come, and of course her orders were law. Literally so, since she was the empress. Ngoc Ha swallowed her fear until it was nothing more than a tiny, festering shard in her heart, and came onboard.

The Turtle's Golden Claw was pleased, of course—almost beyond words—her corridors lit with red, joyous light, the poems scrolling on the walls all about homecomings and the happiness of family reunions. She gave Ngoc Ha the best cabin, right next to the heartroom—grey walls with old-fashioned watercolors of starscapes. Clearly the ship had been working on decorating it for a while, and Ngoc Ha felt, once more, obscurely guilty she couldn't give her daughter more than distant affection.

She had taken an escort with her, and her maid—she could have kept them with her, but they would have brought her no company—not onboard this ship. So she left them in a neighboring room and stared at the walls, trying to calm herself as *The Turtle's Golden Claw* moved away from the First Planet and plunged into deep spaces—the start of their weeklong journey toward the Scattered Pearls Belt.

An oily sheen spread over the watercolors and walls, and everything began throbbing in no rhythm Ngoc Ha could name. She logged into the network, and spent the next day watching vids—operas and family sagas, and reality shows in which the contestants sang in five different harmonies or designed increasingly bizarre rice and algae confections with the help of fine-tuned bots. That way, she didn't have to look at the walls; didn't have to see the shadowy shapes on them; to see them slowly turning—watching her, waiting . . .

"Mother?" A knock at the door, though the avatar could have dropped straight into her cabin. "May I come in?"

Ngoc Ha, too exhausted and drained to care, agreed.

The small avatar of *The Turtle's Golden Claw* materialized next to her, hovering over the bedside table. "Mother, you're not well."

Really. Ngoc Ha bit off the sarcastic reply, and said instead, "I don't like deep spaces." No one did. Unless they were Suu Nuoc, who seemed to have a stomach of iron to go with his blank face. And at least they were normal spaces—not the other, higher-order ones the ship had accessed during her search for Ngoc Minh. "I need to stay busy."

"You do," a voice said, gravely. To her surprise, it was Suu Nuoc—who stood at the open door of her room with two Embroidered Guards by his side. His face was set in a faint frown, revealing nothing. Hard to believe Mother had seen enough in him to—but no, she wouldn't go there. It had no bearing on anything else.

"I have vids," Ngoc Ha said, shaking her head. "Or encirclement games, if you feel like you need an adversary." She hated encirclement games; but she needed a distraction—they'd forced her to cut the vids; to pay attention to what was going on in the cabin . . .

Suu Nuoc shrugged. "You knew Grand Master Bach Cuc."

"A little," Ngoc Ha said, warily.

"How were her relationships with the rest of the court?"

Mother had said something about court intrigues, which had made no sense to Ngoc Ha. Then again, she supposed it was a case of the one-eyed man in the land of the blind—Suu Nuoc was a disaster at anything involving subtlety. "She was like you." She hadn't meant to be so blunt, but the faint smell of ozone, the slight yield to the air, the twisting shapes on the walls—they were doing funny things to her. "Blunt and uninterested in anything that wasn't her mission." And proud, with utter belief in her own capacities as a scientist in a way that could be off-putting.

"I see." Suu Nuoc inclined his head. "But she must have had enemies."

"She was no one," Ngoc Ha said. Oily shadows trailed on the wall, unfolded hands like scissors, legs like knives. They were going to turn, to see her . . . "But her mission—that made her friends and enemies."

"Huu Tam?"

"Maybe." She hadn't had a heart-to-heart talk with Huu Tam since he became the heir—ironic, in a way, but then she and her brother had never been very close.

Unlike her and Ngoc Minh—a memory of fingers, folding her hands around a baby chick, of laughter under a pine tree in a solitary courtyard. She breathed in, and buried the treacherous thought before it could unmake her: She'd never grieved for Ngoc Minh. Why should she, when she'd always believed her sister to be alive?

But sometimes, the hollows left by absence were worse than those left by death.

Focus. The last thing she needed was for this grief to intrude on her interview with Suu Nuoc—who would see her hesitation and interpret it as guilt or as Heaven knew what else. "If Ngoc Minh had come back, things would have changed. But you know this already."

"Yes." Suu Nuoc's face was impassive. "What I want to know is how they would have changed for you."

"I don't know," Ngoc Ha said, and realized it was the truth. Why did Mother want Ngoc Minh back—for a change of heir, with the wolves and tigers at their doors, or simply because she was old, and wanted reconciliation with the Bright Princess, the only child she'd ever sent away? "Who knows what Mother thinks?"

"I did, once," Suu Nuoc said. It was a statement of fact, nothing more.

"Then guess."

"That would be beyond my present attributions."

"Of course," Ngoc Ha said. "Fine. You want to know what I think? I didn't much care, one way or another." Untrue—the thought of seeing Ngoc Minh again was a knot in her stomach that only tightened the more she pulled at it. "I wasn't going to rise higher. We all know it, don't we? I don't have the ruthlessness it takes to become empress." Huu Tam was too amenable to flattery—and his brothers were too weak and too inclined to play favorites. Ngoc Minh . . . Ngoc Minh had been intensely focused, dedicated to what she felt was right. But what was right had not included Mother's empire.

"You might still not be very happy to be relegated to the background again. She was your mother's favorite, wasn't she?" Suu Nuoc's voice was quiet. The shadows on the walls were stretching, turning, reaching for her . . . "Would you have been happy to see her back in your life?"

It wasn't that. She remembered a night like any other, when she had been tearing her hair out over an essay assigned by the Grand Secretary—remembered Ngoc Minh coming to sit by her—the rustle of yellow silk, the smell of sandalwood. She'd been busy by then—establishing her court of hermits and monks and mendicants, fighting the first hints of Mother's disapproval. "You're too serious, l'il sis," Ngoc Minh had said. "This isn't what matters."

Ngoc Ha wished she'd been smart enough then to ask the unspoken question; to ask her what truly mattered.

"Leave her alone," *The Turtle's Golden Claw* said: a growl like a tiger's, sending ripples into the patterns on the wall.

Suu Nuoc looked surprised, as if a pet bird had bitten him to the bone. "You know my orders."

"Yes," *The Turtle's Golden Claw* said. "Go to the Scattered Pearls Belt and find and arrest Quoc Quang. Nowhere in this do I see a justification for what you're doing now, Book of Heaven."

Suu Nuoc's eyes narrowed at the over-familiar choice of nickname. "I do what needs to be done."

The Turtle's Golden Claw did not answer, but the atmosphere in the room tightened like an executioner's garrote. Ngoc Ha, drained, merely watched—were they going to have it out? Such a stupid, wasteful idea to argue with a mindship in deep spaces.

At length, Suu Nuoc looked at Ngoc Ha. "I will leave you then, Your Highness." He bowed and left the room, and the tension in the air vanished like a burst bubble—leaving only the oily sheen and faint background noise of deep spaces around them, a cangue she could not escape.

"Thank you," Ngoc Ha whispered.

"It's nothing, Mother." *The Turtle's Golden Claw*'s avatar materialized in the center of the room, spinning left and right. "Just filial duty."

And what about motherly ones? Ngoc Ha suppressed the thought before it could undo her. No point in rehashing old wounds. "You wanted to find Ngoc Minh," she said. "How—"

The ship spun like glass blown by a master, gaining substance with every spin. "Grand Master Bach Cuc thought that deep spaces could be used—to go further. That there was something—" she stopped, picked her words again, "some place that was as far beyond them as deep spaces are to normal space. Places where time ceased to have meaning, where thirty years ago was still as fresh as yesterday."

"That's—" Ngoc Ha tried to swallow the words before they burnt her throat, and failed. "Esoteric babble. Unproved nonsense. I'm sorry." Grand Master Bach Cuc sounded as though she'd taken lessons from Ngoc Minh—like the Bright Princess, listened to hermits in some remote caves for far too long.

"That's all right." *The Turtle's Golden Claw* sounded disturbingly serene— Ngoc Minh again, standing in the courtyard by her room, smiling as Ngoc Ha shouted at her to behave, to see the plots being spun around her, the growing disenchantment of off icials for an heir who did not follow Master Kong's teachings. "I knew you'd say that. That's why I brought you this."

She wanted nothing of this—nonsense. She recoiled, instinctively, before realizing that *The Turtle's Golden Claw* had given her nothing tangible: just a link to a database that hovered in the air in front of her. It was labeled QUOC TUAN'S PERSONAL FILES: Suu Nuoc's personal name, as grandiloquent as he had been obscure. "You can't."

"Of course I can." *The Turtle's Golden Claw* laughed, childish and almost carefree. "You forget—he stored everything in my databanks. I have the highest access credentials here."

Suu Nuoc would kill her—drag her so far down into the mud she'd never breathe again, with a few well-placed words in Mother's ears. "You can't do that," Ngoc Ha said, again. "I'm a suspect in that investigation."

"Are you?" The avatar of her daughter shifted, for a moment; became the head of a woman who took her breath away—a heartbreakingly familiar face with Mother's thin eyebrows and Ngoc Minh's burning eyes—a gaze that pierced her like a lance of fire.

No, Ngoc Ha thought, no. She had wished many things; some of them unforgivable—but she had never acted against anyone, let alone Grand Master Bach Cuc.

"I will leave you," *The Turtle's Golden Claw* said, and out of courtesy, opened the door and crossed through it rather than gradually fading away. The link remained in Ngoc Ha's field of vision, shifting to a turtle's scale, then a polished disc of jade, and other things of value beyond measure. *The Turtle's Golden Claw* really had a peculiar sense of humor.

Ngoc Ha stared at it for a while, and thought of the last time she had seen her sister—a brief message on the night before the Citadel vanished, asking news from her and assuring her everything was well. She dragged it up from her personal space, where she'd sat on it all those years, and stared at it for a while. Nothing seemed to have changed about Ngoc Minh in the years she'd been away from the First Planet—the same burning intensity, the same eyes that seemed to have seen too much. She had to know about Mother's army on its way to her; had to know that her Citadel would soon be embroiled in a war with no winners; but nothing of that had shown on her face.

Ngoc Ha had not answered that message. She had gone back to bed, telling herself she would think of something, that she would find words that would make it all better, as Ngoc Minh had once done for her. By morning, the Citadel was gone, and Ngoc Minh forever beyond her reach.

Where was the Bright Princess now—hiding somewhere she wouldn't be perceived as a threat to Mother's authority? Dead all those years? No, that wasn't possible. Ngoc Ha would have known—surely there was something, some shared connection remaining between them that would have told her?

And then she looked again at that last communication, and realized, with a wrench in her stomach like the shutting of doors, that Ngoc Minh's face had become that of a stranger.

In the end, as *The Turtle's Golden Claw* had known, Ngoc Ha couldn't help herself. She took the link, and everything that the ship had given her, and started reading through it.

The bulk of the early pieces was Grand Master Bach Cuc's correspondence: her directions and discussions with her team, her memorials to Suu Nuoc, her letters asking scientists on other planets for advice—buried in there, too was an account of *The Turtle's Golden Claw*'s conception, implantation, and birth, which Ngoc Ha gave a wide berth to—no desire to see herself as a subject of Bach Cuc's scientific curiosity, dissected with the same precision she'd put into all her experimental reports.

What interested her were the last communications. The earlier reports had been verbose, obfuscating the lack of progress. These were terse to the point of rudeness—but it wasn't rudeness that leapt off the page—just a slow rising excitement that things were moving, that Bach Cuc's search would succeed at last, that she would be honored by her peers for her breakthrough, her discovery of spaces beyond deep spaces where time and individuality ceased to have meaning.

Esoteric nonsense, Ngoc Ha would have said—except that Grand Master Bach Cuc was one of the most pragmatic people she had ever met. If she believed it . . .

She read the correspondence from end to end, carefully. She wasn't a scientist, but unlike Suu Nuoc her broad education had gone deep into mathematics and physics, and the understanding of the rituals that bound the world as surely as Master Kong's teachings bound people. She could—barely—understand what it had been about from skimming the reports, and from what Bach Cuc had told her, before and after she'd carried *The Turtle's Golden Claw.*

And Bach Cuc had written a few reports already. She'd found a trail from the samples *The Turtle's Golden Claw* had brought back: trace elements that could only come from the Citadel's defenses; clouds of particles from the technology Ngoc Minh had used to blast vases to smithereens in the courtyard of the palace. Bach Cuc had started to draw a plan for following these to a source, hoping to reconstitute the path the Citadel had taken after it had vanished from the world.

Hoping to find Ngoc Minh.

And then something had happened. Was it Quoc Quang? Ngoc Ha remembered the man's despair, his quiet, strong need to convince her that he needed to see Grand Master Bach Cuc. It had been that—the entreaty with no expectations—that had convinced her, more than anything.

What had he said? That in the Scattered Pearls Belt his daughter and Tran Thi Long Lam were working on something to do with the Citadel? She hadn't recorded the conversation for future use, but she remembered the name.

Tran Thi Long Lam. She had the profile on her implants: a scholar from the College of Brushes, the kind of brilliant mind that would never work well within the strictures of the imperial civil service. It was, in many ways, a blessing for her that she'd left to take care of her sick parent. But . . .

Yes, there were several communications from a Tran Thi Long Lam—or, more accurately, from her literary name, the Solitary Wanderer. Addressed to Grand Master Bach Cuc, and never answered—opened and read with a glance, perhaps? They didn't come from a laboratory or a university; or anyone Bach Cuc would have recognized as a peer—she could be a snob when she wanted to, and Lam might be brilliant, but she was also young, without any reputation to her name beyond the abandonment of what Bach Cuc would perceive as her responsibilities to science.

Ngoc Ha gathered all the communications, and stared at them for a while. The first few sentences of the first one ran, "I humbly apologize for disturbing you. A common colleague of ours, Moral Mentor Da Thi from the Laboratory of Applied Photonics, has forwarded me some of your published articles on your research . . . "

No, Grand Master Bach Cuc would not have read very far into this kind of inflammatory statement, which barely acknowledged her as a superior before going on to question her research—the things that were going to make her fame and wealth. But Ngoc Ha was not Bach Cuc.

When Ngoc Ha was done reading, she stared at the wall, barely seeing, for once, the twisting, oily shadows that moved like broken bodies in slow motion. Warn Grand Master Bach Cuc, Quoc Quang had said, and now she understood a little of what he had meant.

Lam had been interested in Bach Cuc's research—possibly because whatever she was doing on her isolated orbital intersected it. She'd read it, carefully, applying everything she knew or thought she knew, and thought it worth writing to Bach Cuc.

Your research is dangerous.

Not because it could be weaponized; not because it was things mankind wasn't meant to know or any arrant outsider nonsense. No, what Lam had meant was rather more primal: that Grand Master Bach Cuc was wrong, and that it would kill her. Something about stability—Ngoc Ha read the second to last letter again—the stability of the samples *The Turtle's Golden Claw* was bringing back to the laboratory. Because they came from spaces where time had different meanings, they would tend to want to go back to those spaces. Lam thought this might happen in a violent, exothermic reaction—that all the coiled energy from the samples would release in one fatal explosion.

No, not quite. That wasn't what she'd said.

"Things disturbed have a tendency to go back to their equilibrium point. In this particular case, I have reasons to believe this would be in a single, massive event rather than multiple small ones. I hold the calculations of this at your disposal, but I enclose an outline of them to convince you . . . "

Things disturbed. She hadn't been saying "be careful, your samples might explode." She had been saying "be careful, do not experiment on your samples." She'd told Grand Master Bach Cuc that the manipulations she was doing in her shielded chamber could prove fatal.

That was the warning Quoc Quang had passed on to Bach Cuc, with enough desperation and enough personal touch to make her pay attention.

Except . . .

Except Grand Master Bach Cuc was proud, wasn't she? Unbearably so. She had listened, but she'd done the wrong thing. Ngoc Ha would have put the project on hold while she worked out the risks, but she wasn't the one whose reputation had been impugned by an uppity young scholar and an unimportant engineer and her drunken failure of a father.

She knew exactly what Bach Cuc had done. She had shown Quoc Quang out with a smile and her thanks—hiding the furious turmoil that must have seized her at receiving such a warning. She'd sat for a while, thinking on things—staring at the wall, just as Ngoc Ha was doing, trying to collect her thoughts, to think on the proper course of action.

And then she'd gone into the shielded chamber. She'd taken off her mem-implants because she'd needed absolute focus on what she was going to do; because she'd believed there might be a danger, but not to the level Lam was describing. Because she'd wanted to show the young outworlder upstart that she was wrong.

And it had killed the Grand Master.

She had to—no, she couldn't tell that to *The Turtle's Golden Claw*—couldn't distress the ship without any evidence.

But she had to tell Suu Nuoc.

The Officer

Suu Nuoc was surprised by the Scattered Pearls Belt. He couldn't have put his finger on what he'd expected—something both larger and less pathetic, more in tune with his mental image of what the Citadel had been?

It wasn't grand, or modern: everything appeared to have been cobbled together from scraps of disused metal, the walls looking like a patchwork of engineering, the communal network so primitive it required hard-wiring implants to have access to it—Suu Nuoc had refused, because who knew what they'd put in if he allowed them access?

Beside him, Ngoc Ha was silent, her escort trailing after her with closed faces. She had walked up to him earlier, on the shuttle taking them from the mindship to the central orbital, and had asked to speak with him in private. What she had then said . . .

He wasn't sure what to think of it. It sounded like the weakest chain of evidence he'd ever seen—wrapped into a compelling story, to be sure, but anyone could spin words, and especially a princess educated by the best scholars of the empire. He'd read the research, and Lam's emails to Grand Master Bach Cuc—and had noticed none of this. But he knew his weaknesses, and unlike scholars, he didn't have any mem-implants to compensate for his lack of education.

He'd thanked Ngoc Ha, and told her he'd think on it. "Don't tell my daughter," she'd said. For some reason, this had shocked him into silence—

only after she'd gone had he realized that it was one of the only times she'd referred to the ship in those affectionate tones.

According to Ngoc Ha, Grand Master Bach Cuc was dead; which he wouldn't admit. It would mean a setback in the search for Bright Princess Ngoc Minh, at a time when they could not afford setbacks. He needed to be sure, before he told anyone of this—Heaven, he wasn't even sure Ngoc Ha was entirely innocent in this. She'd hated her sister: that much was clear from her own words.

Focus. He needed to do his duty to the empress and the empire, and flights of fancy were unhelpful.

The Scattered Pearls Belt was governed by a council of elders, and a local magistrate who, like many of the low-echelon officials, looked stressed and perpetually harried. Yes, he knew of Quoc Quang, had always known he would be in trouble one day—it was the drugs, and the drink; he'd never been the same since his wife's disappearance. Yes, he'd come back recently from a voyage into the heart of the empire, and of course he would be happy to help the honored General Who Read the Book of Heaven in any way required.

The magistrate's obsequiousness, and the missing attempt to defend Quoc Quang, made Suu Nuoc feel faintly ill; but he tried not to let it show on his face. "Bring him to us," he said, more brusquely than he'd meant to, and was perversely glad to see the man flinch.

He watched as the magistrate intercepted a pale-looking clerk, and mentally tallied the time it was going to take to find Quoc Quang with their overstretched resources. Too much. "On second thought, cancel that order. Take us to him. It will be faster."

"He has a daughter, hasn't he?" Ngoc Ha asked, as the magistrate's clerks escorted them to another shuttle.

"Diem Huong," the magistrate said—with a frown. Clearly, he was about to add the daughter's behavior to a list of perceived sins against the empire, too. Coward, and a malicious one at that.

Suu Nuoc wouldn't stand for that. "Are you going to tell us about the daughter's failures, too?" he asked, conversationally.

The magistrate blanched—and Ngoc Ha winced. "No, of course not," he said—Suu Nuoc heard him swallow, once, twice, as his face went the color of ceruse. "It's just that . . . Diem Huong has always been odd."

"Odd?"

"Obsessed," one of the clerks said, a little more gently than the magistrate. "Her mother was on the Citadel. She vanished when Diem Huong was six, and Diem Huong never quite recovered from it." Her eyes were grave, thoughtful. "If I may—"

"Go on," Suu Nuoc said, though he wasn't fooled. The delivery was gentler, and meant more kindly, but it was the same, nevertheless.

Heaven, how he missed the battlefield, sometimes. Soldiers and bots wouldn't prevaricate, and whatever backstabbing might occur was short and clean.

"People break, sometimes," the clerk said. "Diem Huong . . . does her job, correctly. Helps her orbital with the hydroponics system. No one's ever had a complaint against her. But it's an open secret she and Lam, and a couple of other youngsters, were obsessed with the Citadel."

"Lam? Tran Thi Long Lam?" *The Turtle's Golden Claw* asked.

The clerk, startled, looked at the small avatar of the ship—hadn't even noticed it floating by her side. "Yes," she said. "A graduate of the College of Brushes—"

Suu Nuoc tuned her out as she started to list Lam's qualifications. The orbital was proud of Lam, as they hadn't been of either Quoc Quang or his daughter—because Lam was the local girl who had succeeded beyond everyone's wildest dream; granted, she'd had to return home, but everyone understood the necessity of caring for a sick father. Lam was cool-headed and competent and probably managed an important segment of her orbital—a position beneath her, but which she'd taken on without complaining on returning home. He'd seen it a thousand times already, and it was of no interest.

What mattered was Grand Master Bach Cuc, and Bright Princess Ngoc Minh.

He let the clerk drone on as their shuttle moved from the central orbital to the Silver Abalone orbital—focusing again on the messages Lam had sent Grand Master Bach Cuc. Warnings, using a language too obscure for him to make them out. Was Ngoc Ha right? He didn't know. He knew that she was right in her assessment of Bach Cuc: that the Grand Master was proud of her achievements, and hungry for recognition. A young person like Lam, daring to question her . . . No, she wouldn't have listened to her. It was a wonder she'd received Quoc Quang at all, but perhaps she had not dared to refuse someone introduced by Ngoc Ha herself.

It galled him to even entertain the thought, because one did not speak ill of the disappeared or the dead, but he had not cared much for Bac Cuc.

Quoc Quang's compartment turned out to be a small and cozy one— the kitchen showed traces of use so heavy the cleaning bots hadn't quite managed to make them disappear, and a faint smell of sesame oil and fish sauce clung to everything.

It also did not contain Quoc Quang, or his wayward daughter. The aged aunt who lived with them—quailing in the face of the Embroidered Guard—said he had gone out.

"Running away?" *The Turtle's Golden Claw* asked.

Suu Nuoc shook his head. Getting drunk, more likely. "Scour the teahouses," he said. "Can someone access the network?" Without it, everything seemed curiously bare—objects with no context or feelings attached to them. He ran a finger on the wok on the hearth, half-expecting information to pop up in his field of vision—what brand it was, what had last been cooked in it. But there was nothing.

The clerk nodded.

"Anything interesting?"

Silence, for a while. "A message from his daughter," she said at last. "Diem Huong. She says she's gone to work with Lam, at the teahouse."

Diem Huong. Long Lam. Suu Nuoc didn't even pause to consider. "Where is the teahouse?"

"I don't know—" the clerk started, and then another of her colleagues cut her off. "It's the old teahouse," he said. "Where the youngsters hang out, right by the White Turtle Temple on the outer rings."

"Take us there," Suu Nuoc said. "And keep looking for Quoc Quang!"

It was all scattering out—that familiar feeling he had before entering battle, when all the bots he was linked to left in different directions, and the battlefield opened up like the petals of flowers—that instant, frozen in time, before everything became rage and chaos; when he still felt the illusion of control over everything.

But this wasn't battle. This didn't involve ships or soldiers; or at least, not more than one ship. He could handle this.

He just wished he could believe his own lies.

The White Turtle Temple was a surprise, albeit a provincial one: a fragile construction of rafters and glass that stretched all the way to a heightened ceiling, a luxury that seemed unwarranted on an orbital—though the glass was probably shatter-proof, or not even glass. It had a quaint kind of prettiness; and yet . . . and yet, in its simple, affectless setup, it felt more authentic and warm than the hundred more impressive pagodas on the First Planet. When all this was over, Suu Nuoc should come there; should sit, for a while, in front of the statues of Quan Vu and Quan Am, and meditate on the fragile value of life.

The building next to the temple, squat and rectangular, had indeed been a teahouse—some tables were still outside, and the counter was lying in two pieces in the corridor. But that wasn't what raised Suu Nuoc's hackles.

The building glowed.

There was no other word for it. It was a faint blue radiance that seemed to seep through everything, making metal and plastics as translucent as high-quality porcelain—light creeping through every crack, every line of the walls until it seemed to be the glue that held it together. And it was a light that thrummed and throbbed, like . . .

He had seen this somewhere before. He gestured to the Embroidered Guard, had them position themselves on either side of the entrance. It didn't look as though there was any danger they could tackle—"unnatural light" not exactly being in their prerogatives. He'd been too cautious: he should have asked at least one of them to plug into the communal network—they would be blind to local cues. It had been fine when they'd just been on a mission to pick up a witness, but now . . .

He looked again at the light, wishing he knew what it reminded him of. That annoying buzz, just on the edge of hearing—like a ship's engine? But no, that wasn't it. How long had it been spreading? "I want to know if the monks of the temple filed a report," he said.

The magistrate looked at one of his clerks, who shook her head. "Not in the system."

Not so long, then. Perhaps there was still time.

But time for what?

"I can go in," a voice said. "Have a look." *The Turtle's Golden Claw.*

"Out of the question." Ngoc Ha's voice was flat and almost unrecognizable from the small, courtly woman who seldom spoke her mind so bluntly. "You have no idea what's in there."

"I'm not here," *The Turtle's Golden Claw* said. "Not really. It's just a projection—"

"There's enough of you here," Ngoc Ha said. "Bits and pieces hooked into the communal network. That's how you work, isn't it? You can't process this fast, this quickly, if you're not here in some capacity."

"Mother—"

"Tell me you're not here," Ngoc Ha said, relentless. Her hair was shot through with blue highlights—lifted as though in an invisible wind, and her eyes—her eyes seemed to burn. Did everyone look like that? But no, the clerks didn't seem affected to that extent. "Tell me there's no part of you here at all, and then I'll let you go in."

"You can't force me!" *The Turtle's Golden Claw* said. "Grand Master Bach Cuc—"

Ngoc Ha opened her mouth, and Suu Nuoc knew, then, exactly what she was going to say. He found himself moving then—catching the heated words Ngoc Ha was about to fling into her daughter's face and covering them with his own. "The Grand Master is probably dead, Ship. And what killed her might be inside."

There was silence; and that same unnatural light. At length the ship said—bobbing up and down like a torn feather in a storm—"She can't be. She can't—Mother—Book of Heaven—"

"I'm sorry," Ngoc Ha said.

"We're not sure—" Suu Nuoc started.

"Then there's still a chance—"

"Don't you recognize what this is?" Ngoc Ha asked.

"I've seen it before—"

Her voice was harsh, unforgiving. "It's the light of a harmonization arch, General."

She was right. Suu Nuoc suppressed a curse. Harmonization arches were localized around their surrounding frames—the biggest one he'd seen had been twice the size of a man and already buckling under the stress. They certainly never cast a light strong enough to illuminate an entire building. Whatever was going on inside, it was badly out of control.

"I need your help," he said, to *The Turtle's Golden Claw*.

"Yes?"

"Tell me if the illumination is stable."

The ship was silent for a while; but even before she spoke up, Suu Nuoc knew the answer. "No. The intensity has been increasing. And . . . "

More bad news, Suu Nuoc could tell. Why couldn't he have some luck for a change?

"I would need more observations to confirm, but at the rate this is going, it will have spread to the entire orbital in a few hours."

"Do you know what's inside?"

"Not with certainty, no. But I can hazard a guess. Some volatile reaction that should have required containment—except that the explosion has breached the arch," *The Turtle's Golden Claw* said.

Which was emphatically not good for the orbital, whichever way you put it. Suu Nuoc's physics were basic, but even he could intuit that. He took in a deep, trembling breath. The battle joined, again; the familiar ache in his bones and in his mind, telling him it was time to enter the maelstrom where everything was clean-cut and elegantly simple—where he could once more feel the thrill of split-second decisions; of hanging on the sword's edge between life and death.

Except it wasn't a battle; it wasn't enemy soldiers out there—just deep spaces and whatever else Bach Cuc had been working on, all the cryptic reports Suu Nuoc had barely been able to follow. Could he handle this? He was badly out of his depth . . .

But it was for the empress, and the good of the empire, and there was no choice. There had never been any choice.

He gestured to the Embroidered Guard. "Set up a perimeter, but don't get too comfortable. We're going in."

• • •

The Engineer

The world around Diem Huong shifted and twisted, and then vanished—and, for a moment, she hung in a vacuum as deep as the space between stars, small and alone and frightened, on the edge of extinction—and, for a moment, she felt the touch of a presence against her mind, something vast and numinous and terrible, like the wings of some huge bird of prey, wrapping themselves around her until she choked.

And then she came slamming back into her body, into a place she recognized.

Or almost did. It was—and was not—as Diem Huong remembered: the door to Mother's compartment, a mere narrow arch in a recessed corridor, indistinguishable from the other doors. From within came the smell of garlic and fish sauce, strong enough to make her feel six years old again. And yet . . . and yet it was smaller, and diminished from what she remembered; almost ordinary, but loaded with memories that threatened to overwhelm her.

Slowly, gently—not certain it would still remain there, if she moved, if she breathed—she raised a hand, and knocked.

Nothing.

She exhaled. And knocked again—and saw the tips of her fingers slide, for a bare moment, through the metal. A bare moment only, and then it was as solid as before.

She was fading. Going back in time to Lam's lab? To the void and whatever waited for her there?

No use in thinking upon it. She couldn't let fear choke her until she died of it. She braced herself to knock again, when the door opened.

She knew Mother's face by heart; the one on the holos on the ancestral altar, young and unlined and forever frozen into her early forties: the wide eyes, the round cheeks, the skin darkened by sunlight and starlight. She'd forgotten how much of her would be familiar—the smell of sandalwood clinging to her, the graceful movements that unlocked something deep, deep within her—and she was six again and safe; before the betrayal that shattered her world; before the years of grief.

"Can I help you?" Mother asked. She sounded puzzled.

She had to say something, no matter how inane; had to prevent Mother's face from creasing in the same look of suspicion she'd seen in the monk's eyes. Had to. "I'm sorry, but I had to meet you. I'm your daughter."

"Diem Huong?" Mother's voice was puzzled. "What joke is this? Diem Huong is outside playing at a friend's house. She's six years old."

"I know," Diem Huong said. She hadn't meant to say that, but in the face of the woman before her, all that came out was the truth, no matter how inadequate. "I come from another time," she said. "Another place."

"From the future?" Mother's eyes narrowed. "You'd better come in."

Inside, she turned, looked at Diem Huong—every time this happened, Diem Huong would wait with baited breath, afraid that this was it, the moment when Mother would start forgetting her again. "There is a family resemblance," Mother said at last.

"I was born in the year of the Water Tiger, in the Hour of the Rat," Diem Huong said, slowly. "You wanted to name me Thien Bao; Father thought it an inappropriate name for a girl. Please, Mother. I don't have much time, and I'm running out of it."

"We all are," Mother said, soberly. She gestured toward the kitchen. "Have a tea."

"There is no time," Diem Huong said, and then paused, scrabbling for words. "What do you mean, 'we're all running out of time'?"

Mother did not answer. She turned back, at last, and looked at Diem Huong. "Oh, I'm sorry, I hadn't seen you here. What can I do for you?"

"Mother—" the words were out of Diem Huong's mouth before she could think, but they were said so low Mother did not seem to hear them. "You have to tell me. Why are you running out of time?"

Mother shook her head. "Who told you that?"

"You did. A moment ago."

"I did not." Mother's voice was cold. "You imagine things. Why don't you come into the kitchen, and then we can talk." She looked, uncertainly, at the door. She wouldn't remember how Diem Huong had got in—she was wondering if she should call the militia, temporizing because Diem Huong looked innocuous, and perhaps just familiar enough.

Don't you recognize me, Mother? Can't you tell? I'm your daughter, and I need to know.

The corridor they stood in was dark, lit only by the altar to Quan Am in the corner—the bodhisattva's face lifted in that familiar half-smile—how many times had she stared at it on her way in or out, until it became woven into her memories?

"Please tell me," Diem Huong said, slowly, softly. "You said the Citadel still stood. You said you didn't know for how long." She should have started over; should have made up some story about being a distant relative, to explain the family likeness—or even better, something official-sounding, an investigation by a magistrate or something that would scare her enough not to think. But no, she couldn't scare Mother. Couldn't, wouldn't.

Mother's face did not move. Diem Huong could not read her. Was she calling the militia? "Come into the kitchen," she said, finally, and Diem Huong gave in.

She got another puzzled look as Mother busied herself around the small kitchen—withdrawing tea from a cupboard, sending the bots to put together dumplings and cakes that they dropped into boiling water. "I'm sorry," Mother said. "I keep forgetting you were coming today."

"It's nothing," Diem Huong said. The kitchen was almost unfamiliar— she remembered the underside of the table, the feet of chairs, but all of it from a lower vantage. Had she played there, once? But then she saw the small doll on the tiling, and knelt, tears brimming in her eyes. Em Be Be—Little Baby Sister. She remembered *that*; the feel of the plastic hands in hers; the faint sour, familiar smell from clothes that had been chewed on and hugged and dragged everywhere.

Em Be Be.

"Oh, I'm sorry," Mother said. "My daughter left this here, and I was too lazy to clean up."

"It's nothing," Diem Huong said again. She rose, holding the doll like a fragile treasure, her heart twisting as though a fist of ice were closing around it. "Really." She wasn't going to break down and cry in the middle of the kitchen, she really wasn't. She was stronger than this. "Tell me about the Citadel."

Mother was having that frown again—she was in the middle of a conversation that kept slipping out from under her. It was only a matter of time until she called the militia—except that the militia wouldn't remember her call for more than a few moments—or asked Diem Huong to leave, outright—something else she wouldn't remember, if it did happen.

Diem Huong watched the doll in her hands, wondering how long she had before it vanished; how long before she, too, vanished. "Please, elder aunt." She used the endearment; the term for intimates rather than another, more distant one.

"It's going to fall, one way or another," Mother said, slowly, carefully. "The empress's armies are coming here, aren't they?" She put a plate full of dumplings before Diem Huong and stared for a while at the doll. "I have to think of this. We're not defenseless—of course we're not. But the harm . . . " She shook her head. "You don't have children, do you?"

Diem Huong shook her head.

"Sometimes, all you have are bad choices," Mother said.

Diem Huong carefully set the doll aside, and reached for a dumpling— it'd vanish too, because Mother had only baked it for her. All traces of her presence would go away, at some point; all memories of her. "Bad choices," she said. "I understand, believe me." The dumpling smelled of dough and meat and herbs, and of that indefinable tang of childhood, that promise that all would be well in the end; that the compartment was and forever would be safe.

All dust, in the end; all doomed to vanish in the whirlwind.

"Do you?" Mother's voice was distant. Had she forgotten again? But instead, she said, "One day, my daughter will grow up to be someone like you, younger aunt—a strong and beautiful adult. And it will be because I've done what I had to."

"I don't understand," Diem Huong said.

"You don't have to." There were—no.

Mother—

There were tears in Mother's eyes. "No one leaves. We stand, united. Always. For those of us who can."

Mother, no.

Mother smiled, again. "That's all right," she said. "I didn't feel you'd understand, younger aunt. You're too young to have children, or believe in the necessity of holding up the world." And then her gaze unfocused again, slid over Diem Huong again. "Can you remind me what I was saying? I seem to be having these frightful absences."

She was crying; young and vulnerable and so utterly unlike Mother. Diem Huong had wanted . . . reassurances. Explanations. Embraces that would have made everything right with the world. Not—not this. Never this. "I'm sorry," she said, slowly backing away from the kitchen. "I'm really sorry. I didn't mean—"

It was only after she passed it that she realized her arm had gone through the door. She barely had enough time to be worried, because, by the time she reached the street, the Embroidered Guard was massed there, waiting for her with their weapons drawn.

The Empress

Mi Hiep sat in her chambers, thinking of Ngoc Minh, of weapons, and of lost opportunities.

Next to her, a handful of ancestors flickered into existence. They cast no shadow: below them, the ceramic tiles displayed the same slowly changing pattern of mist and pebbles—giving Mi Hiep the impression she stood in a mountain stream on some faraway planet. "There is news," the first emperor said. "Their fleet has jumped."

The La Hoa drive. "How far?" Mi Hiep asked.

"Not far," the twenty-second emperor said, fingering his beardless chin. "A few light-days."

Not mindships, then.

"They're going to jump again," Mi Hiep said, flatly. It wasn't a question.

"Yes," the first emperor said. "They're still outside the empire; but they won't be for long."

"There has been no news from the Scattered Pearls Belt," the twenty-second emperor said, with a disapproving frown. "You shouldn't have sent Suu Nuoc on his own."

Again, and again, the same arguments repeated with the plodding patience of the dead. "I sent Ngoc Ha with him."

"Not enough," the first emperor said.

The door to her chambers opened; let through Lady Linh and Van, the head of the Embroidered Guard; followed by Huu Tam, and two servants bringing tea and dumplings on a lacquered tray. "You wanted to see us," Lady Linh said. She carried the folder Mi Hiep had toyed with, which she laid on the table. In the communal network, it bulged with ghostly files. Linh wouldn't have put anything in it unless she had a good reason.

"You have something," Mi Hiep said, more sharply than she'd intended to.

Huu Tam bowed to her: he didn't look sullen, for once—and Mi Hiep realized the glint in his eyes was all too familiar.

Fear. The bone-deep, paralyzing terror of those on the edge of the abyss.

"I have intelligence," Van said, briefly bowing to Mi Hiep. Van, the head of the Embroidered Guard, was middle-aged now, with a husband and two children, but still as preternaturally sharp as she had been, twenty years ago, when a look from her had sent scholars scattering back to their offices.

"I told her about the fleet," the first emperor said, with a nod to Van. The emperors liked her—she was scary and utterly loyal; and with the kind of contained imagination that didn't challenge their worldviews.

Mi Hiep gestured: the pattern on the floor became a dark red—the color of blood and New Year's lanterns—and the pebbles vanished, replaced by abstract models.

Van opened the folder and spread the first picture on the table before Mi Hiep, over the inlaid nacre dragon and phoenix circling the word "longevity." It was an infrared with several luminous stains; even with the low definition it was easy to see that they didn't all have the same heat signature. "This is what we have on the fleet," she said.

"The different stains are different ships?" Mi Hiep asked. She bent closer, trying to keep her heartbeat at a normal rate. They'd leapt, but not far— they wouldn't be there for a while.

Van took out two other pictures—still infrared, but close-ups in a slightly different band. One was a ship Mi Hiep had already seen—the squat, utilitarian design of Nam engineers, with little heat signature that she could see, everything slightly blurred and unfocused as if she watched through a pane of thick glass. The second one . . . She'd seen the second one, too, before, or its likeliness: twisted and bent and out of shape, something that had once been elegant but was now deformed by the added, pustulous modules.

They take ships, Lady Linh had said. Influence what they see and think, with just a few modules. They took living, breathing beings, with a family, with love—and they turned them into unthinking weapons of war.

"Their ships, and their hijacked mindships." She was surprised at the calm in her voice. She couldn't afford to be angry, not now. Van had laid the last picture on top of the first one, but in the communal network it was easy enough to invert the transparency layers so that she was staring at the fleet again.

Three hijacked mindships, twenty Nam ships. "Do you know anything about the mindships?" Huu Tam asked.

Van shook her head. "We have asked the outlying planets for any reports on missing mindships. One of them fits the profile of *The Lonely Tiger*, a mindship that disappeared near the twenty-third planet. We haven't apprised the family yet because we're not sure."

Not sure. What would it do to them—what kind of destruction would it wreak among them? Mi Hiep thought of *The Turtle's Golden Claw*; but it was different. She'd ordered the ship made for a cause, and that cause outweighed everything else; even the love she might have been able to provide.

"I see." Mi Hiep took a deep breath.

"We need to evacuate," Huu Tam said.

Mi Hiep nodded. "Yes. That too. But first, I need you to capture one of these."

"The mindships?" Van grimaced. "That's possible, but we'll sustain heavy losses."

"Yes," Mi Hiep said. The time for cautiousness—for dancing with diplomats and subtle threats—had long since passed. "I know. But they found a way to turn those against us, and to make them follow the fleet. Did they leap at the same time as the others?"

"Insofar as we can tell, yes," Van said. "Not as far as the others—it was very clear they were waiting for them to play catch-up."

Which meant they weren't as efficient as they could be, yet—that they couldn't harness the full potential of a mindship; leaping any distance they wanted when they wanted. Which was good news, in a way. "They're not up to speed yet," Mi Hiep said. "Which means we can study their shunts, and find a way to break them."

Van looked dubious. "With respect—"

"I know," Mi Hiep said. It wasn't so much the research—Grand Master Bach Cuc hadn't been the only genius scientist she'd had available, and there were plenty of war laboratories knowledgeable in Nam technology. "We don't have much time."

"And we'll pay a horrendous price." Van grimaced. She knew all about the calculus of cruelty, the abacuses that counted losses and gains as distant beads, ones that could not cause grief or sorrow or pain. "I'll send the order. You do realize this is a declaration of war." Huu Tam looked sick, but he said nothing. She hadn't misjudged him: alone of her surviving children he had the backbone to realize what must be done, and to carry it through.

"Then war it is," Mi Hiep said. "Round up the Nam envoys, will you? And send them home." The Galactic outsiders considered them in, but both the Nam and the Dai Viet took a different position: they were their master's voices, and as such, the letters they bore, the words they uttered, were sacred. Their persons were not. But in this case, executions would not achieve anything, and it wasn't as though they had seen much that they could take back to their masters.

Van shrugged. She was more bloodthirsty than Mi Hiep. "As you wish."

The twenty-second emperor fingered the image, frowning. "Are they headed for the imperial shipyards?" he asked.

"Too early to tell with certainty," Lady Linh said. She gestured, and another image—of the ships' trajectories—was overlaid over the old one. "The trajectory is consistent, though."

Mi Hiep watched the red line, weaving its way through the outer reaches of the numbered planets. There was not, nor had there ever been, much choice. "There are ships at anchor, in the shipyards?"

"And Mind-bearers," the simulation of her mother said. "They're heavily pregnant: they won't be in a state to travel."

"They will have to," Huu Tam said. His face was harsh—good, he was learning. One did not become emperor of the Dai Viet by being squeamish. "How many are there?"

"Six."

"They'll fit onboard one of the ships." She spared a thought for what they were about to do; a shred of pity: she'd been pregnant, though not with a ship-mind, and she remembered all too well what it had felt like—deprived of sleep, gravid and unable to move without being short of breath. "Have them evacuate the station. Don't let the ship into deep spaces."

Everything got weird in deep spaces—and something as fragile as a fetus or the seed that would become a ship-mind would probably not bear it. "Probably"—no one had run experiments, or at least no one had admitted to it, though the sixteenth empress—who'd had a fondness for questionable science ethics—had come dangerously close to admitting it in Mi Hiep's hearing.

Lady Linh was looking at something on the network—a list of names. "There are four ships at anchor in the yards," she said. "*The Dragons in the Peach Gardens. The Blackbirds' Bridge. The Crystal Down Below. The Bird that Looked South.*" She moved text around and remained for a while, absorbing information. "The first two were here for refits. The others are young."

Young and vulnerable; still being taught by their mothers—children, in truth. Children whom she would have to send to war. Unless—"What about the military mindships?"

Van grimaced. "They're here already—we sent them a while ago. I've deployed them as protection."

"Good," Mi Hiep said. "Have the women and their birth-masters board *The Dragons in the Peach Gardens.*" An experienced ship was what they needed; not a younger, more panicked one who would be more likely to make mistakes. "Keep the young ships at anchor until the other ships have arrived." They wanted ships and the building facilities of the yard; she had to provide bait. Like Van, she had long since gotten used to making ruthless decisions in a heartbeat: two young ships against a chance to turn the tide—against the protection of dozens of others? It was an easy choice.

"Oh, and one more thing," Mi Hiep said. "The shells for those ship-minds?" The beautiful, lovingly crafted bodies, the shells of ships into which the Minds would be inserted after birth—months and months of painstaking work by the alchemists and the Grand Masters of Design Harmonies, fine-tuning every turn of the corridors to ensure the flow of *khi* would welcome the Mind within its new carapace. "Destroy them."

"Your highness," Van said, shocked. That stopped her, for a moment: she hadn't thought it was possible to shock Van.

To her surprise, it was Huu Tam who spoke. "The empress is right. They've come here for our technologies. Let us leave nothing for them to grasp."

Technologies. Mindships. Weapons. How she wished they had something better—everything she'd feared from Ngoc Minh. If only they had the Bright Princess on their side.

But they didn't, and there was no point in weeping for what was past or hoping for miracles. Whatever Suu Nuoc found in the Scattered Pearls Belt, it would be too late. War had come to her, as it had thirty years ago, and, as she had done in the past, she met it head-on rather than let it cow her into submission. She nodded to Huu Tam. "You understand."

Her son bit his lip, in an all too familiar fashion. "I don't approve," he said. "But I know what has to be done."

Good. If they didn't agree on most things, they could at least agree on this. "Send word to Suu Nuoc," Mi Hiep said, ignoring Huu Tam's grimace. "Tell him we're at war."

The Younger Sister

Suu Nuoc took the head of a detachment of three men and stepped forward, into the maelstrom of light. Ngoc Ha watched him from behind one of the overturned tables—something crackled and popped when he stepped inside, like burning flesh on a grill, but he didn't seem to notice it.

He said something, but the words came through garbled—he moved at odd angles; faster than the eye could see at moments, slow enough to seem frozen at others, every limb seemingly on a different rhythm like those nightmarish collages Ngoc Ha had seen as a child—a narrow, lined eye of an old Dai Viet within the pale, sallow face of a horse, the muzzle of a tiger with the smiling lips and cheeks of a woman, the familiar boundaries shattered until nothing made sense. Children's fancies, they had been, but what she saw now dragged the unease back into daylight, making it blossom like a rotting flower. "Suu Nuoc? Can you hear me?"

The Turtle's Golden Claw was hovering near the boundary, bobbing like a craft in a storm. "There's a differential," she said. "Different timelines all dragged together. If you gave me time—"

"No," Ngoc Ha said. She didn't even have to think; it came welling out of her like blood out of a wound.

Silence. Then *The Turtle's Golden Claw* said, sullenly, "I'm not a child, you know. You can't protect me forever."

"I wasn't trying," Ngoc Ha said, and realized, with a horrible twist in her gut, that this was true. She hadn't abandoned the ship—had played with her, taught her what she knew—but it had always been with that same pent-up resentment, that same feeling that the choice to have this child had been forced upon her, that Ngoc Minh was reaching from wherever she was and deforming every aspect of Ngoc Ha's life again. Thirty years. The Bright Princess had been gone thirty years, and in that time she had tasted freedom.

And loss; but the word came in her thoughts so quickly she barely registered it.

The Turtle's Golden Claw, heedless of her hesitations, was already skirting the boundary, making a small noise like a child humming—except the words were in some strange language, mathematical formulas and folk songs mingled together. "A to the power of four, the fisherman's lament on the water—divide by three times C minus delta, provided delta is negative—the Citadel was impregnable, the Golden Turtle Spirit said, for as long as his claw remained on the crossbow, and the crossbow remained in the Citadel . . ."

But the Citadel had fallen, and her sister was forever silent. Except, perhaps, inside, where all the answers awaited.

Ngoc Ha was hardly aware of moving—hardly aware of her slow crawl toward the boundary, until she stood by the side of *The Turtle's Golden Claw*—her hand trailing on what should have been air—feeling the hairs on her skin rise as if in a strong electrical current.

"Deep spaces," *The Turtle's Golden Claw* said. Her voice came out weird, by turns tinny and booming, as if she couldn't quite make up her mind at which distance she stood.

"Here? That's not possible—"

"Why not?" *The Turtle's Golden Claw* asked, and Ngoc Ha had no answer.

Ngoc Ha pushed; felt her hand go in as though through congealed rice porridge. Deep spaces. Shadows and nightmares, and that sick feeling in her belly; that fear that they would take her, swallow her whole and change her utterly.

And yet . . .

Yet, somewhere within, were people who might know where her sister was.

"Can we go in?" she asked; and felt more than saw the ship smile.

"Of course, Mother."

Inside, it was dark and cool—everything limned with that curious light—everything at odd angles, the furniture showing part of asteroids and metal lodes, and the flames of workshops; and legs and blank polished surfaces; and fragments of flowers lacquered on its surface at the same time—different times, different points of view merged together in a way that made Ngoc Ha's head ache.

She looked at *The Turtle's Golden Claw*, but the ship was unchanged, and her hands were the same, veined and pale. Perhaps whatever had a hold there didn't apply to them, but she felt, in the background, some great pressure; some great presence awakening to their presence—a muzzle raised, questing; eyes like two supernovae turned their way . . .

"Here," *The Turtle's Golden Claw* said, and waited, patiently, for her to follow. She heard muffled noises: Suu Nuoc's voice, coming from far away, saying words she couldn't make out, and noises of metal against metal—and the same persistent hum in the background, and the shadows on the walls, the same as on the ship, stretching and turning and changing into claws . . .

She took a deep, shaking breath. Why had she charged in?

As they went deeper in, the furniture straightened up. Things became . . . almost normal, save that everything seemed still charged with that curious, pent-up electricity. "Time differentials," *The Turtle's Golden Claw* said. "Like the eye of the storm." She whispered something, and after a while Ngoc Ha realized it was the same singsong incantations she'd said outside: "Integrate the quotient over the gradient lines—the princess' blood became pearls at the bottom of the river, and her husband committed suicide at her grave—four times the potential energy at the point of stability, divided by N . . ."

There was a door, ahead, and the light was almost blinding. Little by little—though it felt as if she was making no progress—they walked toward it, even as *The Turtle's Golden Claw* wove her equations together; her curious singsong of old legends and mathematics.

The lab reminded her of Grand Master Bach Cuc's: every surface covered with objects and odd constructs—pieces of electronics, half-baked, discarded ceramics; the light playing over all of them, limning them in blue. It was filled with Suu Nuoc's escort, the Embroidered Guards, standing ill at ease, wedged against bits and pieces of machines.

Ahead, another door: a harmonization arch, the source of all the light, and Suu Nuoc, kneeling by the side of a young, panicked woman who was putting two bits of cabling together. "It's overloading," she said.

"Turn it off," Suu Nuoc said. He glanced up, and nodded at Ngoc Ha as she knelt by her side.

The Turtle's Golden Claw was still humming—more warily, avoiding the edges of the harmonization arch. "You set up an access to deep spaces here?"

"As I said"—the young woman—Lam—took a brief, angry look at the mindship—"I didn't expect this to work!"

"Turn it off," Suu Nuoc said.

"I can't," Lam's voice was hard. "I have someone still inside."

"Diem Huong?" Ngoc Ha asked, and knew she was right. There was something about the arch; about what lay beyond it—there was something in the lab with them, that same vast presence she'd felt earlier, slowly turning toward them. "The disruption is spreading to the orbital."

"Yes," Lam said. "I know. But I'm still not leaving Diem Huong in it."

The Turtle's Golden Claw followed the boundary of the harmonization arch, slowly tracing is contours, whispering words Ngoc Ha could barely hear. "It's not stabilized, that's the issue."

"You can talk," Ngoc Ha said, more sharply than she'd meant to. "Grand Master Bach Cuc didn't stabilize anything either, and it killed her."

"We will not talk of Bach Cuc here," *The Turtle's Golden Claw* snapped.

Lam looked vaguely curious but, through what appeared to be a supreme effort of will, turned her attention back to the door. Through the light Ngoc Ha caught glimpses and pieces—a hand, an arm, a fragment of an altar with incense sticks protruding from it, the face of a yellow-robed monk. Another place, another time. "What was it supposed to be?"

Lam finished clinching together her two cables—making no perceptible difference. She looked up, her face gleaming with blue-tinged sweat. "The Citadel. Diem Huong's always wanted to go back." She snapped her fingers and bots rose up from the floor, though they were in bad shape—missing arms and with live wires trailing from them. "A time machine sounded like a good idea, at the time."

A time machine. Summoning deep spaces on an orbital. "And you thought Grand Master Bach Cuc was imprudent?"

"At least I'm still here," Lam snapped. "Which isn't, I understand, what happened with the Grand Master."

"Please stop arguing about Bach Cuc," Suu Nuoc said, in a low but commanding voice. "And turn this thing off. I don't care about Diem Huong. This is going to destroy the orbital."

"I'm not doing anything until Diem Huong walks out that door," Lam said.

Ngoc Ha stood, watching the door. Watching the light, and the presence without, and her daughter, the mind-ship, prowling around the machine like a tiger. A time machine. A window on the Citadel. On Ngoc Minh and the empire and the distant past—the past that had twisted her life into its present shape and continued to hang over her like the shadow of a sword.

She reached out before she could stop herself—heard, distantly, Suu Nuoc's scream, felt Lam Long's arm pulling at her—but it was too late, she was already touching the arch—she'd expected some irresistible force to drag her in, some irreversible current that would have taken her to Diem Huong and the Citadel, amidst all the hurt she'd been bottling up.

Instead, there was silence.

Calm spread from the machine, like oil thrown on waves; a deafening lack of noise that seemed to still everything and everyone in its wake. And, like a huge beast lumbering toward its den, the presence that had been dogging Ngoc Ha ever since she'd entered the deep spaces turned its eyes toward her, and saw.

I am here.

It was a voice like the fires of stars torn apart, like the thunder of ships' engines, like the call of a bell in a temple beyond time.

I am here.

And it was a voice Ngoc Ha had heard, and never forgotten, one that rose in the holes of her heart, each word a twisting hook that dragged raw, red memories from the depths of the past.

Ngoc Minh.

The Engineer

Diem Huong stood, paralyzed. The Embroidered Guards were staring at her; the commander raising a gun toward her. "There's been a report of an intruder here, harassing Madam Quynh."

Reports whose memories wouldn't last more than a few moments; but sometimes, a few moments was all that it took for a message to travel along a chain of command and—like everyone else—the Embroidered Guards could teleport from the palace to any place in a heartbeat.

Diem Huong could teleport, too, but she was frozen, trying not to stare at the muzzles of five weapons aimed at her. They would shoot, and it didn't take that long for energy arcs to find their mark.

"Look," she said, "I can explain—" If she had enough time, they would forget her—why she was here, why she mattered. If she had enough time.

They all had their weapons raised—trained on her—and the commander was frowning, trying to see what to make of her. He was going to fire. He was going to—

There was only one thing for it.

Run.

Before she could think, she'd started pelting away from them—back toward the compartment, back toward Mother, who wouldn't recognize or acknowledge her, or answer any of her questions.

"Stop—"

At any moment, she would feel it; the energy going through her, the spasms as it traveled through her body—would fall to the floor screaming and twitching like a puppet taken apart—but still, she ran, toward the illusory, unattainable safety of a home that had long since ceased to be hers . . .

Run.

There was a wave of stillness passing over the faces of the soldiers, catching them mid-frown and freezing them in place—an invisible wind that blew through the station, laying icy fingers on her like a caress.

In front of her, the door opened; save that it was wreathed in blue light, like that of the harmonization arch. The wind blew through it, carrying the smell of fried garlic and fish sauce and jasmine rice—so incongruously familiar Diem Huong stopped. Surely that wasn't possible . . .

The wind blew through the door, carrying tatters of light toward it, each gust adding depth and body to the light, until the vague outline of a figure became visible—line after line, a shape drawn by a master's paintbrush— the outline of a face surrounded by a mane of black hair; of silk clothes and jade bracelets as green as forest leaves.

Lam. Had to be. Lam had finally found a way to rescue her.

But it wasn't Lam. The clothes were yellow brocade—for a moment only, and then they became the saffron of monks' robes. The hair was longer than Lam's, the face older and more refined—and the eyes were two pits of unbearable compassion. "Child," the woman said. "Come."

"Who are you?" Diem Huong asked.

The woman laughed; a low, pleasant sound with no edge of threat to it. "I am Ngoc Minh. Come now, there isn't much time."

Ngoc Minh? The Bright Princess? "I don't understand—" Diem Huong said, but Ngoc Minh was extending a hand as translucent as porcelain, and, because nothing else made sense, Diem Huong took it.

For a moment—a dizzying, terrifying moment—she hung again in the blackness, in the void between the stars, brushed by a presence as terrible as a mindship in deep spaces, something that wrapped huge wings around her until she choked—and then it passed, and she realized the terrible presence was the Bright Princess herself; that the wings weren't choking her, but holding her as she flew.

"It's going to be fine," the Bright Princess whispered, in her mind.

"Mother—"

There were no words in the darkness, in the void; just the distant, dispassionate light of stars and the sound of beings calling to each other like spaceships in the deep. There were no words, and no illusions left. Only kindness. And the memory of tears glistening in Mother's eyes.

"Your mother loved you," the Bright Princess said.

It still stands.

But for how long?

It's going to fall, one way or another.

Sometimes, all you have are bad choices. Make a stand, or be conquered. Kill, or be killed. Submit, or have to submit others.

Mother had sent them away—packing off her daughter and her husband, hiding what it had cost her. She had known. She had known the Citadel had no other choice but to vanish; that Ngoc Minh would never fight against her own people. That she would gather, instead, all her powers—all her monks and hermits and their students, for one purpose only: to disappear where no one would ever find them.

"You told her," Diem Huong said. "What was going to happen. What you were going to do."

"Of course," the Bright Princess said. "It's a Citadel, not a dictatorship; not an Imperial Court. My word is law, but I wouldn't have decided something like this without asking everyone to make a choice. The cost was too high."

Too high. Mother had made her bad choice; to have her family survive; to have her daughter grow into adulthood. "Where is she?"

"Nowhere. Everywhere," the Bright Princess whispered. "Beyond your reach, forever, child. She made her choice. Let her be."

I didn't feel you'd understand, younger aunt. You're too young to have children or believe in the necessity of holding up the world.

"I do understand," Diem Huong said, to the darkness, but it was too late. It had always been thirty years too late, and Mother was gone and would not come back no matter how hard she prayed or worked. "I do understand, Mother," she whispered; and she realized, with a shock, that she was crying.

The Empress

Mi Hiep summoned Huu Tam to her quarters; in the gardens outside her rooms, where bots were maintaining the grottos and waterfalls, the pavilions by the side of ponds covered with water lilies and lotuses, the arched bridges covered by willow branches, like a prelude to separation.

"Walk with me, will you?"

Huu Tam was silent, staring at the skies; at the ballet of shuttles in the skies. His attendants walked three steps behind them, affording them both the illusion of privacy.

"We are at war," Mi Hiep said. In the communal network, every place in the gardens was named; everything associated with an exquisite poem. It had been, she remembered, a competition to choose the poems. Ngoc Minh had won in several places, but Mi Hiep couldn't even remember where her daughter's poems would be. She could look it up, of course, but it wouldn't be the same. "You're going to have to take more responsibilities."

Huu Tam snorted. "I'm not a warrior."

Two ghost emperors flickered into life: the first, the Righteously Martial Emperor, who had founded the dynasty in floods of blood, and the twenty-third, the Great Virtue Emperor, who had hidden in his palace while civil war tore apart the empire. "No one is," the twenty-third emperor said.

"I know." Huu Tam's voice was curt.

"You will need Van," Mi Hiep said. Then, carefully, "And Suu Nuoc."

He sucked in a breath and looked away. He wouldn't contradict her—what child gainsaid their parents?—but he didn't agree. "You don't like him. You don't have to." She raised a hand, to forestall any objections. How was she going to make him understand? She had tried, over twenty-six years, and perhaps failed. "You like flattery, child. Always have. It's more pleasant to hear pleasant things about yourself; more pleasant never to be challenged. And more pleasant to surround yourself with friends."

"Who wouldn't?" Huu Tam was defiant.

"A court is not a nest of sycophants," the first emperor said, sternly.

"Flattery will destroy you," the twenty-third emperor—sallow-faced and fearful—whispered. "Look at my life as an example."

Huu Tam said nothing for a while. He would obey her, she knew; he was too well bred and too polite. He wasn't Ngoc Minh, who would have disagreed and stormed off. He would talk to Suu Nuoc, but he wouldn't trust him. She couldn't force him to.

There was a wind in the gardens; a ripple on the surface of the pond bending the lotus flowers, as if a giant hand from the heavens had rifled through them, discarding stems and petals—and the world seemed to pause and hold its breath for a bare moment.

Mi Hiep turned and saw her.

The Bright Princess stood in the octagonal pavilion in the middle of the pond—not so much coalescing into existence, but simply here one moment, as if the Universe had reorganized itself to include her—almost too far away for Mi Hiep to make out the face, though she would have recognized her in a heartbeat—and then, as Mi Hiep held a deep, burning breath, the Bright Princess flickered out of existence, and reappeared an arm's length away from both her and Huu Tam.

Huu Tam's face was pale. "Elder sister," he whispered.

The Bright Princess hadn't changed—still the same face that Mi Hiep remembered; the full cheeks, the burning eyes looking straight at her, refusing to bend to the empress her mother. Her hair was the same, too; not tied in a topknot, but loose, falling all the way to the ground until it seemed to root her to the soil.

"Child," she whispered. "Where are you?" She could see the pavilion through Ngoc Minh's body, and the pink lotus flowers and the darkening heavens over their heads.

Nowhere, whispered the wind. *Everywhere*.

"There are no miracles," Huu Tam whispered.

Yes. No. Perhaps, said the wind. *It doesn't matter.*

Mi Hiep reached out and so did Ngoc Minh—one ghostly hand reaching for a wrinkled one—her touch was the cold between stars; a slight pressure that didn't feel quite real—the memory of a dream on waking up.

Ngoc Minh smiled, and it seemed to fill up the entire world—and suddenly Mi Hiep was young again, watching an infant play in the courtyard, lining up pebbles and frag.ments of broken vases, and the infant looked up and saw her, and smiled, and the en.tire Universe seemed to shift and twist and hurt like salted knives in wounds—and then she was older, and the infant older too, and she tossed and turned in her bed, afraid for her life—and she woke up and asked the army to invade the Citadel. . . .

"Child . . . " I'm sorry, she wanted to say. The emperors had been right—Huu Tam had been right: it had never been about weapons or war, or about technologies she could steal from the Citadel. But simply about this—a mother and her daughter, and all the unsaid words, the unsaid fears—the unresolved quarrel that was all Mi Hiep's fault.

Ngoc Minh said nothing, and merely smiled back.

I forgive you, the wind whispered. *Please forgive me, Mother.*

"What for?"

Greed. Anger. Disobedience. Good-bye, Mother.

"Child . . . " Mi Hiep reached out again, but Ngoc Minh was gone, and only the memory of that smile remained. And then even that was gone, and Mi Hiep was alone again, gasping for breaths that burnt her lungs, as the Universe became a blur around her.

Huu Tam looked at her, shaking. "Mother—"

Mi Hiep shook her head. "Not now, please."

"Empress!" It was Lady Linh and Van, both looking grim. Mi Hiep took a deep breath, waiting for things to right themselves again. Mercifully, none of the ghost emperors had said any words. "What is it?" she asked.

Van made a gesture, and the air between them filled with the image of a ship—battered and pocked through like the surface of an airless moon, with warmth—oxygen?—pouring out of a hole in the hull.

One of the Nam mindships.

"We have one," Van said. "But the rest jumped. Given their previous pattern, they'll be at the imperial shipyards in two days."

Huu Tam threw a concerned look at Mi Hiep—who didn't answer. She didn't feel anything she said would make sense, in the wake of Ngoc Minh's disappearance. "How soon can you work on the ship?"

"We're getting it towed to the nearest safe space," Lady Linh said. "And sending a team of scientists on board, to start work immediately. They'll find out how it was done."

Of course they would. "And the shipyards?" Mi Hiep asked, slowly, carefully—every word feeling as though it broke a moment of magical silence.

"Pulling away, as you ordered." Van gestured again, and pulled an image into the network. The yards, with the shells of mindships clustered among them, and bots pulling them apart in slow motion, dismantling them little by little. As Van gestured, they moved in accelerated time—and everything seemed to disintegrate into nothingness. Other, whole ships moved to take the place of those she'd ordered destroyed: warships, bristling with weapons, and civilian ships, looking small and pathetic next to them, a bulwark against the inevitable. "They've already evacuated the Mind-bearers. The other ships are waiting for them."

There would be a battle—many battles, to slow down the Nam fleet in any way they could—waiting until the empire could gather its defenses; until they could study the hijacked ship and determine how it had been done, and how it could be reversed. And even if it couldn't . . . they still had their own mindships, and the might of their army. "We'll be fine, Mother," Huu Tam, softly. "One doesn't need miracles to fight a war."

No. One needed miracles to avoid one. But Ngoc Minh was gone, her technologies and her Citadel with her, and all that remained of the empress' daughter was the memory of a hand in hers, like the caress of the wind.

Where are you?

Nowhere. Everywhere.

Mi Hiep stood, her face unmoving, and listened to her advisors, steeling herself for what lay ahead—a long, slow slog of unending battles and feints, of retreats and invasions and pincer moves, and the calculus of deaths and acceptable losses. She rubbed her hand, slowly, carefully.

Forgive me, Mother. Good-bye.

Good-bye, child.

And on her hand, the touch of the wind faded away, until it was nothing more than a gentle balm on her heart; a memory to cling to in the days ahead—as they all made their way forward in the days of the war, in an age without miracles.

The Younger Sister

Ngoc Ha stood, caught in the light—her hand thrust through the door, becoming part of the whirlwind of images beyond. She didn't feel any different, more as if her hand had ceased to exist altogether—no sensation coming back from it, nothing.

And then she did feel something—faint at first, but growing stronger with every passing moment—until she recognized the touch of a hand on hers, fingers interlacing with her own.

I am here.

She didn't think, merely pulled, and her hand came back from beyond the harmonization arch and, with it, another hand and an arm and a body.

Two figures coalesced from within the maelstrom. The first, bedraggled and mousy, her topknot askew, her face streaked with tears, could only be the missing engineer.

"Huong," Lam said, sharply; and dropped what she was holding, to run toward her. "You idiot." She was crying, too, and Diem Huong let her drag her away. "You freaking idiot."

But the other one . . . the one whose hand Ngoc Ha was still holding, even now . . .

She had changed, and not changed. She was all of Ngoc Ha's memories—the hands closing hers around the baby chick, the tall, comforting presence who had held her after too many nights frustrated over her dissertations, the sister who had stood on the viewscreen with her last message, assuring her all was well—and yet she was more, too. Her head was well under the harmonization arch, except that there was about her a presence, a sense of vastness that was far greater than her actual size. She was faintly translucent and so were her clothes, shifting from one shape to the next, from yellow brocade to nuns' saffron, the jewelry on her hands and wrists flickering in and out of existence.

"Elder sister." Nothing but formality would come past her frozen lips.

"L'il sis." Ngoc Minh smiled and looked at her. "There isn't much time."

"I don't understand," Ngoc Ha said. "Why are you here?"

"Because you called," Ngoc Minh said. With her free hand, the Bright Princess gestured to *The Turtle's Golden Claw*: the ship had moved to stand by her side, though she said nothing. "Because blood calls to blood, even in the depths of time"

"I—" Ngoc Ha took a deep, trembling breath. "I wanted to find you. Or not to. I wasn't sure."

Ngoc Minh laughed. "You were always so indecisive." Her eyes—her eyes were twin stars, their radiance burning. "As I said—I am here."

"Here?" Ngoc Ha asked. "Where?" The light streamed around her, blurring everything—beyond the arch, the world was still shattered splinters, meaningless fragments.

The Turtle's Golden Claw said, slowly, softly, "This is nowhere, nowhen. Just a pocket of deep spaces. A piece of the past."

Of course. They weren't like Grand Master Bach Cuc, destroyed in the conflagration within her laboratory. But were they any better off?

"Nowhere," Ngoc Minh said, with a nod. She looked, for a moment, past Ngoc Ha at the two engineers huddled together in a corner of the laboratory, holding hands like long-lost friends. "That's where I am, l'il sis. Everywhere. Nowhere. Beyond time, beyond space."

No. "You're dead," Ngoc Ha said, sharply, and the words burnt her throat like tears.

"Perhaps," Ngoc Minh said. "I and the Citadel and the people aboard—" She closed her eyes, and, for a moment, she wasn't huge or beyond time but merely young, and tired, and faced with choices that had destroyed her. "Mother's army and I could have fought each other, spilling blood for every measure of the Citadel. I couldn't do that. Brother shall not fight brother, son shall not slay father, daughter shall not abandon mother. . . . " The familiar litany of righteousness taught by their tutors in days long gone by. "There was a way out."

Death.

"Nowhere. Everywhere," Ngoc Minh said. "If you go far enough into deep spaces, time ceases to have meaning. That's where I took the Citadel."

Time ceases to have meaning. Humanity, too, ceased to have any meaning—Ngoc Ha had read Grand Master Bach Cuc's notes. She'd sent *The Turtle's Golden Claw* there on her own because humans who went this far dissolved, turning into the dust of stars, the ashes of planets. "You're not human," Ngoc Ha said. Not anymore.

"I'm not human either," *The Turtle's Golden Claw* said, gently.

Ngoc Minh merely smiled. "You place too much value on that word."

Because you're my sister. Because—because she was tired, too, of dragging the past behind her; of thirty years of not knowing whether she should mourn or move on; of Mother not giving her any attention beyond her use in finding her sister. Because—

"Did you never think of us?" The words were torn out of Ngoc Ha's mouth before she could think. Did she never see the sleepless nights, the days where she'd carefully molded her face and her thoughts to never see Ngoc Minh—the long years of shaping a life around the wound of her absence?

Ngoc Minh did not answer. Not human. Not anymore. A star storm, somewhere in the vastness of space. Storms did not think whether they harmed you or care whether you grieved.

There isn't much time, she'd said. Of course. Of course no one could live for long, in deep spaces.

"Goodbye, l'il sis. Be at peace." And the Bright Princess withdrew her hand from Ngoc Ha's, turning back toward the light of the harmonization arch, going back to wherever she was, whatever she had turned into. The face she showed now, the one that didn't seem to have changed, was nothing more than a mask, a gift to Ngoc Ha to comfort her. The real Ngoc Minh—and everyone else in the Citadel—didn't wear faces or bodies anymore.

But still, she'd come; for one last glimpse, one last gift. A moment, frozen in time, before the machine was turned off or killed them all.

Be at peace.

If such a thing could ever happen—if memories could be erased, wounds magically healed, lives righted back into the proper shape without the shadow of jealousy and love and loss.

"Wait," Ngoc Ha said, and Bright Princess Ngoc Minh paused and looked back at her, reaching out with a translucent hand, her eyes serene and distant, her smile the same enigmatic one as the bodhisattva statues in the temples.

The hand was wreathed in light; the blue nimbus of the harmonization door; the shadow of deep spaces where she lived, where no one could survive.

Nowhere. Everywhere.

"Wait."

"Mother—" *The Turtle's Golden Claw* said. "You can't—"

Ngoc Ha smiled. "Of course I can," she said; and reached out and clasped her sister's hand to hers.

The Officer

From where he stood rooted to the ground, Suu Nuoc saw it all happen, as if in some nightmare he couldn't wake up from: Ngoc Ha talking with the figure in the doorway, *The Turtle's Golden Claw* screaming, and Lam cursing, the bots surging from the floor at her command, making for the arch.

Too late.

Ngoc Ha reached out and took the outstretched hand. Her topknot had come undone, and her hair was streaming in the wind from the door—for a moment they stood side by side, the two sisters, almost like mirror images of each other, as if they were the same person with two very different paths in life.

"Princess!" Suu Nuoc called—knowing, with a horrible twist in his belly, what was going to happen before it did.

Ngoc Ha turned to look at him, for a fraction of a second. She smiled; and her smile was cold, distant already—a moment only, and then she turned back to look at her sister the Bright Princess, and her other hand wrapped itself around her sister's free hand, locking them in an embrace that couldn't be broken.

And then they were gone, scattering into a thousand shards of light.

"No," *The Turtle's Golden Claw* said. "No. Mother . . . "

No panic. This was not the time for it. With an effort, Suu Nuoc wrenched his thoughts back from the brink of incoherence. Someone needed to be pragmatic about matters, and clearly neither of the two scientists, nor the mindship, was going to provide level-headedness.

"She's gone," he said to *The Turtle's Golden Claw*. "This isn't what we need to worry about. How do we shut off this machine before it kills us all?"

"She's my mother!" *The Turtle's Golden Claw* said.

"I know," Suu Nuoc said, curtly. Pragmatism, again. Someone needed to have it. "You can look for her later."

"There is no later!"

"There always is. Leave it, will you? We have more pressing problems."

"Yes, we do." Lam had come back, and with her was the engineer—Diem Huong, who still looked as though she'd been through eight levels of Hell and beyond, but whose face no longer had the shocked look of someone who had seen things she shouldn't. "You're right. We need to shut this thing down. Come on, Huong. Give me a hand." They crouched together by the machine, handing each other bits and pieces of ceramic and cabling. After a while, *The Turtle's Golden Claw* drifted, reluctantly, to join them, interjecting advice, while the bots moved slowly, drunkenly, piecing things back together as best they could.

Suu Nuoc, whose talents most emphatically did not lie in science or experimental time machines, drifted back to the harmonization arch, watching the world beyond—the collage of pristine corridors and delicately painted temples; the fragments of citizens teleporting from one ship to the next.

The Citadel. What the empress had desperately sought. What she'd thought she desperately needed—and Suu Nuoc had never argued with her, only taken her orders to heart and done his best to see them to fruition.

But now . . . Now he wasn't so sure, anymore, that they'd ever needed any of this.

"It's gone," Diem Huong said, gently. She was standing by his side, watching the door, her voice quiet, thoughtful; though he was not fooled at the strength of the emotions she was repressing. "The Bright Princess took it too far into deep spaces, and it vanished. That's what really happened to it. That's why Grand Master Bach Cuc would never have found it. It only exists in the past, now."

"I know," Suu Nuoc said. Perhaps, if another of the empress's children was willing to touch the arch—but his gut told him it wouldn't work again. Ngoc Ha had been close to Bright Princess Ngoc Minh; too close, in fact—

the seeds of her ultimate fate already sown long before they had come here, to the Scattered Pearls Belt. There was no one else whose touch would call forth the Bright Princess again; even if the empress was willing to sanction the building of another time machine, after it had killed a Master of Grand Design Harmony and almost destroyed an orbital.

"There!" Lam said, triumphantly. She rose, holding two bits of cable at the same time as *The Turtle's Golden Claw* reached for something on the edge of the harmonization arch.

The light went out as if she'd thrown a switch. When it came on again, the air had changed—no longer charged or lit with blue, it was simply the slightly stale, odorless atmosphere of any orbital. And the room, too, shrank back to normal, the furniture simply tables and chairs and screens, rather than the collage of monstrosities Suu Nuoc and his squad had seen on the way in.

Suu Nuoc took a deep, trembling breath, trying to convince himself it was over.

The Turtle's Golden Claw drifted back to the machine—now nothing more than a rectangle with a deactivated harmonization arch, looking small and pathetic, and altogether too diminished to have caused so much trouble. "I'll find her," she said. "Somewhere in deep spaces. . . ."

Suu Nuoc said nothing. He'd have to gather them all; to bring them back to the first planet, so they could be debriefed—so he could explain to the empress why she had lost a second daughter. And—if she still would have him, when it was all accounted for—he would have to help her fight a war.

But, for now, he watched the harmonization arch and remembered what he had seen through it. The past. The Citadel, like some fabled underground treasure. Ghostly apparitions, like myths and fairytales—nothing to build a life or a war strategy on.

The present was all that mattered. The past's grievous wounds had to close or to be ignored, and the future's war and the baying of wolves could only be distant worries. He would stand where he had always stood; by his empress's side, to guide the empire forward for as long as she would have him.

The Citadel was gone, and so were its miracles—but wasn't it for the best, after all?

GYPSY

Carter Scholz

The living being is only a species of the dead, and a very rare species.
—Nietzsche

When a long shot is all you have, you're a fool not to take it.
—Romany saying

1.

The launch of Earth's first starship went unremarked. The crew gave no interviews. No camera broadcast the hard light pulsing from its tail. To the plain eye, it might have been a common airplane.

The media battened on multiple wars and catastrophes. The Arctic Ocean was open sea. Florida was underwater. Crises and opportunities intersected.

World population was something over ten billion. No one was really counting anymore. A few billion were stateless refugees. A few billion more were indentured or imprisoned.

Oil reserves, declared as recently as 2010 to exceed a trillion barrels, proved to be an accounting gimmick, gone by 2020. More difficult and expensive sources—tar sands in Canada and Venezuela, natural-gas fracking—became primary, driving up atmospheric methane and the price of fresh water.

The countries formerly known as the Third World stripped and sold their resources with more ruthless abandon than their mentors had. With the proceeds they armed themselves.

The U.S. was no longer the global hyperpower, but it went on behaving as if. Generations of outspending the rest of the world combined had made this its habit and brand: arms merchant to expedient allies, former and future foes alike, starting or provoking conflicts more or less at need, its constant need being, as always, resources. Its waning might was built on a memory of those vast native resources it had long since expropriated and depleted, and a sense of entitlement to more. These overseas conflicts were problematic and carried wildly unintended consequences. As the President of Venezuela put it just days before his assassination, "It's dangerous to go to war against your own asshole."

The starship traveled out of our solar system at a steep angle to the ecliptic plane. It would pass no planets. It was soon gone. Going South.

SOPHIE (2043)

Trying to rise up out of the cold sinking back into a dream of rising up out of the. Stop, stop it now. Shivering. So dark. So thirsty. Momma? Help me?

Her parents were wealthy. They had investments, a great home, they sent her to the best schools. They told her how privileged she was. She'd always assumed this meant she would be okay forever. She was going to be a poet.

It was breathtaking how quickly it went away, all that okay. Her dad's job, the investments, the college tuition, the house. In two years, like so many others, they were penniless and living in their car. She left unfinished her thesis on Louis Zukofsky's last book, 80 Flowers. *She changed her major to information science, slept with a loan officer, finished grad school half a million in debt, and immediately took the best-paying job she could find, at Xocket Defense Systems. Librarian. She hadn't known that defense contractors hired librarians. They were pretty much the only ones who did anymore. Her student loan was adjustable rate—the only kind offered. As long as the rate didn't go up, she could just about get by on her salary. Best case, she'd have it paid off in thirty years. Then the rate doubled. She lost her apartment. XDS had huge dorms for employees who couldn't afford their own living space. Over half their workforce lived there.*

Yet she was lucky, lucky. If she'd been a couple of years younger she wouldn't have finished school at all. She'd be fighting in Burma or Venezuela or Kazakhstan.

At XDS she tended the library's firewalls, maintained and documented software, catalogued projects, fielded service calls from personnel who needed this or that right now, or had forgotten a password, or locked themselves out of their own account. She learned Unix, wrote cron scripts and daemons and Perl routines. There was a satisfaction in keeping it all straight. She was a serf, but they needed her and they knew it, and that knowledge sustained in her a hard small sense of freedom. It was almost a kind of poetry, the vocabulary of code.

Chirping. Birds? Were there still birds?

No. Tinnitus. Her ears ached for sound in this profound silence. Created their own.

• • •

She was a California girl, an athlete, a hiker, a climber. She'd been all over the Sierra Nevada, had summited four 14,000-footers by the time she was sixteen. She loved the backcountry. Loved its stark beauty, solitude, the life that survived in its harshness: the pikas, the marmots, the mountain chickadees, the heather and whitebark pine and polemonium.

After she joined XDS, it became hard for her to get to the mountains. Then it became impossible. In 2035 the Keep Wilderness Wild Act shut the public out of the national parks, the national forests, the BLM lands. The high country above timberline was surveilled by satellites and drones, and it was said that mining and fracking operators would shoot intruders on sight, and that in the remotest areas, like the Enchanted Gorge and the Muro Blanco, lived small nomadic bands of malcontents. She knew enough about the drones and satellites to doubt it; no one on Earth could stay hidden anywhere for more than a day.

The backcountry she mourned was all Earth to her. To lose it was to lose all Earth. And to harden something final inside her.

One day Roger Fry came to her attention—perhaps it was the other way round—poking in her stacks where he didn't belong. That was odd; the login and password had been validated, the clearance was the highest, there was no place in the stacks prohibited to this user; yet her alarms had tripped. By the time she put packet sniffers on it he was gone. In her email was an invitation to visit a website called Gypsy.

When she logged in she understood at once. It thrilled her and frightened her. They were going to leave the planet. It was insane. Yet she felt the powerful seduction of it. How starkly its plain insanity exposed the greater consensus insanity the planet was now living. That there was an alternative—!

She sat up on the slab. Slowly unwrapped the mylar bodysuit, disconnected one by one its drips and derms and stents and catheters and waldos and sensors. Let it drift crinkling to the floor.

Her breathing was shallow and ragged. Every few minutes she gasped for air and her pulse raced. The temperature had been raised to twenty degrees Celsius as she came to, but still she shivered. Her body smelled a way it had never smelled before. Like vinegar and nail polish. It looked pale and flabby, but familiar. After she'd gathered strength, she reached under the slab, found a sweatshirt and sweatpants, and pulled them on. There was also a bottle of water. She drank it all.

The space was small and dark and utterly silent. No ports, no windows. Here and there, on flat black walls, glowed a few pods of LEDs. She braced her hands against the slab and stood up, swaying. Even in the slight gravity her heart pounded. The ceiling curved gently away a handsbreadth above her head, and the floor curved gently to follow it. Unseen beyond the ceiling was the center of the ship, the hole of the donut, and beyond that the other half of the slowly spinning torus. Twice a minute it rotated, creating a centripetal gravity of one-tenth g. Any slower would be too weak to be helpful. Any faster, gravity would differ at the head and the feet enough to cause vertigo. Under her was the outer ring of the water tank, then panels of aerogel sandwiched within sheets of hydrogenous carbon-composite, then a surrounding jacket of liquid hydrogen tanks, and then interstellar space.

What had happened? Why was she awake?

Look, over seventy plus years, systems will fail. We can't rely on auto-repair. With a crew of twenty, we could wake one person every few years to perform maintenance.

And put them back under? Hibernation is dicey enough without trying to do it twice.

Yes, it's a risk. What's the alternative?

What about failsafes? No one gets wakened unless a system is critical. Then we wake a specialist. A steward.

That could work.

She walked the short distance to the ship's console and sat. It would have been grandiose to call it a bridge. It was a small desk bolted to the floor. It held a couple of monitors, a keyboard, some pads. It was like the light and sound booth of a community theater.

She wished she could turn on more lights. There were no more. Their energy budget was too tight. They had a fission reactor onboard but it wasn't running. It was to fire the nuclear rocket at their arrival. It wouldn't last seventy-two years if they used it for power during their cruise.

Not far from her—nothing on the ship was far from her—were some fifty kilograms of plutonium pellets—not the Pu-239 of fission bombs, but the more energetic Pu-238. The missing neutron cut the isotope's half-life from 25,000 years to eighty-eight years, and made it proportionately more radioactive. That alpha radiation was contained by iridium cladding and a casing of graphite, but the pellets still gave off heat, many kilowatts' worth. Most of that heat warmed the ship's interior to its normal temperature of four degrees Celsius. Enough of it was channeled outward to keep the surrounding water liquid in its jacket, and the outer tanks of hydrogen at fourteen kelvins, slush, maximally dense. The rest of the heat ran a Stirling engine to generate electricity.

First she read through the protocols, which she had written: *Stewards' logs to be read by each wakened steward. Kept in the computers, with redundant backups, but also kept by hand, ink on paper, in case of system failures, a last-chance critical backup. And because there is something restorative about writing by hand.*

There were no stewards' logs. She was the first to be wakened.

They were only two years out. Barely into the Oort cloud. She felt let down. What had gone wrong so soon?

All at once she was ravenous. She stood, and the gravity differential hit her. She steadied herself against the desk, then took two steps to the storage bay. Three-quarters of the ship was storage. What they would need at the other end. What Roger called pop-up civilization. She only had to go a step inside to find a box of MREs. She took three, stepped out, and put one into the microwave. The smell of it warming made her mouth water and her stomach heave. Her whole body trembled as she ate. Immediately she put a second into the microwave. As she waited for it, she fell asleep.

She saw Roger, what must have happened to him after that terrible morning when they received his message: Go. Go now. Go at once.

He was wearing an orange jumpsuit, shackled to a metal table.

How did you think you could get away with it, Fry?

I did get away with it. They've gone.

But we've got you.

That doesn't matter. I was never meant to be aboard.

Where are they going?

Alpha Centauri. (He would pronounce it with the hard K.)

That's impossible.

Very likely. But that's where they're going.

Why?

It's less impossible than here.

When she opened her eyes, her second meal had cooled, but she didn't want it. Her disused bowels protested. She went to the toilet and strained but voided only a trickle of urine. Feeling ill, she hunched in the dark, small space, shivering, sweat from her armpits running down her ribs. The smell of her urine mixed with the toilet's chemicals and the sweetly acrid odor of her long fast.

pleine de l'âcre odeur des temps, poudreuse et noire
full of the acrid smell of time, dusty and black

Baudelaire. Another world. With wonder she felt it present itself. Consciousness was a mystery. She stared into the darkness, fell asleep again on the pot.

• • •

Again she saw Roger shackled to the metal table. A door opened and he looked up.

We've decided.

He waited.

Your ship, your crew, your people—they don't exist. No one will ever know about them.

Roger was silent.

The ones remaining here, the ones who helped you—you're thinking we can't keep them all quiet. We can. We're into your private keys. We know everyone who was involved. We'll round them up. The number's small enough. After all your work, Roger, all their years of effort, there will be nothing but a few pathetic rumors and conspiracy theories. All those good people who helped you will be disappeared forever. Like you. How does that make you feel?

They knew the risks. For them it was already over. Like me.

Over? Oh, Roger. We can make "over" last a long time.

Still, we did it. They did it. They know that.

You're not hearing me, Roger. I said we've changed that.

The ship is out there.

No. I said it's not. Repeat after me. Say it's not, Roger.

BUFFER OVERFLOW. So that was it. Their datastream was not being received. Sophie had done much of the information theory design work. An energy-efficient system approaching Shannon's limit for channel capacity. Even from Alpha C it would be only ten joules per bit.

The instruments collected data. Magnetometer, spectrometers, plasma analyzer, cosmic-ray telescope, Cerenkov detector, et cetera. Data was queued in a transmit buffer and sent out more or less continuously at a low bit rate. The protocol was designed to be robust against interference, dropped packets, interstellar scintillation, and the long latencies imposed by their great distance and the speed of light.

They'd debated even whether to carry communications.

What's the point? We're turning our backs on them.

Roger was insistent: Are we scientists? This is an unprecedented chance to collect data in the heliopause, the Oort cloud, the interstellar medium, the Alpha system itself. Astrometry from Alpha, reliable distances to every star in our galaxy—that alone is huge.

Sending back data broadcasts our location.

So? How hard is it to follow a nuclear plasma trail to the nearest star? Anyway, they'd need a ship to follow. We have the only one.

You say the Earth situation is terminal. Who's going to receive this data? Anybody. Everybody.

So: Shackleton Crater. It was a major comm link anyway, and its site at the south pole of the Moon assured low ambient noise and permanent line of sight to the ship. They had a Gypsy there—one of their tribe—to receive their datastream.

The datastream was broken up into packets, to better weather the long trip home. Whenever Shackleton received a packet, it responded with an acknowledgment, to confirm reception. When the ship received that ACK signal—at their present distance, that would be about two months after a packet was transmitted—the confirmed packet was removed from the transmit queue to make room for new data. Otherwise the packet went back to the end of the queue, to be retransmitted later. Packets were time-stamped, so they could be reassembled into a consecutive datastream no matter in what order they were received.

But no ACK signals had been received for over a year. The buffer was full and new data were being lost. That was why she was awake.

They'd known the Shackleton link could be broken, even though it had a plausible cover story of looking for SETI transmissions from Alpha C. But other Gypsies on Earth should also be receiving. Someone should be acknowledging. A year of silence!

Going back through computer logs, she found there'd been an impact. Eight months ago something had hit the ship. Why hadn't that wakened a steward?

It had been large enough to get through the forward electromagnetic shield. The shield deflected small particles which, over decades, would erode their hull. The damage had been instantaneous. Repair geckos responded in the first minutes. Since it took most of a day to rouse a steward, there would have been no point.

Maybe the impact hit the antenna array. She checked and adjusted alignment to the Sun. They were okay. She took a routine spectrograph and measured the Doppler shift.

0.056 c.

No. Their velocity should be 0.067 c.

Twelve years. It added twelve years to their cruising time.

She studied the ship's logs as that sank in. The fusion engine had burned its last over a year ago, then was jettisoned to spare mass.

Why hadn't a steward awakened before her? The computer hadn't logged any problems. Engine function read as normal; the sleds that held the fuel had been emptied one by one and discarded; all the fuel had been burned—

all as planned. So, absent other problems, the lower velocity alone hadn't triggered an alert. Stupid!

Think. They'd begun to lag only in the last months of burn. Some ignitions had failed or underperformed. It was probably antiproton decay in the triggers. Nothing could have corrected that. Good thinking, nice fail.

Twelve years.

It angered her. The impact and the low velocity directly threatened their survival, and no alarms went off. But loss of comms, *that* set off alarms, that was important to Roger. Who was never meant to be on board. *He's turned his back on humanity, but he still wants them to hear all about it. And to hell with us.*

When her fear receded, she was calmer. If Roger still believed in anything redeemable about humankind, it was the scientific impulse. Of course it was primary to him that this ship do science, and send data. This was her job.

Why Alpha C? Why so impossibly far?

Why not the Moon? The U.S. was there: the base at Shackleton, with a ten-thousand-acre solar power plant, a deuterium mine in the lunar ice, and a twenty-gigawatt particle beam. The Chinese were on the far side, mining helium-3 from the regolith.

Why not Mars? China was there. A one-way mission had been sent in 2025. The crew might not have survived—that was classified—but the robotics had. The planet was reachable and therefore dangerous.

Jupiter? There were rumors that the U.S. was there as well, maybe the Chinese too, robots anyway, staking a claim to all that helium. Roger didn't put much credence in the rumors, but they might be true.

Why not wait it out at a Lagrange point? Roger thought there was nothing to wait for. The situation was terminal. As things spiraled down the maelstrom, anyplace cislunar would be at risk. Sooner or later any ship out there would be detected and destroyed. Or it might last only because civilization was shattered, with the survivors in some pit plotting to pummel the shards.

It was Alpha C because Roger Fry was a fanatic who believed that only an exit from the solar system offered humanity any hope of escaping what it had become.

She thought of Sergei, saying in his bad accent and absent grammar, which he exaggerated for effect: This is shit. You say me Alpha See is best? Absolute impossible. Is double star, no planet in habitable orbit—yes yes, whatever, minima maxima, zone of hopeful bullshit. Ghost Planet Hope. You shoot load there?

How long they had argued over this—their destination.

Gliese 581.

Impossible.

Roger, it's a rocky planet with liquid water.

That's three mistakes in one sentence. Something is orbiting the star, with a period of thirteen days and a mass of two Earths and some spectral lines. Rocky, water, liquid, that's all surmise. What's for sure is it's twenty light-years away. Plus, the star is a flare star. It's disqualified twice before we even get to the hope-it's-a-planet part.

You don't know it's a flare star! There are no observations!

In the absence of observations, we assume it behaves like other observed stars of its class. It flares.

You have this agenda for Alpha C, you've invented these criteria to shoot down every other candidate!

The criteria are transparent. We've agreed to them. Number one: Twelve light-years is our outer limit. Right there we're down to twenty-four stars. For reasons of luminosity and stability we prefer a nonvariable G- or K-class star. Now we're down to five. Alpha Centauri, Epsilon Eridani, 61 Cygni, Epsilon Indi, and Tau Ceti make the cut. Alpha is half the distance of the next nearest.

Bullshit, Roger. You have bug up ass for your Alpha See. Why not disqualify as double, heh? Why this not shoot-down criteria?

Because we have modeled it, and we know planet formation is possible in this system, and we have direct evidence of planets in other double systems. And because—I know.

They ended with Alpha because it was closest. Epsilon Eridani had planets for sure, but they were better off with a closer Ghost Planet Hope than a sure thing so far they couldn't reach it. Cosmic rays would degrade the electronics, the ship, their very cells. Every year in space brought them closer to some component's MTBF: mean time between failures.

Well, they'd known they might lose Shackleton. It was even likely. Just not so soon.

She'd been pushing away the possibility that things had gone so badly on Earth that no one was left to reply.

She remembered walking on a fire road after a conference in Berkeley—the Bay dappled sapphire and russet, thick white marine layer pushing in over the Golden Gate Bridge—talking to Roger about Fermi's Paradox. If the universe harbors life, intelligence, why haven't we seen evidence of it? Why are we alone? Roger favored what he called the Mean Time Between Failures argument. Technological civilizations simply fail, just as the components that make up their technology fail, sooner or later, for reasons as individually insignificant as they are inexorable, and final. Complex systems, after a point, tend away from robustness.

• • •

Okay. Any receivers on Earth will have to find their new signal. It was going to be like SETI in reverse: She had to make the new signal maximally detectable. She could do that. She could retune the frequency to better penetrate Earth's atmosphere. Reprogram the PLLs and antenna array, use orthogonal FSK modulation across the K- and X- bands. Increase the buffer size. And hope for the best.

Eighty-four years to go. My God, they were barely out the front door. My God, it was lonely out here.

The mission plan had been seventy-two years, with a predicted systems-failure rate of under twenty percent. The Weibull curve climbed steeply after that. At eighty-four years, systems-failure rate was over fifty percent.

What could be done to speed them? The nuclear rocket and its fuel were for deceleration and navigation at the far end. To use it here would add—she calculated—a total of 0.0002 c to their current speed. Saving them all of three months. And leaving them no means of planetfall.

They had nothing. Their cruise velocity was unalterable.

All right, that's that, so find a line. Commit to it and move.

Cruise at this speed for longer, decelerate later and harder. That could save a few years. They'd have to run more current through the magsail, increase its drag, push its specs.

Enter the Alpha C system faster than planned, slow down harder once within it. She didn't know how to calculate those maneuvers, but someone else would.

Her brain was racing now, wouldn't let her sleep. She'd been up for three days. These were not her decisions to make, but she was the only one who could.

She wrote up detailed logs with the various options and calculations she'd made. At last there was no more for her to do. But a sort of nostalgia came over her. She wanted, absurdly, to check her email. Really, just to hear some voice not her own.

Nothing broadcast from Earth reached this far except for the ACK signals beamed directly to them from Shackleton. Shackleton was also an IPN node, connecting space assets to the Internet. For cover, the ACK signals it sent to *Gypsy* were piggybacked on bogus Internet packets. And those had all been stored by the computer.

So in her homesick curiosity, she called them out of memory, and dissected some packets that had been saved from up to a year ago. Examined their broken and scrambled content like a torn, discarded newspaper for anything they might tell her of the planet she'd never see again.

M . 3 , S + S D S 0 U 4 : & E S (& % R = & E C ; & 4 @ : 7 , @ 8 V] P > 7)
I9VAT960@,3DY,R!B>2! Warmer than usual regime actively

amplifies tundra thaw Drought melt permafrost thermokarsts methane burn wildfire giants 800 ppm Hot atmospheric ridge NOAA frontrunning collapse Weapon tensions under Islamic media policy arsenals strategic counterinsurgency artillery air component mountain strongholds photorecce altitudes HQ backbone Su-35 SAMs Deals deals deals enter coupon code derivative modern thaws in dawn's pregnant grave Knowing perpendicular sex dating in Knob Lick Missouri teratologys appoint to plaintive technocrat and afar SEX FREE PICS RU.S.SIAN hardcore incest stories motorcycle cop fetish sex toys caesar milfhunters pokemon porn gallery fisting Here Is Links
M0UE"15)705(@25,@0T]-24Y'(0T2F]H;B!!<G%U:6QL82!A;F0@1

Lost, distant, desolate. The world she'd left forever, speaking its poison poetry of ruin and catastrophe and longing. Told her nothing she didn't already know about the corrupt destiny and thwarted feeling that had drawn humankind into the maelstrom *Gypsy* had escaped. She stood and walked furiously the meager length of the curved corridor, stopping at each slab, regarding the sleeping forms of her crewmates, naked in translucent bodysuits, young and fit, yet broken, like her, in ways that had made this extremity feel to them all the only chance.

They gathered together for the first time on the ship after receiving Roger's signal.

We'll be fine. Not even Roger knows where the ship is. They won't be able to find us before we're gone.

It was her first time in space. From the shuttle, the ship appeared a formless clutter: layers of bomb sleds, each bearing thousands of microfusion devices, under and around them a jacket of hydrogen tanks, shields, conduits, antennas. Two white-suited figures crawled over this maze. A hijacked hydrogen depot was offloading its cargo.

Five were already aboard, retrofitting. Everything not needed for deep space had been jettisoned. Everything lacking was brought and secured. Shuttles that were supposed to be elsewhere came and went on encrypted itineraries.

One shuttle didn't make it. They never learned why. So they were down to a sixteen crew.

The ship wasn't meant to hold so many active people. The crew area was less than a quarter of the torus, a single room narrowed to less than ten feet by the hibernation slabs lining each long wall. Dim even with all the LED bays on.

Darius opened champagne. Contraband: No one knew how alcohol might interact with the hibernation drugs.

To Andrew and Chung-Pei and Hari and Maryam. They're with us in spirit.

Some time later the first bomb went off. The ship trembled but didn't move. Another blast. Then another. Grudgingly the great mass budged. Like a car departing a curb, no faster at first. Fuel mass went from it and kinetic energy into it. Kinesis was gradual but unceasing. In its first few minutes it advanced less than a kilometer. In its first hour it moved two thousand kilometers. In its first day, a million kilometers. After a year, when the last bomb was expended, it would be some two thousand astronomical units from the Earth, and Gypsy *would coast on at her fixed speed for decades, a dark, silent, near-dead thing.*

As Sophie prepared to return to hibernation, she took stock. She walked the short interior of the quarter-torus. Less than twenty paces end to end. The black walls, the dim LED pods, the slabs of her crewmates.

Never to see her beloved mountains again. Her dear sawtooth Sierra. She thought of the blue sky, and remembered a hunk of stuff she'd seen on Roger's desk, some odd kind of rock. It was about five inches long. You could see through it. Its edges were blurry. Against a dark background it had a bluish tinge. She took it in her hand and it was nearly weightless.

What is this?

Silica aerogel. The best insulator in the world.

Why is it blue?

Rayleigh scattering.

She knew what that meant: Why the sky is blue. Billions of particles in the air scatter sunlight, shorter wavelengths scatter most, so those suffuse the sky. The shortest we can see is blue. But that was an ocean of air around the planet and this was a small rock.

You're joking.

No, it's true. There are billions of internal surfaces in that piece.

It's like a piece of sky.

Yes, it is.

It was all around her now, that stuff—in the walls of the ship, keeping out the cold of space—allowing her to imagine a poetry of sky where none was.

And that was it. She'd been awake for five days. She'd fixed the datastream back to Earth. She'd written her logs. She'd reprogrammed the magsail deployment for seventy years from now, at increased current, in the event that no other steward was wakened in the meantime. She'd purged her bowels and injected the hibernation cocktail. She was back in the bodysuit, life supports connected. As she went under, she wondered why.

• • •

2.

Gypsy departed a day short of Roger Fry's fortieth birthday. Born September 11, 2001, he was hired to a national weapons laboratory straight out of Caltech. He never did finish his doctorate. Within a year at the Lab he had designed the first breakeven fusion reaction. It had long been known that a very small amount of antimatter could trigger a burn wave in thermonuclear fuel. Roger solved how. He was twenty-four.

Soon there were net energy gains. That's when the bomb people came in. In truth, their interest was why he was hired in the first place. Roger knew this and didn't care. Once fusion became a going concern, it would mean unlimited clean energy. It would change the world. Bombs would have no purpose.

But it was a long haul to a commercial fusion reactor. Meanwhile, bombs were easier.

The smallest had a kiloton of yield, powerful enough to level forty or fifty city blocks; it used just a hundred grams of lithium deuteride, and less than a microgram of antimatter. It was easy to manufacture and transport and deploy. It created little radiation or electromagnetic pulse. Tens of thousands, then hundreds of thousands, were moved to orbiting drop platforms called sleds. Because the minimum yield was within the range of conventional explosives, no nuclear treaties were violated.

Putting them in orbit did violate the Outer Space Treaty, so at first they were more politely called the Orbital Asteroid Defense Network. But when a large asteroid passed through cislunar space a few years later—with no warning, no alert, no response at all—the pretense was dropped, and the system came under the command of the U.S. Instant Global Strike Initiative.

Lots of money went into the production of antimatter. There were a dozen facilities worldwide that produced about a gram, all told, of antiprotons a year. Some of it went into the first fusion power plants, which themselves produced more antiprotons. Most went into bomb triggers. There they were held in traps, isolated from normal matter, but that lasted only so long. They decayed, like tritium in the older nuclear weapons, but much faster; some traps could store milligrams of antiprotons for many months at a time, and they were improving; still, bomb triggers had to be replaced often.

As a defense system it was insane, but hugely profitable. Then came the problem of where to park the profits, since there were no stable markets anywhere. The economic system most rewarded those who created and surfed instabilities and could externalize their risks, which created greater instabilities.

Year after year Roger worked and waited, and the number of bombs grew, as did the number of countries deploying them, and the global resource wars intensified, and his fusion utopia failed to arrive. When the first commercial plants did start operating, it made no difference. Everything went on as before. Those who had the power to change things had no reason to; things had worked out pretty well for them so far.

Atmospheric CO_2 shot past six hundred parts per million. The methane burden was now measured in parts per million, not parts per billon. No one outside the classified world knew the exact numbers, but the effects were everywhere. The West Antarctic ice shelf collapsed. Sea level rose three meters.

Sometime in there, Roger Fry gave up on Earth.

But not on humanity, not entirely. Something in the complex process of civilization had forced it into this place from which it now had no exit. He didn't see this as an inevitable result of the process, but it had happened. There might have been a time when the situation was reversible. If certain decisions had been made. If resources had been treated as a commons. Back when the population of the planet was two or three billion, when there was still enough to go around, enough time to alter course, enough leisure to think things through. But it hadn't gone that way. He didn't much care why. The question was what to do now.

FANG TIR EOGHAIN (2081)

The ancestor of all mammals must have been a hibernator. Body temperature falls as much as fifteen kelvins. A bear's heartbeat goes down to five per minute. Blood pressure drops to thirty millimeters. In humans, these conditions would be fatal.

Relatively few genes are involved in torpor. We have located the critical ones. And we have found the protein complexes they uptake and produce. Monophosphates mostly.

Yes, I know, induced hypothermia is not torpor. But this state has the signatures of torpor. For example, there is a surfeit of MCT1 which transports ketones to the brain during fasting.

Ketosis, that's true, we are in a sense poisoning the subject in order to achieve this state. Some ischemia and refusion damage results, but less than anticipated. Doing it more than a couple of times is sure to be fatal. But for our purposes, maybe it gets the job done.

Anyway it had better; we have nothing else.

Her da was screaming at her to get up. He wasn't truly her father; her father had gone to the stars. That was a story she'd made up long ago; it was better than the truth.

Her thick brown legs touched the floor. Not as thick and brown as she remembered. Weak, pale, withered. She tried to stand and fell back. Try harder, cow. She fell asleep.

She'd tried so hard for so long. She'd been accepted early at university. Then her parents went afoul of the system. One day she came home to a bare apartment. All are zhonghua minzu, *but it was a bad time for certain ethnics in China.*

She lost her place at university. She was shunted to a polytechnic secondary in Guangzhou, where she lived with her aunt and uncle in a small apartment. It wasn't science; it was job training in technology services. One day she overheard the uncle on the phone, bragging: He had turned her parents in, collected a bounty and a stipend.

She was not yet fifteen. It was still possible, then, to be adopted out of country. Covertly, she set about it. Caitlin Tyrone was the person who helped her from afar.

They'd met online, in a science chatroom. Ireland needed scientists. She didn't know or care where that was; she'd have gone to Hell. It took almost a year to arrange it, the adoption. It took all Fang's diligence, all her cunning, all her need, all her cold hate, to keep it from her uncle, to acquire the paperwork, to forge his signature, to sequester money, and finally on the last morning to sneak out of the apartment before dawn.

She flew from Guangzhao to Beijing to Frankfurt to Dublin, too nervous to sleep. Each time she had to stop in an airport and wait for the next flight, sometimes for hours, she feared arrest. In her sleepless imagination, the waiting lounges turned into detention centers. Then she was on the last flight. The stars faded and the sun rose over the Atlantic, and there was Ireland. O! the green of it. And her new mother Caitlin was there to greet her, grab her, look into her eyes. Good-bye forever to the wounded past.

She had a scholarship at Trinity College, in biochemistry. She already knew English, but during her first year she studied phonology and orthography and grammar, to try to map, linguistically, how far she'd traveled. It wasn't so far. The human vocal apparatus is everywhere the same. So is the brain, constructing the grammar that drives the voice box. Most of her native phonemes had Irish or English equivalents, near enough. But the sounds she made of hers were not quite correct, so she worked daily to refine them.

O is where she often came to rest. The exclamative particle, the sound of that moment when the senses surprise the body, same in Ireland as in China— same body, same senses, same sound. Yet a human universe of shadings. The English O was one thing; Mandarin didn't quite have it; Cantonese was closer; but everywhere the sound slid around depending on locality, on country, even on county: monophthong to diphthong, the tongue wandering in the mouth, seeking to settle. When she felt lost in the night, which was often, she sought for that O, round and solid and vast and various and homey as the planet beneath her, holding her with its gravity. Moving her tongue in her mouth as she lay in bed waiting for sleep.

Biochemistry wasn't so distant, in her mind, from language. She saw it all as signaling. DNA wasn't "information," data held statically in helices, it was activity, transaction.

She insisted on her new hybrid name, the whole long Gaelic mess of it—it was Caitlin's surname—as a reminder of the contigency of belonging, of culture and language, of identity itself. Her solid legs had landed on solid ground, or solid enough to support her.

Carefully, arduously, one connector at a time, she unplugged herself from the bodysuit, then sat up on the slab. Too quickly. She dizzied and pitched forward.

Get up, you cow. The da again. Dream trash. As if she couldn't. She'd show him. She gave all her muscles a great heave.

And woke shivering on the carbon deckplates. Held weakly down by the thin false gravity. It was no embracing O, just a trickle of mockery. *You have to do this,* she told her will.

She could smell acetone on her breath. Glycogen used up, body starts to burn fat, produces ketones. Ketoacidosis. She should check ketone levels in the others.

Roger came into Fang's life by way of Caitlin. Years before, Caitlin had studied physics at Trinity. Roger had read her papers. They were brilliant. He'd come to teach a seminar, and he had the idea of recruiting her to the Lab. But science is bound at the hip to its application, and turbulence occurs at that interface where theory meets practice, knowledge meets performance. Where the beauty of the means goes to die in the instrumentality of the ends.

Roger found to his dismay that Caitlin couldn't manage even the sandbox politics of grad school. She'd been aced out of the best advisors and was unable to see that her science career was already in a death spiral. She'd never make it on her own at the Lab, or in a corp. He could intervene to some degree, but he was reluctant; he saw a better way.

Already Caitlin was on U, a Merck pharmaceutical widely prescribed for a new category in DSM-6: "social interoperability disorder." U for eudaimonia- zine. Roger had tried it briefly himself. In his opinion, half the planet fit the diagnostic criteria, which was excellent business for Merck but said more about planetary social conditions than about the individuals who suffered under them.

U was supposed to increase compassion for others, to make other people seem more real. But Caitlin was already too empathic for her own good, too ready to yield her place to others, and the U merely blissed her out, put her in a zone of self-abnegation. Perhaps that's why it was a popular street drug; when some governments tried to ban it, Merck sued them under global trade agreements, for loss of expected future profits.

Caitlin ended up sidelined in the Trinity library, where she met and married James, an older charming sociopath with terrific interoperability. Meanwhile, Roger kept tabs on her from afar. He hacked James's medical records and noted that James was infertile.

It took Fang several hours to come to herself. She tried not to worry; this was to be expected. Her body had gone through a serious near-death trauma. She felt weak, nauseous, and her head throbbed, but she was alive. That she was sitting here sipping warm tea was a triumph, for her body and for her science. She still felt a little stunned, a little distant from that success. So many things could have gone wrong: Hibernation was only the half of it; like every other problem they'd faced, it came with its own set of ancillaries.

When she felt able, she checked on the others. Each sleeper bore implanted and dermal sensors—for core and skin temperature, EKG, EEG, pulse, blood pressure and flow, plasma ions, plasma metabolites, clotting function, respiratory rate and depth, gas analysis and flow, urine production, EMG, tremor, body composition. Near-infrared spectrometry measured hematocrit, blood glucose, tissue O_2 and pH. Muscles were stimulated electrically and mechanically to counteract atrophy. The slabs tipped thirty degrees up or down and rotated the body from supine to prone to provide mechanical loading in all directions. Exoskeletal waldos at the joints, and the soles and fingers, provided periodic range-of-motion stimulus. A range of pharmacological and genetic interventions further regulated bone and muscle regeneration.

Also, twitching was important. If you didn't twitch you wouldn't wake.

Did they dream? She didn't know. EEGs showed periodic variation but were so unlike normal EEGs that it was hard to say. You couldn't very well wake someone to ask, as the first sleep researchers had done.

All looked well on the monitor, except for number fourteen. Reza. Blood pressure almost nonexistent. She got to her feet and walked down the row of slabs to have a look at Reza.

A pursed greyish face sagging on its skull. Maybe a touch of life was visible, some purple in the grey, blood still coursing. Or maybe not.

Speckling the grey skin was a web of small white dots, each the size of a pencil eraser or smaller. They were circular but not perfectly so, margins blurred. Looked like a fungus.

She went back and touched the screen for records. This steward was long overdue for rousing. The machine had started the warming cycle three times. Each time he hadn't come out of torpor, so the machine had shut down the cycle, stabilized him, and tried again. After three failures, it had moved down the list to the next steward. Her.

She touched a few levels deeper. Not enough fat on this guy. Raising the temperature without rousing would simply bring on ischemia and perfusion. That's why the machine gave up. It was a delicate balance, to keep the metabolism burning fat instead of carbohydrates, without burning too much of the body's stores. Humans couldn't bulk up on fat in advance the way natural hibernators could. But she thought she'd solved that with the nutrient derms.

It was the fortieth year of the voyage. They were two light-years from home. Not quite halfway. If hibernation was failing now, they had a serious problem.

Was the fungus a result or a cause? Was it a fungus? She wanted to open the bodysuit and run tests, but any contagion had to be contained.

They'd discussed possible failure modes. Gene activity in bacteria increased in low gravity; they evolved more rapidly. In the presence of a host they became more virulent. Radiation caused mutations. But ultraviolet light scoured the suits every day and should have killed bacteria and fungus alike. Logs showed that the UV was functioning. It wasn't enough.

James—the da, as he insisted Fang call him—had black hair and blue eyes that twinkled like ice when he smiled. At first he was mere background to her; he'd stumble in late from the pub to find Caitlin and Fang talking. Ah, the Addams sisters, he'd say, nodding sagely. Fang never understood what he meant by it. For all his geniality, he kept her at a distance, treated her like a houseguest.

Caitlin was more like an older sister than a mother; she was only twelve years older. It was fun to talk science with her, and it was helpful. She was quick to understand the details of Fang's field, and this dexterity spurred Fang to excel.

After a couple of years, James grew more sullen, resentful, almost abusive. He dropped the suave act. He found fault with Fang's appearance, her habits, her character. The guest had overstayed her welcome. He was jealous.

She couldn't figure out why a woman as good and as smart as Caitlin stayed on with him. Maybe something damaged in Caitlin was called by a like damage in James. Caitlin had lost her father while a girl, as had Fang. When Fang looked at James through Caitlin's eyes, she could see in him the ruins of something strong and attractive and paternal. But that thing was no longer alive. Only Caitlin's need for it lived, and that need had become a reproach to James, who had lost the ability to meet it, and who fled from it.

The further James fled into drink, the more Caitlin retreated into her U, into a quiescence where things could feel whole. All the while, James felt Fang's eyes on him, evaluating him, seeing him as he was. He saw she wasn't buying him. And he saw that Caitlin was alive and present only with Fang. They clung to one another, and were moving away from him.

James was truly good to me, before you knew him.

On U, everyone seems good to you.

No, long before that. When I failed my orals he was a great support.

You were vulnerable. He fed on your need.

You don't know, Fang. I was lost. He helped me, he held on to me when I needed it. Then I had you.

She thought not. She thought James had learned to enjoy preying on the vulnerable. And Caitlin was too willing to ignore this, to go along with it. As Fang finished her years at Trinity, she agonized over how she must deal with this trouble. It was then that the offer arrived from Roger's lab.

Come with me to America.

Oh, Fang. I can't. What about James? What would he do there?

It was James's pretense that he was still whole and competent and functional, when in fact his days were marked out by the habits of rising late, avoiding work in the library, and leaving early for the pub. Any move or change would expose the pretense.

Just you and me. Just for a year.

I can't.

Fang heard alarms. If she stayed and tried to protect Caitlin, her presence might drive James to some extreme. Or Fang might be drawn more deeply into their dysfunction. She didn't know if she could survive that. The thing Fang was best at was saving herself. So she went to America alone.

There was a second body covered with fungus. Number fifteen. Loren.

Either the fungus was contained, restricted to these two, or more likely it had already spread. But how? The bodysuits showed no faults, no breaches. They were isolated from each other, with no pathways for infection. The only possible connection would be through the air supply, and the scrubbers should remove any pathogens, certainly anything as large as a fungus.

In any case, it was bad. She could try rousing another steward manually. But to what purpose? Only she had the expertise to deal with this.

She realized she thought of it because she was desperately lonely. She wanted company with this problem. She wasn't going to get any.

Not enough fat to rouse. Increase glycogen uptake? Maybe, but carbohydrate fasting was a key part of the process.

They had this advantage over natural hibernators: They didn't need to get all their energy from stored body fat. Lipids were dripped in dermally to provide ATP. But body fat was getting metabolized anyway.

Signaling. Perhaps the antisenescents were signaling the fungus not to die. Slowing not its growth but its morbidity. If it were a fungus. Sure it was, it had to be. But confirm it.

After she came to the Lab, Fang learned that her adoption was not so much a matter of her initiative, or of Caitlin's, or of good fortune. Roger had pulled strings every step of the way—strings Fang had no idea existed.

He'd known of Fang because all student work—every paper, test, email, click, eyeblink, keystroke—was stored and tracked and mined. Her permanent record. Corps and labs had algorithms conducting eternal worldwide surveillance for, among so many other things, promising scientists. Roger had his own algorithms: his stock-market eye for early bloomers, good draft choices. He'd purchased Fang's freedom from some Chinese consortium and linked her to Caitlin.

Roger, Fang came to realize, had seen in Caitlin's needs and infirmities a way to help three people: Caitlin, who needed someone to nurture and give herself to, so as not to immolate herself; Fang, who needed that nurturing; and himself, who needed Fang's talent. In other words: Roger judged that Caitlin would do best as the mother of a scientist.

He wasn't wrong. Caitlin's nurture was going to waste on James, who simply sucked it in and gave nothing back. And Fang needed a brilliant, loving, female example to give her confidence in her own brilliance. That's what Caitlin herself had lacked. If Fang had known all this, she'd have taken the terms; she'd have done anything to get out of China. But she hadn't known; she hadn't been consulted. So when she found out, those years later, she was furious. For Caitlin, for herself. As she saw it, Roger couldn't have the mother, so he took the daughter. He used their love and mutual need to get what he wanted, and then he broke them apart. It was cold and calculating and utterly selfish of Roger; of the three of them, only he wasn't damaged by it. She'd almost quit Gypsy in her fury.

She did quit the Lab. She went into product development at Glaxo, under contract to DARPA. That was the start of her hibernation work. It was for battlefield use, as a way to keep injured soldiers alive during transport. When she reflected on this move, she wasn't so sure that Roger hadn't pulled more strings. In any case, the work was essential to Gypsy.

Roger had fury of his own, to spare. Fang knew all about the calm front. Roger reeked of it. He'd learned that he had the talent and the position to do great harm; the orbiting bombs were proof of that. His anger and disappointment had raised in him the urge to do more harm. At the Lab he was surrounded by the means and the opportunity. So he'd gathered all his ingenuity and his rage against humanity and sequestered it in a project large enough and complex enough to occupy it fully, so that it could not further harm him or the world: Gypsy. He would do a thing that had never been done before; and he would take away half the bombs he'd enabled in the doing of it; and the thing would not be shared with humanity. She imagined he saw it as a victimless revenge.

Well, here were the victims.

A day later, *Pseudogymnoascus destructans* was her best guess. Or some mutation of it. It had killed most of the bats on Earth. It grew only in low temperatures, in the four-to-fifteen-degree Celsius range. The ship was normally held at four degrees Celsius.

She could synthesize an antifungal agent with the gene printer, but what about interactions? Polyenes would bind with a fungus's ergosterols but could have severe and lethal side effects.

How could she tweak the cocktail? Some components acted only at the start of the process. They triggered a cascade of enzymes in key pathways to bring on torpor. Some continued to drip in, to reinforce gene expression, to suppress circadian rhythms, and so on.

It was all designed to interact with nonhuman mammalian genes she'd spliced in. Including parts of the bat immune system—*Myotis lucifugus*—parts relevant to hibernation, to respond to the appropriate mRNA signals. But were they also vulnerable to this fungus? *O God, did I do this? Did I open up this vulnerability?*

She gave her presentation, in the open, to DARPA. It was amazing; she was speaking in code to the few Gypsies in the audience, including Roger, telling them in effect how they'd survive the long trip to Alpha, yet her plaintext words were telling DARPA about battlefield applications: suspending wounded soldiers, possibly in space, possibly for long periods, 3D-printing organs, crisping stem cells, and so on.

In Q&A she knew DARPA was sold; they'd get their funding. Roger was right: Everything was dual use.

She'd been up for ten days. The cramped, dark space was wearing her down. Save them. They had to make it. She'd pulled a DNA sequencer and a gene printer from the storage bay. As she fed it *E. coli* and *Mycoplasma mycoides* stock, she reviewed what she'd come up with.

She could mute the expression of the bat genes at this stage, probably without disrupting hibernation. They were the receptors for the triggers that started and stopped the process. But that could compromise rousing. So mute them temporarily—for how long?—hope to revive an immune response, temporarily damp down the antisenescents, add an antifungal. She'd have to automate everything in the mixture; the ship wouldn't rouse her a second time to supervise.

It was a long shot, but so was everything now.

It was too hard for her. For anyone. She had the technology: a complete library of genetic sequences, a range of restriction enzymes, Sleeping Beauty transposase, et cetera. She'd be capable on the spot, for instance, of producing a pathogen that could selectively kill individuals with certain ethnic markers—that had been one project at the Lab, demurely called "preventive." But she didn't have the knowledge she needed for this. It had taken years of research experimentation, and collaboration, to come up with the original cocktail, and it would take years more to truly solve this. She had only a few days. Then the residue of the cocktail would be out of her system and she would lose the ability to rehibernate. So she had to go with what she had now. Test it on DNA from her own saliva.

Not everyone stuck with Gypsy. One scientist at the Lab, Sidney Lefebvre, was wooed by Roger to sign up, and declined only after carefully studying their plans for a couple of weeks. It's too hard, Roger. What you have here is impressive. But it's only a start. There are too many intractable problems. Much more work needs to be done.

That work won't get done. Things are falling apart, not coming together. It's now or never.

Probably so. Regardless, the time for this is not now. This, too, will fall apart.

She wrote the log for the next steward, who would almost surely have the duty of more corpses. Worse, as stewards died, maintenance would be deferred. Systems would die. She didn't know how to address that. Maybe Lefebvre was right. But no: They had to make it. How could this be harder than getting from Guangxhou to Dublin to here?

She prepared to go back under. Fasted the day. Enema, shower. Taps and stents and waldos and derms attached and the bodysuit sealed around her. She felt the cocktail run into her veins.

The lights were off. The air was chill. In her last moment of clarity, she stared into blackness. Always she had run, away from distress, toward something new, to eradicate its pain and its hold. Not from fear. As a gesture of contempt, of power: done with you, never going back. But run to where? No world, no O, no gravity, no hold, nothing to cling to. This was the end of the line. There was nowhere but here. And, still impossibly far, another forty-four years, Alpha C. As impossibly far as Earth.

• • •

3.

Roger recruited his core group face to face. At conferences and symposia he sat for papers that had something to offer his project, and he made a judgment about the presenter. If favorable, it led to a conversation. Always outside, in the open. Fire roads in the Berkeley hills. A cemetery in Zurich. The shores of Lake Como. Fry was well known, traveled much. He wasn't Einstein, he wasn't Feynman, he wasn't Hawking, but he had a certain presence.

The conferences were Kabuki. Not a scientist in the world was unlinked to classified projects through government or corporate sponsors. Presentations were so oblique that expert interpretation was required to parse their real import.

Roger parsed well. Within a year he had a few dozen trusted collaborators. They divided the mission into parts: target selection, engine and fuel, vessel, hibernation, navigation, obstacle avoidance, computers, deceleration, landfall, survival.

The puzzle had too many pieces. Each piece was unthinkably complex. They needed much more help.

They put up a site they called Gypsy. On the surface it was a gaming site, complex and thick with virtual worlds, sandboxes, self-evolving puzzles, and links. Buried in there was an interactive starship-design section, where ideas were solicited, models built, simulations run. Good nerdy crackpot fun.

The core group tested the site themselves for half a year before going live. Their own usage stats became the profile of the sort of visitors they sought: people like themselves: people with enough standing to have access to the high-speed classified web, with enough autonomy to waste professional time on a game site, and finally with enough curiosity and dissidence to pursue certain key links down a critical chain. They needed people far enough inside an institution to have access to resources, but not so far inside as to identify with its ideology. When a user appeared to fit that profile, a public key was issued. The key unlocked further levels and ultimately enabled secure email to an encrypted server.

No one, not even Roger Fry, knew how big the conspiracy was. Ninety-nine percent of their traffic was noise—privileged kids, stoked hackers, drunken Ph.D.s, curious spooks. Hundreds of keys were issued in the first year. Every key increased the risk. But without resources they were going nowhere.

The authorities would vanish Roger Fry and everyone associated with him on the day they learned what he was planning. Not because of the what: a starship posed no threat. But because of the how and the why: Only serious and capable dissidents could plan so immense a thing; the seriousness and the capability were the threat. And eventually they would be found, because every bit of the world's digital traffic was swept up and stored and analyzed. There was a city under the Utah desert where these yottabytes of data were archived in server farms. But the sheer size of the archive outran its analysis and opened a time window in which they might act.

Some ran propellant calculations. Some forwarded classified medical studies. Some were space workers with access to shuttles and tugs. Some passed on classified findings from telescopes seeking exoplanets.

One was an operator of the particle beam at Shackleton Crater. The beam was used, among other purposes, to move the orbiting sleds containing the very bombs Roger had helped design.

One worked at a seed archive in Norway. She piggybacked a capsule into Earth orbit containing seeds from fifty thousand unmodified plant species, including plants legally extinct. They needed those because every cultivated acre on Earth was now planted with engineered varieties that were sterile; terminator genes had been implanted to protect the agro firms' profit streams; and these genes had jumped to wild varieties. There wasn't a live food plant left anywhere on Earth that could propagate itself.

They acquired frozen zygotes of some ten thousand animal species, from bacteria to primates. Hundred thousands more complete DNA sequences in a data library, and a genome printer. Nothing like the genetic diversity of Earth, even in its present state, but enough, perhaps, to reboot such diversity.

At Roger's lab, panels of hydrogenous carbon-composite, made to shield high-orbit craft from cosmic rays and to withstand temperatures of two thousand degrees Celsius, went missing. Quite a lot of silica aerogel as well.

At a sister lab, a researcher put them in touch with a contractor from whom they purchased, quite aboveboard, seventy kilometers of lightweight, high-current-density superconducting cable.

After a year, Roger decided that their web had grown too large to remain secure. He didn't like the number of unused keys going out. He didn't like the page patterns he was seeing. He didn't consult with the others, he just shut it down.

But they had their pieces.

SERGEI (2118)

Eat, drink, shit. That's all he did for the first day or three. Water tasted funny. Seventy-seven years might have viled it, or his taste buds. Life went on, including the ending of it. Vital signs of half the crew were flat. He considered disposing of bodies, ejecting them, but number one, he couldn't be sure they were dead; number two, he couldn't propel them hard enough to keep them from making orbit around the ship, which was funny but horrible; and finally, it would be unpleasant and very hard work that would tire him out. An old man—he surely felt old, and the calendar would back him up—needs to reserve his strength. So he let them lie on their slabs.

The logs told a grim story. They were slow. To try to make up for lost time, Sophie had reprogrammed the magsail to deploy later and to run at higher current. Another steward had been wakened at the original deployment point, to confirm their speed and position, and to validate the decision to wait. Sergei didn't agree with that, and he especially didn't like the handwaving over when to ignite the nuclear rocket in-system, but it was done: They'd gone the extra years at speed and now they needed to start decelerating hard.

CURRENT INJECTION FAILED. MAGSAIL NOT DEPLOYED.

He tapped the screen to cycle through its languages. Stopped at the Cyrillic script, and tapped the speaker, just so he could hear spoken Russian.

So he had to fix the magsail. Current had flowed on schedule from inside, but the sail wasn't charging or deploying. According to telltales, the bay was open but the superconducting cable just sat there. That meant EVA. He didn't like it, but there was no choice. It's what he was here for. Once it was done he'd shower again under that pathetic lukewarm stream, purge his bowels, get back in the Mylar suit, and go under for another, what, eight more years, a mere nothing, we're almost there. Ghost Planet Hope.

He was the only one onboard who'd been a career astronaut. Roger had conveyed a faint class disapproval about that, but needed the expertise. Sergei had been one of the gene-slushed orbital jockeys who pushed bomb sleds around. He knew the feel of zero G, of sunlight on one side of you and absolute cold on the other. He knew how it felt when the particle beam from Shackleton swept over you to push you and the sleds into a new orbit. And you saluted and cut the herds, and kept whatever more you might know to yourself.

Which in Sergei's case was quite a bit. Sergei knew orbital codes and protocols far beyond his pay grade; he could basically move anything in orbit to or from anywhere. But only Sergei, so Sergei thought, knew that. How Roger learned it remained a mystery.

To his great surprise, Sergei learned that even he hadn't known the full extent of his skills. How easy it had been to steal half a million bombs. True, the eternal war economy was so corrupt that materiel was supposed to disappear; something was wrong if it didn't. Still, he would never have dared anything so outrageous on his own. Despite Roger's planning, he was sweating the day he moved the first sled into an unauthorized orbit. But days passed, then weeks and months, as sled followed sled into new holding orbits. In eighteen months they had all their fuel. No traps had sprung, no alarms tripped. Sophie managed to make the manifests look okay. And he wondered again at what the world had become. And what he was in it.

This spacesuit was light, thin, too comfortable. Like a toddler's fleece playsuit with slippers and gloves. Even the helmet was soft. He was more used to heavy Russian engineering, but whatever. They'd argued over whether to include a suit at all. He'd argued against. EVA had looked unlikely, an unlucky possibility. So he was happy now to have anything.

The soles and palms were sticky, a clever off-the-shelf idea inspired by lizards. Billions of carbon nanotubes lined them. The Van der Waals molecular force made them stick to any surface. He tested it by walking on the interior walls. Hands or feet held you fast, with or against the ship's rotational gravity. You had to kind of toe-and-heel to walk, but it was easy enough.

Пойдем. Let's go. He climbed into the hatch and cycled it. As the pressure dropped, the suit expanded and felt more substantial. He tested the grip of his palms on the hull before rising fully out of the hatch. Then his feet came up and gripped, and he stood.

In darkness and immensity stiller than he could comprehend. Interstellar space. The frozen splendor of the galactic core overhead. Nothing appeared to move.

He remembered a still evening on a lake, sitting with a friend on a dock, legs over the edge. They talked as the sky darkened, looking up as the stars came out. Only when it was fully dark did he happen to look down. The water was so still, stars were reflected under his feet. He almost lurched over the edge of the dock in surprise.

The memory tensed his legs, and he realized the galactic core was moving slowly around the ship. Here on the outside of the ship, its spin-induced gravity was reversed. He stood upright but felt pulled toward the stars.

He faced forward. Tenth of a light-year from Alpha, its two stars still appeared as one. They were brighter than Venus in the Earth's sky. They cast his faint but distinct shadow on the hull.

They were here. They had come this far. On this tiny splinter of human will forging through vast, uncaring space. It was remarkable.

A line of light to his left flashed. Some microscopic particle ionized by the ship's magnetic shield. He tensed again at this evidence of their movement and turned slowly, directing his beam over the hull. Its light caught a huge gash through one of the hydrogen tanks. Edges of the gash had failed to be covered by a dozen geckos, frozen in place by hydrogen ice. That was bad.

Worse, it hadn't been in the log. Maybe it was from the impact Sophie had referred to. He would have to see how bad it was after freeing the magsail.

He turned, and toed and heeled his way carefully aft. Now ahead of him was our Sun, still one of the brightest stars, the heavens turning slowly around it. He approached the circular bay that held the magsail. His light showed six large spools of cable, each a meter and a half across and a meter thick. About five metric tons in all, seventy kilometers of thin superconductor wire. Current injection should have caused the spools to unreel under the force of the electric field. But it wasn't getting current, or it was somehow stuck. He was going to have to . . . well, he wasn't sure.

Then he saw it. Almost laughed at the simplicity and familiarity of it. Something like a circuit breaker, red and green buttons, the red one lit. He squatted at the edge of the bay and found he could reach the thing. He felt cold penetrate his suit. He really ought to go back inside and spend a few hours troubleshooting, read the fucking manual, but the cold and the flimsy spacesuit and the immensity convinced him otherwise. He slapped the green button.

It lit. The cable accepted current. He saw it lurch. As he smiled and stood, the current surging in the coils sent its field through the soles of his spacesuit, disrupting for a moment the molecular force holding them to the hull. In that moment, the angular velocity of the rotating ship was transmitted to his body and he detached, moving away from the ship at a stately three meters per second. Beyond his flailing feet, the cables of the magsail began leisurely to unfurl.

As he tumbled the stars rolled past. He'd seen Orion behind the ship in the moment he detached, and as he tumbled he looked for it, for something to grab on to, but he never saw it or the ship again. So he didn't see the huge coil of wire reach its full extension, nor the glow of ionization around the twenty-kilometer circle when it began to drag against the interstellar medium, nor how the ship itself started to lag against the background stars. The ionization set up a howl across the radio spectrum, but his radio was off, so he didn't hear that. He tumbled in silence in the bowl of the heavens at his fixed velocity, which was now slightly greater than the ship's. Every so often the brightness of Alpha crossed his view. He was going to get there first.

4.

Their biggest single problem was fuel. To cross that enormous distance in less than a human lifetime, even in this stripped-down vessel, required an inconceivable amount of energy. Ten to the twenty first joules. Two hundred fifty trillion kilowatt hours. Twenty years' worth of all Earth's greedy energy consumption. The mass of the fuel, efficient though it was, would be several times the mass of the ship. And to reach cruising speed was only half of it; they had to decelerate when they reached Alpha C, doubling the fuel. It was undoable.

Until someone found an old paper on magnetic sails. A superconducting loop of wire many kilometers across, well charged, could act as a drag brake against the interstellar medium. That would cut the fuel requirement almost in half. Done that way, it was just possible, though out on the ragged edge of what was survivable. This deceleration would take ten years.

For their primary fuel, Roger pointed to the hundreds of thousands of bombs in orbit. His bombs. His intellectual property. Toss them out the back and ignite them. A Blumlein pulse-forming line—they called it the "bloom line"—a self-generated magnetic vise, something like a Z-pinch— would direct nearly all the blast to exhaust velocity. The vise, called into being for the nanoseconds of ignition, funneled all that force straight back. Repeat every minute. Push the compression ratio up, you won't get many neutrons.

In the end they had two main engines: first, the antiproton-fusion monster to get them up to speed. It could only be used for the first year; any longer and the antiprotons would decay. Then the magsail would slow them most of the way, until they entered the system.

For the last leg, a gas-core nuclear rocket to decelerate in the system, which required carrying a large amount of hydrogen. They discussed scooping hydrogen from the interstellar medium as they traveled, but Roger vetoed it: not off the shelf. They didn't have the time or means to devise a new technology. Anyway, the hydrogen would make, in combination with their EM shield, an effective barrier to cosmic rays. Dual use.

And even so, everything had to be stretched to the limit: the mass of the ship minimized, the human lifetime lengthened, the fuel leveraged every way possible.

The first spacecraft ever to leave the solar system, *Pioneer 10*, had used Jupiter's gravity to boost its velocity. As it flew by, it stole kinetic energy from the planet; its small mass sped up a lot; Jupiter's stupendous mass slowed unnoticeably.

They would do the same thing to lose speed. They had the combined mass of two stars orbiting each other, equal to two thousand Jupiters. When *Gypsy* was to arrive in 2113, the stars in their mutual orbit would be as close together as they ever got: eleven astronomical units. *Gypsy* would fly by the B star and pull one last trick: Retrofire the nuclear rocket deep in its gravity well; that would multiply the kinetic effect of the propellant severalfold.

And then they'd repeat that maneuver around A. The relative closeness of elevenAU was still as far as Earth to Saturn, so even after arrival, even at their still-great speed, the dual braking maneuver would take over a year.

Only then would they be moving slowly enough to aerobrake in the planet's atmosphere, and that would take a few dozen passes before they could ride the ship down on its heatshield to the surface.

If there was a planet. If it had an atmosphere.

ZIA (2120)

As a child he was lord of the dark—finding his way at night, never stumbling, able to read books by starlight; to read also, in faces and landscapes, traces and glimmers that others missed. Darkness was warmth and comfort to him.

A cave in Ephesus. In the Q'uran, Surah Al-Kahf. The sleepers waking after centuries, emerging into a changed world. Trying to spend old coins.

After the horror of his teen years, he'd found that dark was still a friend. Looking through the eyepiece of an observatory telescope, in the Himalayan foothills, in Uttar Pradesh. Describing the cluster of galaxies, one by one, to the astronomer. *You see the seventh? What eyes!*

Nothing moved but in his mind. Dreams of tenacity and complication. Baffling remnants, consciousness too weak to sort. Every unanswered question of his life, every casual observation, every bit of mental flotsam, tossed together in one desperate, implicate attempt at resolving them all. Things fell; he lunged to catch them. He stood on street corners in an endless night, searching for his shoes, his car, his keys, his wife. His mother chided him in a room lit by incandescent bulbs, dim and flickering like firelight. Galaxies in the eyepiece faded, and he looked up from the eyepiece to a blackened sky. He lay waking, in the dark, now aware of the dream state, returning with such huge reluctance to the life of the body, that weight immovable on its slab.

His eyelid was yanked open. A drop of fluid splashed there. A green line swept across his vision. He caught a breath and it burned in his lungs.

He was awake. Aboard *Gypsy*. It was bringing him back to life.

But I'm cold. Too cold to shiver. Getting colder as I wake up.

How hollow he felt. In this slight gravity. How unreal. It came to him, in the eclipsing of his dreams and the rising of his surroundings, that the gravity of Earth might be something more profound than the acceleration of a mass, the curvature of spacetime. Was it not an emanation of the planet, a life force? All life on Earth evolved in it, rose from it, fought it every moment, lived and bred and died awash in it. Those tides swept through our cells, the force from Earth, and the gravity of the sun and the gravity of the moon. What was life out here, without that embrace, that permeation, that bondage? Without it, would they wither and die like plants in a shed?

The hollowness came singing, roaring, whining, crackling into his ears. Into his throat and nose and eyes and skin it came as desiccation. Searing into his mouth. He needed to cough and he couldn't. His thorax spasmed.

There was an antiseptic moistness in his throat. It stung, but his muscles had loosened. He could breathe. Cold swept from his shoulders down through his torso and he began to shiver uncontrollably.

When he could, he raised a hand. He closed his eyes and held the hand afloat in the parodic gravity, thinking about it, how it felt, how far away it actually was. At last, with hesitation, his eyes opened and came to focus. An old man's hand, knobby, misshapen at the joints, the skin papery, sagging and hanging in folds. He couldn't close the fingers. How many years had he slept? He forced on his hand the imagination of a clenched fist. The hand didn't move.

Oh my god the pain.

Without which, no life. Pain too is an emanation of the planet, of the life force.

It sucked back like a wave, gathering for another concussion. He tried to sit up and passed out.

Nikos Kakopoulos was a short man, just over five feet, stocky but fit. The features of his face were fleshy, slightly comic. He was greying, balding, but not old. In his fifties. He smiled as he said he planned to be around a hundred years from now. His office was full of Mediterranean light. A large Modigliani covered one wall. His money came mostly from aquifer rights. He spent ten percent of it on charities. One such awarded science scholarships. Which was how he'd come to Roger's attention.

So you see, I am not such a bad guy.

Those foundations are just window dressing. What they once called greenwash.

Zia, said Roger.

Kakopoulos shrugged as if to say, Let him talk, I've heard it all. To Zia he said: They do some good after all. They're a comfort to millions of people.

Drinking water would be more of a comfort.

There isn't enough to go round. I didn't create that situation.

You exploit it.

So sorry to say this. Social justice and a civilized lifestyle can't be done both at once. Not for ten billion people. Not on this planet.

You've decided this.

It's a conclusion based on the evidence.

And you care about this why?

I'm Greek. We invented justice and civilization.

You're Cypriot. Also, the Chinese would argue that. The Persians. The Egyptians. Not to mention India.

Kakopoulos waved away the first objection and addressed the rest. Of course they would. And England, and Germany, and Italy, and Russia, and the U.S. They're arguing as we speak. Me, I'm not going to argue. I'm going to a safe place until the arguing is over. After that, if we're very lucky, we can have our discussion about civilization and justice.

On your terms.

On terms that might have some meaning.

What terms would those be?

World population under a billion, for starters. Kakopoulos reached across the table and popped an olive into his mouth.

How do you think that's going to happen? asked Zia.

It's happening. Just a matter of time. Since I don't know how much time, I want a safe house for the duration.

How are you going to get up there?

Kakopoulous grinned. When the Chinese acquired Lockheed, I picked up an X-33. It can do Mach 25. I have a spaceport on Naxos. Want a ride?

The VTOL craft looked like the tip of a Delta IV rocket, or of a penis: a blunt, rounded conic. Not unlike Kakopoulos himself. Some outsize Humpty Dumpty.

How do you know him? Zia asked Roger as they boarded.

I've been advising him.

You're advising the man who owns a third of the world's fresh water?

He owns a lot of things. My first concern is for our project. We need him.

What for?

Roger stared off into space.

He immiserates the Earth, Roger.

We all ten billion immiserate the Earth by being here.

Kakopoulos returned.

Make yourselves comfortable. Even at Mach 25, it takes some time.

It was night, and the Earth was below their window. Rivers of manmade light ran across it. Zia could see the orange squiggle of the India-Pakistan border, all three thousand floodlit kilometers of it. Then the ship banked and the window turned to the stars.

Being lord of the dark had a touch of clairvoyance in it. The dark seldom brought surprise to him. Something bulked out there and he felt it. Some gravity about it called to him from some future. Sun blazed forth behind the limb of the Earth, but the thing was still in Earth's shadow. It made a blackness against the Milky Way. Then sunlight touched it. Its lines caught light: the edges of panels, tanks, heat sinks, antennas. Blunt radar-shedding angles. A squat torus shape under it all. It didn't look like a ship. It looked like a squashed donut to which a junkyard had been glued. It turned slowly on its axis.

My safe house, said Kakopoulos.

It was, indeed, no larger than a house. About ten meters long, twice that across. It had cost a large part of Kakopoulos's considerable fortune. Which he recouped by manipulating and looting several central banks. As a result, a handful of small countries, some hundred million people, went off the cliff-edge of modernity into an abyss of debt peonage.

While they waited to dock with the thing, Kakopoulos came and sat next to Zia.

Listen, my friend—

I'm not your friend.

As you like, I don't care. I don't think you're stupid. When I said my foundations make people feel better, I meant the rich, of course. You're Pakistani?

Indian actually.

But Muslim. Kashmir?

Zia shrugged.

Okay. We're not so different, I think. I grew up in the slums of Athens after the euro collapsed. The histories, the videos, they don't capture it. I imagine Kashmir was much worse. But we each found a way out, no? So tell me, would you go back to that? No, you don't have to answer. You wouldn't. Not for anything. You'd sooner die. But you're not the kind of asshole who writes conscience checks. Or thinks your own self is wonderful enough to deserve anything. So where does that leave a guy like you in this world?

Fuck you.

Kakopoulos patted Zia's hand and smiled. I love it when people say fuck you to me. You know why? It means I won. They've got nothing left but their fuck you. He got up and went away.

The pilot came in then, swamp-walking the zero G in his velcro shoes, and said they'd docked.

The ship massed about a hundred metric tons. A corridor circled the inner circumference, floor against the outer hull, most of the space taken up by hibernation slabs for a crew of twenty. Once commissioned, it would spin on its axis a few times a minute to create something like lunar gravity. They drifted around it slowly, pulling themselves by handholds.

This, Kakopoulos banged a wall, is expensive. Exotic composites, all that aerogel. Why so much insulation?

Roger let "expensive" pass unchallenged. Zia didn't.

You think there's nothing more important than money.

Kakopoulos turned, as if surprised Zia was still there. He said, There are many things more important than money. You just don't get any of them without it.

Roger said, Even while you're hibernating, the ship will radiate infrared.

That's one reason you'll park at a Lagrange point, far enough away not to attract attention. When you wake up and start using energy, you're going to light up like a Christmas tree. And you're going to hope that whatever is left on Earth or in space won't immediately blow you out of the sky. The insulation will hide you somewhat.

At one end of the cramped command center was a micro-apartment.

What's this, Nikos?

Ah, my few luxuries. Music, movies, artworks. We may be out here awhile after we wake up. Look at my kitchen.

A range?

Propane, but it generates 30,000 BTU!

That's insane. You're not on holiday here.

Look, it's vented, only one burner, I got a great engineer, you can examine the plans—

Get rid of it.

What! Kakopoulos yelled. Whose ship is this!

Roger pretended to think for a second. Do you mean who owns it, or who designed it?

Do you know how much it cost to get that range up here?

I can guess to the nearest million.

When I wake up I want a good breakfast!

When you wake up you'll be too weak to stand. Your first meal will be coming down tubes.

Kakopoulos appeared to sulk.

Nikos, what is your design specification here?

I just want a decent omelette.

I can make that happen. But the range goes.

Kakopoulous nursed his sulk, then brightened. Gonna be some meteor, that range. I'll call my observatory, have them image it.

Later, when they were alone, Zia said: All right, Roger. I've been very patient.

Patient? Roger snorted.

How can that little pustule help us?

That's our ship. We're going to steal it.

Later, Zia suggested that they christen the ship the Fuck You.

Eighty years later, Zia was eating one of Kakopoulos's omelettes. Freeze-dried egg, mushrooms, onion, tarragon. Microwaved with two ounces of water. Not bad. He had another.

Mach 900, asshole, he said aloud.

Most of the crew were dead. Fungus had grown on the skin stretched like drums over their skulls, their ribs, their hips.

He'd seen worse. During his mandatory service, as a teenager in the military, he'd patrolled Deccan slums. He'd seen parents eating their dead children. Pariah dogs fat as sheep roamed the streets. Cadavers, bones, skulls, were piled in front of nearly every house. The cloying carrion smell never lifted. Hollowed-out buildings housed squatters and corpses equally, darkened plains of them below fortified bunkers lit like Las Vegas, where the driving bass of party music echoed the percussion of automatic weapons and rocket grenades.

Now his stomach rebelled, but he commanded it to be still as he swallowed some olive oil. Gradually the chill in his core subsided.

He needed to look at the sky. The ship had two telescopes: a one-meter honeycomb mirror for detail work and a wide-angle high-res CCD camera. Zoomed fully out, the camera took in about eighty degrees. Ahead was the blazing pair of Alpha Centauri A and B, to the eye more than stars but not yet suns. He'd never seen anything like them. Brighter than Venus, bright as the full moon, but such tiny disks. As he watched, the angle of them moved against the ship's rotation.

He swept the sky, looking for landmarks. But the stars were wrong. What had happened to Orion? Mintaka had moved. The belt didn't point to Sirius, as it should. A brilliant blue star off Orion's left shoulder outshone Betelgeuse, and then he realized. *That* was Sirius. Thirty degrees from where it should be. Of course: It was eight light-years from Earth. They had come half that distance, and, like a nearby buoy seen against a far shore, it had changed position against the farther stars.

More distant stars had also shifted, but not as much. He turned to what he still absurdly thought of as "north." The Big Dipper was there. The Little Dipper's bowl was squashed. Past Polaris was Cassiopeia, the zigzag W, the queen's throne. And there a new, bright star blazed above it, as if that W had grown another zag. Could it be a nova? He stared, and the stars of Cassiopeia circled this strange bright one slowly as the ship rotated. Then he knew: The strange star was Sol. Our Sun.

That was when he felt it, in his body: They were really here.

From the beginning Roger had a hand—a heavy, guiding hand—in the design of the ship. Not for nothing had he learned the Lab's doctrine of dual use. Not for nothing had he cultivated Kakopoulos's acquaintance. Every feature that fitted the ship for interstellar space was a plausible choice for Kak's purpose: hibernators, cosmic-ray shielding, nuclear rocket, hardened computers, plutonium pile and Stirling engine.

In the weeks prior to departure, they moved the ship to a more distant orbit, too distant for Kak's X-33 to reach. There they jettisoned quite a bit of the ship's interior. They added their fusion engine, surrounded the vessel with fuel

*sleds, secured antiproton traps, stowed the magsail, loaded the seed bank and a
hundred other things.*

They were three hundred AU out from Alpha Centauri. Velocity was
one-thousandth c. The magsail was programmed to run for two more
years, slowing them by half again. But lately their deceleration had shown
variance. The magsail was running at higher current than planned. Very
close to max spec. That wasn't good. Logs told him why, and that was worse.

He considered options, none good. The sail was braking against the
interstellar medium, stray neutral atoms of hydrogen. No one knew for sure
how it would behave once it ran into Alpha's charged solar wind. Nor just
where that wind started. The interstellar medium might already be giving
way to it. If so, the count of galactic cosmic rays would be going down and
the temperature of charged particles going up.

He checked. Definitely maybe on both counts.

He'd never liked this plan, its narrow margins of error. Not that he had
a better. That was the whole problem: no plan B. Every intricate, fragile,
untried part of it had to work. He'd pushed pretty hard for a decent margin
of error in this deceleration stage and the subsequent maneuvering in the
system—what a tragedy it would be to come to grief so close, within sight
of shore—and now he saw that margin evaporating.

Possibly the sail would continue to brake in the solar wind. If only they
could have tested it first.

Zia didn't trust materials. Or, rather: He trusted them to fail.
Superconductors, carbon composite, silicon, the human body. Problem was,
you never knew just how or when they'd fail.

One theory said that a hydrogen wall existed somewhere between
the termination shock and the heliopause, where solar wind gave way to
interstellar space. Three hundred AU put *Gypsy* in that dicey zone.

It would be prudent to back off the magsail current. That would lessen
their decel, and they needed all they could get, they had started it too late,
but they also needed to protect the sail and run it as long as possible.

Any change to the current had to happen slowly. It would take hours or
possibly days. The trick was not to deform the coil too much in the process,
or create eddy currents that could quench the superconducting field.

The amount of power he had available was another issue. The plutonium
running the Stirling engine had decayed to about half its original capacity.

He shut down heat in the cabin to divert more to the Stirling engine.
He turned down most of the LED lighting, and worked in the semi-dark,
except for the glow of the monitor. Programmed a gentle ramp up in current.

Then he couldn't keep his eyes open.

• • •

At Davos, he found himself talking to an old college roommate. Carter Hall III was his name; he was something with the U.N. now, and with the Council for Foreign Relations—an enlightened and condescending asshole. They were both Harvard '32, but Hall remained a self-appointed Brahmin, generously, sincerely, and with vast but guarded amusement, guiding a Sudra through the world that was his by birthright. Never mind the Sudra was Muslim.

From a carpeted terrace they overlooked a groomed green park. There was no snow in town this January, an increasingly common state of affairs. Zia noted but politely declined to point out the obvious irony, the connection between the policies determined here and the retreat of the snow line.

Why Zia was there was complicated. He was persona non grata with the ruling party, but he was a scientist, he had security clearances, and he had access to diplomats on both sides of the border. India had secretly built many thousands of microfusion weapons and denied it. The U.S. was about to enter into the newest round of endless talks over "nonproliferation," in which the U.S. never gave up anything but insisted that other nations must.

Hall now lectured him. India needed to rein in its population, which was over two billion. The U.S. had half a billion.

Zia, please, look at the numbers. Four-plus children per household just isn't sustainable.

Abruptly Zia felt his manners fail.

Sustainable? Excuse me. Our Indian culture is four thousand years old, self-sustained through all that time. Yours is two, three, maybe five hundred years old, depending on your measure. And in that short time, not only is it falling apart, it's taking the rest of the world down with it, including my homeland.

Two hundred years, I don't get that, if you mean Western—

I mean technology, I mean capital, I mean extraction.

Well, but those are very, I mean if you look at your, your four thousand years of, of poverty and class discrimination, and violence—

Ah? And there is no poverty or violence in your brief and perfect history? No extermination? No slavery?

Hall's expression didn't change much.

We've gotten past all that, Zia. We—

Zia didn't care that Hall was offended. He went on:

The story of resource extraction has only two cases, okay? In the first case, the extractors arrive and make the local ruler an offer. Being selfish, he takes it and he becomes rich—never so rich as the extractors, but compared to his people, fabulously, delusionally rich. His people become the cheap labor used to extract the resource. This leads to social upheaval. Villages are moved, families destroyed. A few people are enriched, the majority are ruined. Maybe there is an uprising against the ruler.

In the second case the ruler is smarter. Maybe he's seen some neighboring ruler's head on a pike. He says no thanks to the extractors. To this they have various responses: make him a better offer, find a greedier rival, hire an assassin, or bring in the gunships. But in the end it's the same: A few people are enriched, most are ruined. What the extractors never, ever do in any case, in all your history, is take no for an answer.

Zia, much as I enjoy our historical discussions—

Ah, you see? There it is—your refusal to take no. Talk is done, now we move forward with your agenda.

We have to deal with the facts on the ground. Where we are now.

Yes, of course. It's remarkable how, when the mess you've made has grown so large that even you must admit to it, you want to reset everything to zero. You want to get past "all that." All of history starts over, with these "facts on the ground." Let's move on, move forward, forget how we got here, forget the exploitation and the theft and the waste and the betrayals. Forget the, what is that charming accounting word, the externalities. Start from the new zero.

Hall looked weary and annoyed that he was called upon to suffer such childishness. That well-fed yet kept-fit form hunched, that pale skin looked suddenly papery and aged in the Davos sunlight.

You know, Zia prodded, greed could at least be more efficient. If you know what you want, at least take it cleanly. No need to leave whole countries in ruins.

Hall smiled a tight, grim smile, just a glimpse of the wolf beneath. He said: Then it wouldn't be greed. Greed never knows what it wants.

That was the exact measure of Hall's friendship, to say that to Zia. But then Zia knew what he wanted: out.

As he drifted awake, he realized that, decades past, the ship would have collected data on the Sun's own heliopause on their way out. If he could access that data, maybe he could learn whether the hydrogen wall was a real thing. What effect it might—

There was a loud bang. The monitor and the cabin went dark. His mind reached into the outer darkness and it sensed something long and loose and broken trailing behind them.

What light there was came back on. The computer rebooted. The monitor displayed readings for the magsail over the past hour: current ramping up, then oscillating to compensate for varying densities in the medium, then a sharp spike. And then zero. Quenched.

Hydrogen wall? He didn't know. The magsail was fried. He tried for an hour more to get it to accept current. No luck. He remembered with some distaste the EVA suit. He didn't want to go outside, to tempt that darkness, but he might have to, so he walked forward to check it out.

The suit wasn't in its cubby. Zia turned and walked up the corridor, glancing at his torpid crewmates. The last slab was empty.

Sergei was gone. The suit was gone. You would assume they'd gone together, but that wasn't in the logs. *I may be some time.* Sergei didn't strike him as the type to take a last walk in the dark. And for that he wouldn't have needed the suit. Still. You can't guess what anyone might do.

So that was final: no EVA: the magsail couldn't be fixed. From the console, he cut it loose.

They were going far too fast. Twice what they'd planned. Now they had only the nuclear plasma rocket for deceleration, and one fuel tank was empty, somehow. Even though the fuel remaining outmassed the ship, it wasn't enough. If they couldn't slow below the escape velocity of the system, they'd shoot right through and out the other side.

The ship had been gathering data for months and had good orbital elements for the entire system. Around A were four planets, none in a position to assist with flybys. Even if they were, their masses would be little help. Only the two stars were usable.

If he brought them in a lot closer around B—how close could they get? one fiftieth AU? one hundredth?—and if the heat shield held—it should withstand 2500 degrees Celsius for a few hours—the ship could be slowed more with the same amount of fuel. The B star was closest: It was the less luminous of the pair, cooler, allowing them to get in closer, shed more speed. Then repeat the maneuver at A.

There was a further problem. Twelve years ago, as per the original plan, Alpha A and B were at their closest to one another: eleven AU. The stars were now twenty AU apart and widening. So the trip from B to A would take twice as long. And systems were failing. They were out on the rising edge of the bathtub curve.

Power continued erratic. The computer crashed again and again as he worked out the trajectories. He took to writing down intermediate results on paper in case he lost a session, cursing as he did so. Materials. We stole our tech from the most corrupt forces on Earth. Dude, you want an extended warranty with that? He examined the Stirling engine, saw that the power surge had compromised it. He switched the pile over to backup thermocouples. That took hours to do and it was less efficient, but it kept the computer running. It was still frustrating. The computer was designed to be redundant, hardened, hence slow. Minimal graphics, no 3D holobox. He had to think through his starting parameters carefully before he wasted processor time running a simulation.

Finally he had a new trajectory, swinging in perilously close to B, then A. It might work. Next he calculated that, when he did what he was about to do, seventy kilometers of magsail cable wouldn't catch them up and foul them. Then he fired the maneuvering thrusters.

What sold him, finally, was a handful of photons.

This is highly classified, said Roger. He held a manila file folder containing paper. Any computer file was permeable, hackable. Paper was serious.

The data were gathered by an orbiting telescope. It wasn't a photograph. It was a blurred, noisy image that looked like rings intersecting in a pond a few seconds after some pebbles had been thrown.

It's a deconvolved cross-correlation map of a signal gathered by a chopped pair of Bracewell baselines. You know how that works?

He didn't. Roger explained. Any habitable planet around Alpha Centauri A or B would appear a small fraction of an arc-second away from the stars, and would be at least twenty-two magnitudes fainter. At that separation, the most sensitive camera made, with the best dynamic range, couldn't hope to find the planet in the stars' glare. But put several cameras together in a particular phase relation and the stars' light could be nulled out. What remained, if anything, would be light from another source. A planet, perhaps.

Also this, in visible light.

An elliptical iris of grainy red, black at its center, where an occulter had physically blocked the stars' disks.

Coronagraph, said Roger. Here's the detail.

A speck, a single pixel, slightly brighter than the enveloping noise.

What do you think?

Could be anything. Dust, hot pixel, cosmic ray. . . .

It shows up repeatedly. And it moves.

Roger, for all I know you photoshopped it in.

He looked honestly shocked. Do you really think I'd . . .

I'm kidding. But where did you get these? Can you trust the source?

Why would anyone fake such a thing?

The question hung and around it gathered, like sepsis, the suspicion of some agency setting them up, of some agenda beyond their knowing. After the Kepler exoplanet finder went dark, subsequent exoplanet data—like all other government-sponsored scientific work—were classified. Roger's clearance was pretty high, but even he couldn't be sure of his sources.

You're not convinced, are you.

But somehow Zia was. The orbiting telescope had an aperture of, he forgot the final number, it had been scaled down several times owing to budget cuts. A couple of meters, maybe. That meant light from this far-off dim planet fell on it at a rate of just a few photons per second. It made him unutterably lonely to think of those photons traveling so far. It also made him believe in the planet.

Well, okay, Roger Fry was mad. Zia knew that. But he would throw in with Roger because all humanity was mad. Perhaps always had been. Certainly for the past century-plus, with the monoculture madness called modernity. Roger at least was mad in a different way, perhaps Zia's way.

He wrote the details into the log, reduced the orbital mechanics to a cookbook formula. Another steward would have to be awakened when they reached the B star; that would be in five years; his calculations weren't good enough to automate the burn time, which would depend on the ship's precise momentum and distance from the star as it rounded. It wasn't enough just to slow down; their exit trajectory from B needed to point them exactly to where A would be a year later. That wouldn't be easy; he took a couple of days to write an app to make it easier, but with large blocks of memory failing in the computer, Sophie's idea of a handwritten logbook no longer looked so dumb.

As he copied it all out, he imagined the world they'd left so far behind: the billions in their innocence or willed ignorance or complicity, the elites he'd despised for their lack of imagination, their surfeit of hubris, working together in a horrible *folie à deux*. He saw the bombs raining down, atomizing history and memory and accomplishment, working methodically backward from the cities to the cradles of civilization to the birthplaces of the species—the Fertile Crescent, the Horn of Africa, the Great Rift Valley—in a crescendo of destruction and denial of everything humanity had ever been—its failures, its cruelties, its grandeurs, its aspirations—all extirpated to the root, in a fury of self-loathing that fed on what it destroyed.

Zia's anger rose again in his ruined, aching body—his lifelong pointless rage at all that stupidity, cupidity, yes, there's some hollow satisfaction being away from all that. Away from the noise of their being. Their unceasing commotion of disruption and corruption. How he'd longed to escape it. But in the silent enclosure of the ship, in this empty house populated by the stilled ghosts of his crewmates, he now longed for any sound, any noise. He had wanted to be here, out in the dark. But not for nothing. And he wept.

And then he was just weary. His job was done. Existence seemed a pointless series of problems. What was identity? Better never to have been. He shut his eyes.

In bed with Maria, she moved in her sleep, rolled against him, and he rolled away. She twitched and woke from some dream.

What! What! she cried.

He flinched. His heart moved, but he lay still, letting her calm. Finally he said, What was that?

You pulled away from me!

Then they were in a park somewhere. Boston? Maria was yelling at him, in tears. Why must you be so negative!

He had no answer for her, then or now. Or for himself. Whatever "himself" might be. Something had eluded him in his life, and he wasn't going to find it now.

He wondered again about what had happened to Sergei. Well, it was still an option for him. He wouldn't need a suit.

Funny, isn't it, how one's human sympathy—Zia meant most severely his own—extends about as far as those like oneself. He meant true sympathy; abstractions like justice don't count. Even now, missing Earth, he felt sympathy only for those aboard *Gypsy*, those orphaned, damaged, disaffected, dispossessed, Aspergerish souls whose anger at that great abstraction, The World, was more truly an anger at all those fortunate enough to be unlike them. We were all so young. How can you be so young, and so hungry for, and yet so empty of life?

As he closed his log, he hit on a final option for the ship, if not himself. If after rounding B and A the ship still runs too fast to aerobrake into orbit around the planet, do this. Load all the genetic material—the frozen zygotes, the seed bank, the whatever—into a heatshielded pod. Drop it into the planet's atmosphere. If not themselves, some kind of life would have some chance. Yet as soon as he wrote those words, he felt their sting.

Roger, and to some degree all of them, had seen this as a way to transcend their thwarted lives on Earth. They were the essence of striving humanity: Their planning and foresight served the animal's desperate drive to overcome what can't be overcome. To escape the limits of death. Yet transcendence, if it meant anything at all, was the accommodation to limits: a finding of freedom within them, not a breaking of them. Depositing the proteins of life here, like a stiff prick dropping its load, could only, in the best case, lead to a replication of the same futile striving. The animal remains trapped in the cage of its being.

5.

An old, old man in a wheelchair. Tube in his nose. Oxygen bottle on a cart. He'd been somebody at the Lab once. Recruited Roger, among many others, plucked him out of the pack at Caltech. Roger loathed the old man but figured he owed him. And was owed.

They sat on a long, covered porch looking out at hills of dry grass patched with dark stands of live oak. The old man was feeling pretty spry after he'd thumbed through Roger's papers and lit the cigar Roger offered him. He detached the tube, took a discreet puff, exhaled very slowly, and put the tube back in.

Hand it to you, Roger, most elaborate, expensive form of mass suicide in history.

Really? I'd give that honor to the so-called statecraft of the past century.

Wouldn't disagree. But that's been very good to you and me. That stupidity gradient.

This effort is modest by comparison. Very few lives are at stake here. They might even survive it.

How many bombs you got onboard this thing? How many megatons?

They're not bombs, they're fuel. We measure it in exajoules.

Gonna blow them up in a magnetic pinch, aren't you? I call things that blow up bombs. But fine, measure it in horsepower if it makes you feel virtuous. Exajoules, huh? He stared into space for a minute. Ship's mass?

One hundred metric tons dry.

That's nice and light. Wonder where you got ahold of that. But you still don't have enough push. Take you over a hundred years. Your systems'll die.

Seventy-two years.

You done survival analysis? You get a bathtub curve with most of these systems. Funny thing is, redundancy works against you.

How so?

Shit, you got Sidney Lefebvre down the hall from you, world's expert in failure modes, don't you know that?

Roger knew the name. The man worked on something completely different now. Somehow this expertise had been erased from his resume and his working life.

How you gone slow down?

Magsail.

I always wondered, would that work.

You wrote the papers on it.

You know how hand-wavy they are. We don't know squat about the interstellar medium. And we don't have superconductors that good anyway. Or do we?

Roger didn't answer.

What happens when you get into the system?

That's what I want to know. Will the magsail work in the solar wind? Tarasenko says no.

Fuck him.

His math is sound. I want to know what you know. Does it work?

How would I know. Never got to test it. Never heard of anyone who did. Tell me, Dan.

Tell you I don't know. Tarasenko's a crank, got a Ukraine-sized chip on his shoulder.

That doesn't mean he's wrong.

The old man shrugged, looked critically at the cigar, tapped the ash off its end.

Don't hold out on me.

Christ on a crutch, Roger, I'm a dead man. Want me to spill my guts, be nice, bring me a Havana.

There was a spell of silence. In the sunstruck sky a turkey vulture wobbled and banked into an updraft.

How you gone build a magsail that big? You got some superconductor scam goin?

After ten years of braking we come in on this star, through its heliopause, at about 500 kilometers per second. That's too fast to be captured by the system's gravity.

Cause I can help you there. Got some yttrium futures.

If we don't manage enough decel after that, we're done.

Gas-core reactor rocket.

We can't carry enough fuel. Do the math. Specific impulse is about three thousand at best.

The old man took the tube from his nose, tapped more ash off the cigar, inhaled. After a moment he began to cough. Roger had seen this act before. But it went on longer than usual, into a loud climax.

Roger . . . you really doin this? Wouldn't fool a dead man?

I'm modeling. For a multiplayer game.

That brought the old man more than half back. Fuck you too, he said. But that was for any surveillance, Roger thought.

The old man stared into the distance, then said: Oberth effect.

What's that?

Here's what you do, the old man whispered, hunched over, as he brought out a pen and an envelope.

ROSA (2125)

After she'd suffered through the cold, the numbness, the chills, the burning, still she lay, unready to move, as if she weren't whole, had lost some essence—her anima, her purpose. She went over the whole mission in her mind, step by step, piece by piece. Do we have everything? The bombs to get us out of the solar system, the sail to slow us down, the nuclear rocket, the habitat . . . what else? What have we forgotten? There is something in the dark.

What is in the dark? Another ship? Oh my God. If we did it, they could do it, too. It would be insane for them to come after us. But they are insane. And we stole their bombs. What would they *not* do to us? Insane and vengeful as they are. They could send a drone after us, unmanned, or manned by a suicide crew. It's just what they would do.

She breathed the stale, cold air and stared up at the dark ceiling. Okay, relax. That's the worst-case scenario. Best case, they never saw us go. Most likely, they saw but they have other priorities. Everything has worked so far. Or you would not be lying here fretting, Rosa.

Born Rose. Mamá was from Trinidad. Dad was Venezuelan. She called him Papá against his wishes. Solid citizens, assimilated: a banker, a realtor. Home was Altadena, California. There was a bit of Irish blood and more than a dollop of Romany, the renegade uncle Tonio told Rosa, mi mestiza.

They flipped when she joined a chapter of La Raza Nueva. Dad railed: A terrorist organization! And us born in countries we've occupied! Amazed that Caltech even permitted LRN on campus. The family got visits from Homeland Security. Eggs and paint bombs from the neighbors. Caltech looked into it and found that of its seven members, five weren't students. LRN was a creation of Homeland Security. Rosa and Sean were the only two authentic members, and they kept bailing out of planned actions.

Her father came to her while Homeland Security was on top of them, in the dark of her bedroom. He sat on the edge of the bed, she could feel his weight there and the displacement of it, could smell faintly the alcohol on his breath. He said: My mother and my father, my sisters, after the invasion, we lived in cardboard refrigerator boxes in the median strip of the main road from the airport to the city. For a year.

He'd never told her that. She hated him. For sparing her that, only to use it on her now. She'd known he'd grown up poor, but not that. She said bitterly: Behind every fortune is a crime. What's yours?

He drew in his breath. She felt him recoil, the mattress shift under his weight. Then a greater shift, unfelt, of some dark energy, and he sighed. I won't deny it, but it was for family. For you! with sudden anger.

What did you do?

That I won't tell you. It's not safe.

Safe! You always want to be safe, when you should stand up!

Stand up? I did the hardest things possible for a man to do. For you, for this family. And now you put us all at risk—His voice came close to breaking.

When he spoke again, there was no trace of anger left. You don't know how easily it can all be taken from you. What a luxury it is to stand up, as you call it.

Homeland Security backed off when Caltech raised a legal stink about entrapment. She felt vindicated. But her father didn't see it that way. The dumb luck, he called it, of a small fish. Stubborn in his way as she.

Sean, her lovely brother, who'd taken her side through all this, decided to stand up in his own perverse way: He joined the Army. She thought it was dumb, but she had to respect his argument: It was unjust that only poor Latinos joined. Certainly Papá, the patriot, couldn't argue with that logic, though he was furious.

Six months later Sean was killed in Bolivia. Mamá went into a prolonged, withdrawn mourning. Papá stifled an inchoate rage.

She'd met Roger Fry when he taught her senior course in particle physics; as "associated faculty" he became her thesis advisor. He looked as young as she. Actually, he was four years older. Women still weren't exactly welcome in high-energy physics. Rosa—not cute, not demure, not quiet—was even less so. Roger, however, didn't seem to see her. Gender and appearance seemed to make no impression at all on Roger.

He moved north mid-semester to work at the Lab but continued advising her via email. In grad school she followed his name on papers, R. A. Fry, as it moved up from the tail of a list of some dozen names to the head of such lists. "Physics of milli-K Antiproton Confinement in an Improved Penning Trap." "Antiprotons as Drivers for Inertial Confinement Fusion." "Typical Number of Antiprotons Necessary for Fast Ignition in LiDT." "Antiproton-Catalyzed Microfusion." And finally, "Antimatter Induced Continuous Fusion Reactions and Thermonuclear Explosions."

Rosa applied to work at the Lab.

She didn't stop to think, then, why she did it. It was because Roger, of all the people she knew, appeared to have stood up and gone his own way and had arrived somewhere worth going.

They were supposed to have landed on the planet twelve years ago.

Nothing was out there in the dark. Nothing had followed. They were alone. That was worse.

She weighed herself. Four kilos. That would be forty in Earth gravity. Looked down at her arms, her legs, her slack breasts and belly. Skin grey and loose and wrinkled and hanging. On Earth she'd been chunky, glossy as an apple, never under sixty kilos. Her body had been taken from her, and this wasted, frail thing put in its place.

Turning on the monitor's camera she had another shock. She was older than her mother. When they'd left Earth, Mamá was fifty. Rosa was at least sixty, by the look of it. They weren't supposed to have aged. Not like this.

She breathed and told herself it was a luxury to be alive.

• • •

Small parts of the core group met face to face on rare occasions. Never all at once—they were too dispersed for that and even with travel permits it was unwise—it was threes or fours or fives at most. There was no such thing as a secure location. They had to rely on the ubiquity of surveillance outrunning the ability to process it all.

The Berkeley marina was no more secure than anywhere else. Despite the city's Potemkin liberalism, you could count, if you were looking, at least ten cameras from every point within its boundaries, and take for granted there were many more, hidden or winged, small and quick as hummingbirds, with software to read your lips from a hundred yards, and up beyond the atmosphere satellites to read the book in your hand if the air was steady, denoise it if not, likewise take your body temperature. At the marina the strong onshore flow from the cold Pacific made certain of these feats more difficult, but the marina's main advantage was that it was still beautiful, protected by accumulated capital and privilege—though now the names on the yachts were mostly in hanzi characters—and near enough to places where many of them worked, yet within the tether of their freedom—so they came to this rendezvous as often as they dared.

I remember the old marina. See where University Avenue runs into the water? It was half a mile past that. At neap tide you sometimes see it surface. Plenty chop there when it's windy.

They debated what to call this mad thing. Names out of the history of the idea—starships that had been planned but never built—Orion, Prometheus, Daedalus, Icarus, Longshot, Medusa. Names out of their imagination: Persephone, Finnegan, Ephesus. But finally they came to call it—not yet the ship, but themselves, and their being together in it—Gypsy. It was a word rude and available and they took it. They were going wandering, without a land, orphaned and dispossessed, they were gypping the rubes, the hateful inhumane ones who owned everything and out of the devilry of ownership would destroy it rather than share it. She was okay with that taking, she was definitely gypsy.

She slept with Roger. She didn't love him, but she admired him as a fellow spirit. Admired his intellect and his commitment and his belief. Wanted to partake of him and share herself. The way he had worked on fusion, and solved it. And then, when it was taken from him, he found something else. Something mad, bold, bad, dangerous, inspiring.

Roger's voice in the dark: I thought it was the leaders, the nations, the corporations, the elites, who were out of touch, who didn't understand the gravity of our situation. I believed in the sincerity of their stupid denials—of global warming, of resource depletion, of nuclear proliferation, of population *pressure. I thought them stupid. But if you judge them by their actions instead of their rhetoric, you can see that they understood it perfectly and accepted the gravity of it very early. They simply gave it up as unfixable. Concluded that law and democracy and civilization were hindrances to their continued power. Moved quite purposely and at speed toward this dire world they foresaw, a world in which, to have the amenities even of a middle-class life—things like clean water, food, shelter, energy, transportation, medical care—you would need the wealth of a prince. You would need legal and military force to keep desperate others from seizing it. Seeing that, they moved to amass such wealth for themselves as quickly and ruthlessly as possible, with the full understanding that it hastened the day they feared.*

She sat at the desk with the monitors, reviewed the logs. Zia had been the last to waken. Four and a half years ago. Trouble with the magsail. It was gone, and their incoming velocity was too high. And they were very close now, following his trajectory to the B star. She looked at his calculations and thought that he'd done well; it might work. What she had to do: fine-tune the elements of the trajectory, deploy the sunshield, prime the fuel, and finally light the hydrogen torch that would push palely back against the fury of this sun. But not yet. She was too weak.

Zia was dead for sure, on his slab, shriveled like a nut in the bodysuit; he had gone back into hibernation but had not reattached his stents. The others didn't look good. Fang's log told that story, what she'd done to combat the fungus, what else might need to be done, what to look out for. Fang had done the best she could. Rosa, at least, was alive.

A surge of grief hit her suddenly, bewildered her. She hadn't realized it till now: She had a narrative about all this. She was going to a new world and she was going to bear children in it. That was never a narrative she thought was hers; hers was all about standing up for herself. But there it was, and as the possibility of it vanished, she felt its teeth. The woman she saw in the monitor-mirror was never going to have children. A further truth rushed upon her as implacable as the star ahead: The universe didn't have that narrative, or any narrative, and all of hers had been voided in its indifference. What loss she felt. And for what, a story? For something that never was?

Lying next to her in the dark, Roger said: I would never have children. I would never do that to another person.

You already have, Rosa poked him.

You know what I mean.

The universe is vast, Roger.

I know.
The universe of feeling is vast.
No children.
I could make you change your mind.

She'd left Roger behind on Earth. No regrets about that; clearly there was no place for another person on the inside of Roger's life.

The hydrogen in the tanks around the ship thawed as they drew near the sun. One tank read empty. She surmised from logs that it had been breached very early in the voyage. So they had to marshal fuel even more closely.

The orbital elements had been refined since Zia first set up the parameters of his elegant cushion shot. It wasn't Rosa's field, but she had enough math and computer tools to handle it. Another adjustment would have to be made in a year when they neared the A star, but she'd point them as close as she could.

It was going to be a near thing. There was a demanding trade-off between decel and trajectory; they had to complete their braking turn pointed exactly at where A would be in a year. Too much or too little and they'd miss it; they didn't have enough fuel to make course corrections. She ran Zia's app over and over, timing the burn.

Occasionally she looked at the planet through the telescope. Still too far away to see much. It was like a moon of Jupiter seen from Earth. Little more than a dot without color, hiding in the glare of A.

It took most of a week to prep the rocket. She triple-checked every step. It was supposed to be Sergei's job. Only Sergei was not on the ship. He'd left no log. She had no idea what had happened, but now it was her job to start up a twenty-gigawatt gas-core fission reactor. The reactor would irradiate and superheat their hydrogen fuel, which would exit the nozzle with a thrust of some two million newtons.

She fired the attitude thrusters to derotate the ship, fixing it in the shadow of the sunshield. As the spin stopped, so did gravity; she became weightless.

Over the next two days, the thermal sensors climbed steadily to one thousand degrees Celsius, twelve hundred, fifteen hundred. Nothing within the ship changed. It remained dark and cool and silent and weightless. On the far side of the shield, twelve centimeters thick, megawatts of thermal energy pounded, but no more than a hundred watts reached the ship. They fell toward the star and she watched the outer temperature rise to two thousand.

Now, as the ship made its closest approach, the rocket came on line. It was astounding. The force pulled her out of the chair, hard into the crawlspace beneath the bolted desk. Her legs were pinned by her sudden body weight, knees twisted in a bad way. The pain increased as G-forces grew. She reached backward, up, away from this new gravity, which was orthogonal to the floor. She clutched the chair legs above her and pulled until her left foot was freed from her weight, and then fell back against the bay of the desk, curled in a fetal position, exhausted. A full G, she guessed. Which her body had not experienced for eighty-four years. It felt like much more. Her heart labored. It was hard to breathe. Idiot! Not to think of this. She clutched the chair by its legs. Trapped here, unable to move or see while the engine thundered.

She hoped it didn't matter. The ship would run at full reverse thrust for exactly the time needed to bend their trajectory toward the farther sun, its nuclear flame burning in front of them, a venomous, roiling torrent of plasma and neutrons spewing from the center of the torus, and all this fury not even a spark to show against the huge sun that smote their carbon shield with its avalanche of light. The ship vibrated continuously with the rocket's thunder. Periodic concussions from she knew not what shocked her.

Two hours passed. As they turned, attitude thrusters kept them in the shield's shadow. If it failed, there would be a quick hot end to a long cold voyage.

An alert whined. That meant shield temperature had passed twenty-five hundred. She counted seconds. The hull boomed and she lost count and started again. When she reached a thousand she stopped. Some time later the whining ceased. The concussions grew less frequent. The temperature was falling. They were around.

Another thirty minutes and the engines died. Their thunder and their weight abruptly shut off. She was afloat in silence. She trembled in her sweat. Her left foot throbbed.

They'd halved their speed. As they flew on, the sun's pull from behind would slow them more, taking away the acceleration it had added to their approach. That much would be regained as they fell toward the A star over the next year.

She slept in the weightlessness for several hours. At last she spun the ship back up to one-tenth G and took stock. Even in the slight gravity her foot and ankle were painful. She might have broken bones. Nothing she could do about it.

Most of their fuel was spent. At least one of the hydrogen tanks had suffered boil-off. She was unwilling to calculate whether enough remained for the second maneuver. It wasn't her job. She was done. She wrote her log. The modified hibernation drugs were already in her system, prepping her for a final year of sleep she might not wake from. But what was the alternative?

It hit her then: Eighty-four years had passed since she climbed aboard this ship. Mamá and Papá were dead. Roger too. Unless perhaps Roger had been wrong and the great genius of humanity was to evade the ruin it always seemed about to bring upon itself. Unless humanity had emerged into some unlikely golden age of peace, longevity, forgiveness. And they, these Gypsies and their certainty, were outcast from it. But that was another narrative, and she couldn't bring herself to believe it.

6.

They'd never debated what they'd do when they landed.

The ship would jettison everything that had equipped it for interstellar travel and aerobrake into orbit. That might take thirty or forty glancing passes through the atmosphere, to slow them enough for a final descent, while cameras surveyed for a landing site. Criteria, insofar as possible: easy terrain, temperate zone, near water, arable land.

It was fruitless to plan the details of in-situ resource use while the site was unknown. But it would have to be Earth-like because they didn't have resources for terraforming more than the immediate neighborhood. All told, there was fifty tons of stuff in the storage bay—prefab habitats made for Mars, solar panels, fuel cells, bacterial cultures, seed bank, 3D printers, genetic tools, nanotech, recyclers—all meant to jump-start a colony. There was enough in the way of food and water to support a crew of sixteen for six months. If they hadn't become self-sufficient by then, it was over.

They hadn't debated options because they weren't going to have any. This part of it—even assuming the planet were hospitable enough to let them set up in the first place—would be a lot harder than the voyage. It didn't bear discussion.

SOPHIE (2126)

Waking. Again? Trying to rise up out of that dream of sinking back into the dream of rising up out of the. Momma? All that okay.

Soph? Upsa daise. Пойдем. Allons.

Sergei?

She was sitting on the cold, hard deck, gasping for breath.

Good girl, Soph. Get up, sit to console, bring spectroscope online. What we got? Soph! Stay with!

She sat at the console. The screen showed dimly, through blurs and maculae that she couldn't blink away, a stranger's face: ruined, wrinkled, sagging, eyes milky, strands of lank white hair falling from a sored scalp. With swollen knuckles and gnarled fingers slow and painful under loose sheathes of skin, she explored hard lumps in the sinews of her neck, in her breasts, under her skeletal arms. It hurt to swallow. Or not to.

The antisenescents hadn't worked. They'd known this was possible. But she'd been twenty-five. Her body hadn't known. Now she was old, sick, and dying after unlived decades spent on a slab. Regret beyond despair whelmed her. Every possible future that might have been hers, good or ill, promised or compromised, all discarded the day they launched. Now she had to accept the choice that had cost her life. Not afraid of death, but sick at heart thinking of that life, hers, however desperate it might have been on Earth—any life—now unlivable.

She tried to read the logs. Files corrupted, many lost. Handwritten copies blurry in her sight. Her eyes weren't good enough for this. She shut them, thought, then went into the supply bay, rested there for a minute, pulled out a printer and scanner, rested again, connected them to the computer, brought up the proper software. That all took a few tiring hours. She napped. Woke and affixed the scanner to her face. Felt nothing as mild infrared swept her corneas and mapped their aberrations. The printer was already loaded with polycarbonate stock, and after a minute it began to hum.

She put her new glasses on, still warm. About the cataracts she could do nothing. But now she could read.

They had braked once, going around B. Rosa had executed the first part of the maneuver, following Zia's plan. His cushion shot. But their outgoing velocity was too fast.

Sergei continued talking in the background, on and on as he did, trying to get her attention. She felt annoyed with him, couldn't he see she was busy?

Look! Look for spectra.

She felt woozy, wandering. Planets did that. They wandered against the stars. How does a planet feel? Oh yes, she should look for a planet. That's where they were going.

Four. There were four planets. No, five—there was a sub-Mercury in close orbit around B. The other four orbited A. Three were too small, too close to the star, too hot. The fourth was Earth-like. It was in an orbit of 0.8 AU, eccentricity 0.05. Its mass was three-quarters that of Earth. Its year was about two hundred sixty days. They were still 1.8 AU from it, on the far side of Alpha Centauri A. The spectroscope showed nitrogen, oxygen, argon, carbon dioxide, krypton, neon, helium, methane, hydrogen. And liquid water.

Liquid water. She tasted the phrase on her tongue like a prayer, a benediction.

It was there. It was real. Liquid water.

But then there were the others. Fourteen who could not be roused. Leaving only her and Sergei. And of course Sergei was not real.

So there was no point. The mission was over however you looked at it. She couldn't do it alone. Even if they reached the planet, even if she managed to aerobrake the ship and bring it down in one piece, they were done, because there was no more they.

The humane, the sensible thing to do now would be to let the ship fall into the approaching sun. Get it over quickly.

She didn't want to deal with this. It made her tired.

Two thirds of the way there's a chockstone, a large rock jammed in the crack, for protection before the hardest part. She grasps it, gets her breath, and pulls round it. The crux involves laybacking and right arm pulling. Her arm is too tired. Shaking and straining she fights it. She thinks of falling. That was bad, it meant her thoughts were wandering.

Someday you will die. Death will not wait. Only then will you realize you have not practiced well. Don't give up.

She awoke with a start. She realized they were closing on the sun at its speed, not hers. If she did nothing, that was a decision. And that was not her decision to make. All of them had committed to this line. Her datastream was still sending, whether anyone received it or not. She hadn't fallen on the mountain, and she wasn't going to fall into a sun now.

The planet was lost in the blaze of Alpha A. Two days away from that fire, and the hull temperature was climbing.

The A sun was hotter, more luminous, than B. It couldn't be approached as closely. There would be less decel.

This was not her expertise. But Zia and Rosa had left exhaustive notes, and Sophie's expertise was in winnowing and organizing and executing. She prepped the reactor. She adjusted their trajectory, angled the cushion shot just so.

Attitude thrusters halted the ship's rotation, turned it to rest in the sunshield's shadow. Gravity feathered away. She floated as they freefell into light.

Through the sunshield, through the layers of carbon, aerogel, through closed eyelids, radiance fills the ship with its pressure, suffusing all, dispelling the decades of cold, warming her feelings to this new planet given life by this sun; eyes closed, she sees it more clearly than Earth—rivers running, trees tossing in the wind, insects chirring in a meadow—all familiar but made strange by this deep, pervasive light. It might almost be Earth, but it's not. It's a new world.

Four million kilometers from the face of the sun. Twenty-five hundred degrees Celsius.

Don't forget to strap in.

Thank you, Rosa.

At periapsis, the deepest point in the gravity well, the engine woke in thunder. The ship shuddered, its aged hull wailed and boomed. Propellant pushed hard against their momentum, against the ship's forward vector, its force multiplied by its fall into the star's gravity, slowing the ship, gradually turning it. After an hour, the engine sputtered and died, and they raced away from that radiance into the abiding cold and silence of space.

Oh, Sergei. Oh, no. Still too fast.

They were traveling at twice the escape velocity of the Alpha C system. Fuel gone, having rounded both suns, they will pass the planet and continue out of the system into interstellar space.

Maneuver to planet. Like Zia said. Take all genetic material, seeds, zygotes, heatshield payload and drop to surface, okay? Best we can do. Give life a chance.

No fuel, Sergei. Not a drop. We can't maneuver, you hear me?

Пойдем.

Her mind is playing tricks. She has to concentrate. The planet is directly in front of them now, but still nine days away. Inexorable, it will move on in its orbit. Inexorable, the ship will follow its own divergent path. They will miss by 0.002 AU. Closer than the Moon to the Earth.

Coldly desperate, she remembered the attitude thrusters, fired them for ten minutes until all their hydrazine was exhausted. It made no difference.

She continued to collect data. Her datastream lived, a thousand bits per hour, her meager yet efficient engine of science pushing its mite of meaning back into the plaintext chaos of the universe, without acknowledgment.

The planet was drier than Earth, mostly rock with two large seas, colder, extensive polar caps. She radar-mapped the topography. The orbit was more eccentric than Earth's, so the caps must vary, and the seas they fed. A thirty-hour day. Two small moons, one with high albedo, the other dark.

What are they doing here? Have they thrown their lives away for nothing? Was it a great evil to have done this? Abandoned Earth?

But what were they to do? Like all of them, Roger was a problem solver, and the great problem on Earth, the problem of humanity, was unsolvable; it was out of control and beyond the reach of engineering. The problems of *Gypsy* were large but definable.

We were engineers. Of our own deaths. These were the deaths we wanted. Out here. Not among those wretched and unsanctified. We isolates.

She begins to compose a poem a day. Not by writing. She holds the words in her mind, reciting them over and over until the whole is fixed in memory. Then she writes it down. A simple discipline, to combat her mental wandering.

> *In the eye of the sun*
> *what is not burned to ash?*
>
> *In the spire of the wind*
> *what is not scattered as dust?*
>
> *Love? art?*
> *body's rude health?*
> *memory of its satisfactions?*
>
> *Antaeus*
> *lost strength*
> *lifted from Earth*
>
> *Reft from our gravity*
> *we fail*
>
> *Lime kept sailors hale*
> *light of mind alone*
> *with itself*
> *is not enough*

The scope tracked the planet as they passed it by. Over roughly three hours it grew in size from about a degree to about two degrees, then dwindled again. She spent the time gazing at its features with preternatural attention, with longing and regret, as if it were the face of an unattainable loved one.

It's there, Sergei, it's real—Ghost Planet Hope—and it is beautiful— look, how blue the water—see the clouds—and the seacoast—there must be rain, and plants and animals happy for it—fish, and birds, maybe, and worms, turning the soil. Look at the mountains! Look at the snow on their peaks!

This was when the science pod should have been released, the large reflecting telescope ejected into planetary orbit to start its years-long mission of measuring stellar distances. But that was in a divergent universe, one that each passing hour took her farther from.

We made it. No one will ever know, but we made it. We came so far. It was our only time to do it. No sooner, we hadn't developed the means. And if we'd waited any longer, the means would have killed us all. We came through a narrow window. Just a little too narrow.

She recorded their passing. She transmitted all their logs. Her recent poems. The story of their long dying. In four and a quarter years it would reach home. No telling if anyone would hear.

So long for us to evolve. So long to walk out of Africa and around the globe. So long to build a human world. So quick to ruin it. Is this, our doomed and final effort, no more than our grieving for Earth? Our mere mourning?

Every last bit of it was a long shot: their journey, humanity, life itself, the universe with its constants so finely tuned that planets, stars, or time itself, had come to be.

Fermi's question again: If life is commonplace in the universe, where is everyone? How come we haven't heard from anyone? What is the mean time between failures for civilizations?

Not long. Not long enough.

Now she slept. Language was not a tool used often enough even in sleep to lament its own passing. Other things lamented more. The brilliance turned to and turned away.

She remembers the garden behind the house. Her father grew corn—he was particular about the variety, complained how hard it was to find Silver Queen, even the terminated variety—with beans interplanted, which climbed the cornstalks, and different varieties of tomato with basil interplanted, and lettuces—he liked frisee. And in the flower beds alstroemeria, and wind lilies, and *Eschscholzia*. He taught her those names, and the names of Sierra flowers—taught her to learn names. We name things in order to love them, to remember them when they are absent. She recites the names of the fourteen dead with her, and weeps.

She'd been awake for over two weeks. The planet was far behind. The hibernation cocktail was completely flushed from her system. She wasn't going back to sleep.

ground
rose
sand

elixir
cave

root
dark

golden

sky-born
lift
earth
fall

The radio receiver chirps. She wakes, stares at it dumbly.

The signal is strong! Beamed directly at them. From Earth! Words form on the screen. She feels the words rather than reads them.

We turned it around. Everything is fixed. The bad years are behind us. We live. We know what you did, why you did it. We honor your bravery. We're sorry you're out there, sorry you had to do it, wish you . . . wish . . . wish . . . Good luck. Good-bye.

Where are her glasses? She needs to hear the words. She needs to hear a human voice, even synthetic. She taps the speaker.

The white noise of space. A blank screen.

She is in the Sierra, before the closure. Early July. Sun dapples the trail. Above the alpine meadow, in the shade, snow deepens, but it's packed and easy walking. She kicks steps into the steeper parts. She comes into a little flat just beginning to melt out, surrounded by snowy peaks, among white pine and red fir and mountain hemlock. Her young muscles are warm and supple and happy in their movements. The snowbound flat is still, yet humming with the undertone of life. A tiny mosquito lands on her forearm, casts its shadow, too young even to know to bite. She brushes it off, walks on, beyond the flat, into higher country.

thistle daisy cow-parsnip strawberry clover
mariposa-lily corn-lily ceanothus elderberry marigold

mimulus sunflower senecio goldenbush dandelion
mules-ear iris miners-lettuce sorrel clarkia
milkweed tiger-lily mallow veronica rue
nettle violet buttercup ivesia asphodel
ladyslipper larkspur pea bluebells onion
yarrow cinquefoil arnica pennyroyal fireweed
phlox monkshood foxglove vetch buckwheat
goldenrod groundsel valerian lovage columbine
stonecrop angelica rangers-buttons pussytoes everlasting
watercress rockcress groundsmoke solomons-seal bitterroot
liveforever lupine paintbrush blue-eyed-grass gentian
pussypaws butterballs campion primrose forget-me-not
saxifrage aster polemonium sedum rockfringe
sky-pilot shooting-star heather alpine-gold penstemon

Forget me not.

THE PAUPER PRINCE
AND THE EUCALYPTUS JINN

Usman T. Malik

When the Spirit World appears in a sensory Form, the Human Eye confines it. The Spiritual Entity cannot abandon that Form as long as Man continues to look at it in this special way. To escape, the Spiritual Entity manifests an Image it adopts for him, like a veil. It pretends the Image is moving in a certain direction so the Eye will follow it. At which point the Spiritual Entity escapes its confinement and disappears.

Whoever knows this and wishes to maintain perception of the Spiritual, must not let his Eye follow this illusion.

This is one of the Divine Secrets.

—from The Meccan Revelations *by Muhiyuddin Ibn Arabi*

For fifteen years my grandfather lived next door to the Mughal princess Zeenat Begum. The princess ran a tea stall outside the walled city of Old Lahore in the shade of an ancient eucalyptus. Dozens of children from Bhati Model School rushed screaming down muddy lanes to gather at her shop, which was really just a roadside counter with a tin roof and a smattering of chairs and a table. On winter afternoons it was her steaming cardamom-and-honey tea the kids wanted; in summer it was the chilled Rooh Afza.

As Gramps talked, he smacked his lips and licked his fingers, remembering the sweet rosewater sharbat. He told me that the princess was so poor she had to recycle tea leaves and sharbat residue. Not from customers, of course, but from her own boiling pans—although who really knew, he said, and winked.

I didn't believe a word of it.

"Where was her kingdom?" I said.

"Gone. Lost. Fallen to the British a hundred years ago," Gramps said. "She never begged, though. Never asked anyone's help, see?"

I was ten. We were sitting on the steps of our mobile home in Florida. It was a wet summer afternoon and rain hissed like diamondbacks in the grass and crackled in the gutters of the trailer park.

"And her family?"

"Dead. Her great-great-great grandfather, the exiled King Bahadur Shah Zafar, died in Rangoon and is buried there. Burmese Muslims make pilgrimages to his shrine and honor him as a saint."

"Why was he buried there? Why couldn't he go home?"

"He had no home anymore."

For a while I stared, then surprised both him and myself by bursting into tears. Bewildered, Gramps took me in his arms and whispered comforting things, and gradually I quieted, letting his voice and the rain sounds lull me to sleep, the loamy smell of him and grass and damp earth becoming one in my sniffling nostrils.

I remember the night Gramps told me the rest of the story. I was twelve or thirteen. We were at this desi party in Windermere thrown by Baba's friend Hanif Uncle, a posh affair with Italian leather sofas, crystal cutlery, and marble-topped tables. Someone broached a discussion about the pauper princess. Another person guffawed. The Mughal princess was an urban legend, this aunty said. Yes, yes, she too had heard stories about this so-called princess, but they were a hoax. The descendants of the Mughals left India and Pakistan decades ago. They are settled in London and Paris and Manhattan now, living postcolonial, extravagant lives after selling their estates in their native land.

Gramps disagreed vehemently. Not only was the princess real, she had given him free tea. She had told him stories of her forebears.

The desi aunty laughed. "Senility is known to create stories," she said, tapping her manicured fingers on her wineglass.

Gramps bristled. A long heated argument followed and we ended up leaving the party early.

"Rafiq, tell your father to calm down," Hanif Uncle said to my baba at the door. "He takes things too seriously."

"He might be old and set in his ways, Doctor sahib," Baba said, "but he's sharp as a tack. Pardon my boldness but some of your friends in there . . . " Without looking at Hanif Uncle, Baba waved a palm at the open door from which blue light and Bollywood music spilled onto the driveway.

Hanif Uncle smiled. He was a gentle and quiet man who sometimes invited us over to his fancy parties where rich expatriates from the Indian subcontinent opined about politics, stocks, cricket, religious fundamentalism, and their successful Ivy League–attending progeny. The shyer the man the louder his feasts, Gramps was fond of saying.

"They're a piece of work all right," Hanif Uncle said. "Listen, bring your family over some weekend. I'd love to listen to that Mughal girl's story."

"Sure, Doctor sahib. Thank you."

The three of us squatted into our listing truck and Baba yanked the gearshift forward, beginning the drive home.

"Abba-ji," he said to Gramps. "You need to rein in your temper. You can't pick a fight with these people. The doctor's been very kind to me, but word of mouth's how I get work and it's exactly how I can lose it."

"But that woman is wrong, Rafiq," Gramps protested. "What she's heard are rumors. I told them the truth. I lived in the time of the pauper princess. I lived through the horrors of the eucalyptus jinn."

"Abba-ji, listen to what you're saying! Please, I beg you, keep these stories to yourself. Last thing I want is people whispering the handyman has a crazy, quarrelsome father." Baba wiped his forehead and rubbed his perpetually blistered thumb and index finger together.

Gramps stared at him, then whipped his face to the window and began to chew a candy wrapper (he was diabetic and wasn't allowed sweets). We sat in hot, thorny silence the rest of the ride and when we got home Gramps marched straight to his room like a prisoner returning to his cell.

I followed him and plopped on his bed.

"Tell me about the princess and the jinn," I said in Urdu.

Gramps grunted out of his compression stockings and kneaded his legs. They occasionally swelled with fluid. He needed water pills but they made him incontinent and smell like piss and he hated them. "The last time I told you her story you started crying. I don't want your parents yelling at me. Especially tonight."

"Oh, come on, they don't *yell* at you. Plus I won't tell them. Look, Gramps, think about it this way: I could write a story in my school paper about the princess. This could be my junior project." I snuggled into his bed sheets. They smelled of sweat and medicine, but I didn't mind.

"All right, but if your mother comes in here, complaining—"

"She won't."

He arched his back and shuffled to the armchair by the window. It was ten at night. Cicadas chirped their intermittent static outside, but I doubt Gramps heard them. He wore hearing aids and the ones we could afford crackled in his ears, so he refused to wear them at home.

Gramps opened his mouth, pinched the lower denture, and rocked it. Back and forth, back and forth. Loosening it from the socket. *Pop!* He removed the upper one similarly and dropped both in a bowl of warm water on the table by the armchair.

I slid off the bed. I went to him and sat on the floor by his spidery, white-haired feet. "Can you tell me the story, Gramps?"

Night stole in through the window blinds and settled around us, soft and warm. Gramps curled his toes and pressed them against the wooden leg of his armchair. His eyes drifted to the painting hanging above the door, a picture of a young woman turned ageless by the artist's hand. Soft muddy eyes, a knowing smile, an orange dopatta framing her black hair. She sat on a brilliantly colored rug and held a silver goblet in an outstretched hand, as if offering it to the viewer.

The painting had hung in Gramps's room for so long I'd stopped seeing it. When I was younger I'd once asked him if the woman was Grandma, and he'd looked at me. Grandma died when Baba was young, he said.

The cicadas burst into an electric row and I rapped the floorboards with my knuckles, fascinated by how I could keep time with their piping.

"I bet the pauper princess," said Gramps quietly, "would be happy to have her story told."

"Yes."

"She would've wanted everyone to know how the greatest dynasty in history came to a ruinous end."

"Yes."

Gramps scooped up a two-sided brush and a bottle of cleaning solution from the table. Carefully, he began to brush his dentures. As he scrubbed, he talked, his deep-set watery eyes slowly brightening until it seemed he glowed with memory. I listened, and at one point Mama came to the door, peered in, and whispered something we both ignored. It was Saturday night so she left us alone, and Gramps and I sat there for the longest time I would ever spend with him.

This is how, that night, my gramps ended up telling me the story of the Pauper Princess and the Eucalyptus Jinn.

The princess, Gramps said, was a woman in her twenties with a touch of silver in her hair. She was lean as a sorghum broomstick, face dark and plain, but her eyes glittered as she hummed the Qaseeda Burdah Shareef and swept the wooden counter in her teashop with a dust cloth. She had a gold nose stud that, she told her customers, was a family heirloom. Each evening after she was done serving she folded her aluminum chairs, upended the stools on the plywood table, and took a break. She'd sit down by the trunk of the towering eucalyptus outside Bhati Gate, pluck out the stud, and shine it with a mint-water-soaked rag until it gleamed like an eye.

It was tradition, she said.

"If it's an heirloom, why do you wear it every day? What if you break it?

What if someone sees it and decides to rob you?" Gramps asked her. He was about fourteen then and just that morning had gotten Juma pocket money and was feeling rich. He whistled as he sat sipping tea in the tree's shade and watched steel workers, potters, calligraphers, and laborers carry their work outside their foundries and shops, grateful for the winter-softened sky.

Princess Zeenat smiled and her teeth shone at him. "Nah ji. No one can steal from us. My family is protected by a jinn, you know."

This was something Gramps had heard before. A jinn protected the princess and her two sisters, a duty imposed by Akbar the Great five hundred years back. Guard and defend Mughal honor. Not a clichéd horned jinn, you understand, but a daunting, invisible entity that defied the laws of physics: it could slip in and out of time, could swap its senses, hear out of its nostrils, smell with its eyes. It could even fly like the tales of yore said.

Mostly amused but occasionally uneasy, Gramps laughed when the princess told these stories. He had never really questioned the reality of her existence; lots of nawabs and princes of pre-Partition India had offspring languishing in poverty these days. An impoverished Mughal princess was conceivable.

A custodian jinn, not so much.

Unconvinced thus, Gramps said:

"Where does he live?"

"What does he eat?"

And, "If he's invisible, how does one know he's real?"

The princess's answers came back practiced and surreal:

The jinn lived in the eucalyptus tree above the tea stall.

He ate angel-bread.

He was as real as jasmine-touched breeze, as shifting temperatures, as the many spells of weather that alternately lull and shake humans in their variegated fists.

"Have *you* seen him?" Gramps fired.

"Such questions." The Princess shook her head and laughed, her thick, long hair squirming out from under her chador. "Hai Allah, these kids." Still tittering, she sauntered off to her counter, leaving a disgruntled Gramps scratching his head.

The existential ramifications of such a creature's presence unsettled Gramps, but what could he do? Arguing about it was as useful as arguing about the wind jouncing the eucalyptus boughs. Especially when the neighborhood kids began to tell disturbing tales as well.

Of a gnarled bat-like creature that hung upside down from the warped branches, its shadow twined around the wicker chairs and table fronting the counter. If you looked up, you saw a bird nest—just another huddle of zoysia grass and bird feathers—but then you dropped your gaze and the creature's malignant reflection juddered and swam in the tea inside the chipped china.

"Foul face," said one boy. "Dark and ugly and wrinkled like a fruit."

"Sharp, crooked fangs," said another.

"No, no, he has razor blades planted in his jaws," said the first one quickly. "My cousin told me. That's how he flays the skin off little kids."

The description of the eucalyptus jinn varied seasonally. In summertime, his cheeks were scorched, his eyes red rimmed like the midday sun. Come winter, his lips were blue and his eyes misty, his touch cold like damp roots. On one thing everyone agreed: if he laid eyes on you, you were a goner.

The lean, mean older kids nodded and shook their heads wisely.

A goner.

The mystery continued this way, deliciously gossiped and fervently argued, until one summer day a child of ten with wild eyes and a snot-covered chin rushed into the tea stall, gabbling and crying, blood trickling from the gash in his temple. Despite several attempts by the princess and her customers, he wouldn't be induced to tell who or what had hurt him, but his older brother, who had followed the boy inside, face scrunched with delight, declared he had last been seen pissing at the bottom of the eucalyptus.

"The jinn. The jinn," all the kids cried in unison. "A victim of the jinn's malice."

"No. He fell out of the tree," a grownup said firmly. "The gash is from the fall."

"The boy's incurred the jinn's wrath," said the kids happily. "The jinn will flense the meat off his bones and crunch his marrow."

"Oh shut up," said Princess Zeenat, feeling the boy's cheeks, "the eucalyptus jinn doesn't harm innocents. He's a defender of honor and dignity," while all the time she fretted over the boy, dabbed at his forehead with a wet cloth, and poured him a hot cup of tea.

The princess's sisters emerged from the doorway of their two-room shack twenty paces from the tea stall. They peered in, two teenage girls in flour-caked dopattas and rose-printed shalwar kameez, and the younger one stifled a cry when the boy turned to her, eyes shiny and vacuous with delirium, and whispered, "He says the lightning trees are dying."

The princess gasped. The customers pressed in, awed and murmuring. An elderly man with betel-juice-stained teeth gripped the front of his own shirt with palsied hands and fanned his chest with it. "The jinn has overcome the child," he said, looking profoundly at the sky beyond the stall, and chomped his tobacco paan faster.

The boy shuddered. He closed his eyes, breathed erratically, and behind him the shadow of the tree fell long and clawing at the ground.

The lightning trees are dying. The lightning trees are dying.

So spread the nonsensical words through the neighborhood. Zipping from bamboo door-to-door; blazing through dark lovers' alleys; hopping from one beggar's gleeful tongue to another's, the prophecy became a proverb and the proverb a song.

A starving calligrapher-poet licked his reed quill and wrote an elegy for the lightning trees.

A courtesan from the Diamond Market sang it from her rooftop on a moonlit night.

Thus the walled city heard the story of the possessed boy and his curious proclamation and shivered with this message from realms unknown. Arthritic grandmothers and lithe young men rocked in their courtyards and lawns, nodding dreamily at the stars above, allowing themselves to remember secrets from childhood they hadn't dared remember before.

Meanwhile word reached local families that a child had gotten hurt climbing the eucalyptus. Angry fathers, most of them laborers and shopkeepers with kids who rarely went home before nightfall, came barging into the Municipality's lean-to, fists hammering on the sad-looking officer's table, demanding that the tree be chopped down.

"It's a menace," they said.

"It's hollow. Worm eaten."

"It's haunted!"

"Look, its gum's flammable and therefore a fire hazard," offered one versed in horticulture, "and the tree's a pest. What's a eucalyptus doing in the middle of a street anyway?"

So they argued and thundered until the officer came knocking at the princess's door. "The tree," said the sad-looking officer, twisting his squirrel-tail mustache, "needs to go."

"Over my dead body," said the princess. She threw down her polish rag and glared at the officer. "It was planted by my forefathers. It's a relic, it's history."

"It's a public menace. Look, bibi, we can do this the easy way or the hard way, but I'm telling you—"

"Try it. You just try it," cried the princess. "I will take this matter to the highest authorities. I'll go to the Supreme Court. That tree—" she jabbed a quivering finger at the monstrous thing "—gives us shade. A fakir told my grandfather never to move his business elsewhere. It's blessed, he said."

The sad-faced officer rolled up his sleeves. The princess eyed him with apprehension as he yanked one of her chairs back and lowered himself into it.

"Bibi," he said not unkindly, "let me tell you something. The eucalyptus was brought here by the British to cure India's salinity and flooding problems. Gora sahib hardly cared about our ecology." His mustache drooped from his thin lips. The strawberry mole on his chin quivered. "It's not indigenous, it's a pest. It's not a blessing, it repels other flora and fauna and guzzles groundwater by the tons. It's not ours," the officer said, not looking at the princess. "It's alien."

It was early afternoon and school hadn't broken yet. The truant Gramps sat in a corner sucking on a cigarette he'd found in the trash can outside his school and watched the princess. Why wasn't she telling the officer about the jinn? That the tree was its home? Her cheeks were puffed from clenching her jaws, the hollows under her eyes deeper and darker as she clapped a hand to her forehead.

"Look," she said, her voice rising and falling like the wind stirring the tear-shaped eucalyptus leaves, "you take the tree, you take our good luck. My shop is all I have. The tree protects it. It protects us. It's family."

"Nothing I can do." The officer scratched his birthmark. "Had there been no complaint . . . but now I have no choice. The Lahore Development Authority has been planning to remove the poplars and the eucalyptus for a while anyway. They want to bring back trees of Old Lahore. Neem, pipal, sukhchain, mulberry, mango. This foreigner—" he looked with distaste at the eucalyptus "—steals water from our land. It needs to go."

Shaking his head, the officer left. The princess lurched to her stall and began to prepare Rooh Afza. She poured a glittering parabola of sharbat into a mug with trembling hands, staggered to the tree, and flung the liquid at its hoary, clawing roots.

"There," she cried, her eyes reddened. "I can't save you. You must go."

Was she talking to the jinn? To the tree? Gramps felt his spine run cold as the blood-red libation sank into the ground, muddying the earth around the eucalyptus roots. Somewhere in the branches, a bird whistled.

The princess toed the roots for a moment longer, then trudged back to her counter.

Gramps left his teacup half-empty and went to the tree. He tilted his head to look at its top. It was so high. The branches squirmed and fled from the main trunk, reaching restlessly for the hot white clouds. A plump chukar with a crimson beak sat on a branch swaying gently. It stared back at Gramps, but no creature with razor-blade jaws and hollow dust-filled cheeks dangled from the tree.

As Gramps left, the shadows of the canopies and awnings of shops in the alley stretched toward the tree accusatorially.

That night Gramps dreamed of the eucalyptus jinn.

It was a red-snouted shape hurtling toward the heavens, its slipstream body glittering and dancing in the dark. Space and freedom rotated above it, but as it accelerated showers of golden meteors came bursting from the stars and slammed into it. The creature thinned and elongated until it looked like a reed pen trying to scribble a cryptic message between the stars, but the meteors wouldn't stop.

Drop back, you blasphemer, whispered the heavens. *You absconder, you vermin. The old world is gone. No place for your kind here now. Fall back and do your duty.*

And eventually the jinn gave up and let go.

It plummeted: a fluttering, helpless, enflamed ball shooting to the earth. It shrieked as it dove, flickering rapidly in and out of space and time but bound by their quantum fetters. It wanted to rage but couldn't. It wanted to save the lightning trees, to upchuck their tremulous shimmering roots and plant them somewhere the son of man wouldn't find them. Instead it was imprisoned, captured by prehuman magic and trapped to do time for a sin so old it had forgotten what it was.

So now it tumbled and plunged, hated and hating. It changed colors like a fiendish rainbow: mid-flame blue, muscle red, terror green, until the force of its fall bleached all its hues away and it became a pale scorching bolt of fire.

Thus the eucalyptus jinn fell to its inevitable dissolution, even as Gramps woke up, his heart pounding, eyes fogged and aching from the dream. He groped in the dark, found the lantern, and lit it. He was still shaking. He got up, went to his narrow window that looked out at the moon-drenched Bhati Gate a hundred yards away. The eight arches of the Mughal structure were black and lonely above the central arch. Gramps listened. Someone was moving in the shack next door. In the princess's home. He gazed at the mosque of Ghulam Rasool—a legendary mystic known as the Master of Cats—on its left.

And he looked at the eucalyptus tree.

It soared higher than the gate, its wild armature pawing at the night, the oily scent of its leaves potent even at this distance. Gramps shivered, although heat was swelling from the ground from the first patter of raindrops. More smells crept into the room: dust, trash, verdure.

He backed away from the window, slipped his sandals on, dashed out of the house. He ran toward the tea stall but, before he could as much as cross the chicken yard up front, lightning unzipped the dark and the sky roared.

The blast of its fall could be heard for miles.

The eucalyptus exploded into a thousand pieces, the burning limbs crackling and sputtering in the thunderstorm that followed. More lightning splintered the night sky. Children shrieked, dreaming of twisted corridors with shadows wending past one another. Adults moaned as timeless gulfs shrank and pulsed behind their eyelids. The walled city thrashed in sweat-soaked sheets until the mullah climbed the minaret and screamed his predawn call.

In the morning the smell of ash and eucalyptol hung around the crisped boughs. The princess sobbed as she gazed at her buckled tin roof and smashed stall. Shards of china, plywood, clay, and charred wicker twigs lay everywhere.

The laborers and steel workers rubbed their chins.

"Well, good riddance," said Alamdin electrician, father of the injured boy whose possession had ultimately proved fleeting. Alamdin fingered a hole in his string vest. "Although I'm sorry for your loss, bibi. Perhaps the government will give you a monthly pension, being that you're royal descent and all."

Princess Zeenat's nose stud looked dull in the grey after-storm light. Her shirt was torn at the back, where a fragment of wood had bitten her as she scoured the wreckage.

"He was supposed to protect us," she murmured to the tree's remains: a black stump that poked from the earth like a singed umbilicus, and the roots lapping madly at her feet. "To give us shade and blessed sanctuary." Her grimed finger went for the nose stud and wrenched it out. "Instead—" She backpedaled and slumped at the foot of her shack's door. "Oh, my sisters. My sisters."

Tutting uncomfortably, the men drifted away, abandoning the pauper princess and her Mughal siblings. The women huddled together, a bevy of chukars stunned by a blood moon. Their shop was gone, the tree was gone. Princess Zeenat hugged her sisters and with a fierce light in her eyes whispered to them.

Over the next few days Gramps stood at Bhati Gate, watching the girls salvage timber, china, and clay. They washed and scrubbed their copper pots. Heaved out the tin sheet from the debris and dragged it to the foundries. Looped the remaining wicker into small bundles and sold it to basket weavers inside the walled city.

Gramps and a few past patrons offered to help. The Mughal women declined politely.

"But I can help, I really can," Gramps said, but the princess merely knitted her eyebrows, cocked her head, and stared at Gramps until he turned and fled.

The Municipality officer tapped at their door one Friday after Juma prayers.

"Condolences, bibi," he said. "My countless apologies. We should've cut it down before this happened."

"It's all right." The princess rolled the gold stud tied in a hemp necklace around her neck between two fingers. Her face was tired but tranquil. "It was going to happen one way or the other."

The officer picked at his red birthmark. "I meant your shop."

"We had good times here—" she nodded "—but my family's long overdue for a migration. We're going to go live with my cousin. He has an orange-and-fig farm in Mansehra. We'll find plenty to do."

The man ran his fingernail down the edge of her door. For the first time Gramps saw how his eyes never stayed on the princess. They drifted toward her face, then darted away as if the flush of her skin would sear them if they lingered. Warmth slipped around Gramps's neck, up his scalp, and across his face until his own flesh burned.

"Of course," the officer said. "Of course," and he turned and trudged to the skeletal stump. Already crows had marked the area with their pecking, busily creating a roost of the fallen tree. Soon they would be protected from horned owls and other birds of prey, they thought. But Gramps and Princess Zeenat knew better.

There was no protection here.

The officer cast one long look at the Mughal family, stepped around the stump, and walked away.

Later, the princess called to Gramps. He was sitting on the mosque's steps, shaking a brass bowl, pretending to be a beggar. He ran over, the coins jingling in his pocket.

"I know you saw something," she said once they were seated on the hemp charpoy in her shack. "I could see it in your face when you offered your help."

Gramps stared at her.

"That night," she persisted, "when the lightning hit the tree." She leaned forward, her fragrance of tealeaves and ash and cardamom filling his nostrils. "What did you see?"

"Nothing," he said and began to get up.

She grabbed his wrist. "Sit," she said. Her left hand shot out and pressed something into his palm. Gramps leapt off the charpoy. There was an electric sensation in his flesh; his hair crackled. He opened his fist and looked at the object.

It was her nose stud. The freshly polished gold shimmered in the dingy shack.

Gramps touched the stud with his other hand and withdrew it. "It's so cold."

The princess smiled, a bright thing that lit up the shack. Full of love, sorrow, and relief. But relief at what? Gramps sat back down, gripped the charpoy's posts, and tugged its torn hemp strands nervously.

"My family will be gone by tonight," the princess said.

And even though he'd been expecting this for days, it still came as a shock to Gramps. The imminence of her departure took his breath away. All he could do was wobble his head.

"Once we've left, the city might come to uproot that stump." The princess glanced over her shoulder toward the back of the room where shadows lingered. "If they try, do you promise you'll dig under it?" She rose and peered into the dimness, her eyes gleaming like jewels.

"Dig under the tree? Why?"

"Something lies there which, if you dig it up, you'll keep to yourself." Princess Zeenat swiveled on her heels. "Which you will hide in a safe place and never tell a soul about."

"Why?"

"Because that's what the fakir told my grandfather. Something old and secret rests under that tree and it's not for human eyes." She turned and walked to the door.

Gramps said, "Did you ever dig under it?"

She shook her head without looking back. "I didn't need to. As long as the tree stood, there was no need for me to excavate secrets not meant for me."

"And the gold stud? Why're you giving it away?"

"It comes with the burden."

"What burden? What *is* under that tree?"

The princess half turned. She stood in a nimbus of midday light, her long muscled arms hanging loosely, fingers playing with the place in the hemp necklace where once her family heirloom had been; and despite the worry lines and the callused hands and her uneven, grimy fingernails, she was beautiful.

Somewhere close, a brick truck unloaded its cargo and in its sudden thunder what the princess said was muffled and nearly inaudible. Gramps thought later it might have been, "The map to the memory of heaven."

But that of course couldn't be right.

"The princess and her family left Lahore that night," said Gramps. "This was in the fifties and the country was too busy recovering from Partition and picking up its own pieces to worry about a Mughal princess disappearing from the pages of history. So no one cared. Except me."

He sank back into the armchair and began to rock.

"She or her sisters ever come back?" I said, pushing myself off the floor with my knuckles. "What happened to them?"

Gramps shrugged. "What happens to all girls. Married their cousins in the north, I suppose. Had large families. They never returned to Lahore, see?"

"And the jinn?"

Gramps bent and poked his ankle with a finger. It left a shallow dimple. "I guess he died or flew away once the lightning felled the tree."

"What was under the stump?"

"How should I know?"

"What do you mean?"

"I didn't dig it up. No one came to remove the stump, so I never got a chance to take out whatever was there. Anyway, bache, you really should be going. It's late."

I glanced at my Star Wars watch. Luke's saber shone fluorescent across the Roman numeral two. I was impressed Mama hadn't returned to scold me to bed. I arched my back to ease the stiffness and looked at him with one eye closed. "You're seriously telling me you didn't dig up the secret?"

"I was scared," said Gramps, and gummed a fiber bar. "Look, I was told not to remove it if I didn't have to, so I didn't. Those days we listened to our elders, see?" He grinned, delighted with this unexpected opportunity to rebuke.

"But that's cheating," I cried. "The gold stud. The jinn's disappearance. You've explained nothing. That . . . that's not a good story at all. It just leaves more questions."

"All good stories leave questions. Now go on, get out of here. Before your mother yells at us both."

He rose and waved me toward the door, grimacing and rubbing his belly—heartburn from Hanif Uncle's party food? I slipped out and shut the door behind me. Already ghazal music was drifting out: *Ranjish hi sahih dil hi dukhanay ke liye aa*. Let it be heartbreak; come if just to hurt me again. I knew the song well. Gramps had worn out so many cassettes that Apna Bazaar ordered them in bulk just for him, Mama joked.

I went to my room, undressed, and for a long time tossed in the sheets, watching the moon outside my window. It was a supermoon kids at school had talked about, a magical golden egg floating near the horizon, and I wondered how many Mughal princes and princesses had gazed at it through the ages, holding hands with their lovers.

This is how the story of the Pauper Princess and the Eucalyptus Jinn comes to an end, I thought. In utter, infuriating oblivion.

I was wrong, of course.

• • •

In September 2013, Gramps had a sudden onset of chest pain and became short of breath; 911 was called, but by the time the medics came his heart had stopped and his extremities were mottled. Still they shocked him and injected him with epi-and-atropine and sped him to the hospital where he was pronounced dead on arrival.

Gramps had really needed those water pills he'd refused until the end.

I was at Tufts teaching a course in comparative mythology when Baba called. It was a difficult year. I'd been refused tenure and a close friend had been fired over department politics. But when Baba asked me if I could come, I said of course. Gramps and I hadn't talked in years after I graduated from Florida State and moved to Massachusetts, but it didn't matter. There would be a funeral and a burial and a reception for the smattering of relatives who lived within drivable distance. I, the only grandchild, must be there.

Sara wanted to go with me. It would be a good gesture, she said.

"No," I said. "It would be a terrible gesture. Baba might not say anything, but the last person he'd want at Gramps's funeral is my white girlfriend. Trust me."

Sara didn't let go of my hand. Her fingers weren't dainty like some women's—you're afraid to squeeze them lest they shatter like glass—but they were soft and curled easily around mine. "You'll come back soon, won't you?"

"Of course. Why'd you ask?" I looked at her.

"Because," she said kindly, "you're going home." Her other hand plucked at a hair on my knuckle. She smiled, but there was a ghost of worry pinching the corner of her lips. "Because sometimes I can't read you."

We stood in the kitchenette facing each other. I touched Sara's chin. In the last few months there had been moments when things had been a bit hesitant, but nothing that jeopardized what we had.

"I'll be back," I said.

We hugged and kissed and whispered things I don't remember now. Eventually we parted and I flew to Florida, watching the morning landscape tilt through the plane windows. Below, the Charles gleamed like steel, then fell away until it was a silver twig in a hard land; and I thought, *The lightning trees are dying.*

Then we were past the waters and up and away, and the thought receded like the river.

We buried Gramps in Orlando Memorial Gardens under a row of pines. He was pale and stiff limbed, nostrils stuffed with cotton, the white shroud rippling in the breeze. I wished, like all fools rattled by late epiphanies, that I'd had more time with him. I said as much to Baba, who nodded.

"He would have liked that," Baba said. He stared at the gravestone with the epitaph *I have glimpsed the truth of the Great Unseen* that Gramps had insisted be written below his name. A verse from Rumi. "He would have liked that very much."

We stood in silence and I thought of Gramps and the stories he took with him that would stay untold forever. There's a funny thing about teaching myth and history: you realize in the deep of your bones that you'd be lucky to become a mote of dust, a speck on the bookshelf of human existence. The more tales you preserve, the more claims to immortality you can make.

After the burial we went home and Mama made us chicken karahi and basmati rice. It had been ages since I'd had home-cooked Pakistani food and the spice and garlicky taste knocked me back a bit. I downed half a bowl of fiery gravy and fled to Gramps's room where I'd been put up. Where smells of his cologne and musty clothes and his comings and goings still hung like a memory of old days.

In the following week Baba and I talked. More than we had in ages. He asked me about Sara with a glint in his eyes. I said we were still together. He grunted.

"Thousands of suitable Pakistani girls," he began to murmur, and Mama shushed him.

In Urdu half-butchered from years of disuse I told them about Tufts and New England. Boston Commons, the Freedom Trail with its dozen cemeteries and royal burial grounds, the extremities of weather; how fall spun gold and rubies and amethyst from its foliage. Baba listened, occasionally wincing, as he worked on a broken power drill from his toolbox. It had been six years since I'd seen him and Mama, and the reality of their aging was like a gut punch. Mama's hair was silver, but at least her skin retained a youthful glow. Baba's fistful of beard was completely white, the hollows of his eyes deeper and darker. His fingers were swollen from rheumatoid arthritis he'd let fester for years because he couldn't afford insurance.

"You really need to see a doctor," I said.

"I have one. I go to the community health center in Leesburg, you know."

"Not a free clinic. You need to see a specialist."

"I'm fifty-nine. Six more years and then." He pressed the power button on the drill and it roared to life. "Things will change," he said cheerfully.

I didn't know what to say. I had offered to pay his bills before. The handyman's son wasn't exactly rich, but he was grown up now and could help his family out.

Baba would have none of it. I didn't like it, but what could I do? He had pushed me away for years. *Get out of here while you can*, he'd say. He marched me to college the same way he would march me to Sunday classes at Clermont Islamic Center. *Go on*, he said outside the mosque, as I clutched the siparas to my chest. *Memorize the Quran. If you don't, who will?*

Was that why I hadn't returned home until Gramps's death? Even then I knew there was more. Home was a morass where I would sink. I had tried one or two family holidays midway through college. They depressed me, my parents' stagnation, their world where nothing changed. The trailer park, its tired residents, the dead-leaf-strewn grounds that always seemed to get muddy and wet and never clean. A strange lethargy would settle on me here, a leaden feeling that left me cold and shaken. Visiting home became an ordeal filled with guilt at my indifference. I was new to the cutthroat world of academia then and bouncing from one adjunct position to another was taking up all my time anyway.

I stopped going back. It was easier to call, make promises, talk about how bright my prospects were in the big cities. And with Gramps even phone talk was useless. He couldn't hear me, and he wouldn't put on those damn hearing aids.

So now I was living thousands of miles away with a girl Baba had never met.

I suppose I must've been hurt at his refusal of my help. The next few days were a blur between helping Mama with cleaning out Gramps's room and keeping up with the assignments my undergrads were emailing me even though I was on leave. A trickle of relatives and friends came, but to my relief Baba took over the hosting duties and let me sort through the piles of journals and tomes Gramps had amassed.

It was an impressive collection. Dozens of Sufi texts and religious treatises in different languages: Arabic, Urdu, Farsi, Punjabi, Turkish. Margins covered with Gramps's neat handwriting. I didn't remember seeing so many books in his room when I used to live here.

I asked Baba. He nodded.

"Gramps collected most of these after you left." He smiled. "I suppose he missed you."

I showed him the books. "Didn't you say he was having memory trouble? I remember Mama being worried about him getting dementia last time I talked. How could he learn new languages?"

"I didn't know he knew half these languages. Urdu and Punjabi he spoke and read fluently, but the others—" He shrugged.

Curious, I went through a few line notes. Thoughtful speculation on ontological and existential questions posed by the mystic texts. These were not the ramblings of a senile mind. Was Gramps's forgetfulness mere aging? Or had he written most of these before he began losing his marbles?

"Well, he did have a few mini strokes," Mama said when I asked. "Sometimes he'd forget where he was. Talk about Lahore, and oddly, Mansehra. It's a small city in Northern Pakistan," she added when I raised an eyebrow. "Perhaps he had friends there when he was young."

I looked at the books, ran my finger along their spines. It would be fun, nostalgic, to go through them at leisure, read Rumi's couplets and Hafiz's *Diwan*. I resolved to take the books with me. Just rent a car and drive up north with my trunk rattling with a cardboard box full of Gramps's manuscripts.

Then one drizzling morning I found a yellowed, dog-eared notebook under an old rug in his closet. Gramps's journal.

Before I left Florida I went to Baba. He was crouched below the kitchen sink, twisting a long wrench back and forth between the pipes, grunting. I waited until he was done, looked him in the eye, and said, "Did Gramps ever mention a woman named Zeenat Begum?"

Baba tossed the wrench into the toolbox. "Isn't that the woman in the fairy tale he used to tell? The pauper Mughal princess?"

"Yes."

"Sure he mentioned her. About a million times."

"But not as someone *you* might have known in real life?"

"No."

Across the kitchen I watched the door of Gramps's room. It was firmly closed. Within hung the portrait of the brown-eyed woman in the orange dopatta with her knowing half smile. She had gazed down at my family for decades, offering us that mysterious silver cup. There was a lump in my throat but I couldn't tell if it was anger or sorrow.

Baba was watching me, his swollen fingers tapping at the corner of his mouth. "Are you all right?"

I smiled, feeling the artifice of it stretch my skin like a mask. "Have you ever been to Turkey?"

"Turkey?" He laughed. "Sure. Right after I won the lottery and took that magical tour in the Caribbean."

I ignored the jest. "Does the phrase 'Courtesan of the Mughals' mean anything to you?"

He seemed startled. A smile of such beauty lit up his face that he looked ten years younger. "Ya Allah, I haven't heard that in forty years. Where'd you read it?"

I shrugged.

"It's Lahore. My city. That's what they called it in those books I read as a kid. Because it went through so many royal hands." He laughed, eyes gleaming with delight and mischief, and lowered his voice. "My friend Habib used to call it *La-whore*. The Mughal hooker. Now for Allah's sake, don't go telling your mother on me." His gaze turned inward. "Habib. God, I haven't thought of him in ages."

"Baba." I gripped the edge of the kitchen table. "Why don't you ever go back to Pakistan?"

His smile disappeared. He turned around, slammed the lid of his toolbox, and hefted it up. "Don't have time."

"You spent your teenage years there, didn't you? You obviously have some attachment to the city. Why didn't you take us back for a visit?"

"What would we go back to? We have no family there. My old friends are probably dead." He carried the toolbox out into the October sun, sweat gleaming on his forearms. He placed it in the back of his battered truck and climbed into the driver's seat. "I'll see you later."

I looked at him turn the keys in the ignition with fingers that shook. He was off to hammer sparkling new shelves in other people's garages, replace squirrel-rent screens on their lanais, plant magnolias and palms in their golfing communities, and I could say nothing. I thought I understood why he didn't want to visit the town where he grew up.

I thought about Mansehra and Turkey. If Baba really didn't know and Gramps had perfected the deception by concealing the truth within a lie, there was nothing I could do that wouldn't change, and possibly wreck, my family.

All good stories leave questions, Gramps had said to me.

You bastard, I thought.

"Sure," I said and watched my baba pull out and drive away, leaving a plumage of dust in his wake.

I called Sara when I got home. "Can I see you?" I said as soon as she picked up.

She smiled. I could hear her smile. "That bad, huh?"

"No, it was all right. I just really want to see you."

"It's one in the afternoon. I'm on campus." She paused. In the background birds chittered along with students. Probably the courtyard. "You sure you're okay?"

"Yes. Maybe." I upended the cardboard box on the carpet. The tower of books stood tall and uneven like a dwarf tree. "Come soon as you can, okay?"

"Sure. Love you."

"Love you too."

We hung up. I went to the bathroom and washed my face. I rubbed my eyes and stared at my reflection. It bared its teeth.

"Shut up," I whispered. "He was senile. Must have been completely insane. I don't believe a word of it."

But when Sara came that evening, her red hair streaming like fall leaves, her freckled cheeks dimpling when she saw me, I told her I believed, I really did. She sat and listened and stroked the back of my hand when it trembled as I lay in her lap and told her about Gramps and his journal.

It was an assortment of sketches and scribbling. A talented hand had drawn pastures, mountaintops, a walled city shown as a semicircle with half a dozen doors and hundreds of people bustling within, a farmhouse, and rows of fig and orange trees. Some of these were miniatures: images drawn as scenes witnessed by an omniscient eye above the landscape. Others were more conventional. All had one feature in common: a man and woman present in the center of the scenery going about the mundanities of their lives.

In one scene the man sat in a mosque's courtyard, performing ablution by the wudu tap. He wore a kurta and shalwar and Peshawari sandals. He was in his early twenties, lean, thickly bearded, with deep-set eyes that watched you impassively. In his hands he held a squalling baby whose tiny wrinkled fist was clenched around a stream of water from the tap. In the background a female face, familiar but older than I remembered, loomed over the courtyard wall, smiling at the pair.

The man was unmistakably Gramps, and the woman . . .

"Are you kidding me?" Sara leaned over and stared at the picture. "That's the woman in the portrait hanging in his room?"

"He lied to me. To us all. She was my grandma."

"Who *is* she?"

"Princess Zeenat Begum," I said quietly.

Gramps had narrated the story of his life in a series of sketches and notes. The writing was in third person, but it was clear that the protagonist was he.

I imagined him going about the daily rituals of his life in Lahore after Princess Zeenat left. Dropping out of school, going to his father's shop in the Niche of Calligraphers near Bhati Gate, learning the art of khattati, painting billboards in red and yellow, fusing the ancient art with new slogans and advertisements. Now he's a lanky brown teenager wetting the tip of his brush, pausing to look up into the sky with its sweeping blue secrets. Now he's a tall man, yanking bird feathers and cobwebs away from a eucalyptus stump, digging under it in the deep of the night with a flashlight in his hand.

And now—he's wiping his tears, filling his knapsack with necessaries, burying his newly discovered treasure under a scatter of clothes, hitching the bag up his shoulders, and heading out into the vast unseen. All this time, there's only one image in his head and one desire.

"He was smitten with her. Probably had been for a long time without knowing it," I said. "Ruthlessly marked. His youth never had a chance against the siren call of history."

"Hold on a sec. What was under the tree again?" Sara said.

I shook my head. "He doesn't say."

"So he lied again? About not digging it up?"

"Yes."

"Who was he looking for?"

I looked at her. "My grandmother and her sisters."

We read his notes and envisioned Gramps's journey. Abandoning his own family, wandering his way into the mountains, asking everyone he met about a fig-and-orange farm on a quiet fir-covered peak in the heart of Mansehra. He was magnetized to the displaced Mughal family not because of their royalty, but the lack thereof.

And eventually he found them.

"He stayed with them for years, helping the pauper princess's uncle with farm work. In the summer he calligraphed Quranic verses on the minarets of local mosques. In wintertime he drew portraits for tourists and painted road signs. As years passed, he married Zeenat Begum—whose portrait one summer evening he drew and painted, carried with him, and lied about— and became one of them."

I looked up at Sara, into her gentle green eyes glittering above me. She bent and kissed my nose.

"They were happy for a while, he and his new family," I said, "but then, like in so many lives, tragedy came knocking at their door."

Eyes closed, I pictured the fire: a glowering creature clawing at their windows and door, crisping their apples, billowing flames across the barn to set their hay bales ablaze. The whinnying of the horses, the frantic braying of cattle and, buried in the din, human screams.

"All three Mughal women died that night," I murmured. "Gramps and his two-year-old son were the only survivors of the brushfire. Broken and bereft, Gramps left Mansehra with the infant and went to Karachi. There he boarded a freighter that took them to Iran, then Turkey, where a sympathetic shopkeeper hired him in his rug shop. Gramps and his son stayed there for four years."

What a strange life, I thought. I hadn't known my father had spent part of his childhood in Turkey and apparently neither had he. He remembered nothing. How old was he when they moved back? As I thought this, my heart constricted in my chest, filling my brain with the hum of my blood.

Sara's face was unreadable when I opened my eyes. "Quite a story, eh?" I said uneasily.

She scratched the groove above her lips with a pink fingernail. "So he digs up whatever was under the tree and it decides him. He leaves everything and goes off to marry a stranger. This is romantic bullshit. You know that, right?"

"I don't know anything."

"Left everything," she repeated. Her mouth was parted with wonder. "You think whatever he found under the stump survived the fire?"

"Presumably. But where he took it—who can say? Eventually, though, they returned home. To Lahore, when Gramps had recovered enough sanity, I guess. Where his father, now old, had closed shop. Gramps helped him reopen. Together they ran that design stall for years."

It must have been a strange time for Gramps, I thought. He loved his parents, but he hated Bhati. Even as he dipped his pen in ink and drew spirals and curlicues, his thoughts drew phantom pictures of those he had lost. Over the years, he came to loathe this art that unlocked so many memories inside him. And after his parents died he had neither heart nor imperative to keep going.

"He was done with the place, the shop, and Lahore. So when a friend offered to help him and his teenage son move to the States, Gramps agreed."

I turned my head and burrowed into Sara's lap. Her smell filled my brain: apple blossom, lipstick, and Sara.

She nuzzled my neck. The tip of her nose was cold. "He never talked to you about it? Never said what happened?"

"No."

"And you and your family had no idea about this artistic side of him? How's that possible?"

"Don't know," I said. "He worked at a 7-Eleven in Houston when he and Baba first came here. Never did any painting or calligraphy, commissioned or otherwise. Maybe he just left all his talent, all his dreams in his hometown. Here, look at this."

I showed her the phrase that spiraled across the edges of a couple dozen pages: *My killer, my deceiver, the Courtesan of the Mughals.* "It's Lahore. He's talking about the city betraying him."

"How's that?"

I shrugged.

"How weird," Sara said. "Interesting how broken up his story is. As if he's trying to piece together his own life."

"Maybe that's what he was doing. Maybe he forced himself to forget the most painful parts."

"Lightning trees. Odd thing to say." She looked at me thoughtfully and put the journal away. "So, you're the last of the Mughals, huh?" She smiled to show she wasn't laughing.

I chortled for her. "Seems like it. The Pauper Prince of New England."

"Wow. You come with a certificate of authenticity?" She nudged her foot at the book tower. "Is it in there somewhere?"

It was getting late. Sara tugged at my shirt, and I got up and carried her to bed, where we celebrated my return with zest. Her face was beautiful in the snow shadows that crept in through the window.

"I love you, I love you," we murmured, enchanted with each other, drunk with belief in some form of eternity. The dark lay quietly beside us, and, smoldering in its heart, a rotating image.

A dim idea of what was to come.

I went through Gramps's notes. Many were in old Urdu, raikhta, which I wasn't proficient in. But I got the gist: discourses and rumination on the otherworldly.

Gramps was especially obsessed with Ibn Arabi's treatise on jinns in *The Meccan Revelations*. The Lofty Master Arabi says, wrote Gramps, that the meaning of the lexical root J-N-N in Arabic is "concealed." Jinn isn't just another created being ontologically placed between man and angel; it is the *entirety* of the hidden world.

"Isn't that fucking crazy?" I said to Sara. We were watching a rerun of *Finding Neverland*, my knuckles caked with butter and flakes of popcorn. On the screen J. M Barrie's wife was beginning to be upset by the attention he lavished upon the children's mother, Sylvia. "It kills the traditional narrative of jinns in *A Thousand and One Nights*. If one were to pursue this train of thought, it would mean relearning the symbolism in this text and virtually all others."

Sara nodded, her gaze fixed on the TV. "Uh huh."

"Consider this passage: 'A thousand years before Darwin, Sufis described the evolution of man as rising from the inorganic state through plant and animal to human. But the mineral consciousness of man, that dim memory of being buried in the great stone mother, lives on.'"

Sara popped a handful of popcorn into her mouth. Munched.

I rubbed my hands together. "'Jinns are carriers of that concealed memory, much like a firefly carries a memory of the primordial fire.' It's the oddest interpretation of jinns I've seen."

"Yeah, it's great." Sara shifted on the couch. "But can we please watch the movie?"

"Uh-huh."

I stared at the TV. Gramps thought jinns weren't devil-horned creatures bound to a lamp or, for that matter, a tree.

They were flickers of cosmic consciousness.

I couldn't get that image out of my head. Why was Gramps obsessed with this? How was this related to his life in Lahore? Something to do with the eucalyptus secret?

The next morning I went to Widener Library and dug up all I could about Arabi's and Ibn Taymeeyah's treatment of jinns. I read and pondered, went back to Gramps's notebooks, underlined passages in *The Meccan Revelations*, and walked the campus with my hands in my pockets and my heart in a world long dissipated.

"Arabi's cosmovision is staggering," I told Sara. We were sitting in a coffee shop downtown during lunch break. It was drizzling, just a gentle stutter of grey upon grey outside the window, but it made the brick buildings blush.

Sara sipped her mocha and glanced at her watch. She had to leave soon for her class.

"Consider life as a spark of consciousness. In Islamic cosmology the jinn's intrinsic nature is that of wind and fire. Adam's—read, man's—nature is water and clay, which are more resistant than fire to cold and dryness. As the universe changes, so do the requirements for life's vehicle. Now it needs creatures more resistant and better adapted. Therefore, *from the needs of sentient matter rose the invention that is us.*"

I clenched my hand into a fist. "This interpretation is pretty fucking genius. I mean, is it possible Gramps was doing real academic work? For example, had he discovered something in those textbooks that could potentially produce a whole new ideology of creation? Why, it could be the scholarly discovery of the century."

"Yes, it's great." She rapped her spoon against the edge of the table. Glanced at me, looked away.

"What?"

"Nothing. Listen, I gotta run, okay?" She gave me a quick peck on the cheek and slid out of her seat. At the door she hesitated, turned, and stood tapping her shoes, a waiting look in her eyes.

I dabbed pastry crumbs off my lips with a napkin. "Are you okay?"

Annoyance flashed in her face and vanished. "Never better." She pulled her jacket's hood over her head, yanked the door open, and strode out into the rain.

It wasn't until later that evening, when I was finalizing the spring calendar for my freshman class, that I realized I had forgotten our first-date anniversary.

Sara hadn't. There was a heart-shaped box with a pink bow sitting on the bed when I returned home. Inside was a note laying atop a box of Godiva Chocolates:

Happy Anniversary. May our next one be like your grandfather's fairy tales.

My eyes burned with lack of sleep. It was one in the morning and I'd had a long day at the university. Also, the hour-long apology to Sara had drained me. She had shaken her head and tried to laugh it off, but I took my time, deeming it a wise investment for the future.

I went to the kitchen and poured myself a glass of ice water. Kicked off my slippers, returned to the desk, and continued reading.

I hadn't lied to Sara. The implications of this new jinn mythology were tremendous. A new origin myth, a bastardized version of the Abrahamic creationist lore. Trouble was these conclusions were tenuous. Gramps had speculated more than logically derived them. Arabi himself had touched on these themes in an abstract manner. To produce a viable theory of this alternate history of the universe, I needed more details, more sources.

Suppose there were other papers, hidden manuscripts. Was it possible that the treasure Gramps had found under the eucalyptus stump was truly "the map to the memory of heaven"? Ancient papers of cosmological importance never discovered?

"Shit, Gramps. Where'd you hide them?" I murmured.

His journal said he'd spent quite a bit of time in different places: Mansehra, Iran. Turkey, where he spent four years in a rug shop. The papers could really be anywhere.

My eyes were drawn to the phrase again: the Courtesan of the Mughals. I admired how beautiful the form and composition of the calligraphy was. Gramps had shaped the Urdu alphabet carefully into a flat design so that the conjoined words *Mughal* and *Courtesan* turned into an ornate rug. A calligram. The curves of the meem and ghain letters became the tassels and borders of the rug, the laam's seductive curvature its rippling belly.

Such artistry. One shape discloses another. A secret, symbolic relationship.

There, I thought. The secret hides in the city. The clues to the riddle of the eucalyptus treasure are in Lahore.

I spent the next few days sorting out my finances. Once I was satisfied that the trip was feasible, I began to make arrangements.

Sara stared at me when I told her. "Lahore? You're going to Lahore?"

"Yes."

"To look for something your grandpa may or may not have left there fifty-some years ago?"

"Yes."

"You're crazy. I mean it's one thing to talk about a journal."

"I know. I still need to go."

"So you're telling me, not asking. Why? Why are you so fixed on this? You know that country isn't safe these days. What if something happens?" She crossed her arms, lifted her feet off the floor, and tucked them under her on the couch. She was shivering a little.

"Nothing's gonna happen. Look, whatever he left in Lahore, he wanted me to see it. Why else write about it and leave it in his journal which he knew would be found one day? Don't you see? He was really writing to me."

"Well, that sounds self-important. Why not your dad? Also, why drop hints then? Why not just tell you straight up what it is?"

"I don't know." I shrugged. "Maybe he didn't want other people to find out."

"Or maybe he was senile. Look, I'm sorry, but this is crazy. You can't just fly off to the end of the world on a whim to look for a relic." She rubbed her legs. "It could take you weeks. Months. How much vacation time do you have left?"

"I'll take unpaid leave if I have to. Don't you see? I need to do this."

She opened her mouth, closed it. "Is this something you plan to keep doing?" she said quietly. "Run off each time anything bothers you."

"What?" I quirked my eyebrows. "Nothing's bothering me."

"No?" She jumped up from the couch and glared at me. "You've met my mother and Fanny, but I've never met your parents. You didn't take me to your grandfather's funeral. And since your return you don't seem interested in what we have, or once had. Are you *trying* to avoid talking about us? Are we still in love, Sal, or are we just getting by? Are we really together?"

"Of course we're together. Don't be ridiculous," I mumbled, but there was a constriction in my stomach. It wouldn't let me meet her eyes.

"Don't patronize me. You're obsessed with your own little world. Look, I have no problem with you giving time to your folks. Or your gramps's work. But we've been together for three years and you still find excuses to steer me away from your family. This cultural thing that you claim to resent, you seem almost proud of it. Do you see what I mean?"

"No." I was beginning to get a bit angry. "And I'm not sure you do either."

"You're lying. You know what I'm talking about."

"Do I? Okay, lemme try to explain what my problem is. Look at me, Sara. What do you see?"

She stared at me, shook her head. "I see a man who doesn't know he's lost."

"Wrong. You see a twenty-eight-year-old brown man living in a shitty apartment, doing a shitty job that doesn't pay much and has no hope of tenure. You see a man who can't fend for himself, let alone a wife and kids—"

"No one's asking you to—"

"—if he doesn't do something better with his life. But you go on believing all will be well if we trade families? Open your damn eyes." I leaned against the TV cabinet, suddenly tired. "All my life I was prudent. I planned and planned and gave up one thing for another. Moved here. Never looked back. Did whatever I could to be what I thought I needed to be. The archetypal fucking immigrant in the land of opportunities. But after Gramps died . . . " I closed my eyes, breathed, opened them. "I realize some things are worth more than that. Some things are worth going after."

"Some things, huh?" Sara half smiled, a trembling flicker that took me aback more than her words did. "Didn't your grandfather give up everything—his life, his family, his country—for love? And you're giving up . . . love for . . . what exactly? Shame? Guilt? Identity? A fucking manventure in a foreign land?"

"You're wrong," I said. "I'm not—"

But she wasn't listening. Her chest hitched. Sara turned, walked into the bedroom, and gently closed the door, leaving me standing alone.

I stomped down Highland Avenue. It was mid-October and the oaks and silver maples were burning with fall. They blazed yellow and crimson. They made me feel sadder and angrier and more confused.

Had our life together always been this fragile? I wondered if I had missed clues that Sara felt this way. She always was more aware of bumps in our relationship. I recalled watching her seated at the desk marking student papers once, her beautiful, freckled face scrunched in a frown, and thinking she would never really be welcome in my parents' house. Mama would smile nervously if I brought her home and retreat into the kitchen. Baba wouldn't say a word and somehow that would be worse than an outraged rejection. And what would Gramps have done? I didn't know. My head was messed up. It had been since his death.

It was dusk when I returned home, the lights in our neighborhood floating dreamily like gold sequins in black velvet.

Sara wasn't there.

The bed was made, the empty hangers in the closet pushed neatly together. On the coffee table in the living room under a Valentine mug was yet another note. She had become adept at writing me love letters.

I made myself a sandwich, sat in the dark, and picked at the bread. When I had mustered enough courage, I retrieved the note and began to read:

Salman,

I ~~wrote~~ tried to write this several times and each time my hand shook and made me write things I didn't want to. It sucks that we're such damn weaklings, the both of us. I'm stuck in love with you and you ~~are~~ with me. At least I hope so. At least that's the way I ~~feel~~ read you. But then I think about my mother and my heart begins racing.

You've met my family. Mom likes you. Fanny too. They think you're good for me. But you've never met my dad. You don't know why we ~~never~~ don't talk about him anymore.

He left Mom when Fanny and I were young. I don't remember him, although sometimes I think I can. When I close my eyes, I see this big, bulky shadow overwhelm the doorway of my room. There's this bittersweet smell, gin and sweat and tobacco. I remember not feeling afraid of him, for which I'm grateful.

But Dad left us Mom and he broke her. In especially bitter moments she would say it was another woman, but I don't think so. At least I never saw any proof of that in my mother's eyes when she talked about him. (In the beginning she talked a LOT about him.) I think he left her because he wanted more from life and Mom didn't understand pick that up. I think she didn't read his unhappiness in time. That's the vibe I get.

Does that excuse what he did? I don't think so. My mother's spent all her life trying to put us back together and she's done okay, but there are pieces of herself she wasn't able to find. In either me, or Fanny, or in anyone else.

I don't want that to happen to me. I don't want to end up like my mother. That's pretty much it. If you didn't love me, I'd understand. I'd be hurt, but I could live with it. But living with this uncertainty, never knowing when you might get that wanderlust I've seen in your eyes lately, is impossible for me. There's so much I want to say to you. Things you need to know if we're to have a future together. But the last thing I want to do is force you.

So I'm leaving. I'm going to stay at Fanny's. Think things through. It will be good for both of us. It will help me get my head straight and will let you do whatever you want to get your fucking demons out. So fly free. Go to Pakistan. Follow your goddamn heart or whatever. Just remember I won't wait all my life.

You know where to find me.

Love,
Sara

I put down the letter and stared out the window. Night rain drummed on the glass. I tapped my finger to its tune, fascinated by how difficult it was to keep time with it. A weight had settled on my chest and I couldn't push it off.

If an asshole weeps in the forest and no one is around to witness, is he still an asshole?

Nobody was there to answer.

For most of the fifteen-hour flight from New York to Lahore I was out. I hadn't realized how tired I was until I slumped into the economy seat and woke up half-dazed when the flight attendant gently shook my shoulder.

"Lahore, sir." She smiled when I continued to stare at her. The lipstick smudge on her teeth glistened. "Allama Iqbal International Airport."

"Yes," I said, struggling up and out. The plane was empty, the seats gaping. "How's the weather?"

"Cold. Bit misty. Fog bank's coming, they said. Early this year."

That didn't sound promising. I thanked her and hurried out, my carry-on clattering against the aisle armrests.

I exited the airport into the arms of a mid-November day and the air was fresh but full of teeth. The pale sea-glass sky seemed to wrap around the airport. I hailed a cab and asked for Bhati Gate. As we sped out of the terminal, whiteness seethed on the runway and blanketed the horizon. The flight attendant was right. Fog was on the way.

At a busy traffic signal the cabbie took a right. Past army barracks, the redbrick Aitchison College, and colonial-era Jinnah Gardens we went, until the roads narrowed and we hiccuped through a sea of motorbikes, rickshaws, cars, and pedestrians. *TERRORISTS ARE ENEMIES OF PEACE*, said a large black placard on a wall that jutted out left of a fifty-foot high stone gate. The looming structure had a massive central arch with eight small arches above it. It had a painting of the Kaaba on the right and Prophet Muhammad's shrine on the left with vermilion roses embossed in the middle. Another sign hung near it: *WELCOME TO OLD LAHORE BY THE GRACE OF ALLAH.*

We were at Bhati Gate.

The cab rolled to a stop in front of Kashi Manzil. A tall, narrow historical-home-turned-hotel with a facade made of ochre and azure faience tiles. A wide terrace ran around the second floor and a small black copper pot hung from a nail on the edge of the doorway awning.

I recognized the superstition. Black to ward off black. Protection against the evil eye.

Welcome to Gramps's world, I thought.

I looked down the street. Roadside bakeries, paan-and-cigarette shops, pirated DVD stalls, a girls' school with peeling walls, and dust, dust everywhere; but my gaze of course went to Bhati and its double row of arches.

This was the place my grandfather had once gazed at, lived by, walked through. Somewhere around here used to be a tea stall run by a Mughal princess. Someplace close had been a eucalyptus from which a kid had fallen and gashed his head. A secret that had traveled the globe had come here with Gramps and awaited me in some dingy old alcove.

That stupid wanderlust in your eyes.

Sara's voice in my brain was a gentle rebuke.

Later, I thought fiercely. *Later.*

• • •

The next day I began my search.

I had planned to start with the tea stalls. Places like this have long memories. Old Lahore was more or less the city's ancient downtown and people here wouldn't forget much. Least of all a Mughal princess who ran a tea shop. Gramps's journal didn't much touch on his life in the walled city. I certainly couldn't discern any clues about the location of the eucalyptus treasure.

Where did you hide it, old man? Your shack? A friend's place? Under that fucking tree stump?

If Gramps was correct and the tree had fallen half a century ago, that landmark was probably irretrievable. Gramps's house seemed the next logical place. Trouble was I didn't know where Gramps had lived. Before I left, I'd called Baba and asked him. He wasn't helpful.

"It's been a long time, son. Fifty years. Don't tax an old man's memory. You'll make me senile."

When I pressed, he reluctantly gave me the street where they used to live and his childhood friend Habib's last name.

"I don't remember our address, but I remember the street. Ask anyone in Hakiman Bazaar for Khajoor Gali. They'll know it."

Encircled by a wall raised by Akbar the Great, Old Lahore was bustling and dense. Two hundred thousand people lived in an area less than one square mile. Breezes drunk with the odor of cardamom, grease, and tobacco. The place boggled my mind as I strolled around taking in the niche pharmacies, foundries, rug shops, kite shops, and baked mud eateries.

I talked to everyone I encountered. The tea stall owner who poured Peshawari kahva in my clay cup. The fruit seller who handed me sliced oranges and guavas and frowned when I mentioned the pauper princess. Rug merchants, cigarette vendors, knife sellers. No one had heard of Zeenat Begum. Nobody knew of a young man named Sharif or his father who ran a calligraphy-and-design stall.

"Not around my shop, sahib." They shook their heads and turned away.

I located Khajoor Gali—a winding narrow alley once dotted by palm trees (or so the locals claimed) now home to dusty ramshackle buildings hunched behind open manholes—and went door to door, asking. No luck. An aged man with henna-dyed hair and a shishamwood cane stared at me when I mentioned Baba's friend Habib Ataywala, and said, "Habib. Ah, he and his family moved to Karachi several years ago. No one knows where."

"How about a eucalyptus tree?" I asked. "An ancient eucalyptus that used to stand next to Bhati Gate?"

Nope.

Listlessly I wandered, gazing at the mist lifting off the edges of the streets and billowing toward me. On the third day it was like slicing through a hundred rippling white shrouds. As night fell and fairy lights blinked on the minarets of Lahore's patron saint Data Sahib's shrine across the road from Bhati, I felt displaced. Depersonalized. I was a mote drifting in a slat of light surrounded by endless dark. Gramps was correct. Old Lahore had betrayed him. It was as if the city had deliberately rescinded all memory or trace of his family and the princess's. Sara was right. Coming here was a mistake. My life since Gramps's death was a mistake. Seeing this world as it *was* rather than through the fabular lens of Gramps's stories was fucking enlightening.

In this fog, the city's fresh anemia, I thought of things I hadn't thought about in years. The time Gramps taught me to perform the salat. The first time he brought my palms together to form the supplicant's cup. *Be the beggar at Allah's door*, he told me gently. *He loves humility. It's in the mendicant's bowl that the secrets of Self are revealed.* In the tashahuud position Gramps's index finger would shoot from a clenched fist and flutter up and down.

"This is how we beat the devil on the head," he said.

But what devil was I trying to beat? I'd been following a ghost and hoping for recognition from the living.

By the fifth day I'd made up my mind. I sat shivering on a wooden bench and watched my breath flute its way across Khajoor Gali as my finger tapped my cell phone and thousands of miles away Sara's phone rang.

She picked up almost immediately. Her voice was wary. "Sal?"

"Hey."

"Are you all right?"

"Yes."

A pause. "You didn't call before you left."

"I thought you didn't want me to."

"I was worried sick. One call after you landed would've been nice."

I was surprised but pleased. After so much disappointment, her concern was welcome. "Sorry."

"Jesus. I was . . . " She trailed off, her breath harsh and rapid in my ear. "Find the magic treasure yet?"

"No."

"Pity." She seemed distracted now. In the background water was running. "How long will you stay there?"

"I honest to God don't know, but I'll tell you this. I'm fucking exhausted."

"I'm sorry." She didn't sound sorry. I smiled a little.

"Must be around five in the morning there. Why're you up?" I said.

"I was . . . worried, I guess. Couldn't sleep. Bad dreams." She sighed. I imagined her rubbing her neck, her long fingers curling around the muscles, kneading them, and I wanted to touch her.

"I miss you," I said.

Pause. "Yeah. Me too. It's a mystery how much I'm used to you being around. And now that . . . " She stopped and exhaled. "Never mind."

"What?"

"Nothing." She grunted. "This damn weather. I think I'm coming down with something. Been headachy all day."

"Are you okay?"

"Yeah. It'll go away. Listen, I'm gonna go take a shower. You have fun."

Was that reproach? "Yeah, you too. Be safe."

"Sure." She sounded as if she were pondering. "Hey, I discovered something. Been meaning to tell you, but . . . you know."

"I'm all ears."

"Remember what your gramps said in the story. Lightning trees?"

"Yes."

"Well, lemme text it to you. I mentioned the term to a friend at school and turned out he recognized it too. From a lecture we both attended at MIT years ago about fractal similarities and diffusion-limited aggregation."

"Fractal what?" My phone beeped. I removed it from my ear and looked at the screen. A high-definition picture of a man with what looked like a tree-shaped henna tattoo on his left shoulder branching all the way down his arm. Pretty.

I put her on speakerphone. "Why're you sending me pictures of henna tattoos?"

She was quiet, then started laughing. "That didn't even occur to me, but, yeah, it does look like henna art."

"It isn't?"

"Nope. What you're seeing is a Lichtenberg figure created when branching electrical charges run through insulating material. Glass, resin, human skin—you name it. This man was hit by lightning and survived with this stamped on his flesh."

"What?"

"Yup. It can be created in any modern lab using nonconducting plates. Called electric treeing. Or lightning trees."

The lightning trees are dying.

"Holy shit," I said softly.

"Yup."

I tapped the touch screen to zoom in for a closer look. "How could Gramps know about this? If he made up the stories, how the fuck would he know something like this?"

"No idea. Maybe he knew someone who had this happen to them."

"But what does it mean?"

"The heck should I know. Anyways, I gotta go. Figured it might help you with whatever you're looking for."

"Thanks."

She hung up. I stared at the pattern on the man's arm. It was reddish, fernlike, and quite detailed. The illusion was so perfect I could even see buds and leaves. A breathtaking electric foliage. A map of lightning.

A memory of heaven.

I went to sleep early that night.

At five in the morning the Fajar call to prayer woke me up. I lay in bed watching fog drift through the skylight window, listening to the mullah's sonorous azaan, and suddenly I jolted upright.

The mosque of Ghulam Rasool, the Master of Cats.

Wasn't that what Gramps had told me a million years ago? That there was a mosque near Bhati Gate that faced his house?

I hadn't seen *any* mosques around.

I slipped on clothes and ran outside.

The morning smelled like burnished metal. The light was soft, the shape of early risers gentle in the mist-draped streets. A rooster crowed in the next alley. It had drizzled the night before and the ground was muddy. I half slipped, half leapt my way toward the mullah's voice rising and falling like an ocean heard in one's dream.

Wisps of white drifted around me like twilit angels. The azaan had stopped. I stared at the narrow doorway next to a rug merchant's shop ten feet away. Its entrance nearly hidden by an apple tree growing in the middle of the sidewalk, the place was tucked well away from traffic. Green light spilled from it. Tiny replicas of the Prophet's Mosque in Medina and Rumi's shrine in Turkey were painted above the door.

Who would put Rumi here when Data Sahib's shrine was just across the road?

I took off my shoes and entered the mosque.

A tiny room with a low ceiling set with zero-watt green bulbs. On reed mats the congregation stood shoulder to shoulder in two rows behind a smallish man in shalwar kameez and a turban. The Imam sahib clicked the mute button on the standing microphone in front, touched his earlobes, and Fajar began.

Feeling oddly guilty, I sat down in a corner. Looked around the room. Ninety-nine names of Allah and Muhammad, prayers and Quranic verses belching from the corners, twisting and pirouetting across the walls.

Calligrams in the shape of a mynah bird, a charging lion, a man prostrate in sajdah, his hands out before him shaping a beggar's bowl filled with alphabet vapors. Gorgeous work.

Salat was over. The namazis began to leave. Imam sahib turned. In his hands he held a tally counter for tasbih. *Click click!* Murmuring prayers, he rose and hobbled toward me.

"Assalam-o-alaikum. May I help you, son?" he said in Urdu.

"Wa Laikum Assalam. Yes," I said. "Is this Masjid Ghulam Rasool?"

He shook his head. He was in his seventies at least, long noorani beard, white hair sticking out of his ears. His paunch bulged through the striped-flannel kameez flowing past his ankles. "No. That mosque was closed and martyred in the nineties. Sectarian attacks. Left a dozen men dead. Shia mosque, you know. Used to stand in Khajoor Gali, I believe."

"Oh." I told myself I'd been expecting this, but my voice was heavy with disappointment. "I'm sorry to bother you then. I'll leave you to finish up."

"You're not local, son. Your salam has an accent," he said. "Amreekan, I think. You look troubled. How can I help you?" He looked at me, took his turban off. He had a pale scar near his left temple shaped like a climbing vine.

I watched him. His hair was silver. His sharp eyes were blue, submerged in a sea of wrinkles. "I was looking for a house. My late grandfather's. He lived close to the mosque, next door to a lady named Zeenat Begum. She used to run a tea stall."

"Zeenat Begum." His eyes narrowed, the blues receding into shadow. "And your grandfather's name?" he asked, watching the last of the worshippers rise to his feet.

"Sharif. Muhammad Sharif."

The oddest feeling, a sort of déjà vu, came over me. Something had changed in the air of the room. Even the last namazi felt it and glanced over his shoulder on his way out.

"Who did you say you were again?" Imam sahib said quietly.

"Salman Ali Zaidi."

"I see. Yes, I do believe I can help you out. This way."

He turned around, limping, and beckoned me to follow. We exited the mosque. He padlocked it, parted the bead curtain in the doorway of the rug shop next door, stepped in.

When I hesitated, he paused, the tasbih counter clicking in his hands. "Come in, son. My place is your place."

I studied the rug shop. It was located between the mosque and a souvenir stall. The awning above the arched doorway was grey, the brick voussoirs and keystone of the arch faded and peeling. The plaque by the entrance said *Karavan Kilim*.

Kilim is a kind of Turkish carpet. What was a kilim shop doing in Old Lahore?

He led me through a narrow well-lit corridor into a hardwood-floored showroom. Mounds of neatly folded rugs sat next to walls covered in rectangles of rich tapestries, carpets, and pottery-filled shelves. Stunning illustrations and calligraphy swirled across the high wooden ceiling. Here an entranced dervish whirled in blue, one palm toward the sky and one to the ground. There a crowd haloed with golden light held out dozens of drinking goblets, an Urdu inscription spiraling into a vast cloud above their heads: *They hear his hidden hand pour truth in the heavens.*

A bald middle-aged man dressed in a checkered brown half-sleeve shirt sat behind a desk. Imam Sahib nodded at him. "My nephew Khalid."

Khalid and I exchanged pleasantries. Imam sahib placed the tasbih counter and his turban on the desk. I gazed around me. "Imam sahib," I said. "This is a Turkish carpet shop. You run an imported rug business in your spare time?"

"Turkish design, yes, but not imported. My apprentices make them right here in the walled city." Without looking back, he began walking. "You can call me Bashir."

We went to the back of the shop, weaving our way through rug piles into a storeroom lit by sunlight from a narrow window. Filled to the ceiling with mountains of fabric rolls and broken looms, the room smelled of damp, rotten wood, and tobacco. In a corner was a large box covered with a bedsheet. Bashir yanked the sheet away and a puff of dust bloomed and clouded the air.

"Sharif," said the merchant Imam. "He's dead, huh?"

"You *knew* him?"

"Of course. He was friends with the Mughal princess. The lady who used to give us tea."

"How do you know that?" I stared at him. "Who are you?"

His eyes hung like sapphires in the dimness, gaze fixed on me, one hand resting atop the embossed six-foot-long metal trunk that had emerged. He tilted his head so the feeble light fell on his left temple. The twisted pale scar gleamed.

"The boy who fell from the eucalyptus tree," I whispered. "He gashed his head and the princess bandaged it for him. You're him."

The old man smiled. "Who I am is not important, son. What's important is this room where your grandfather worked for years."

Speechless, I gaped at him. After days of frustration and disappointment, I was standing in the room Gramps had occupied decades ago, this dingy store with its decaying inhabitants. I looked around as if at any moment Gramps might step out from the shadows.

"He was the best teacher I ever had," Bashir said. "We used to call him the Calligrapher Prince."

He flashed a smile. It brightened Bashir the merchant's tired, old face like a flame.

I watched this man with his wispy moonlight hair and that coiled scar who had kept my grandfather's secret for half a century. We sat around a low circular table, dipping cake rusk into mugs of milk chai sweetened with brown sugar. It was eight in the morning.

Bashir gripped his cup with both hands and frowned into it.

"My father was an electrician," he said. "By the time he was fifty he'd saved enough to buy a carpet shop. With lots of construction going on, he was able to get this shop dirt cheap.

"Rugs were an easy trade back in the seventies. You hired weavers, most of 'em immigrants from up north, and managed the product. We didn't have good relations with neighboring countries, so high demand existed for local rugs and tapestries without us worrying about competition. After the dictator Zia came, all that changed. Our shop didn't do well, what with rugs being imported cheap from the Middle East and Afghanistan. We began to get desperate.

"Right about then a stranger came to us."

It began, Bashir said, the evening someone knocked on their door with a rosy-cheeked child by his side and told Bashir's father he was looking for work. Bashir, then in his late teens, stood behind his baba, watching the visitor. Wary, the rug merchant asked where they hailed from. The man lifted his head and his face shone with the strangest light Bashir had seen on a human countenance.

"It swept across his cheeks, it flared in his eyes, it illuminated the cuts and angles of his bones," said Bashir, mesmerized by memory. "It was as if he had been touched by an angel or a demon. I'll never forget it."

"From thousands of miles away," said the man quietly. "From many years away."

It was Gramps, of course.

Bashir's father didn't recognize him, but he knew the man's family. Their only son, Muhammad Sharif, had been abroad for years, he'd heard. Lived in Iran, Turkey, Allah knew where else. Sharif's aged father still lived on Khajoor Gali in Old Lahore, but he'd shut down his design stall in the Niche of Calligraphers years ago.

"Sharif had been back for a few months and he and his son were living with his father. Now they needed money to reopen their shop." Bashir smiled. "Turned out your grandfather was an expert rug weaver. He said he learned it in Turkey near Maulana Rumi's shrine. My father offered him a job and he accepted. He worked with us for three years while he taught kilim weaving to our apprentices.

"He was young, hardly a few years older than I, but when he showed me his notebook, I knew he was no ordinary artist. He had drawn mystical poetry in animal shapes. Taken the quill and created dazzling worlds. Later, when my father put him before the loom, Sharif produced wonders such as we'd never seen."

Merchant Bashir got up and plodded to a pile of rugs. He grabbed a kilim and unrolled it across the floor. A mosaic of black, yellow, and maroon geometries glimmered.

"He taught me rug weaving. It's a nomadic art, he said. Pattern making carries the past into the future." Bashir pointed to a recurrent cross motif that ran down the kilim's center. "The four corners of the cross are the four corners of the universe. The scorpion here—" he toed a many-legged symmetric creature woven in yellow "—represents freedom. Sharif taught me this and more. He was a natural at symbols. I asked him why he went to Turkey. He looked at me and said, 'To learn to weave the best kilim in the world.'"

I cocked my head, rapt. I had believed it was grief that banished Gramps from Pakistan and love that bade him return. Now this man was telling me Gramps went to Turkey purposefully. How many other secrets had my grandfather left out?

"I didn't know he was a rug weaver," I said.

"Certainly was. One of the best we ever saw. He knew what silk on silk warping was. Don't weave on a poor warp. Never work on a loom out of alignment. He knew all this. Yet, *he* didn't consider himself a weaver. He learned the craft to carry out a duty, he said. His passion was calligraphy. All this you see—" Bashir waved a hand at the brilliant kilims and tapestries around us, at the twists and curlicues of the verses on the walls, the wondrous illustrations "—is his genius manifested. The Ottoman Turkish script, those calligrams in our mosque, the paintings. It's all him and his obsession with the Turkish masters."

"He ever say why he left Pakistan or why he returned?"

Bashir shrugged. "We never asked. As long as it wasn't criminal, we didn't care."

"Why'd you call him the Calligrapher Prince?"

The old man laughed. "It was a nickname the apprentices gave him and it stuck. Seemed so fitting." Bashir lifted his cup and swallowed the last mouthful of tea along with the grounds. I winced. "Sharif was courteous and diligent. Hardly went home before midnight and he helped the business run more smoothly than it had in years, but I knew he was waiting for something. His eyes were always restless. Inward."

In the evenings when the shop had closed Sharif drew and carved keenly. For hours he engraved, his cotton swabs with lacquer thinner in one hand, his burin and flat gravers in the other. What he was making was no secret. Bashir watched the process and the product: a large brass trunk with a complex inlay in its lid. A labyrinthine repoussé network gouged into the metal, spiraling into itself. Such fine work it took one's breath away.

"Never, never, never," said Bashir, "have I seen such a thing of beauty evolve in a craftsman's hand again."

Sharif's concentration was diabolical, his hands careful as nature's might have been as it designed the ornate shells of certain mollusks or the divine geometry of certain leaves.

"What are you making and why?" Bashir had asked his master.

Sharif shrugged. "A nest for ages," he said, and the rug merchant's son had to be content with the baffling reply.

Two years passed. One evening Bashir's father got drenched in a downpour and caught pneumonia, which turned aggressive. Despite rapid treatment, he passed away. Bashir took over the shop. In his father's name, he turned their old house into a small Quran center (which would eventually become Bhati's only mosque). He ran the rug shop honestly and with Sharif's help was able to maintain business the way it had been.

At the end of his third year Sharif came to Bashir.

"My friend," he said. "I came here for a purpose. Something precious was given to me that is not mine to keep. It must wait here in the protection of the tree, even as I go help my father reopen his calligraphy stall."

The young rug merchant was not surprised. He had glimpsed his master's departure in his face the night he arrived. But what was that about a tree?

Sharif saw his student's face and smiled. "You don't remember, do you? Where your shop is now the eucalyptus tree used to stand."

Bashir was stunned. He had forgotten all about the tree and the incident with the jinn. It was as if a firm hand had descended and swept all memory of the incident from his brain, like a sand picture.

He waited for Sharif to go on, but the Calligrapher Prince rose, grasped Bashir's hand, and thrust two heavy envelopes into it.

"The first one is for you. Enough money to rent space for my trunk."

"You're not taking it with you?" Bashir was dumbfounded. The trunk with its elaborate design was worth hundreds, maybe thousands of rupees.

"No. It must stay here." Sharif looked his student in the eye. "And it must not be opened till a particular someone comes."

"Who?" said Bashir, and wished he hadn't. These were curious things and they made his spine tingle and his legs shake. A strange thought entered his head: *A burden the mountains couldn't bear settles on me tonight.* It vanished quick as it had come.

Sharif's voice was dry like swiftly turning thread when he said, "Look at the name on the second envelope."

And his heart full of misgivings, fears, and wonder—most of all, wonder—Bashir did.

I give myself credit: I was calm. My hands were steady. I didn't bat an eye when I took the yellowed envelope from Merchant Bashir's hands.

"It is yours," said Bashir. "The envelope, the secret, the burden." He wiped his face with the hem of his kameez. "Fifty years I carried it. Allah be praised, today it's passed on to you."

A burden the mountains couldn't bear settles on me tonight.

I shivered a little.

"It's cold," Bashir said. "I will turn the heat on and leave you to peruse the contents of the envelope alone. I'll be in the tea stall two shops down. Take as long as you wish."

"You kept your word," I said softly. "You didn't open the envelope."

Bashir nodded. "I asked Sharif how in God's name he could trust me with it when I didn't trust myself. A secret is like a disease, I said. It begins with an itch in a corner of your flesh, then spreads like cancer, until you're overcome and give in. He just smiled and said he knew I wouldn't open it." The rug weaver dabbed a kerchief at his grimy cheeks. "Maybe because he had such faith in me, it helped keep wicked desire at bay."

Or maybe he knew *you wouldn't,* I thought, holding the envelope, feeling my pulse beat in my fingertips. *Just like he knew the name of the rightful owner decades before he was born.*

My name.

Through the back window I watched Bashir tromp down the street. The mist had thickened and the alley was submerged in blue-white. A steady whine of wind and the occasional thump as pedestrians walked into trashcans and bicycle stands. A whorl of fog shimmered around the streetlight on the far corner.

I turned and went to the counter. Picked up the envelope. Sliced it open. Inside was a sheaf of blank papers. I pulled them out and a small object swept out and fell on the floor. I reached down and picked it up, its radiance casting a twitching halo on my palm.

It was a silver key with a grooved golden stud for a blade, dangling from a rusted hoop.

Impossible.

My gaze was riveted on the golden stud. It took a considerable amount of effort to force my eyes away, to pocket the key, rise, and shamble to the storeroom.

It was dark. Fog had weakened the daylight. Broken looms with their limp warp strings and tipping beams gaped. I crossed the room and stood in front of the brass trunk. The padlock was tarnished. Round keyhole. I retrieved the key and stared at it, this centuries-old gold stud—if one were to believe Gramps—fused to a silver handle.

The instruction was clear.

I brushed the dust away from the lid. A floral design was carved into it, wreathed with grime but still visible: a medallion motif in a gilt finish with a Quranic verse running through its heart like an artery.

"Those who believe in the Great Unseen," I whispered. In my head Baba smiled and a row of pine trees cast a long shadow across Gramps's tombstone where I had last read a similar epitaph.

I inserted the Mughal key into the padlock, turned it twice, and opened the trunk.

A rug. A rolled-up kilim, judging by its thinness.

I stared at it, at the lavish weave of its edges that shone from light *within* the rolled layers. Was there a flashlight inside? Ridiculous idea. I leaned in.

The kilim smelled of sunshine. Of leaves and earth and fresh rainfall. Scents that filled my nostrils and tapped my taste buds, flooded my mouth with a sweet tang, not unlike cardamom tea.

My palms were sweating despite the cold. I tugged at the fat end of the rug and it fell to the floor, unspooling. It was seven by five feet, its borders perfectly even, and as it raced across the room, the storeroom was inundated with colors: primrose yellow, iris white, smoke blue. A bright scarlet sparked in the air that reminded me of the sharbat Mama used to make during Ramadan.

I fell back. Awestruck, I watched this display of lights surging from the kilim. Thrashing and gusting and slamming into one another, spinning faster and faster until they became a dancing shadow with many rainbow arms, each pointing earthward to their source—the carpet.

The shadow pirouetted once more and began to sink. The myriad images in the carpet flashed as it dissolved into them, and within moments the room was dark. The only evidence of the specter's presence was the afterglow on my retina.

I breathed. My knees were weak, the base of my spine thrummed with charge. A smell like burning refuse lingered in my nostrils.

What was that?

A miracle, Gramps spoke in my head softly.

I went to the carpet. It was gorgeous. Multitudes of figures ran in every shape around its edges. Flora and fauna. Grotesques and arabesques. They seethed over nomadic symbols. I traced my finger across the surface. Cabalistic squares, hexagrams, eight-pointed stars, a barb-tailed scorpion. A concoction of emblems swirled together by the artisan's finger until it seemed the carpet crawled with arcana I'd seen in ancient texts used mostly for one purpose.

Traps, I thought. *For what?*

I peered closer. The central figures eddied to form the armature of a tower with four jagged limbs shot into the corners of the rug where they were pinned down with pieces of glass. Four curved symmetric pieces, clear with the slightest tinge of purple. Together these four quarter-circles stuck out from the corners of the kilim as if they had once belonged to a cup.

They shimmered.

"What are you," I whispered. The carpet and the embedded glass said nothing. I hesitated, the soles of my feet tingling, then bent and looked inside the upper right shard.

A man looked back at me, his face expressionless, young, and not mine.

"Salam, beta," Gramps said in Urdu, still smiling. "Welcome."

The age of wonders shivered and died when the world changed.

In the summer of 1963, however, an eighteen-year-old boy named Sharif discovered a miracle as he panted and dug and heaved an earthen pot out from under a rotten eucalyptus stump.

It was night, there were no streetlamps, and, by all laws holy, the dark should have been supreme. Except a light emanated from the pot.

Sharif wiped his forehead and removed the pot's lid. Inside was a purple glass chalice glowing with brightness he couldn't look upon. He had to carry it home and put on dark shades before he could peer in.

The chalice was empty and the light came from the glass itself.

Trembling with excitement, the boy wrapped it in a blanket and hid it under the bed. The next day when his parents were gone, he poured water into it and watched the liquid's meniscus bubble and seethe on the kitchen table. The water was the light and the light all liquid.

The fakir had warned the Mughal princess that the secret was not for human eyes, but since that fateful night when the boy had first glimpsed the eucalyptus jinn, saw his fetters stretch from sky to earth, his dreams had been transformed. He saw nightscapes that he shouldn't see. Found himself in places that shouldn't exist. And now here was an enchanted cup frothing with liquid light on his kitchen table.

The boy looked at the chalice again. The churning motion of its contents hypnotized him. He raised it, and drank the light.

Such was how unfortunate, young Sharif discovered the secrets of Jaam-e-Jam.

The Cup of Heaven.

Legends of the Jaam have been passed down for generations in the Islamic world. Jamshed, the Zoroastrian emperor of Persia, was said to have possessed a seven-ringed scrying cup that revealed the mysteries of heaven to him. Persian mythmakers ascribed the centuries-long success of the empire to the magic of the Cup of Heaven.

And now it was in Sharif's hand.

The Mother of Revelations. It swept across the boy's body like a fever. It seeped inside his skin, blanched the marrow of his bones, until every last bit of him understood. He knew what he had to do next, and if he could he would destroy the cup, but that wasn't his choice anymore. The cup gave him much, including foreknowledge with all the knots that weave the future. Everything from that moment on he *remembered* already.

And now he needed to conceal it.

So Sharif left for the rest of his life. He went to Mansehra. Found the Mughal princess. Married her. He made her very happy for the rest of her brief life, and on a sunny Friday afternoon he took his goggling, squalling son with him to pray Juma in a mosque in the mountains, where he would stay the night for worship and meditation.

Even though he knew it was the day appointed for his wife's death.

There was no thought, no coercion, no struggle. Just the wisdom of extinction, the doggedness of destiny that steered his way. He and his son would return to find their family incinerated. Sharif and the villagers would carry out their charred corpses and he would weep; he was allowed that much.

After, he took his son to Turkey.

For years he learned rug weaving at a master weaver's atelier. His newfound knowledge demanded he rein in the Cup of Heaven's contents till the time for their disclosure returned. For that he must learn to prepare a special trap.

It took his fingers time to learn the trick even if his brain knew it. Years of mistakes and practice. Eventually he mastered the most sublime ways of weaving. He could apply them to create a trap so elegant, so fast and wise that nothing would escape it.

Sharif had learned how to weave the fabric of light itself.

Now he could return to his hometown, seek out the shadow of the eucalyptus tree, and prepare the device for imprisoning the cup.

First, he designed a kilim with the holy names of reality woven into it. Carefully, with a diamond-tipped glasscutter, he took the Jaam-e-Jam apart into four pieces and set them into the kilim. Next, he snared waves of light that fell in through the workshop window. He looped the peaks and troughs and braided them into a net. He stretched the net over the glass shards and warped them into place. He constructed a brass trunk and etched binding symbols on its lid, then rolled up the kilim and placed it inside.

Last, a special key was prepared. This part took some sorting out—he had to fetch certain particles farther along in time—but he succeeded; and finally he had the key. It was designed to talk to the blood-light in one person only, one descended from Sharif's line and the Mughal princess's.

Me.

Incredulous, I gazed at my dead grandfather as he told me his last story.

His cheeks glowed with youth, his eyes sharp and filled with truth. His hair was black, parted on the left. Maybe the glass shone, or his eyes, but the effect was the same: an incredible halo of light, near holy in its alienness, surrounded him. When he shook his head, the halo wobbled. When he spoke, the carpet's fringe threads stirred as if a breeze moved them, but the voice was sourceless and everywhere.

"Today is the sixteenth of November, 2013," he had said before launching into narration like a machine. "You're twenty-eight. The woman you love will be twenty-five in three months. As for me"—he smiled—"I'm dead."

He was telling me the future. Prescience, it seemed, had been his forte. And now I knew how. The Cup of Heaven.

"Is it really you?" I said when he was done, my voice full of awe.

Gramps nodded. "More a portion of my punishment than me."

"What does that mean? What other secrets were in the cup? Tell me everything, Gramps," I said, "before I go crazy."

"All good stories leave questions. Isn't that what I will say?" He watched me, serious. "You should understand that I'm sorry. For bringing you here. For passing this on to you. I wish I'd never dug under that tree. But it is the way it is. I was handed a responsibility. I suppose we all get our burdens."

The air in the room was thick and musty. Our eyes were locked together. *He lured me here*, I thought. My hands were shaking and this time it was with anger. Rage at being manipulated. All those stories of princesses and paupers, those lies he told for years while all the time he knew exactly what he was doing and how he was preparing me for this burden, whatever it was.

Gramps's spirit, or whoever he was in this current state, watched me with eyes that had no room for empathy or guilt. Didn't he care at all?

"I do, son," he said gently. He was reading my mind or already knew it—I wasn't clear which—and that angered me more. "I haven't gotten to the most important part of the story."

"I don't care," I said in a low voice. "Just tell me what was in the cup."

"You need to know this." His tone was mechanical, not my gramps's voice. The person I knew and loved was not here. "The Jaam gave me much. Visions, power, perfect knowledge, but it cost me too. Quite a bit. You can't stare into the heart of the Unseen and not have it stare back at you."

He swept a hand around himself. For the first time I noticed the halo wasn't just hovering behind his head; it was a luminescent ring blooming from his shoulders, encircling his neck, wrapping around his body.

"It wasn't for me to decide the cup's fate, so I hid it away. But because the Unseen's presence ran like a torrent from it I paid more than a man should ever have to pay for a mistake. I was told to dig up the secret and hide it, not to gaze at its wonders or partake of its mysteries. My punishment hence was remembering the future and being powerless to prevent it. I would lose everything I remembered about the love of my life. Starting from the moment I dug under the eucalyptus, I would *forget* ever having been with your grandmother. My lovely, luckless Zeenat.

"Once the task was complete and I handed over the trunk to Bashir, my memories began to go. With time, my mind confabulated details to fill in the gaps and I told myself and everyone who'd ask that I had married a woman who died during childbirth. By the time we moved to America, all I remembered was this nostalgia and longing to discover a secret I thought I'd never pursued: the pauper princess and her magical jinn."

When he stopped, the outline of his face wavered. It was the halo blazing. "What you see before you"—with a manicured finger Gramps made a circle around his face—"is an impression of those lost years. My love's memory wrenched from me."

He closed his eyes, letting me study the absence of age on his face. If he were telling the truth, he was a figment of his own imagination, and I . . . I was crazy to believe any of this. This room was a delusion and I was complicit in it, solidifying it.

Maybe that was why he forgot. Maybe the human mind couldn't marry such unrealities and live with them.

"What about the journal? If you forgot everything, how could you draw? How could you write down details of your life?"

Gramps, his apparition, opened his eyes. "Senility. When my organic memory dissolved, fragments of my other life came seeping back in dreams."

So he wrote the journal entries like someone else's story. He had visions and dreams, but didn't know whose life was flooding his head, filling it with devastating images, maybe even ushering in his death earlier than it otherwise might have come.

I leaned back and watched the threads of the carpet twist. The woven tower shot into the sky with hundreds of creatures gathered around it, looking at its top disappear into the heavens.

"I want to see the cup." My voice rose like a razor in the dark, cutting through the awkwardness between us. "I want to see the contents."

"I know." He nodded. "Even such a warning as you see before you wouldn't deter you."

"If the cup's real, I will take it with me to the States, where historians and mythologists will validate its authenticity and . . . "

And what? Truly believe it was a magical cup and place it in the Smithsonian? *The cup's secret isn't for human eyes,* Gramps had said. But what else are secrets for if not discovery? That is their nature. Only time stands between a mystery and its rightful master.

Gramps's fingers played with the halo, twisting strands of luminosity like hair between his fingers. "You will have the secret, but before you drink from it, I want you to do something for me."

He snapped his fingers and threads of light sprang from the halo, brightening as they came apart. Quickly he noosed them until he had a complicated knot with a glowing center and a string dangling at the end.

He offered it to me. "Pull."

Warily, I looked at the phosphorescent string. "Why?"

"Before you gaze inside the cup, you will have a taste of my memories. After that you decide your own demons."

I reached out a hand to the glass shard, withdrew, extended it again. When my fingers touched it, I flinched. It was warm. Slowly, I pushed my hand into the glass. It was like forcing it through tangles of leaves hot from the sun.

The string reddened. Its end whipped back and forth. I pinched it, pulled, and the light string rocketed toward me, the brilliant corpuscle at its center thrashing and unraveling into reality.

I gasped. A fat worm of peacock colors was climbing my hand, wrapping itself around my wrist.

"Gramps! What is this?" I shouted, twisting my arm, but the creature was already squirming its way up my arm, its grooves hot against my flesh, leaving shadows of crimson, mauve, azure, muddy green, and yellow on my skin. I could smell its colors. Farm odors. Damp foliage. Herbal teas. Baba's truck with its ancient vomit-stained upholstery and greasy wheel covers. My mother's hair. Sara's embrace.

I shuddered. The worm's body was taut across the bridge of my nose, its two ends poised like metal filings in front of my eyes.

"These," Gramps said, "are the stingers of memory."

The worm's barbs were like boulders in my vision. As I watched them, terrified, they vibrated once.

Then plunged into my eyes.

• • •

In the cup was everything, Gramps said. He meant it.

What the teenage boy saw went back all the way until he was destroyed and remade from the complete memory of the universe. From the moment of its birth until the end. Free of space, time, and their building blocks, the boy experienced all at once: a mausoleum of reality that wrapped around him, plunged into which he floated through the Unseen.

And I, a blinking, tumbling speck, followed.

Gramps watched the concussion of first particles reverberate through infinity. He watched instantaneous *being* bloom from one edge of existence to the other; watched the triumph of fire and ejective forces that shook creation in their fists. He observed these phenomena and knew all the realms of the hidden by heart.

Matter has always been conscious. That was the secret. Sentience is as much its property as gravity and it is always striving toward a new form with better accommodation.

From the needs of sentient matter rose the invention that humans are.

Gramps gripped the darkness of prebeing and billowed inside the cracks of matter. When I tried to go after him, an awful black defied me. To me belonged just a fraction of his immersion.

I sat on a molten petal of creation as it solidified, and watched serpentine fractals of revelation slither toward me. Jinns are carrier particles of sentience, they murmured. Of the universe's memory of the Great Migration.

My prehuman flesh sang on hearing these words. Truths it had once known made music in my body, even if I didn't quite remember them.

The Great Migration?

The first fires and winds created many primordials, the fractals said.

You mean jinns?

Beings unfettered by the young principles of matter and energy. As the world began to cool, new rules kicked in. The primordials became obsolete. Now the selfish sentience needed resistant clay-and-water creatures to thrive upon. For humans to exist, the primordials had to migrate.

They complied?

They dug tunnels into space-time and left our corner of existence so it could evolve on its own. Before they departed, however, they caged the memory of their being here, for if such a memory were unleashed upon the world, matter would rescind its newest form and return to the essence. Things as we know them would cease to exist.

So they made the cup, I said. *To imprison the memories of a bygone age.*

Before they passed into shadow, whispered the fractals, they made sure the old ways would be available. In case the new ones proved fleeting.

An image came to me then: a dazzling array of fantastical creatures—

made of light, shadow, earth, inferno, metal, space, and time—traveling across a brimming grey land, their plethora of heads bowed. As they plodded, revolved, and flew, the dimensions of the universe changed around them to accommodate this pilgrimage of the phantastique. Matter erupted into iridescent light. Flames and flagella bloomed and dissolved. Their chiaroscuric anatomies shuttered as the primordials made their way into the breath of the unknown.

The flimsy speck that was I trembled. I was witnessing a colossal sacrifice. A mother of migrations. What should a vehicle of sentience do except bow before its ageless saviors?

In the distance, over the cusp of the planets, a primordial paused, its mammoth body shimmering itself into perception. As I watched it, a dreadful certainty gripped me: this was how Gramps was trapped. If I didn't look away immediately, I would be punished too, for when have human eyes glimpsed divinity without forsaking every sight they hold dear?

But I was rooted, stilled by the primordial's composition. Strange minerals gleamed in its haunches. From head to tail, it was decorated with black-and-white orbs like eyes. They twitched like muscles and revolved around its flesh until their center, a gush of flame riding bony gears, was visible to me. Mirages and reveries danced in it, constellations of knowledge ripe for the taking. Twisted ropes of fire shot outward, probing for surface, oscillating up and down.

My gaze went to a peculiar vision bubbling inside the fiery center. I watched it churn inside the primordial, and in the briefest of instants I knew what I knew.

As if sensing my study, the creature began to turn. Fear whipped me forward, a reverential awe goading me closer to these wonders undiluted by human genes, unpolluted by flesh, unmade by sentience.

Sentience is everything, sentience the mystery and the master, I sighed as I drifted closer.

But then came a shock wave that pulsed in my ears like a million crickets chirping. I rode the blast force, grief stricken by this separation, spinning and flickering through string-shaped fractures in reality, like gigantic cracks in the surface of a frozen lake. Somewhere matter bellowed like a swamp gator and the wave rushed at the sound. Tassels of light stirred in the emptiness, sputtering and branching like gargantuan towers—

Lightning trees, I thought.

—and suddenly I was veering toward them, pitched up, tossed down, slung across them until there was a whipping sound like the breaking of a sound barrier, and I was slipping, sliding, and falling through.

• • •

My eyes felt raw and swollen. I was choking.

I gagged and squirmed up from the carpet as the light worm crawled up my throat and out my left nostril. It rushed out, its segments instantly melting and fading to roseate vapors. The vapors wafted in the darkness like Chinese lanterns, lighting up discarded looms and moth-eaten rug rolls before dissipating into nothing.

I stared around, fell back, and lay spread-eagled on the carpet. The nostril through which the worm had exited was bleeding. A heavy weight had settled on my chest.

A memory came to me. Of being young and very small, standing at the classroom door, nose pressed against the glass, waiting for Mama. She was running late and the terror in me was so powerful, so huge, that all I could do was cry. Only it wasn't just terror, it was feeling abandoned, feeling insignificant, and knowing there wasn't a damn thing I could do about it.

Footsteps. I forced myself through the lethargy to turn on my side. Bashir the rug merchant stood outlined against the rectangle of light beyond the doorway. His face was in shadow. The blue of his eyes glinted.

"You all right, son?"

My heart pounded so violently I could feel it in every inch of my body. As if I were a leather-taut drum with a kid hammering inside and screaming.

"I don't know." I tottered upright, breathed, and glanced at the carpet. The light was gone and it was ordinary. Gramps was gone too. The cup's pieces in the corners were dull and empty.

Just glass.

I looked at Bashir. "I saw my grandfather."

"Yes." The rug merchant's shadow was long and alien on the carpet. "What will you do now that he's gone?"

I stared at him. His bright sapphire eyes, not old but ancient, watched me. He was so still. Not a hair stirred on his head. I wiped my mouth and finally understood.

"You're not the boy who fell," I said quietly. "The eucalyptus jinn. That's you."

He said nothing but his gaze followed me as I stepped away from the carpet, from this magical rectangle woven a half century ago. How long had he guarded the secret? Not the carpet, but the cup? How long since Bashir the rug merchant had died and the eucalyptus jinn had taken his form?

"A very long time," Bashir said in a voice that gave away nothing.

Our eyes met and at last I knew burden. Left behind by the primordial titans, here was a messenger of times past, the last of his kind, who had kept this unwanted vigil for millennia. Carrying the responsibility of the cup, silently waiting for the end of days. Was there place in this new world for him or that damned chalice? Could there be a fate worse than death?

I stood before the caged shards of the Jaam. Gramps might have traversed the seven layers of heaven, but during my brief visit into the Unseen I'd seen enough to understand the pricelessness of this vehicle. Whatever magic the cup was, it transcended human logic. Were it destroyed, the last vestige of cosmic memory would vanish from our world.

"Whatever you decide," the jinn said, "remember what you saw in the ideograms of the Eternum."

For a moment I didn't understand, then the vision returned to me. The mammoth primordial with its flaming core and the glimpse of what churned between its bonelike gears. My heartbeat quickened.

If what I saw was true, I'd do anything to protect it, even if it meant destroying the most glorious artifact the world would ever know.

The jinn's face was kind. He knew what I was thinking.

"What about the shop?" I asked, my eyes on the damaged looms, the dead insects, the obsolete designs no one needed.

"Will go to my assistant," he said. "Bashir's nephew."

I looked at him. In his eyes, blue as the deepest ocean's memory, was a lifetime of waiting. No, several lifetimes.

Oblivion. The eucalyptus jinn courted oblivion. And I would give it to him.

"Thank you," he said, smiling, and his voice was so full of warmth I wanted to cry.

"You miss the princess. You protected their family?"

"I protected only the cup. The Mughal lineage just happened to be the secret's bearer," said the eucalyptus jinn, but he wouldn't meet my eyes.

Which was why he couldn't follow them when they left, until Gramps went after them with the cup. Which was also why he couldn't save them from the fire that killed them. Gramps knew it too, but he couldn't or wouldn't do anything to change the future.

Was Gramps's then the worst burden of all? It made my heart ache to think of it.

We looked at each other. I stepped toward the brass trunk and retrieved the key with the gold stud from the padlock. Without looking at the jinn, I nodded.

He bowed his head, and left to fetch me the instruments of his destruction.

The city breathed fog when I left the rug shop. Clouds of white heaved from the ground, silencing the traffic and the streets. Men and women plodded in the alleys, their shadows quivering on dirt roads. I raised my head and imagined stars pricking the night sky, their light so puny, so distant, it made one wistful. Was it my imagination or could I smell them?

The odd notion refused to dissipate even after I returned to the inn and packed for the airport. The colors of the world were flimsy. Things skittered in the corners of my eyes. They vanished in the murmuring fog when I looked at them. Whatever this new state was, it wasn't disconcerting. I felt warmer than I had in years.

The plane bucked as it lifted, startling the passengers. They looked at one another and laughed. They'd been worried about being grounded because of weather. I stared at the ground falling away, away, the white layers of Lahore undulating atop one another, like a pile of rugs.

My chin was scratchy, my flesh crept, as I brought the hammer down and smashed the pieces of the cup.

I leaned against the plane window. My forehead was hot. Was I coming down with something? Bereavement, PTSD, post-party blues? But I *had* been through hell. I should expect strange, melancholic moods.

The flame twitched in my hand. The smell of gasoline strong in my nose. At my feet the carpet lay limp like a terrified animal.

"Coffee, sir?" said the stewardess. She was young and had an angular face like a chalice. She smiled at me, flashing teeth that would look wonderful dangling from a hemp string.

"No," I said, horrified by the idea, and my voice was harsher than I'd intended. Startled, she stepped back. I tried to smile, but she turned and hurried away.

I wiped my sweaty face with a paper napkin and breathed. Weird images, but I felt more in control, and the feeling that the world was losing shape had diminished. I unzipped my carry-on and pulled out Gramps's journal. So strange he'd left without saying goodbye.

That ghost in the glass was just a fragment of Gramps's memories, I told myself. *It wasn't him.*

Wasn't it? We are our memories. This mist that falls so vast and brooding can erase so much, but not the man. Will I remember Gramps? Will I remember *me* and what befell me in this strange land midway between the Old World and the New?

That is a question more difficult to answer, for, you see, about ten hours ago, when I changed planes in Manchester, I realized I am beginning to forget. Bits and pieces, but they are disappearing irrevocably. I have already forgotten the name of the street where Gramps and the princess once lived. I've even forgotten what the rug shop looked like. What was its name?

Karavan Kilim! An appropriate name, that. The word is the etymologic root for *caravan*. A convoy, or a party of pilgrims.

At first, it was terrifying, losing memories like that. But as I pondered the phenomenon, it occurred to me that the erasure of my journey to Old

Lahore is so important the rest of my life likely depends on it. I have come to believe that the colorlessness of the world, the canting of things, the jagged movements of shadows is the peeling of the onionskin which separates men from the worlds of jinn. An unfractured reality from the Great Unseen. If the osmosis persisted, it would drive me mad, see?

That was when I decided I would write my testament while I could. I have been writing in this notebook for hours now and my fingers are hurting. The process has been cathartic. I feel more anchored to our world. Soon, I will stop writing and put a reminder in the notebook telling myself to seal it in an envelope along with Gramps's journal when I get home. I will place them in a deposit box at my bank. I will also prepare a set of instructions for my lawyer that, upon my death, the envelope and its contents be delivered to my grandson who should then read it and decide accordingly.

Decide what? You might say. There's no more choice to make. Didn't I destroy the carpet and the cup and the jinn with my own hands? Those are about the few memories left in my head from this experience. I remember destroying the rug and its contents. So vivid those memories, as if someone painted them inside my head. I remember my conversation with the jinn; he was delighted to be banished forever.

Wasn't he?

This is making me think of the vision I had in—what did the jinn call it?—the Eternum.

The root J-N-N has so many derivatives. *Jannah*, paradise, is the hidden garden. *Majnoon* is a crazy person whose intellect has been hidden. My favorite, though, is *janin*.

The embryo hidden inside the mother.

The jinn are not gone from our world, you see. They've just donned new clothes.

My beloved Terry, I saw your face printed in a primordial's flesh. I know you, my grandson, before you will know yourself. I also saw your father, my son, in his mother's womb. He is so beautiful. Sara doesn't know yet, but Neil will be tall and black-haired like me. Even now, his peanut-sized mass is drinking his mother's fluids. She will get migraines throughout the pregnancy, but that's him borrowing from his mom. He will return the kindness when he's all grown up. Sara's kidneys will fail and my fine boy will give his mother one, smiling and saying she'll never be able to tell him to piss off again because *her* piss will be formed through his gift.

My Mughal children, my pauper princes, you and your mother are why I made my decision. The Old World is gone, let it rest. The primordials and other denizens of the Unseen are obsolete. If memory of their days threatens the world, if mere mention of it upsets the order of creation, it's too dangerous to be left to chance. For another to find.

So I destroyed it.

The historian and the bookkeeper in me wept, but I'd do it a thousand times again if it means the survival of our species. Our children. No use mourning what's passed. We need to preserve our future.

Soon, I will land in the US of A. I will embrace the love of my life, kiss her, take her to meet my family. They're wary, but such is the nature of love. It protects us from what is unseen. I will teach my parents to love my wife. They will come to know what I already know. That the new world is not hostile, just different. My parents are afraid and that is okay. Someday I too will despise your girlfriends (and fear them), for that's how the song goes, doesn't it?

Meanwhile, I'm grateful. I was witness to the passing of the Great Unseen. I saw the anatomy of the phantastique. I saw the pilgrimage of the primordials. Some of their magic still lingers in the corners of our lives, wrapped in breathless shadow, and that is enough. We shall glimpse it in our dreams, taste it in the occasional startling vision, hear it in a night bird's song. And we will believe for a moment, even if we dismiss these fancies in the morning.

We will believe. And, just like this timeless gold stud that will soon adorn my wife's nose, the glamour of such belief will endure forever.

WHAT HAS PASSED SHALL IN KINDER LIGHT APPEAR

Bao Shu
(translated by Ken Liu)

1.

My parents named me "Xie Baosheng," hoping I would live a life full of precious memories. I was born on the day the world was supposed to end.

Mom and Dad told me how strange flashing lights appeared in the sky all over the globe, accompanied by thunder and lightning, as though the heavens had turned into a terrifying battlefield. Scientists could not agree on an explanation: some said extraterrestrials had arrived; some suggested the Earth was passing through the galactic plane; still others claimed that the universe was starting to collapse. The apocalyptic atmosphere drove many into church pews while the rest shivered in their beds.

In the end, nothing happened. As soon as the clock struck midnight, the world returned to normality. The crowds, teary-eyed, embraced each other and kissed, thankful for God's gift. Many petitioned for that day to be declared the world's new birthday as a reminder for humanity to live more honestly and purely, and to treasure our existence.

The grateful mood didn't last long, and people pretty much went on living as before. The Arab Spring happened, followed by the global financial crisis. Life had to go on, and we needed to resolve troubles both big and small. Everyone was so busy that the awkward joke about the end of the world never came up again. Of course, I had no memory of any of this: I was born on that day. I had no impressions of the next few years, either.

My earliest memory was of the Opening Ceremony of the Olympics. I was only four then, but nonetheless caught up in the excitement all around me.

Mom and Dad told me, *China is going to host the Olympics!*

I had no idea what the "Olympics" were, just that it was an occasion worth celebrating. That night, Mom took me out. The streets were packed and she held me up so that I could see, overhead, immense footprints formed by fireworks. One after another, they appeared in the night sky, as if some giant was walking above us. I was amazed.

The neighborhood park had a large projection screen, and Mom brought me there to see the live broadcast. I remembered there were many, many people and it was like a big party. I looked around and saw Qiqi. She was wearing a pink skirt and a pair of shoes that lit up; two braids stuck out from the top of her head like the horns of a goat. Smiling sweetly, she called out: "Bao *gege*!"

Qiqi's mother and Mom were good friends from way back, before they both got married. I was only a month older than Qiqi and had almost certainly seen her lots of times before that night, but I couldn't remember any of those occasions. The Opening Ceremony of the Olympics was the first memory I could really recall with Qiqi in it—it was the first time I understood what *pretty* meant. After we ran into Qiqi and her parents, our two families watched the live broadcast together. While the adults conversed, Qiqi and I sat next to a bed of flowers and had our own chat. Later, an oval-shaped, shiny gigantic basket appeared on the screen.

What's that? I asked.

It's called the Bird's Nest, Qiqi said.

There were no birds inside the Nest, but there was an enormous scroll with flickering animated images that were very pretty. Qiqi and I were entranced.

How do they make those pictures? Qiqi asked.

It's all done with computers, I said. *My dad knows how to do it. Someday, I'll make a big picture, too, just for you.*

Qiqi looked at me, her eyes full of admiration. Later, a little girl about our age sang on the screen, and I thought Qiqi was prettier than her.

That was one of the loveliest, most magical nights of my life. Later, I kept on hoping China would host the Olympics again, but it never happened. After I became a father, I told my son about that night, and he refused to believe China had once been so prosperous.

I had no clear memories of kindergarten, either. Qiqi and I went to the same English-immersion kindergarten, in which half the classes were conducted in English, but I couldn't recall any of it—I certainly didn't learn any English.

I did remember watching *Pleasant Goat and Big Big Wolf* with Qiqi. I told her that I thought she was like Beauty, the cute lamb in the cartoon. She said I was like Grey Wolf.

If I'm Grey Wolf, I said, *you must be Red Wolf.* Red Wolf was Grey Wolf's wife.

She pinched me, and we fought. Qiqi was always ready to hit me to get her way, but she also cried easily. I only pushed back a little bit and she started sobbing. I was terrified she might tattle on me and rushed to the fridge to get some red-bean-flavored shaved ice for her, and she broke into a smile. We went on watching *Chibi Maruko Chan* and *The Adventures of Red Cat and Blue Rabbit* while sharing a bowl of shaved ice.

We played and fought, fought and played, and before we knew it, our childhood had escaped us.

Back then, I thought Qiqi and I were so close that we'd never be apart. However, before we started elementary school, Qiqi's father got a promotion at work and the whole family had to move to Shanghai. Mom took me to say good-bye. While the adults became all misty-eyed, Qiqi and I ran around, laughing like it was just some regular playdate. Then Qiqi got on the train and waved at me through the window like her parents were doing, and I waved back. The train left and took Qiqi away.

The next day, I asked Mom, "When's Qiqi coming back? How about we all go to Tiananmen Square next Sunday?"

But Qiqi wasn't back the next Sunday, or the one after that. She disappeared from my life. I didn't get to see her again for many years, until my memories of her had blurred and sunk into the depths of my heart.

In elementary school, I made a good friend—everyone called him "Heizi" because he was dark and skinny. Heizi and I lived in the same neighborhood, and his family was in business—supposedly his dad had made his fortune by flipping real estate. Heizi wasn't a good student and often asked to copy my homework; to show his gratitude, he invited me over to his house to play. His family owned a very cool computer hooked up to an ultra-high-def LCD screen that took up half a wall—fantastic for racing or fighting games, though the adults didn't let us play for long. But when we were in the third grade, SARS was going around and some kid in the neighborhood got sick, so we all had to be taken out of school and quarantined at home. We ended up playing games the whole day, every day. Good times.

During those months in the shadow of SARS, the adults had gloomy expressions and sighed all the time. Everyone hoarded food and other consumables at home and seldom went out—when they did, they wore face masks. They also forced me to drink some kind of bitter Chinese medicine soup that supposedly provided immunity against SARS. I was old enough to understand that something terrible was going on in China and the rest of the world, and felt scared. That was my first experience of the dread and panic of a world nearing doom. One time, I overheard Mom and Dad discussing some rumor that tens of thousands of people had died from SARS, and I ended up suffering a nightmare. I dreamt that everyone around me had died so that I was the only one left, and the United States was taking advantage of the SARS crisis to attack China, dropping bombs everywhere . . . I woke up in a cold sweat.

Of course, nothing bad really happened. The SARS crisis ended up not being a big deal at all.

But it was a start. In the days still to come, my generation would experience events far more terrifying than SARS. We knew nothing of the future that awaited us.

2.

During the SARS crisis, I dreamt of an American attack on China because the U.S. had just conquered Iraq and Afghanistan, and managed to catch Saddam. They were also looking for a man named bin Laden, and it was all over the news. I watched the news during dinnertime and I remember being annoyed at America: *Why are the Americans always invading other countries?* I felt especially bad for Saddam: a pitiable old man captured by the Americans and put on trial. And they said he was going to be executed. How terrible! I kept hoping the Americans would lose.

Amazingly, my wish came true. Not long after SARS, the news reports said that something called the Iraqi Republican Guard had mobilized and rescued Saddam. Saddam led the resistance against the American invasion and somehow managed to chase the U.S. out of Iraq. In Afghanistan, a group called Tali-something also started an uprising and waged guerrilla war against the American troops in the mountains. Bin Laden even succeeded in planning a shocking attack that brought down two American skyscrapers using airliners. The Americans got scared and retreated in defeat.

Two years later, I started middle school. Heizi and I were in the same school but different classes.

My first year coincided with another apocalypse predicted by an ancient calendar—I had no idea back then why there were so many apocalyptic legends; maybe everyone felt living in this world wasn't safe. Those were also the years when the world economy was in a depression and lots of places had difficulties: Russia, a new country called Yugoslavia, Somalia. . . . The desperate Americans even decided to bomb our embassy in Belgrade. People were so angry that college students marched to the American embassy and threw rocks at the windows.

However, the life of middle-school students was very different. The costume drama *Princess Pearl* was really popular and they showed it all the time on TV. Everyone in my class became addicted, and all we could talk about was the fate of Princess Xiaoyanzi. We didn't understand politics and paid very little attention to those world events.

Gradually, though, the effects of the worldwide depression became apparent in daily life. Real estate prices kept crashing; Heizi's father lost money in his property deals and turned to day-trading stocks, but he was still losing money. Although prices for everything were falling, wages dropped even faster. Since no one was buying the high-tech gadgets, they stopped making them. The huge LCD screen in Heizi's home broke, but they couldn't find anything similar in the market and had to make do with a clumsy CRT monitor: the screen was tiny and convex, which just looked weird. My father's notebook computer was gone, replaced by a big tower that had much worse specs—supposedly this was all due to the depressed American economy. Over time, websites failed one after another, and the new computer games were so bad that it was no longer fun to mess around on the computer. Street arcades became popular, and kids our age went to hang out at those places while the adults began to practice traditional Chinese meditation.

There was one benefit to all this "progress": the sky over Beijing became clear and blue. I remembered that, when I was little, every day was filled with smog and it was difficult to breathe. Now, however, other than during sandstorm season, you could see blue sky and white clouds all the time.

In the summer of my second year in middle school, Qiqi returned to Beijing for a visit and stayed with my family. She was tall and slender, almost five-foot three inches, and wore a pair of glasses. With her graceful manners and big eyes, she was closer to a young woman than a girl and I still thought she was pretty. When she saw me, she smiled shyly, and instead of calling me "Bao *gege*" like a kid, she addressed me by my given name: "Baosheng." She had lost all traces of her Beijing accent and spoke in the gentle tones of southern China, which I found pleasing. I tried to reminisce with her about the Olympics and watching *Pleasant Goat and Big Big Wolf.* Disappointingly, she told me she couldn't remember much.

I overheard Mom and Dad saying that Qiqi's parents were in the middle of a bitter divorce and were fighting over every bit of property and Qiqi's custody. They had sent Qiqi away to Beijing to avoid hurting her while they tore into each other. I could tell that Qiqi was unhappy because I heard her cry in her room the night she arrived. I didn't know how to help her except to take her around to eat good food and see interesting sights, and to distract her with silly stories. Although Qiqi was born in Beijing, she was so young when she left that she might as well have been a first-time visitor. That whole summer, she rode behind me on my bicycle, and we toured every major avenue and narrow *hutong* in the city.

We grew close again, but it wasn't the same as our childhood friendship; rather, our budding adolescence colored everything. It wasn't love, of course, but it was more than just friendship. Qiqi got to know my good friends, too. Heizi, in particular, came over to my home much more frequently now that a young woman was living there. One time, Heizi and I took Qiqi to hike the Fragrant Hills. Heizi paid a lot of attention to Qiqi: helping her up and down the rocky steps and telling her jokes. While Qiqi and Heizi chatted happily, I felt annoyed. That was when I first noticed I didn't like others intruding between Qiqi and me, not even Heizi.

Near the end of summer break, Qiqi had to go back to Shanghai. Since neither of my parents was free that day, I took her to the train station. The two of us squeezed onto the train half an hour before departure time, and I made up my mind and took from my backpack a gift-wrapped parcel I had prepared ahead of time.

Hesitantly, I said, "Um, this . . . is a . . . present for . . . for you."

Qiqi was surprised. "What is it?"

"Um . . . why don't you . . . open it . . . um . . . later? No!—"

But it was too late. Qiqi had torn open the package and was staring wide-eyed at the copy of *High-Difficulty Mathematical Questions from the High School Entrance Examination with Solutions and Explanations*.

"Well, you told me you had trouble with math . . . " I struggled to explain. "I like this book . . . I figured . . . um . . . you might find it helpful. . . . "

Qiqi was laughing so hard that tears were coming out of her eyes. I felt like the world's biggest idiot.

"Whoever heard of giving a girl a test-prep manual as a gift?" Still laughing, Qiqi opened the book to the title page. Her face froze as she read the Pushkin poem I had copied out:

Life's deceit may Fortune's fawning
Turn to scorn, yet, as you grieve,
Do not anger, but believe
In tomorrow's merry dawning.

When your heart is rid at last
Of regret, despair, and fear,
In the future, what has passed
Shall in kinder light appear.[1]

After the poem, I had written two lines:

To my friend Zhao Qi: May you forget the unhappy parts of life and live each day in joy. Love life and embrace ideals!

I felt very foolish.

Qiqi held the book to her chest and gave me a bright smile, but tears were spilling out of the corners of her eyes.

3.

Qiqi left and my life returned to its familiar routines. But my heart would not calm down.

When Qiqi visited, she brought a book called *Season of Bloom, Season of Rain*, which was popular among middle school girls back then. She had wrapped the book's cover carefully in poster paper and written the title on it in her neat, elegant handwriting. Curious, I had flipped through it but didn't find it interesting. Qiqi left the book behind when she returned to Shanghai, and I hid it in the deepest recess of my desk because I was afraid Mom would take it away. The book still held Qiqi's scent, and I pulled it out from time to time to read until I finished it. Afterward, I couldn't help but compare myself and Qiqi to the high school students involved in the novel's complicated love triangles: Was I more like this guy or that one? Was Qiqi more like this girl or that girl? One time, I brought up the topic with Heizi and he almost died from laughing.

Just because boys weren't into romance novels didn't mean we weren't interested in the mysterious emotions portrayed in them. Anything having to do with love was popular among my classmates: everyone copied love poems, sang romantic ballads, and watched *Divine Eagle, Gallant Lovers*, imagining we were also star-crossed martial arts heroes and heroines. "Matchmaking" by astrology became a popular game. Once, one of the girls in my class, Shen Qian, and I were assigned classroom cleanup duty together, and somehow that inspired everyone to think of us as a couple. I vociferously denied this, not realizing that this only made the game even more fun for others. I resorted to ignoring Shen Qian altogether, but this only led all our classmates to postulate that we were having a "lovers' spat." I didn't know what to do.

In the end, Shen Qian came to my rescue. She made no secret of her interest in a high school boy known for his wit and generated a ton of juicy gossip—as a result, rumors about Shen Qian and me naturally died out.

Shen Qian's early attempt at romance soon ended when parents and teachers intervened, alarmed by this distraction from our academic development. Afterward, she acted aloof and cold to all of us, but spent her time reading books that appeared profound and abstruse: contemplative essays about Chinese culture, collected works of obscure philosophy, and the like. Everyone now said that Shen Qian was going to become a famous writer. However, her class compositions often took original and rebellious points of view that led to criticism from the teachers.

Despite the rumors about us, I didn't grow closer to Shen Qian; instead, I became even more convinced of the depth of my feelings for Qiqi. I thought: *She might not be the prettiest girl and she's far away in Shanghai, but I like her, and I'm going to be good to her.* Unfortunately, with thousands of kilometers dividing us, I only heard news about her from occasional phone calls between our mothers. After the divorce, Qiqi lived with her mother, and though they were poor, Qiqi did well academically and managed to place into one of the best high schools in the city.

Oh, one more thing: During my middle school years, a short man named Deng Xiaoping rose to prominence and became a member of the Central Committee. Although Jiang Zemin was still the General Secretary, Deng held all the real power. Deng started a series of reforms aimed at nationalizing industry, and he justified his policies with many novel theories: "Socialism with Chinese Characteristics"; "it doesn't matter whether it is a white cat or a black cat; a cat that catches mice is a good cat"—and so on. Lots of people became rich by taking advantage of the new opportunities, but many others sank into poverty. Because the economy was doing so poorly, the small company Dad worked for had to shut down, but with the Deng-initiated reforms, he got a job with a state-owned enterprise that guaranteed we'd at least have the basic necessities. Honestly, compared to the rest of the world, China wasn't doing too badly. For example, I heard there was a financial crisis in Southeast Asia that affected the world; Russia's economy collapsed and even college students had to become streetwalkers; there was a civil war in Yugoslavia and a genocide in Africa; the United States had pulled out of Iraq but maintained a blockade and sanctions. . . .

None of this had much to do with my life, of course. The most important things in my life were studying, cramming for the college entrance examination, and sometimes thinking about Qiqi.

During my first year in high school, many people had "pen pals," strangers they corresponded with. This wasn't all that different from the web-based chats we used to have when we were little, but the practice seemed a bit more literary. I missed Qiqi so much that I decided to write her a letter in English—full of grammatical errors, as you might imagine— with the excuse that I was doing so to improve my English skills. Email would have been easier, but computers had disappeared from daily life, and so I had no choice but to write an actual letter. As soon as I dropped it into the mailbox I regretted my rash act, but it was too late. The following two weeks crept by so slowly they felt like years.

Qiqi answered! She'd certainly made more of that English-immersion kindergarten experience than I had: her letter was much better. Leaving aside the content, even her handwriting was pretty, like a series of notes on a musical score. I had to read that letter with a dictionary by my side, and I ended up practically memorizing it. I did feel my English improved a great deal as a result.

Qiqi's letter was pretty short, just over a page. She mentioned that the math book I had given her more than a year earlier had been helpful, and she was grateful. She also recommended *New Concept English* to me, and told me some simple facts about her school. But I was most pleased by her last paragraph, in which she asked about my school, Heizi, and so on. Her meaning couldn't be clearer: she was looking forward to another letter from me.

We corresponded in English regularly after that. We never said anything all that interesting: school, ideals in life, things like that. But the very fact that we were writing to each other made me incredibly happy. Just knowing that someone far away, practically on the other side of the world, was thinking about you and cared about you was an indescribably wonderful feeling. Qiqi told me that her mother had gotten married again. Her stepfather had a child of his own and was rather cold to her. She didn't feel that her home was her home anymore, and wanted to leave for college as soon as possible so that she could be independent.

I finished high school without much trouble and did really well on my college entrance examination, so I could pick from several schools. Summoning my courage, I called Qiqi and asked her what schools she was picking. She said she didn't want to stay in Shanghai, and filled out Nanjing University with a major in English as her first choice.

I wanted to go to Nanjing as well: one, I wanted to be with Qiqi; and two, I wanted to be away from my parents and try to make it on my own. But my parents absolutely would not allow it and insisted that I stay in Beijing. We had a huge fight, but in the end I gave in and filled out Peking University with a major in Chinese as my top choice. Heizi never made it into a good high school and couldn't get into college at all, so he joined a department store as a sales clerk. Still, all of us believed that we had bright futures ahead of us.

4.

Compared to the close supervision we were under back in high school, college was practically total freedom. Although the school administrators, *in loco parentis*, weren't keen on the idea of students dating, they basically looked the other way. Boys and girls paired up quickly, and the Chinese Department was known as a hotbed of romance. Several of my roommates soon had beautiful girlfriends, and I was very envious.

Shen Qian also got into Peking University, majoring in Politics. Our high school classmates all predicted we would end up together, but Shen Qian soon published some outrageous poems and articles in the school paper and became part of the artsy, literary, avant-garde crowd. Other than occasionally seeing each other at gatherings of old high school friends, she and I ran in completely different circles.

Qiqi and I continued our correspondence, but we no longer needed writing in English as an excuse. We wrote to each other every week and our letters ran on for dozens of pages, covering everything silly, interesting, or even boring in our lives. Sometimes I had to use extra stamps. I really wanted to make our relationship formal, but just couldn't get up the courage.

By the time we were second-years, the name of some boy began to appear in Qiqi's letters. She mentioned him so casually—without even explaining who he was—as though he was already a natural part of her life. I asked her about him, and Qiqi wrote back saying he was the class president: handsome, fluent in English, and also in the Drama Club with her.

Reading her response, I was not happy. I tried writing a reply but couldn't find the words. I would have pulled out my cell phone to call her, but by then no one used cell phones anymore. China Mobile had long since gone out of business, and the cell phone in my desk—a birthday present from my father when I turned ten—was just a useless piece of antique junk.

I went downstairs to use the public phone. Every residential hall had only one phone, and the woman who picked up on the other end was the matron for Qiqi's residential hall. She interrogated me for a long while before she agreed to go get Qiqi. I waited and waited. One of Qiqi's roommates eventually picked up.

"Qiqi is out with her boyfriend."

I dropped the phone and ran to the train station to buy a ticket to Nanjing. I was at the door of her residential hall at noon the next day.

Qiqi came down the stairs like a graceful bird in a white pleated skirt, her hair tied back in neat braids. She appeared to be glowing with the warm sunlight. Other than a few pictures through the mail, we hadn't seen each other since that summer in middle school. She was no longer a girl, but a tall, vivacious young woman. She didn't look too surprised to see me; instead, she lowered her eyes and chuckled, as though she knew I would be here.

That afternoon, she took me to the famous No-Sorrow Lake, where we rented a boat and rowed it to the center of the jade-green water. She asked me whether I had seen a popular Japanese TV drama called *Tokyo Love Story*.

I had heard about the show, but since my roommates and I didn't own a TV, I had only seen some clips when I visited my parents and read some summaries in the TV guide. But I didn't want to show my ignorance.

"Yes," I said.

"So . . . who do you like?" Qiqi asked, very interested.

"I . . . I like Satomi." Honestly, I wasn't even sure who the characters were.

Qiqi was surprised. "Satomi? I can't stand her. Why do you like her?"

My heart skipped a beat. "Uh . . . Satomi is the female lead, right? She has such a pretty smile."

"What are you talking about? The female lead is Rika Akana!"

"Wait! I read the synopsis, and they said that Satomi grew up with the male lead, and then the two of them ended up together . . . doesn't that make her the female lead?"

"That's ludicrous." Qiqi laughed. I loved the way she wrinkled her nose. "Why would you think such a thing?"

"Because . . . because I feel that people who knew each other when they were young ought to end up together. For example . . . uh. . . . " I couldn't continue.

"For example?" She grinned.

"You and me," I blurted out.

Qiqi tilted her head and looked at me for a while. "What a silly idea." She slapped me.

It wasn't a real slap, of course—it was so light it was more like a caress. Her slender fingers slid across my face and I shivered as though they were charged with electricity. My heart leapt wildly and I grabbed her hand. Qiqi didn't pull away. I stood up and wanted to pull her into an embrace, except I had forgotten we were on a boat, and so—

The boat capsized, and as Qiqi screamed, we tumbled into the water.

We giggled like fools as we climbed back into the boat. Qiqi was now my girlfriend.

Later, she told me that the class president really was interested in her, but she had never cared for him. She wrote about him in her letters to me on purpose to see if she could finally get me to express myself clearly. She didn't quite anticipate that I would be so worried I'd come all the way to Nanjing—as she said this, I could tell how pleased she was.

We held hands and visited all the big tourist attractions of Nanjing that day: Xuanwu Lake, Qinhuai River, Confucius Temple, Sun Yat-sen's Mausoleum . . . I spent the day in a honey-flavored daze.

For the remainder of our time in college, we only got to see each other occasionally during breaks, but we wrote to each other even more often and were completely in love. My parents, after finding out about Qiqi and me, were pleased because of the friendship between our families. Mom spoke of Qiqi as her future daughter-in-law and joked that she and Qiqi's mother had arranged for our marriage before we were even born. We planned to find jobs in the same city after graduation and then get married.

5.

Just as happiness appeared to be within reach, it shattered into a million pieces.

The economies of Russia, Ukraine, and some other countries collapsed so completely that the unimaginable happened: a man named Gorbachev emerged as a powerful leader and convinced more than a dozen independent states to join together to form a new country called the "Union of Soviet Socialist Republics," dedicated to the implementation of socialism. The new country became very powerful very quickly and thwarted the Americans at every turn, instantly adding tension to the international situation. The Soviet Union then encouraged revolutions in Eastern Europe—and even Germany, whose eastern and western halves weren't at the same level of economic development, split into two countries, with East Germany joining the Soviet bloc.

In China, Deng's planned economic reforms weren't successful and the economy continued to deteriorate. More and more people grew unhappy with the government. The machinery of the state was corrupt, ossified, authoritarian, and full of misadministration. College students still remembered how prosperous and strong the country had been when they were children, and comparing the past to the present filled them with rage. Rumors were full of tales of corrupt officials, of misappropriation of state funds for private gain, of attempts to fill public administration posts with family members and loyal minions—although few could explain clearly the root causes of the problems, everyone appeared to agree on the solution in debates and discussions: the country was in trouble and the political system had to be fundamentally reformed to implement real democracy. The incompetent leaders had to go! A political manifesto composed some twenty years earlier, simply called "Charter '08," began to spread secretly among college students.

Right before my graduation, the factional struggles within the Communist Party grew even more intense. It was said that the leader of the reformists, Zhao Ziyang, had been relieved of his duties and placed under house arrest. The news was like the spark that set off a powder keg, and the long-repressed rage among the population erupted in a way that shocked everyone. Students at all the major universities in Beijing went into the streets to march and protest, and with the support of Beijing's citizens they occupied Tiananmen Square, which drew the attention of the world. A city of tents sprouted in the square, and some protestors even erected a statue of the Goddess of Liberty in front of the Gate of Heavenly Peace itself.

The drafter of Charter '08, Liu Xiaobo, returned to China from overseas. He made a speech at the square vowing to go on a hunger strike until there was true reform. The whole nation was inspired. Young people began to arrive from everywhere in China and the mass movement gained momentum. Even ordinary citizens in Beijing mobilized to support the students. Heizi, for example, often came by on his tricycle to bring us food and water.

"Eat and drink!" he shouted. "You need your strength to fight those fucking bums sitting in Zhongnanhai."

Shen Qian had published some provocative essays in the past and she was a fan of Liu Xiaobo. Her influence among the students made her one of the leaders in the movement. She came by to discuss with me how to motivate the students in the Chinese Department to play a more active role. Stimulated by her fervor, I felt I had to do something for the country, and in the famous triangular plaza at the heart of Peking University's campus, I made a speech denouncing the corrupt, bureaucratic student council and calling for all students to free themselves from government control and to form a democratic, independent, self-governing body. Amazingly, many professors and students applauded my speech, and a few days later the Students' Autonomous Federation came into existence. Shen Qian was elected one of the standing committee members, and because she felt I had some talent, she asked me to join the Federation's publicity department. Thus I became a core member of the movement. I felt as though my talent had finally been properly recognized.

We created a command center in the square where our daily routines resembled those of a mini-government: receiving student representatives from all across the country, announcing various proclamations and programs, issuing open letters, and engaging in vigorous debate over everything as though the future of the entire nation depended on us. News that our compatriots in Hong Kong and Taiwan were also supporting us and donating funds filled us with even more zeal. We laughed, we cried, we screamed, we sang, all the while dreaming of forging a brand-new future for China with our youth and passion.

One day, at the beginning of June, I was in a crude tent at the edge of the command center writing a new program for the movement. The weather was humid and hot, and I was drenched in sweat. Suddenly, I heard Shen Qian call out, "Baosheng, look who's here to see you!"

I emerged from the tent. Qiqi was standing there in a sky-blue dress, carrying a small pack on her back and looking tired from her journey. Overcome by joy and surprise, I couldn't speak, and Shen Qian made fun of us.

Since Shen Qian had never met Qiqi before, she gave her a careful once-over and said, "So this is Baosheng's mysterious girlfriend. . . . "

Qiqi blushed.

Finally, after getting rid of Shen Qian, I peppered Qiqi with questions: "How did you get here? Did you come with other students from Nanjing University? That's great! I heard about the protests in Nanjing, too. Who's in charge of your group? I've just drafted a new program for the movement and it would be useful to get some feedback—"

"Is this all you have to say to me after all this time?" Qiqi interrupted.

"Of course not! I've really missed you." I hugged her, laughing, but soon turned serious again. "But the movement is running out of steam and the students are splitting into factions. . . . The hunger strike isn't sustainable, and I've been discussing with Liu Xiaobo how to develop the movement and extend it. . . . Come, take a look at my draft—"

"Baosheng," Qiqi interrupted again. "I stopped by your home. Your mother asked me to come and talk to you."

A bucket of cold water had been poured onto the fire in me. "Oh," I said, and nothing more.

"Your mother is really worried about you. . . . " Qiqi's voice was gentle. "It's almost time for you to receive your post-graduation job assignment. You know how important that is. Stop messing around with these people. Come home with me."

"Qiqi, how can you say such a thing?" I was disappointed as well as angry. " 'Messing around'? Look at the tens of thousands of students assembled in this square! Look at the millions of citizens beyond them! All of Beijing—no, all of China—has boiled over. Everyone is fighting for the future of our country. How can we go back to studying in a classroom?"

"What can you possibly accomplish? You'll never overcome the government. They have the army! Also, some of your proposals are too radical; they're impossible—"

"What do you mean, *impossible*?" I was very unhappy with her. "The army serves the people. The soldiers will never point their guns at us. Some of the students are talking to them already. Don't worry. I've heard that the bureaucrats in the central leadership are terrified. They'll soon be willing to compromise."

Qiqi sighed and sat down, looking miserably at me.

We talked and talked, but there was no resolution. In the end, I refused to leave the square, and Qiqi stayed with me. That night, we slept in the same tent. We talked about the national and international situation and the movement's prospects, but we couldn't agree on anything and started to argue. Eventually, we stopped talking about these matters and simply held each other.

We reminisced about our childhood together, and then I could no longer hold back. I kissed her, first her face, then her lips. That was the first time we really kissed. Her lips were soft and chapped, which broke my heart. I kissed her deeply and would not let go . . .

In the dark, it happened naturally. With so many young people in the square, our lovemaking was an open secret. Normally I despised such behavior, and felt that couples who engaged in it tarnished the sacred nature of our protest. But now that it was happening to me, I couldn't resist, and felt our actions were a natural part of the movement itself. Maybe some nameless anxiety about the future also made us want to seize this last moment of total freedom. Every motion, every gesture was infused with awkwardness and embarrassment. We were clumsy and raw, but passion, the irresistible power of youthful passion, eventually brought that fumbling, ridiculous process to a conclusion of sweet intimacy that surpassed understanding.

6.

The next day, we heard the news that troops had arrived just outside Beijing to enforce martial law. A vanguard had already entered the city, preparing to clear the square.

Should we retreat? The command center held a meeting and opinions were divided. Liu Xiaobo advocated retreat to prevent the loss of lives. Due to Qiqi's influence, I also supported Liu's suggestion. But the commander-in-chief, Chai Ling, was indignant and refused to budge. She even called us cowards and said that we must resist to the utmost, even with our lives. Her words inspired all the other attendees and those advocating retreat were silenced. In the end, most of the students stayed to follow Chai Ling's orders.

That night was especially hot. Qiqi and I couldn't fall asleep, and so we lay outside the tent, whispering to each other. "You were right," I said. "Chai Ling is too stubborn. I don't think any good will come of this. I'll tell Liu Xiaobo tomorrow that we're going home."

"All right." She leaned her head against my shoulder and fell asleep. I followed soon after.

I startled awake with the noise of the crowd all around me. The stars in the summer sky overhead were eerily bright. It took me a moment to realize that all the lamps on the square were extinguished and darkness engulfed us, which was why the stars shone so bright and clear. People were shouting all around us and loudspeakers squawked. I couldn't understand what was going on.

"Baosheng!" Someone ran at us with a flashlight and the glare made me squint. A blurry figure came closer: Shen Qian. She was sobbing as she said, "Hurry! You have to leave! The army is clearing the square."

"What? Where's Chai Ling? She's supposed to be in charge!"

"That bitch was the first to run away! Go, go! I still have to find Liu Xiaobo."

Later, I found out that a large number of armed police had come into the square with batons to break down the tents, beating any students who resisted. But we couldn't see anything at the time and everything around us was utter chaos. I didn't know what to do, so I grabbed Qiqi by the hand and tried to follow the flow of the crowd.

A few students from the provinces ran past us, screaming, "Tanks! Tanks! Someone got crushed by the tanks!" They collided into us and separated Qiqi from me.

I heard Qiqi calling my name and ran toward her, shouting her name. But I tripped over a tent and couldn't get up for some seconds while others ran over me, kicking me back down. By the time I finally struggled up, I could no longer hear Qiqi and didn't know where she was. Helpless, I tried to continue in the same direction I'd been headed. A chaotic crowd surrounded me, but there was no Qiqi. I screamed her name. Then someone started singing "The Internationale" and everyone joined in. I couldn't even hear my own voice.

Caught up in the tumultuous crowd, I left Tiananmen Square.

In this manner, we were forcefully removed from the square—at least no shots were fired. However, elsewhere in the city, there were more violent encounters between the army and the protestors, and gunshots were heard from time to time. I returned home, hoping against hope, but Qiqi had not been there. Ignoring the objections of my parents, I ran back toward the city center.

By then it was dawn, and scattered tanks and soldiers could be seen in the streets. Bloody corpses lined the roads, many of them young students. I felt as though I was in the middle of a battlefield and terror seized me. But the idea that something had happened to Qiqi terrified me even more. Like a crazy man, I looked everywhere for her.

At noon, I ran into one of my friends from the command center. He brought me to a secret gathering, where I found Shen Qian and Liu Xiaobo. Many were wounded, and Shen Qian, her face drained of blood, shivered as Liu held her. I asked them if they had seen Qiqi.

Shen Qian started to sob. My heart sank into an icy abyss.

Tearfully, Shen Qian explained that Qiqi had found them as the square was being cleared, and they retreated together. They encountered a column of soldiers at an intersection, and, not fully understanding the situation, they denounced the soldiers. The soldiers responded by firing upon them and a few of the students fell. They turned to run again, only realizing after a while that Qiqi was no longer with them. Shen retraced their steps and found Qiqi lying in a pool of blood, not moving. They had wanted to save Qiqi, but the soldiers were chasing them and they had no choice but to keep running.

She was sobbing so hard by now that she could no longer speak.

I demanded that Shen Qian tell me the exact location and then dashed madly toward the address. At the intersection, I saw the smoking, burnt remnant of an army truck. Inside was the charred corpse of a soldier. In a pool of blood next to the intersection lay a few more bodies, but I didn't see Qiqi. Forcing down my nausea, I searched all around, though I was hoping to find nothing.

But then I saw Qiqi's sky-blue dress under one of the wheels of the army truck. Blood had stained it purple, and protruding from the skirt was a section of her perfect calf, ending in a bloody mess.

Shivering, I approached. An overwhelming stench of blood filled my nose. I felt the sky and the earth spin around me and could no longer stand up. Everything was speeding away from me, leaving only an endless darkness that descended over me, extinguishing my last spark of consciousness.

By the time I woke up, it was dark again. I heard the sound of occasional gunshots in the distance. A column of soldiers passed no more than two meters from me, but they ignored me, probably thinking I was just another corpse. I lay still, stunned, and for a moment I forgot what had happened—until the terrifying memory returned and crushed me with despair.

I couldn't blame Chai Ling, or the students who had run into Qiqi and me and separated us from each other, or even the soldiers. I knew that the real culprit responsible for Qiqi's death was me, because I didn't listen to her.

That night, I became a walking corpse. I dared not look at Qiqi's body again. Wandering the city on my own, I paid no attention to the fearsome soldiers or the criminals who took advantage of the chaos to loot and rob. Several times I saw people fall down near me and die, but somehow, miraculously, I was spared. The world had turned into a nightmare from which I could not awaken.

The next day, as a long column of tanks rolled down the Avenue of Eternal Peace, I stepped in front of them. Passersby watched, stunned. I wanted the tanks to crush me beneath their treads. . . .

But I didn't die. Plainclothes officers grabbed me and pulled me off the street. I was thrown into a dark room and interrogated for a few days. By then I had recovered some of my senses and managed to tell them what had happened. I was certain I would be sentenced to death or at least be locked away for years. My heart had already died, and I didn't care.

Unexpectedly, after a few months of detention, I was released without even a trial. My punishment was quite light: expulsion from Peking University.

7.

By the time I was released, order had been restored. After the violent crackdown that ended the protests, the government became unexpectedly magnanimous. General Secretary Jiang stepped down, and although Deng Xiaoping retained power, the reformist Zhao Ziyang became the new General Secretary, and another reformist leader with a good reputation, Hu Yaobang, also took up an important political post. Most of the participants in the protests were not punished. Even Liu Xiaobo was allowed to continue teaching at a university, though he would no longer be permitted to leave the country. The government's final summary of the protests was this: the university students made legitimate demands; however, international forces took advantage of them.

Supposedly, the international forces were working against the entire socialist camp, not just China. They stirred up trouble in Eastern Europe, too, hoping to encircle and contain the Soviet Union. In the end, the Western powers failed utterly in this plan. The Soviet Union not only survived, but also installed socialist governments in Czechoslovakia, Poland, and several other Eastern European countries. These satellites formed the Warsaw Pact with the Soviet Union to counteract the power of NATO. The U.S. and the U.S.S.R. thus began a "Cold War."

After my release from prison, Qiqi's mother came to our home and demanded to know where her daughter was. During the interim months, she had almost gone mad with the lack of any news about Qiqi. She came to Beijing only to find that I had been locked up as well.

I fell to my knees in front of her and tearfully confessed that I was responsible for Qiqi's death. At first she refused to believe me, but then she kicked and beat me until my parents pulled her off. She collapsed to the ground and sobbed inconsolably.

Qiqi's mother never forgave me, and she broke off all contact with my family. Later, I went to Shanghai a few times, but she refused to see me. I heard that she had fallen on hard times and I tried to send her some money and necessities, but she always returned my packages unopened.

On the day of Qiqi's death, my mental state had broken down so completely that I didn't even remember to collect her body. Now it was too late even to give her a decent burial. No doubt she had been cremated en masse with the other unclaimed corpses. A spirited young woman in the spring of her life had disappeared from the world, and it was as if she had never existed.

No, that was not quite true. I did find a purple hairclip in my pocket. I remembered Qiqi taking it off the night we were in the tent together, and I had pocketed it without thinking. This was my last memento of her.

I found everything in my home that held memories of Qiqi and put them together on the desk: the hairclip, bundles of letters, little presents we had given each other, a few photographs of the two of us, and that copy of *Season of Bloom, Season of Rain*. Every day, I sat in front of this shrine and tried to relive all the moments we had shared, as though she was still by my side. I spent half a year like this—maybe I had gone a bit mad.

At the Spring Festival, as the family gathered for New Year's dinner, my mother broke down in tears. She said she couldn't bear to see me like this. She wanted me to stop living in the past and go on with my life. I sat at the table dully for a long while.

I steeled myself and carefully packed up all the objects on my desk and placed them at the bottom of my trunk. I kept the bundle with me always but seldom looked at those mementos again. Life had to go on, and I did not want to experience that heart-rending pain and sense of guilt anew.

Though I was expelled from school, General Secretary Zhao indicated that he was interested in a more enlightened administration that would let bygones be bygones, and the professors in my department who sympathized with my plight managed to give me my diploma through back channels. I couldn't find a job, though. When I was younger, companies recruited on campus for graduates, but after the reforms, all jobs were assigned by the state. Since my record was stained by my participation in the protests, I was no longer part of the system and no job would be assigned to me.

Heizi had also lost his job because of his support for the students. The two of us got together and figured we'd try our luck at starting a business. Back then, Zhao Ziyang was pushing through price reforms aimed at addressing the transition from market economy to planned economy, and prices for everything had skyrocketed. Everybody around the country was hoarding and life was becoming harder for the average person. Since many everyday goods were in short supply, the government started to issue ration tickets for food, clothing, and so on, to limit the amount anyone could purchase. If we were clever and bought and sold goods at the right times, we stood to make a good profit.

Heizi and I planned to go to Guangdong in the south, which was more developed than the rest of China. Although my parents didn't want me to be so far away from home, they were glad to see me trying to get my life back on track and gave us their life savings as starting capital. There were many opportunities in those days, and Heizi and I quickly brought some T-shirts back to Beijing, which we sold at a significant markup. Not only did we recoup all our capital, we even managed to make tens of thousands in profit. And thus we became two so-called "profiteers" who traveled all over China, searching for opportunities. Sometimes Heizi and I struck gold, but other times we were so poor we didn't know where our next meal would come from.

After spending a few years traveling around and interacting with all segments of society, I realized how immature we had been back at Tiananmen. China was an overladen freight train burdened with the weight of the past as well as the present. A few students fervently shouting slogans could not change the complicated conditions of the country. But how might things be improved? I had no answers. All I knew was that although China had recovered its tranquility and the people appeared to be focused only on the concerns of daily life, there were strong currents and countercurrents of competing social interests. Together, they formed a powerful hidden whirlpool that might pull the nation into an abyss that no one wanted to see. Yet the process wasn't something that could be controlled by anyone or any authority. No one could control history. We were all simply parts of a great vortex that was greater than any individual.

Two years after Heizi and I started our business, I bumped into Shen Qian while searching for something to buy in Guangzhou. After the protests, I stayed away from the literary elites and rarely got to see her, although I had heard that she became Liu Xiaobo's lover. Although Liu was married, Shen Qian was willing to be his mistress because she truly loved him. Later, the rumors said Liu had divorced his wife and I thought he would marry Shen Qian. I certainly didn't expect to find her so far from Beijing.

Meeting an old friend a long way from home always made me emotional. Reminded of Qiqi, I felt my eyes grow wet. Shen Qian told me that she had arrived in Guangzhou hoping to stay with an old friend and get back on her feet, but the friend was nowhere to be found and she didn't know what to do. I promised I'd help her.

I took Shen Qian to a restaurant to welcome her to Guangzhou. We talked about the old times, but both of us avoided any mention of Tiananmen. After a few rounds of drinks, Shen Qian's lips loosened and she told me tearfully about how Liu Xiaobo had taken advantage of her trust. He had promised to divorce his wife and marry her, but she caught him with another student. They had a fight and broke up. . . . As she told her story, she kept on drinking, straight from the bottle, and I couldn't stop her. Later, she began to sing loudly, and everybody in the restaurant stared at us. I quickly paid the bill and hurried her out of there.

Shen Qian was so drunk that I had to hold her up. Since she had nowhere else to stay, I brought her back to my room. I left her to recover in my bed while I slept on the floor.

The next morning, I needed to get out early to browse the markets, and so I left without waking up Shen Qian. By the time I got back, I expected she would be gone. However, when I came in the door, I saw that my messy room had been cleaned up and everything was neatly and logically arranged. There was a new cloth on the small kitchen table, and Shen Qian, in an apron, was carrying a plate of steaming scrambled eggs with tomatoes out of the kitchen.

We looked at each other; she smiled shyly.

I knew that my life was about to start a new chapter.

8.

Shen Qian continued to stay in my rental unit. She made the place feel like home, a feeling I had long missed. And so the two of us, both with pasts that we wanted to forget, leaned against each other for warmth. Heizi had just gotten married, and after finding out that Shen Qian and I were together, he was very happy for us. He treated Shen Qian as though we were already married.

Since Shen Qian couldn't find a job, she helped us with our business. She was nothing like the young radical student rebel she had been. After all she had gone through, she had abandoned her dreams of revolutions and literary fame and turned all her attention to family. Who was to say this wasn't a self as true as her former image?

Half a year later, my mother came to Guangzhou for a visit and my relationship with Shen Qian could no longer be kept a secret. My mother didn't like Shen Qian at first, but after living with us for a while, she began to accept this future daughter-in-law and urged us to get married. Society was turning more conservative by then, and since we were no longer so young, we returned to Beijing to apply for a marriage license. At our wedding, a few old classmates joked that they always knew we would end up together.

After a year, Shen Qian gave birth to our son, Xiaobao. The wounds of the past were gradually healing. Though I couldn't say we were happy or that everything was perfect, our life wasn't without warmth or simple pleasures.

The leadership in Beijing was now deepening the economic reforms and gradually pushing planned economy to displace the market. One of the policies was a dual-price system, which involved one price for goods set by the economic planning authorities and another price set by the market. Many officials with the right connections could become "official profiteers" by buying goods at the low planned economy price and selling them on the market at an enormous profit. Low-level peddlers like Heizi and me, on the other hand, suffered due to our lack of connections. Business became harder and harder. One time, we managed to acquire a bunch of color televisions, but the official profiteers were a step ahead of us and cornered the market. We had no choice but to sell at a loss. We ended up owing a bunch of money and had to close up shop and head back to Beijing.

One of Heizi's uncles was a shift foreman at a factory, and he managed to get Heizi a job as a driver there. By carrying private goods for people on official trips, Heizi made good money. I couldn't find any such opportunity, and I was exhausted after years spent struggling in business. I decided to return to university, and began to prepare to take the examination for graduate school.

As a graduate of Peking University, I thought the exam would be a piece of cake. But after being away from a classroom for so many years, it wasn't easy to get back into the right mind-set. I took the exam two years in a row and couldn't pass. Since Xiaobao was getting older and our savings were nearing depletion, we relied on help from my parents. Shen Qian finally managed to get a job at a newspaper, which at least guaranteed us a base salary and benefits like housing and healthcare.

Then she began to complain about my lack of accomplishments.

"Look at you! When we got together, I thought you had some business savvy and might make it big. But in the end, you're just a bookworm who can't even manage to get into grad school. The Chinese Women's Volleyball Team has won the world championship three times, which is as many times as you've failed!"

Faced with this nagging tirade, I felt lost. What had happened to that passionate, idealistic, revolutionary leader I once knew?

Of course I knew that wasn't Shen Qian's fault. This was what happened after life subjected us to its endless grind. The world wasn't a fairy tale or the setting for an adventure—even if it were, we would not be the protagonists. No matter what ideals and hopes we once harbored, the most we could hope to accomplish, in the end, was to survive.

Since I was feeling low during that time, I sought refuge in fiction and got into *wuxia* fantasies. The remake of *Legend of the Condor Heroes*, produced in Hong Kong, was very popular on TV. I had seen an older version when I was little but thought the remake was better, even though the budget clearly wasn't as big. I borrowed *wuxia* books by Jin Yong, Gu Long, Liang Yusheng—I would have read Huang Yi's books, too, but I couldn't find them anywhere.[2]

Xiaobao was now old enough that he spent every day practicing "Eighteen Stages to Subdue a Dragon" along with the heroes on TV. Shen Qian got mad and told me that I was rotting our child's mind. I had to switch to reading something else.

Science fiction was also popular. Ye Yonglie's *Little Know-it-All Roams the Future* sold millions of copies, and Zheng Wenguang's *Toward Sagittarius* was flying off the shelves. I gradually became a fan—only science fiction could liberate me from the weight of daily life and allow me to enjoy a little pleasure. It was too bad that there were so few Chinese science fiction books, and not many foreign works were being translated. I soon finished all the ones I could find.

Inspired by my reading, I tried my hand at writing and ended up with a book called *Little Know-it-All Roams the Universe*, which was a sequel to Ye Yonglie's famous work. At first, I passed the draft among friends, but then I got to know a young man named Yao Haijun who helped me obtain Mr. Ye's permission and found me a publisher. The story gained me a bit of fame and I was called a "rising star of science fiction." Encouraged, I wrote another book called *Little Know-it-All Roams the Body*, which was meant to teach readers some interesting facts about the human body. Unfortunately, this book caused a lot of controversy: some argued that I was stealing too much from Ye Yonglie; some suggested I was tarnishing Chinese science fiction with portrayals that encouraged lascivious thoughts; still others claimed that my work was an example of capitalist liberalism and contained metaphors criticizing the Communist Party. . . .[3]

I was writing at a fairly turbulent time when ideological debates were on the rise. There were even sporadic student movements again. The central leadership probably wanted to create the opportunity for another purge, so they initiated an effort to cleanse society of "spiritual pollution." I became a target and was severely criticized. Luckily, the government wasn't interested in having the "pollution-cleaning" spin out of control, and I wasn't punished much. However, it was impossible for me to be published anymore. I had to go back to the textbooks and prepare for the graduate school examination again.

It was only later that I understood how fortunate I had been. The country was also undergoing a movement of "intensive crackdown." This involved every aspect of life: purse-snatchers were handed death sentences, while public dancing carried a charge of indecency. Liu Xiaobo found himself in trouble because he had several lovers and was executed by firing squad. When she heard the news, Shen Qian was depressed for a long time.

After the intensive crackdown, society grew even more conservative. Many things that used to be common became crimes: cohabitating without being married, kissing in public, wearing revealing clothes, and so forth. Given the shift in mainstream culture, I dared not write about sensitive areas again. Thus did my career as an author come to an end.

9.

Just as weal can lead to woe, misfortune can also lead to lucky breaks. A prominent professor turned out to be a fan of my novels and specifically requested me during the admission process. As a result, I became his graduate student and returned to school the next year.

At my mentor and advisor's suggestion, I chose Sartre's existentialism as my topic. Although many people had been studying it, most explanations were half-baked. After so many years wasted drifting in society, I treasured the opportunity to study in depth. I read many foreign books in the original languages—taught myself French—and published a few papers that were well received. Eventually, with my advisor's recommendation, I was given the precious opportunity to study overseas at a famous university in America at the government's expense.

This was the first and last time in my life I lived outside China. Visiting this country on the other side of the Pacific that people both loved and hated was quite an experience. The university was in New York, the greatest city on Earth. When I was little, I saw a ton of TV shows and movies set in New York: *Beijinger in New York, Godzilla* . . . and I had long wanted to visit. The sights and sounds of the city—skyscrapers, overpasses, highways, subways—were overwhelming.

I remembered the Beijing of my childhood as a prosperous city comparable to New York, but for some reason, after a few decades, New York remained a modern metropolis while Beijing had declined precipitously. I saw in America many goods that had long ceased to be findable in China: Coca-Cola, KFC, Nescafé . . . These were the brands I grew up with and I indulged in a bit of nostalgia. I finally understood why so many people preferred to leave China for the U.S. and not return.

However, I could also see signs that America was on the decline. At the time of my visit, a new blockbuster had just been released: *Star Wars Episode IV: A New Hope.* I remembered seeing Episodes I through III when I was little and had always wanted to find out what would happen next. To re-experience the wonder of my childhood memories, I bought an expensive ticket. But Episode IV turned out to be far less spectacular than the previous three, and the special effects were so bad that you could almost see the strings on the spaceships. I was really disappointed. Apparently the Cold War had drained America's resources into the arms race and the economy wasn't doing so well.

Unlike in the past, opportunities for exchanges between America and China were growing scarce. It was almost impossible to visit America on your own, and even government-sponsored trips were rare. There were only a handful of Chinese from the mainland in the entire university. To celebrate my arrival, they held a party for me, and as we enjoyed our French fries, they asked me how things were in China. Since it took almost a full month for international mail to reach the recipient and phone calls were extremely inconvenient, they got most of their information about China from English-language news reports, which tended to be so narrow in scope that it was like trying to understand a beach by observing a few pebbles. We reminisced about how when we were little we could chat with friends on the other side of the globe just by opening a window over the web, and it felt like another age, another world.

While we were discussing rumors about the transition of power from Deng Xiaoping to Hua Guofeng, a dark horse about whom little was known, the doorbell rang. A woman stood up and said, *Oh, it must be so-and-so*—but I didn't catch the name. She went and opened the door and a woman came in, limping with the aid of a cane. I gave her a curious glance, and when I saw her face, I froze.

She looked at me, unable to speak.

It was a dream. A dream.

Qiqi, my Qiqi.

In a moment, everything around me—no, the entire universe—disappeared. Only Qiqi and I remained between heaven and earth. We gazed at each other, our eyes saying what our lips could not. Fate had played a cruel game with us. After the trials and tribulations of more than ten years, we had found each other again on the other side of the Pacific.

Trembling, we came together and held on to each other for dear life. Tears poured from our eyes as sobs wracked our bodies. The others realized that something extraordinary was happening and left so that we could be alone together.

Qiqi told me that when she was shot that night, she lost consciousness. When she woke up, she saw a car passing by and screamed for help. A few foreigners from the car came to her aid, but she passed out again. . . . The car turned out to belong to an American news crew who had planned to film a live report, but the danger of the situation had forced them to retreat, which was when they saw Qiqi. They brought her back to the American embassy, where the embassy doctors dressed her wounds.

Later, Qiqi met Chai Ling and the others hiding in the embassy. They told her that I had died. Chai Ling and the rest were wanted by the authorities and, while Qiqi was still recovering, their request for political asylum was approved. Under the protection of the embassy, Qiqi left Beijing, a city of sorrow, and came with the others to New York.

At first, Qiqi didn't know what conditions were like in China, and she dared not make contact with anyone in the country lest they suffer as a result. After a few years, Qiqi managed to return to Shanghai once to visit her mother, who told her that I had gotten married in Guangzhou. Not wanting to disturb my life, she told her mother not to let me know that she was still alive.

The bullets had left her with a permanent handicap and deprived her of the ability to become a mother. Helpless in this country, she married an old man who abused her. After her divorce, she managed to apply for and win a scholarship and came to study in this university.

We spent the whole night recounting to each other our experiences during the intervening years, and we held each other and cried. What should have been the most wonderful decade of our lives had been lost to the vicissitudes of fate. I said, "I'm so sorry," countless times, but what was the use? I vowed to devote the rest of my life to making it up to her, to giving her the happiness that should have been hers.

Naturally, ignoring the gossip, we moved in together. We barely spent any time apart, trying to make up for our lost youth. Qiqi had her green card. As long as I stayed with her, I should be able to remain in the United States. Since conditions in China had deteriorated further and China was now engaged in a war with Vietnam, Qiqi told me not to go back. But I couldn't just forget about Shen Qian and my son. Ever since I started grad school, Shen Qian had been living like a single mother, struggling to keep the whole family afloat, pinning her hopes on my success. To simply abandon her felt to me an unforgivable betrayal.

Although Qiqi and I had recovered some measure of our happiness, my heart was conflicted. But I was a coward. All I cared about was the joy of the present, and I dared not think about the choice I had to make.

10.

I stayed for more than a year in New York. After our lives had settled down somewhat, I threw myself into my work. I read many books of literary theory, politics, and philosophy, and felt my understanding grow by leaps and bounds. Often, I pushed Qiqi's wheelchair and took walks with her in Battery Park, where we both gazed at the distant figure of the Statue of Liberty and debated the fate of China and the future of the world.

My American advisor thought highly of my paper. He told me there was a teaching position open to those with a literary background that might be a good fit for me. If I got the job, I could stay and finish my Ph.D. Excited, I handed in my application right away. But then I received the letter from Shen Qian.

There isn't a wall in the world that doesn't have a crack. Even divided by the Pacific, rumors about Qiqi and me had managed to make their way back to China. Shen Qian was polite but firm in her letter, demanding an explanation. I finally decided to make a short trip back to China to clarify the situation with her.

Qiqi originally wanted to accompany me, but I asked her to stay put for now. Having her show up at the door with me might be too much for Shen Qian, and I wanted to talk to her alone. We said good-bye at the airport, and Qiqi, in a bright green jacket, leaned against the railing with her cane and watched me go through border control. I turned back to look at her.

Even decades later, the sight of her watching me—like the woman from that old legend who turned to stone waiting for her husband by the sea— would remain with me like a brand burned into my heart.

Back in China, Shen Qian was happy to see me. She made no mention of the question she'd asked me in her letter. Wearing her apron, she busied herself about the kitchen preparing my favorite dishes, many of which were not available in the U.S.: sautéed shredded pork with soybean paste, pork with bamboo shoots, steamed chicken with mushrooms . . . At dinner, she didn't ask me about my life in the U.S. and only talked about the domestic news: ration tickets were now required for most goods; farmers were no longer allotted individual plots of land, but had to work collectively in communes; her newspaper was in the middle of a debate about the proper authority for Marxist philosophy. Xiaobao was playing at my feet, absolutely delighted with the toy robot I had brought him. Faced with my innocent son and tender wife, I just couldn't bring myself to say the word "divorce."

That night, as we lay in bed, Shen Qian held me and passionately kissed me. I could feel her body trembling. Steeling myself, I gently pushed her away. "Qian, I need to tell you something."

"What's the rush?" Her arms went around my neck again as she murmured, "The night is still young. Why don't we first—"

"I want a divorce," I blurted out before I lost my nerve.

Her body stiffened. "Stop it. That's not funny."

"I'm not kidding. Qiqi is in America, and we . . . " I couldn't continue, but Shen Qian understood.

"You've decided?" She sat up.

"Yes."

"I understand." As she continued, her eyes flared with anger and her voice gradually grew harsh. "I know you were living with Zhao Qi. I know you used to be a couple. I knew that ten years ago! But what about me? What about all the years I've put into this marriage? Without me slaving away to take care of you and your son, do you think you could have gotten the chance to leave China? To see your old lover? Now that you've finally made it, do you think you can discard me like a pair of old shoes?"

"No! Listen . . . I will make it up to you . . . I will pay. . . . " I had planned a whole pretty speech but couldn't remember any of the words. What I did say sounded so cold, so heartless. I was disgusted by my own hypocrisy and clumsiness.

Shen Qian laughed mirthlessly. She slid off the bed and, without even putting on her shoes, headed out.

"Where are you going? It's the middle of the night." Afraid that she might leave the apartment, I got up as well.

She went onto the balcony and locked the door behind her. She stood facing me with her hands behind her. Her white nightgown trembled with her breath and she looked like a ghost in the night. I was terrified that she was going to jump.

"Don't, please!" I begged. "Let's talk about this."

"What are you afraid of?" Shen Qian said mockingly. "If I died, wouldn't that be perfect for you and Zhao Qi? Don't worry, I'm not going to grant your wish."

She raised her arms and tossed something over the edge of the balcony. I saw pieces of paper drifting in the wind, falling like snowflakes.

My passport, and other documents.

Behind me, Xiaobao, who had been awakened by our argument, started to cry.

Shen Qian left with Xiaobao and went to her parents' home. The next day, her parents and uncle came to our place to scream at me, and I had no choice but to hide in my room. It was impossible to keep something like this secret, and soon all my neighbors and colleagues at the university had heard the news. The rumors mutated as they spread: some were saying that I had found a wealthy, powerful woman overseas, and I was going to abandon my wife and child like one of those villains in the old folk operas. The denunciations were so oppressive that I couldn't even leave home without feeling fingers pointed at me behind my back. Even my mentor, for whom

I held deep respect and affection, gave me a tongue-lashing, and I could say nothing in my defense. My father fell ill because of what was happening.

This was how life made you helpless. If you tried to swim against its currents, you'd feel resistance at every step. I regretted coming back—it would have been easier if I'd had the strength to stay overseas. But now it was impossible to leave. To replace my passport would require a great deal of paperwork, and now that my reputation was ruined, I couldn't even get a recommendation letter from my department. I was stuck: I lacked the strength to continue the struggle, yet I was unwilling to give up.

It took half a year before the situation changed. In the end, as much as Shen Qian hated me, she wasn't going to shackle us together for the rest of our lives. She agreed to a divorce but demanded full custody of our son. I agreed, and also promised her monetary compensation. Finally, after everything was resolved, I placed a long-distance call to Qiqi, and she was overjoyed by the news. Since I still couldn't leave the country for the time being, she said she would come back the next month so that we could get married in China and then leave together.

I waited and waited for her flight, but it never arrived.

The next month, the era of Mao Zedong began.

11.

For years, the government had been following a policy of "buy rather than build." This created the false appearance of prosperity in the economy but hollowed out China's industrial infrastructure. The gap between the wealthy and the poor grew, and anger at the government grew along with it. Everywhere, a specter-like name haunted China, a name that grew gradually in prominence. People said, *This man will bring China fresh hope.*

He was called Mao Zedong. A few years earlier, he had held the post of Secretary of the Sichuan Provincial Committee in the provincial capital of Chongqing, and his various policies—known by the slogan "Sing Red Songs, Strike Black Forces" and involving public displays of Communist zeal and intensive government intervention—had made Chongqing into a prosperous city. Many ordinary citizens, especially poor peasants in the rural areas, supported him. The paramount leader of China, Hua Guofeng, was deeply influenced by Mao Zedong, and once Hua had gotten into power, he initiated the Great Proletariat Cultural Revolution, which sought to mobilize the people to bring down the capitalist roaders within the Communist Party. The mass movements swept the entire country, and political power within China was redistributed overnight. Deng

Xiaoping, Ye Jianying, Hu Yaobang, and others in their faction all fell from prominence, and with the entire country behind him, Mao Zedong was elected Chairman of the Communist Party.

After he became the Chairman, Mao continued the Cultural Revolution, focusing on criticizing Deng and opposing rightist tendencies, especially Deng's "foreigners' slave" political philosophy. He abolished Deng's policy of keeping China open to outside influences and essentially cut China off from the rest of the world. Soon after, the United States terminated all diplomatic relations with China. I could no longer go to America, and Qiqi could not come to China.

And so, once again, history divided us.

During the early stages of the Cultural Revolution, the personality cult of Mao was extreme, but the movement itself wasn't too violent. With my mentor's recommendation, I became an instructor at the university after grad school. Although colleges were no longer admitting students and the social status of intellectuals had declined, it was at least possible to make a living by writing theory papers on Marxism-Leninism, criticizing traditional Confucian philosophy, and reinterpreting Chinese history through a Communist lens as directed by the central leadership. The Cultural Revolution also interrupted the divorce proceedings, and so Shen Qian and I ended up living together again, doing our best to get along.

Year after year, we went to work, we came home, and we studied the required political readings. The Revolution was going well, as was proclaimed in public at every opportunity, but life itself had become as still as a pool of dead water. During those years, even bright-colored clothing was forbidden. No forms of culture or entertainment were permitted—since they were all corrupted by feudal, American-capitalist, or Soviet-revisionist influences—except for the eight model revolutionary operas. One time, I found a dirty, ragged copy of *Harry Potter and the Philosopher's Stone* abandoned in a public bathroom and tears filled my eyes. I took it home and read it in secret several times. But, in the end, terrified of being accused of harboring contraband, I burned it.

Sometimes, as I studied the latest directives from the paramount leader, I would think: *What happened to all the eras I have lived through? When I was a young man, the streets were packed with bellbottoms and "profiteers"; when I was a teenager, TV dramas from Hong Kong and Taiwan filled the airwaves; when I was a child, it was possible to play games on the web, to go and see the latest movies from Hollywood, and there were the Olympics and 3D films. . . . Did those times really exist? Where did they come from, and where have they gone? Or was all this just a dream?*

Maybe everything was simply a game played by time. What was time?

What was there besides nothingness? Before us had been nothingness, and after us will be nothingness.

Sometimes, in the middle of the night, I thought of the woman I loved on the other shore of the Pacific and pain wracked my body. Those days when I was half-mad with love, when I was a stranger in a strange land—they felt so real and yet so much like a fantasy. What would have happened if I had listened to Qiqi and stayed in America? Would I be happier than now? Or would I simply be mired in an even deeper illusion?

At least I would then be with the person I loved.

In reality, America was no paradise, either. *The People's Daily* explained that because the United States was addicted to militarism, it had sunk into the quagmire of the Vietnam War. Racial conflicts within America were intensifying and the crisis in the Middle East was causing an oil shortage. The capitalists were likely not going to last much longer, and American radical leftist movements were gaining momentum.

The Soviet camp, meanwhile, was growing stronger every day. The Cold War grew heated, and on almost every continent proxy wars were fought between the two superpowers. Ballistic nuclear submarines patrolled the sea depths, and every warhead they carried was capable of destroying an entire city. Even more missiles rested in their silos, awaiting the order that would launch them soaring though the air to rain destruction upon us. Death itself roamed overhead, poised to send all of humanity into hell. Regardless of whether you were Chinese or American, you were headed for the same place.

Sometimes, I recalled the rumors about the end of the world from my childhood. Maybe the prophecy had been true—except that perhaps the apocalypse didn't arrive in a single instant, but took decades or even centuries to descend. Or perhaps the world had already been destroyed by the time I was born, and all that I had experienced was nothing but a shadow of a fantasy that was slowly dissipating. Who knew what the truth was?

In the fourth year of the Cultural Revolution, I received a letter from the U.S. The very sight of the American stamps on it frightened me—corresponding with foreigners was an activity subject to intense scrutiny. However, the letter's contents seemed harmless enough, consisting of a few words of greeting cobbled together with some revolutionary language in an unnatural manner.

Comrade Xie Baosheng:
First, let us express together our fondest wish that the brightest, reddest sun in our hearts, Chairman Mao, live ten thousand years! As the Chairman wrote in his poem, "The seas roil with rage, and the continents shake in fury!" In America, under the leadership of Mao Zedong Thought,

the civil rights movement and leftist revolutionaries have made the
capitalists of Wall Street tremble before the awakened power of the
people! Chairman Mao was absolutely correct when he wrote that the
revolutionary conditions are not just good, but great!

All right, then, how are you doing? . . .

Of course the letter came from Qiqi. It had been delivered to my department, where the head of the workers' propaganda team[4] intercepted it. This man read the letter suspiciously and then looked up at me, glaring.

He slammed his hand down on the desk. "Xie Baosheng, the people's eyes can see everything! Now, confess the number of foreign contacts you have! What kind of secrets exist between you and the woman who wrote this letter?"

I laughed. "That's enough of that. You know everything there is to know about Qiqi and me. Now hand me the letter."

By an incredible stroke of luck, I was talking to my old friend Heizi. Formerly just an ordinary factory worker, he had been turned by the Cultural Revolution into a member of the workers' propaganda team that, pursuant to directives issued by the Chairman, came to supervise my university. In this manner, a man who had never even gone to college became the most important person in one of China's most prestigious universities. Without him, the letter would have gotten me into deep trouble.

Heizi handed the letter to me and told me to burn it after reading. I read Qiqi's words over and over until I figured out what she was trying to say between the lines. First, she explained that she had obtained her degree and was now teaching Chinese literature at an American college. Second, she was still unmarried and wanted to come visit me in China. I sighed and wiped my eyes. It had been five years since my parting from Qiqi, and she still wanted me. But what could I do? Even if she returned, the most we could hope for was to be like the hero and heroine in *The Second Handshake*, an underground novel we passed around in handwritten copies, who could only gaze at each other, knowing that they could never be together.

In the end, it didn't matter what I thought. I had no way of sending a letter to Qiqi.

I hid her letter in a stack of documents I took home. I didn't want Shen Qian to find it, but I also couldn't bear to burn it. Finally, I decided to conceal it between the pages of the copy of *Season of Bloom, Season of Rain* that had once belonged to Qiqi. Although the book itself was also an example of feudal, capitalist, and revisionist thinking, I just couldn't imagine getting rid of it. I wrapped the book in a bundle of old clothes and kept it at the bottom of the trunk.

• • •

12.

Rationally, I knew that Qiqi shouldn't come back, but a corner of my selfish heart continued to harbor the hope that she would. Around that time, President Nixon visited China, hoping to form an alliance with China against the Soviet Union. As the Sino–American relationship improved, hope reignited within me. However, somehow Nixon and Mao couldn't come to an agreement, and the Americans were so angry that they took revenge by manipulating the U.N. Security Council to expel the People's Republic of China and hand its seat at the U.N. to Taiwan as the "legitimate" representative for all of China. What little connection had existed between the U.S. and China was completely cut off.

Qiqi didn't return, and I received no more news about her.

In the sixth year of the Cultural Revolution, my father passed away. A few days before his death, China launched the satellite *The East Is Red*. It had been many years since China had sent an artificial satellite into orbit, and the occasion was marked with a great celebration. As my father lay dying, he held my hand and muttered, "When I was young, China had so many satellites in space I lost count. We even had manned spaceships and a space station. But this single little satellite is now seen as some remarkable achievement. What has happened to the world?"

I had no response. That world of my childhood, a world that had once existed, now felt even more impossible than science fiction. My father closed his eyes and let out his last breath.

To be fair, there were some advances in technology. The next year, the Americans managed to land on the moon with the Apollo mission—an unprecedented achievement—and the Stars and Stripes flew on lunar soil, shocking the world. This was not good news for China. Chairman Mao had come up with the proposal that China should lead the revolution of the Third World against the developed nations and the Soviet Union. As a result, bilateral relations between China and the U.S. and China and the Soviet Union were tense. China was also in a border conflict with the Soviet Union over Zhenbao Island and was completely isolated internationally. I only heard about the American moon landing by secretly listening to banned American radio broadcasts.

Two years later, my son was old enough to be called a young man. His generation was different from mine. They had no memory of the relative openness of Deng's reformist years and grew up under a barrage of propaganda centered on Mao Zedong Thought. They had little exposure to

Western culture, and no knowledge of China's traditional culture, either. They worshipped Chairman Mao with true zeal and believed it was their duty to die to protect his revolutionary path. They passionately declared that they would fight until they broke through the walls of the Kremlin, until they leveled the White House, until they liberated all of humankind.

My son disliked the name "Xiaobao," which meant "Precious," because it wasn't revolutionary enough. He renamed himself "Weidong," which meant "Defend the East." He became a Red Guard, and before he had even graduated from high school, he wanted to quit school and go on revolutionary tours around the country with his friends, sharing the experience of rebelling against authority with other Red Guards. Shen Qian and I did not like the idea at all, but this was something promoted by the leadership in Beijing. As soon as we started to object, our son brought out the Little Red Book and denounced us as though we were class enemies. We had no choice but to let him go.

None of us knew that a more violent storm lay in waiting.

The Red Guard movement grew, and young men and women turned on their teachers as "reactionary academic authorities." At every school, Red Guards held mass rallies called "struggle sessions" to torture and denounce these enemies of the revolution. My mentor, a famous professor who had studied overseas, naturally became a target, and I was brought along to the struggle sessions as a secondary target. Half of the hair on our heads was shaved off; tall, conical hats were stuck on top; and then our arms were pulled back and held up to force us to bow down to the revolutionary masses who hurled abuse at us. My mentor was beaten and tortured until he collapsed and lost consciousness. Only then did the mass rally end.

I held my old teacher and called his name, but he didn't wake up. Heizi helped me bring him to the hospital, but it was too late. He died a few days later.

The Red Guards were not satisfied with having murdered my mentor. They imprisoned me and demanded that I confess to all my past sins—what they really had in mind was my participation in the Tiananmen protests twenty years ago. I debated them by putting my academic skills to good use: "I was protesting against the dark path Deng Xiaoping wanted for China. We spoke loudly, wrote openly, and demanded true revolutionary democracy. This was absolutely in line with Mao Zedong Thought. We were supported by the masses of Beijing, the ordinary workers and laborers who also participated in the movement. How could you call such protests counterrevolutionary?"

The Red Guards lacked sufficient experience in this style of argument to win against me. They couldn't get me for having foreign contacts, either, because I had burned or buried anything having to do with America, and there was now no proof of my relationship with Qiqi. But ultimately, I was probably saved because of my friendship with Heizi.

After I was finally released and allowed to go home, I found out that Shen Qian had been taken away by the revolutionary rebels who had taken over her newspaper.

Someone at the newspaper, it turned out, had revealed Shen Qian's long-ago affair with Liu Xiaobo in a big character poster. Liu Xiaobo was without a doubt one of the worst counterrevolutionary rightists—he had once claimed that China could only be saved by three centuries of Western colonization; had drafted the capitalist legalistic screed "Charter '08"; and had been utterly corrupt in his sexual relationships. Although he was dead, his influence continued to linger. Since Shen Qian had been his lover for several years, she must have known many of his secrets. The revolutionary rebels salivated at the prospect of interrogating one of Liu's mistresses. They held her in a "cowshed"—a prison set up at the newspaper—and demanded that she write her confession.

Shen Qian was locked away for a whole week and I was not allowed to see her. By the time she returned, her hair had all been shaven off and her face and arms were littered with scars. She stared at me dully, as though she no longer recognized me. Finally, she recovered and sobbed uncontrollably as I held her.

She never told me what she suffered during her interrogation and I never asked. However, not long after, many people who had once known Liu Xiaobo were imprisoned and interrogated, and the rumor was that Shen Qian's confession had been used as the foundation for accusations against them. I knew it was wrong to blame Shen Qian. In this age, survival was the only goal, and conscience was a luxury few could afford.

In this manner, both Shen Qian and I were stamped with the label of counterrevolutionaries. By the time our son returned from his revolutionary tour, he found his parents to be bona fide, irredeemable class enemies. This meant that he was also considered impure. To remedy the situation, he went to the school and hung big character posters denouncing Shen Qian and me, and revealed some so-called "sins" that he knew we had committed. While others watched, he slapped me in the face and declared that he was no longer my son. He turned around and walked away, proud of his steadfast revolutionary ardor. I almost fainted from rage.

After our son left, we were angry for a few days, but then began to worry. We asked around for news about him but heard nothing for a couple of months. Then Heizi's son, Xiaohei, came to visit.

"Um, Uncle Xie . . . I have to tell you something. Please sit down."

Xiaohei and my son were good friends. I realized something was wrong. I took a deep breath and said, "Go ahead."

"Weidong . . . he . . . "

My heart sank and the world seemed to wobble around me. But I insisted that he continue.

My son and Xiaohei had joined a faction of Red Guards called the "April 14th Brigade." He had been promoted to squad leader, but because of my status and his mother's, he was demoted and almost expelled. To show that he had completely cast us away and was a dedicated revolutionary, my son decided to take on the most dangerous tasks and always led every charge. A few days ago, his faction fought a battle against another faction at the university; my son rushed ahead with an iron bar, but the other side had obtained rifles from the army, and with a bang, my son's chest exploded and he collapsed to the ground. . . .

The world blacked out around me before Xiaohei could finish.

13.

The death of our son destroyed the only hope left for Shen Qian and me. Our hair turned white almost overnight. My mother died from the shock and grief. Although Shen Qian and I weren't even fifty, we looked much older. We sat in our home with nothing to say to each other.

I didn't know how we survived those dark years. I didn't really want to recall the time. Like two fish tossed ashore, Shen Qian and I lay gasping, trying to keep each other's gills wet with the foam from our mouths. But eventual suffocation was our certain fate.

One year later, the Cultural Revolution ended.

Mao decided to retire behind the scenes and Liu Shaoqi became the President of China. Working with Premier Zhou Enlai, Liu tried to lead an economic recovery by instituting limited free markets and allocating land to individual families instead of collective farming by communes. Slowly, the country recovered, and colleges opened their doors again to new students. Intellectuals were treated better, and after a few years, Shen Qian and I were rehabilitated and no longer labeled rightists.

The ten years of the Cultural Revolution had decimated academia, and my department lacked qualified faculty. I had the respect of my colleagues and years of experience, but since I wasn't a member of the Communist Party (due to my political history), I was passed over for promotions. Summoning my courage, I wrote a letter to the authorities demanding the country make better use of the few intellectuals it had left, but I heard nothing.

A year later, when I had already given up all hope, my fortunes took an abrupt turn: I was promoted to full professor and given membership in the Communist Party. Even more amazingly, I was elected the department chair by a landslide.

In my new position of power, I began to get to know some elite intellectuals. One time, I met Guo Moruo, President of the Chinese Academy of Sciences. He told me in confidence that Premier Zhou Enlai had read my letter and given the directive to promote me despite my flawed background. Guo told me to work hard and not disappoint the Premier. Sometime later, the Premier visited our school and asked specifically to meet me. Anxiously, I expressed my gratitude to him, and the Premier laughed. "Comrade Baosheng, I know you're a talented man. The country is trying to get back on her feet and we have to focus on science and technology. Didn't you once write science fiction? Why not write more and get our young people interested in science again?"

Since the Premier and Guo Moruo had both given the green light, the novels I had written were reissued in new editions. Readers had not had access to such books in a long time and the response was overwhelming. Magazines began to approach me and commission new stories, and eventually I published a few collections. Fans began to call me a "famous writer."

I knew very well that these new stories were nowhere near as good as my old ones. I no longer dared to write about politically sensitive subjects, and these new offerings were affected works that praised the regime without articulating anything new. But who said the world was fair? I knew I was unlikely to accomplish anything great during what remained of my career. I decided I would use the little bit of influence I had to try to help talented young people, and to that end, I began to actively participate in social functions.

The good times didn't last. Soon, the country hit another rough patch. China conducted another nuclear test, and once again, both the Soviet Union and the United States imposed sanctions. Food shortages became rampant and everyone's rations were reduced. The streets were full of hungry people, and it was said that even Chairman Mao had stopped eating meat.

But even so, those of us in the big cities were lucky. Heizi told me that people were starving to death in the countryside. But since no news of this kind could be published, no one knew the truth. We didn't dare to speculate or say much, either. Although the Cultural Revolution was over, the political climate was still very severe. Rumor had it that when Marshal Peng Dehuai dared to offer some opinions critical of official policy at the Lushan Conference, he was severely punished.

The next year, Shen Qian died. No, not from starvation. She had liver cancer. As the wife of a high-status intellectual, she could have received treatment that would have prolonged her life, but she refused it.

"We stuck with each other . . . all these years. . . . Life has been so exhausting, hasn't it? We are like those two fish . . . in that Daoist parable . . . rather than struggling to keep each other alive on land, wouldn't it have been better . . . if we had never known each other at all, but lived free in the rivers and lakes? Don't be sad. . . . I'm not sad to go. . . . "

I held her hand, and tears made it impossible to speak. I remembered something from our youth: back then, everyone in middle school said we were a pair because we had classroom cleanup duty, but I didn't like her, and she didn't like me. When we worked together, it was very awkward because we refused to talk to each other. One time, I was standing on a chair to wash the windows and started to fall. She rushed over to help and I ended up falling on her. As we both limped to see the school nurse, the absurdity of the situation struck us and we laughed as we blamed each other. . . . That faded memory now felt like a preview of our time together.

"I really want to . . . hear that old song again." Shen Qian's voice was fading. "I haven't heard it in such a long time. Can you . . . sing for me?"

I knew the song she was talking about: "Rain, Hail, or Shine," by the Taiwanese singer Wakin Chau. We used to sing it all the time when we were in high school. I had forgotten most of the lyrics, and the best I could do was to recall a few fragments about love, about the pain and pleasure that dreams brought us, about regrets. I sang, my voice trembling, tears flowing down my face, and my cracked voice not sounding musical at all.

But Shen Qian moved her lips along with mine. She could no longer make any noise, but she was lost in the silent music of yesteryear. The rays of the setting sun shone through the window and fell upon her, covering her gaunt face with a golden glow.

We sang together like that for a long, long time.

14.

The years of starvation finally came to an end. The Soviet Union and China repaired their broken bond and trade began to grow. The Soviet Union provided us with a great deal of assistance and the domestic economy slowly recovered. But I was now almost sixty and felt much older. I resigned from the position of department chair, thinking I'd use what little time was left to write a few books. But I was nominated assistant dean of the university and became a standing committee member for the China Writers Association. In addition, I was picked as a delegate to the National People's Congress. I was too busy to write.

One day, I received a call from Mao Dun, the Minister of Culture.

"The Premier has asked you to attend a diplomatic function. There's a group of avant-garde Western writers visiting and he thinks you know one of them."

"Who?"

"I don't know the details. I'll send a car for you."

That evening, a car took me to the Beijing Hotel, which had one of the country's best Western-style restaurants. Many important people were in attendance, including the Premier himself, who gave a welcome address. As I surveyed the foreign visitors, I recognized the writer I was supposed to know right away. I couldn't believe my eyes.

After a series of boring speeches and a formal dinner, finally the time came to mingle and converse. I walked up to that man and said, in my terrible French, "*Bonsoir, Monsieur Sartre.*"

He gazed at me curiously through his thick glasses and gave me a friendly smile.

I switched to English and introduced myself. Then I told him how much I admired *L'être et le néant* and how I had written papers on it. I had never expected to see him in China.

"Well." Sartre quirked an eyebrow at me. "I never expected anyone in China to be interested in my work."

I lowered my voice. "Before the Cultural Revolution, your work was very popular in China. Many people were utterly entranced by your words, though they—myself included—could not claim to truly understand your philosophy. However, I've always tried to understand the world through it."

"I'm honored to hear that. But you shouldn't think so highly of my words. Your own thoughts about the world are the most precious thing— really, thinking itself is the only thing that is important. I must admit I'm surprised. I would have expected you to be a socialist."

I smiled bitterly. "Socialism is our life, but this form of life has turned me and many others into existentialists. Perhaps in that way the two are connected."

"What is your thought on existentialism?"

"To quote you, '*L'existence précède l'essence.*' The world appears out of an essenceless abyss. Other than time, it depends on nothing, and it has no meaning. All meaning comes after the world itself, and it is fundamentally absurd. I agree with this. The existence of the world is . . . absurd."

I paused, and then, gaining courage, continued with the puzzle that had plagued me for years. "Look at our world! Where does it come from? Where is it headed? When I was born, the Internet had connected all parts of the globe, and high-speed railways crisscrossed the country. The store shelves were full of anything one might desire, and there were countless novels, films, TV shows. . . . Everyone dreamt of a more wonderful future. But now? The web and mobile phones have long disappeared, and so has television. We appear to live in a world that is moving backward. Is this not absurd? Perhaps it is because our existence has no essence at all."

"Sir," said a smiling Sartre, "I think I understand what is troubling you. But I don't understand why you think this state is absurd."

"If the existence of the world has meaning, the world must advance, don't you think? Otherwise what is the point of generation struggling after generation? The world appears to be a twisted shadow of some reality."

Sartre shook his head. "I know that the Chinese once had a philosopher named Zhuangzi. He told this story: if you give a monkey three nuts in the morning and four nuts in the evening, the monkey will be unhappy. But if you give the monkey four nuts in the morning and only three in the evening, the monkey will be ecstatic. In your view, is the monkey foolish?"

"Uh . . . yes. Zhuangzi's monkey is a byword for foolishness among the Chinese."

A mocking glint came into Sartre's eyes. "But how are we different from the monkey in that story? Are we in pursuit of some 'correct' order of history? If you switch happiness and misfortune around in time, will everything appear 'normal' to you? If evil exists in history, does it disappear merely by switching the order of events around?"

I felt like I was on the verge of understanding something, but I couldn't articulate it.

Sartre continued, "*Progress* is not a constant. It is merely a temporary phase of this universe. I'm no scientist, but the physicists tell us that the universe expands and then collapses and then expands again, not unlike the cosmic cycles envisioned by your Daoist philosophers. Time could easily flow in another direction . . . or in one of countless directions. Perhaps events can be arranged in any of a number of different sequences, because time may choose from an infinite set of options. Remember the aphorism of Heraclitus: 'Time is a child playing dice; the kingly power is a child's.'

"But so what? Whichever direction time takes, what meaning does all this have? The world exists. Its existence precedes essence because its very existence is steeped in nothingness. It is absurd regardless of the order of the events within it. Perhaps you're right—had time picked another direction, the universe would be very different: humanity would progress from darkness to light, from sorrow to joy, but such a universe would not be any better. In the end, joy belongs to those who are born in times of joy, and suffering belongs to those born in times of suffering. In the eyes of God, it makes no difference.

"Some say that if war were to break out between the Soviet Union and the United States, the world would end. But I say the apocalypse has long since arrived. It has been with us since the birth of the world, but we have become inured to it by familiarity. The end of the world comes not with the destruction of everything, but with the fact that nothing that happens around us has any meaning. The world has returned to primordial chaos, and we have nothing."

Sartre stopped, as though expecting me to say something. My mind was utterly confused, and after a long while, I said, "What, then, is the hope for humanity?"

"Hope has always existed and always will," he said solemnly. "But hope is not the future because time does not have an inevitable direction. Hope is now: in existence itself, in nothingness. The truth of nothingness is freedom. Man has always had the freedom to choose, and this is the only comfort and grace offered to humanity."

"I understand that's your theory. But do you really think the freedom to choose belongs to humanity?" My voice grew sharper. "Thirty years ago, I was separated from the woman I loved on the other side of an ocean. Then I returned here. I do not know where she is or whether she is still alive. Can I choose to go find her? A few years back, tens of millions of people died from starvation in this country. If possible, they would all have chosen to survive. But could they have survived? Let me tell you something: many honorable and great men and women chose Communism, believing it would save humanity from suffering, but have you seen the results of their choice? Have you seen what has happened to China? The freedom of mankind is but a fantasy, a cheap consolation. Our state is despair."

Sartre was silent for a while. Then he said, "Perhaps you're right. But the meaning of freedom is that you can always choose, though there is no promise that your choice will become reality. Maybe this is a cheap consolation, but other than this, we have nothing."

I don't know if I really understood Sartre, or maybe even he couldn't express himself clearly. He stayed in China for more than a month and we saw each other often. He said he would try to think about what I said and write a new book, but then he left China and I never saw him again.

15.

The next few years were a golden age for the People's Republic. The Cultural Revolution was a distant memory and the later anti-rightist movements were also deemed historical errors. As the cultural sphere grew more animated and open, dissent was tolerated and many different opinions could be voiced.

The central leadership adjusted the socialist economic model through new democratic reforms that permitted some measure of private enterprise. The Soviet Union and China entered a honeymoon period, and with Soviet aid, China announced a new five-year plan of full-scale development. Everywhere people were excited and threw themselves into their work with passion. Once again, we began to hope for a better future.

But hope did not last. After the Cuban Missile Crisis, the Cold War heated up again. An American plot overthrew Cuba's Castro and the dictator Batista came into power. The Communist forces were driven from the Americas, and then the Korean Peninsula became a new flashpoint. Along the 38th parallel, both sides amassed forces, and war broke out without anybody knowing who had fired the first shot. China could not help but become involved, and young men from China had to go to Korea to fight for the survival of the Republic.

This was the first time in living memory that China and the United States fought directly. The Americans had picked a moment in China's history when China was at her weakest, when she needed peace and recovery the most. Every sign indicated that China was going to lose. Incredibly, however, the Chinese Volunteers, who possessed nothing except courage, pushed back the American assault and forced the American army to a standstill along the 38th parallel. This was not achieved without great cost. It was said that hundreds of thousands, perhaps even millions, gave their lives. I didn't know the exact figure, but considering that even Chairman Mao's son died in battle, one could imagine how desperate and fierce the fighting was.

The war caused the economy to collapse. Prices soared and more hardships were added to people's lives. Dissatisfaction with the government grew and a name long forbidden began to surface in conversations: Chiang Kai-shek.

He was a hardened anti-Communist. Although the situation across the Taiwan Strait had long been tense due to the mainland's overwhelming advantage over the island, Taiwan's leaders had always pursued a policy of de facto independence, only passively resisting any mainland advances. But twenty years ago, after Chiang Kai-shek came to power, he declared that he would reclaim the mainland. Since the war in Korea had reached a stalemate, the Americans encouraged Chiang to join the conflict. He thus declared his intention to carry out his old promise.

With American support, Taiwan's fighters and warships encroached upon the mainland coast and pamphlets were dropped in Guangzhou, Shanghai, and other cities. Taiwan's army entered Burma and harassed the border with China. It was said that parts of Yunnan Province had already fallen to Chiang's forces. Tibet declared independence and would no longer heed orders from Beijing. Bandits under the flag of the "Nationalist Army" killed and looted the rural countryside. Spies in various cities began to put up anti-Communist posters.

The government responded by cracking down on counterrevolutionaries, but the effects appeared slight. Rumors were rampant and the population grew restless. The central leadership signed a cease-fire with the Americans and pulled the army back into China in an attempt to stabilize the domestic situation.

Chiang Kai-shek then launched an all-out assault, and the peace across the Taiwan Strait that had lasted my entire lifetime ended as the Chinese Civil War began.

With the help of the American Seventh Fleet, the Nationalist Army landed in Guangdong. They headed north and conquered Nanjing. The central leadership pulled the troops that had returned from Korea to the southern front, but the troops were tired of fighting and surrendered to the Nationalists en masse, raising the flag of the Republic of China, a blue sky with a white sun. In little more than a year, all territories south of the Yangtze had fallen to the Nationalists, and even the north appeared to be teetering on the precipice.

During that time, through my connections in the Soviet Union, I unexpectedly received a copy of Sartre's new book, which recorded his impressions of China. Sartre also sent me a long letter in which he discussed some further thoughts about our conversations. It was highly technical and rather hard to read. However, near the end, an almost casually tossed-off line shocked me:

"Recently, a Chinese-American scholar came to Paris to visit me. Her name is Zhao Qi, and she has been away from China for many decades. . . . "

Qiqi! My Qiqi! The world spun around me. I forced myself to be calm and continued to read.

"She is an excellent scholar, and she wishes to return to her homeland to do what she can to help. I mentioned you to her, and she said she would like to visit you in Beijing."

The letter went on to discuss other matters I did not care about.

For a long while, my mind was utter chaos. When I finally calmed down, I figured out what Sartre really meant. During the month we spent together, I told him about Qiqi and asked for his help to find out news about her if he ever visited the United States. The reason he had crafted his letter to make it sound as if Qiqi and I were strangers was an attempt to protect us in the event the letter were read by others.

The important news was that Qiqi was going to return to Beijing to find me. This was actually a consequence of the present crisis. The reason that

Qiqi couldn't return to China before was because of the Cold War, but if the political situation changed, the barrier between us would be lifted.

Sartre's real message to me was simple: *If you want to see Qiqi again, find a way to stay in Beijing!*

16.

While I waited excitedly in Beijing, another piece of shocking news arrived: Chiang Kai-shek proclaimed that the Republic of China was reasserting its sovereignty over the entire country. The capital would be returned to Nanjing, and Beijing renamed Beiping. He vowed to cross the Yangtze and slaughter every last Communist until China was unified.

The next day, Heizi came to find me, holding a pamphlet in his hand. "What is wrong with you? Why are you still here?"

"Where am I supposed to go?" I was baffled.

"Don't you know?" Heizi handed the pamphlet to me. "A Nationalist airplane dropped this earlier today."

I read the pamphlet. Basically, it said that the Nationalists were winning victory after victory in their advance north and they would soon conquer Beiping. Everyone would be pardoned, with the exception of a list of major war criminals. The pamphlet went on to urge Communist officers and soldiers to surrender.

"What does this have to do with me?" I asked.

"Look at the back."

I flipped the sheet of paper over. It was a list of "Major Communist War Criminals." I glanced through the names: Mao Zedong, Zhou Enlai, Liu Shaoqi . . . There were at least a hundred names, and most were important figures in the Party or the government. The penultimate name was Guo Moruo, my old friend. The last name on the list was even more familiar: *Xie Baosheng.*

"What . . . is my name doing here?"

"Of course you're on there," said Heizi. "Have you forgotten who you are? You've been the dean of the university, the Secretary-General of the China Federation of Literary and Art Circles, standing committee member of the Chinese People's Political Consultative Conference, and you are always showing up at state banquets. As far as the cultural sphere is concerned, you and Guo Moruo are the two biggest fish."

"Those are just honorary titles. I've never done anything."

"It really doesn't matter. They need a name on there to show they mean business, and it might as well be yours." Heizi sighed. "I heard that Chiang

Kai-shek has started purges in the south. Anybody connected with the Communists is executed, and he's killed enough people to make the rivers to flow red. He hung many of the bodies from lampposts to instill terror. Since you're on the list, if Beijing were to fall. . . . You'd better get out."

I smiled bitterly. "I think it's too late for that. What are your plans?"

"My wife and I will follow our son, of course. Xiaohei is still in the army. In fact, he's a member of the guard for the central leadership. He's already arranged for us to go to the Northeast. We leave in two days. Old friend, I really think you need to plan for this."

A few days later, the Nationalists were almost at the city. Artillery shells were already exploding in Beijing. Someone passed me a copy of an article published in a newspaper in Nanjing, which was supposed to describe the "Crimes of Communist Bandit Leaders." The section on me claimed I had betrayed Liu Xiaobo after my arrest post-Tiananmen; that I had served as a tool of the regime during the Cultural Revolution; that after coming into power, I had abused my authority to suppress anyone who disagreed with me; that I had written science fiction novels spreading propaganda about Communism and advocating corrupt sexual practices; that I had emboldened and invigorated the totalitarian system. . . . In a word, I must be executed to pacify the people's anger.

I had to laugh at this. Here was I, thinking I had accomplished nothing in my life, but in this article I was an amazing villain with extraordinary powers.

That night, a squad of fully armed soldiers woke me by banging on the door. They were members of the guard for the central leadership and the officer in charge was Xiaohei.

"Uncle Xie, we are here with orders to escort you out of the city."

"Where are you going?"

"The commander of Beijing's peripheral defenses has betrayed us," Xiaohei said. "That bastard surrendered and the Nationalists are now attacking the city. To avoid the destruction of the city's cultural artifacts and ancient buildings, the central leadership has decided to retreat. We've got to go now."

"No. I'm too old to run. I'll wait here. Whatever happens is fate."

"Uncle Xie, you're on the list of war criminals. If you stay here, you'll die for sure."

He continued trying to change my mind, but I refused to budge. One of his soldiers got impatient and pointed his gun at me. "Xie Baosheng, if you don't leave, then you're trying to betray the revolution and surrender to the enemy. I'll kill you right now."

Xiaohei pushed the gun barrel down. "Uncle Xie, I'm sorry, but we're under strict orders. You must leave with us. If you don't come willingly, we'll have to resort to cruder measures."

I sighed. "Fine. Give me a few minutes to pack some things."

An hour later, deep in the night, the soldiers and I got into a jeep and drove west. Many buildings along the way had already collapsed from artillery fire and the road was filled with pits. Electricity had been shut off and all the streetlights were dark. Other than columns of soldiers, I saw almost no pedestrians. Tanks passed by from time to time and I could hear the distant rumble of cannons.

I was reminded of another bloody night forty years ago.

The car drove past Tiananmen along the Avenue of Eternal Peace. Under the cold light of the moon, I saw that on this square that had once held tens of thousands of idealistic young hearts, the Great Hall of the People and the Monument to the People's Heroes had both been reduced to heaps of rubble. A bare flagstaff stood in the middle of the square, but the red flag with five golden stars was no longer flying from it; instead, it lay crumpled on the ground. A few soldiers were working on the Gate of Heavenly Peace itself, taking down the portrait of Chairman Mao so that it could be carried away. I still couldn't believe I was witnessing the end of the country in which I was born.

I thought I had been through too much ever to be moved by the shifting vicissitudes of fortune. But I was wrong. In that moment, my eyes grew blurry. Tiananmen became an old watercolor painting, dissolving in my hot tears. One time, the entire country celebrated the founding of the People's Republic with a parade through this very square; one time, students from around the country gathered here to demand democracy; one time, Chairman Mao stood here and surveyed the Red Guards—where were they now? Had it all been a dream?

Equally broken lay the dream of reuniting with Qiqi. I had waited so long in this city for her, but by the time she managed to return to her homeland, in which corner of China would I find myself? Perhaps we would never meet again until death. . . .

No one spoke. The car bumped along and left war-torn Beijing, heading for the Western Hills.

17.

A lamp is lit on the mountain in the east,
The light falls on the mountain in the west.
The plain between them is smooth and vast,
But I can't seem to find you. . . .

The Loess Plateau of central China lay before us. The yellow earth, deposited by dust storms over the eons, stretched to the horizon. Thousands of years of erosion had carved countless canyons and channels in it, like the wrinkles left by time on our faces. The barren terraced fields bore silent testimony to the hardships endured by the people eking out a living on this ancient land. Baota Mountain, the symbol of the town of Yan'an, stood not far from us, and the Yellow River flowed past the foot of it. The folk song echoed between the canyons, lingering for a long time.

"People enjoy love songs, even in a place like this," said Heizi. "Oh, do you remember that popular song about the Loess Plateau from when we were young? Back then, I was so curious what the place really looked like. I never got to see it until now, when it's become my home. Fate is really funny sometimes."

For the last few years, as the civil war raged on, I had followed the People's Liberation Army first to Hebei, and then to the liberated regions in the center of the country, and finally here, to Yan'an, where I unexpectedly bumped into my old friend. Heizi had been in the Northeast until he followed his son here, but his wife had died during the Siege of Changchun.

Although the PLA had begun the civil war with a series of crushing defeats, under the leadership of Lin Biao, Peng Dehuai, and Liu Bocheng, the PLA soon rallied and pushed back. Chiang Kai-shek became the President of the Republic of China in Nanjing, but his dream of unifying China couldn't be realized. The more he tried to "exterminate" the Communists, the more his own hold on power appeared to waver. The Communists managed to hold on to some liberated zones in northern China, and the two sides settled into a seesawing stalemate. Since both factions were tired of the fighting, they declared a cease-fire and began negotiations in Chongqing, hoping to form a new coalition government. But since neither side was willing to compromise, the talks went nowhere.

While China was embroiled in this civil war, extreme militarists came to power in Japan and launched an invasion of China. They advanced quickly and forced Chiang Kai-shek to leave Nanjing and move the capital temporarily to Chongqing. The Japanese then invaded the Philippines and opened a new Pacific front against the American forces stationed there. The Americans were completely unprepared and fled before the might of Japan. In distant Europe, a madman named Hitler rose to prominence in Germany with the support of the army and instantly declared war on the Soviet Union. The German forces reclaimed East Germany and invaded France. The whole world had descended into the first truly global war in history.

The Cold War dissolved before this new threat. The Americans and the Soviets, erstwhile enemies, formed an alliance against the new Axis Powers of Germany, Italy, and Japan. Meanwhile, in China, the Nationalists and the Communists had to put aside their differences to fight together for the survival of the Chinese people against the Japanese slaughter. Thus did history turn over a new page.

After arriving in Yan'an, I didn't want anything more to do with administration or politics. I dedicated myself to collecting folk songs and preserving traditional arts, which I enjoyed. Although my life was no longer comfortable—I lived in a traditional cave dwelling and subsisted on coarse grains just like all the local peasants—I counted myself lucky. It was a time of war, after all.

While Heizi and I reminisced, a young student ran up the mountainous path toward us.

"Teacher! Someone is here looking for you!" He struggled to catch his breath.

"Who?" I didn't even get up. I was too old to be excited.

"An old lady. I think she's from America."

I jumped up and grabbed him. "An old lady? What's her name? How old is she?"

"Um . . . I'm not sure. I guess over sixty? She's talking with the dean of the Arts Academy. The dean said you know her."

From America . . . over sixty . . . an old lady . . . my Qiqi. She's here. She's finally here!

I started to run. But I was too old; I couldn't catch my breath and I felt dizzy. I had to slow down and Heizi caught up to me.

"Do you really think it's Qiqi?" he asked.

"Of course it is. Heizi, slap me! I want to be sure I'm not dreaming."

Like a true friend, Heizi slapped me in the face, hard. I put my hand against my cheek, savoring the pain, and laughed.

"Don't get too excited," said Heizi. "Zhao Qi is your age, isn't she? She's not a pretty young lady anymore. It's been decades since you've seen her. You might be disappointed."

"That's ridiculous. Look at all of us. We're like candle stubs sputtering in our last moments of glory. Seeing her one more time before I die would be more than enough."

Heizi chuckled. "You might be old, but you're still in good health—I bet the parts of your body that matter still work pretty well. How about this? If you two are going to get married, I want to be the witness."

I laughed and felt calmer. We chatted as we descended the mountain, and then my heart began to leap wildly again as I approached the Arts Academy.

• • •

18.

I didn't recognize her.

She was Caucasian. Although her hair was turning white, I could tell it had once been blonde. Blue eyes stared at me thoughtfully out of an angled, distinctive face. Although she was not young, she was still beautiful.

I was deeply disappointed. That foolish student hadn't even clarified whether he was talking about a Chinese or a foreigner.

"Hello," the woman said. Her Chinese was excellent. "Are you Mr. Xie Baosheng?"

"I am. May I ask your name?"

"I'm Anna Louise Strong, a writer."

I recognized the name. She was a leftist American author who had lived in Beijing and written several books about the China of the Mao era. She was friends with both Mao Zedong and Zhou Enlai. Though I knew who she was, I had never met her. I heard she had moved back to the U.S. around the time Shen Qian died. Why was she looking for me?

Anna looked uncomfortable and I felt uneasy. She hesitated, and then said, "I have something important to tell you, but perhaps it's best to speak in private."

I led her to my cave. Anna retrieved a bundle from her suitcase, which she carefully unwrapped. Anxiously, I watched as she set a crude brown ceramic jar down on the table.

Solemnly, she said, "This holds the ashes of Miss Zhao Qi."

I stared at the jar, unable to connect this strange artifact with the lovely, graceful Qiqi of my memory.

"What are you saying?" I asked. I simply could not make sense of what she was telling me.

"I'm sorry, but . . . she's dead."

The air in the cave seemed to solidify. I stood rooted in place, unable to speak.

"Are you all right?" Anna asked.

After a while, I nodded. "I'm fine. Oh, would you like a cup of water?" I was surprised I could think about such irrelevant details at that moment.

I had imagined the scene of our reunion countless times, and of course I had imagined the possibility that Qiqi was already dead. I always thought I would howl, scream, fall to the ground, or even faint. But I was wrong. I was amazed by how calmly I accepted the news. Maybe I had always known there would be no happily-ever-after in my life.

"When?" I asked.

"Three days ago, in Luochuan."

Anna told me that Qiqi had been looking for me for years. Although I had some notoriety as a war criminal, because I was part of the Communist army and always on the march, it was impossible to locate me. Once war broke out with Japan, the Nationalists and the Communists both became American allies and it was no longer difficult to travel to China. Qiqi finally heard that I was in Yan'an and bought a ticket on the boat crossing the Pacific. On the voyage, she met Anna and the two became friends. On the long ride across the ocean, she told Anna our story.

Anna and Qiqi arrived in Hong Kong, but as most of eastern China had fallen to Japanese occupation, they had to get on another boat to Guangxi, from whence they passed through Guizhou and Sichuan, and then continued north through Shaanxi to arrive finally in Yan'an.

"But Zhao Qi was no longer a young woman," Anna said, "and with her handicap, the journey was very tough on her. By the time she arrived in Xi'an, she fell ill, and yet she forced herself to go on so that she wouldn't slow us down. In Luochuan, her condition deteriorated. . . . Because of the war, we couldn't get the medicine she needed. . . . We tried everything, but we couldn't save her." Anna stopped, unable to continue.

"Don't blame yourself. You did your best." I tried to console her.

Anna looked at me strangely, as if unable to comprehend my calmness.

"Why don't you tell me what her life in America was like following our separation?" I asked.

Anna told me that after I left, Qiqi continued her studies in the U.S., waiting for me. She wrote to me several times but never received any replies. Once she was awarded her Ph.D., she taught in college and then remarried. Ten years ago, after her husband died, she wanted to return to China, but the civil war put those plans on hold. Finally, only days from Yan'an, she died. Since they couldn't carry her body through the mountains, they had to cremate her. Thus I was deprived of the chance to see her one last time—

"No," I interrupted. I picked up the jar of ashes. "Qiqi and I are together now, and we'll never be apart again. Thank you."

I ignored Anna's stare as I held the jar against my chest and muttered to myself. Tears flowed down my face, the tears of happiness.

CODA

The setting sun, red as blood, floated next to the ancient pagoda on Baota Mountain. It cast its remaining light over northern China, veiling everything in a golden-red hue. The Yan River sparkled in the distance, and I could see a few young soldiers, barely more than boys, playing in the water.

I sat under a tree; Qiqi sat next to me, resting her head on my shoulder.

The pendulum of life appeared to have returned to the origin. After all we had witnessed and endured, she and I had traversed countless moments, both bitter and sweet, and once again leaned against each other. It didn't matter how much time had passed us by. It didn't matter if we were alive or dead. It was enough that we were together.

"I'm not sure if you know this," I said. "After your mother died during the Cultural Revolution, I helped to arrange her funeral. She had suffered some because of her relationship to you, but she died relatively peacefully. In her last moments, she asked me to tell you to stay away from China and try to live a good life. But I always knew you would return. . . .

"Do you remember Heizi? He's in Yan'an, too. Even at his age, he's as goofy as when he was a boy. Last month, he told me that if you came back, we'd all go climb Baota Mountain together, just like when we were kids. Don't worry, the mountain is not very high. I can carry you if you have trouble with your leg. . . .

"It's been twenty years since my mother's death. There used to be two jade bracelets that had been in my family for generations. My mother planned to give one each to you and me. Later, she gave one to Shen Qian, but the Red Guards broke it because it was a feudal relic. . . . I hid the other, hoping to give it to you. Have a look. I hope you like it."

I opened the bundle that had been on my back and took out a smooth jade bracelet. In the sun's last rays, it glowed brightly.

"You want to know what else is in the bundle?" I chuckled. "Lots of good things. I've been carrying them around for years. It hasn't been easy to keep them safe. Look."

I took out the treasures of my memory one by one: the English letters Qiqi had written to me in high school; the *New Concept English* cassette tapes she gave me; the posters for *Tokyo Love Story*; a lock of hair I begged from her after we started dating; the purple hairclip she wore to Tiananmen Square; a few photographs of us taken in New York; the "revolutionese" letter she sent me during the Cultural Revolution. . . .

I examined each object carefully, remembering. It was like gazing through a time telescope at moments as far away as galaxies, or perhaps like diving into the sea of history in search of forgotten treasures in sunken ships. The distant years had settled deep into the strata of time, turning into indistinct fossils. But perhaps they were also like seeds that would germinate after years of quiescence and poke through the crust of our souls. . . .

Finally, at the bottom of the bundle, I found the copy of *Season of Bloom, Season of Rain*. She left it in my home after visiting my family during middle school, but I hadn't read it in years. More than fifty years later, the pages had turned yellow and brittle. I held it in my hand and caressed the cover wrap Qiqi had made, admiring her handwriting. The smooth texture of the poster paper felt strangely familiar, as though I was opening a tunnel into the past.

I opened the book, thinking I would read a few pages. But my hand felt something strange. I looked closely: there was something trapped between the poster paper wrap and the original cover of the book.

Carefully, I unwrapped the poster paper, but I had underestimated the fragility of the book. The cover was torn off and a rectangular card fell out like a colorful butterfly. It fluttered to the ground after a brief dance in the sunlight.

I picked it up.

It was a high-definition photograph, probably taken with a digital camera. Fireworks exploded in the night sky, and in the distant background was a glowing screen on which you could make out the shape of some magnificent stadium. I recognized it: the Bird's Nest. In the foreground were many people dressed in colorful clothes holding balloons and Chinese flags and cotton candy and popcorn. Everyone was laughing, pointing, strolling. . . .

In the middle of the photograph were two children about four years old. One was a boy in a grey jacket, the other a girl in a pink dress. They stood together, holding hands. Illuminated by the fireworks exploding overhead, the smiles on their flushed faces were pure and innocent.

I stared at the photograph for a long time and then flipped it over. I saw a graceful line of handwritten characters:

Beauty is about to go home. Take care, my Grey Wolf.

More than fifty years earlier, Qiqi had hidden this present to me in a book she had "forgotten." I had never unwrapped it.

I remembered the last conversation I had with Anna.

"What did she say before she died?"

"She was delirious . . . but she said she would return to the past you two shared, to the place where she met you for the first time, and wait for you. I don't know what she meant."

"Maybe all of us will return there someday."

"Where?"

"To the origin of the universe, of life, of time. . . . To the time before the world began. Perhaps we could choose another direction and live another life."

"I don't understand."

"I don't, either. Maybe our lives are lived in order to comprehend this mystery, and we'll understand only at the end."

"It's time, isn't it?" I asked Qiqi. "We'll go back together. Would you like that?"

Qiqi said nothing.

I closed my eyes. The world dissolved around me. Layer after layer peeled back, and era after era emerged and returned to nothingness. Strings of shining names fell from the empyrean of history, as though they had never existed. We were thirty, twenty, fifteen, five . . . not just me and Qiqi, but also Shen Qian, Heizi, and everyone else. We returned to the origin of our lives, turned into babies, into fetuses. In the deepest abyss of the world, the beginning of consciousness stirred, ready to choose new worlds, new time lines, new possibilities. . . .

The sun had fallen beneath the horizon in the east, and the long day was about to end. But tomorrow the sun would rise in the west again, bathing the world in a kinder light. On the terraced fields along the slope of the mountain, millions of poppy flowers trembled, blooming, burning incomparably bright in the last light of dusk.

⊷⊶

AUTHOR'S POSTSCRIPT:

Many interesting works have been written about the arrow of time. This one is perhaps a bit distinct: while each person lives their life forward, the sociopolitical conditions regress backward.

This absurd story has a fairly realist origin. One time, on an Internet discussion board, someone made the comment that if a certain prominent figure in contemporary Chinese politics came to power, the Cultural Revolution would happen again. I didn't agree with him at the time, but I did think: *What would it be like if my generation has to experience the conditions of the Cultural Revolution again in our forties or fifties?* More broadly, I wondered what life would be like if society moved backward in history.

The frame of this story might be seen as a reversed arrow of time, but strictly speaking, what has been reversed isn't time, only the trends of history.

This story was written as a work of entertainment, and so it should not be read as some kind of political manifesto. If one must attribute a political message to it, it is simply this: I hope that all the historical tragedies our nation has experienced will not repeat in the future.

[1] TRANSLATOR'S NOTE: English translation courtesy of Anatoly Belilovsky, © 2014. Used here with permission.

[2] TRANSLATOR'S NOTE: In our timeline, Jin Yong, Gu Long, and Liang Yusheng are three of the acnkowledged masters of *wuxia* fantasy, and most

of their best works were written before 1980. Huang Yi's works rose to prominence later, in the 1990s.

[3] TRANSLATOR'S NOTE: This is a bit of an inside joke for Chinese sf fans. In our timeline, Yao Haijun is the assistant chief editor for *Science Fiction World*, China's most prominent sci-fi magazine. Bao Shu, the author of this story, began his career as a fanfic author in the universe of Liu Cixin's "Three Body" series.

[4] TRANSLATOR'S NOTE: In our timeline, "workers' Mao Zedong Thought propaganda teams" were a unique creation of the Cultural Revolution. They consisted of teams of ordinary workers installed at colleges and high schools to take over the administrative functions and to put a stop to the bloody Red Guard factional wars. For the most part, they stabilized the chaos introduced by the early stages of the Cultural Revolution.

THE LAST WITNESS

K. J. Parker

I remember waking up in the middle of the night. My sister was crying. She was five years old, I was eight. There was a horrible noise coming from downstairs, shouting, banging. We crept to the top of the stairs (really it was just a glorified ladder) and I peered down. I couldn't see all that well, because the fire had died down and the lamps weren't lit. I saw my father; he'd got his walking stick in his hand, which was odd because why would he need it indoors? My mother was yelling at him; you're stupid, you're so stupid, I should have listened to my family, they said you were useless and you are. Then my father swung the stick at her. I think he meant to hit her head, but she moved and he caught her on the side of the left arm. Oddly, instead of backing away she went forward, toward him. He staggered and fell sideways, onto the little table with the spindly legs; it went *crunch* under his weight, and I thought; he's broken it, he's going to be in so much trouble. Then my sister screamed. My mother looked up at us, and I saw the knife in her hand. She yelled, "Go to *bed*!" She yelled at us all the time. We were always getting under her feet.

I also remember a night when I couldn't sleep. I was about six. Mummy and Daddy were having a horrible row downstairs, and it made me cry. I cried so much I woke up my brother. Forget it, he told me, they're always rowing, go to sleep. I couldn't stop crying. Something bad's going to happen, I said. I think he thought so too, and we crept to the top of the stairs and looked down, the way we used to spy on the guests-for-dinner. I saw Daddy knock Mummy to the ground with his stick, and then Uncle Sass (he wasn't really our uncle) jumped out from behind the chimney corner and stabbed Daddy with a knife. Then Mummy saw us and yelled at us to go back to bed.

I also remember the night my husband died.

I remember that job very clearly.

I remember, when I was growing up, we lived on the edge of the moor, in a little house in a valley. About five miles north, just above the heather-line, were these old ruins. I used to go there a lot when I was a boy. Mostly the grass had grown up all over them, but in places the masonry still poked out, like teeth through gums. It must have been a big city once—of course, I didn't know about cities then—and there was this tall square pillar; it stood about ten feet and it was leaning slightly. Between the wind and the rain and the sheep itching against it, there wasn't much left to see of the carvings; rounded outlines that were probably meant to be people doing things, and on one side, where the slight lean sheltered it a tiny bit from the weather, there were these markings that I later realized must have been writing. I can picture them in my mind to this day; and when I became rich and had some spare time I searched the Studium library, which is the finest in the world (the memory of the human race, they call it) but I never found anything remotely like that script, or any record of any city on our moors, or any race or civilization who'd ever lived there.

I remember the first time I met them. When you've been in this business as long as I have, clients tend to merge together, but these ones stand out in my mind. There was an old man and a younger one; father and son or uncle and nephew, I never did find out. The old man was big, broad and bony, with a long face and a shiny dome of a head, nose like a hawk's beak, very bright blue sunken eyes, big ears sticking out like handles. The young man was just like him only red-haired and much smaller; you could have fitted him comfortably inside the old man, like those trick dolls from the East. He didn't talk much.

We heard all about you, the old man said, the stuff you can do. Is it true?

Depends what you've heard, I told him. Most of what people say about me is garbage.

I think he expected me to be more businesslike. Is it true, he said, that you can read people's minds?

No, I told him, I can't do that, nobody can, not even the Grand Masters. That would be magic, and there's no such thing. What I can do (I said quickly, before I tried his patience too far) is get inside people's heads and take their memories.

They both looked at me. That's what we'd heard, the old man said, but we weren't sure if we could believe it. And anyhow, isn't that mind reading?

So many of them say that. I don't know how I do it, I told them, and neither does anyone else. None of the professors at the Studium could explain it. According to them, it's not possible. All I know is, I can see my way into someone's head—literally, I stare at him hard, and the wall of his skull seems to melt away, and then it seems to me that I'm standing in a library. On three sides of me there are shelves, floor to ceiling, spaced about nine inches apart; on the shelves are thousands and thousands of scrolls of parchment, like in the Old Library at Marshand. Each scroll is in a brass cylinder, with a number and the first line of the text embossed on the cap. Don't ask me how, but I know what's in each one. I reach out my hand—I actually have to lift my arm and reach out physically—and it seems to me that I pull down the scroll I want from the shelf and unscrew the cap; then I walk over to the window (there's always a window) because the light's better there, and there's a chair. I sit down and unroll the scroll and look at it, at which point the memory becomes mine, just exactly as though it had happened to me. Then I roll up the scroll and put it under my arm; the moment I've done that, the whole illusion fades, I'm back where I started, and no time has passed. The memory stays in my head, but the client or the victim will have forgotten it completely and forever; won't even remember that he ever had that memory to begin with, if you see what I mean. Anyway, I said, that's what I do. That's all I can do. But I'm the only man alive who can do it, and as far as I know, nobody's ever been able to do it before.

The old man was dead quiet for maybe five heartbeats, and his face was frozen. And you do this for money? he said.

I nodded. For a great deal of money, yes.

I could see he didn't believe me. That's pretty remarkable, he said, and it does sound quite a lot like magic. Is there any way—?

I can prove it? I gave him my unsettling grin. Sure, I said. I can't prove it to you, of course, but I can prove it, to someone else who you trust. I'll have to damage you a bit, I'm afraid. Up to you.

He actually went pale when I said that. He asked me to explain, so I did. I told him, think of a memory you share with someone else. I'll take that memory out of your head. Then I'll describe it, and the person you shared it with will confirm that it's authentic. Of course, you'll have forgotten it forever, so please choose something you don't particularly value.

He gave me that horrified look. You're sure you don't read minds, he said. I told him, I was sure. Can't be done, I told him. Not possible.

Well, he whispered with the young man for a moment or so, and then he told me about an afternoon in early autumn, twenty years ago. A boy falls out of an apple tree and cuts his forehead. He starts crying, and the noise disturbs an old black sow asleep in the shade; the sow jumps up and trots away snorting; the boy stops crying and laughs.

I recited what he'd told me back to him, slowly and carefully. He gives me a worried grin. Will it hurt? He's joking. I nod, tell him I'm afraid so, yes. Before he can answer, I'm inside his head.

(This is where I'm uncertain. What I see, every time I go through, is always the same. It's very much like the Old Library at the Studium, except that the shelves are a much darker wood—oak, I think, rather than red cedar—and the window is to the left, not the right, and the ceiling has plaster moldings, but vine and grape clusters rather than geometric patterns, and the line of the floorboards is north-south, not east-west. Maybe it's just that my mind has taken the Old Library as a sort of template and embellished it a bit, and that's what I'd prefer to believe. Another explanation, however, has occurred to me. What if someone else once found themselves in this place I go to, and it made such an impression on him that when he got given the job of designing the Old Library, he based his design on what he'd once seen?)

The usual. I always know which scroll to pick, which is just as well, because although there's writing on the scroll-caps, it's in letters I can't read, though I do believe I've seen something similar before, on a worn old stone somewhere; anyhow, they're no help at all. I grab the scroll, undo the cap, tease out the parchment with thumbnail and forefinger; over to the chair, sit down; a boy falls out of an apple tree—ah yes, I remember it as though it were yesterday. There are dark clouds in the sky and I can smell the rain that's just about to fall. I tread on a windfall apple and it crunches under my foot. The cut on the boy's head is on the left side, about an inch long. I feel contempt, because he's crying. I roll up the parchment, and—

It does hurt the client, so I'm told. Not as bad as amputation or childbirth, but much worse than having a tooth pulled.

The old man had gone white, and was leaning back in his chair as though he'd been spread on it, like butter on bread. I ignored him. I turned to the young man and described the memory, slowly, in exact detail, stuff that wasn't in the old man's summary. His eyes opened very wide and he nodded.

You sure? I asked him. Quite sure, he said. That's just how I remember it.

I'd left out the contempt. I have my faults, but I'm not a bad person really.

I turned to the old man. He looked blank. I don't remember that at all, he said.

Indeed. Memory is such a slippery thing, don't you think? You think you remember something clear as daylight, but then it turns out you've been wrong all along; it was autumn, not winter, the horse was brown, not white, there were two men, not three, you heard the door slam after he came out, not before. Unreliable; but my unreliable memory is good enough to get you condemned to death in a court of law, provided I sound convincing and nobody spots the inconsistencies. And, furthermore, after a while memory is all there is—once a city stood here, or hereabouts; once there was a man called such-and-such who did these glorious or deplorable things; once your people slaughtered my people and drove them out of their own country. Only forget, and who's to say any of it ever happened? What's forgotten might as well never have existed.

Think of that. If there are no witnesses, did it really ever happen?

You know, of course. Even after the last witness has died, you still remember what you did.

That's why you need me.

So I told them my terms of business. I remember the expression on the old man's face when I got specific about money. The young man gave him an oh-for-crying-out-loud look, and he pulled himself together. You must be a rich man by now, the old man said. I just grinned.

Right then, I said, tell me what you want.

The old man hesitated. Just a minute, he said. You can take the memory out of someone's head, fine. So, do you remember it?

Of course, I told him. I just proved that.

Yes, he said, but afterwards. Does it stick or just fade away?

I kept my face straight. It sticks, I said. I have one of those special memories, I told him. Show me a page of figures, just a quick glance; five years later, I can recite it all perfectly. I remember everything.

He didn't like that one little bit. So I pay you to get rid of one witness, and in his place I get another one. With perfect recall. That's not a good deal.

I scowled at him. Total confidence, I said. I never tell. I'd rather die.

Sure, he said. You say that now. But what if someone gets hold of you and tortures you? They can make anybody talk, sooner or later.

I sighed. Oddly enough, I said, you're not the first person to think of that. Trust me, it's not a problem. It just isn't.

He was looking extremely unhappy, but I couldn't be bothered with all that. Take it or leave it, I said. That's how I do business. If you don't like it, don't hire me. I couldn't care less.

The young man leant across and whispered something in his ear. He whispered back. I could tell they were within an ace of getting really angry with each other. I made a big show of yawning.

The old man straightened his back and glowered at me. We'll trust you, he said. It's like this.

Believe me, I've heard it all, seen it all. I remember it all. Everything. If you can imagine it, I've got it tucked away in the back of my mind somewhere, vivid as if it were yesterday, sharp and clear as if I were standing there. Murder, rape, every kind of physical injury, every variation and subspecies of the malicious, the perverted, the degrading, the despicable; sometimes as victim, sometimes as perpetrator, surprisingly often as both. And, given the slippery nature of memory, does that mean I've actually suffered those things, *done* those things? Might as well have. Close enough, good enough. Do I wake up screaming at night? Well, no. Not since I learned how to distill poppies.

Turned out all they wanted me to fix was some trivial little fraud. There were two sets of accounts for the Temple charitable fund, and by mistake the younger man had let the auditor see the wrong ledger. No big deal. The auditor had told the old man, thirty per cent and I'll forget I ever saw anything.

I was relieved. The way they'd been carrying on, I expected a triple murder at the very least. I remembered to look grave and professional. I can handle that for you, I told them. But—

But?

I smiled. The price just went up, I said. And then I explained; as well as a really good memory, I'm blessed with an aptitude for mental arithmetic. If they were stewards of the White Temple charitable fund and they stood to save thirty per cent of their depredations through my intervention, the very least I could charge them was double the original estimate.

The old man looked shocked. So much dishonesty and bad faith in this world, his face seemed to say. That wasn't an estimate, he said, it was a fixed fee. You fixed it.

I grinned. It was an estimate, I said. Maybe your memory's playing tricks on you.

We haggled. In the end, we settled on three times the original estimate. When I haggle, I haggle rough.

They hadn't asked how I would go about doing it. They never do.

Actually, it was a piece of cake. The auditor was a priest, and it's easy as pie to get a few moments alone with a priest. You go to confession.

"Bless me, Father," I said, "for I have sinned."

A moment's silence from the other side of the curtain. Then: "Go on," he said.

"I have things on my conscience," I said. "Terrible things."

"Tell me."

Oh, boy. Where to start? "Father," I said, "do we need to have this curtain? I don't feel right, talking to a bit of cloth."

I'd surprised him. "It's not a requirement," he said mildly. "In fact, it's there to make it easier for you to speak freely."

"I'd rather see who I'm talking to, if that's all right," I said.

So he pulled the curtain back. He had pale blue eyes. He was a nice old man.

I looked straight at him. "If I close my eyes," I said, "I can see it just as it happened."

"Tell me."

"If I tell you, will it go away?"

He shook his head. "But you'll know you've been forgiven," he said. "That's what counts."

So I told him, a round half-dozen memories. I think one of them was actually one of mine. He kept perfectly still. I think he'd forgotten to breathe. When I stopped talking, he said, "You did that?"

"I remember it as though it were yesterday."

"My son—" he said, and then words must have failed him. I could see he was suffering. I'm no angel, but I couldn't see any point in crucifying the old boy any further. I did the stare, and there I was inside his head, and it's never easy but these days it's nice and quick. I got what I came for, along with everything I'd just said to him, and then we were sitting opposite and he had this blank look on his face—

"Father?" I said.

He blinked twice. "My son," he said. I felt sorry for him. He'd just come round out of a daze, with no idea of who I was or why the curtain was drawn. "Well?" I said.

"Say six *sempiternas* and a *sacramentum in parvo*," he replied, without turning a hair. "And don't do it again."

I admire a professional. "Thank you, Father," I said, and left.

My family and I never quite saw eye to eye. You know how it is. They had strong views about morality and duty and the reason why we're here; so did I, but they didn't coincide all that often. My family gradually came to the conclusion that they didn't like me very much. I can sympathize. As I think I've said, I'm no angel. Of course the faults weren't all on one side, they never are. But most of them were on mine. No point in denying that.

I remember how it all started. My sister and I were on our way back from town; we'd been sent to take five fleeces to the mill, but instead of hurrying straight back like we'd been told, we hung around until it was nearly dark. That meant we'd be late, a very serious crime, unless we took the forbidden short cut through Hanger copse—so naturally, that's what we did, and we made good time. We were through the thick of the wood and coming out into the fields. There was no path in Hanger, so there were places where you had to make your own way by pushing through. I ducked under this spindly little copper beech and bent a low branch out of the way;

I remember telling myself, don't let go of the branch or it'll spring back and smack her in the eye. Then it occurred to me that letting go and smacking her in the face would be a good joke (I was, what, nine, ten years old) so I did just that. I didn't look round. I heard this terrible scream.

The stupid branch had hit her in the eye all right. It was all blood, welling up and pumping out of this impossible hole in her face. Then she covered it with her hands, still yelling. I realized what I'd done. I felt—well, you can imagine. Actually, no, you can't.

"Stop yelling," I said. "It's only a scratch. Here, let me look."

She shied away, like the calf you can't catch. "You did it on purpose."

"Don't be stupid."

"You did it on purpose. I know. I saw you."

I hate the truth sometimes. "I didn't," I said. "It was an accident. I'm sorry. It wasn't my fault."

You can't really lie to someone who knows the facts. She'd seen me; holding back the branch just long enough to give her the impression it was safe to take the next step forward, then opening my hand, relaxing my grip, like an archer loosing an arrow, deliberate, precise, accurate. She'd witnessed it, she understood what I'd done, and she was going to tell on me.

I remember stooping down. There was this stone. You could kill someone with a stone like that.

"I can't see," she said. "You did it on purpose. You did."

I think I would have killed her, there and then. I was looking at her, I remember, not as my sister, a human being, but as a target—just there, I'd decided, above the ear; that's where the old man in the village got kicked by the horse, and he died just like that. I was staring at the exact spot; and then the side of her head seemed to melt away—

And that's a curious thing, because at that age I'd never seen a library, never even seen a book; heard of them, vaguely, like you've heard of elephants, but no idea what they looked like or how you used them. Goes without saying, I couldn't read. But I could; at least, I could read the books inside her head, well enough to find what I needed, the moment when I let go of the bent branch and it came swinging at her, filling her field of vision and blotting it out in red. I knew what to do, too. It came perfectly naturally, like milking a goat or killing a chicken. Like I'd been doing it all my life.

"Are you all right?" I said.

"My face hurts," she sobbed. "I can't see."

"What happened?"

"A branch jumped back and hit me in the eye."

"I'm sorry. I'm so sorry."

"Not your fault."

I remembered I was still holding the stone. I opened my fingers and let it drop. "It'll be all right," I remember telling her. "We'll get you home and then it'll all be just fine. You'll see."

It turned out that I was the hero of that story. They couldn't save the eye, of course. It was too far gone. But everyone said how well I'd handled the situation, how calm I was, how grown-up and sensible. And what the hell: why not? The bad thing had already happened, it was gone, past repair. If the truth had come out, it'd have torn our family apart, just think of all the damage it'd have done, to all of us, right down the line forever. There's too much unhappiness in the world as it is.

Anyhow, I think that was me. Pretty sure.

After all, what is truth but the consensus of memories of reliable witnesses? I think He (the fire-god, the Invincible Sun, whoever, whatever; I've had so many genuine mystical experiences, all totally convincing, most of them hopelessly contradictory) put me on this Earth as a sort of antidote to the truth—you know, like dock leaves and nettles. Under certain circumstances, I can do this amazing thing. I can reshape the past. I can erase truth. It sounds pretentious, but I regard it as my mission in life. Truth is like love; it's universally lauded and admired, and most of the time it just causes pain and makes trouble for people. Obviously, I can't be there for everybody, and there are some things so big and blatantly obvious that I can't do anything about them—the Second Social War, for example, or the Great Plague. But I stand for the wonderful revelation that the past is not immutable and the truth is not absolute. This ought to inspire people and give them hope. It doesn't, of course, because the essence of my work is that nobody knows about it, apart from the people who commission me (and half of them don't remember doing so, for obvious reasons), and they ain't telling.

The memory of a priest, however, is a real bitch. People confess to priests. I guess being a priest is the closest anybody normal ever gets to being me. They have to open their minds and their memories to all the poisonous waste of Mankind—imagine being a priest with a memory like mine, it'd kill you. They have their faith, of course, which is a wonderful thing. It must be like those gravel beds they build in watercourses, to filter out all the crap. Breaking into a priest's memory is, therefore, not something I enjoy.

Now I think I've given you the impression that I'm rather better at my job than I really am. I've let you think that I go in, get precisely what I want, and get out again, completely unaware of and unaffected by anything else that might be in there. If only. True, I only read—well, the titles of the scrolls, the list of contents, the index. That's bad enough. Each entry in the ledger (I'm beginning to realize how inadequate my library metaphor is; sorry) embodies a minuscule but intensely compressed summary. Your eye rests on it for a split second, and immediately you get the gist of it. I can skim down the average man's lifetime of memories in the time it takes you to read a page of your household accounts. But every entry is like a tiny, incredibly detailed picture, and I have (so to speak) exceptional eyesight.

Furthermore, some memories leak. They're so bright and sharp and vivid that they stand out, your eye's drawn to them, you can't help looking at them. I try and mind my own business, of course I do, but some things—

Like the men who murder their wives and the women who murder their children, the men who poison wells and kill whole towns, the rapists and the sadists and the broad rainbow spectrum of human maladjustment; and they go to their priests to get rid of it, and the priests take away the sins of the world and file them in their archives, and then I come along. I really don't like doing priests. It's like walking barefoot through a dark room with broken glass on the floor. Oh, and I did that once, or someone did. No fun at all.

I went to where I was supposed to be meeting them. The young man was there; no sign of the old man. He was sitting on a bench in front of the Blue Star Temple, reading a book. He looked up as my shadow fell across the page. "Well?" he said.

"All done."

He frowned at me, as though I were a spelling mistake. "How do I know that?"

I get tired sometimes. "You don't. Instead, you trust me and my colossal reputation among respected leaders of the community."

"You'll be wanting your money."

"Yes."

He moved his feet, and I saw a fat leather satchel. "You lunatic," I said. "I can't walk home carrying that. I wouldn't get a hundred yards."

"I got here just fine."

"You don't live where I do."

He shrugged. "Your problem," he said. "Well? Do you want to count it?"

I smiled at him. "People don't double-cross me," I said. "They simply wouldn't dare."

An unpleasant thought must have crossed his mind just then. "No, I don't suppose they would. Anyway, it's all there."

I leaned forward to take hold of the strap but he shifted his feet again. "We can trust you, can't we?"

"Of course."

"I mean," he went on, "we're not killers, my dad and I, or we'd have had that old fool's head bashed in. But there comes a point where you have to look beyond your principles, don't you know. I just thought I'd mention that."

I put the back of my hand against his calf and moved it sideways. Then I pulled the satchel out. It was reassuringly heavy. "Don't worry," I said. "I'm an honorable man."

"Really."

I stood up. I remember thinking: no, don't do it, there's no call for that sort of behavior. "And I do try to give value for money," I said. "I want my customers to think they've got what they paid for. It's good for business."

"Right. Well, goodbye."

"So if I sense that a customer isn't satisfied," I went on, "I throw in something extra, for goodwill. He's not your father."

His eyes were very wide. "You what? What did you say?"

"Goodbye."

Actually, I was lying, though of course he had no way of knowing that. So what? He asked for it. The truly splendid, insidious thing about it is, when his father and mother eventually die and only he is left, the last surviving witness to those events, it *will be* true—in his mind, the only archive. So you see, I can create truth as well as delete it. Clever old me.

Several of my clients, misguided souls who thought they wanted to get to know me better, have asked me how I got into this line of work in the first place. I tell them I can't remember.

There was this spot of trouble when I was seventeen. As I my have mentioned, I'm no angel. There was a small difficulty, and I had to leave home in rather a hurry. Luckily, it was a dark night and the people looking for me didn't know the countryside around our place as well as I did; their dogs were rubbish, too. I took the precaution of bringing along the clothes I'd been wearing the previous day and stuffing them inside a hollow tree I knew I'd be passing on the way out, so to speak. Fortuitously, it stood on the banks of the river. Stupid dogs all crowded round the tree, jumping up and yelling their heads off, while I swam upstream a bit, hopped out, and went on my way rejoicing. The men who were after me were livid, as you can imagine—I wasn't there to see, of course, but I remember the looks on their faces quite clearly. Gave me the best laugh I'd had in ages.

Still, once the warm inner glow of profound cleverness had worn off, I reflected on my position and found it largely unsatisfactory. There I was, sopping wet, one angel thirty to my name, no place to go, no friends, no identity. Naturally, I wasn't the first person in history to find himself in that state. After all, that's how cities came about in the first place; it's what they're for.

The nearest city was only twenty miles away. I knew it quite well, so it was useless; somebody would recognize me, and word would get about. My angel thirty would've been just enough to buy me a seat on the stage to the next city down the coast, but I decided not to risk it, since coachmen sometimes remember names and faces. As things had turned out, I'd left home in a pair of wooden-soled hemp slippers, the kind you wear for slopping about the house in. There wasn't much left of them by the time I dared risk stopping and thinking. They certainly weren't in a fit state to carry me eighty miles on bad roads, assuming I was prepared to take the chance of staying on the road, which I wasn't. Remember when you could buy a decent pair of boots for an angel thirty? You could back then, but first you have to find a shoemaker, for which you need a city. One damn thing after another.

I find that when you're in a deep pit of doubt and perplexity, Fate jumps in and provides you with an answer, almost invariably the wrong one. As in this case. First thing I saw when the sun rose was a farmhouse, practically rearing up on its hind legs at me out of the early morning mist. I thought: there'll be boots in there. I'll walk up to the door and offer to buy a pair. Easy as that.

Idiot. A stranger hobbling up out of nowhere wanting to buy footwear would tend to snag in the memory, particularly out in the wild, where nothing ever happens. I had good reason to wish not to be memorable. The hell with it, I thought. I was by now more or less resigned to the fact that I'm no angel; what's one more minor transgression? Be a man. Steal the stupid boots.

Sad fact. It's not enough to be a thief. You need to be a good thief. I'm not. My problem is, I don't look where I'm going. I try, ever so hard; but sooner or later there'll be a chair or a table or a tin plate or a bowl of apples that I somehow contrive to overlook. Crash it goes on the hard flagstone floor, and that's that. Here we go again.

The farmer was an old man, feeble, with a bad leg. I could've taken him easily. His son and his four grandsons were a different matter. What they were doing, hanging around the house when the sun was well up and they should've been out grafting, I have no idea. They didn't approve of thieves. There was an apple tree just outside the back door, with a low branch sticking out practically at a right angle. They had, they assured me, plenty of rope, not to mention a dung heap. And besides, they said, who'd miss me?

The human memory is a wonderful thing. They say that when you die, at the moment of departure, your entire life flashes past your eyes in a fraction of a second. This isn't actually true; but all sorts of stuff crowds into your mind when you're standing on the bed of a cart with a rope round your neck; among them, in my case, the circumstances of my sister's accident. To be honest, I hadn't given it much thought in the intervening time—tried to put it out of my mind, I guess, and who can blame me?—but it came right back to me at that precise moment, and I remember thinking, I wish I could do that trick where I went into her mind and pulled the memory out, it'd be really useful right now if I could do that. And suddenly I found I could.

False modesty aside, it was a tour de force. Six men and five women, one after the other, in a matter of seconds. I've done bigger jobs since, but that's with the benefit of considerable experience. For what was only my second go at it, I did remarkably well. Incentive helps, of course. It wasn't the neatest work I ever did, I had to hurt them quite a lot—like I cared—the pain kept them off balance and sort of woozy, which helped considerably. When I'd finished, we were left with this tableau; a kid standing on a cart under the apple tree, with six men and five women crowded round. No rope, I'd chucked that into the nettles. How we all got there, a total mystery to everybody except me.

I cleared my throat. I think my voice must've been a bit high and croaky, but I did my best. "Well, thanks for that," I remember saying. "I'd better be getting along."

One of the grandsons helped me down off the cart. He had a sort of dazed look. I took a long stride, and felt the dewy wet grass under my feet. "I almost forgot," I said. "The boots."

The old man looked at me. "What?"

"The boots," I repeated. "Really kind of you." He was still holding them in his hand; evidence, I guess. I reached out, took them, and pulled them on. Lousy fit, but what can you do? "Thanks again," I said, and walked quickly away. You learn not to look back. It takes some doing, but it's worth the effort.

I'm not the sort of man that people tend to remember. Just look at me and you'll agree. I'm about five seven, thickset, small nose, small ears, low forehead, leg-of-pork forearms, the typical farm boy up from the country. I slip out of people's minds as easily as a wriggling fish. People hardly notice me, in the street, in a crowded room. Most of the time, I might as well not be there.

Remember what I told you about why I don't like doing priests? For three days afterwards, I wandered around feeling useless and stupid, like having a headache but without the pain. I knew there was something on my mind, but I couldn't figure out what it was. I filled the time in with chores. I bought a new (to me) pair of boots. I fixed the leak in the roof—at that time I was living in the roofspace above a grain store; one wall had cracked and was bulging out in a disturbing fashion, so it was empty until the owners raised the money to repair it; the rats had the ground floor, I had the penthouse. I mended both my shirts where they'd started to fray. Stuff like that.

And then, on my way to the market early, to see if I could buy some windfall apples cheap, I met a man I knew slightly. I pretended I hadn't seen him. He called out my name. I stopped.

"Long time no see," he said.

"I've been busy," I told him.

He nodded. "Working?"

"Yes."

"Splendid. Get paid?"

"Yes."

"In funds, then."

I sighed a little sigh. "Yes."

"Destiny," he said, and grinned. "Back of the Sincerity & Trust, one hour after sunset. Be there."

I walked away without saying a word.

I sometimes wonder if I'm like that hero in the old legends whose strength was as the strength of ten, but only as long as the sun was in the sky. In my case, strength of will. All that day, while the Invincible Sun rode the heavens, blessing us poor mortals with the sacrament of His light, I was utterly determined. I wasn't going. No force on Earth would get me within a mile of the Sincerity until noon tomorrow. Throughout the morning I felt the power within me grow; at midday, I was solid as a rock. I stayed that way till halfway through the afternoon, and as the shadows began to lengthen I kept checking up on myself, to see if my strength of purpose was going to hold out—and it did, right up till the first red streaks began to show in the sky. I don't know, maybe I'm more like a werewolf or something like that. Maybe it's the darkness that affects me, or more precisely the yellow glow of lighted windows. They call to me; come inside, they say, where it's warm and friendly. I noticed to my surprise that I was only two blocks from the Sincerity. The light was fading rapidly. I quickened my pace and walked the other way.

I believe it happens a lot in deserts. You walk and walk and keep on walking, and suddenly you realize you've gone in a circle and you're back where you started from. In this case, just across the street from the back door of the Sincerity at one hour after sunset.

About half of them I knew, if only slightly. The usual crowd. They'd already started. A tall, thin elderly man I didn't know had the dice. He was trying to make six. A man I knew well tapped me on the shoulder, nodded, and said, "Bet?"

I shook my head. "Just here to watch."

He laughed. "Ten angels. I'll give you five to one."

"Bet."

The thin old man made his six. My ten angels had become fifty. I nearly always start off with a win.

So there I was, at dawn the next day, considerably poorer than the day I was born, but blessed with a useful skill with which I could earn money. Just as well, really.

I remembered that I had an appointment to see a prospective customer. I headed back home, washed, shaved, put on my clean shirt and my new boots. I'll say this for myself, I've got this gambling thing well under control now. As soon as I run out of money, I stop; I never ever play with markers or get into debt. Someone once told me I gamble so as to get rid of all the money I make. There may be something in that. If I'd kept what I've made over the years, right now I'd have more money than the government.

Disgustingly bright and early (I'm not a morning person) I walked out into Cornmarket, heading west. On the corner of Sheep Street and Coppergate I realized someone was following me. I didn't look 'round. I guess I'd detected him by the way his footsteps kept perfect time with my own—it sounds a bit paranoid, but I have experience in these matters, believe me. I did my best not to do anything that would let him know I'd noticed him.

I had two options. Either I could keep to the main streets, where there were plenty of people, or I could lead him off the beaten track down into the little dark alleys between Coppergate and Lower Town, where I stood a reasonable chance of losing him or jumping him. Like a fool, I chose the latter. In my defense, I would like to point out that I have the memories of God only knows how many fights, together comprising a better combat education that you'd get in any military academy anywhere. I know about that sort of thing.

Rather too much, in fact. Out back of the carpet warehouse in Tanners Yard there's an old gateway with two massive pillars; I'd noticed it a long time ago, with just such a contingency in mind. I led him there, ducked in between the pillars, and vanished. He stopped and looked round to see where I'd gone. As soon as his back was turned, I was on him like the proverbial snake.

The law in these parts disapproves of carrying weapons of any sort in public places, but since when is three feet of waxed string a weapon? Answer: when you slip it over a man's head, cross the ends over at the base of his neck, and pull hard. My trouble is, I don't know my own strength.

I was so stunned and disgusted with myself that I was almost too late to get inside his head before all the lights went out. It was a scramble. I know from experience, it's not pleasant to be in there when someone dies. I had just enough time to grab what I wanted and run.

Sure enough (I stood over him, looking down); he'd been hired by one of my satisfied customers, for five angels. I ask you, five angels. It's about time the hired killers in this town got organized.

Well, it's inevitable. When I consume the memory of the last surviving witness, I become the last surviving witness, and there's nobody to clear out my head cleanly and humanely. You can't blame them; I don't. My set scale of fees includes a levy, to cover the inconvenience and mental trauma of monotonously regular attempts on my life.

But I don't hold it against my clients. I can't afford to.

When you've been inside someone's head, you know him, intimately; what he looks like is substantially irrelevant and uninteresting. I turned him over with my foot. Age thirty-five (I already knew that), the big, hollow frame of an ex-soldier who hasn't been eating too well lately. He had red hair and blue eyes. So what?

I always reckon that you gain something from pretty well every experience, however bad it may be. From him (whoever he was) I took away a picture of dawn in the Claygess Mountains, a rapturous explosion of light, blue skies, green fir trees, and snow. Just thinking of it makes me feel clean. That and a move whereby, when someone's behind you and strangling you, a slight rearrangement of the feet and shift of your center of balance enables you to throw them over your shoulder like a sack of feathers. If he'd remembered it a trifle earlier, he'd probably have made it. Ah, well.

By a curious coincidence, the man who'd hired him to kill me was the man I was on my way to meet. He was surprised to see me.

"You said you had a job for me," I said.

"Changed my mind."

"Ah." I nodded slowly. "In that case, there's just the matter of my consultancy fee."

He looked at me. Sometimes I think I'm not the only one who can see inside people's heads. "Fine," he said. "How much?"

"Five hundred angels."

He licked his lips. "Five hundred."

"Yes."

"Draft? On the Gorgai brothers? I haven't got that much in cash."

I know the Gorgai brothers better than they know themselves. "All right," I said.

I stood over him while he wrote, then thanked him politely and left. I felt happy; I was back in the money again. Happiness in this world is by definition a transitory state, and two small tumbling ivory cubes put me back where I'd started from twelve hours later, but at least I had the memory of being rich, for a little while. Only memory endures. I learned that the hard way.

Two days later I had another client, a genuine one who paid. It was a something-and-nothing job, really rather touching; he was fifty-six and rich and wanted to marry again, but there was this one memory of his dead wife that really broke him up, and could I help? Of course. To me, it was just an image of a moderately pretty girl in old-fashioned clothes arranging flowers, in a bay window in an old house in the country. When I'd finished he gave me that blank look: *I know who you are and why you're here, but I have no idea why it was so important.* It sort of offends me that when I do my best work, the customer hasn't a clue how much I've done for him. It's like painting a masterpiece for a blind patron.

I distinctly remember the next time I met the old man and his son.

I was fast asleep, and then I hit the floor and woke up. The last time I fell out of bed, I was four (I remember it well).

I opened my eyes, and saw a ring of faces looking down at me. Two of them I recognized. The old man said, "Get him up."

Two of the other faces grabbed my arms and hauled me upright. They were strong and not very gentle. I know half a dozen ways of dealing with a situation like that, but those memories came from men twice my weight, and besides, I wasn't in the mood.

"You betrayed us," the old man said.

I was stunned. "Me? God, no, I'd never do a thing like that. Never."

For that I got a fist like oak in my solar plexus. "Who did you tell?" the old man asked. Stupid. I couldn't answer, because I had no breath in my body. "Who did you tell?" the old man repeated. I tried to breathe in, but I was all blocked up inside. I saw him nod, and someone hit me again. "What did you do with the money you stole from us?"

I shook my head. "I never stole from you, I wouldn't dare." Then someone threw a rope over the crossbeam of the rafters directly overhead. *Oh*, I thought.

"One more time," the old man said. "Who did you tell?"

I couldn't speak, so I mouthed the word: *nobody*. Someone behind me dropped the noose over my head.

"Get on with it," the old man said. I tried to think of something to say, a lie, something he'd want to hear, but—here's an interesting fact for you. When you're winded so bad you can't breathe, you can't lie, your imagination simply blanks out and making stuff up is impossible, you just can't do it. You don't have the strength, simple as that.

Someone hauled on the rope. I felt my feet lift off the ground. I felt this excruciating pain. And then—

But I'm getting ahead of myself.

This clerk came to see me, a boy, seventeen at most, with a long turkey neck and big ears. He worked for them, the old man and his son. They were pleased with the job I'd done for them, and would I help them out with another little problem? You'll recall that I was broke again at this point. Depends what it is, I replied. The clerk said he didn't know the details, but to meet them outside the Flawless Diamonds of Orthodoxy at third watch that evening. What about the curfew? I asked. The boy just grinned nervously and gave me a piece of paper. It was a draft on the Merchant Union, two hundred angels.

"He betrayed us," the old man told me. It was dark and bitter cold, and I'd come out without my scarf (now I come to think of it, I'd traded my scarf for a loaf of bread). "He'll deny it, of course. He'd rather die than tell. That's what we need you for."

The rest you know. They picked the lock and we all trooped up the stairs quiet as little mice; they woke him up by pulling him out of bed onto the floor. He claimed he was innocent and hadn't betrayed them or stolen from them, not a bent stuiver. After a while, they threw a rope over a rafter and hung him. I was inside his mind when he died. He'd been telling the truth. He was a lawyer, by the way, acting for the Temple oversight committee.

"Well?" the old man asked me.

"Nothing," I told him. "He was telling the truth. He didn't betray you. He didn't steal anything." I paused. "I could've told you that anyhow. There was no need—"

I got frowned at for that, so I shut up. Customers always think they know best. "You sure?"

"Positive," I said. "If he'd had that on his mind, I'd have seen it. But there wasn't anything."

I got the feeling he didn't believe me. Stupid. Why would I lie? Well, obviously, if I meant to blackmail them or sell them out to their enemies, but I wouldn't do that, because it'd be unprofessional. I may be no angel but I have standards. Of course, they had no way of knowing that.

"Get out," the old man said. "And keep yourself available. We may want you again."

"You've just made me accessory to a murder," I said. "I'm not pleased about that."

He shook his head. "Not murder," he said. "Suicide. And don't you ever talk back to me. Got that?"

I considered the evidence of my own eyes. There's this man, hanging from a rafter. The only chair in the room is lying on its side, right under his dangling feet. No sign of forced entry, or anyway, there won't be, ten minutes from now. Sure looks like suicide, and the only evidence to the contrary is a memory. "Point taken," I said. It's amazing how many people construe that as *yes*. "Suicide," I said. "Silly me. I'll go now."

"Hold on." The younger man was looking at me. "Before he goes, he can make himself useful."

The old man looked at him; he was nodding stupidly at the hired men. Oh, come on, I thought, there's six of them. "That's a point," the old man said.

"You can't afford it," I told him.

He grinned at me. "Reduced rate for quantity. Or you could be feeling really depressed and sad."

Oh, I thought. Sad enough to jump off the Haymarket Bridge, and (as the man said) who would miss me? Fair enough. "Tell you what," I said. "This one's on the house."

The young man grinned. The old man said he wouldn't hear of it. The laborer is worthy of his hire. So I did all six of them for fifteen angels each.

Not that it mattered all that much. Forty-eight hours later I was broke again.

The point being; I died in that room. I know I did, because I remember it clear as day.

I died, but here I am. Explain that, if you can. Simple. I died, and I was born again, just like it says in the Testament. Proof positive. I have difficulty with the faith aspect of it, but the plain facts admit of no other explanation. Blessed are those who have seen and yet have believed.

We call them the Temple trustees and everybody knows who we mean, but their proper name is the Guardians of the Perpetual Fund for the Proliferation of Orthodoxy. They're serious men, and they own all the best grazing land from the Hog's Back right out to the Blackwater, as well as half the prime real estate in the Capital and a whole lot of other nice things, all of which came into the possession of the Fund through the bequests and endowments of former Guardians. The income from these assets is divided between the Commissioners of the Fabric, who maintain and improve the Temple buildings throughout the empire, and the Social Fund, which pays for the soup kitchens and the way stations and the diocesan free schools, not to mention the traveling doctors and the Last Chance advocates who defend prisoners on capital charges who haven't got the money to hire a real lawyer. I seem to remember someone telling me that about a third of the wealth of the empire passes through the trustees' hands, and that the trustees themselves are chosen from the select few who have the brains to do the job and so much money of their own that they have no possible incentive to steal; in fact, you have to pay an annual fee equivalent to the cost of outfitting and maintaining a regiment in the field in order to belong to the College of Guardians, and there's a waiting list a mile long. It's probably quite true. When you're that rich, money is just a way of keeping score.

That was the sort of people I was dealing with; rich, powerful men, peers of the gods, the sort who make and alter truth—What is truth? Truth is what you know, if you're one of them. Truth is what you own. If the whim takes you, you can say, "On the banks of the Blackwater there's a city constructed entirely of marble." Actually, no, there isn't. "Oh, yes, there is. I had it built, last week." Or: "There never was a war between the Blemyans and the Aram Chantat." You go to the Temple library to look up the references to refute this idiotic statement, and all the relevant books are missing all the relevant pages. Or: "Who? There's no such person." Indeed. Men like gods who can ordain the future, regulate the present, and amend the past—pretty well everything worthwhile that ever happened in history was done by men like that; they built cities, instituted trade and manufacture, fostered the sciences and the arts, and endowed charities. *Let it be so*, they said, and it was so. And, quite rightly, what they paid for, they own: the freeholds, the equity. And us. Without them, we'd be dressed in animal skins and living in caves. I believe in them, the way I believe in the Invincible Sun—which is to say, I acknowledge their existence, and their authority, and their power. Doesn't mean I have to like them. Or Him, for that matter.

When I was nineteen, not long after I left home, I met this girl. I can close my eyes and picture her exactly, as though Euxis the Mannerist had painted her on the inside of my eyelids. Not that Euxis would've accepted the commission, since he only ever painted incarnations of perfection, absolute physical beauty—and she was hardly that. Pretty, yes, but—my mother had a saying, *she's prettier than she looks*. And anyway, Euxis wasn't all that good. He couldn't do hands worth spit.

The good thing about the way she looked was that she inspired no interest in the handsome, rich, charming young men who could've taken her away from me just by noticing her. Don't get me wrong, she wasn't that sort of girl, but I know perfectly well that some things are outside one's control. Beauty, of course, is one of them. Alongside the rich, in the pantheon of gods, are the beautiful. They too can change the world, a smile here, a frown there. They can inspire and kill love as easily as a rich man can endow a hospital or arrange a murder, and they do it because they can. But I worshipped her because she was no goddess, and if only there were someone else who could do what I can do, I'd pay him anything he asked for to get her out of my mind. She died, you see, and when I went down on my knees and prayed to the gods to bring her back to life, they just ignored me. Forget her, they told me, move on. I can only assume they were trying to be funny. Anyhow, I won't forget that in a hurry, believe me.

My next job for the old man and his son was quick, easy, and safe, or so they told me. A business associate of theirs was to be entrusted with certain sensitive information in order to carry out a certain confidential transaction on their behalf. Once the deal had been done, I was to remove the whole episode from his memory. He had (they told me) been fully informed about my special abilities, and had readily agreed to the procedure. He would just sit there, perfectly still and quiet, while I did my thing. In spite of this, I would be paid the same fee I'd received for more arduous work.

At the time I was not well off for money, as a result of some unsatisfactory experiments into certain aspects of probability theory. One of the worst things about poverty is that when people like the old man call on you, you're actually glad to see them. Delighted, I told them, and thank you for your valued custom. They told me a time and a place. I promised I'd be there, and went away to wash my other shirt, because a smart appearance creates a good impression.

If they're worth the money, you don't notice them, not until they're right on top of you and there's nothing you can do. These two—I wish I knew their names, so that I could hire them myself if I ever need any help with violence. One of them was vaguely familiar, I may have caught a glimpse of him in the street at some point over the last few days (I never forget a face) and thought nothing of it; the other one I'd never seen before in my life. They hit me with a short wooden club and dropped a sack over my head, and that was that.

When the sack came off, I barely noticed, because the room was dark. I was vaguely aware of the shape of a man not far away. I was sitting down, but my hands and feet were tied. I heard a man's voice, not the man whose shape I could just make out. It said, "This thing you do."

I waited. Someone nudged the back of my head with a sharp object. "Yes?" I said.

"The person you do it to," the voice went on. "Do they know about it?"

"It hurts," I replied. "But they don't necessarily realize it's me doing it. They may think it's a heart attack, or something like that."

"So it hurts a lot."

"Yes."

Pause for mature consideration. Then I screamed, because someone was holding a red-hot iron to the back of my neck. "As bad as that?"

It took me a moment to catch my breath. "Different sort of pain, I think," I said. "But purely in terms of quantity, about that, yes."

"Mphm." I heard movement behind me, and the cherry-red end of an iron rod appeared in front of my eyes. "Can you make it a bit less painful, if you really try hard?"

"No," I said. From a slight intake of breath, I guessed I'd said the wrong thing. "Of course, I can remove the memory of the pain. That's easy."

(A slight overstatement; like saying the sea is a bit damp. But I can do that, yes.)

"Ah." He liked me again. The red-hot iron went away, though probably only as far as a charcoal brazier. "So you can do it to someone and he won't know about it."

"Yes."

"Splendid." Slight pause. "Now, I'm going to ask you that again, and this time, if you were lying, tell the truth. You can do it to someone and he won't know?"

"Yes. You have my word."

I'd said something funny. "Fair enough," said the voice. "The word of a gentleman is always good enough for me. Now, then. You work for—" And he mentioned two names. They weren't the names I knew the old man and his son by, but I'd done a little research. "Yes," I said, and braced myself for another touch of the hot iron.

"Relax," the voice said. "I'm not going to ask you to betray confidences, I know you wouldn't do that." Pause. "Not for some time, and by then you'd be no good for anything. But I am going to ask you to do something that isn't in the best interests of your employers. I'm going to ask you to bleach something out of their minds. Would that be awkward for you, ethically speaking?"

Believe it or not, I did actually think about it before answering. Not for terribly long. "No," I said, "that wouldn't be a problem." Silence, so I expanded a little. "My duty to my client is not to divulge things he doesn't want known. That's it, as far as I'm concerned."

"Particularly if he never knows about it."

"Particularly, yes."

The voice laughed gently. "Because if nobody knows about it, it never happened. Splendid. I believe your usual charge is a thousand angels."

Wonderful, what people believe. But I have nothing against good honest faith. We could do with more of it in this world. "That's right, yes."

"Two thousand angels, since there are two of them, father and son."

I was beginning to warm to him. "That's right, yes."

"The rest of you, out." Shuffling noises. The man in front of me stood up and walked away. A door closed. "Now I'm going to tell you what I need you to remove. I know I can trust your discretion, because you're a gentleman. Listen carefully."

Burns on the back of the neck are no fun at all; every time you turn your head, you stretch them, and it hurts. Something to remember him by.

Still, two thousand angels. I lay awake (on my face; I can only get to sleep lying on my side) all that night thinking of what I could do with two thousand angels. Buy a large farm, fully stocked, and hire a good bailiff. Or invest in shipping, which is going to be the next big thing, or copper mines in Scheria (or maybe not; too much of a gamble for my taste). Give up work for good. Get rich. Become a god.

Two days to go before I next saw the old man and his son; in the meanwhile, I had a piffling little job to get out of the way. Two hundred angels practically for nothing.

He was an inoffensive old boy, well into his eighties, living in a smart house overlooking the bay—he'd been a ship's captain, and he liked to see the sails in the harbor. His servant brought me green tea in a little porcelain bowl, and some wafer-thin biscuits that tasted of honey and cinnamon. I sat on a big carved rosewood chair made for someone twice my size. It was all very civilized.

He told me about his son; a good boy, very clever, took after his mother. My client had just bought his own ship, after a lifetime of hard work and being careful with money. Naturally, he wanted his son to come and work with him, but the boy had set his heart on being a musician. He could play the flute very well (but all technique and no feeling). It was what his mother would have wanted, he kept on saying. My client was heartbroken, because the whole idea of the ship was so he could pass it on to his son and heir. There were harsh words, and the boy slammed out of the house. He got a job playing the flute in a teahouse down by the docks; and there he died, on account of slow reflexes when the furniture started to fly. I think about him every day, the old man said, and it's killing me.

Well, I thought, what do you expect? Serves you right for meddling with love. You'll get no sympathy from me. But he'd been very polite and given me a nice cup of tea, and two hundred angels was two hundred angels more than I had in the world, and I am, after all, a professional. "How can I help?" I asked.

"I want to forget him," he said. "I want to forget he was ever born."

I got up. I think I said thank you for the tea. I told him, sorry, I can't help you, I'm really sorry and I wish there was something I can do, but I can't. He accepted it quietly, like the prisoner who's pleaded guilty. Because he was such a nice old fellow, I tried really hard to keep the loathing off my face, at least until the door closed behind me.

(Sometimes I wonder, what if none of this is really me? What if—for an obscene amount of money—I was at some point hired to take over someone's entire life, from birth, every memory, the lot; and what if every memory I think is mine is really that other man's, a complete and coherent narrative, utterly vivid and real in my head, perfect and irrefutably valid, subject to corroboration and proof from external sources, except that it actually happened to somebody else? I guess it's one of those fantasies you spin to keep yourself going; like, my parents aren't really my parents, really I'm the son of a duke, stolen from his cot by tinkers, and one day my real father will turn up and claim me, and take me back to my real life, the one I should have had all along?)

On my way to meet the old man and his son, I ran into someone I knew.

By the time I saw him, it was too late for evasive action. I looked round to see if there was anyone to hear if I yelled for help—no such luck; I was taking my usual shortcut through the Caulkers' Yards. Maximum privacy. Serves me right for being too lazy to walk down Crowngate.

He smiled at me. "Been looking for you," he said.

Too big to fight, too nimble to evade. "I've got your money," I said.

"No," he said. "You haven't."

"I'll have it for you by tonight, that's a promise."

"Two angels sixteen," he said. "I want it now."

"Be reasonable," I started to say, but then he kicked me in the groin and I fell down. I twisted as I went down and landed on my shoulder, absorbing most of the impact in muscle. After a while, it becomes second nature.

"But it's all right," he said, and kicked me in the ribs. "I'm patient, I can wait." Another kick. His heart wasn't in it, though, I could tell. "Here, tonight, fourth watch. Three angels."

Of course. Interest on two angels sixteen. He's not very good at basic arithmetic, but he doesn't need to be. "No problem," I whispered. "I'll be here."

"You'd better be." He gave me a look of infinite contempt. "It's so easy for you rich bastards, never had to do a day's work in your lives. Plenty more where that came from. You think you're so much better. You make me sick." A third kick, for luck; this time with feeling. "And don't ever borrow money from me again."

I waited till he'd gone, and picked myself up slowly. It took a while. To be fair to myself, I'd only borrowed from him because he'd just won everything I had, well, everything I had left. Over the years he's had enough money out of me to pay the revenues for Moesia province, including the charcoal levy. But he dresses like trash and lives in a coal cellar. Beats me what he spends it all on.

Fortunately he'd done no irreparable visible damage. I dusted myself off and limped the rest of the way as quickly as I could manage. I'm proud to say I was on time for my appointment, in spite of everything.

My victim was a fine-looking man, about forty years old, tall and broad-shouldered, with a farmer's tan. He was reclining on a couch, with a silver goblet at his elbow and a plate of those minced-up fish nibbles in wafer-thin crispy pastry shells. He didn't stand up when I entered the room, but there was a sort of involuntary movement which told me he'd considered it before deciding it wouldn't be appropriate.

The young man was wearing one of those fashionable silk robes; it was far too big for him and, in a moment of inspiration, I realized it was one of his father's hand-me-downs. The old man was wearing quilted wool (in summer, dear God) with frayed cuffs and elbows. The rich, bless them.

"This is the man I was telling you about," the old man said. "It won't take two minutes, and it doesn't hurt."

My victim frowned beautifully. "And he won't remember anything?"

I cleared my throat, but the old man answered for me. "He remembers all right," he said, "but he won't say anything. And besides, look at him. Who'd believe him?"

Uncalled for; I was wearing my good shirt, which fortunately hadn't come to harm to anything like the same extent as I had. "I take my clients' confidences very seriously," I said. I don't think anybody heard me.

"Up to you," my victim said. "It's your risk, after all."

The young man pulled a miserable face, which got him a scowl from his father. "We might as well get on with it," the old man said.

My victim shrugged. "What do I do?"

"Nothing," the old man said. "Just sit there."

I knew exactly what to look for, so it was a nice, easy job, in and out. I confess, my mind wasn't really on it, preoccupied as I was with the job I had to do on the old man and his son immediately afterwards, which would be much harder. I remembered to wipe the memory of the pain I'd caused him—he actually yelled out loud, with his eyes shut—and then straight on to do the old man and his son, while he was recovering from the shock.

By now you should have a pretty good idea of how I operate, so I won't bore you with a blow-by-blow; we can get a bit ahead of ourselves, to the point where I was shown out into the street (not the same one I'd come in by; the servants' entrance opened onto the stable yard, which led to a long mews, which opened into a winding high-walled alley that led eventually to Haymarket). I was in a pretty good mood. I'd done a pretty spectacularly impressive job on the old man and his son, professionally speaking, one of the highlights of my career so far—if my profession had learned journals and more than one practitioner, I could have written it up in a paper and been invited to speak at seminars. I'd got out of there in one piece. And I had money. I had a draft on the Diocesan Loan from the old man, and an escrow note from my other customer which I was now clear to cash in; a vast amount of money, enough for a new beginning, a clean slate, the wherewithal to be born again, washed in the blood of the Invincible Sun. It made me smile to think I'd been beaten up only an hour earlier for a tenth of one per cent of what I now possessed. If there'd been a puddle in the alley, I'd have walked on its surface without wetting my boots.

It was bleachingly hot in Haymarket, with the sunlight reflected off the broad white marble frontages. I walked up as far as the Stooping Victory, turned left into Palace Yard, called in at the Diocesan Loan, who settled my note without giving any indication that I was visible. Then down the steps opposite the Mercury Fountain to the Stamnite Brotherhood, who confirmed that the escrow on my note had been lifted and paid me out in twenty-angel pieces, fresh from the Mint, the edges of the flans still slightly sharp. Two doors down from the Stamnites is the Social and Beneficent Order, the only bank in the Capital I'd trust as far as I could sneeze them. I paid in the lot, less five angels. And if I write a note on any of it in the next ten days, I told them, don't honor it, tear it up. Yes, sir, as though I'd made a perfectly reasonable request. Not their place to understand, just to do as they're told; the proper attitude of acolytes towards gods, after all.

(Bear in mind what I told you earlier, about my amazing strength of mind. The point being, it was just before noon by this stage, when the Sun is nearing His highest point, and my strength was therefore as the strength of ten. Where I usually go wrong is getting paid in the evening.)

The rest of the day—the rest of my life—was my own. I wandered down to the Old Market, sat at a table under a plane tree outside one of those high-class teashops and ordered green tea and a honeycake. I needed to sit down; the implications of what I'd just done—the proper word, actually, would be "achieved"—were only just starting to percolate through. I'd been paid for a big job, got my hands on enough money, and instead of rushing out and gambling the lot away as quickly as I could, I'd put it away safe in a bank, with measures in place to stop me getting at it. I'd done it quickly and without thinking, the way an experienced killer does a murder. That's the key, where irrevocable actions are concerned. Don't stop to think about it until it's done and too late.

They brought me my tea. When I tried to pay, they looked at me; sorry, we don't have change for a five-angel. I remembered I was a god. Send someone to the moneychangers, I said. It's fine, I'm not in a hurry.

While I was waiting for my change, I tried hard to think seriously about the morning's momentous events. But I couldn't; not deliberately, like that. Instead, my mind skidded off and started to wander, and I thought about the good-looking man, my willing victim. Now here's a thing about what I do. I don't peek. Really. Why the hell should I want to take on more memories than I have to? But it's a bit like lawyers. Apparently, when they enter a room where there are documents, they automatically read them, quickly, at a glance, upside down even; it's second nature, they can't help it, and it's amazing how much they can read of a document just by looking at it. Same, I think, with me. I don't deliberately browse the other memories. I just glance, while looking for the one I'm after. But even a glance takes in a lot. Like those freaks or geniuses or whatever (actually, I'm one of them) who can see a painting, say, for a fraction of a second out of the corner of their eyes, and a week later describe the whole scene to you in precise detail.

The point being, as I sat in my shady seat drinking my delicious tea, I could recall with total clarity some of the glimpses I'd taken of the good-looking man's memory. It was probably because I was in a hurry and preoccupied; I hadn't made a conscious effort not to. The closest thing—I'm no great shakes at explaining, you can tell—would be getting through brambles. If you're patient and careful, you pick your way, carefully lifting the flailing tendrils out of the way, tenderly disengaging the ones that hook into you, and you come out unscathed. If you just bustle through, you get scratched to hell and your coat's covered in leaves and bits of briar.

There was a memory that just seemed to leap out and flood my mind. I was a soldier, and I was in a trench. I could smell the clay, which was wet and sticky underfoot. We were trying to climb out of the trench, but the sides were too steep and the clay was too hard to get a toehold in. I was shouting, because I was the officer and we were supposed to be attacking; I really didn't want anything to do with it, because I was terrified and worn out, and as far as I could see the job was impossible. But I was yelling, Come on, you bone-idle, chickenshit sons of bitches (and my fingers were clawing at the clay, but I couldn't get a grip); the men were scrambling, jumping—frantic, as if my shouting were wild dogs snapping at their legs, as if they were desperately trying to run away, not charge into battle; and the more they tried, the more I had to try too. I remember I got my left foot braced on a small chunk of stone sticking out of the trench wall. I put my weight on it and boosted myself up, clawed for a handhold, couldn't find one. My foot was slipping off the stone, which was tapered, not the right shape; it came off like a cam completing its stroke, and I slithered three feet down the trench wall, with my face in the clay. There was blood in my mouth and my lower lip was hard as a rock, I was sure I must've ripped my nose and chin off. I landed on my right ankle, badly; felt it turn over under my full weight, and something gave, and it hurt so much I screamed. I tried to stand up, but my leg just folded; and someone behind me used my head as a stepping-stone—the hobnails on his soles getting traction on my scalp—and flung himself at the lip of the trench; I saw him hanging by his fingertips, dragging himself up until his chin was over the top; and then he dropped back, a dead weight, and landed on my outstretched leg, and there was a crack as the bone broke; and there was an arrow in his forehead, clean through the bone, just above the left eyebrow.

I must've passed out at that point, because the memory ended abruptly. Thank you so much for that, I thought. Just what I needed.

Describing it like I've just done makes it sound like I lived through it all, half an hour or a quarter of an hour or however long it took. Not so. All over and done with in the time it takes to touch a tea-bowl to your lower lip. I put down the bowl and frowned. Sudden unsolicited episodes of memory aren't exactly uncommon—well, you do it all the time, don't you?—and I've learned to take them in my stride, as far as that's possible. But there was something else about that one, quite apart from its rather grisly subject matter. The grisliness was neither here nor there. I've got far worse stuff than that stowed away in my head. Rather, it was a sort of familiarity—no, wrong word, hopelessly wrong, giving you entirely the wrong idea, I'm so useless with language. All my memories are familiar, of course they are. You know that thing they call déjà vu? Like that, always. But this one—it's like that time (can't remember if it was me or someone else) when I walked into the house of someone I'd never met before, and there on the table was a candlestick, and I was absolutely certain I'd seen it before. I picked it up (my host gave me a funny look, but I didn't care) and examined it, looking for details of decoration and design; I very nearly said to him, you bastard, you stole my candlestick. But before I did that, I remembered that the one

I had back home, sitting on the upturned water barrel that serves me as a table, was one of a pair; the one I was looking at was my candlestick's twin, hence the familiarity.

Like that—

I drank my tea. To push the analogy where it was reluctant to go, it felt like I'd managed to acquire the twin memory of one I already had—but it doesn't work like that, does it? And besides, I have perfect recall, and I couldn't remember another episode in a clay trench in the war. I was absolutely certain I'd never broken my leg; that's not the sort of thing you forget, even if you're capable of forgetting—

(I assume I'm incapable of forgetting, because I've never been aware of having done so. Exactly. Circular argument.)

The honeycake wasn't bad, though I wish they wouldn't overdo it by piling on the cinnamon. The man came back with my change. I left a two-stuiver tip. You can afford to be generous when you've got more money than God.

A hero like me (my weakness is heroic; it's a recurring theme in the mythologies of most cultures) fears nothing but fear itself; I'm shit-scared of fear, the very thought of it makes me go all to pieces. As the sun went down, I had this overwhelming urge to barricade myself in my loft, chain myself to the rafters, anything to keep from going out into the gathering darkness to where the dice fall and the cards are dealt. But I'd given my word of honor, so I had to go. If you can't trust a god, who can you trust?

Don't answer that.

I stopped off at a certain low-profile all-night dealership on the way, but I was still early; he didn't turn up until well after curfew. I stepped out from behind a pillar, and he didn't see me until it was too late.

I drew my sword and hit him between the shoulder blades with the pommel-nut. I recommend this move; you knock all the air out of a man's body without causing permanent damage. He's helpless, you can do what you like. I grabbed him and turned him round, then brought the pommel-nut down as hard as I could on his collarbone. It's one of the most painful things you can do to anybody. His mouth opened, and no sound came out. I stepped back to half measure and touched the point of the blade to his neck. "I've brought you your money," I said.

He was staring at me. He made me feel like I was unimaginably horrifying, the sort of thing you can't see without losing your mind. I liked that. I gave him a little prod with the sword, almost enough to draw blood but not quite. "Three angels," I said. "Hold out your hand."

He couldn't. He was too numb from the pain. So I came forward, grabbed his hand, pulled it toward me, and opened the balled fingers. Tucked inside my palm were the coins. I released them into his hand and closed his fingers around them.

"Pleasure doing business with you," I said.

The plan was to kick him in the nuts, to keep him busy while I withdrew, but there was no need. I slid the sword back into its scabbard under my coat, turned, and walked away. After I'd gone a few yards I turned and looked. He was still standing there, frozen. Not sensible, to stay perfectly still for any length of time in that neighborhood, if you've got money on your person. But so what? Am I my brother's keeper?

How do you suppose you'd feel if, after many trials and tribulations and having endured many sorrows along the way, you arrived at the satisfactory culmination of your adventures, with every loose end tied off and all outstanding issues dealt with finally and symmetrically? As though your life were a perfectly told story, concluded with a magnificent flourish?

I went home, pausing only to dump the sword down a well (not the sort of thing you'd want to be caught with on the streets at night, even if you're a god). I realized I was starving hungry, but there was nothing to eat apart from a stale quarter-loaf and a sliver of cheese rind. Forget it, I told myself; tomorrow you'll be out of here forever. Then I remembered I couldn't touch my money for another ten days—ah, well. That gave me ten days to select a gentleman's residence and deal with the legal formalities; in the meantime, I still had a whole angel, enough to buy plenty of good, wholesome food for a fortnight. I was very nearly out of lamp oil, so I snuffed the lamp and sat there in the dark most of the night, waiting to be reborn.

I think I fell asleep just before dawn, because when the knock on the door woke me up, I was groggy and stupid, and the light through the hole in the roof was very early morning, by its tone and angle. I got up off the floor and staggered to answer the door.

There was this woman. She looked at me, but didn't say what she was thinking. Instead, she said, "Excuse me, but are you the man who takes away memories?"

She was probably about forty-five, or a bit older; not younger. She had a thin face, and clothes that had cost a fair bit of money a long time ago. Someone had put in a lot of time and effort keeping them neat and clean over the years. "Yes," I said, "but I'm retired now. Sorry."

"It's my daughter," she said. "It's so bad, and I don't know what to do."

I looked at her. I can't read minds, but I've been in business a long time, so I can guess. "You'd better come in," I said.

"I haven't got much money."

"No," I said, "I don't suppose you have."

I was right. Three days earlier, her daughter had been raped by three men on her way back from Temple. Since then she hadn't said a word, hadn't eaten anything, just sat and stared at something nobody else could see. Her mother had six angels, but she was sure she could borrow another six. She was terribly afraid her daughter was going to die.

I looked at her. "Do I know you?" I said.

She shrugged. "I don't think so."

"Don't worry about it," I said. "I have this terrible memory."

She didn't try to answer that. "Will you help her?" she said. "Please?"

The bad thing about being a god is that people pray to you. I said nothing. I think that hurt her more than a sharp blow to the collarbone. I'm no angel, but I do feel things. "If it's the money," she said, "I can go to a moneylender or something. Please?"

I sighed, and I remember thinking, maybe this is how it is for the Invincible Sun, who takes away the sins of the world. Easy, glib phrase, that—you say it twice a day at Offices, but have you stopped to think what it actually means? I have. The idea is He takes your sins, the loathsome and unbearable things you've done, and *he transfers them to Himself*; it's as if He'd done them, not you, for all practical purposes He has done them, and all the guilt and pain and self-disgust are His now, not yours, and you're free and clear. Just imagine how much love and goodness it'd take to make anyone do a thing like that.

Still, I don't suppose He *enjoys* it; and accordingly, I don't have to either.

"I can give you half an hour," I said, rather ungraciously. "Where do you live?"

On the way there, I asked her who'd told her about me. She said she couldn't remember.

The daughter was a skinny, stupid-looking little thing, which made me wonder who the hell could be bothered; a question that would of course be answered very soon. I took the mother to one side. You do realize, I told her, that if I wipe this memory, she won't be able to identify the men or testify against them; they'll get off scot-free, and that's not right. She just looked at me. Fair enough. Justice (which doesn't exist) is not to be confused with retribution. Justice would be making it so that the bad thing had never even happened. Justice is mine, saith the Invincible Sun.

I sat down on a three-legged stool opposite the girl and stared at her until the side of her head melted and I could see in. There were the usual rows of shelves, with the memories stacked on them. No trouble at all finding the one I was after. It was right there in front of me. I reached for it and took it down.

—and there she was, the skinny girl, standing next to me. She had a long, thin nose that reminded me of someone, and no lobes to her ears. She was staring at me—not eye to eye, she was gazing at the side of my head. Get out of it, I shouted at her—I mouthed the words but could make no sound. Stop doing that. Get out of my mind. She turned her head and looked at me, frowning, as if I were logically impossible. She said something, but I couldn't hear it. Her lips were thin and practically colorless, and I couldn't read them. It's for your own good, you stupid girl, I tried to tell her. She couldn't understand me. She reached for the scroll in my hand, but I pulled it away. I could feel her looking through the wall of my skull. It hurt like hell. I yelled, and got out of there.

The girl had her eyes tight shut, and she was screaming. Her mother pulled me off the stool and dragged me away. She was shouting, stop it, what have you done to her? Then the girl stopped yammering; I pulled my arm out of the mother's sharklike grip and ran out into the street. People turned and looked at me. I kept running. I remember thinking, when He does it, they're grateful. I get yelled at. There's no justice.

The plan had been to spend the morning cruising elegantly round the various auctioneers and real-estate agents. I didn't do that. Instead, I went home, wedged my one chair against the door, and sat crouched in a corner.

The memory of the rape (which was bad enough, God knows) had somehow fused with the moment when I found the skinny girl standing next to me. I wanted to hide, but you can't when it's yourself you're trying to run away from. Just as well I'd dumped that sword, or I'd have tried to cut my own head off. Any damn thing, just to make it stop.

Which it did, of its own accord, a long and unquantifiable amount of time later. What cured it, I think, was a little voice in my head, apparently unaffected by the mayhem going on all around (like the farmer in the valley just over the ridge from the battle, who goes on serenely plowing while thirty thousand men die, half a mile away) that kept repeating; I know that woman, I'm sure I've seen her before, I never forget a face—

And then I sort of slid into another of the memories I'd taken from the good-looking man the day before. This time it was a nice one. He was sitting on the grass beside a river—I knew the place, an old abandoned iron mine high up on the moor, sounds grim but actually it's beautiful when the heather's out and the sun's shining. He was with another man and two pretty girls, and they were all dressed in the gentrified walking outfits that were in fashion about twenty years ago. There was a big wicker basket; cold chicken, ham, garlic sausage, fluffy white rolls; a stone bottle floated in the river to keep it cool, a string round its neck to keep it from floating away, anchored to a wooden peg driven into the turf of the bank. I made a joke (which I didn't quite catch); the girls laughed, but the other man scowled— he didn't like that I was amusing them, and that made me want to smile. He was my best friend and a brother officer, but all's fair in love and war.

Around noon, I suddenly remembered that I was still hungry. I've never been so pleased to be hungry in all my life.

To reconcile my unkempt appearance with my desire to buy an expensive house, I told them I was a gold miner just back from the Mesoge. I don't think they believed me but it was an acceptable lie; they recognized it, the way governments recognize each other without necessarily approving. I showed them a letter from the Social and Beneficent, which confirmed that I was indeed a rich man, whose funds would be available to draw on in nine days' time. They liked me ever so much more after that.

The first place they took me to see, I didn't even bother going inside. Sorry, I told them, but I don't have a dog. And if I did, I wouldn't be so cruel as to keep it cramped up in something that small.

The next place was just off the Park, opposite the side gate of the Baths of Genseric. There was a high brick wall with a tiny wicket gate in it; go through that and you're suddenly in this beautiful formal garden, with a fountain and little box-hedge-enclosed diamonds planted out in sweet herbs and lavender. The house itself was early Formalist, with those tiny leaded-pane windows and two ornate columns flanking the front door. The price they were asking seemed a trifle on the cheap side; it turned out they were acting as agents for the Treasury, the house having been confiscated from the estate of a recently executed traitor. I had, how shall I put it, certain connections with that case (here's a hint; they hanged the wrong man). Thanks but no thanks.

The third one was just right. It was on the riverbank; the main entrance was actually from a landing-stage, and we arrived by boat. As soon as I walked through the door I felt at home. There was something about the place that made me feel right somehow, as though I'd been away for too long but was back again where I ought to be. I sat down on the window seat in the back kitchen and looked out over the river. I could see a boat, one of those flat-bottomed barges they use for hauling lumber and ore down from the moors to the City. It lay low in the water, and gulls were mobbing the crew as they lounged and ate barley cakes in the bows. I grinned and reached for my tea.

Which wasn't there, of course, although my fingers closed with exact precision on where the tea-bowl should have been—where it had been, twenty-one years ago, when I sat in the bay window of my best friend's house, the second day of his first home leave from the war—

I jumped up, remembering to duck my head so as not to crack it against the overhanging beam, which I hadn't noticed when I sat down (but I knew it was there, just as I know where my fingers are) and ran out of the house. The agent was outside, leaning against a pillar, eating an apple. Not this one, I told him. He smiled. Of course not, he said. Let's go and look at something else.

The next day, the man from the Knights of Poverty took me out to see a place he was sure I'd like, about ten miles north of the city. True, it was just a farmhouse; but in the big hay meadow stood the derelict but still fundamentally sound shell of a fine old manor house. I could live in the farm while the big house was done up, which wouldn't take long (by an extraordinary coincidence, his brother-in-law the builder lived in the village) and then I'd have exactly the home I wanted, created to my precise specifications, for a tenth of what it'd have cost to buy anything similar that still had a roof. We saw the ruin first. It was a tall galleon of bleak, untidy stone rearing up out of a sea of nettles. It certainly had potential, the way a granite boulder is potentially a masterpiece of portrait sculpture. It looked as much like a house as I do, but the Knight assured me his brother-in-law would have it shipshape in ten minutes flat. Then we looked round the farmhouse: one big room downstairs, a combination bedroom and hayloft above it. I grew up in a smaller version. Oh, and there were a hundred and ninety acres of good pasture, if I was interested in that sort of thing. Five hundred angels. I offered him four and he accepted open-mouthed, as though he'd just cut open a fish and found a giant ruby. I asked him, who used to live in the big house? He didn't know. It was a long time ago, and everyone had died or moved away.

The best thing about living in the farmhouse was nobody knowing I was there. I had taken pains to leave no forwarding addresses, and I'd made the Knights promise they'd never heard of me, if anyone came asking.

The second best thing was the house itself, with its paved yard, three barns, well, and stable. I walked into the village and bought a dozen chickens; an old woman and a very young boy brought them on a handcart that afternoon, by which time I'd fixed up the end of the smallest barn as a poultry shed. I left the chickens pecking weeds out from between the flags in the yard and hiked out east to look for my neighbor; he turned out to be a short, broad, harassed-looking man about my age, who sold me a half-ton of barley and told his eldest boy to cart it over that evening. By nightfall, I had chicken-feed and chickens to feed it to; I ground a big cupful of the barley in a rusty hand-mill I found in the middle barn, to make bread for myself the next day. I'd forgotten how tiring it is working one of those things. After an hour, my arm and neck ached and I still had half the grain to do. I was happy, for the first time in years; relaxed, peaceful, as I'd assumed only a god could be.

Over the next two weeks I bought two dozen good ewes at the fair, and a pony and cart, and a dog. I was busy patching up the hedges and fences. The Knight's brother-in-law came asking for money. He found me in the long pasture, splitting rails out of a crooked ash I'd felled the previous day, and asked me if I knew where the owner was. Who? The rich city gent who'd bought the big house. Oh, him, I said, and sent him down to the farmhouse. He left a note. I wrote a reply and a draft on the Bank, walked down to the village when it was too dark to work, and slipped it under his door. Two days later I was driving the sheep to new pasture and happened to pass the ruin. It was almost invisible under new white pine scaffolding, like a city under siege. I gave it a wide berth.

That night the fox got in and killed all my chickens. I remember sitting cross-legged in the yard, surrounded by feathered wrecks, bawling like a child.

Then they tracked me down, and a carriage arrived to take me to the City. Get lost, I told the driver, I'm retired, I'm a gentleman of leisure now. He looked at my clothes and the hammer and fencing pliers stuck through my belt and the wire burns on my hands, and went away to report to his superiors.

Then the young man—the old man's son—rode out to see me. They needed me, he said. He understood that I'd given up regular practice, but he was sure I'd make an exception. The fee was a thousand angels. I'm retired, I said, I'm a gentleman farmer. I have all the money I could possibly want.

He looked at me as though I was mad. We need you, he said. Things have taken a turn for the worse. My father is seriously concerned.

He'd interrupted me while I was driving in a fence post. I'd been working since dawn, and the sledge felt like it weighed three hundredweight. I'm retired, I repeated. Sorry, but I don't do that stuff any more.

My father says you've got to come now, he said. Maybe I haven't made myself clear. This is important.

So's this, I told him. And I'm retired. Sorry.

He scowled at me. We've been doing some research, he said. About you. We found out some interesting things. He grinned; it made him look like a dog. You've led an eventful life, haven't you?

I thought about smashing his skull with the hammer, and decided against it. Probably it was a weak decision. If I'd killed him and melted away into the countryside (wouldn't be the first time I'd done that) I'd have had to give up the money and the farm and my apotheosis, but I'd have been free and clear, for a little while. I could have gone anywhere, been anybody, done anything. A weak and tired decision; I traded freedom and infinite potential for a little comfort.

Who told you? I said.

He shook his head. I'm hardly likely to tell you, am I? Anyway, there it is. You can refuse if you like, but if you do, you'll regret it. Come on, he added. We can't afford to waste time.

I put it to him that blackmailing me would be a very bad idea, given that I knew enough about him and his father to destroy the entire world. But he just gave me an impatient look, because he knew as well as I did that if I went to the authorities, I wouldn't live long enough to testify; and, as a relatively new, arriviste god, with no friends or connections among the senior pantheon, my absence wouldn't arouse much comment.

He'd come in a covered two-seater chaise. It wasn't designed to carry two people long distances on poor roads. I comfort myself with the reflection that he must have suffered even more than I did, every time we went over a pothole.

Consider it this way. The present is a split second, so tiny and trivial as to be immaterial. Everything else, everything real and substantial, is a coral reef of dead split seconds, forming the islands and continents of our reality. Every moment is a brick in the wall of the past, building enormous structures that have identity and meaning, cities we live in. The future is wet shapeless clay, the present is so brief it barely exists, but the past houses and shelters us, gives us a home and a name; and the mortar that binds those bricks, that stops them from sliding apart into a nettle-shrouded ruin, is memory.

I had no way of knowing, of course, exactly which of my past misdemeanors he'd contrived to unearth. But—last time I counted, and that was a while back, thirty-six of them carried the death penalty in the relevant jurisdiction, and I'd long since lost count of the things I'd done which would land me in jail or the galleys or the hulks or the slate quarries if anyone ever brought them home to me. The issue is confused, of course, by all the crimes I remember vividly but didn't do; even so, I was and am uncomfortably aware that my past (so long as memory sustains it) isn't so much a city as a condemned cell. Don't get me wrong; I'm not fundamentally a bad person. They'll hang you for any damn thing in some of the places I've been, Boc Auxine or Perigeuna; failure to salute the flag, sneezing during the Remembrance Festival. But I've had my moments. As previously noted, no angel.

Someone opened the chaise door and I poked my head out. Not somewhere I recognized, though it was fairly obvious what sort of place it was. Mile-high tenement blocks crowded round a little square yard; two single-story sheds north and south, and in the middle a circle of black ash ringed with big sooty stones; to the right a fifty-gallon barrel with one charred side. You've got it; a wheelwright's yard, of which there are probably forty in the City, maybe more—the ruts in the streets are hard on wheels and axles. I guessed we weren't there to have the chaise fixed, however.

The young man led me into the shed on the north side. The shutters were down, but there was a big fire still glowing on the forge hearth. The old man was sitting awkwardly on an anvil, with five men standing behind him; they needed no explanation. Opposite the old man, kneeling on the hard stone floor, was a little thin man, anywhere between forty and fifty-five. He had a black eye and a cut lip, ugly bruise on his cheek, hair matted with blood from one of those scalp wounds that just keep on bleeding. He was nursing his left hand in his right; someone had flattened his fingertips on the anvil with a big hammer. He had that still, quiet look.

The old man glanced up as I came in, then turned his attention back to the poor devil kneeling on the floor. This man, he said, stole from us. He was a clerk in the counting-house, we looked after him, trusted him, and he stole from us. And he won't tell us what he's done with our money.

I looked at the clerk, who shook his head. It's not true, he said (it was hard to make out the words, his mouth was too badly damaged), I never stole anything. The young man rolled his eyes, as though the clerk were a naughty boy with jam round his mouth insisting he knew nothing about the missing cake.

Fine, I said, we can settle this quite easily. I braced myself; it was going to be a difficult, nasty job, and I was out of practice.

I did the old man first. I'm ashamed to admit that I was a bit cavalier about going in. I've found you can modulate—is that the word?—the level of discomfort you cause when you look through the side of someone's head; on this occasion, I didn't bother too much. The memories I wanted were easy enough to find—half of the things he'd found out about me weren't even true. I bundled them up, wiped the memory of the pain, and got out fast. Same for his son. Then I did the clerk. Then out again. By this time I was feeling shattered, sweat running down my face and inside my shirt, as though I'd just run up a steep hill with a hay bale hanging from each hand.

"He's telling the truth," I said. "He never stole from you, and he hasn't got your money."

The old man opened his mouth, then closed it again. The young man called me a liar and various other things; his father sighed and told him to be quiet.

The clerk's head had rolled forward onto his chest; he was asleep. "You'd better untie him and dump him in an alley somewhere," I went on. "I've taken away all his memories of what you've done to him, he'll wake up and have no idea how he got in this state, it'll save you having to kill him." I smiled. "Now, then," I said, "I don't think we discussed my fee. The usual rate?"

The old man gave me a puzzled look, then wrote out a draft for three hundred angels. I didn't argue. "Well," I said, "it's been a pleasure working for you, but as I told your son, I'm retired now, so we won't be seeing each other again. Rest assured you can rely on my discretion. Don't bother giving me a lift, I can walk."

I got out of there as quickly as I could, and headed straight for the Sword of Justice, simply because it was nearest and I badly needed a drink. So badly, in fact, that I stuck to black tea with honey and pepper, because some things you need you shouldn't always get. I was sipping it when a man I used to know came up and told me they'd got a game going out back, if I was interested.

I looked at him and grinned. "Sorry," I said, "I'm broke. Look at me," I added.

He did so, noting the farm clothes and the worn-out boots. "Screw you, then," he replied pleasantly, and left me in peace.

How was it, I hear you ask, that I came to develop my unique talent and establish a career as the Empire's leading consulting memory engineer?

It's a classic success story. There I was, an ignorant farm boy on the run from the law, turning up in the big city with nothing but the rags on his back and a dream of a better life. An early but significant demonstration of my powers came about when hunger drove me to the back door of the old Industry and Enterprise in Sheep Street—remember it? It's gone now, of course, pulled down to make space for the new cattle pens. The door was open, and I could see through into the kitchen, where they were roasting chickens on a spit. There didn't seem to be anybody about, so I nipped in and helped myself.

I was cheerfully stuffing my face when the landlord loomed up out of the shadows and kicked me halfway across the room. Then he picked up a cleaver. I swear it was instinct; I stared right through his skull, picked out the sight of me tiptoeing in and grabbing a chicken, and darted back out again. There was the landlord, cleaver in hand, puzzled frown on face. Who the hell are you? he asked me. Got any work? I answered. No, get lost. I nodded (I'd stuck the chicken down the front of my shirt) and headed back into the street as fast as I could go.

For someone who'd had to work for his living, this episode was a revelation to me; a flawless modus operandi, fully formed and perfected, like suddenly waking up one morning to find that you'd learned the silversmith's trade overnight, in a dream. I refined it a bit, of course. I know, they say *if it ain't broke don't fix it*, but I modified the original pattern to leave out the getting-kicked-across-the-room stage, and in the event it worked just as well without it. Instead, I'd go into teashops when there were no other customers, eat and drink as much as I liked, then cause the owner to forget me completely. Same with dosshouse-keepers and landladies of furnished accommodation: as soon as they asked me for rent, they'd never seen me before in their lives. I got into a few scrapes, it's true, but that's all done and forgotten about now. In due course, I refined my business model and started getting jobs that actually paid money; eventually, lots of money, which somehow never stayed with me very long, but that's not the point. I was a success. I made something of myself, and there's not many men from my background who can say that.

So why, I hear you ask, did I turn my back on all that, a lifetime of achievement, not to mention the money, in order to go scurrying back to my grubby roots and relapse into peasant farming?

Actually, I should think that was obvious. I was terrified. Ever since I'd done that job on the girl who was raped, I knew something was terribly wrong. I'd tried to figure out what had happened, couldn't—no matter. I'm not a scholar or a scientist, just an honest artisan practicing his trade. But when the trade gets dangerous and not worth the risk, I stop. Simple: if I don't go back there, it can't hurt me. And I was horribly sure that if I did go back, I'd get hurt.

I could remember it all perfectly; the skinny girl, standing next to me. She had a long, thin nose, and no lobes to her ears. She was staring at me—not eye to eye, she was gazing at the side of my head. Get out of it, I shouted at her—I mouthed the words but could make no sound. Stop doing that. Get out of my mind. She turned her head and looked at me, frowning, as if I were a spelling mistake. She said something, but I couldn't hear it. Her lips were thin and practically colorless, and I couldn't read them. It's for your own good, you stupid girl, I tried to tell her. She couldn't understand me. She reached for the scroll in my hand, but I pulled it away. I could feel her looking through the wall of my skull. It hurt like hell. I yelled, and got out quick—

So what's the chance, I kept asking myself, that there's someone else out there with the same knack or talent I've got; a skinny girl, nobody really, but she can see through the walls of skulls into the library inside? Except that wasn't what I'd encountered, was it? I met her inside her own head, conscious of me; she'd tried to get at my memories, but I'd been too quick for her and got away before she could break in. Conclusion: she could do what I can do, but there was more to it than that. She was aware of me gatecrashing her mind; she was actually there, in person, and nearly managed to snatch the scroll out of my hand.

And still only young, twenty or so; not much older than I was when I started. Give her a few years to come to terms with her ability and put on a bit of mental muscle—what other tricks could she do, I wondered? What sort of monster had I blundered into?

I owed her a drink, of course. If it hadn't been for the scare she'd put into me, I'd never have found the strength to quit the job and get out of the City. That change was definitely an improvement, no question at all about it.

I cashed the old man's draft and got them to write a letter of credit to the Social and Beneficent; another couple of hundred couldn't do any harm, after all, even if I was highly unlikely ever to need it. Then I caught the carrier's cart to my village and walked the rest of the way. It had been raining, and the wet grass soaked my trousers up to the knees. I walked past the ruin—they'd roofed it over with wooden shingles, over which I'd specified a single continuous sheet of burnished copper, but they hadn't got round to that yet. I peered at it from a distance, too far away to make out what the builders' men were saying, and cut through the woods to get home. The smell of the wet grass was wonderful. It was nearly dark by then. The back door was slightly ajar, just as I'd left it. I went inside and groped for the lamp and the tinderbox. I was just about to wind the tinderbox handle when light filled the room.

Two of them; I can picture them to this day—one lifting the shutter of a dark lantern, the other rising gracefully to his feet and leveling the crossbow he'd been cradling on his knees. He was the one who messed it all up, of course, because as he stood up he got between his target and the light, giving me plenty of time to back out and slam the door in his face; I felt it quiver as the bolt hit it. I was almost as stupid as he was. I wasted a good second looking round for something to wedge the door with, instead of legging it straightaway into the friendly, conspiratorial dark. But I got smart as soon as I felt his weight slam against the door; I let go, allowing him to sprawl out and trip over his feet, while I scampered across the yard toward the hay barn. The only reason I went that way was a vague memory of where I'd left a hayfork, which was the only weapon I had that wasn't in the house.

The trouble with a vague memory is it doesn't help you find things in the pitch dark. Furthermore, while I was groping about in the hay, I trod on that damned loose floorboard, the one that creaks like a soul in torment. The sound carried wonderfully in the still night air. I froze. Not tactics, terror. Then I heard the scrape of a hobnail on the slate lintel.

It reminded me of a night, many years earlier, when I'd crept through a dark garden towards the wall of a house and looked up at a narrow window. The architect who built that house had no daughters, or he wouldn't have allowed the window of the best east-facing bedroom, looking out over the rose garden, to be so easily accessible by drainpipe.

I was quite athletic in those days, but just as clumsy as I am now. The heel of my boot dragged on the stone windowsill, making a noise that sounded like morning shift in the slate quarries. I froze and counted to twenty; her mother's maid slept in the next room, and was no friend of mine. But twenty came and went, no banging doors or raised voices. I hauled myself over the sill and got my feet down on a good, discreet Vesani rug.

But something was wrong. She should have been there. I was alone in someone else's house. Suddenly, I felt like a burglar.

Fortuitously, I knew about burglary, thanks to a paying customer. I knew how to walk quietly, and what to watch out for. I crept through the dressing room into her bedroom. It was dark. I knew its geography, of course. I have a blind man's memories of how to navigate in the dark. I found the bed, and my fingertips told me it was made up. I stood there, feeling incredibly stupid. Then the door opened, and the light almost blinded me.

I should explain that I'd been away for nearly six months, for my health. I hadn't dared write, and all the time I was away I'd been out of my mind with worry. The first thing I did when I got back was leave the agreed sign—a hand-and-flower, chalked on the foot of the sundial at the end of the rose garden; when I came back the next night, her countersign was there, with two crosses, meaning *in two days' time*. So she was still there, still wanted to see me, but her room was empty.

Framed in the light was a man I knew only too well, though we'd never met face to face or spoken to each other. At that time, her father was a senator and a wealthy merchant, doing extremely well in the cotton and linen business; this was several years before the crash came and it turned out that the only money he had was what he'd embezzled from Party funds. He was a big man, bald, with the arms and shoulders of a country blacksmith, and his attitude towards me, as far as I could gather, was basically agnostic; he couldn't quite bring himself to believe that I existed, but he had lurking suspicions. He was alone, but all that signified was a sensible disinclination to share the next few minutes with any witnesses.

I'd already turned to run for it, but he said, "No, wait," and there was something in the way he said it—not anger, just sadness. I stayed where I was and he came up close and held the lamp so he could see my face. "You're shorter than I expected," he said.

"Where is she?"

For a moment I thought he was going to go for me. The little, isolated part of my mind that arranges tactical details was busy taking note of the fact that he was holding the lamp in his right hand and his left hand was empty; no weapon, so either he was unarmed or he'd have to shift the lamp to his left to draw; or if he planned on killing me with his bare hands, he'd have to lead with his left, and his feet were all wrong for that, unless he was a natural southpaw—But then he shook his head, and the look on his face made me go cold. "She's dead," he said.

It's so easy to say: in that moment, I died. Grand overstatement. Melodrama. I wish I had the words, but I don't.

He went on: "There was a problem with the pregnancy. It was blood poisoning."

All I could do was repeat: "Pregnancy."

He made this noise. It was a big, cold laugh. "You didn't know?"

"No. I—" I ran out of words and just stood there.

"Ah." He nodded slightly. "Interesting. She assumed you'd guessed and run out on her because of it. Well, it killed her. It took a long time. They gave her poppy extract, but the pain was—" He stopped and shrugged. "You killed my daughter."

This tactical part of my mind—I wonder, do other people have the same thing, or is it just me? If it's just me, is it somehow connected with the special thing I do? I've often wondered. In any event, at that moment it was busy again. It was telling me: his wife, her mother, died five years ago, and he has no close family; I could wipe her out of his memory and spare him the pain, it was the least I could do. But that wouldn't work. He was a man in public office, with about a million acquaintances, all of them properly sympathetic. It wouldn't really help matters if I got him a reputation for having been driven insane by grief.

"I was going to kill you," he said. He was looking straight at me, the way an arrow looks at a target. "But I think I'll let you live. It'd be crueller."

He was right about that. Being dead is bad enough. Being dead and still having to walk around and eat is so much worse.

Hence the sudden and immediate twist of pain when I heard that nail-on-stone noise. No bad thing, really; it prevented me from ignoring the sound or mistaking it for something else. Saved my life, actually. Now there's irony.

My tactical planner was giving me instructions; get down, keep still, make yourself small. I had no weapon and chances were the owner of the hobnailed boot was a much better fighter than me, but I had the advantage of the dark; I knew where he was, but he didn't know where I was. He was, of course, between me and the door. I've been in worse situations.

Then I had a stroke of luck. He uncovered his dark lantern. He saw me and I saw him.

I went in through the side of his head like a slingstone. As I'd assumed, the old man had sent him; my reluctance and intention to retire had made me an unacceptable risk, no longer outweighed by my potential usefulness. Fine. I wiped that; then, in an excess of spite of which I am not proud, I wiped a whole lot more—his name, most of his past, more or less everything in easy reach. When I came out of his head, he was standing there looking stupid. There was a hay rake leaning up against the wall. I grabbed it and broke it over his head. I felt sorry for him, and ashamed of myself.

He'd dropped the lantern, but it hadn't gone out; a lit lantern on the floor of a hay barn is nobody's friend. I grabbed it, and then it did go out. I went to the door and threw it away. One down.

I stood in the doorway and tried to be sensible. Defeating one hired man wasn't victory in any meaningful sense. If the old man had decided it was time for me to die, I could defeat a thousand of his foot soldiers in tense little duels and still be no safer. My own stupid fault. By buying a house and putting down roots, I'd made myself an easy target—one of the very few stupid things I'd never done before. I don't know. Maybe there's a secret part of me that won't be satisfied until I've completed the set.

Time to go. As I walked quietly up to the road, I cursed myself for cashing that two-hundred-angel draft. It'd be suicide to go anywhere near the Social and Beneficent, or even to write a draft; they'd track me down and that'd be that. My only hope lay in anonymity and distance.

I started walking. About a week later, I stopped and asked where I was. They looked at me as if I were crazy and said, Scheria. Just my luck.

• • •

Don't get me wrong. There are worse places than Scheria. Four of them, at least.

I never had the time or the energy to learn a musical instrument; but I had the unhappy privilege of attending the great Clamanzi in his last illness, which was horribly exacerbated by memories of how badly he'd treated his wife. The poor man only had days to live, and it was certain he'd never play the flute again. It wasn't really stealing, more a case of rescuing a glorious thing and keeping it safe.

Partly out of respect, I'd never even picked up a flute since that day; but it was all there, in my head. My tactical adviser suggested that the old man's people wouldn't be looking for a traveling musician. And, whatever their other faults as a nation, the Scherians are fond of music.

I'm ashamed to say, I stole the flute. I heard its music as I was walking down a village street. Pretty tune, I thought; then it stopped, and maybe its beauty reminded me of Clamanzi, I don't know. I waited; it started again, and I traced it to a house in the corner of a little square. I went away and came back after dark. The blind man I mentioned just now helped me find the flute—it had been left lying around on the kitchen table, some people are just so careless. My flute now.

To practice, I walked up into the hills. As well as the flute, I'd found a new loaf on that kitchen table, and there are plenty of sweet-water springs draining off the peat. I allowed myself three days to learn the flute. Took me about half an hour, in the event. The rest of the time I took to eat that loaf, I just enjoyed myself, playing music.

I say *myself*; I can't really claim any credit. I'm the first to admit I don't have an artistic bone in my body. So please don't make the mistake of thinking that listening to me was like listening to Clamanzi. I had the fingering, the breath control, the education, the technique—but no passion, no soul. Correction: I had *my* soul, which is a pretty inferior example of the type and certainly not something you'd want to listen to. No angel; I think we've established that. But I could pipe a tune, as well as most and better than some, and a piper can always earn a few stuivers in Scheria. Not that there's much in those parts you'd want to spend it on.

The hell with it; I walked to the next town, sat down in front of the mercantile, and started to play. Not even a hat at my feet—I didn't actually possess a hat—just music, for its own sake. To begin with, people were reluctant, because there was no obvious place to drop their coins. But once two or three stuivers were gathered together in a little cluster that ceased to be a problem. The store owner came out and I thought he was going to move me on; instead, he brought me out a bowl of tea and a loaf of bread, quietly so as not to disturb me. I only stopped when my lips got sore, by which time the pile of coins was too big to hold comfortably in one hand. Best part of a quarter angel; more than a skilled man earns in a week.

I slept, by invitation, in the storekeeper's comfortable hayloft, and started playing again as soon as it was light. It helped that I can remember every tune I ever heard. On the third day it rained; but that wasn't a problem, because the local lord-of-the-manor sent a cart for me. He had guests for dinner, and if I wasn't busy . . . A month later, I'd moved to Cerauno, which is the third largest city in Scheria, and was playing indoors, to people who'd come specially to hear me, and who handed in their coins at the door rather than dropping them on the ground. Three months later, I was rich. Again.

I seem to have this knack of hauling myself up by my bootstraps, usually when my mind is on other things.

Practically every night in Cerauno I dreamed about the skinny girl. Sometimes she was in the dark looking for me, with a knife; sometimes I met her in the street or beside the river. Sometimes she had a knife, other times it would be a rope or an axe. The one constant was that she wanted to kill me.

I heard the news of the coup back home from the ambassador himself, no less, at a reception. He confessed that he was terrified at the thought of being recalled, since he was clearly identified with the old regime. I asked him who was behind it all; he looked around to make sure nobody was listening, and whispered a few names. Two of them (father and son) I recognized.

I reminded myself that I was a professional, and my clients' secrets were sacrosanct, even if the clients in question had sent assassins to murder me. If I were you, I told the ambassador, I'd stay here where it's safe. Those clowns won't last long, sooner or later they'll cut each other's throats and everything will go back to normal. Don't go back, whatever you do. He gave me a sad smile. My wife and daughter are still there, he said, in the City.

I thought about that while pretending to sip my tea, though the bowl was empty. If he refused to go back, they'd kill his family. If he went back, they'd kill him and his family as well, because now they were in power they could afford to be particular about loose ends. I know; it was only my opinion, and what do I know about high-level politics? But I'd come to like the ambassador; he'd fallen asleep in the front row of one of my recitals, on a night when I was particularly uninspired—he clearly had taste, and I like that in a man.

He turned away to grab one of those rice-cakes-filled-with-pureed-seaweed that the Scherians fondly imagine are edible. I stared at the side of his head, and then he turned back. He was frowning.

Tell me, ambassador, I said. Are you married?

He looked at me as if I'd just asked him for the square root of seven. No, he said.

I smiled at him. If I were you, I said, I'd stay here in Scheria where it's safe. He nodded. I might just do that, he said.

As soon as I could, I left the reception, went home to my comfortable lodgings in fashionable Peace Square, and was violently sick. I can only assume it was the pureed seaweed.

I'd been in Scheria for about six months when I started hearing rumors. News from the Old Country was hard to come by; my only reliable source was my friend the ambassador (Scheria didn't recognize the new regime, so he stayed on; he was invited to receptions, but had to borrow money to live on) and all he knew came from refugees and exiles. Apart from what he told me, I heard the usual wild and improbable stuff, a mixture of impossible atrocity stories and political gossip, scurrilous in tone and often biologically impossible. But just occasionally I heard something that rang true. For instance: I heard that the society charlatan who used to claim he could read minds had mysteriously disappeared just before the coup, but lately there was a new mind-reader who'd taken over his old practice; she was in favour with the regime, who made no secret of her supposed powers. They used her for interrogations and to administer a particularly terrifying form of punishment—artificially induced amnesia. The victim, so the rumor went, was left with no memories whatsoever, not even his name. It was the proverbial fate worse than death, and apparently the new government kept her extremely busy. Her? Oh, yes, my informants assured me, this mind-reader's a woman, actually just a young girl, but nasty as a sackful of adders. Also, they've put a price on the old mind-reader's head; ten thousand angels dead, twenty-five thousand if they get him alive. Of course, it's all nonsense, but—

And my mother used to tell me I'd never amount to anything. Twenty-five thousand angels. It's enough to make your head spin. No human being could conceivably be worth that. It made me wish I still had a family, so I could turn myself in and make them all rich.

I remember the first time I saw her.

I remember it two ways; in one version, I'm sitting on a low wall, talking to my best friend. The other way, I'm standing. Apart from that, it's the same, up to the point where I say, "I think I know her brother," in a soft whisper. From then on, the two versions diverge.

In one version, I just stand there, bashful and hopeless. In the other, I go up to her, introduce myself. She gives me that look nice girls are supposed to give to importunate strangers. Then I ask if her brother is so-and-so, who was at the Studium at such-and-such a time. Why, yes, she says, and smiles, and he's mentioned you.

In the other version, I reflect bitterly on my lack of education, which meant I'd never been at some fancy school with the brothers of pretty girls. Meanwhile I watch my best friend exercise his legendary charm, and think: oh well.

Footnotes: at this time, I'd been in the City for just under a year. I'd started exercising my talent in a controlled and profitable manner; I was making a lot of money, and spending it on playing the part of an affluent merchant's son—no attempt to hide the taint of trade, but a surprising number of genuine young noblemen are happy to associate with parvenus, if they're witty and presentable and prepared to buy the drinks and pay for the damage. Nobody asked me searching questions about my antecedents, because it was assumed they couldn't possibly be more disgraceful than a rich wine-merchant for a father. My friend had recently left the military academy and was loosely associated with a good regiment (but not in such a way as to cut unduly into his free time).

She had a friend, who I didn't like much. The four of us went to various social events. It wasn't a happy time for me.

The news that I'd been supplanted in my profession didn't bother me much, per se; I had no intention of resuming my practice if I could possibly avoid it. I much preferred flute-playing, and Scheria was starting to grow on me, like some sort of lichen. It was my supplanter herself who bothered me, that and the price on my head. If I was safe anywhere, it was Scheria— war hadn't been formally declared, but the border was closed, and one of my compatriots would've been noticed and dealt with very quickly; the Scherians are good at that sort of thing. Even so, twenty-five thousand angels has a sort of inner momentum that tends to transcend politics. One thing was certain. I didn't dare go back and investigate this woman, even if I'd wanted to.

Instead, I played the flute. I'm not sure what got into me. Maybe it was the worry and the stress, or perhaps it was just Clamanzi getting used to my mouth and fingers. I got better and better. It helped that I was encouraged to tackle a wider repertoire—the great Scherian classics, Gorgias, Procopius, Cordusa; you can't put an infinite amount of soul into the folk tunes I'd picked up back home, but if you put together Clamanzi's technique and Procopius's flute sonatas, there's a sort of alchemical reaction that refuses to be confined by the spiritual poverty of the intermediary, even when he's me. Also, people who know about music say that the great performer draws on his experience, which is just another word for memories; of those I had plenty. Even the greatest virtuoso—even Clamanzi—can only draw on his own experience, which limits him. Unless he happens to have a head stuffed full of other people's lives, sorrows, joys, wickedness, weakness, and misery. I reached a point where I could let the music and the memories talk to each other. A hundred strangers provided the soul, Clamanzi operated the keys, I stood there while it happened, bowed when it was over, and took the money. I remember one reception, where I'd played for a bunch of ambassadors and ministers. Some fool came up to me, an old man, he looked like he'd been crying. He told me he'd heard the great Clamanzi play that sonata twenty years ago and had avoided hearing it since, because he was afraid to spoil the memory; but I had been better than Clamanzi, I'd found new depths, new resonances—

I'm afraid I was quite rude to him.

There was one piece I flatly refused to play; Chirophon's *Lyrical Dances*, which was what the band played at a dance we all went to, around the time my best friend's regiment was posted south. It was while they were playing the second movement and the four of us were sitting it out on the veranda that I realized how much she loved him. I remember there was a beautiful glass decanter on the table; I looked at it and saw that if I broke it on the side of the table, I could cut his throat with the sharp edge of the neck before he had a chance to defend himself. I reached for it, my fingertips registered the smooth, cold surface; and I realized that there was a better way. Which is how I come to have his memories of her as well as my own. On the way back from the dance I stole them all; and the next day his regiment marched for the southern frontier. A month later he wrote to me; he was getting love letters from some female he'd never heard of—hot stuff, he said, you had to wear gloves to read them. He thought it was a huge joke, and should he write back? Write care of me, I replied; I'll deliver the letter and take a look at her for you. I don't know if he ever got that, because he was killed very soon afterwards.

The politics took a turn for the worse; enough to scare the Scherians into peace talks. A high-level delegation from the new regime would visit Scheria in the hope of preventing further escalation, and all that sort of thing. Naturally, there would be events, receptions. Naturally, I would be hired to play for them.

I got as far as packing a bag. Two bags, five—I realized I had far too much stuff I couldn't bear to be parted from, which was another way of saying that this time, I wasn't prepared to run away.

So I did the next best thing. I went to see my friend the director of the Conservatory—in Scheria, the country's top musician is an ex officio member of the Council of State, can you believe that? He was pleased to see me, sent for tea and honeycakes. "You saved me a job," he said. "I need to talk to you about the gala recital for the peace delegation."

I gave him a weak grin. "It's sort of about that," I said. "I can't do it."

He looked at me as though I'd just cut off his fingers. "Not funny," he said. I took a deep breath. "There are some things about me that maybe you ought to know," I told him.

And I explained. The story of my life. He sat perfectly still until I'd finished, and for a moment or so after that. Then he said, "But you haven't actually done anything wrong in Scheria."

I frowned. "Not yet."

"Don't mess with me," he snapped. "Since you got here, you've been a blameless, productive member of society. Yes? I need you to tell me the truth."

I nodded. "Apart from lying about who I am."

"That's not a crime," he said quickly, "unless you're on oath. So, the plain fact is, in Scheria you're clean."

I nodded. "Like that matters," I said. "Weren't you listening? As far as this delegation's concerned, I'm an enemy of the State. Also, I have information about two of the delegates that would kill them very dead if it ever got loose. Think about that."

He thought, though not for very long. "You wouldn't consider—"

"No. I'm definite on that. I don't tell."

He shrugged. "Before you go, do me a favor and make me forget you told me that, because it's my duty as a Counselor to go to my colleagues and inform them that you have vital information that could win us the war, and all they have to do is torture you till you spit it out." He frowned. "You can really do that? That's amazing."

For a moment I didn't know what to say. "Thanks," I said. "But the point remains. As soon as they see me, they'll hit the roof. They'll assume—"

Suddenly he grinned. "Yes," he said. "Won't they just." He leaned forward and gave me a slap on the back that loosened three teeth. "How does it feel to be a secret weapon?"

It goes to show how stress mucks up your intellect; I hadn't seen it in that light before. "All right," I conceded. "But the moment that old devil sets eyes on me, my life won't be worth spit."

"We'll protect you." He nodded several times; habit of his. "Oh, you bet we will." He stopped and shook himself like a wet dog; I saw he was sweating, but he was better now. "Right," he said, "that's that dealt with. Onwards. I was thinking, we start off with the Nicephorus quartet in C."

I went home—I had a nice place, opposite the Power and Glory Stairs—bolted the door, shuttered the windows, and lit the lamp. The first thing I saw was this mirror.

I bought it for half an angel, and I got a bargain; a genuine silver-backed glass mirror, Mezentine, about three hundred years old, there's only five or six in all of Scheria. The man who sold it to me grinned: present for the wife? Daughter? Girlfriend? I just smiled at him. I bought a mirror—the best that money could buy—to remind myself of something.

It was not long after she died, and I was called out to a surgeon, a household name. I can't tell you what it was about, not relevant. But in his house he had a mirror, a cheap brass-plate job, entirely out of place in his sumptuously decorated home. He saw me looking at it and told me the story; how, when he was a young Army sawbones, he got caught up in some actual fighting and took an arrow in the gut. He knew that unless he got the loathsome thing out quick, he'd be dead, also that there was nobody competent to do the job within thirty miles. So he set up that mirror where he could see it clearly, and operated on himself. He nearly killed himself, and he was sick as a dog for a month, but he survived, and had kept the mirror ever since, to remind himself that he was a genius for whom anything was possible.

And that, of course, set me thinking.

I was in the money at that time, so I bought myself a mirror; silver-backed glass, Mezentine, about three hundred years old, I paid twenty angels for it at an auction. I hired a carpenter to build a special cradle for it, so it could be swiveled about and adjusted to exactly the angle I wanted. Then, one night, I barred all the doors and windows and lit a hundred oil lamps—I wanted to be able to see what I was doing. I had no idea if what I planned on doing was possible—just like my client the surgeon, I guess; as with him, though, it was a matter of life and death, because I knew I couldn't carry on much longer, not with those memories inside my head.

I fiddled with the mirror until I had a clear view of the side of my own head. Then I stared, really hard—and I was in.

Exactly the same usual thing: a library, with shelves of scrolls. I knew, as I always do, which one to reach for. I picked it out, unrolled it. The page was blank.

Two days later, I sold the mirror. I got thirty angels for it, from a collector. Born lucky, I guess.

• • •

My friend the director and I eventually compromised on the Procopius concerto and the overture to *The Triumph of Compassion* (the Euxinus arrangement, not the Theodotus). I cancelled all my engagements for a week, and practiced till I could barely stand up. Not that I needed to, but it helped me feel like I was doing something. I'm guessing that, to this day, there's a company of the Third Lancers who cover their ears and whimper every time the band strikes up the *Triumph* overture; the poor devils ordered to guard me night and day must've heard the wretched thing a couple of hundred times.

(In case you're wondering, I didn't wipe my friend's memory after all; he got squeamish. He said he'd rather change his mind than have someone change it for him. I was mildly offended, but made nothing of it. I figure a friend has the right to offend you at least once.)

The concert was held in the auditorium of the Silver Star Temple, my second favorite after the Imperial; I wondered why, since it seats less than a thousand, until I remembered that at the Silver Star, there's an underground passage from the green room straight to the stage; the performers are out of sight of the audience until the screens actually come down. At the Imperial, you walk down the main aisle, and a man with a knife who didn't care about his future could have a go at you, and there'd be nobody to stop him. The choice of venue was considerate, but mildly terrifying; but the acoustic at the Silver Star is just right for the Procopius, especially the slow second movement.

The other thing about the stage at the Silver Star is that you're quite high up, which means you're on a dead level sight line with the best seats in the house (six rows from the front)—you can see them and they can see you. I remember peering out into the sea of faces just before I took my stand. I found them quite easily: the old man and his son. They were talking to each other, heads turned, not looking at the stage. Then, as I lifted the flute to my lips, the old man looked up and saw me, and he went white as a sheet. Then it was my cue, six bars in, and I forgot about everything else and started to play.

Clamanzi was at the top of his form that day. Actually, I don't rate the *Triumph* overture all that much—melodrama—but the Procopius is one of the supreme achievements of the human race (so very strange, that a really nasty piece of work like Procopius could have produced something so sublime) and I defy anybody who claims to be any better than an animal not to be completely carried away by it. I wasn't really aware of anything else until I'd played that last long string of dying thirds. Then, when the music stopped, in the split second of dead silence you always get before the applause starts, I sort of woke up and looked down at the audience. I was looking for the old man and his son, but my attention was distracted. I saw another familiar face, in the row above them.

Familiar in more than one sense . . .

Familiar, because I'd seen her before; once in the flesh, more times than I could count in dreams. But also familiar, because for the first time I realized who she reminded me of. It was the way she was sitting, the angle of her face, slightly away, chin slightly lifted. Nobody could ever call the skinny girl a beauty, but at that angle the resemblance was unmistakable.

I can't remember how I got off the stage or back to the green room, but I remember sitting in a corner refusing tea and wine, and my friend the director bounding up to me like a friendly dog and yapping at me—wonderful, amazing, all the superlatives, except that he actually meant them; and especially the *Triumph*, my God, I never realized a human being could play like that. I frowned at him. I couldn't remember having played the *Triumph* overture—the Procopius, yes, but everything after that was just a blur. I muttered something or other and told him I'd like to be left in peace, please. He wasn't offended. Of course, he said, and made sure nobody spoke to me.

She was here; well, why was I surprised? Naturally, the enemy would bring their secret weapon. I had enough confidence in the Scherian authorities to assume that they knew what she could do and had taken the necessary measures to make sure she didn't do it to anybody who mattered—except that I'd been up there on stage, with her staring at me. A moment of panic; then I was able to reassure myself. I could remember every memory I'd acquired during my time with the old man and his son—

Presumably. But how the hell would I know?

No: be logical. I could remember things that would get their necks stretched in two minutes flat; therefore, she hadn't been at me. Quick mental geometry: how far was the stage from the eighth row of the auditorium? I didn't actually know, and for me, distance isn't really a problem, I can see through a man's head at any distance where I can clearly make out his face. But maybe the girl had problems with distance, maybe she was short-sighted. She had that slight squint, which would fit. And her mother . . .

I caught myself thinking that before I realized the implications; her mother was short-sighted too, when I knew her, twenty years ago.

Except that I'd met her mother, whom I'd never seen before (and I never forget a face), and the other woman had died twenty years ago, in childbirth.

I remember, I was alone in the green room by that stage, though presumably there was a half-company of guards outside in the corridor. I closed my eyes and tried to think. But my father and mother never showed any signs, perish the thought.

And then I reflected; be all that as it may, the reason she's here is to hurt you, of that you can be certain. And that takes priority over all other considerations. Doesn't it?

About twenty. Any age between nineteen and twenty-three. I've always been hopeless at guessing women's ages.

I slept badly—nightmares—and awoke to find that I'd been awarded an extra thousand angels, the Order of the Headless Spear, and full Scherian citizenship by a grateful Council. Well, I thought, that's nice.

My friend the director was in meetings all morning, but he made time to come and see me.

"That girl," I said, before he could sit down. "The one with the delegation. Have you any idea who she is?"

He nodded grimly. "We objected," he said, "but they insisted. It was a deal-breaker. But she's not allowed in to any of the sessions."

"She's here to kill me," I said.

He blinked. I could tell he believed me. "She couldn't get past the guards," he said.

I sighed. "You don't understand how it works," I told him. "She could get past an army. And you'd have fifty thousand soldiers who couldn't remember their own names."

He hadn't thought of that. "What can we do?"

I shrugged. "No idea," I said.

He frowned. Then he looked up. "We can poison her," he said.

He wasn't joking. "You can't." I'd spoken very quickly. "You'd start a war."

"There's poisons and poisons," he replied, and I felt cold all over. "All right, maybe not kill her. But a really bad stomach upset—"

In spite of everything I couldn't help laughing, at the thought of it.

"Trust me," he went on, "I've had a dicky tummy for years, while it's happening you simply can't think about anything else. A really bad dose of the shits will neutralize any power on Earth. We've got a man at Intelligence who specializes in that sort of thing. Leave it with me, it'll be just fine."

He dosed the lot of them, for good measure. My guess is, he dressed it up in a dish of the notorious Scherian pork terrine, a national delicacy that'll do for anybody who hasn't been brought up on it since childhood. The rest of the delegation was up and about after a day or so. The girl (my friend reported cheerfully) had taken it particularly hard, probably because she was so thin and delicate, and would be confined to the shithouse for at least a week.

Woe to the conquered, I thought. Less extreme than killing her, as effective, considerably less humane.

Except that it did kill her. The delegation withdrew from the negotiations for a whole day without any explanation, then announced that one of their advisers, a young woman, had contracted food poisoning and sadly passed away. It would have been her wish, they said, that the negotiations proceed; so they proceeded.

There was a bleak little funeral, which I insisted on attending, though I had no right to do so—except, possibly, that the body they were burying was my daughter, and of course I couldn't tell anyone that. My daughter, killed on my orders, for the single reason that she took after her father. Possibly. No way of proving it, naturally. And that which can't be proven can't be regarded as true.

But I saw them set up a long wooden box on a trestle, stack logs all round it, splash around some oil and apply fire. There was that unmistakable roast-pork smell, which they try and mask with scenty stuff, but it never really works. The old man and his son were there, of course. They kept looking at me. It occurred to me, later, that I could've wiped their heads there and then, and been rid of them. Later. At the time, I was preoccupied with other things.

They postponed the war, bless them; it would happen one day, inevitably as the leaves fall from the trees, but it wouldn't be soon. There was another concert, followed by a reception. I stood in a corner, trying to be invisible. Sure enough, the old man and his son headed straight for me.

You haven't told anyone. It was a statement of fact, which I confirmed. I pointed out that they'd sent men to kill me, driven me from my own country, and put a fortune on my head. They acknowledged as much, and warned me to keep my mouth shut and never, ever go home. They managed to make me feel as if it were all my fault. But they didn't mention the skinny girl, and neither did I.

The head of the delegation, who was also the provisional head of the provisional government (call him the provisional dictator) made a point of congratulating me on my performance and issuing a standing invitation to perform in the City, any time I felt like it. Clearly the old man and his son were as good at keeping secrets as me.

Then they went home; and I was mortally afraid that I'd lose my guards—they were picked men from the Prefect's Battalion, and there were probably other things they should have been doing. But my friend the director made out a case for me being a national treasure—I was eligible, apparently, now

I was a citizen—which entitled me to maximum security, in case I was stolen, defaced, vandalized, or damaged. He made loads of jokes about it afterwards, which I managed to take in good part. I went back to work, to full houses and embarrassing applause; I didn't mind. I was playing better than ever, and enjoying every minute of it. As for money—I can honestly say I lost interest in it, the way fish aren't particularly interested in the sea.

I moved; from the center of town out to the northern suburbs, where you could look out of your window and see meadows and woods. I never had time to do more than look at them. On the rare occasions when I was at home, I was totally occupied in learning and practicing new pieces, or rehearsing with orchestras in the massive barn I'd had built in the grounds. People talked about me; they found it strange that I never did anything besides work, no time for pleasures, no wine, no women. I never tried to explain to anyone, understandably enough.

It was late one night. I'd been up since dawn, going through a new concerto I'd commissioned from a promising young composer. A wonderful thing; the more I played it, the more I found in it, and it struck me that if I hadn't existed, if I'd never been born and never lived a life that brought me to that place at that time in exactly that way, it might never have been written. The young man, almost obscenely talented, was only interested in the money, which he said he needed really badly, for his sister's dowry or his mother's operation, or whatever. I paid him double, because the concerto was so good, even though I knew the money would shorten his life (which it did: dead of liver failure at age twenty-six) and cheat the world of what he might have written. What can you do?

I'd reached the point where I couldn't play any more, so I packed up my flute and locked it away, made myself a last bowl of tea, and shuffled off to bed. I fell asleep straight away, and slipped into one of the old nightmares. Disappointing, because I hadn't been getting them since the delegation went home. I woke up in a sweat, and saw that the lamp was lit, and there was someone in the room with me.

She was eating an apple. I saw the lamplight reflected in her eyes. "Hello," she said.

I found it hard to breathe. "Are you going to kill me?" I asked.

"Silly," she said. "You'd be dead already."

I tried to sit up, but she frowned at me, so I stayed where I was. "You know who I am," she said.

"Yes," I replied. "I—" Words are useless. "I helped you once."

That made her laugh. She put down the apple on the bed, by my feet. "So I'm told," she said. "But I don't believe it. You're my father."

I nodded. "I guessed," I said.

"Because I have the same talent as you." She picked something up off the bed. It was a knife. One of mine, actually.

"How did you get past the guards?"

She smiled. "I feel sorry for them," she said. "But I guess they signed on of their own free will. They were in the way."

"You wiped their minds."

"Yes."

I was waiting for the tactical officer inside my head to suggest something, but nothing came. "That was a horrible thing to do."

"You've done worse."

"To save my life," I said. "I never tried to harm you."

"You had them put something nasty in my food," she replied, as though correcting an obvious flaw in my logic. "It didn't kill me, but it made me very ill. So I suggested how would it be if we told everybody I died, then he'd assume he'd succeeded, and I'd be safe. So that's what we did." She took another bite from the apple. "I gather you came to my funeral. Did you cry?"

"No."

She nodded. "I told them I wanted to stay behind, after they went home. I've got a few jobs to do while I'm here, and then I'll head back." She paused, as if waiting for something. "Why haven't you tried to get inside my head?"

"I wish you no harm," I told her.

"That's a good one." She took another bite from the apple, then threw the core into the corner of the room. "You never mean any harm, do you? You didn't mean to blind your sister. Except you did. You held the branch back on purpose."

"How do you know that?"

She shrugged. "I know everything about you," she said. "More than you do."

"You've been inside my head."

Then she really laughed. She made a noise like a donkey. "You have no idea, have you? How much trouble you've caused. Well, of course you haven't, you saw to that. You ran away."

"People were trying to kill me."

"I don't mean that, stupid." She took a deep breath, then let it go slowly. "You know what," she said. "Once I made you a promise. I think I'll break it. Well? If I do, will you forgive me?"

I looked at her. "You never promised me anything."

"It's rude to call someone a liar. Well? Are you going to forgive me or not?"

I shrugged. "Does it matter?"

"Fine." She sat up straight, put down the knife, and folded her hands in her lap. "I made you a promise, about five years ago. You don't remember, do you?"

I shook my head.

"I came to see you," she said. "You don't remember, but I do. You were living in a nice suite of rooms next door but two to the Old Theatre. There was a marble staircase, and a big oak door with a shutter in it. You had a servant, I think he was Cimbrian. You made him wear a white tunic with brass buttons." She paused and grinned at me. "Remember?"

"I remember."

"The big door opened into a sort of hall," she went on, "with a marble floor, white and red, in a chessboard pattern. There were three couches and a brass table. Oh, yes, and a sort of palm tree thing in a big clay pot. And you had a parrot, in a cage."

"Go on," I said.

"You were sitting on one of the couches, and you had a barber to shave you. He was a tall man with red hair, left-handed. His name was Euja, I know, because you said, Thank you, Euja, that's all for today. Remember?"

"Yes."

She nodded approvingly. "You told me to sit down and you rang a bell, for tea. It came in a red-and-white porcelain pot, and there was a dragon on the bottom of the bowl. Is that right?"

"Yes."

"You waited till the servant had poured the tea, then you asked me politely what you could do for me. You must've thought I was a customer. I was fifteen. I told you, I'm your daughter."

I stared at her—her eyes, not the side of her head. "Go on."

"I told you things about my mother, things I'd heard from the people who brought me up. They were servants from my mother's family. They died when I was six, in the plague, and the woman's sister had me then. But I told you things, about her, and you realized I was telling the truth."

"Go on."

She smiled at me. "I told you how poor we were, because all the money my mother's father left for me had gone. I knew you were rich. I asked you for money."

My mouth was dry. "What did I say?"

She frowned. "You looked at me for a long time. Then you asked how I'd found you. I said, I'd heard about you; how you could go inside people's heads and take away memories. That's how I knew. I could do it too. Of course," she went on, "I couldn't be sure until I told you the secret things, about my mother. You recognized them all, and then I was certain. But I made sure."

"You looked—"

"In your head, yes. I saw my mother's bedroom, just as my nurse described it. And anyway, I recognized you, from her memories. You were much younger then, of course. But your voice was the same."

My feet and knees had gone cold. "So," I said, "you asked me for money. What did I say?"

She was silent for a long time. "You said you wouldn't give me anything, but I could earn four thousand angels. If I'd do a simple job for you. Then you took a piece of paper from the brass table and wrote out a draft and showed it to me."

"I wanted you to take away a memory," I said. "Well?"

"Of course. What other possible use could I be?"

I closed my eyes. "What did you take from me?"

I heard her say, "This."

I remembered it all, very clearly. I remembered hearing my younger sister crying, upstairs in the loft. I remember hearing my mother yelling at my father, the usual hateful stuff. Not again, I thought. I'd just come in from putting the chickens away; it was raining, and I was still wearing a coat, the big homespun that my uncle had left behind when he came to visit. I wanted to get to the fire—I was wet and cold—but that would mean going through the main room, which was where my mother and father were fighting. I decided I'd have to stay where I was until they stopped.

Then they came out past the chimney corner; I could see them, but they hadn't seen me. My father staggered a little; I knew what that meant, he'd been drinking, and when he was drunk he did stupid things. I saw him reach in the corner for his stick, a heavy blackthorn cudgel I knew only too well. He took a step forward, and I knew he was about to hit my mother. She screamed at him, you're stupid, you're so stupid, I should have listened to my family, they said you were useless and you are. He swung at her, aiming for her head. Long practice made her duck and swerve, and he hit her on the arm. She tried to back away, but her foot caught in the rucked-up rug and she tripped forward, toward him. He was about to hit her again, and my inner tactician told me that this time he'd get her, because she was off-balance and couldn't get out of the way. I suddenly remembered that in my right hand was the knife I'd taken with me to cut the twine on the neck of the feed sack. I stepped forward, in between them, and whether my father walked into the knife or whether I stabbed him, I simply don't know.

My mother was staring at him. I'd let go of the knife; it was still stuck in him. He opened his mouth, but all that came out was blood. She grabbed the knife and pulled it out, and then he fell over, crushing the little table. Nobody falls like that unless they're dead.

She stood there for a moment or so, with the knife in her hand, looking at me; then I heard my sister's voice, up at the top of the ladder. My mother swung round and screamed, "Go to *bed*!"

I tried to say something, but I couldn't. I remember the look on her face. On the advice of my internal tactical officer I took a long step back, out of her reach.

He was going to kill you, I said.

Don't be so stupid, she snapped at me. He would never—

He hit you with the stick. He—

I remember her knuckles were white around the knife handle. I knew, in that moment; like me, inside her head was a little voice advising her on distances and angles, how long a step she'd need to take to reach me, how to drive the knife home without letting me parry or ward her off. I took two long strides back, then turned and ran—

"You paid me," she said, "to remove that. I've been keeping it safe for you all this time, like a trustee. I think you should have it back now."

I think I actually raised a hand in front of me. "No," I said. "Please, take it back. I don't think I could bear to live with it."

Then she grinned. "Oh, there's more," she said.

I remembered the day my father found my sister. He'd gone into the barn to get his billhook, and there she was, hanging from the crossbeam. He'd tried to cut her down, but in his shock and grief he'd cut himself to the bone; he ran into the house for something to bind the cut with, and I was there. Come with me, he shouted. I remembered seeing her. I remembered cutting her down, and how she landed like a hay bale tossed from the loft, and how he swore at me. I remembered the note she left, written on the flyleaf of the Book, because there was nothing else in the house to write on; how everybody hated her because she was so ugly, because of her missing eye. It was after that that my father started drinking.

I remembered the day I came home. I found my mother sitting in the kitchen. I remembered thinking how dirty the place was, not like it used to be, everything neat and clean. I got your letter, I told her.

She looked at me. I hadn't seen her since the night my father died, when she'd called out all the neighbors to look for me, because I'd murdered my father and ought to be hung.

I need you to do something for me, she said.

● ● ●

"That's enough," I said. "Whatever it is you think I've done to you, that's enough."

The girl gave me a quizzical look. "You killed my mother," she explained. "It's not nearly enough."

I need you to do something for me, she said.

I waited. It was as though she expected me to guess what it was. Well? I asked.

You can do that trick, she said. I've been hearing all about you. You're making ever so much money in the City.

If it's money, I said, but she scowled at me. You can take away memories.

Yes, I said.

Fine. I want you to go inside my mind and take out every memory of you. Everything. I want it so I don't know you ever existed. Can you do that? And your brother and sister too, I want them to forget you. Take it all away, then get out and never come back. That's all.

"I think I may take after her," she said. "Strong. Single-minded."

"How the hell are you doing this?" I said. "I couldn't. I can only take them away, I can't put them back."

"I guess I'm better than you," she said. "Better than you in every way. That wouldn't be so hard." She raised an eyebrow. "Do you remember? How I came to you when I was fifteen, and all you wanted was to get rid of those memories? But you had money, and we needed it so badly. And you never told me—" She stopped for a moment. "You never told me what I was going to see. And I've had it inside me ever since. You forced it on me, like rape. I would never—"

"All right," I said. "So, what do you want me to do?"

Her eyes widened. "I want you to remember," she said.

I remembered the letter. It was barely legible, written in cheap oak-gall ink on wrapping paper. This is to let you know, it said, that she died but the kid survived. Her father paid my husband and me to take the child away, but the money he gave us has all run out and we're poor and we need money. You have a daughter. She's five now. You can have her, if you like.

I remembered sending a draft for twenty angels, which was all I had; but I didn't go. I couldn't bear to. And I burned the letter, with the name and the address. Because I didn't want her daughter, I wanted—

"You never meant me to see that," she said. "But I did. And then you asked me to wipe me out of your mind as well, as though I'd never been born." She looked at me again. "How could you do that? Like mother, like son?"

I said, "I'll give you ten thousand angels. It's all I've got."

"I could get twice as much for you," she replied, "but then you'd die, and that'd be letting you off easy. And you're forgetting, you've got lots of money back in the City, with the Social and Beneficent. I want all that, as well."

I wrote her two drafts. She read them carefully, to make sure they were in order. Then she folded them and tucked them into her sleeve. "What's so sad about it," she said, "is that all the really bad things you ever did were done for love—killing your father and my mother, I mean, blinding your sister was just stupid. You're really very stupid, aren't you? That's what your mother called your father." She examined me, as if she were considering buying me. "Are you happy?" she said. "Now, I mean. Here and now."

"Yes," I said. "Or I was."

She tutted. "Can't have that," she said. "I think that playing the flute's given you more happiness than anything else in your life, and that was someone else's, wasn't it? I don't think you can be allowed to keep it. I think I'll have it instead."

I felt the burning pain, just above my ear. "Sorry," she said. "Actually, I can do it without hurting, but it takes a little bit more effort, and I couldn't be bothered. Don't worry," she went on, "you can still remember what it was like being a famous musician. I've just taken what you took. That's fair, isn't it?"

Instinctively, I tried to remember how to hold a flute, how you shape your lips, the spread of the fingers. All gone. I had no idea.

"I remember wondering," she was saying, "why you didn't have me wipe my mother out of your head. Those memories must've been painful, but you kept them. No, don't explain," she added, "I'd like to think it was some last spark of decency in you, and anything you say will probably disappoint me. I don't want to have to punish you any more than I have already. I'm not a cruel person, you understand. It's just that you disgust me so much. I wish you were a spider, so I could squash you."

I looked at her; at the spot just above her ugly, lobeless ear. "What else can you do?" I said. "Apart from memories."

She grinned. "Oh, lots of things. I can put ideas in people's heads—like, for instance, I once met a really nasty man who had this special talent that allowed him to make stupid amounts of money. So I gave him this urge to gamble it all away. That's justice, don't you think?"

I shook my head. "That wasn't you."

"Maybe. Maybe not. How could you ever know for sure?" She laughed. "And now I think it's time you did something for me. Call it twenty years' worth of birthday presents from my father."

I remember—I don't know whose memory it was, mine or someone else's—the time I got beaten up in the dockyards, late at night. I think it must've been me, because it was over some trivial gambling debt. I remember the point where they were still hitting me, but I'd stopped feeling it, and I was just bone weary, I wanted to lie down and go to sleep but they wouldn't let me.

"Let me guess," I said.

So I went into her mind, and there she was standing over me while I took down the scrolls from the shelves, watching to make sure I didn't stick my nose in to anything else while I was there. Then I remembered going to see *me*, how badly I treated her, as though she had some horrible contagious disease. Then she pushed me out again; I found myself back in my bed, and she was staring at me.

I took a deep breath. "It's all right," I said. "Nothing bad's happened. Just go home."

She frowned. "Did I know you?" she said.

"No," I told her. "Don't lose the bits of paper in your sleeve, they're valuable. Don't think about anything. Just go home."

Which she did; and so did I, back to the City, where I belonged.

Not straightaway, of course. I got my friend the director to arrange for me to be smuggled safely over the border; then I walked (no money, remember?) all the way to the City. I was scared stiff I'd be recognized, but luckily I didn't run into anybody who remembered me. I went to the house where the old man and his son lived. I feel guilty about what I did to their guards and some of the servants, but they were in the way. I feel no guilt at all about what I did to the old man and his son.

Very soon afterwards, the new regime collapsed—as was inevitable, with its two leading lights reduced to vegetables. A few months later, they held proper elections again. After the inauguration of the new Consul and his cabinet, there was a grand reception at the Palace; entertainment was provided by a talented young flautist. Nobody knows where she suddenly appeared from, but people who should know compare her favorably with Clamanzi at his best. I've followed her career with interest, though from a distance; I've never actually heard her play. People who know her say that's she's happy, completely caught up in her music. I'm glad about that.

Of course, I don't live in the City these days. I moved to Permia, bought a large farm, I'm completely retired now. In case you're wondering: before I left the City, I stole a spade and went to a place on the moors, south of town, and dug up a big steel box full of gold coins. I knew where to look for it, thanks to the clerk who stole it from the old man and his son—I never break a professional confidence, but I don't always tell the truth. No angel, you might say. Ah, well.

I don't want to detain you any longer than necessary, but I'd just like to share a few insights with you, as the world's greatest living authority on suffering. I reckon I can claim that honor. I've caused more suffering, endured more suffering, witnessed, experienced, inflicted, savored, analyzed, enjoyed, dissected, wallowed in more suffering than anybody else who's ever lived. I have been in the mind of my enemy, my victim, my persecutor, your enemy, your victim, your persecutor; I know pain like fish know water, like birds know air. Suffering has fed and clothed me most of my life, I've sunk my roots deep into it and sucked it up into me; pain and suffering have made me what I am. To be quite honest, I'm sick and tired of it.

Along the way, I guess I've lost my edge a bit—like blacksmiths whose fingertips get burned so much they lose the fine touch. I'm not sure I can tell whose pain is which any more. Is the child crying in the street me or just some stranger? Answer: to make a distinction is to miss the point entirely. To try and rationalize all this in terms of right, wrong, good, evil, is just naïve; the very worst things we do, after all, we do for love, and the very worst pain we feel comes from love. She was right about that. In my opinion, love is the greatest and most enduring enemy, because love gives rise to the memories that kill us, slowly, every day. I think a man who never encounters love might quite possibly live forever. He'd have to, because if he died, who the hell would ever remember him?

INHUMAN GARBAGE

Kristine Kathryn Rusch

Detective Noelle DeRicci opened the top of the waste crate. The smell of rott id the faint smell of urine and feces. A woman's body curled on top of the compost pile as if she had fallen asleep.

She hadn't, though. Her eyes were open.

DeRicci couldn't see any obvious cause of death. The woman's skin might have been copper colored when she was alive, but death had turned it sallow. Her hair was pulled back into a tight bun, undisturbed by whatever killed her. She wore a grey and tan pantsuit that seemed more practical than flattering.

DeRicci put the lid down, and resisted the urge to remove her thin gloves. They itched. They always itched. Because she used department gloves rather than buying her own, and they never fit properly.

She rubbed her fingers together, as if something from the crate could have gotten through the gloves, and turned around. Nearly one hundred identical containers lined up behind it. More arrived hourly from all over Armstrong, the largest city on Earth's Moon.

The entire interior of the warehouse smelled faintly of organic material gone bad. She was only in one section of the warehouse. There were dozens of others, and at the end of each, was a conveyer belt that took the waste crate, mulched it, and then sent the material for use in the Growing Pits outside Armstrong's dome.

The crates were cleaned in a completely different section of the warehouse, and then sent back into the city for reuse.

Not every business recycled its organic produce for the Growing Pits, but almost all of the restaurants and half of the grocery stores did. DeRicci's apartment building sent organic food waste into bins that came here as well.

The owner of the warehouse, Najib Ansel, stood next to the nearest row of crates. He wore a blue smock over matching blue trousers, and blue booties on his feet. Blue gloves stuck out of his pocket, and a blue mask hung around his neck.

"How did you find her?" DeRicci asked.

Ansel nodded at the ray of blue light that hovered above the crate, then toed the floor.

"The weight was off," he said. "The crate was too heavy."

DeRicci looked down.

"I take it you have sensors in the floor?" she asked.

"Along the orange line."

She didn't see an orange line. She moved slightly, then saw it. It really wasn't a line, more a series of orange rectangles, long enough to hold the crates, and too short to measure anything beside them.

"So you lifted the lid . . . " DeRicci started.

"No, sir," Ansel said, using the traditional honorific for someone with more authority.

DeRicci wasn't sure why she had more authority than he did. She had looked him up on her way here. He owned a multimillion-dollar industry, which made its fortune charging for waste removal from the city itself, and then reselling that waste at a low price to the Growing Pits.

She had known this business existed, but she hadn't paid a lot of attention to it until an hour ago. She had felt a shock of recognition when she saw the name of the business in the download that sent her here: *Ansel Management* was scrawled on the side of every waste container in every recycling room in the city.

Najib Ansel had a near monopoly in Armstrong, and had warehouses in six other domed communities. According to her admittedly cursory research, he had filed for permits to work in two new communities just this week. So the fact he was in standard worker gear, just like his employees, amazed her. She would have thought a mogul like Ansel would be in a gigantic office somewhere making deals, rather than standing on the floor of the main warehouse just outside Armstrong's dome.

Even though he used the honorific, he didn't say anything more. Clearly, Ansel was going to make her work for information.

"Okay," DeRicci said. "The crate was too heavy. Then what?"

"Then we activated the sensors, to see what was inside the crate." He looked up at the blue light again. Obviously that was the sensor.

"Show me how that works," she said.

He rubbed his fingers together—probably activating some kind of chip. The light came down and broadened, enveloping the crate. Information flowed above it, mostly in chemical compounds and other numbers. She was amazed she recognized that the symbols were compounds. She wondered where she had picked that up.

"No visuals?" she asked.

"Not right away." He reached up to the holographic display. The numbers kept scrolling. "You see, there's really nothing out of the ordinary here. Even her clothes must be made of some kind of organic material. So my people couldn't figure out what was causing the extra weight."

"You didn't find this, then?" she asked.

"No, sir," he said.

"I'd like to talk with the person who did," she said.

"She's over there." He nodded toward a small room off to the side of the crates.

DeRicci suppressed a sigh. Of course he cleared the employee off the floor. Anything to make a cop's job harder.

"All right," DeRicci said, not trying to hide her annoyance. "How did your 'people' discover the extra weight?"

"When the numbers didn't show anything," he said, "they had the system scan for a large piece. Sometimes, when crates come in from the dome, someone dumps something directly into the crate without paying attention to weight and size restrictions."

Those were hard to ignore. DeRicci vividly remembered the first time she tried to dump something of the wrong size into a recycling crate. She dumped a rotted roast she had never managed to cook (back in the days when she actually believed she could cook). She'd put it into the crate behind her then-apartment building. The damn crate beeped at her, and when she didn't remove the roast fast enough for the stupid thing, it actually started to yell at her, telling her that she wasn't following the rules. There was a way to turn off the alarms, but she and her building superintendent didn't know it. Clearly, someone else did.

"So," DeRicci said, "the system scanned, and . . . ?"

"Registered something larger," he said somewhat primly. "That's when my people switched the information feed to visual, and got the surprise of their lives."

She would wager. She wondered if they thought the woman was sleeping. She wasn't going to ask him that question; she'd save it for the person who actually found the body. "When did they call you?" she asked.

"After they visually confirmed the body," he said.

"Meaning what?" she asked. "They saw it on the feed or they actually lifted the lid?"

"On the feed," he said.

"Where was this?" she asked.

He pointed to a small booth that hovered over the floor. The booth clearly operated on the same tech that the flying cars in Armstrong used. The booth was smaller than the average car, however, and was clear on all four sides.

Only the bottom appeared to have some kind of structure, probably to hide all the mechanics.

"Is someone in the booth?" she asked.

"We always have someone monitoring the floor," he said, "but I put someone new up there, so that the team which discovered the body can talk to you."

DeRicci supposed he had put the entire team in one room, together, so that they could align their stories. But she didn't say anything like that. No sense antagonizing Ansel. He was helping her.

"We're going to need to shut down this part of your line," she said. "Everything in this part of the warehouse will need to be examined."

To her surprise, he didn't protest. Of course, if he had protested, she would have had him shut down the entire warehouse.

Maybe he had dealt with the police before.

"So," she said, "who actually opened the lid on this container?"

"I did," he said quietly.

She hadn't expected that. "Tell me about it."

"The staff contacted me after they saw the body."

"On your links?" she asked. Everyone had internal links for communication, and the links could be set up with varying degrees of privacy. She would wager that the entire communication system inside Ansel Management was on its own dedicated link.

"Yes," he said. "The staff contacted me on my company link."

"I'd like to have copies of that contact," she said.

"Sure." He wasn't acting like someone who had anything to hide. In fact, he was acting like someone who had been through this before.

"What did your staff tell you?" she asked.

His lips turned upward. Someone might have called that expression a smile, but it wasn't. It was rueful.

"They told me that there was a woman in crate A1865."

DeRicci made a mental note about the number. Before this investigation was over, she'd learn everything about this operation, from the crate numbering system to the way that the conveyer to the actual mulching process.

"That's what they said?" she asked. "A woman in the crate?"

"Crate A1865," he repeated, as if he wanted that detail to be exactly right.

"What did you think when you heard that?" DeRicci asked.

He shook his head, then sighed. "I—we've had this happen before, Detective. Not for more than a year, but we've found bodies. Usually homeless people in the crates near the Port, people who came into Armstrong and can't get out. Sometimes we get an alien or two sleeping in the crates. The Oranjanie view rotting produce as a luxury, and they look human from some angles."

The Port of Armstrong was the main spaceport onto the Moon, and also functioned as the gateway to Earth. Member species of the Earth Alliance had to stop in Armstrong first, before traveling to Earth. Some travelers never made it into Earth's protected zone, and got stuck on the Moon itself.

Right now, however, she had no reason to suspect alien involvement in this crime. She preferred working human-on-human crime. It made the investigation so much easier.

"You've found human bodies in your crates before," she clarified.

"Yeah," he said.

"And the police have investigated?"

"All of the bodies, alien and human," he said. "Different precincts, usually, and different time periods. My grandmother started this business over a hundred years ago. She found bodies even way back then."

DeRicci guessed it would make sense to hide a body in one of the crates. Or someone would think it made sense.

"Do you think that bodies have gotten through the mulching process?" It took her a lot of strength not to look at the conveyer belt as she asked that question.

"I don't think a lot got through," he said. "I know some did. Back in my grandmother's day. She's the one who set up the safeguards. We might have had a few glitches after the safeguards were in place, before we knew how well they worked, but I can guarantee nothing has gone through since I started managing this company twenty-five years ago."

DeRicci tried not to shudder as she thought about human flesh serving as compost at the Growing Pits. She hated Moon-grown food, and she had a hunch she was going to hate it more after this case.

But she had to keep asking questions.

"You said you can guarantee it," she repeated.

He nodded.

"What if someone cut up the body?" she asked.

He grimaced. "The pieces would have to be small to get past our weight and size restrictions. Forgive me for being graphic, but no full arms or legs or torsos or heads. Maybe fingers and toes. We have nanoprobes on these things, looking for human DNA. But the probes are coating the lining of the crates. If someone buried a finger in the middle of some rotting lettuce, we might miss it."

She turned so that he wouldn't see her reaction. She forced herself to swallow some bile back, and wished she had some savings. She wanted to go home and purge her refrigerator anything grown on the Moon, and buy expensive Earth-grown produce.

But she couldn't afford that, not on a detective's salary.

"Fair enough," she said, surprised she could sound so calm when she was so thoroughly grossed out. "No full bodies have gone through in at least twenty-five years. But you've seen quite a few. How many?"

"I don't know," he said. "I'd have to check the records."

That surprised her. It meant there were enough that he couldn't keep track. "Any place where they show up the most often?"

"The Port," he said. "There's a lot of homeless in that neighborhood."

Technically, they weren't homeless. They were people who lived on the city's charity. A lot of small cubicle sized rooms existed on the Port blocks, and anyone who couldn't afford their own home or ended up stranded and unemployable in the city could stay in one of the cubicles for six months, no questions asked.

After six months, they needed to move to long-term city services, which were housed elsewhere. She wanted to ask if anyone had turned up in those neighborhoods, but she'd do that after she looked at his records.

"I'm confused," she said. "Do these people crawl into the crates and die?"

The crate didn't look like it was sealed so tightly that the person couldn't get oxygen.

"Some of them," he said. "They're usually high or drunk."

"And the rest?" she asked.

"Obviously someone has put them there," he said.

"A different someone each time, I assume," she said.

He shrugged. "I let the police investigate. I don't ask questions."

"You don't ask questions about dead people in your crates?"

His face flushed. She had finally gotten to him.

"Believe it or not, Detective," he snapped, "I don't like to think about it. I'm very proud of this business. We provide a service that enables the cities on the Moon to not only have food, but to have *great* food. Sometimes our system gets fouled up by crazy people, and I *hate* that. We've gone to great lengths to prevent it. That's why you're here. Because our systems *work*."

"I didn't mean to offend you," she lied. "This is all new to me, so I'm going to ask some very ignorant questions at times."

He looked annoyed, but he nodded.

"What part of town did this crate come from?" she asked.

"The Port," he said tiredly.

She should have expected that, after he had mentioned the Port a few times.

"Was the body in the crate when it was picked up at the Port?" she asked.

"The weight was the same from Port to here," he said. "Weight gets recorded at pick-up but flagged near the conveyer. The entire system is automated until the crates get to the warehouse. Besides, we don't have the ability to investigate anything inside Armstrong. There are a lot of regulations on things that are considered garbage inside the dome. If we violate those, we'll get black marks against our license, and if we get too many black marks in a year, we could lose that license."

More stuff she didn't know. City stuff, regulatory stuff. The kinds of things she always ignored.

And things she would probably have to investigate now.

"Do you know her?" DeRicci asked, hoping to catch him off balance.

"Her?" He looked confused for a moment. Then he looked at the crate, and his flush grew deeper. "You mean, *her*?"

"Yes," DeRicci said. Just from his reaction she knew his response. He didn't know the woman. And the idea that she was inside one of his crates upset him more than he wanted to say.

Which was probably why he was the person talking to DeRicci now.

"No," he said. "I don't know her, and I don't recognize her. We didn't run any recognition programs on her either. We figured you all would do that."

"No one touched her? No one checked her for identification chips?"

"I'm the one who opened the crate," he said. "I saw her, I saw that her eyes were open, and then I closed the lid. I leave the identifying to you all."

"Do you know all your employees, Mr. Ansel?"

"By name," he said.

"By look," she said.

He shook his head. "I have nearly three hundred employees in Armstrong alone."

"But you just said you know their names. You know all three hundred employees by name?"

He smiled absently, which seemed like a rote response. He'd responded to this kind of thing before.

"I have an eidetic memory," he said. "If I've seen a name, then I remember it."

"An eidetic memory for names, but not faces? I've never heard of that," DeRicci said.

"I haven't met all of my employees," he said. "But I go over the pay amounts every week before they get sent to the employees' accounts. I see the names. I rarely see the faces."

"So you wouldn't know if she worked here," DeRicci said.

"Here?" he asked. "Here I would know. I come here every day. If she worked in one of the other warehouses or in transport or in sales, I wouldn't know that."

"Did this crate go somewhere else before coming to this warehouse?" DeRicci asked.

"No," Ansel said. "Each crate is assigned a number. That number puts it in a location, and then when the crate fills, it gets swapped out with another. The crate comes to the same warehouse each time, without deviation. And since that system is automated, as I mentioned, I know that it doesn't go awry."

"Can someone stop the crate in transit and add a body?"

"No," he said. "I can show you if you want."

She shook her head. That would be a good job for her partner, Rayvon Lake. Rayvon still hadn't arrived, the bastard. DeRicci would have to report him pretty soon. He had gotten very lax about crime scenes, leaving them to her. He left most everything to her, and she hated it.

He was a lazy detective—twenty years in the position—and he saw her as an upstart who needed to be put in her place.

She wouldn't have minded if he did his job. Well, that wasn't exactly true. She would have minded. She hated people who disliked her. But she wouldn't be considering filing a report on him if he actually did the work he was supposed to do.

She would get Lake to handle the transport information by telling him she wasn't smart enough to understand it. It would mean that she'd have to suffer through an explanation later in the case, but maybe by then, she'd either have this thing solved or she'd have a new partner.

A woman could hope, after all.

"One of the other detectives will look into the transport process," DeRicci said. "I'm just trying to cover the basics here, so we start looking in the right place. Can outsiders come into this warehouse?"

"And get into one of our crates?" Ansel asked. "No. Look."

He touched the edge of the lid, and she heard a loud snap.

"It's sealed shut now," he said.

She didn't like the sound of that snap.

"If I were in there," she asked, "could I breathe through that seal?"

"Yes," he said. "For about two days, if need be. But it doesn't seal shut like that until it leaves the transport and crosses the threshold here at the warehouse. So there's no way anyone could crawl in here at the warehouse."

"All right," DeRicci said. "So, let me be sure I understand you. The only place that someone could either place a body into a crate or crawl into it on their own is on site."

"Yes," Ansel said. "We try to encourage composting, so we allow bypassers to stuff something into a crate. We search for non-organic material at the site, and flag the crates with non-organic material so they can be cleaned."

"Clothing is organic?" DeRicci asked.

"Much of it, yes," Ansel said. "Synthetics aren't good hosts for nanoproducts, so most people wear clothing made from recycled organic material."

DeRicci's skin literally crawled. She hadn't known that. She wasn't an organic kind of woman. She preferred fake stuff, much to the dismay of her friends.

"All right," she said. "I'm going to talk with your people in a minute. I'll want to know what they know. And I'll need to see your records on previous incidents."

She didn't check to see if he had sent her anything on her links. She didn't want downloads to confuse her sense of the crime scene. She liked to make her own opinions, and she did that by being thorough.

Detectives like Rayvon Lake gathered as much information as possible, multitasking as they walked through a crime scene. She believed they missed most of the important details while doing that, and that led to a lot of side roads and wasted time. And, if she could prove it (if she had time to prove it), a lot of false convictions. She had caught Lake twice trying to close a case by accusing an innocent person who was convenient, rather than doing the hard legwork required of a good investigator.

Ansel fluttered near her for a moment. She inclined her head toward the room where the staff had gathered, knowing she was inviting him to contaminate her witnesses even more, but she had a hunch none of them were going to be useful to the investigation anyway.

"Before you go," she said, just in case he didn't take the hint, "could you unseal this crate for me?"

"Oh, yes, sorry," he said, and ran his fingers along the side again. It snapped one more time, then popped up slightly.

DeRicci thanked him, and pulled back the lid. The crate was deep—up to DeRicci's ribs—and filled with unidentifiable bits of rotting food. The woman lay on top of them, hands cradled under her cheek, feet tucked together.

DeRicci couldn't imagine anyone just curling up here, even at the bidding of someone else. But people did strange things for strange reasons, and she wasn't going to rule it out.

She put the lid down and then looked at the warehouse again. She would need the numbers, but she suspected thousands of crates went through Ansel's facilities around the Moon daily. Done properly, it would be a perfect way to dispose of bodies and all kinds of other things that no one wanted to see. She wondered how many others knew about this facility and how it worked.

She suspected she would have to find out.

Getting the crime scene unit to a warehouse outside of the dome took more work than Ethan Broduer liked to do. Fortunately, he was a deputy coroner, which meant he couldn't control the crime scene unit. Someone with more seniority had to handle requisitioning the right vehicle from the Police

Department yards outside the dome, and making certain the team had the right equipment.

Broduer came to the warehouse via train. The ride was only five minutes long, but it made him nervous. He was born inside the dome, and he hated leaving it for any reason at all, especially for a reason involving work. So much of his work had to do with temperature and conditions, and if the body had been in an airless environment at all, it had an impact on every aspect of his job.

He was relieved when he arrived at the warehouse and learned that the body had never gone outside of an Earth Normal environment. However, he was annoyed to see that he would be working with Noelle DeRicci. She was notoriously difficult and demanding, and often asked coroners to redo something or double-check their findings. She'd caught him in several mistakes, which he found embarrassing. Then she had had the gall to tell him that he should probably double-check all of his work, considering its shoddy quality.

She stood next to a crate, the only one of thousands that was open. She was rumpled—she was always rumpled—and her curly black hair looked messier than usual.

When she saw him approach, she glared at him.

"Oh, lucky me," she said.

Broduer bit back a response. He'd been recording everything since he got off the train inside the warehouse's private platform, and he didn't want to show any animosity toward DeRicci on anything that might go to court.

"Just show me the body and I'll get to work," he said.

She raised her eyebrows at the word "work," and she didn't have to add anything to convey her meaning. She didn't think Broduer worked at all.

"My biggest priority at the moment is an identification," DeRicci said.

And his biggest priority was to do this investigation right. But he didn't say that. Instead he looked at the dozens of crates spread out before him. "Which one am I dealing with?" he asked, pleased that he could sound so calm in the face of her rudeness.

She placed a hand on the crate behind her. He was pleased to see that she wore gloves. He had worked with her partner Rayvon Lake before, and Lake had to be reminded to follow any kind of procedure.

But Broduer didn't see Lake anywhere.

"Have you had cases involving the waste crates before?" DeRicci asked Broduer.

"No," he said, not adding that he tried to pass anything outside the dome onto anyone else, "but I've heard about cases involving them. I guess it's not that uncommon."

"Hmm," she said looking toward a room at the far end of the large warehouse. "And here I thought they were."

Broduer was going to argue his point when he realized that DeRicci wasn't talking to him now. She was arguing with someone she had already spoken to.

"Can you get me information on that?" DeRicci asked Broduer.

He hated it when detectives wanted him to do their work for them. "It's in the records."

DeRicci made a low, growly sound, like he had irritated her beyond measure.

So he decided to tweak her a bit more. "Just search for warehouses and recycling and crates—"

"I know," she said. "I was hoping your office already had statistics."

"I'm sure we do, Detective," he said, moving past her, "but you want me to figure out what killed this poor creature, right? Not dig into old cases."

"I think the old cases might be relevant," she said.

He shrugged. He didn't care what was or wasn't relevant to her investigation. His priority was dealing with this body. "Excuse me," he said, and slipped on his favorite pair of gloves. Then he raised the lid on the crate.

The woman inside was maybe thirty. She had been pretty, too, before her eyes had filmed over and her cheeks sunk in. She had clearly died in an Earth Normal environment, and she hadn't left that environment, as advertised. He would have to do some research to figure out if the presence of rotting food had an impact on the body's decomposition, but that was something to worry about later.

Then Broduer glanced up. "I'll have information for you in a while," he said to DeRicci.

"Just give me a name," she said. "We haven't traced anything."

He didn't want to move the body yet. He didn't even want to touch it, because he was afraid of disturbing some important evidence.

The corpse's hands were tucked under her head, so he couldn't just run the identification chips everyone had buried in their palms. So he used the coroner's office facial recognition program. It had a record of every single human who lived in Armstrong, and was constantly updated with information from the arrivals and departures sections of the city every single day.

"Initial results show that her name is Sonja Mycenae. She was born here, and moved off-Moon with her family ten years ago. She returned one month ago to work as a nanny for . . . . "

He paused, stunned at the name that turned up.

"For?" DeRicci pushed.

Broduer looked up. He could feel the color draining from his face. "Luc Deshin," he said quietly. "She works for Luc Deshin."

Luc Deshin.

DeRicci hadn't expected that name.

Luc Deshin ran a corporation called Deshin Enterprises that the police department flagged and monitored continually. Everyone in Armstrong knew Deshin controlled a huge crime syndicate that trafficked in all sorts of illegal and banned substances. The bulk of Deshin's business had moved off-Moon, but he had gotten his start as an average street thug, rising, as those kids often do, through murder and targeted assassination into a position of power, using the deaths of others to advance his own career.

"Luc Deshin needed a nanny?" DeRicci sounded confused.

"He married a few years ago," Broduer said, as he bent over the body again. "I guess they had kids."

"And didn't like the nanny." DeRicci whistled. "Talk about a high stress job."

She glanced at the room filled with employees who found the body. There was a lot of work to be done here, but none of it was as important as catching Deshin by surprise with this investigation. If he killed this Sonja Mycenae, then he would be expecting the police's appearance. But he might not expect them so soon.

Or maybe he had always used the waste crates to dump his bodies. No one had ever been able to pin a murder on him.

Perhaps this was why.

She needed to leave. But before she did, she sent a message to Lake. Only she sent it using the standard police links, not the encoded link any other officer would use with her partner. She wanted it on record that Lake hadn't shown up yet.

Rayvon, you need to get here ASAP. There are employees to interview. I'm following a lead, but someone has to supervise the crime scene unit. Someone sent Deputy Coroner Broduer and he doesn't have supervisory authority.

She didn't want for Lake's response. Before he said anything, she sent another message to her immediate supervisor, Chief of Detectives Andrea Gumiela, this time through an encoded private link.

This case has ties to Deshin Enterprises, DeRicci sent. I'm going there now, but we need a good team on this. It's not some random death. It needs to be done perfectly. Between Broduer and Lake, we're off to a bad start.

She didn't wait for Gumiela to respond either. In fact, after sending that message, DeRicci shut off all but her emergency links.

She didn't want Gumiela to tell her to stay on site, and she didn't want to hear Lake's invective when he realized she had essentially chastised him in front of the entire department.

"Make sure no one leaves," DeRicci said to Broduer.

He looked up, panicked. "I don't have the authority."

"Pretend," she snapped, and walked away from him.

She needed to get to Luc Deshin, and she needed to get to him now.

Luc Deshin grabbed his long-waisted overcoat and headed down the stairs. So a police detective wanted to meet with him. He wished he found such things unusual. But they weren't. The police liked to harass him. Less now than in the past. They'd had a frustrating time pinning anything on him.

He always found it ironic that the crimes they accused him of were crimes he'd never think of committing, and the crimes he had committed—long ago and far away—were crimes they had never heard of. Now, all of his activities were legal. Just-inside-the-law legal, but legal nonetheless. Or so his cadre of lawyers kept telling the local courts, and the local judges—at least the ones he would find himself in front of—always believed his lawyers.

So, a meeting like this, coming in the middle of the day, was an annoyance, and nothing more.

He used his trip down the stairs to stay in shape. His office was a penthouse on the top floor of the building he'd built to house Deshin Enterprises years ago. He used to love that office, but he liked it less since he and his wife Gerda brought a baby into their lives.

He smiled at the thought of Paavo. They had adopted him—sort of. They had drawn up some legal papers and wills that the lawyers assured him would stand any challenge should he and Gerda die suddenly.

But Deshin and Gerda had decided against an actual adoption given Deshin's business practices and his reputation in Armstrong. They were worried some judge would deem them unfit, based on Deshin's reputation.

Plus, Paavo was the child of two Disappeareds, making the adoption situation even more difficult. The Earth Alliance's insistence that local laws prevailed when crimes were committed meant that humans were often subjected to alien laws, laws that made no sense at all. Many humans didn't like being forced to lose a limb as punishment for chopping down an exotic tree, or giving up a child because they'd broken food laws on a different planet. Those who could afford to get new names and new identities did so rather than accept their punishment under Earth Alliance law. Those people Disappeared.

Paavo's parents had Disappeared within weeks of his birth, leaving him to face whatever legal threat those aliens could dream up.

Paavo, alone, at four months.

Fortunately, Deshin and Gerda had sources inside Armstrong's family services, which they had cultivated for just this sort of reason. Both Deshin and Gerda had had difficult childhoods—to say the least. They knew what it was like to be unwanted.

Their initial plan had been to bring several unwanted children into their home, but after they met Paavo, a brilliant baby with his own special needs, they decided to put that plan on hold. If they could only save Paavo, that would be enough.

Just a month into life with the baby, and they knew that any more children would take a focus that, at the moment at least, Paavo's needs wouldn't allow.

Deshin reached the bottom of the stairwell, ran a hand through his hair, and then walked through the double doors. His staff kept the detective in the lobby.

She was immediately obvious, even though she wasn't in uniform. A slightly disheveled woman with curly black hair and a sharp, intelligent face, she wasn't looking around like she was supposed to. Most new visitors to Deshin Enterprises either pretended to be unimpressed with the real marble floors, the imported wood paneling, and the artwork that constantly shifted on the walls and ceiling. Or the visitors gaped openly at all of it.

This detective did neither. Instead, she scanned the people in the lobby—all staff, all there to guard him and keep an eye on her.

She would be difficult. He could tell that just from her body language. He wasn't used to dealing with someone from the Armstrong Police Department who was intelligent *and* difficult to impress.

He walked toward her, and as he reached her, he extended his hand.

"Detective," he said warmly. "I'm Luc Deshin."

She wiped her hands on her stained shirt, and just as he thought she was going to take his hand in greeting, she shoved her hands into the pockets of her ill-fitting black pants.

"I know who you are," she said.

She deliberately failed to introduce herself, probably as a power play. He could play back, ask to see the badge chip embedded in the palm of her hand, but he didn't feel like playing. She had already wasted enough of his time.

So he took her name, Noelle DeRicci, from the building's security records, and declined to look at her service record. He had it if he needed it.

"What can I do for you, Detective?" He was going to charm her, even if It took a bit of strength to ignore the games.

"I'd like to speak somewhere private," she said.

He smiled. "No one is near us, and we have no recording devices in this part of the lobby. If you like, we can go outside. There's a lovely coffee shop across the street."

Her eyes narrowed. He watched her think: did she ask to go to his office and get denied, or did she just play along?

"The privacy is for you," she said, "but okay. . . . "

She sounded dubious, a nice little trick. A less secure man would then invite her into the office. Deshin waited. He learned that middle managers—and that was what detectives truly were—always felt the press of time. He never had enough time for anything and yet, as the head of his own corporation, he also had all the time in the universe.

"I'm here about Sonja Mycenae," she said.

Sonja. The nanny he had fired just that morning. Well, fired wasn't an accurate term. He had deliberately avoided firing her. He had eliminated her position.

He and Gerda had decided Sonja wasn't affectionate enough toward their son. In fact, she had seemed a bit cold toward him. And once Deshin and Gerda started that conversation about Sonja's attitudes, they realized they didn't like having someone visit their home every day, and they didn't like giving up any time with Paavo. Both Gerda and Deshin had worried, given their backgrounds, that they wouldn't know how to nurture a baby, but Sonja had taught them training mattered a lot less than actual love.

"I understand she works for you," the detective said.

"She work*ed* for me," he said.

Something changed in the detective's face. Something small. He felt uneasy for the first time.

"Tell me what this is about, Detective," he said.

"It's about Sonja Mycenae," she repeated.

"Yes, you said that. What exactly has she done?" he asked.

"Why don't you tell me why she no longer works for you," the detective said.

"My wife and I decided that we didn't need a nanny for our son. I called Sonja to the office this morning, and let her know that, effective immediately, her employment was terminated through no fault of her own."

"Do you have footage of that conversation?" the detective asked.

"I do, and it's protected. You'll need permission from both of us or a warrant before I can give it to you."

The detective raised her eyebrows. "I'm sure you can forgo the formalities, Mr. Deshin."

"I'm sure that many people do, Detective," he said, "however, it's my understanding that an employee's records are confidential. You may get a warrant if you like. Otherwise, I'm going to protect Sonja's privacy."

"Why would you do that, Mr. Deshin?"

"Believe it or not, I follow the rules." He managed to say that without sarcasm.

The detective grunted as if she didn't believe him. "What made you decide to terminate her position today?"

"I told you," Deshin said, keeping his voice bland even though he was getting annoyed. "My wife and I decided we didn't need a nanny to help us raise our son."

"You might want to share that footage with me without wasting time on a warrant, Mr. Deshin," the detective said.

"Why would I do that, Detective? I'm not even sure why you're asking about Sonja. What has she done?"

"She has died, Mr. Deshin."

The words hung between them. He frowned. The detective had finally caught him off guard. For the first time, he did not know how to respond. He probably needed one of his lawyers here. Any time his name came up in an investigation, he was automatically the first suspect.

But in this case, he had nothing to do with Sonja's death. So he would act accordingly, and let the lawyers handle the mess.

"What happened?" he asked softly.

He had known Sonja since she was a child. She was the daughter of a friend. That was one of the many reasons he had hired her, because he had known her. Even then, she hadn't turned out as expected. He remembered an affectionate happy girl. The nanny who had come to his house didn't seem to know how to smile at all. There had been no affection in her.

And when he last saw her, she'd been crying and pleading with him to keep her job. He actually had to have security drag her out of his office.

"We don't know what happened," the detective said.

That sentence could mean a lot. It could mean they didn't know what happened at all or that they didn't know if her death was by natural causes or by murder. It could also mean that they didn't know exactly what or who caused the death, but that they suspected murder. Since he was facing a detective and not a beat officer, he knew they suspected murder.

"Where did it happen?" Deshin asked.

"We don't know that either," the detective said.

He snapped, "Then how do you know she's dead?"

Again, that slight change in the detective's face. Apparently he had finally hit on the correct question.

"Because workers found her in a waste crate in a warehouse outside the dome."

"Outside the dome . . . ?" That didn't make sense to him. Sonja hadn't even owned an environmental suit. She had hated them with a passion. "She died outside the dome?"

"I didn't say that, Mr. Deshin," the detective said.

He let out a breath. "Look, Detective, I'm cooperating here, but you need to work with me. I saw Sonja this morning, eliminated her position, and watched her leave my office. Then I went to work. I haven't gone out of the building all day."

"But your people have," the detective said.

He felt a thin thread of fury, and he suppressed it. Everyone assumed that his people murdered other people according to some whim. That simply was not true.

"Detective," he said calmly. "If I wanted Sonja dead, why would I terminate her employment this morning?"

"I have only your word for that," the detective said. "Unless you give me the footage."

"And I have only your word that she's dead," he said.

The detective pressed her hands together, then separated them. A hologram appeared between them—a young woman, looking as if she had fallen asleep in a meadow. Until he looked closely, and saw that the "meadow" was bits of food, and the young woman's eyes were open and filmy.

It was Sonja.

"My God," he said.

"If you give me the footage," the detective said, "and it confirms what you say, then you'll be in the clear. If you wait, then we're going to assume it was doctored."

Deshin glared at her. She was good—and she was right. The longer he waited, the less credibility he would have.

"I'm going to consult with my attorneys," he said. "If they believe this information has use to you and it doesn't cause me any legal liabilities, then you will receive it from them within the hour."

The detective crossed her arms. "I suggest you send it to me now. I promise you I will not look at anything until you or your attorneys say I can."

It was an odd compromise, but one that *would* protect him. If she believed he would doctor the footage, then having the footage in her possession wouldn't harm him.

But he didn't know the laws on something this arcane.

"How's this, detective," he said. "My staff will give you a chip with the information on it. You may not put the chip into any device or watch it until I've consulted with my attorneys. You will wait here while I do so."

"Seems fine to me," the detective said. "I've got all the time in the world."

• • •

She didn't, of course. DeRicci was probably getting all kinds of messages on her links from Lake and Gumiela and Broduer and everyone else, telling her she was stupid or needed or something.

She didn't care. She certainly wasn't going to turn her links back on. She was close to something. She had actually surprised the Great Luc Deshin, Criminal Mastermind.

He pivoted, and moved three steps away from her. He was clearly contacting someone on his links, but using private encoded links.

A staff member approached, a woman DeRicci hadn't seen before. The woman, dressed in a black suit, extended a hand covered with gold rings.

"If you'll come this way, Detective DeRicci . . . "

DeRicci shook her head. "Mr. Deshin promised me a chip. I'm staying here until I get it."

The woman opened her other hand. In it was a chip case the size of a thumbnail. The case was clear, and inside, DeRicci saw another case—blue, with a filament thinner than an eyelash.

"Here is your chip, Detective," the woman said. "I've been instructed to take you—"

"I don't care," DeRicci said. "I'll take the chip, and I'll wait right here. You have my word that I won't open either case, and I won't watch anything until I get the okay."

The woman's eyes glazed slightly. Clearly, she was seeing if that was all right.

Then she focused on DeRicci, and bowed her head slightly.

"As you wish, Detective."

She handed DeRicci the case. It was heavier than it looked. It probably had a lot of protections built in, so that she couldn't activate anything through the case. Not that she had the technical ability to do any of that, even if she wanted to.

She sighed. She had a fluttery feeling that she had just been outmaneuvered.

Then she made herself watch Deshin. He seemed truly distressed at the news of Sonja Mycenae's death. If DeRicci had to put money on it, she would say that he hadn't known she was dead and he hadn't ordered the death. But he was also well known for his business acumen, his criminal savvy, and his ability to beat a clear case against him. A man didn't get a reputation like that by being easy to read.

She closed her fist around the chip case, clasped her hands behind her back, and waited, watching Luc Deshin the entire time.

• • •

Deshin hadn't gone far. He wanted to keep an eye on the detective. He'd learned in the past that police officers had a tendency to wander, and observe things they shouldn't. He had staff in various parts of the lobby to prevent the detective from doing just that.

Through private, encoded links, he had contacted his favorite attorney, Martin Oberholtz. For eight years, Oberholtz had managed the most delicate cases for Deshin—always knowing how far the law could bend before it broke.

BEFORE I TELL YOU WHAT TO DO, Oberholtz was saying on their link, I WANT TO SEE THE FOOTAGE.

IT'LL TAKE TIME, Deshin sent.

ACH, Oberholtz sent. I'LL JUST BILL YOU FOR IT. SEND IT TO ME.

I ALREADY HAVE, Deshin sent.

I'LL BE IN CONTACT SHORTLY, Oberholtz sent, and signed off.

Deshin walked to the other side of the lobby. He didn't want to vanish because he didn't want the detective to think he was doing something nefarious.

But he was unsettled. That meeting with Sonja had not gone as he expected.

Over the years, Deshin had probably fired two hundred people personally, and his staff had fired even more. And that didn't count the business relationships he had terminated. Doing unpleasant things didn't bother him. They usually followed a pattern. But the meeting that morning hadn't followed a pattern that he recognized.

He had spoken quite calmly to Sonja, telling her that he and Gerda had decided to raise Paavo without help. He hadn't criticized Sonja at all. In fact, he had promised her a reference if she wanted it, and he had complimented her on the record, saying that her presence had given him and Gerda the confidence to handle Paavo alone.

He hadn't said that the confidence had come from the fact that Sonja had years of training and she missed the essential ingredient—affection. He had kept everything as neutral and positive as possible, given that he was effectively firing her without firing her.

Midway through his little speech, her eyes widened. He had thought she was going to burst into tears. Instead, she put a shaking hand to her mouth, looking like she had just received news that everything she loved in the world was going to be taken away from her.

He had a moment of confusion—had she actually cared that much about Paavo?—and then he decided it didn't matter; he and Gerda really did want to raise the boy on their own, without any outside help.

"Mr. Deshin," Sonja had said when he finished. "Please, I beg you, do not fire me."

"I'm not firing you, Sonja," he had said. "I just don't have a job for you any longer."

"Please," she said. "I will work here. I will do anything, the lowest of the low. I will do jobs that are disgusting or frightening, anything, Mr. Deshin. Please. Just don't make me leave."

He had never had an employee beg so strenuously to keep her job. It unnerved him. "I don't have any work for you."

"Please, Mr. Deshin." She reached for him and he leaned back. "Please. Don't make me leave."

That was when he sent a message along his links to security. This woman was crazy, and no one on his staff had picked up on it. He felt both relieved and appalled. Relieved that she was going nowhere near Paavo again, and appalled that he had left his beloved little son in her care.

The door opened, and then Sonja screamed "No!" at the top of her lungs. She grabbed at Deshin, and one of his security people pulled her away.

She kicked and fought and screamed and cried all the way through the door. It closed behind her, leaving him alone, but he could still hear her yelling all the way to the elevator.

The incident had unsettled him.

It still unsettled him.

And now, just a few hours later, Sonja was dead.

That couldn't be a coincidence.

It couldn't be a coincidence at all.

It took nearly fifteen minutes before Luc Deshin returned. DeRicci had watched him pace on the other side of the lobby, his expression grim.

It was still grim when he reached her.

He nodded at the chip in her hand. "My staff tells me that you have a lot of information on that chip. In addition to the meeting in my office, you'll see Sonja's arrival and her departure. You'll also see that she left through that front door. After she disappeared off our external security cameras, no one on my staff saw her again."

He was being very precise. DeRicci figured his lawyer had told him to do that.

"Thank you," she said, closing her fingers around the case. "I appreciate the cooperation."

"You're welcome," Deshin said, then walked away.

She watched him go. Something about his mood had darkened since she originally spoke to him. Because of the lawyer? Or something else?

It didn't matter. She had the information she needed, at least for the moment.

She would deal with Deshin later if she needed to.

• • •

Deshin took the stairs back to his office. He needed to think, and he didn't want to run into any of his staff on the elevator. Besides, exercise kept his head clear.

He had thought Sonja crazy after her reaction in his office. But what if she knew her life was in danger if she left his employ? Then her behavior made sense. He wasn't going to say that to the detective, nor had he mentioned it to his lawyer. Deshin was going to investigate this himself.

As he reached the top floor, he sent a message to his head of security, Otto Koos: MY OFFICE. NOW.

Deshin went through the doors and stopped, as he always did, looking at the view. He had a three hundred sixty -degree view of the City of Armstrong. Right now, the dome was set at Dome Daylight, mimicking midday sunlight on Earth. He loved the look of Dome Daylight because it put buildings all over the city in such clear light that it made them look like a beautiful painting or a holographic wall image.

He crossed to his desk, and called up the file on Sonja Mycenae, looking for anything untoward, anything his staff might have missed.

He saw nothing.

She had worked for a family on Earth who had filed monthly reports with the nanny service that had vetted her. The reports were excellent. Sonja had then left the family to come to the Moon, because, apparently, she had been homesick.

He couldn't find anything in a cursory search of that file which showed any contradictory information.

The door to his office opened, and Koos entered. He was a short man with broad shoulders and a way of walking that made him look like he was itching for a fight.

Deshin had known him since they were boys, and trusted Koos with his life. Koos had saved that life more than once.

"Sonja was murdered after she left us this morning," Deshin said.

Koos glanced at the door. "So that was why Armstrong PD was here."

"Yeah," Deshin said, "and it clarifies her reaction. She knew something bad would happen to her."

"She was a plant," Koos said.

"Or something," Deshin said. "We need to know why. Did anyone follow her after she left?"

"You didn't order us to," Koos said, "and I saw no reason to keep track of her. She was crying pretty hard when she walked out, but she never looked back and as far as I could tell, no one was after her."

"The police are going to trace her movements," Deshin said. "We need to as well. But what I want to know is this: What did we miss about this woman? I've already checked her file. I see nothing unusual."

"I'll go over it again," Koos said.

"Don't go over it," Deshin said, feeling a little annoyed. After all, he had just done that, and he didn't need to be double-checked. "Vet her again, as if we were just about to hire her. See what you come up with."

"Yes, sir," Koos said. Normally, he would have left after that, but he didn't. Instead, he held his position.

Deshin suppressed a sigh. Something else was coming his way. "What?"

"When you dismissed her and she reacted badly," Koos said, "I increased security around your wife and child. I'm going to increase it again, and I'm going to make sure you've got extra protection as well."

Deshin opened his mouth, but Koos put up one finger, stopping him.

"Don't argue with me," Koos said. "Something's going on here, and I don't like it."

Deshin smiled. "I wasn't going to argue with you, Otto. I was going to thank you. I hadn't thought to increase security around my family, and it makes sense."

Koos nodded, as if Deshin's praise embarrassed him. Then he left the office.

Deshin watched him go. As soon as he was gone, Deshin contacted Gerda on their private links.

Koos might have increased security, but Deshin wanted to make sure everything was all right.

He used to say that families were a weakness, and he never wanted one. Then he met Gerda, and they brought Paavo into their lives.

He realized that families *were* a weakness, but they were strength as well.

And he was going to make sure his was safe, no matter what it took.

It had taken more work than Broduer expected to get the body back to the coroner's office. Just to get the stupid crate out of the warehouse, he'd had to sign documentation swearing he wouldn't use it to make money at the expense of Ansel Management.

"Company policy," Najib Ansel had said with an insincere smile.

If Broduer hadn't known better, he would have thought that Ansel was just trying to make things difficult for him.

But things had become difficult for Broduer when DeRicci's partner, Rayvon Lake, arrived. Lake had been as angry as Broduer had ever seen him, claiming that DeRicci—who was apparently a junior officer to Lake—had been giving him orders.

Lake had shouted at everyone, except Broduer. Broduer had fended a shouting match off by holding up his hands and saying, "I'm not sure what killed this girl, but I don't like it. It might contaminate everything. We have to get her out of here, now."

Lake, who was a notorious germophobe (which Broduer found strange in a detective), had gulped and stepped back. Broduer had gotten the crate to the warehouse door before Ansel had come after him with all the documentation crap.

Maybe Ansel had done it just so that he wouldn't have to talk with Lake. Broduer would have done anything to avoid Lake—and apparently just had.

Broduer smiled to himself, relieved to be back at the coroner's office. The office was a misnomer—the coroners had their own building, divided into sections to deal with the various kinds of death that happened in Armstrong.

Broduer had tested out of the alien section after two years of trying. He hated working in an environmental suit, like he so often had to. Weirdly (he always thought) humans started in the alien section and had to get a promotion to work on human cadavers. Probably because no one really wanted to see the interior of a Sequev more than once. No human did, anyway.

There were more than a dozen alien coroners, most of whom worked with human supervisors since many alien cultures did not investigate cause of death. Armstrong was a human-run society on a human-run Moon, so human laws applied here, and human laws always needed a cause of death.

Broduer had placed Sonja Mycenae on the autopsy table, carefully positioning her before beginning work, and he'd been startled at how well proportioned she was. Most people had obvious flaws, at least when a coroner was looking at them. One arm a little too long, a roll of fat under the chin, a misshapen ankle.

He hadn't removed her clothing yet, but as far as he could tell from the work he'd done with her already, nothing was unusual.

Which made her unusual all by herself.

He also couldn't see any obvious cause of death. He had noted, however, that full rigor mortis had already set in. Which was odd, since the decomposition, according to the exam his nanobots had already started, seemed to have progressed at a rate that put her death at least five hours earlier. By now, under the conditions she'd been stored in, she should have still been pliable—at least her limbs. Rigor began in the eyes, jaw, and neck then spread to the face and through the chest before getting to the limbs. The fingers and toes were always the last to stiffen up.

That made him suspicious, particularly since liver mortis also seemed off.

He would have thought, given how long she had been curled inside that crate, that the blood would have pooled in the side of her body resting on top of the compost heap. But no blood had pooled at all.

He had bots move the autopsy table into one of the more advanced autopsy theaters. He wanted every single device he could find to do the work.

He suspected she'd been killed with some kind of hardening poison. They had become truly popular with assassins in the last two decades, and had just recently been banned from the Moon. Hardening poisons killed quickly by absorbing all the liquid in the body and/or by baking it into place. It was a quick death, but a painful one, and usually the victim's muscles frozen in place, so she couldn't even express that pain as it occurred.

He put on a high-grade environmental suit in an excess of caution. Some of the hardening poisons leaked out of the pores and then infected anyone who touched them.

What he had to determine was if Sonja Mycenae had died of one of those, and if her body had been placed in a waste crate not just to hide the corpse, but to infect the food supply in Armstrong. Because the Growing Pits inspections looked at the growing materials—the soil, the water, the light, the atmosphere, and the seeds. The inspectors would also look at the fertilizer, but if it came from a certified organization like Ansel Management, then there would only be a cursory search of materials.

Hardening poisons could thread their way into the DNA of a plant—just a little bit, so that, say, an apple wouldn't be quite as juicy. A little hardening poison wouldn't really hurt the fruit of a tree (although that tree might eventually die of what a botanist would consider a wasting disease), but a trace of hardening poison in the human system would have an impact over time. And if the human continued to eat things with hardening poisons in them, the poisons would build up, until the body couldn't take it any more.

A person poisoned in that way wouldn't die like Sonja Mycenae had; instead, the poison would overwhelm the standard nanohealers that everyone had installed, that person would get sick, and organs would slowly fail. Armstrong would have a plague but not necessarily know what caused it.

He double-checked his gloves, then let out a breath. Yes, he knew he was being paranoid. But he thought about these things a lot—the kinds of death that could happen with just a bit of carelessness, like sickness in a dome, poison through the food supply, the wrong mix in the air supply.

He had moved from working with living humans to working with the dead primarily because his imagination was so vivid. Usually working with the dead calmed him. The regular march of unremarkable deaths reminded him that most people would die of natural causes after a hundred and fifty or more years, maybe longer if they took good care of themselves.

Working with the dead usually gave him hope.

But Sonja Mycenae was making him nervous.

And he didn't like that at all.

• • •

Deshin had just finished talking with Gerda when Koos sent him an encoded message:

Need to talk as soon as you can.

Now's fine, Deshin sent.

He moved away from the windows, where he'd been standing as he made sure Gerda was okay. She actually sounded happy, which she hadn't since Sonja moved in.

She said she no longer felt like her every move was being judged.

Paavo seemed happier too. He wasn't crying as much, and he didn't cling as hard to Gerda. Instead, he played with a mobile from his bouncy chair and watched her cook, cooing most of the time.

Just that one report made Deshin feel like he had made the right choice with Sonja.

Not that he had had a doubt—at least about her—after her reaction that morning. But apparently a tiny doubt had lingered about whether or not he and Gerda needed the help of a nanny. Gerda's report on Paavo's calmness eased that. Deshin knew they would have hard times ahead—he wasn't deluding himself—but he also knew that they had made the right choice to go nanny-free.

He hadn't told Gerda what happened to Sonja, and he wouldn't, until he knew more. He didn't want to spoil Gerda's day.

The door to Deshin's office opened, and Koos entered, looking upset. "Upset" was actually the wrong word. Something about Koos made Deshin think the man was afraid. Then Deshin shook that thought off: he'd seen Koos in extremely dangerous circumstances and the man had never seemed afraid.

"I did what you asked," Koos said without preamble. "I started vetting her all over again."

Deshin leaned against the desk, just like he had done when he spoke to Sonja. "And?"

"Her employers on Earth are still filing updates about her exemplary work for them."

Deshin felt a chill. "Tell me that they were just behind in their reports."

Koos shook his head. "She's still working for them."

"How is that possible?" Deshin asked. "We vetted her. We even used a DNA sample to make sure her DNA was the same as the DNA on file with the service. And we collected it ourselves."

Koos swallowed. "We used the service's matching program."

"Of course we did," Deshin said. "They were the ones with the DNA on file."

"We could have requested that sample, and then run it ourselves."

That chill Deshin had felt became a full-fledged shiver. "What's the difference?"

"Depth," Koos said. "They don't go into the same kind of depth we would go into in our search. They just look at standard markers, which is really all most people would need to confirm identity."

His phrasing made Deshin uncomfortable. "She's not who she said she was?"

Koos let out a small sigh. "It's more complicated than that."

More complicated. Deshin shifted. He could only think of one thing that would be more complicated.

Sonja was a clone.

And that created all kinds of other issues.

But first, he had to confirm his suspicion.

"You checked for clone marks, right?" Deshin asked. "I know you did. We always do."

The Earth Alliance required human clones to have a mark on the back of their neck or behind their ear that gave their number. If they were the second clone from an original, the number would be "2."

Clones also did not have birth certificates. They had day of creation documents. Deshin had a strict policy for Deshin Enterprises: every person he hired had to have a birth certificate or a document showing that they, as a clone, had been legally adopted by an original human and therefore could be considered human under the law.

When it came to human clones, Earth Alliance and Armstrong laws were the same: clones were property. They were created and owned by their creator. They could be bought or sold, and they had no rights of their own. The law did not distinguish between slow-grow clones, which were raised like any naturally born human child, and fast-grow clones, which reached full adult size in days, but never had a full-grown human intelligence. The laws were an injustice, but only clones seemed to protest it, and they, as property, had no real standing.

Koos's lips thinned. He didn't answer right away.

Deshin cursed. He hated having clones in his business, and didn't own any, even though he could take advantage of the loopholes in the law.

Clones made identity theft too easy, and made an organization vulnerable.

He always made certain his organization remained protected.

Or he had, until now.

"We did check like we do with all new hires." Koos's voice was strangled. "And we also checked her birth certificate. It was all in order."

"But now you're telling me it's not," Deshin said.

Koos's eyes narrowed a little, not with anger, but with tension.

"The first snag we hit," he said, "was that we were not able to get Sonja Mycenae's DNA from the service. According to them, she's currently employed, and not available for hire, so the standard service-subsidized searches are inactive. She likes her job. I looked: the job is the old one, not the one with you."

Deshin crossed his arms. "If that's the case, then how did we get the service comparison in the first place?"

"At first, I worried that someone had spoofed our system," Koos said. "It hadn't. There was a redundancy in the service's files that got repaired. I checked with a tech at the service. The tech said they'd been hit with an attack that replicated everything inside their system. It lasted for about two days."

"Let me guess," Deshin said. "Two days around the point we'd hired Sonja."

Koos nodded.

"I'm amazed the tech admitted it," Deshin said.

"It wasn't their glitch," Koos said. "It happened because of some government program."

"Government?" Deshin asked.

"The Earth Alliance required some changes in their software," Koos said. "They made the changes and the glitch appeared. The service caught it, removed the Earth Alliance changes, and petitioned to return to their old way of doing things. Their petition was granted."

Deshin couldn't sit still with this. "Did Sonja know this glitch was going to happen?"

Koos shrugged. "I don't know what she knew."

Deshin let out a small breath. He felt a little off-balance. "I assume the birth certificate was stolen."

"It was real. We checked it. I double-checked it today," Koos said.

Deshin rubbed his forehead. "So, was the Sonja Mycenae I hired a clone or is the clone at the other job? Or does Sonja Mycenae have a biological twin?"

Koos looked down, which was all the answer Deshin needed. She was a clone.

"She left a lot of DNA this morning," Koos said. "Tears, you name it. We checked it all."

Deshin waited, even though he knew. He knew, and he was getting furious.

"She had no clone mark," Koos said, "except in her DNA. The telomeres were marked."

"Designer Criminal Clone," Deshin said. A number of criminal organizations, most operating outside the Alliance, made and trained Designer Criminal Clones for just the kind of thing that had happened to Deshin.

The clone, who replicated someone the family or the target knew casually, would slide into a business or a household for months, maybe years, and steal information. Then the clone would leave with that information on a chip, bringing it to whoever had either hired that DCC or who had grown and trained the clone.

"I don't think she was a DCC," Koos said. "The markers don't fit anyone we know."

"A new player?" Deshin asked.

Koos shrugged. Then he took one step forward. "I'm going to check everything she touched, everything she did, sir. But this is my error, and it's a serious one. It put your business and more importantly your family in danger. I know you're going to fire me, but before you do, let me track down her creator. Let me redeem myself."

Deshin didn't move for a long moment. He had double-checked everything Koos had done. *Everything.* Because Sonja Mycenae—or whatever that clone was named—was going to work in his home, with his family.

"Do you think she stole my son's DNA?" Deshin asked quietly.

"I don't know. Clearly she didn't have any with her today, but if she had handlers—"

"She wouldn't have had trouble meeting them, because Gerda and I didn't want a live-in nanny." Deshin cursed silently. There was more than enough blame to go around, and if he were honest with himself, most of it belonged to him. He had been so concerned with raising his son, that he hadn't taken the usual precautions in protecting his family.

"I would like to retrace all of her steps," Koos said. "We might be able to find her handler."

"Or not," Deshin said. The handler had killed her the moment she had ceased to be useful. The handler felt he could waste a slow-grow clone, expensive and well trained, placed in the household of a man everyone believed to be a criminal mastermind.

Some mastermind. He had screwed up something this important.

He bit back anger, not sure how he would tell Gerda. *If* he would tell Gerda.

Something had been planned here, something he hadn't figured out yet, and that planning was not complete. Sonja (or whatever her name was) had confirmed that with her reaction to her dismissal. She was terrified, and she probably knew she was going to die.

He sighed.

"I will quit now if you'd like me to," Koos said.

Deshin wasn't ready to fire Koos.

"Find out who she answered to. Better yet, find out who made her," Deshin said. "Find her handler. We'll figure out what happens to you after you complete that assignment."

Koos nodded, but didn't thank Deshin. Koos knew his employer well, knew that the thanks would only irritate him.

Deshin hated to lose Koos, but Koos was no longer one hundred percent trustworthy. He should have caught this. He should have tested Sonja's DNA himself.

And that was why Deshin would put new security measures into place for his business and his family. Measures he designed.

He'd also begin the search for the new head of security.

It would take time.

And, he was afraid, it would take time to find out what exactly Sonja (or whatever her name was) had been trying to do inside his home.

That had just become his first priority.

Because no one was going to hurt his family.

No matter what he had to do to protect them.

Broduer had six different nanoprobes digging into various places on the dead woman's skin, when a holographic computer screen appeared in front of him, a red warning light flashing.

He moaned slightly. He hated the lights. They got sent to his boss automatically, and often the damn lights reported something he had done wrong.

Well, not wrong, exactly, but not according to protocol.

The irony was, everything he had done in this autopsy so far had been exactly according to protocol. The body was on an isolated gurney, which was doing its own investigation; they were in one of the most protected autopsy chambers in the coroner's office; and Broduer was using all the right equipment.

He even had on the right environmental suit for the type of poison he suspected killed the woman.

He cursed, silently and creatively, wishing he could express his frustration aloud, but knowing he couldn't, because it would become part of the permanent record.

Instead, he glared at the light and wished it would go away. Not that he could make it go away with a look.

The light had a code he had never seen before. He put his gloved finger on the code, and it created a whole new screen.

This body is cloned. Please file the permissions code to autopsy this clone or cease work immediately.

"The hell . . . ?" he asked, then realized he had spoken aloud, and he silently cursed himself. Some stupid supervisor, reviewing the footage, would think he was too dumb to know a cloned body from a real body.

But he had made a mistake. He hadn't taken DNA in the field. He had used facial recognition to identify this woman, and he had told DeRicci who the woman was based not on the DNA testing, but on the facial recognition.

Of course, if DeRicci hadn't pressed him to give her an identification right away, he would have followed procedure.

Broduer let out a small sigh, then remembered what he had been doing.

There was still a way to cover his ass. He had been investigating whether or not this woman died of a hardening poison, and if that poison had gotten into the composting system. He would use that as his excuse, and then mention that he needed to continue to find cause of death for public health reasons.

Besides, someone should want to know who was killing clones and putting them into the composting. Not that it was illegal, exactly. After all, a dead clone was organic waste, just like rotted vegetables were.

He shuddered, not wanting to think about it. Maybe someone should tell the Armstrong City Council to ban the composting of any human flesh be it original or cloned.

He sighed. He didn't want to be the one to do it. He'd slip the suggestion into his supervisor's ear and hope that she would take him up on it.

He pinged his supervisor, telling her that it was important she contact him right away.

Then he bent over the body, determined to get as much work done as possible before someone shut this investigation down entirely.

DeRicci sat in her car in the part of Armstrong Police Department parking lot set aside for detectives. She hadn't used the car all day, but it was the most private place she could think of to watch the footage Deshin had given her.

She didn't want to take the footage inside the station until she'd had a chance to absorb it. She wasn't sure how relevant it was, and she wasn't sure what her colleagues would think of it.

Or, if she were being truthful with herself, she didn't want Lake anywhere near this thing. He had some dubious connections, and he might just confiscate the footage—not for the case, but for reasons she didn't really want to think about.

So she stayed in her car, quietly watching the footage for the second time, taking mental notes. Because something was off here. People rarely got that upset getting fired from a job, at least not in front of a man known to be as dangerous as Luc Deshin.

Besides, he had handled the whole thing well, made it sound like not a firing, more like something inevitable, something that Sonja Mycenae's excellent job performance helped facilitate. The man was impressive, although DeRicci would never admit that to anyone else.

When DeRicci watched the footage the first time, she had been amazed at how calmly Deshin handled Mycenae's meltdown. He managed to stay out of her way, and he managed to get his security into the office without making her get even worse.

Not that it would be easy for her to be worse. If DeRicci hadn't known that Sonja Mycenae was murdered shortly after this footage was taken, DeRicci would have thought the woman unhinged. Instead, DeRicci knew that Mycenae was terrified.

She had known that losing her position would result in something awful, mostly likely her death.

But why? And what did someone have on a simple nanny with no record, something bad enough to get her to work in the home of a master criminal and his wife, bad enough to make her beg said criminal to keep the job?

DeRicci didn't like this. She particularly did not like the way that Mycenae disappeared off the security footage as she stepped outside of the building. She stood beside the building and sobbed for a few minutes, then staggered away. No nearby buildings had exterior security cameras, and what DeRicci could get from the street cameras told her little.

She would have to get the information from inside police headquarters.

Um, Detective?

DeRicci sighed. The contact came from Broduer, on her links. He was asking for a visual, which she was not inclined to give him. But he probably had something to show her from the autopsy.

She activated the visual, in two dimensions, making his head float above the car's control panel. Broduer wore an environmental suit, but he had removed the hood that had covered his face. It hung behind his skull like a half-visible alien appendage.

News for me, Ethan? she asked, hoping to move him along quickly. He could get much too chatty for her tastes.

Well, you're not going to like any of it. He ran a hand through his hair, messing it up. It looked a little damp, as if he'd been sweating inside the suit.

DeRicci waited. She didn't know how she could like or dislike any news about the woman's death. It was a case. A sad and strange case, but a case nonetheless.

She died from a hardening poison, Broduer sent. I've narrowed it down to one of five related types. I'm running the test now to see which poison it actually is.

Poison. That took effort. Not in the actual application—many poisons were impossible to see, taste, or feel—but in the planning.

Someone wanted this woman dead, and then they wanted to keep her death secret.

That's a weird way to kill someone, DeRicci sent.

Broduer looked concerned. Over the woman? He usually saw corpses as a curiosity, not as someone to empathize with. That was one of the few things DeRicci liked about Broduer. He could handle a job as a job.

It is a weird way to kill someone, Broduer sent. Then he glanced over his shoulder as if he expected someone to enter his office and yell at him. The thing is, one of these types of poisons could contaminate the food supply.

What? she sent. Or maybe she said that out loud. Or both. She felt cold. Contaminate the food supply? With a body?

She wasn't quite sure of the connection, but she didn't like it.

She hadn't like the corpse in the compost part of this case from the very first.

Broduer took an obvious deep breath and his gaze met hers. She stabilized the floating image, so she wasn't tracking him as he moved up, down, and across the control panel.

If, he sent, the poison leaked from the skin and got into the compost, then it would be layered onto the growing plants, which would take in the poison along with the nutrients. It wouldn't be enough to kill anyone, unless someone'd been doing this for a long time.

DeRicci shook her head. Then I don't get it. How is this anything other than a normal contamination?

If a wannabe killer wants to destroy the food supply, he'd do stuff like this for months, Broduer sent. People would start dying mysteriously. Generally, the old and the sick would go first, or people who are vulnerable in the parts of their bodies this stuff targets.

Wouldn't the basic nanohealers take care of this problem? DeRicci was glad they weren't doing this verbally. She didn't want him to know how shaken she was.

If it were small or irregular, sure, he sent. But over time? No. They're not made to handle huge contaminations. They're not

EVEN DESIGNED TO RECOGNIZE THESE KINDS OF POISONS. THAT'S WHY THESE POISONS CAN KILL SO QUICKLY.

DeRicci suppressed a shudder.

GREAT, she sent. HOW DO WE INVESTIGATE FOOD CONTAMINATION LIKE THAT?

THAT'S YOUR PROBLEM, DETECTIVE, Broduer sent back, somewhat primly. I'D SUGGEST STARTING WITH A SEARCH OF RECORDS, SEEING IF THERE HAS BEEN A RISE IN DEATHS IN VULNERABLE POPULATIONS.

CAN'T YOU DO THAT EASIER THAN I CAN? She sent, even though she knew he would back out. It couldn't hurt to try to get him to help.

NOT AT THE MOMENT, he sent, I HAVE A JOB TO DO.

She nearly cursed at him. But she managed to control herself. A job to do. The bastard. *She* had a job to do too, and it was just as important as his job.

This was why she hated working with Broduer. He was a jerk.

WELL, she sent, LET ME KNOW THE TYPE OF POISON FIRST, BEFORE I GET INTO THAT PART OF THE INVESTIGATION. YOU SAID THERE WERE FIVE, AND ONLY ONE COULD CONTAMINATE THE FOOD SUPPLY. YOU THINK THAT'S THE ONE WE'RE DEALING WITH?

I DON'T KNOW YET, DETECTIVE, he sent. I'LL KNOW WHEN THE TESTING IS DONE.

WHICH WILL TAKE HOW LONG?

He shrugged. NOT LONG, I HOPE.

GREAT, she sent again. She wanted to push him, but pushing him sometimes made him even more passive/aggressive about getting work done.

WELL, YOU WERE RIGHT, SHE SENT. I DIDN'T LIKE IT. NOW I'M OFF TO INVESTIGATE EVEN MORE CRAP.

UM, NOT YET, Broduer sent.

NOT YET? Who was this guy and why did he think he could control everything she did. She clenched her fists. Pretty soon, she would tell this idiot exactly what she thought of him, and that wouldn't make for a good working relationship.

UM, YEAH, he sent. THERE'S ONE OTHER PROBLEM.

She waited, her fists so tight her fingernails were digging into the skin of her palm.

He looked down. I, UM, MISIDENTIFIED YOUR WOMAN.

YOU WHAT? He had been an idiot about helping her, and then he told her that he had done crappy work? This man was the absolutely worst coroner she'd ever worked with (which was saying something) and she was going to report him to the Chief of Detectives, maybe even to the Chief of Police, and get him removed from his position.

Yeah, Broduer sent. She's, um, not Sonja Mycenae.

You said that, DeRicci sent. Already, her mind was racing. Misidentifying the corpse would cause all kinds of problems, not the least of which would be problems with Luc Deshin. Who the hell is she, then?

Broduer's skin had turned grey. He clearly knew he had screwed up big time. She's a clone of Sonja Mycenae.

A *what*? DeRicci rolled her eyes. That would have been good to know right from the start. Because it meant the investigation had gone in the wrong direction from the moment she had a name.

A clone. I'm sorry, Detective.

You should be, DeRicci sent. I shouldn't even be on this investigation This isn't a homicide.

Well, technically, it's the same thing, Broduer sent.

Technically, it isn't, DeRicci sent. She'd had dozens of clone cases before, and no matter how much she argued with the Chief of Detectives, Andrea Gumiela, it didn't matter. The clones weren't human under the law; their deaths fell into property crimes, generally vandalism or destruction of valuable property, depending on how much the clone was worth or how much it cost to create.

But, Detective, she's a human being . . .

DeRicci sighed. She believed that, but what she believed didn't matter. What mattered was what the law said and how her boss handled it. And she'd been through this with Gumiela. Gumiela would send DeRicci elsewhere.

Gumiela hadn't seen the poor girl crying and begging for her life in front of Deshin. Gumiela hadn't seen the near-perfect corpse, posed as if she were sleeping on a pile of compost.

Wait a minute, DeRicci sent. You told me about the poisoning first because . . . ?

Because, Detective, she might not be human, but she might have been a weapon or weaponized material. And that would fall into your jurisdiction, wouldn't it?

Just when she thought that Broduer was the worst person she had ever worked with, he manipulated a clone case to keep it inside DeRicci's Detective Division.

I don't determine jurisdiction, she sent, mostly because this was on the record, and she didn't want to show her personal feelings on something that might hit court and derail any potential prosecution.

But check, would you? Broduer sent. Because someone competent should handle this.

She wasn't sure what "this" was: the dead clone or the contamination.

JUST SEND ME ALL THE INFORMATION, DeRicci sent, AND LET ME KNOW THE MINUTE YOU CONFIRM WHICH HARDENING POISON KILLED THIS CLONE.

I'LL HAVE IT SOON, Broduer sent and signed off.

DeRicci leaned back in the car seat, her cheeks warm. She had gone to Luc Deshin for nothing.

Or had she?

Which Sonja Mycenae had Deshin fired that morning? The real one? Or the clone?

DeRicci let herself out of the car. She had to talk to Gumiela. But before she did, she needed to find out where the real Mycenae was—and fast.

Deshin wasn't certain how to tell Gerda that Sonja had been a plant, placed in their home for a reason he didn't know yet.

He wandered his office, screens moving with him as he examined the tracker he had placed in Sonja. Then he winced. Every time he thought of the clone as Sonja, he felt like a fool. From now on, he would just call her the clone, because she clearly wasn't Sonja.

So he examined the information from the tracker he had placed in the clone's palm the moment she was hired. She hadn't known he had inserted it. He had done it when he shook her hand, using technology that didn't show up on any of the regular scans.

He wished he had been paranoid enough to install a video tracker, but he had thought—or rather, Gerda had thought—that their nanny needed her privacy in her off time.

Of course, that had been too kind. Deshin should have tracked the clone the way he tracked anyone he didn't entirely trust.

Whenever the clone had been with Paavo, Deshin had always kept a screen open. He'd even set an alert in case the clone took Paavo out of the house without Gerda accompanying them. That alert had never activated, because Gerda had always been nearby when the clone was with Paavo. Deshin was grateful for that caution now. He had no idea what serious crisis they had dodged.

He was now searching through all the other information in the tracker— where the clone had gone during her days off, where she had spent her free time. He knew that Koos had been, in theory, making sure she had no unsavory contacts—or at least, Deshin had tasked Koos with doing that. Now, Deshin was double-checking his head of security, making certain that he had actually done his job.

The first thing Deshin had done was make certain that the clone hadn't gone to the bad parts of town. According to the tracker, she hadn't. Her apartment was exactly where she had claimed it was, and as far as he could tell, all she had done in her off hours was shop for her own groceries, eaten at a local restaurant, and gone home.

He had already sent a message to one of the investigative services he used. He wanted them to search the clone's apartment. He wanted video and DNA and all kinds of trace. He wanted an investigation of her finances and a look at the things she kept.

He also didn't want anyone from Deshin Enterprises associated with that search. He knew that his investigative service would keep him out of it. They had done so before.

He had hired them to search before he had known she was a clone. He had hired them while he was waiting for his attorney to look at the footage he had given that detective. With luck, they'd be done with the search by now.

But he had decided to check the tracker himself, looking for anomalies.

The only anomaly he had found was a weekly visit to a building in downtown Armstrong. On her day off, she went to that building at noon. She had also been at that building the evening Deshin had hired her. He scanned the address, looking for the businesses that rented or owned the place. The building had dozens of small offices, and none of the businesses were registered with the city.

He found that odd: usually the city insisted that every business register for tax purposes. So he traced the building's ownership. He went through several layers of corporate dodges to find something odd: the building's owner wasn't a corporation at all.

It was the Earth Alliance.

He let out a breath, and then sank into a nearby chair.

Suddenly everything made sense.

The Earth Alliance had been after him for years, convinced he was breaking a million different Alliance laws and not only getting away with it, but making billions from the practice. Ironically, he had broken a lot of Alliance laws when he started out, and he still had a lot of sketchy associates, but *he* hadn't broken a law in years and years.

Still, it would have been a coup for someone in Alliance government to bring down Luc Deshin and his criminal enterprises.

The Alliance had found it impossible to plant listening devices and trackers in Deshin's empire. The Alliance was always behind Deshin Enterprises when it came to technology. And Deshin himself was innately cautious—

Or he had thought he was, until this incident with the clone.

They had slipped her into his home. They might have had a hundred purposes in doing so—as a spy on his family, to steal familial DNA, to set up tracking equipment in a completely different way than it had been done before.

And for an entire month, they had been successful.

He was furious at himself, but he knew he couldn't let that emotion dominate his thoughts. He had to take action, and he had to do so now.

He used his links to summon Ishiyo Cumija to his office. He'd been watching her for some time. She hadn't been Koos's second in command in the security department. She had set up her own fiefdom, and once she had mentioned to Deshin that she worried no one was taking security seriously enough.

At the time, he had thought she was making a play for Koos's job. Deshin *still* thought she was making a play for Koos's job on that day, but she might have been doing so with good reason.

Now, she would get a chance to prove herself.

While Deshin waited for her, he checked the clone's DNA and found that strange clone mark embedded into her system. He had never seen anything like it. The Designer Criminal Clones he'd run into had always had a product stamp embedded into their DNA. This wasn't a standard DCC product stamp. It looked like something else.

He copied it, then opened Cumija's file, accessed the DNA samples she had to give every week, and searched to see if there was any kind of mark. His system always searched for the DCC product stamps, but rarely searched for other examples of cloning, including shortened telomeres.

Shortened telomeres could happen naturally. In the past, he'd found that searching for them gave him so many false positives—staff members who were older than they appeared, employees who had had serious injuries—that he decided to stop searching for anything but the product marks.

He wondered now if that had been a mistake.

His search of Cumija's DNA found no DCC product mark, and nothing matching the mark his system had found in the clone's DNA.

As the search ended, Cumija entered the office.

She was stunningly beautiful, with a cap of straight hair so black it almost looked blue, and dancing black eyes. Until he met Cumija, he would never have thought that someone so very attractive would function well in a security position, but she had turned out to be one of his best bodyguards.

She dressed like a woman sexually involved with a very rich man. Her clothing always revealed her taut nut-brown skin and her fantastic legs. Sometimes she looked nearly naked in the clothing she had chosen. Men and women watched her wherever she went, and dismissed her as someone decorative, someone being used.

On this day, she wore a white dress that crossed her breasts with an X, revealing her sides, and expanding to cover her hips and buttocks. Her matching white shoes looked as deadly as the shoes that she had used to kill a man trying to get to Deshin one afternoon.

"That nanny we hired turns out to have been a clone," Deshin said without greeting.

"Yes, I heard." Cumija's voice was low and sexy in keeping with her appearance.

"Has Koos made an announcement?" Deshin asked. Because he would have recommended against it.

"No," she said curtly, and Deshin almost smiled. She monitored everything Koos did. It was a great trait in a security officer, a terrible trait in a subordinate—at least from the perspective of someone in Koos's position.

Deshin said, "I need you to check the other employees—*you*, and you *only*. I don't want anyone to know what you're doing. I have the marker that was in the cloned Sonja Mycenae's DNA. I want you to see if there's a match. I also want a secondary check for Designer Criminal Clone marks, and then I want you to do a slow search of anyone with abnormal telomeres."

Cumija didn't complain, even though he was giving her a lot of work. "You want me to check everyone," she said.

"Yes," he said. "Start with people who have access to me, and then move outward. Do it quickly and quietly."

"Yes, sir," she said.

"Report the results directly to me," he said.

She nodded, thanked him, and left the office.

He stood there for a moment, feeling a little shaken. If the Alliance was trying to infiltrate his organization, then he wouldn't be surprised if there were other clones stationed in various areas, clones he had missed.

After Cumija checked, he would have Koos do the same check, and see if he came up with the same result.

Deshin went back to his investigation of the building the clone had visited regularly. He had no firm evidence of Earth Alliance involvement. Just suspicions, at least at the moment. And regular citizens of the Alliance would be stunned to think their precious Alliance would infiltrate businesses using slow-grow clones, and then disposing of them when they lost their usefulness. But Deshin knew the Alliance had done all kinds of extra-legal things to protect itself over the centuries. And somewhere, Deshin had been flagged as a threat to the Alliance.

He had known that for some time. He had always expected some kind of infiltration of his business. But the infiltration of his home was personal.

And it needed to stop.

• • •

Ethan Broduer looked at the information pouring across his screen, and let out a sigh of relief. The hardening poison wasn't one of the kinds that could leach through the skin. He still had to test the compost to see if the poison had contaminated it, but he doubted that.

The liver mortis told him she had died elsewhere, and then been placed in the crate. And given how fast this hardening poison acted, the blood wouldn't have been able to pool for more than a few minutes anyway.

He stood and walked back into the autopsy room. Now that he knew the woman had died of something that wouldn't hurt him if he came in contact with her skin or breathed the air around her, he didn't need the environmental suit.

Hers was the only body in this autopsy room. He had placed her on her back before sending the nanobots into her system. They were still working, finding out even more about her.

He knew now she was a slow-grow clone, which meant she had lived some twenty years, had hopes, dreams, and desires. As a forensic pathologist who had examined hundreds of human corpses—cloned and non-cloned—the *only* difference he had ever seen were the telomeres and the clone marks.

Slow-grow clones were human beings in everything but the law.

He could make the claim that fast-grow clones were too, that they had the mind of a child inside an adult body, but he tried not to think about that one. Because it meant all those horrors visited on fast-grow clones meant those horrors were visited on a human being that hadn't seen more than a few years of life, an innocent in all possible ways.

He blinked hard, trying not to think about any of it. Then he stopped beside her table. Lights moved along the back of it, different beams examining her, trying to glean her medical history and every single story her biology could tell. Now that it was clear the poison which killed her wouldn't contaminate the dome, no one would investigate this case. No one would care.

No one legally *had* to care.

He sighed, then shook his head, wondering if he could make one final push to solve her murder. Detective DeRicci had asked for a list of bodies found in the crates. Broduer would make her that list after all, but before he did, he would see if those bodies were "human" or clones.

If they were clones, then there was a sabotage problem, some kind of property crime—hell, it wasn't his job to come up with the charge, not when he gave her the thing to investigate.

But maybe he could find something to investigate, something that would have the side benefit of giving some justice to this poor woman, lying alone and unwanted on his autopsy table.

"I'm doing what I can," he whispered, and then wished he hadn't spoken aloud.

His desire to help her would be in the official record. Then he corrected himself: There would be no official record, since she wasn't officially a murder victim.

He was so sorry about that. He'd still document everything he could. Maybe in the future, the laws would change. Maybe in the future, her death would matter as more than a statistic.

Maybe, in the future, she'd be recognized as a person, instead of something to be thrown away, like leftover food.

The Chief of Detectives, Andrea Gumiela, had an office one floor above DeRicci's, but it was light years from DeRicci's. DeRicci's office was in the center of a large room, sectioned off with dark movable walls. She could protect her area by putting a bubble around it for a short period of time, particularly if she were conducting an interview that she felt wouldn't work in one of the interview rooms, but there was no real privacy and no sense of belonging.

DeRicci hated working out in the center, and hoped one day she would eventually get an office of her own. The tiny aspirations of the upwardly mobile, her ex-husband would have said. She couldn't entirely disagree. He had the unfortunate habit of being right.

And as she looked at Gumiela's office, which took up much of the upper floor, DeRicci knew she would never achieve privacy like this. She wasn't political enough. Some days she felt like she was one infraction away from being terminated.

Most days, she didn't entirely care.

Andrea Gumiela, on the other hand, was the most political person DeRicci had ever met. Her office was designed so that it wouldn't offend anyone. It didn't have artwork on the walls, nor did it have floating imagery. The décor shifted colors when someone from outside the department entered.

When someone was as unimportant as DeRicci, the walls were a neutral beige, and the desk a dark woodlike color. The couch and chairs at the far end of the room matched the desk.

But DeRicci had been here when the Governor-General arrived shortly after her election, and the entire room shifted to vibrant colors—the purples and whites associated with the Governor-General herself.

The shift, which happened as the Governor-General was announced, had disturbed DeRicci, but Gumiela managed it as a matter of course. She was going to get promoted some day, and she clearly hoped the Governor-General would do it.

"Make it fast," Gumiela said as DeRicci entered. "I have meetings all afternoon."

Gumiela was tall and heavyset, but her black suit made her look thinner than she was—probably with some kind of tech that DeRicci didn't want to think about. Gumiela's red hair was piled on top of her head, making her long face seem even longer.

"I wanted to talk with you in person about that woman we found in the Ansel Management crate," DeRicci said.

Gumiela, for all her annoying traits, did keep up on the investigations.

"I thought Rayvon Lake was in charge of that case," Gumiela said.

DeRicci shrugged. "He's not in charge of anything, sir. Honestly, when it comes to cases like this, I don't even like to consult him."

Gumiela studied her. "He's your partner, Detective."

"Maybe," DeRicci said, "but he doesn't investigate crimes. He takes advantage of them."

"That's quite a charge," Gumiela said.

"I can back it with evidence," DeRicci said.

"Do so," Gumiela said, to DeRicci's surprise. DeRicci frowned. Had Gumiela paired them so that DeRicci would bring actual evidence against Lake to the Chief's office? It made an odd kind of sense. No one could control Lake, and no one could control DeRicci, but for different reasons. Lake had his own tiny fiefdom, and DeRicci was just plain contrary.

"All right," DeRicci said, feeling a little off balance. She hadn't expected anything positive from Gumiela.

And then Gumiela reverted to type. "I'm in a hurry, remember?"

"Yes, sir, sorry, sir," DeRicci said. This woman always set her teeth on edge. "The woman in the crate, she was killed with a hardening poison. For a while, Broduer thought she might have been put there to contaminate the food supply, but it was the wrong kind of poison. We're okay on that."

Gumiela raised her eyebrows slightly. Apparently she hadn't heard about the possible contamination. DeRicci had been worried that she had.

"Good . . . " Gumiela said in a tone that implied . . . *and . . . ?*

"But, I got a list from him, and sir, someone is dumping bodies in those crates all over the city, and has been for at least a year, maybe more."

"No one saw this pattern?" Gumiela asked.

"The coroner's office noticed it," DeRicci said, making sure she kept her voice calm. "Ansel Management noticed it, but the owner, Najib Ansel, tells me that over the decades his family has owned the business, they've seen all kinds of things dumped in the crates."

"Bodies, though, bodies should have caught our attention," Gumiela said. Clearly, DeRicci had Gumiela's attention now.

"No," DeRicci said. "The coroner got called in, but no one called us."

"Well, I'll have to change this," Gumiela said. "I'll—"

"Wait, sir," DeRicci said. "They didn't call us for the correct legal reasons."

Gumiela turned her head slightly, as if she couldn't believe she had heard DeRicci right. "What reasons could those possibly be?"

"The dead are all clones, sir." DeRicci made sure none of her anger showed up in the tone of her voice.

"Clones? Including this one?"

"Yes, sir," DeRicci said. "And they were all apparently slow-grow. If they had been considered human under the law, we would have said they were murdered."

Gumiela let out an exasperated breath. "This woman, this poisoned woman, she's a clone?"

"Yes, sir." DeRicci knew she only had a moment here to convince Gumiela to let her continue on this case. "But I'd like to continue my investigation, sir, because—"

"We'll send it down to property crimes," Gumiela said.

"Sir," DeRicci said. "This pattern suggests a practicing serial killer. At some point, he'll find legal humans, and then he'll be experienced—"

"What is Ansel Management doing to protect its crates?" Gumiela said.

DeRicci felt a small surge of hope. Was Gumiela actually considering this? "They have sensors that locate things by weight and size. They believe they've reported all the bodies that have come through their system in the last several years."

"They believe?" Gumiela asked.

"There's no way to know without checking every crate," DeRicci said.

"Well, this is a health and safety matter. I'll contact the Armstrong City Inspectors and have them investigate all of the recycling/compost plants."

DeRicci tried not to sigh. This wasn't going her way after all. "I think that's a good idea, sir, but—"

"Tell me, Detective," Gumiela said. "Did you have any leads at all on this potential serial before you found out that the bodies belonged to clones?"

DeRicci felt her emotions shift again. She wasn't sure why she was so emotionally involved here. Maybe because she knew no one would investigate, which meant no one would stop this killer, if she couldn't convince Gumiela to keep the investigation in the department.

"She worked as a nanny for Luc Deshin," DeRicci said. "He fired her this morning."

"I thought this was that case," Gumiela said. "His people probably killed her."

"I considered that," DeRicci said. "But he wouldn't have gone through the trouble of firing her if he was just going to kill her."

Gumiela harrumphed. Then she walked around the furniture, trailing her hand over the back of the couch. She was actually considering DeRicci's proposal—and she knew DeRicci had a point.

"Do you know who the original was?" Gumiela asked.

DeRicci's heart sank. She hadn't wanted Gumiela to ask this question. DeRicci hadn't recognized the name, but Lake had. He had left a message on DeRicci's desk—a message that rose up when she touched the desk's surface (the bastard)—which said, *Why do we care that the daughter of an off-Moon crime lord got murdered?*

DeRicci then looked up the Mycenae family. They were a crime family and had been for generations, but Sonja herself didn't seem to be part of the criminal side. She had attended the best schools on Earth, and actually had a nanny certificate. She had renounced her family both visibly and legally, and was trying to live her own life.

"The original's name is Sonja Mycenae," DeRicci said.

"The Mycenae crime family." Gumiela let out a sigh. "There's a pattern here, and one we don't need to be involved in. Obviously there's some kind of winnowing going on in the Earth-Moon crime families. I'll notify the Alliance to watch for something bigger, but I don't think you need to investigate this."

"Sir, I know Luc Deshin thought she was Sonja Mycenae," DeRicci said. "He didn't know she was a clone. That means this isn't a crime family war—"

"We don't know what it is, Detective," Gumiela said. "And despite your obvious interest in the case, I'm moving you off it. I have better things for you to do. I'll send this and the other cases down to Property, and let them handle the investigation."

"Sir, please—"

"Detective, you have plenty to do. I want that report on Rayvon Lake by morning." Gumiela nodded at her.

DeRicci's breath caught. Gumiela was letting her know that if she dropped this case, she might get a new partner. And maybe, she would guarantee that Lake stopped polluting the department.

There was nothing DeRicci could do. This battle was lost.

"Thank you, sir," she said, not quite able to keep the disappointment from her voice.

Gumiela had already returned to her desk.

DeRicci headed for the door. As it opened, Gumiela said, "Detective, one last thing."

DeRicci closed the door and faced Gumiela, expecting some kind of reprimand or so type of admonition.

"Have you done the clone notification?" Gumiela asked.

Earth Alliance law required any official organization that learned of a clone to notify the original, if at all possible.

"Not yet, sir," DeRicci said. She had held off, hoping that she would keep the case. If she had, she could have gone to the Mycenae family, and maybe learned something that had relevance to the case.

"Don't," Gumiela said. "I'll take care of that too."

"I don't mind, sir," DeRicci said.

"The Mycenae require a delicate touch," Gumiela said. "It's better if the notification goes through the most official of channels."

DeRicci nodded. She couldn't quite bring herself to thank Gumiela. Or even to say anything else. So she let herself out of the office.

And stopped in the hallway.

For a moment, she considered going back in and arguing with Gumiela. Because Gumiela wasn't going to notify anyone about the clone. Gumiela probably believed crime families should fight amongst themselves, so the police didn't have to deal with them.

DeRicci paused for a half second.

If she went back in, she would probably lose her job. Because she would tell Gumiela exactly what she thought of the clone laws, and the way that Property would screw up the investigation, and the fact that *people* were actually dying and being placed in crates.

But, if DeRicci lost her job, she wouldn't be able to investigate anything.

The next time, she got a clone case, she'd sit on that information for as long as she could, finish the investigation, and maybe make an arrest. Sure, it might not hold up, but she could get one of the other divisions to search the perpetrator's home and business, maybe catch him with something else.

This time, she had screwed up. She'd followed the rules too closely. She shouldn't have gone to Gumiela so soon.

DeRicci would know better next time.

And she'd play dumb when Gumiela challenged her over it.

Better to lose a job after solving a case, instead of in the middle of a failed one.

DeRicci sighed. She didn't feel better, but at least she had a plan.

Even if it was a plan she didn't like at all.

The place that the clone frequented near the Port was a one-person office, run by a man named Cade Faulke. Ostensibly, Faulke ran an employment consulting office, one that helped people find jobs or training for jobs. But it didn't take a lot of digging to discover that was a cover for a position with Earth Alliance Security.

From what little Deshin could find, it seemed that Faulke worked alone, with an android guard—the kind that usually monitored prisons. Clearly, no one expected Faulke to be investigated: the android alone would have been a tip-off to anyone who looked deeper than the thin cover that Faulke had over his name.

Deshin wondered how many other Earth Alliance operatives worked like that inside of Armstrong. He supposed there were quite a few, monitoring various Earth Alliance projects. Projects like, apparently, his family.

Deshin let out a sigh. He wandered around his office, feeling like it had become a cage. He clenched and unclenched his fists. Sometimes he hated the way he had restrained himself to build his business and his family. Sometimes he just wanted to go after someone on his own, squeeze the life out of that person, and then leave the corpse, the way someone had left that clone.

Spying on Deshin's family. Gerda and five-month-old Paavo had done nothing except get involved with him.

And, he would wager, that Sonja Mycenae's family would say the same thing about her.

He stopped. He hadn't spoken to the Mycenae family in a long time, but he owed them for an ancient debt.

He sent an encoded message through his links to Aurla Mycenae, the head of the Mycenae and Sonja's mother, asking for a quick audience.

Then Deshin got a contact from Cumija: *Five low-level employees have the marker. None of them have access to your family or to anything important inside Deshin Enterprises. How do you want me to proceed?*

Send me a list, he sent back.

At that moment, his links chirruped, announcing a massive holomessage so encoded that it nearly overloaded his system. He accepted the message, only to find out it was live.

Aurla Mycenae appeared, full-sized, in the center of his floor. She wore a flowing black gown that accented her dark eyebrows and thick black hair. She had faint lines around her black eyes. Otherwise she looked no older than she had the last time he saw her, at least a decade ago.

"Luc," she said in a throaty voice that hadn't suited her as a young woman, but suited her now. "I get this sense this isn't pleasure."

"No," he said. "I thought I should warn you. I encountered a slow-grow clone of your daughter Sonja."

He decided not to mention that he had hired that clone or that she had been murdered.

Mycenae exhaled audibly. "Damn Earth Alliance. Did they try to embed her in your organization?"

"They succeeded for a time," he said.

"And then?"

So much for keeping the information back. "She turned up dead this morning."

"Typical," Mycenae said. "They've got some kind of operation going, and they've been using clones of my family. You're not the first to tell me this."

"All slow-grow?" Deshin asked.

"Yes," Mycenae said. "We've been letting everyone know that anyone applying for work from our family isn't really from our family. I never thought of contacting you because I thought you went legit."

"I have," Deshin lied. He had gone legit on most things. He definitely no longer had his fingers in the kinds of deals that the Mycenae family was famous for.

"Amazing they tried to embed with you, then," Mycenae said.

"She was nanny to my infant son," he said, and he couldn't quite keep the fury from his voice.

"Oh." Mycenae sighed. "They want to use your family like they're using mine. We're setting something up, Luc. We've got the Alliance division doing this crap tracked, and we're going to shut it down. You want to join us?"

Take on an actual Earth Alliance Division? As a young man, he would have considered it. As a man with a family and a half-legitimate business, he didn't dare take the risk.

"I trust you to handle it, Aurla," he said.

"They have your family's DNA now," she said, clearly as a way of enticement.

"It's of no use to them in the short term," he said, "and by the time we reach the long term, you'll have taken care of everything."

"It's not like you to trust anyone, Luc."

And, back when she had known him well, that had been true. But now, he had to balance security for himself and his business associates with security for his family.

"I'm not trusting you per se, Aurla," he said. "I just know how you operate."

She grinned at him. "I'll let you know when we're done."

"No need," he said. "Good luck."

And then he signed off. The last thing he wanted was to be associated in any way with whatever operation Aurla ran. She was right: it wasn't like him to trust anyone. And while he trusted her to destroy the division that was hurting her family, he didn't trust her to keep him out of it. Too much contact with Aurla Mycenae, and Deshin might find himself arrested as the perpetrator of whatever she was planning. Mycenae was notorious for betraying colleagues when her back was against the wall.

The list came through his links from Cumija. She was right: the employees were low-level. He didn't recognize any of the names and had to look them up. None of them had even met Deshin.

Getting the clone of Sonja embedded into his family was some kind of coup.

He wouldn't fire anyone yet. He wanted to see if Koos came up with the same list. If he did, then Deshin would move forward.

But these employees were tagged, just like Sonja's clone had been. He decided to see if they had been visiting Faulke as well.

And if they had, Faulke would regret ever crossing paths with Deshin Enterprises.

Detective DeRicci left Andrea Gumiela's office. Gumiela felt herself relax. DeRicci was trouble. She hated rules and she had a sense of righteousness that often made it difficult for her to do her job well. There wasn't a lot of righteousness in the law, particularly when Earth Alliance law trumped Armstrong law.

Gumiela had to balance both.

She resisted the urge to run a hand through her hair. It had taken a lot of work to pile it just so on top of her head, and she didn't like wasting time on her appearance, as important as it was to her job. Of course, the days when it was important were either days when a major disaster hit Armstrong or when someone in her department screwed up.

She certainly hoped this clone case wouldn't become a screw-up.

She put a hand over her stomach, feeling slightly ill. She had felt ill from the moment DeRicci mentioned Mycenae and Deshin. At that moment, Gumiela knew who had made the clone and who was handling it.

She also knew who was killing the clones—or at least, authorizing the deaths.

DeRicci was right. Those deaths presaged a serial killer (or, in Gumiela's unofficial opinion, already proved one existed). Or worse, the deaths suggested a policy of targeted killings that Gumiela couldn't countenance in her city.

Technically, Gumiela should contact Cade Faulke directly. He had contacted her directly more than once to report a possible upcoming crime. She had used him as an informant, which meant she had used his clones as informants as well.

And those clones were ending up dead.

She choked back bile. Some people, like DeRicci, would say that Gumiela had hands as dirty as Faulke's. But she hadn't known he was killing the clones when they ceased being useful or when they crossed some line. She also hadn't known that he had been poisoning them using such a painful method. And he hadn't even thought about the possible contamination of the food supply.

Gumiela swallowed hard again, hoping her stomach would settle.

Technically, she should contact him and tell him to cease that behavior.

But Gumiela had been in her job a long time. She knew that telling someone like Faulke to quit was like telling an addict to stop drinking. It wouldn't happen, and it couldn't be done.

She couldn't arrest him either. Even if she caught him in the act, all he was doing was damaging property. And that might get him a fine or two or maybe a year or so in jail, if the clone's owners complained. But if DeRicci was right, the clone's owners were the Earth Alliance itself. And Faulke worked for the Alliance, so technically, *he* was probably the owner, and property owners could do whatever they wanted with their belongings.

Except toss them away in a manner that threatened the public health.

Gumiela sat in one of the chairs and leaned her head back, closing her eyes, forcing herself to think. She had to do something, and despite what she had said to DeRicci, following procedure was out of the question. She needed to get Faulke out of Armstrong, only she didn't have the authority to do so.

But she knew who did.

She sat up. Long ago, she'd met Faulke's handler, Ike Jarvis. She could contact him.

Maybe he would work with her.

It was worth a try.

Otto Koos led his team to the building housing Cade Faulke's fake business. The building was made of some kind of polymer that changed appearance daily. This day's appearance made it seem like old-fashioned red brick Koos hadn't seen since his childhood on Earth.

Five Ansel Management crates stood in their protected unit in the alley behind the building. They had a cursory lock with a security code that anyone in the building probably had.

It was as much of a confession as he needed.

But the boss would need more. Luc Deshin had given strict orders for this mission—no killing.

Koos knew he was on probation now—maybe forever. He had missed the Mycenae clone, and, after he had done a quick scan of the employees, discovered he had missed at least five others. At least they hadn't been anywhere near the Deshin family.

The Mycenae clone had. Who knew what kind of material the Alliance had gathered?

Faulke knew. Eventually, Koos would know too. It just might take some time.

He had brought ten people with him to capture Faulke. The office had an android guard, though, the durable kind used in prisons. Koos either had to disable it or get it out of the building.

He'd failed the one time he'd tried to disable those things in the past. He was opting for getting it out of the building.

Ready? he sent to two of his team members.

Yes, they sent back at the same time.

Go! he sent.

They were nowhere near him, but he knew what they were going to do. They were going to start a fight in front of the building that would get progressively more violent. And then they'd start shooting up the area with laser pistols.

Other members of his team would prevent any locals from stopping the fight, and the fight would continue until the guard came down. Then Koos would sneak in the back way, along with three other members of his team.

They were waiting now. They had already checked the back door— unlocked during daylight hours. They were talking as if they had some kind of business with each other.

At least they weren't shifting from foot to foot like he wanted to do.

Instead, all he could do was stare at that stamp for Ansel Management.

It hadn't been much work to pick up the Mycenae clone and stuff her into one of the crates.

If Deshin hadn't given the no-kill order, then Koos would have stuffed Faulke into one of the crates, dying, but alive, so that he knew what he had done.

Koos would have preferred that to Deshin's plan.

But Koos wasn't in charge. And he had to work his way back into Deshin's good graces.

And he would do that.

Starting now.

Gumiela had forgotten that Ike Jarvis was an officious prick. He ran intelligence operatives who worked inside the Alliance. Generally, those operatives didn't operate in human-run areas. In fact, they shouldn't operate in human-run areas at all.

Earth Alliance Intelligence was supposed to do the bulk of its work *outside* the Alliance.

Gumiela had contacted him on a special link the Earth Alliance had set up for the Armstrong Police Department, to be used only in cases of Earth Alliance troubles or serious Alliance issues.

She figured this counted.

Jarvis appeared in the center of the room, his three-dimensional image fritzing in and out either because of a bad connection or because of the levels of encoding this conversation was going through.

He looked better when he appeared and disappeared. She preferred it when he was slightly out of focus.

"This had better be good, Andy," Jarvis said, and Gumiela felt her shoulders stiffen. No one called her Andy, not even her best friends. Only Jarvis had come up with that nickname, and somehow he seemed to believe it made them closer.

"I need you to pull Cade Faulke," she said.

"I don't pull anyone on your say so." Jarvis fritzed again. His image came back just a little smaller, just a little tighter. So the problem was on his end.

If she were in a better mood, she would smile. Jarvis was short enough without doctoring the image. He had once tried to compensate for his height by buying enhancements that deepened his voice. All they had done was ruin it, leaving him sounding like he had poured salt down his throat.

"You pull him or I arrest him for attempted mass murder," she said, a little surprised at herself.

Jarvis moved and fritzed again. Apparently he had taken a step backwards or something, startled by her vehemence.

"What the hell did he do?" Jarvis asked, not playing games any longer.

"You have Faulke running slow-grow clones in criminal organizations, right?" she asked.

"Andy," he said, returning to that condescending tone he had used earlier, "I can't tell you what I'm doing."

"Fine," she snapped. "I thought we had a courteous relationship, based on mutual interest. I was wrong. Sorry to bother you, Ike—"

"Wait," he said. "What did he do?"

"It doesn't matter," she said. "You get to send Earth Alliance lawyers here to talk about the top-secret crap to judges who might've died because of your guy's carelessness."

And then she signed off.

She couldn't do anything she had just threatened Jarvis with. The food thing hadn't risen to the level where she could charge Faulke, and that was if she could prove that he had put the bodies into the crates himself. He had an android guard, which the Chief of Police had had to approve—those things weren't supposed to operate inside the city—and that guard had probably done all the dirty work. They would just claim malfunction, and Faulke would be off the hook.

Jarvis fritzed back in, fainter now. The image had one meter sideways, which meant he was superimposed over one of her office chairs. The chair cut through him at his knees and waist. Obviously, he had no idea where his image had appeared, and she wasn't about to tell him or move the image.

"Okay, okay," Jarvis said. "I've managed to make this link as secure as I possibly can, given my location. Guarantee that your side is secure."

Gumiela shrugged. "I'm alone in my office, in the Armstrong Police Department. Good enough for you?"

She didn't tell him that she was recording this whole thing. She was tired of being used by this asshole.

"I guess it'll have to be. Yes, Faulke is running the clones that we have embedded with major criminal organizations on the Moon."

"If the clones malfunction—" She chose that word carefully "—what's he supposed to do?"

"Depends on how specific the clone is to the job, and how important it is to the operation," he said. "Generally, Faulke's supposed to ship the clone back. That's why Armstrong PD approved android guards for his office."

"There aren't guards," she said. "There's only one."

Jarvis's image came in a bit stronger. "What?"

"Just one," she said, "and that's not all. I don't think your friend Faulke has sent any clones back."

"I can check," Jarvis said.

"I don't care what you do for your records. According to ours—" and there she was lying again "—he's been killing the clones that don't work out and putting them in composting crates. Those crates go to the Growing Pits, which grow fresh food for the city."

"He *what?*" Jarvis asked.

"And to make matters worse, he's using a hardening poison to kill them, a poison our coroner fears might leach into our food supply. We're checking on that now. Although it doesn't matter. The intent is what matters, and clearly your man Faulke has lost his mind."

Jarvis cursed. "You're not making this up."

It wasn't a question.

"I'm not making this up," she said. "I want him and his little android friend out of here within the hour, or I'm arresting him, and I'm putting him on trial. Public trial."

"Do you realize how many operations you'll ruin?"

"No," she said, "and I don't care. Get him out of my city. It's only a matter of time before your crazy little operative starts killing legal humans, not just cloned ones. And I don't want him doing it here."

Jarvis cursed again. "Can I get your help—"

"No," she said. "I don't want anyone at the police department involved with your little operation. And if you go to the chief, I'll tell her that you have thwarted my attempts to arrest a man who threatens the entire dome. Because, honestly, Ike *baby*, this is a courtesy contact. I don't have to do you any favors at all, especially considering what kind of person, if I can use that word, you installed in my city. Have you got that?"

"Yes, Andrea, I do," he said, looking serious.

Andrea. So he had heard her all those times. And he had ignored her, the bastard. She made note of that too.

"One hour," she said, and signed off.

Then she wiped her hands on her skirt. They were shaking just a little. Screw him, the weasely little bastard. She'd send someone to that office now, to escort Jarvis's horrid operative out of Armstrong.

She wanted to make sure that asshole left quickly, and didn't double back.

She wanted this problem out of her city, off her Moon, and as far from her notice as possible. And that, she knew, was the best she could do without upsetting the department's special relationship with the Alliance.

She hoped her best would be good enough.

Up the back stairs, into the narrow hallway that smelled faintly of dry plastic, Koos led the raid, his best team members behind him. They fanned out in the narrow hallway, the two women first, signaling that the hallway was clear. Koos and Hala, the only other man on this part of the team skirted past them, and through the open door of Faulke's office.

It was much smaller than Koos expected. Faulke was only three meters from him. Faulke was scrawny, narrow-shouldered, the kind of man easily ignored on the street.

He reached behind his back—probably for a weapon—as Koos and Hala held their laser rifles on him.

"Don't even try," Koos said. "I have no compunction shooting you."

Faulke's eyes glazed for a half second—probably letting his android guard know he was in trouble—then an expression of panic flitted across his face before he managed to control it.

The other members of Koos's team had already disabled the guard.

"Who are you?" Faulke asked.

Koos ignored him, and spoke to his team. "I want him bound. And make sure you disable his links."

One of the women slipped in around Koos, and put light cuffs around Faulke's wrists and pasted a small rectangle of Silent-Seal over his mouth.

YOU CAN'T GET AWAY WITH THIS, Faulke sent on public links. YOU HAVE NO IDEA WHO I AM—

And then his links shut off.

Koos grinned. "You're Cade Faulke. You work for Earth Alliance Intelligence. You've been running clones that you embed into businesses. Am I missing anything?"

Faulke's eyes didn't change, but he swallowed hard.

"Let's get him out of here," Koos said.

They encircled him, in case the other tenants on the floor decided to see what all the fuss was about. But no one opened any doors. The neighborhood was too dicey for that. If anyone had an ounce of civic feeling, they would have gone out front to stop the fight that Koos had staged below.

And no one had.

He took Faulke's arm, surprised at how flabby it was. Hardly any muscles at all.

No wonder the asshole had used poison. He wasn't strong enough to subdue any living creature on his own.

"You're going to love what we have planned for you," Koos said as he dragged Faulke down the stairs. "By the end of it all, you and I will be old friends."

This time Faulke gave him a startled look.

Koos grinned at him, and led him to the waiting car that would take them to the Port. It would be a long time before anyone heard from Cade Faulke again.

If they ever did.

DeRicci hated days like today. She had lost a case because of stupid laws that had no bearing on what really happened. A woman had been murdered, and DeRicci couldn't solve the case. It would go to Property, where it would get stuck in a pile of cases that no one cared about, because no one would be able to put a value on this particular clone. No owner would come forward. No one would care.

And if DeRicci hadn't seen this sort of thing a dozen times, she would have tried to solve it herself in her off time. She might still hound Property, just to make sure the case didn't get buried. Maybe she'd even use Broduer's lies. She might tell Property that whoever planted the clone had tried to poison the city. That might get some dumb Property detective off his butt.

She, on the other hand, was already working on the one good thing to come out of this long day. She was compiling all the documents on every single thing that Rayvon Lake had screwed up in their short tenure as partners.

Even she hadn't realized how much it was.

She would have a long list for Gumiela by the end of the day, and this time, Gumiela would pay attention.

Or DeRicci would threaten to take the clone case to the media. DeRicci had been appalled that human waste could get into the recycling system; she would wager that the population of Armstrong would too.

One threat like that, and Gumiela would have to fire Lake.

It wasn't justice. It wasn't anything resembling justice.

But after a few years in this job, DeRicci had learned only one thing: Justice didn't exist in the Earth Alliance.

Not for humans, not for clones, not for anyone.

And somehow, she had to live with it.

She just hadn't quite figured out how.

Deshin arrived home, exhausted and more than a little unsettled. The house smelled of baby powder and coffee. He hadn't really checked to see how the rest of Gerda's day alone with Paavo had gone. He felt guilty about that.

He went through the modest living room to the baby's room. He and Gerda didn't flash their wealth around Armstrong, preferring to live quietly. But he had so much security in the home that he was still startled the clone had broken through it.

Gerda was sitting in a rocking chair near the window, Paavo in her arms. She put a finger to her lips, but it did no good.

His five-month-old son twisted, and looked at Deshin with such aware eyes that it humbled him. Deshin knew that this baby was twenty times smarter than he would ever be. It worried him, and it pleased him as well.

Paavo smiled and extended his pudgy arms. Deshin picked him up. The boy was heavier than he had been just a week before. He also needed a diaper change.

Deshin took him to the changing table, and started, knowing just from the look on her face that Gerda was exhausted too.

"Long day?" he asked.

"Good day," she said. "We made the right decision."

"Yes," he said. "We did."

He had decided on the way home not to tell her everything. He would wait until the interrogation of Cade Faulke and the five clones was over. Koos had taken all six of them out of Armstrong in the same ship.

And the interrogations would even start until Koos got them out of Earth Alliance territory, days from now.

Deshin had no idea what would happen to Faulke or the clones after that. Deshin was leaving that up to Koos. Koos no longer headed security for Deshin Enterprises in Armstrong, but he had served Deshin well today. He would handle some of the company's work outside the Alliance.

Not a perfect day's work, not even the day's work Deshin had expected, but a good one nonetheless. He probably had other leaks to plug in his organization, but at least he knew what they were now.

His baby raised a chubby fist at Deshin as if agreeing that action needed to be taken. Deshin bent over and blew bubbles on Paavo's tummy, something that always made Paavo giggle.

He giggled now, a sound so infectious that Deshin wondered how he had lived without it all his life.

He would do everything he could to protect this baby, everything he could to take care of his family.

"He trusts you," Gerda said with a tiny bit of amazement in her voice.

Most people never trusted Deshin. Gerda did, but Gerda was special.

Deshin blew bubbles on Paavo's tummy again, and Paavo laughed.

His boy did trust him.

He picked up his newly diapered son, and cradled him in his arms. Then he kissed Gerda.

The three of them, forever.

That was what he needed, and that was what he ensured today.

The detective could poke around his business all she wanted, but she would never know the one thing that calmed Deshin down.

Justice had been done.

His family was safe.

And that was all that mattered.

⋖◆⋗

THE BONE SWANS OF AMANDALE

C. S. E. Cooney

Dora Rose reached her dying sister a few minutes before the Swan Hunters did. I watched it all from my snug perch in the old juniper, and I won't say I didn't enjoy the scene, what with the blood and the pathos and everything. If only I had a handful of nuts to nibble on, sugared and roasted, the kind they sell in paper packets on market day when the weather turns. They sure know how to do nuts in Amandale.

"Elinore!" Dora Rose's voice was low and urgent, with none of the fluting snootiness I remembered. "Look at me. Elinore. How did they find you? We all agreed to hide—"

Ah, the good stuff. Drama. I lived for it. I scuttled down a branch to pay closer attention.

Dora Rose had draped the limp girl over her lap, stroking back her black, black hair. White feathers everywhere, trailing from Elinore's shoulders, bloodied at the breast, muddied near the hem. Elinore must've been midway between a fleshing and a downing when that Swan Hunter's arrow got her.

"Dora Rose." Elinore's wet red hand left a death smear on her sister's face. "They smoked out the cygnets. Drove them to the lake. Nets—horrible nets. They caught Pope, Maleen, Conrad—even Dash. We tried to free them, but more hunters came, and I . . ."

Turned herself into a swan, I thought, *and flew the hellfowl off.* Smart Elinore.

She'd not see it that way, of course. Swan people fancied themselves a proud folk, elegant as lords in their haughty halls, mean as snakes in a tight corner. Me, I preferred survivors to heroes. Or heroines, however comely.

"I barely escaped," Elinore finished.

From the looks of that gusher in her ribs, I'd guess "escaped" was a gross overstatement. But that's swans for you. Can't speak but they hyperbolize. Every girl's a princess. Every boy's a prince. Swan Folk take their own metaphors so seriously they hold themselves lofty from the vulgar throng. Dora Rose explained it once, when we were younger and she still deigned to chat with the likes of me: "It's not that we think less of anyone, Maurice. It's just that we think better of ourselves."

"Dora Rose, you mustn't linger. They'll be tracking me . . . "

Elinore's hand slipped from Dora Rose's cheek. Her back arched. Her bare toes curled under, and her hands clawed the mossy ground. From her lips burst the most beautiful song—a cascade of notes like moonlight on a waterfall, like a wave breaking on boulders, like the first snow melt of spring. All swan girls are princesses, true, but if styling themselves as royalty ever got boring, they could always go in for the opera.

Elinore was a soprano. Her final, stretched notes pierced even me. Dora Rose used to tell me that I had such tin ears as could be melted down for a saucepan, which at least might then be flipped over and used for a drum, thus contributing in a trivial way to the musical arts.

So maybe I was a little tone-deaf. Didn't mean I couldn't enjoy a swan song when I heard one.

As she crouched anxiously over Elinore's final aria, Dora Rose seemed far remote from the incessantly clever, sporadically sweet, gloriously vain girl who used to be my friend. The silvery sheen of her skin was frosty with pallor. As the song faded, its endmost high note stuttering to a sigh that slackened the singer's white lips, Dora Rose whispered, "Elinore?"

No answer.

My nose twitched as the smell below went from dying swan girl to freshly dead carcass. Olly-olly-in-for-free. As we like to say.

Among my Folk, carrion's a feast that's first come, first served, and I was well placed to take the largest bite. I mean, I *could* wait until Dora Rose lit on outta there. Not polite to go nibbling on someone's sister while she watched, after all. Just not done. Not when that someone had been sort of a friend. (All right—unrequited crush. But that was kid stuff. I'm over it. Grown up. Moved on.)

I heard the sound before she did. Ulia Gol's ivory horn. Not good.

"Psst!" I called from my tree branch. "Psst, Dora Rose. Up here!"

Her head snapped up, twilight eyes searching the tangle of the juniper branches. This tree was the oldest and tallest in the Maze Wood, unusually colossal for its kind, even with its trunk bent double and its branches bowing like a willow's. Nevertheless, Dora Rose's sharp gaze caught my shadowy shape and raked at it like fingernails. I grinned at her, preening my whiskers. Always nice to be noticed by a Swan Princess. Puts me on my mettle.

"Who is it?" Her voice was hoarse from grief and fear. I smelled both on her. Salt and copper.

"Forget me so quickly, Ladybird?" Before she could answer, I dove nose-first down the shaggy trunk, fleshing as I went. By the time I hit ground,

I was a man. Man-shaped, anyway. Maybe a little undersized. Maybe scraggly, with a beard that grew in patches, a nose that fit my face better in my other shape, and eyes only a mother would trust—and only if she'd been drunk since breakfast.

"Maurice!"

"The Incomparable," I agreed. "Your very own Maurice."

Dora Rose stood suddenly, tall and icy in her blood-soaked silver gown. I freely admit to a dropped jaw, an abrupt excess of saliva. She'd only improved with time; her hair was as pale as her sister's had been dark, her eyes as blue as Lake Serenus where she and her Folk dwelled during their winter migrations. The naked grief I'd sensed in her a few moments ago had already cooled, like her sister's corpse. Swan Folk have long memories but a short emotional attention span.

Unlike Rat Folk, whose emotions could still get the better of them after fifteen years . . .

"What are you doing in the Maze Wood?" The snootiness I'd missed was back in her voice. Fabulous.

"Is that what this is?" I peered around, scratching behind my ear. She always hated when I scratched. "I thought it was the theater. *The Tragedy of the Bonny Swans. The Ballad of the Two Sisters* . . . "

Her eyes narrowed. "Maurice, of all the times to crack your tasteless jokes!"

Aaaarooooo! The ivory horn again. This time Dora Rose heard it, too. Her blue eyes flashed black with fury and terror. She hesitated, frozen between flesh and feather, fight and flight. I figured I'd help her out. Just this once. For old time's sake.

"Up the tree," I suggested. "I'll give you a boost."

She cast a perturbed look at dead Elinore, grief flickering briefly across her face. Rolling my eyes, I snapped, "Up, Princess! Unless you want to end the same, here and now."

"Won't the hounds scent me there?"

Dora Rose, good girl, was already moving toward me as she asked the question. Thank the Captured God. Start arguing with a swan girl, and you'll not only find yourself staying up all night, you'll also suffer all the symptoms of a bad hangover in the morning—with none of the fun parts between.

"This old tree's wily enough to mask your scent, my plume. If you ask nicely. We're good friends, the juniper and I."

I'd seen enough Swan Folk slaughtered beneath this tree to keep me tethered to it by curiosity alone. All right, so maybe I stayed with the mildly interested and not at all pathological hope of meeting Dora Rose again, in some situation not unlike this one, perhaps to rescue her from the ignominy of such a death. But I didn't tell her that. Not while her twin sister lay dead on the ground, her blood seeping into the juniper's roots. By the time Elinore had gotten to the tree, it'd've been too late for me to attempt anything, anyway. Even had I been so inclined.

And then, Dora Rose's hand on my shoulder. Her bare heel in my palm. And it was like little silver bells ringing under my skin where she touched me.

Easy, Maurice. Easy, you sleek and savvy rat, you. Bide.

Up she went, and I after her, furring and furling myself into my more compact but no less natty shape. We were both safe and shadow-whelmed in the bent old branches by the time Mayor Ulia Gol and her Swan Hunters arrived on the scene.

If someone held a piece of cheese to my head and told me to describe Ulia Gol in one word or starve, I'd choose *magnificent*. I like cheese too much to dither.

At a guess, I'd say Ulia Gol's ancestry wasn't human. Ogre on her mama's side. Giant on her daddy's. She was taller than Dora Rose, who herself would tower over most mortal men, though Dora Rose was long-lined and lean of limb whereas Ulia Gol was a brawny woman. Her skin was gold as a glazed chicken, her head full of candy-pink curls as was the current fashion. Her breasts were like two mozzarella balls ripe for the gnawing, with hips like two smoked hams. A one-woman banquet, that Ulia Gol, and she knew it, too. The way to a mortal's heart is through its appetite, and Ulia Gol prided herself on collecting mortal hearts. It was a kind of a game with her. Her specialty. Her sorcery.

She had a laugh that reached right out and tickled your belly. They say it was her laugh that won her the last election in Amandale. It wasn't. More like a mob-wide love spell she cast on her constituents. I don't know much about magic, but I know the smell of it. Amandale stinks of Ulia Gol. Its citizens accepted her rule with wretched adoration, wondering why they often woke of a night in a cold sweat from foul dreams of their Mayor feasting on the flesh of their children.

On the surface, she was terrifyingly jovial. She liked hearty dining and a good, hard day at the hunt. Was known for her fine whiskey, exotic lovers, intricate calligraphy, and dabbling in small—totally harmless, it was said—magics, mostly in the realm of the Performing Arts. Was a little too enthusiastic about taxes, everyone thought, but mostly used them to keep Amandale in good order. Streets, bridges, schools, secret police. That sort of thing.

Mortal politics was the idlest of my hobbies, but Ulia Gol had become a right danger to the local Folk, and that directly affected me. Swans weren't the only magic creatures she'd hunted to extinction in the Maze Wood. Before this latest kick, Ulia Gol had ferreted out the Fox Folk, those that fleshed to mortal shape, with tails tucked up under their clothes. Decimated the population in this area. You might ask how I know—after all, Fox Folk don't commune with Rat Folk any more than Swan Folk do. We just don't really talk to each other.

But then, I always was extraordinary. And really nosy.

Me, I suspected Ulia Gol's little hunting parties had a quite specific purpose. I think she knew the Folk could recognize her as inhuman. Mortals, of course, had no idea what she was. What mortals might do if they discovered their Mayor manipulated magic to make the ballot box come out in her favor? Who knew? Mortals in general are content to remain divinely stupid and bovinely docile for long periods of time, but when their ire's roused, there is no creature cleverer in matters of torture and revenge.

Ulia Gol adjusted her collar of rusty fox fur. It clashed terribly with her pink-and-purple riding habit, but she pulled it off with panache. Her slanted beaver hat dripped half a dozen black-tipped tails, which bounced as she strode into the juniper tree's clearing. Two huge-jowled hounds flanked her. She caught her long train up over her arm, her free hand clasping her crossbow with loose proficiency.

"Ha!" shouted Ulia Gol over her shoulder to someone out of my sightlines. "I thought I got her." She squatted over dead Elinore, studying her. "What do you think of this one, Hans? Too delicate for the glockenspiel, I reckon. Too tiny for the tuba. The cygnets completed our wind and percussion sections. Those two cobs and yesterday's pen did for the brass. We might as well finish up the strings here."

A man emerged from a corridor in the Maze Wood. He led Ulia Gol's tall roan mare and his own grey gelding, and looked with interest on the dead swan girl.

"A pretty one," he observed. "She'll make a fine harp, Madame Mayor, unless I miss my guess."

"Outstanding! I love a good harp song. But I always found the going rates too dear; harpists are so full of themselves." Her purple grin widened. "Get the kids in here."

The rest of her Swan Hunters began trotting into the Heart Glade on their plump little ponies. Many corridors, as you'd expect in a Maze Wood of this size, dead-ended in thorn, stone, waterfall, hedge, cliff edge. But Ulia Gol's child army must've had the key to unlocking the maze's secrets, for they came unhesitatingly into the glade and stood in the shadow of the juniper tree where we hid.

Aw, the sweetums. Pink-cheeked they were, the little killers, green-caped, and all of them wearing the famous multicolored, beaked masks of Amandale. Mortals are always fixed in their flesh, like my rat cousins who remain rats no matter what. Can't do furrings, downings, or scalings like the Folk can. So they make do with elaborate costumes, body paint, millinery, and mass exterminations of our kind. Kind of adorable, really.

Ulia Gol clapped her hands. Her pink curls bounced and jounced. The foxtails on her beaver hat swung blithely.

"Dismount!" Her Hunters did so. "Whose turn is it, my little wretches?" she bawled at them. "Has to be someone fresh! Someone who's bathed in mare's milk by moonlight since yesterday's hunt. Now—who's clean? Who's my pure and pretty chanticleer today? Come, don't make me pick one of you!"

Oh, the awkward silence of children called upon to volunteer. A few heads bowed. Other masks lifted and looked elsewhere as if that act rendered them invisible. Presently one of the number was pushed to the forefront, so vehemently it fell and scraped its dimpled knees. I couldn't help noticing that this child had been standing at the very back of the crowd, hugging itself and hoping to escape observation.

Fat chance, kiddling. I licked my lips. I knew what came next. I'd been watching this death dance from the juniper tree for weeks now.

Ulia Gol grinned horribly at the fallen child. "Tag!" she boomed. "You're it." Her heavy hand fell across the child's shoulders, scooting it closer to the dead swan girl. "Dig. Dig her a grave fit for a princess."

The child trembled in its bright green hunter's cape. Its jaunty red mask was tied askew, like a deformed cardinal's head stitched atop a rag doll. The quick desperation of its breath was audible even from the heights where we perched, me sweating and twitching, Dora Rose tense and pale, glistening faintly in the dimness of the canopy.

Dora Rose lay on her belly, arms and legs wrapped around the branch, leaning as far forward as she dared. She watched the scene with avid eyes, and I watched her. She wouldn't have known why her people had been hunted all up and down the lake this autumn. Even when the swans began disappearing a few weeks ago, the survivors hadn't moved on. Swan Folk were big on tradition; Lake Serenus was where they wintered, and that was that. To establish a new migratory pattern would've been tantamount to blasphemy. That's swans for you.

I might have gone to warn them, I guess. Except that the last time she'd seen me, Dora Rose made it pretty clear that she'd rather wear a gown of graveyard nettles and pluck out her own feathers for fletching than have to endure two minutes more in my company. Of course, we were just teenagers then.

I gave the old juniper tree a pat, muttering a soundless prayer for keepsafe and concealment. Just in case Dora Rose'd forgotten to do as much in that first furious climb. Then I saw her lips move, saw her silver fingers stroking the shaggy branch. Good. So she, too, kept up a running stream of supplication. I'd no doubt she knew all the proper formulae; Swan Folk are as religious as they are royal. Maybe because they figure they're the closest things to gods as may still be cut and bleed.

"WHY AREN'T YOU DIGGING YET?" bellowed Ulia Gol, hooking my attention downward.

A masterful woman, and so well coiffed! How fun it was to watch her make those children jump. In my present shape, I can scare grown men out of their boots, they're that afraid of plague-carriers in these parts. The Folk are immune to plague, but mortals can't tell a fixed rat from one of us to save their lives.

Amandale itself was mostly spared a few years back when things got really bad and the plague bells ringing death tolls in distant towns at last fell silent. Ulia Gol spread the rumor abroad that it was her mayoral prowess that got her town through unscathed. Another debt Amandale owed her.

How she loomed.

"Please, Madame Mayor, please!" piped the piccolo voice from behind the cardinal mask. It fair vibrated with apprehension. "I—I cannot dig. I have no shovel!"

"Is that all? Hans! A shovel for our shy red bird!"

Hans of the gray gelding trudged forward with amiable alacrity. I liked his style. Reminded me of me. He was not tall, but he had a dapper air. One of your blonds was Hans, high-colored, with a crooked but entirely proportionate nose, a gold-goateed chin, and boots up to the thigh. He dressed all in red, except for his green cape, and he wore a knife on his belt. A fine big knife, with one edge curved and outrageously serrated.

I shuddered deliciously, deciding right there and then that I would follow him home tonight and steal his things while he slept.

The shovel presented, the little one was bid a third time to dig.

The grave needed only be a shallow one for Ulia Gol's purposes. This I had apprehended in my weeks of study. The earth hardly needed a scratch in its surface. Then the Swan Princess (or Prince, or heap of stiffening cygnets, as was the case yesterday) was rolled in the turned dirt and partially covered. Then Ulia Gol, towering over her small trooper with the blistered hands, would rip the mask off its face and roar, "Weep! If you love your life weep, or I'll give you something to weep about!"

Unmasked, this afternoon's child proved to be a young boy. One of the innumerable Cobblersawl brood unless I missed my guess. Baker's children. The proverbial dozen, give or take a miscarriage. Always carried a slight smell of yeast about them.

Froggit, I think this little one's name was. The seven-year-old. After the twins but before the toddlers and the infant.

I was quite fond of the Cobblersawls. Kids are so messy, you know, strewing crumbs everywhere. Bakers' kids have the best crumbs. Their poor mother was often too harried to sweep up after the lot of them until bedtime. Well after the gleanings had been got.

Right now, dreamy little Froggit looked sick. His hands begrimed with dirt and Elinore's blood, his brown hair matted with sweat, he covered her corpse well and good. Now, on cue, he started sobbing. Truth be told, he hadn't needed Ulia Gol's shouting to do so. His tears spattered the dirt, turning spots of it to mud.

Ulia Gol raised her arms like a conductor. Her big, shapely hands swooped through the air like kestrels.

"Sing, my children! You know the ditty well enough by now, I trust! This one's female; make sure you alter the lyrics accordingly. One-two-three and—"

One in obedience, twenty young Swan Hunters lifted up their voices in wobbly chorus. The hounds bayed mournfully along. I hummed, too, under my breath.

When they'd started the Swan Hunt a few weeks ago, the kids used to join hands and gambol around the juniper tree all maypole-like at Ulia Gol's urging. But the Mayor since discovered that her transformation spell worked just as well if they all stood still. Pity. I missed the dancing. Used to give the whole scene a nice theatrical flair.

Poor little swan girl
Heart pierced through
Buried 'neath the moss and dew
Restless in your grave you'll be
At the foot of the juniper tree
But your bones shall sing your song
Morn and noon and all night long!

The music cut off with an abrupt slash of Ulia Gol's hands. She nodded once in curt approval. "Go on!" she told Froggit Cobblersawl. "Dig her back up again!"

But here Froggit's courage failed him. Or perhaps found him. For he scrubbed his naked face of tears, smearing worse things there, and stared up with big brown eyes that hated only one thing worse than himself, and *that* was Ulia Gol.

"No," he said.

"Hans," said Ulia Gol, "we have another rebel on our hands."

Hans stepped forward and drew from its sheath that swell knife I'd be stealing later. Ulia Gol beamed down at Froggit, foxtails falling to frame her face.

"Master Cobblersawl." She clucked her tongue. "Last week, we put out little Miss Possum's eyes when she refused to sing up the bones. Four weeks before that, we lamed the legs of young Miss Greenpea. A cousin of yours, I think? On our first hunt, she threw that shovel right at Hans and tried to run away. But we took that shovel and we made her pay, didn't we, Master Cobblersawl? And with whom did we replace her to make my hunters twenty strong again? Why, *yourself*, Master Cobblersawl. Now what, pray, Master Cobblersawl, do you think we'll do to *you*?"

Froggit did not answer, not then. Not ever. The next sound he made was a wail, which turned into a shriek, which turned into a swoon. "No" was the last word Froggit Cobblersawl ever spoke, for Hans put his tongue to the knife.

After this, they corked up the swooning boy with moss to soak the blood, and called upon young Ocelot to dig the bones. They'd have to replace the boy later, as they'd replaced Greenpea and Possum. Ulia Gol needed twenty for her sorceries. A solid twenty. No more, no less.

Good old Ocelot. The sort of girl who, as exigency demanded, bathed in mare's milk every night there was a bit of purifying moonlight handy. Her father was Chief Gravedigger in Amandale. She, at the age of thirteen-and-a-half, was his apprentice. Of all her fellow Swan Hunters, Ocelot had the cleanest and most callused hands. Ulia Gol's favorite.

She never flinched. Her shovel scraped once, clearing some of the carelessly spattered dirt from the corpse. The juniper tree glowed silver.

Scraped twice. The green ground roiled white as boiling milk.

Scraped thrice.

It was not a dead girl Ocelot freed from the dirt, after all. Not even a dead swan.

I glanced at Dora Rose to see how she was taking it. Her blue eyes were wide, her gaze fixed. No expression showed upon it, though. No sorrow or astonishment or rage. Nothing in her face was worth neglecting the show below us for, except the face itself. I could drink my fill of that pool and still die of thirst.

But I'd gone down that road once already. What separated us rats from other Folk was our ability to *learn*.

I returned my attention to the scene. When Ocelot stepped back to dust off her hands on her green cape, the exhumed thing that had been Elinore flashed into view.

It was, as Hans had earlier predicted, a harp.

And a large harp it was, of shining white bone, strung with black strings fine as hair, which Ulia Gol bent to breathe upon lightly. Shimmering, shuddering, the harp repeated back a refrain of Elinore's last song.

"It works," Ulia Gol announced with tolling satisfaction. "Load it up on the cart, and we'll take it back to Orchestra Hall. A few more birds in the bag and my automatized orchestra will be complete!"

Back in our budding teens, I'd elected to miss a three-day banquet spree with my rat buddies in post-plague Doornwold, Queen's City. (A dead city now, like the Queen herself.) Why? To attend instead, at Dora Rose's invitation, a water ballet put on by the Swan Folk of Lake Serenus.

I know, right? The whole affair was dull as a tidy pantry, lemme tell you. When I tried to liven things up with Dora Rose a little later, just a bit of flirt and fondle on the silver docks of Lake Serenus, I got myself soundly slapped. Then the Swan Princess of my dreams told me that my attentions were not only unsolicited and unwelcome but grossly, criminally, heinously repellent— her very words—and sent me back to sulk in my nest in Amandale.

You should've seen me. Tail dragging. Whiskers drooping. Sniveling into my fur. Talk about *heinously* repellent. I couldn't've been gladder my friends had all scampered over to the new necropolis, living it up among the corpses of Doornwold. By the time they returned, I had a handle on myself. Started up a dialogue with a nice, fat rat girl. We had some good times. Her name was Moira. That day on the docks was the last I saw Dora Rose up close for fifteen years.

Until today.

Soft as I was, by the time the last of the Swan Hunters trotted clear of the Heart Glade on their ponies, I'd decided to take Dora Rose back to my nest in Amandale. I had apartments in a warren of condemned tenements by the Drukkamag River docks. Squatters' paradise. Any female should rightly have spasmed at the chance; my wainscoted walls were only nominally chewed, my furniture salvaged from the alleyways of Merchant Prince Row, Amandale's elite. The current mode of decoration in my neighborhood was shabby chic. Distressed furniture? Mine was so distressed, it could've been a damsel in a past life.

But talking Dora Rose down from the juniper tree proved a trifle dicey. She wanted to return to Lake Serenus right away and search for survivors.

"Yeah, you and Huntsman Hans," I snorted. "He goes out every night with his nets, hoping to bag another of your Folk. Think he'll mistake you, with your silver gown and your silver skin, for a ruddy-kneed mortal milkmaid out for a skinny dip? Come on, Dora Rose! You got more brains than that, even if you *are* a bird."

I was still in my rat skin when I told her this. She turned on me savagely, grabbing me by the tail, and shook me, hissing as only swans and cobras can hiss. I'd've bitten her, but I was laughing too hard.

"Do you have a better idea, Maurice? Maybe you would be happiest if I turned myself in to Ulia Gol right now! Is that what I should do?"

I fleshed myself to man-shape right under her hands. She dropped me quickly, cheeks burning. Dora Rose did not want to see what she'd've been holding me by once I changed form. I winked at her.

"I got a lot of ideas, Dora Rose, but they all start with a snack and a nap."

Breathing dangerously, she shied back, deeper into the branches. Crossed her arms over her chest. Narrowed her lake-blue eyes. For a swan, you'd think her mama was a mule.

"Come on, Ladybird," I coaxed, scooting nearer—but not too near—my own dear Dora Rose. "You're traumatized. That's not so strong a word, is it, for what you've been through today?"

Her chin jutted. Her gaze shifted. Her lips were firm, not trembling. Not a trembler, that girl. I settled on a nice, thick branch, my legs dangling in the air.

"Damn it, Dora Rose, your twin sister's just been turned into a harp! Your family, your friends, your Folk—all killed and buried and dug back up again as bone instruments. And for what?" I answered myself, since she wouldn't. "So that Mayor Ulia Gol, that skinflint, can cheat Amandale's Guild of Musicians of their entertainment fees. She wants an orchestra that plays itself—so she's sacrificing swans to the juniper tree."

Her mouth winced. She was not easy to faze, my Dora Rose. But hey, she'd had a tough day, and I was riding her hard.

"You'd be surprised," I continued, "how many townspeople support Mayor Gol and her army of Swan Hunters. Everyone likes music. So what's an overextended budget to do?"

Dora Rose unbent so far as to roll her eyes. Taking this as a sign of weakening, I hopped down from the juniper tree.

"Come home with me, Ladybird," I called up. "There's a candy shop around the corner from my building. I'll steal you enough caramels to make you sick. You can glut your grief away, and then you can sleep. And in the morning, when you've decided it's undignified to treat your only ally—no matter his unsavory genus—so crabbily, we'll talk again."

A pause. A rustle. A soundless silver falling. Dora Rose landed lightly on her toe-tips. Above us, an uneasy breeze jangled the dark green needles of the juniper tree. There was a sharp smell of sap. The tree seemed to breathe. It did that, periodically. The god inside its bark did not always sleep.

Dora Rose's face was once more inscrutable, all grief and rage veiled behind her pride. "Caramels?" she asked.

Dora Rose once told me, years ago, that she liked things to taste either very sweet or very salty. Caramels, according to her, were the perfect food.

"Dark chocolate sea-salt caramels," I expounded with only minimal drooling. "Made by a witch named Fetch. These things are to maim for, Dora Rose."

"You remembered." She sounded surprised. If I'd still been thirteen (Captured God save me from ever being thirteen again), I might've burst into tears to be so doubted. Of course I remembered! Rats have exceptional memories. Besides—in my youth, I'd kept a strict diary. Mortal-style.

I was older now. I doffed my wharf boy's cap and offered my elbow. In my best Swan Prince imitation, I told her, "Princess, your every word is branded on my heart."

I didn't do it very well; my voice is too nasal, and I can't help adding overtones of innuendo. But I think Dora Rose was touched by the effort. Or at least, she let herself relax into the ritual of courtesy, something she understood in her bones. Her bones. Which Ulia Gol wanted to turn into a self-playing harpsichord to match Elinore's harp.

Over. My. Dead. Body.

Oh, all right. My slightly dented body. Up to and no further than a chunk off the tail. After that, Dora Rose would be on her own.

"Come on," I said. "Let's go."

She took my elbow. She even leaned on it a smidge, which told me how exhausted and stricken she was beneath her feigned indifference. I refrained from slavering a kiss upon her silver knuckles. Just barely.

The next morning, thanks to a midnight raid on Hans's wardrobe, I was able to greet Dora Rose at my dapper best. New hose, new shining thigh-high boots, new scarlet jerkin, green cape and linen sark.

New curved dagger with serrated edge, complete with flecks of Froggit Cobblersawl's drying tongue meat on it.

I'd drawn the line at stealing Hans's blond goatee, being at some loss as how best to attach it to my own chin. But I did not see why *he* should have one when I couldn't. I had, therefore, left it at the bottom of his chamber pot should he care to seek it there.

Did the Swan Princess gaze at me in adoration? Did she stroke my fine sleeve or fondle my blade? Not a bit of it. She sat on the faded cushion of my best window seat, playing with a tassel from the heavy draperies and chewing on a piece of caramel. Her blue stare went right through me. Not blank, precisely. Meditative. Distant. Like I wasn't important enough to merit even a fraction of her full attention.

"What I cannot decide," she said slowly, "is what course I should take.

Ought I to fly at Ulia Gol in the open streets of Amandale and dash her to the ground? Ought I to forsake this town entirely, and seek shelter with some other royal bevy? If," she added with melancholy, "they would have me. This I doubt, for I would flee to them with empty hands and under a grave mantle of sorrow. Ought I to await at the lake for Hans's net and Hans's knife and join my Folk in death, letting my transformation take me at the foot of the juniper tree?"

That's swans for you. Fraught with "oughts." Stop after three choices, each bleaker and more miserably elegant than the last. Vengeance, exile, or suicide. Take your pick. I sucked my tongue against an acid reply, taking instead a cube of caramel and a deep breath. Twitched my nose. Smoothed out the wrinkles of distaste. Went to crouch on the floor by the window seat. (This was *not*, I'll have you know, the same as kneeling at her feet. For one thing, I was balancing on my heels, not my knees.)

"Seems to me, Dora Rose," I suggested around a sticky, salty mouthful, "that what you want in a case like this—"

"Like this?" she asked, and I knew she was seeing her sister's hair repurposed for harp strings. "There has never *been* a case like mine, Maurice, so do not *dare* attempt to eclipse the magnitude of my despair with your filthy comparisons!"

I loved when she hissed at me. No blank stare now. If looks could kill, I'd be skewered like a shish kebab and served up on a platter. I did my best not to grin. She'd've taken it the wrong way.

Smacking my candy, I said in my grandest theatrical style, even going so far as to roll my R's, "In a case, Dora Rose, where magic meets music, where both are abused and death lacks dignity, where the innocent suffer and a monster goes unchecked, it seems reasonable, I was going to say, to consult an expert. A magical musician, perhaps, who has suffered so much himself he cannot endure to watch the innocent undergo like torment."

Ah, rhetoric. Swans, like rats, are helpless against it. Dora Rose twisted the braid at her shoulder, and lowered her ivory lashes. Early morning light wormed through my dirty windowpane. A few grey glows managed to catch the silver of her skin and set it gleaming.

My hands itched. In this shape, what I missed most was the sensitivity of my whiskers; my palms kept trying to make up for it. I leaned against the wall and scratched each palm vigorously in their turn with my dandy nails. Even in mortal form, these were sharp and black. I was vain about my nails and kept them polished. I wanted to run them though that fine, pale Swan Princess hair.

"Maurice." Miraculously, Dora Rose was smiling. A contemptuous smile, yes, but a smile nonetheless. "You're not saying you know a magical musician? You?"

Implicit in her tone: *You wouldn't know music if a marching band dressed ranks right up your nose.*

I drew myself to my not very considerable height, and I tugged my scarlet jerkin straight, and I said to her, I said to Dora Rose, I said, "He happens to be my best friend!"

"Ah."

"I saved his life down in Doornwold five years ago. The first people to repopulate the place were thieves and brigands, you know, and he wasn't at all equipped to deal with . . . Well. That's how I met Nicolas."

She cocked an eyebrow.

"And then we met again out back of Amandale, down in the town dump. He, uh, got me out of a pickle. A pickle jar, rather. One that didn't have air holes. This was in my other shape, of course."

"Of course," she murmured, still with that trenchant silver smile.

"Nicolas is very shy," I warned her. "So don't you go making great big swan eyes at him or anything. No sudden movements. No hissing or flirting or swooning over your sweet little suicide plans. He had a rough childhood, did Nicolas. Spent the tenderest years of his youth under the Hill, and part of him never left it."

"He has lived in Faerie but is not of it?" Now both Dora Rose's eyebrows arched, winging nigh up to her hairline. "Is he mortal or not?"

I shrugged. "Not Folk, anyway—or not entirely. Maybe some blood from a ways back. Raven, I think. Or Crow. A drop or two of Fox. But he can't slip a skin to scale or down or fur. Not Faerieborn, either, though from his talk it seems he's got the run of the place. Has more than mortal longevity, that's for sure. Among his other gifts. Don't know how old he is. Suspect even *he* doesn't remember, he's been so long under the Hill. What he is, is bright to my nose, like a perfumery or a field of wildflowers. Too many scents to single out the source. But come on, Dora Rose; nothing's more boring than describing a third party where he can't blush to hear! Meet him and sniff for yourself."

Nicolas lived in a cottage in the lee of the Hill. I say Hill, and I mean Hill. As fairy mounds go, this was the biggest and greenest, smooth as a bullfrog and crowned at the top with a circle of red toadstools the size of sycamores that glowed in the dark.

It's not an easy Hill. You don't want to look at it directly. You don't want to stray too near, too casually, or you'll end up asleep for a hundred years, or vanished out of life for seven, or tithed to the dark things that live under the creatures living under the Hill.

But Nicolas dwelled there peaceably enough, possibly because no one who ever goes there by accident gets very far before running off in the opposite direction, shock-haired and shrieking. Those who approach on *purpose* sure as hellfowl aren't coming to bother the poor musician who lives in the Hill's shadow. They come because they want to go *under*, to seek their fortunes, to beg of the Faerie Queen some boon (poor sops), or to exchange the dirt and drudgery of their mortal lives for some otherworldly dream.

We Folk don't truck much with Faerie. We belong to earth, wind, water, and sun just as much as mortals do, and with better right. For my part, anything that stinks of that glittering, glamorous Hillstuff gives me the heebie-jeebies. With the exception of Nicolas.

I left Dora Rose (not without her vociferous protestations) hiding in some shrubbery, and approached the cottage at a jaunty swagger. I didn't bang. That would be rude, and poor Nicolas was so easily startled. Merely, I scratched at the door with my fine black nails. At the third scratch, Nicolas answered. He was dressed only in his long red underwear, his red-and-black hair standing all on end. He was sleepy-eyed and pillow-marked, but he smiled when he saw me and opened wide his door.

"Maurice, Maurice!" he cried in his voice that would strike the sirens dumb. "But I did not expect this! I do not have a pie!" and commenced bustling about his larder, assembling a variety of foods he thought might please me.

He knew me so well! The vittles consisted of a rind of old cheese, a heel of hard bread, the last of the apple preserves, and a slosh of sauerkraut. Truly a feast! Worthy of a Rat King! (If my Folk had kings. We don't. Just as all swans are royalty, we rats are every last one of us a commoner and godsdamned proud of it.) Salivating with delight, I dove for the proffered tray. There was only one chair at the table. Leaving it to me, Nicolas sank to a crouch by the hearth. I grazed with all the greed of a man-and-rat who's breakfasted solely on a single caramel. He watched with a sweet smile on his face, as if nothing had ever given him more pleasure than to feed me.

"Nicolas, my friend," I told him, "I'm in a spot of trouble."

The smile vanished in an instant, replaced by a look of intent concern. Nicolas hugged his red wool-clad knees to his chest and cocked his head, bright black eyes inquiring.

"See," I said, "a few weeks back, I noticed something weird happening in the Maze Wood just south of town? Lots of mortal children trooping in and out of the corridors, dressed fancy. Two scent hounds. A wagon. All led by Henchman Hans and no less a person than the Mayor of Amandale herself. I got concerned, right? I like to keep an eye on things."

Nicolas's own concern darkened to a frown, a sadness of thunderclouds gathering on his brow. But all he said was, "You were snooping, Maurice!"

"All right, all right, Nicolas, so what if I was? Do you have any ale?"

Nicolas pulled a red-and-black tuft of his hair. "Um, I will check! One moment, Maurice!" He sprang off the ground with the agility of an eight-year-old and scurried for a small barrel in a corner by the cellar door. He set his ear to it as if listening for the spirit within.

"It's from the Hill," he warned softly.

I smacked my lips. "Bring it on!"

Faerie ale was the belchiest. Who said I wasn't musical? Ha! Dora Rose'd never heard me burp out "The Lay of Kate and Fred" after bottoms-upping a pint of this stuff. Oh, crap. Dora Rose. She was still outside, awaiting my signal. Never keep a Swan Princess in the bushes. She'd be bound to get antsy and announce herself with trumpets. I accepted the ale and sped ahead with my tale.

"So I started camping out in that old juniper tree, right? You know the one? *The* juniper tree. In the Heart Glade."

"Oh, yes." Nicolas lowed that mournful reply, half-sung, half-wept. "The poor little ghost in the tree. He was too long trapped inside it. The tree became his shrine, and the ghost became a god. That was in the long, long ago. But I remember it all like yesterday. I go to play my pipe for him when I get too lonely. Sometimes, if the moon is right, he sings to me."

Awright! Now we were getting somewhere! Dora Rose should be hearing this, she really should. But if I brought her in now, poor Nicolas'd clam up like a corpse on a riverbank.

"Hey, Nicolas?" I gnawed into a leathery apple. "You have any idea why Ulia Gol'd be burying a bunch of murdered Swan Folk out by the juniper tree, singing a ditty over the bodies, and digging them up again? Or why they should arise thereafter as self-playing instruments?"

Nicolas shook his head, wide-eyed. "No. Not if Ulia Gol did it. She'd have no power there."

I spat out an apple seed. It flew across the room, careening off a copper pot. "Oh, right. Uh, I guess what I meant was . . . if she got a child to do it. A child with a shovel. First to bury the corpse, then weep over it, then dig it up again. While a chorus of twenty kiddlings sang over the grave."

Nicolas hugged himself harder, shivering. "Maurice! They are not doing this? Maurice—they would not use the poor tree so!"

I leaned in, heel of bread in one hand, rind of cheese in the other. "Nicolas. Ulia Gol's murdered most of a bevy of Swan Folk. You know, the one that winters at Lake Serenus? Cygnet, cob, and pen—twenty of them, dead as dead can be. She's making herself an orchestra of bone instruments that play themselves so she won't have to shell out for professional musicians. Or at least that's her excuse this time. But you remember last year, right? With the foxes?"

Nicolas flinched.

"And before that," I went on, "didn't she go fishing all the talking trout from every single stream and wishing well? Are you sensing a pattern? 'Cause no one else seems to be—except for yours truly, the Incomparable Maurice. Now there's only one swan girl left. One out of a whole bevy. And she's . . . she's my . . . The point is, Nicolas, we *must* do something."

Nearly fetal in his corner by the ale barrel, Nicolas hid his face, shaking his head behind his hands. Before I could press him further, a silvery voice began to sing from the doorway.

> *"The nanny-goat said to the little boy*
> *Baa-baa, baa-baa I'm full*
> *I'm a bale of hay and a grassy glade*
> *All stuffed, all stuffed in wool*
>
> *I can eat no more, kind sir, kind sir*
> *Baa-baa, baa-baa my song*
> *Not a sock, not a rock, not a fiddle-fern*
> *I'll be full all winter long."*

By the end of the first verse, Nicolas had lifted his head. By the end of the second, he'd drawn a lanyard out of the collar of his long underwear. From this lanyard hung a slender silver pipe that dazzled the eye, though no sun shone in that corner of the cottage. When Dora Rose got to the third verse, he began piping along.

> *"The little boy said to the nanny goat*
> *Baa-baa, baa-baa all day*
> *You'll want to be fat as all of that*
> *When your coat comes off in May!"*

By the time they reached the bridge of their impromptu set, I was dancing around the cottage in an ecstatic frenzy. The silver pipe's sweet trills drove my limbs to great leaps and twists. Dora Rose danced, too, gasping for breath as she twirled and sang simultaneously. Nicolas stood in the center of the cottage, tapping his feet in time. The song ended, and Nicolas applauded, laughing for joy. Dora Rose gave him a solemn curtsy, which he returned with a shy bow. But as he slipped the silver pipe back beneath his underwear, I watched him realize that underwear was all he wore. Shooting a grey and stricken look my way, pretty much making me feel like I'd betrayed him to the headsman, he jumped into his tiny cot and pulled a ratty blanket over his head. Dora Rose glanced at me.

"Uh, Nicolas?" I said. "Me and Dora Rose'll just go wait outside for a few minutes. You come on out when you got your clothes on, okay?"

"She's a *swan*!" Nicolas called from under his cover. I patted a lump that was probably his foot.

"She needs your help, Nicolas. Her sister got turned into a harp yesterday. All her family are dead now. She's next."

At that point, Dora Rose took me by the ear and yanked me out of the cottage. I cringed—but not too much lest she loosen her grip. Dora Rose rarely touched me of her own volition.

"How dare you?" she whispered, the flush on her face like a frosted flower. "The *Pied Piper*? He could dance any Folk he pleased right to the death and you *pushed* him? Maurice!"

"Aw, Dora Rose," I wheedled, "he's just a little sensitive is all. But he's a good friend—the best! He'd never hurt me. Or mine." She glared at me. I help up my hands. "My, you know, friends. Or whatever."

Dora Rose shook her head, muttering, "I am friendly with a magical musician, he tells me. Who's familiar with Faerie. Who knows about the Folk. He'll help us, he tells me." Her blue eyes blazed, and I quivered in the frenzy of her full attention. "You never said he was the *Pied Piper*, Maurice!"

I set my hands on my hips and leaned away. Slightly. She still had a grip on my ear, after all. "Because I knew you'd react like this! Completely unreasonable! Nicolas wouldn't hurt a fly half-drowned in a butter dish! So he's got a magic pipe, so what? The *Faerie Queen* gave it to him. Faerie Queen says, 'Here, darling, take this; I made it for you,' you don't go refusing the thing. And once you have it, you don't leave it lying around the house for someone else to pick up and play. It's his *livelihood*, Dora Rose! And it's a weapon, too. We'll use it to protect you, if you'll let us."

Her eyebrows winged up, two perfect, pale arches. Her clutch on my ear began to twist. I squeaked out, "On another note, Dora Rose, forgive the pun"—she snorted as I'd meant her to, and I assumed my most earnest expression, which on my face could appear just a trifle disingenuous—"I have to say, your idea about singing nursery rhymes to calm him down was pretty great! Poor Nicolas! All he sees whenever he looks at a woman is the Faerie Queen. Scares him outta his wits. Can't hardly speak, after. He's good with kids, though. Kid stuff. Kid songs. You were right on track with that *baa-baa* tune of yours. He's like a child himself, really . . . "

Dora Rose released my ear. More's the pity.

"Maurice!" She jabbed a sharp finger at my nose, which was sharp enough to jab back. "One of these days!"

That was when Nicolas tiptoed from the cottage, sort of slinky-bashful. He was dressed in his usual beggar's box motley, with his coat of bright rags and two mismatched boots. He had tried to flatten his tufted hair, but it stuck up defiantly all around his head. His black eyes slid to the left of where Dora Rose stood.

"Hi," he said, scuffing the ground.

"It is a fine thing to meet you, Master Nicolas," she returned with courtly serenity. "Bevies far and wide sing of your great musicianship. My own mother"—I saw a harsh movement in her pale throat as she swallowed—"watched you play once, and said she never knew such joy."

"I'm sorry about your family," Nicolas whispered. "I'm sure the juniper tree didn't want to do it. It just didn't understand." His eyes met mine briefly, pleading. I gave him an encouraging *go-ahead* nod. Some of this story I knew already, but Nicolas could tell it better. He'd been around before it was a story, before it was history. He'd been alive when it was a current event.

Nicolas straightened his shoulders and cleared his throat.

"Your Folk winters at Lake Serenus. But perhaps, keeping mostly to yourselves, you do not know the story of the Maze Wood surrounding the lake. The tree at the center of the wood is also . . . also at the center of, of your family's slaughter . . . You see, before he was the god in the tree, he was only a small boy. His stepmother murdered him. His little stepsister buried his bones at the roots of a sapling juniper and went every day to water his grave with her tears.

"To comfort her, the boy's ghost and the juniper tree became one. The young tree was no wiser than the boy—trees understand things like rain and wind and birds. So the ghost and the tree together transformed the boy's bones into a beautiful bird, hoping this would lighten his sister's heart and fly far to sing of his murder.

"That was in the long, long ago. Later, but still long ago, the villagers of what was then a tiny village called Amandale began to worship the ghost in the tree. The ghost became a god. Those whose loved ones had been murdered would bring their bones there. The god would turn these wretched bones to instruments that sang the names of their murderers so loudly, so relentlessly, that the murderers were brought to justice just to silence the music.

"Many generations after this, these practices and even the god itself were all but forgotten. The juniper tree's so old now all it remembers are bones and birds, tears and songs. But the Mayor of Amandale must have read the story somewhere in the town archives. Learned of this old magic, the miracle. And then the Mayor, then she . . . she . . . "

A small muscle in Nicolas's jaw jumped. Suddenly I saw him in a different light, as if he, like his silver pipe, had an inner dazzle that needed no sunlight to evoke it. That dazzle had an edge on it like a broken bottle. Handle this man wrong, and he would cut you, though he wept to do it.

"The Mayor," said the Pied Piper, "is abusing the juniper tree's ancient sorrow. It is wrong. Very wrong."

This time he met Dora Rose's gaze directly, his black eyes bright and cold. "She is no better than the first little boy's killer. She has hunted your Folk to their graves. As birds and murder victims in one, they make the finest instruments. The children of Amandale helped her to do this while their parents stood by. *They are all complicit.*"

"Not all," I put in. Credit where it's due. "Three children stood against her. Punished for it, of course."

Nicolas gave me a nod. "They will be spared."

"Spared?" Dora Rose echoed. But Nicolas was already striding off toward the Maze Wood with his pace that ate horizons. Me and Dora Rose, we had to follow him at a goodly clip.

"This," I whispered to her from one corner of my grin, "is gonna be good."

The maze part of the Maze Wood is made of these long and twisty walls of thorn. It's taller than the tallest of Amandale's four watchtowers and thicker than the fortress wall, erected a few hundred years ago to protect the then-new cathedral of Amandale. But Brotquen, the jolly golden Harvest Goddess in whose honor the cathedral had been built, went out of style last century. Now Brotquen Cathedral is used to store grain—not so big a step down from worshipping it, if you ask me—and I'm quite familiar with its environs. Basically the place is a food mine for yours truly and his pack, Folk and fixed alike. And the stained glass windows are pretty, too.

Like Nicolas said, the Maze Wood's been there before Brotquen, before her cathedral, before the four towers and the fortress wall. It was sown back in the olden days when the only god in these parts was the little one in the juniper tree. I don't know if the maze was planted to honor that god or to confuse it, keep its spirit from wandering too far afield in the shape of a fiery bird, singing heartbreaking melodies of its murder. Maybe both.

Me and the Maze Wood get along all right. Sure, it's scratched off some of my fur. Sure, its owls and civets have tried making a meal of me. But nothing under these trees has got the better of me yet. I know these woods almost as well as I know the back streets of Amandale. I'm a born explorer, though at heart I'm city rat, not woodland. That's what squirrels are for. "Think of us as rats in cute suits," a squirrel friend of mine likes to say. Honestly, I don't see that squirrels are all that adorable myself.

But as well as I knew the Maze Wood, Nicolas *intuited* it.

He moved through its thorny ways like he would the "Willful Child's Reel," a song he could play backwards and blindfolded. Nicolas took shortcuts through corridors I'd never seen and seemed to have some inner needle pointing always to the Heart Glade the way some people can find true north. In no time at all, we came to the juniper tree.

Nicolas went right up to it and flung himself to the ground, wrapping his arms as far about the trunk as he could reach. There he sobbed with all the abandon of a child, like Froggit had sobbed right before they cut out his tongue.

Dora Rose hung back. She looked impassive, but I thought she was embarrassed. Swans don't cry.

After several awkward minutes of this, Nicolas sat up. He wiped his face, drew the silver pipe from his shirt, and played a short riff as if to calm himself. I jittered at the sound, and Dora Rose jumped, but neither of us danced. He didn't play for us that time but for the tree.

The juniper tree began to glow, as it had glowed yesterday when the Swan Hunters sang up Elinore's bones. The mossy ground at the roots turned white as milk. Then a tiny bird, made all of red-and-gold fire, shot out of the trunk to land on Nicolas's shoulder. Nicolas stopped piping but did not remove the silver lip from his mouth. Lifting its flickering head, the bird opened its beak and began to sing in a small, clear, plaintive voice:

> *"Stepmother made a simple stew*
> *Into the pot my bones she threw*
> *When father finished eating me*
> *They buried my bones at the juniper tree*
>
> *Day and night stepsister weeps*
> *Her grief like blood runs red, runs deep*
> *Kywitt! Kywitt! Kywitt! I cry*
> *What a beautiful bird am I!"*

Nicolas's expression reflected the poor bird's flames. He stroked its tiny head, bent his face, and whispered something in its ear. "He's telling the god about your dead Folk," I said to Dora Rose with satisfaction. "Now we'll really see something!"

I should've been born a prophet, for as soon as Nicolas stopped speaking, the bird toppled from his shoulder into his outstretched palm and lay there in a swoon for a full minute before opening its beak to scream. Full-throated, human, anguished.

I covered my ears, wishing they really had been made of tin. But Dora Rose stared as if transfixed. She nodded once, slowly, as if the ghost bird's scream matched the sound she'd been swallowing all day.

The juniper tree blazed up again. The glowing white ground roiled like a tempest-turned sea. Gently, so gently, Nicolas brought his cupped hands back up to the trunk, returning the bird to its armor of shaggy bark. As the fiery bird vanished into the wood, the tree itself began to sing. The Heart Glade filled with a voice that was thunderous and marrow-deep.

"Swan bones changed to harp and fife
Sobbing music, robbed of life
String and drum and horn of bone
Leave them not to weep alone

Set them in a circle here
None for three nights interfere
From my branches let one hang
Swan in blood and bone and name

Bring the twenty whose free will
Dared to use my magic ill
Dance them, drive them into me
Pick the fruit from off this tree!"

The light disappeared. The juniper sagged and seemed to sigh. Nicolas put his pipe away and bowed his head.

Dora Rose turned to me, fierceness shining from her.

"Maurice," she said, "you heard the tree. We must bring the bones here. I must hang for three days. You must keep Ulia Gol and Hans away from the Heart Glade for that time, and bring those twenty young Swan Hunters to me. Quickly! We have no time to waste."

And here the heart-stricken and love-sore child I once was rose up from the depths of me like its very own bone instrument.

"Must I, Ladybird?"

Did I sound peevish? I hardly knew. My voice cracked like a boy soprano whose balls'd just dropped, thus escaping the castrating knife and opium bath and a life of operatic opulence. Peevish, yes. Peevish it was.

"Must I really? So easy, don't you think, to steal an orchestra right out from under an ogre's nose? To keep Ulia Gol from tracking it back here. To lure twenty children all into the Maze Wood without a mob of parents after us. That'll take more than wiles, Princess. That'll take tactics. And why

should I do any of this, eh? For you, Dora Rose? For the sake of a friend? What kind of friend are you to me?"

Nicolas stared from me to Dora Rose, wide-eyed. He had placed a hand over his pipe and kneaded it nervously against his chest. Dora Rose also stared, her face draining of excitement, of grief nearly avenged, of bright rage barely contained. All I saw looking into that shining oval was cool, contemptuous royalty. That was fine. Let her close herself off to me. See if that got her my aid in this endeavor.

"I'm gonna ask you something." I drew closer, taking her slack silver hand in mine. I even pressed it between my itching palms. "If it were *me*, Dora Rose, if I'd come to Lake Serenus before your courtly bevy and said to you, 'Dear Princess, Your Highness, my best old pal! Mayor Ulia Gol's exterminating the Rat Folk of Amandale. She's trapping us and torturing us and making bracelets of our tails. Won't you help me stop her? For pity's sake? For what I once was to you, even if that was only a pest?'

"What would you have said to me, Dora Rose, if I had come to you so?"

Dora Rose turned her face away, but did not remove her hand. "I would have said nothing, Maurice. I would have driven you off. Do you not know me?"

"Yes, Dora Rose." I squeezed her hand, happy that it still held mine. Was it my imagination, or did she squeeze back? Yup. That was definitely a squeeze. More like a vise, truth be told. I loved a vise. Immediately I began feeling more charitable. That was probably her intention.

"Elinore now," I reflected, "*Elinore* would've intervened on my behalf." Dora Rose's head turned cobra-quick. Had she fangs enough and time, I'd be sporting several new apertures in my physiognomy. I went on anyway. "The nice sister, that Elinore. Always sweet as a Blood Haven peach—for all she loathed me tail to toe. You Swan Folk would've come to our aid on *Elinore*'s say so, mark my words, Dora Rose."

"Then," said Dora Rose with freezing slowness, her grip on my hand yet sinewy and relentless, "you will help me for the sake of my dead twin, Maurice? For the help my sister Elinore would have given you had our places been reversed?"

I sighed. "Don't you know me, Ladybird? No. I wouldn't do it for Elinore. Not for gold or chocolate. Not for a dozen peachy swan girls and their noblesse oblige. I'll do it for *you*, of course. Always did like you better than Elinore."

"You," scoffed Dora Rose with a curling lip, flinging my hand from hers, "are the only one who ever did, Maurice."

I shrugged. It was true.

"As a young cygnet, I feared this was because our temperaments were too alike."

I snorted, inordinately pleased. "Yeah, well. Don't go telling my mama I act like a Swan Princess. She'll think she didn't raise me right."

From his place near the juniper tree, Nicolas cleared his throat. "Are we, are we all friends again? Please?" He smoothed one of his long brown hands over the bark. "There's so much to be done, and all of it so dark and sad. Best to do it quickly, before we drown in sorrow."

Dora Rose dropped him a curtsy and included me in it with a dip of her chin. My heart leapt in my chest. Other parts of me leapt, too, but I won't get into that.

"At your convenience, Master Piper," said she. "Maurice."

"Dark work? Sad?" I cried. "No such thing! Say, rather, a lark! The old plague days of Doornwold'll be nothing to it! My Folk scurry at the chance to run amuck. If you hadn't've happened along, Dora Rose, with your great tragedy and all, I'd've had to invent an excuse to misbehave. Of such stuff is drama made! Come on, you two. I have a plan."

We threw Nicolas's old tattercoat over Dora Rose's silver gown and urchined up her face with mud. I stuffed her pale-as-lace hair under my wharf boy's cap and didn't even mind when she turned and pinched me for pawing at her too ardently. Me in the lead, Dora Rose behind, Nicolas bringing up the rear, we marched into Amandale like three mortal-born bumpkins off for a weekend in the big city.

Dwelling by the Hill, Nicolas had lived as near neighbor to Amandale for I don't know how many years. But he was so often gone on his tours, in cities under the Hill that made even the Queen's City seem a hermit's hovel, that he wandered now through Amandale's busy gates with widening and wonder-bright eyes. His head swiveled like it sat on an owl's neck. The woebegone down-bend of his lips began a slow, gladdening, upward trend that was heartbreaking to watch. So I stole only backward glances, sidelong like.

"Maurice." He hurried to my side as we passed a haberdashery.

"Yes, Nicolas?"

"You really live here?"

"All my life."

"Does it," he stooped to speak directly in my ear, "does it ever stop *singing*?"

I grinned over at Dora Rose, who turned her face away to smile. "If by *singing* you mean *stinking*, then no. This is a typical day in Amandale, my friend. A symphony of odors!" He looked so puzzled that I took pity and explained, "According to the princess over there, I'm one who can only ever hear music through my nose."

"Ah!" Nicolas's black eyes beamed. "I see. Yes! You're a synesthete!"

Before I could reply, a fire-spinner out front of Cobblersawl's Cakes and Comfits caught his eye, and Nicolas stopped walking to burst into wild applause. The fire-spinner grinned and embarked upon a particularly intricate pattern of choreography.

No one was exempt, I realized. Not me, and not the pretty fire-spinner. Not even Dora Rose. Plainly it was impossible to keep from smiling at Nicolas when Nicolas was pleased about something. I nudged Dora Rose.

"Hear that, Ladybird? I'm a synesthete!"

"Maurice, if you ever met a synesthete, you'd probably try to eat it."

"Probably. Would it look anything like you?"

Dora Rose did not dignify this with a response but whacked the back of my head, and her tiny smile twisted into something perilously close to a grin. We ducked into the bakery, pulling Nicolas after us so he wouldn't start piping along to the fire-spinner's sequences, sending her off to an early death by flaming poi.

One of the elder Cobblersawl children—Ilse, her name was—stood at the bread counter, looking bored but dutiful. A softhearted lass, our Ilse. Good for a scrap of cheese on occasion. Not above saving a poor rodent if said rodent happened to be trapped under her big brother's boot. She'd not recognize me in this shape, of course, but she might have a friendly feeling for me if I swaggered up to her with a sparkle in my beady little eyes and greeted her with a wheedling, "Hallo, Miss . . . "

She frowned. "No handouts. Store policy."

"No, you misunderstand. We're looking for . . . for Froggit? Young Master Froggit Cobblersawl? We have business with him." Dora Rose poked me between my shoulder blades. Her nails were as sharp as mine. "If you please?" I squeaked.

Ilse's frown deepened to a scowl. "Froggit's sick."

I bet he was. I'd be sick, too, if I'd swallowed half my tongue.

"Sick of . . . politics maybe?" I waggled my eyebrows.

A smell came off the girl like vaporized cheddar. Fear. Sweaty, stinky, delicious fear.

"If you're from the Mayor," Ilse whispered, "tell her that Mama spanked Froggit for not behaving as he ought. We know we're beholden. We know we owe the fancy new shop to her. And—and our arrangement to provide daily bread to the houses on Merchant Prince Row is entirely due her benevolence. Please, Papa cried so hard when he heard how Froggit failed us. We were so proud when his name came up in the Swan Hunter lottery. Really, it's such an honor, we know it's an honor, to work for the Mayor on our very own orchestra, but—it's just he's so young. He didn't understand.

Didn't know, didn't know better. But I'm to take his place next hunt. I will be the twentieth hunter. I will do what he couldn't. I promise." She unfisted her hands and opened both palms in supplication. "Please don't take him to prison. Don't disappear him like you did . . . "

She swallowed whatever she was about to say when Dora Rose stepped forward. Removing my cap, she shook out that uncanny hair of hers and held Ilse's gaze. Silence swamped the bakery as Ilse realized we weren't Ulia Gol's not-so-secret police.

"I want to thank him," Dora Rose said. "That is all. The last swan they killed was my sister."

"Oh," Ilse whimpered. "Oh, you shouldn't be here. You really shouldn't be here."

"Please," said Dora Rose.

Her shaking fingers glimmering by the light pouring off the swan girl's hair, Ilse pointed out a back door. We left the bakery as quickly as we could, not wanting to discomfit her further, or incite her to rouse the alarm.

The exit led into a private courtyard behind the bakery. Froggit was back by the whitewashed outhouse, idly sketching cartoons upon it with a stubby bit of charcoal. Most of these involved the Mayor and Hans in various states of decay, although in quite a few of them, the Swan Huntress Ocelot played a putrescent role. Froggit's shoulder blades scrunched when our shadows fell over him, but he did not turn around.

I opened my mouth to speak, but it was Nicolas who dropped to the ground at Froggit's side, crossing his legs like a fortune-teller and studying the outhouse wall with rapt interest.

"But this is extraordinary! It must be preserved! They will have to remove this entire apparatus to a museum. What, in the meantime, is to be done about waterproofing?" Nicolas examined the art in minute detail, his nose almost touching the graffitied boards. "What to do, what to do," he muttered.

Taking his charcoal stub, Froggit scrawled, "BURN IT!" in childish writing over his latest cartoon. Then he scowled at Nicolas, who widened his eyes at him. Nicolas began nodding, at first slowly, then with increasing vigor.

"Oh, yes! Indeed! Yes, of course! Art is best when ephemeral, don't you think? How your admirers will mourn its destruction. How they will paint their faces with the ashes of your art. And you will stand so"—Nicolas hopped up to demonstrate—"arms crossed, with your glare that is like the glare of a tiger, and they will sob and wail and beg you to draw again—*just once more, please, Master Froggit*—but you shall break your charcoal and their hearts in one snap. Yes! You will take all this beauty from them, as they have taken your tongue. I see. It is stunning. I salute you."

So saying, Nicolas drew out his pipe and began a dirge.

When he finished many minutes later, me and Dora Rose collapsed on the ground, sweating from the excruciatingly stately waltz we'd endured together. Well, *she'd* endured. I rather enjoyed it, despite never having waltzed in my life, least of all in a minor key.

Froggit himself, who much to his consternation had started waltzing with an old rake, let it fall against the outhouse wall and eyeballed the lot of us with keen curiosity and not a little apprehension. What did he see when he looked at us, this little boy without a tongue?

Nicolas sat in the mud again. This made Froggit, still standing, the taller of the two, and Nicolas gazed up at him with childlike eyes.

"Don't be afraid. It's my silver pipe. Magic, you see. Given me by Her Gracious Majesty, Empress of Faerie, Queen of the Realms Beneath the Hill. It imparts upon me power over the creatures of land, sea, air, and fire. Folk and fixed, and everything between. But when I pass into the Hill, my pipe has no power. Under the Hill it is not silver but bone that sings to the wild blood of the Faerieborn. Had I a bone pipe, I might dance them all to their deaths, those Shining Ones who cannot die. But I have no pipe of bone. Just this."

Nicolas's face took on a taut look. Almost, I thought, one of unbearable longing. His knuckles whitened on his pipe. Then he shook himself and dredged up a smile from unfathomable depths, though it was a remote, pathetic, tremulous thread of a thing.

"But here, above the Hill," he continued as if he'd never paused, "it is silver that ensorcels. Silver that enspells. I could pipe my friend the rat Maurice into the Drukkamag River and drown him. See that Swan Princess over there? Her I could pirouette right off a cliff, and not even her swanskin wings could save her. You, little boy, I could jig you up onto a rooftop and thence into the sky, whence you'd fall, fall, fall. But I will not!" Nicolas added as Froggit's round brown eyes flashed wider. "Destroy an artist such as yourself? Shame on me! How could I even think it? I have the greatest respect for you, Master Froggit!"

But Froggit, after that momentary alarm, seemed unafraid. In fact, he began to look envious. He pointed first to the silver pipe, then to his charcoal caricature of Mayor Ulia Gol, dripping gore and missing a few key limbs.

His wide mouth once more woebegone, Nicolas burst out, "Oh, but she is wicked! Wicked! She has an ogre's heart and a giant's greed. She is a monster, and we must rid this world of monsters. For what she did to the juniper tree, that alone deserves a pair of iron shoes baked oven-bright, and four and twenty blackbirds to pluck out her eyes. But for what she has done to *you* . . . and to the swans and the foxes and the trout. Oh! I would break my pipe upon her throat if I . . . But."

Drawing a shaky breath, Nicolas hid his thin face in rigid hands.

"No. I shall not be called upon for that. Not this time. Not today. No. No, Nicolas, you may stay your hand and keep to your music for now. Maurice the Incomparable has a plan. The role of Nicolas promises to be quite small this time. Just a song. Just the right little song. Or the wrong one. The wrongest song of all."

Froggit sat beside Nicolas and touched a trembling hand to his shoulder. Nicolas didn't take his hands from his face, but suddenly bright black eyes peeped between his fingers.

"Your part is bigger than mine, Master Froggit. If you'll play it. Throw in with us. You have no tongue to speak, but you have hands to help, and we'd be proud to have your help."

Froggit stared. At the huddled Piper. At proud Dora Rose standing like a silver statue in the small courtyard. At my grin that had the promise of carnage behind it. Back to Nicolas, whose hands fell away to reveal an expression so careworn and sorrowful and resolute that it terrified me, who knew what it meant. I rubbed my hands together, licking my lips. The boy took up his charcoal stub and wrote two words on the outhouse boards.

One was "Greenpea." The other "Possum."

I stepped in, before Nicolas asked if this were a recipe for the boy's favorite stew and spun off on another tangent about the virtues of Faerie spices versus mortal.

"Of course your friends are invited, Master Froggit!" I said. "Couldn't do it without 'em! You three and we three, all together now." I hooked Dora Rose's elbow and drew her nearer. She complied, but not without a light kick to my ankle. "Your job today, Master Froggit, is to take our resident Swan Princess around to meet Miss Greenpea and Miss Possum. They've sacrificed a pair of legs and eyes between them, haven't they, by refusing to help murder swans?"

Froggit nodded, his soft jaw clenching. What with the swelling of his truncated tongue, that must've meant a whopping mouthful of pain. Boy should've been born a rat!

"You're just what we need. Old enough to know the town, young enough to be ignored. Embittered, battle-scarred, ready for war. Listen up, Master Froggit. You and your friends and Dora Rose are gonna be the ones to, uh, *liberate* those pretty bone instruments from Orchestra Hall. You must do this, and you must return them to the Maze Wood tonight. It all has to be timed perfectly. Dora Rose will tell you why. Can you do this thing?"

Dora Rose put her hand on Froggit's shoulder when his panicked glance streaked to her. "Fear not, princeling," she said, as though soothing a cygnet. "Have not we wings and wits enough between us?"

Before the kid could lose his nerve, I sped on, "Me and Nicolas will be the distraction. We're gonna set Amandale hopping, starting this afternoon. No one will have time to sniff you out, I promise—no matter what shenanigans you four get up to. We'll meet you back in the Maze Wood in three nights' time, with the rest of . . . of what we need. You know where. The juniper tree."

Froggit nodded. His brown eyes filled with tears, but they did not fall. I looked at Dora Rose, who was twisting her hair back up under my wharf boy's cap and refreshing the dirt on her face.

"Help her," I told the kid, too quietly for Dora Rose to overhear. "She'll need you. Tonight most of all."

Froggit watched my face a moment more, then nodded with firm decision. His excitement smelled like ozone. He shoved his charcoal stub into his pocket and stood up, wiping his palms on his cutoff trousers. Solemnly, he offered his hand to Nicolas, who clasped it in both of his, then transferred it over to Dora Rose. She smiled down, and Froggit's gaze on her became worshipful, if worship could hold such bitter regret. I knew that look.

Stupid to be jealous of a tongueless, tousled, char-smudged bed wetter. Bah.

"Take care of each other," Nicolas admonished them.

And so, that Cobblersawl kid and my friend the Swan Princess-in-disguise made their way down a dark alley that teemed with the sort of refuse I relished. Until they disappeared from my sight.

"Shall we?" Nicolas's voice was soft and very dreadful behind me.

"Play on, Pied Piper," said I.

Nicolas set silver lip to scarlet mouth and commenced the next phase of our plan.

Have you ever seen a rat in a waste heap? The rustle of him, the nibble, the nestle, the scrabble and scrape. How he leaps, leaps straight up as if jerked by a string from the fathoms of that stinking stuff, should a clamor startle him? How swift he is. How slinking sly. Faster than a city hawk who makes her aerie in the clock towers and her dinner of diseased pigeons. A brief bolt of furry black lightning he is, with onyx for eyes and tiny red rubies for pupils.

Now imagine this natty rat, this rattiest of rats, with his broken tail, his chewed-looking fur, imagine him as he often is, with a scrap of something vile in his mouth, imagine him right in front of you, sitting on your pillow and watching you unblinkingly as you yawn yourself awake in the morning.

Imagine him.

Then multiply him.

There is a reason more than one of us is called a swarm.

Amandale, there will be no Swan Hunt for you today. Nor will bread be baked, nor cakes be made, nor cookies, biscuits, doughnuts, nor pies. The smell arising from your ovens, Amandale, is singed fur and seared rodent meat, and all your dainty and delectable desserts bear teeth marks.

No schools remain in session. What teacher can pontificate on topics lofty and low when rats sit upon her erasers, scratch inside the stiff desks, run to and from the windowsills, and chew through whole textbooks in their hunger for equations, for history, for language and binding glue and that lovely woody wood pulp as soft and sweet as rose petals?

The blacksmith's hand is swollen from the bite he received last night as he reached for the bellows to stoke his fire. The apple seller has fled from fear of what he found in his apple barrels. The basket maker burns in his bed with fever from an infected breakfast he bolted without noticing it had been shared already by the fine fellows squatting in his larder. I'm afraid the poor chimney sweep is scarred for life. And no, I don't mean that metaphorically.

The Wheelbarrow Mollys and the Guild of Bricklayers are out in the streets with their traps and their terriers. Poor fools, the futility! They might get a few dozen of us, maybe a few hundred. They might celebrate their catch that night with ales all around. But what's a few? We are thousands. Tens of thousands. Millions. The masses. We have come from our hidey-holes and haystacks. We are out in force.

So what if the local butcher flaunts his heap of fresh sausage stuffing, product of today's rat-catching frenzy? We're not above eating our own when we taste as good as sausages! And we're not above petty vengeance, either. You, smug butcher, you won't sleep cold tonight. No, sir. You'll sleep enfolded in the living fur of my family, Folk and fixed alike, united, yellow of tooth and spry of whisker. Resolved.

In the midst of mothers bellowing at those of us sniffing bassinets and cradles, of fathers shrieking like speared boars as they step into boots that bite back, of merchants sobbing and dairymaids cursing and monks chanting prayers of exorcism, there is a softer sound, too, all around. A sound only we rats can hear.

Music.

It is the Pied Piper, and he plays for us.

He's there in a corner, one rat on his boot-top, two in his pocket. That's me right there, scurrying and jiving all up and down his arms and shoulders, like a nervous mama backstage of her darling's first ballet recital. Oh, this is first-rate. This is drama! And I am the director.

Amandale, you do not see Nicolas, the red in his black hair smoldering like live embers in a bed of coal, his black eyes downcast and dreamy, his one rat-free boot tapping time. He's keeping us busy, keeping us brave, making us hop and heave to.

Amandale, you do not see Nicolas, playing his song, doing his best to destroy you for a day.

Or even for three.

On the second Night of the Rats (as the citizens of Amandale called our little display), Mayor Ulia Gol summoned a town meeting in Orchestra Hall.

Sometime after lunch that day, I'd fleshed back into man-shape, with two big plugs of cotton batting in my ears. This made me effectively deaf, but at least I wasn't dancing. The point was to stick as close to Ulia Gol as possible without ending up in a rat catcher's burlap bag. To that end I entrenched myself in the growing mob outside the mayoral mansion and slouched there for hours till my shadow stretched like a giant from the skylands. As reward for my patience, I witnessed the moment Henchman Hans brought Ulia Gol news that the rat infestation had destroyed her bone orchestra.

"All that's left, Madame Mayor," moaned poor Hans (I'm not great at reading lips, but I got the gist), "is bits of bone and a few snarls of black hair."

Ulia Gol's florid face went as putridly pink as her wig. Her shout was so loud I heard her through the cotton batting all the way to my metatarsals. "Town meeting—tonight—eight o' clock—Orchestra Hall—OR ELSE!"

I ran back to report to Nicolas, who laughed around the lip of his pipe. Slapping my forehead, I cried, "Clever, clever! Why didn't I think of it? Manufacture false evidence; blame the rats! It'll keep thief-hunters out of the Maze Wood for sure. Did you think that up, Nicolas?"

Pink-cheeked, Nicolas shook his head and kept playing.

"Wasn't Dora Rose," I mused. "She'd view leaving fragments behind as sacrilege. One of our stalwart recruits, then. Froggit? He's great, but he's kind of young for that level of . . . Or, I suppose it could've been Possum's idea. Don't know her so well. Always thought her one of your sweet, quiet types, Possum." Readjusting my cotton batting, I mulled on the puzzle before settling on my final hypothesis.

"Greenpea. Greenpea, I'll grant you, has the brain for such a scheme. What a firecracker! Back when the Swan Hunt started, she was the most vocal opposition in town. Has a kindness for all animals, does Greenpea. Nearly took Hans's head off with the shovel when he tried to make her dig up that first murdered cob. Ulia Gol took it back from her, though. Broke both her legs so bad the surgeon had to cut 'em off at the knee. Fear of festering, you see. Least, that's what he said. But he's Ulia Gol's creature, badly gone as Hans. Yup, I'll bet the hair and bone were Greenpea's notion. Little minx. I'd like to take her paw and give it a shake. Oh, but hey, Nicolas! We'd best get a move on. You haven't eaten all day, and the sun's nearly down. Mayor Ulia Gol's called a town meeting in a few hours regarding the rat conundrum. I'll fur down and find a bench to hide under. That way I'll be ready for you."

Slipping the silver pipe under his patched tunic, Nicolas advised, "Don't get stomped."

By this time, the rats of Amandale were in such a frenzy it wouldn't much matter if he stopped playing for an hour or two. Most of the Folk rats would come to their senses and slip out of town while the getting was good. Likely they'd spend the next few weeks with wax stoppers in their ears and a great distaste for music of any kind. But they'd be back. By and by, they'd all come back.

The fixed rats, now . . . Smart beasts they may be, those inferior little cousins of mine, but their brains have only ever been the size of peas. Good thing they reproduce quickly's all I'm saying. 'Cause for the sake of drama and Dora Rose—they are going down.

The Mayor of Amandale began, "This meeting is now in—" when an angry mother shot to her feet and shouted over her words. It was the chandler, wailing toddler held high overhead like a trophy or oblation. "Look at my Ruby! Look at her! See that bite on her face? That'll mark her the rest of her natural life." "Won't be too long," observed a rouged bawd. "Wounds like that go bad as runoff from a graveyard."

The blacksmith added, "That's if the rats don't eat her alive first."

The noise in Orchestra Hall surged. A large, high-ceilinged chamber it was, crammed with padded benches and paneled in mahogany. Front and center on the raised stage stood Mayor Ulia Gol, eyes squinting redly as she gaveled the gathering to order.

"Friends! Friends!" Despite the red look in her eyes, her voice held that hint of laughter that made people love her. "Our situation is dire, yes. We are all distressed, yes. But I must beg you now, each and every one of you, to take a deep breath."

She demonstrated.

Enchantment in the expansion and recession of her bosom. Sorcery in her benevolent smile. Hypnosis in the red beam of her eye, pulsing like a beating heart. The crowd calmed. Began to breathe. From my place beneath the bench, I twitched my fine whiskers. Ulia Gol was by far her truer self in the Heart Glade, terrorizing the children of Amandale into murdering Swan Folk. This reassuring woman was hardly believable. A stage mirage. The perfect politician.

"There," cooed the Mayor, looking downright dotingly upon her constituents, "that's right. Tranquility in the face of disaster is our civic duty. Now, in order to formulate appropriate measures against this rodent incursion as well as set in motion plans for the recovery of our wounded"— she ticked off items on her fingers—"and award monetary restitution to the hardest-hit property owners, we must keep our heads. I am willing to work with you. *For* you. That's why you elected me!"

Cool as an ogre picking her teeth with your pinkie finger. No plan of mine could stand long against a brainstorming session spearheaded by Ulia Gol at her glamoursome best. But I had a plan. And she didn't know about it. So I was still a step ahead.

Certain human responses can trump even an ogre's fell enchantments, no matter how deftly she piles on those magical soporific agents. It was now or never. Taking a deep breath of my own, I darted up the nearest trouser leg—

And bit.

The scream was all I ever hoped a scream would be.

Benches upturned. Ladies threw their skirts over their heads. The man I'd trespassed upon kicked a wall, trying to shake me out of his pants. I slid and skittered and finally flew across the room. Something like or near or in my rib cage broke, because all of a sudden the simple act of gasping became a pain in my *everything*.

Couldn't breathe. Couldn't breathe. Couldn't . . .

There came a wash of sound. Scarlet pain turned silver. My world became a dream of feathers. I saw Dora Rose, all downed up in swanskin, swimming across Lake Serenus. Ducking her long, long neck beneath the waves. Disappearing. Emerging as a woman, silver and naked-pale, with all her long hair gleaming down. She could dance atop the waves in this form, barefoot and unsinkable, a star of the Lake Serenus Water Ballet.

I came to myself curled in the center of the Pied Piper's palm. He had the silver pipe in his other hand as if he'd just been playing it. Orchestra Hall had fallen silent.

This was Nicolas as I'd never seen him. This was Nicolas of the Realms Beneath the Hill. His motley rags seemed grander the way he wore them than Ulia Gol's black satin robes with the big pink toggles and purple flounce. His hair was like the flint-and-fire crown of some Netherworld King. Once while drunk on Faerie ale he'd told me—in strictest confidence, of course—that since childhood the Faerie Queen had called him "Beautiful Nicolas" and seated him at her right hand during her Midnight Revels. I'd snorted to hear that, replying, "Yeah, right. *Your* ugly mug?" which made him laugh and laugh. I'd been dead serious, though; I know what beautiful looks like, and its name is *Dora Rose*, not *Nicolas*. But now I could see how the Faerie Queen might just have a point. So. Yeah. Kudos to her. I suppose.

Nicolas's smile flashed from his dark face like the lamp of a lighthouse. His black eyes flickered with a fiendish inner fire.

"Ladies and Gentlemen of Amandale!" Sweeping himself into a bow, he managed to make both pipe and rat natural parts of his elegance, as if we stood proxy for the royal scepter and orb he'd misplaced.

"Having had word of your problem, I came straightway to help. We are neighbors of sorts; I live in the lee of the Hill outside your lovely town. You may have heard my name." Nicolas paused, just long enough. Impeccable timing. "I am the Pied Piper. I propose to pipe your rats away."

So saying, he set me on the floor and brought up his pipe again.

I danced—but it was damned difficult. Something sharp inside me poked other, softer parts of me. I feared the coppery wetness foaming the corners of my mouth meant nothing salubrious for my immediate future. Still, I danced. How could I help it? He played for me.

Nicolas, who at his worst was so sensitive he often achieved what seemed a kind of feverish telepathy, was eerily attuned to my pain. His song shifted, ever so slightly. Something in my rib cage clicked. He played a song not only for me but for my bones as well. And my bones danced back into place.

Burning, burning.

Silver swanfire starfall burning.

Jagged edges knitted. Bones snapped back together. Still I danced. And inside me, his music danced, too, healing up my hurts.

Nicolas took his mouth from the pipe. "I am willing, good Citizens of Amandale, to help you. As you see, rats respond to my music. I can make them do what I wish! Or what you wish, as the case may be."

On cue, released from his spell, I made a beeline for a crack in the wall. A sharp note from his pipe brought me up short, flipped me over, and sent me running back in the other direction. I can't sweat, but I did feel the blood expanding my tail as my panicked body heated up.

"For free?" called the chandler, whose wounded babe had finally stopped wailing for fascination of Nicolas's pipe.

"For neighborliness?" cackled the bawd.

Nicolas scooped me up off the floor. He made it look like another bow.

"Alas, no. Behold me in my rags; I cannot afford charity. But for a token fee only, I will do this for you!"

Me he dangled by the engorged tail. *Them* he held by the balls. Oh, he had them. Well-palmed and squeezing. (Hoo-boy, did that bring back a great memory! There'd been this saucy rat girl named Melanie a few years back, and did she ever know how to do things with her paws . . .)

Mayor Ulia Gol slinked out from behind her podium. Bright-eyed and treacherous and curious as a marten in a chicken hut, she toyed with her gavel. Her countenance was welcoming, even coquettish.

"A Hero from the Hill!" She laughed her deep laughter that brought voters to the ballot box by the hordes. "Come to rescue our troubled Amandale in its time of need."

"Just a musician, Madame Mayor." Nicolas's dire and delicate voice was pitched to warm the cockles and slicken the thighs. "But better than average perhaps—at least where poor, dumb animals are concerned."

"And, of course, musicians must be paid!" Her lip curled.

"Exterminators too."

Ulia Gol had reached him. She walked right up close and personal, right to his face, and inhaled deeply. She could smell the Hill on him, I knew, and those tantalizing hints of Folk in his blood, and the long-lost echoes of the mortal he may once have been. The red glint in her eye deepened drunkenly. His scent was almost too much for her. Over there in his corner of the hall, Hans watched the whole scene, green to the gills with jealousy. It clashed with his second-best suit.

Ulia Gol's expression slid from one of euphoria to that of distaste as she remembered me. Crouched in Nicolas's open hand, I hunkered as small as I could make myself. I was not a very big rat. And she did have a gavel, you see, for all she was letting it swing from the tips of her fingers.

In a velveted boom that carried her words to the far end of the hall, she asked, "What is your price, my precious piper?"

"I take my pay in coin, Madame Mayor."

I swear they heard his whisper all across Amandale that night. Nicolas had a whisper like a kiss, a whisper that could reach out and ring the bells of Brotquen Cathedral so sweetly.

"One thousand gold canaries upon completion of the job. If you choose, you may pay me in silver nightingales, though I fear the tripled weight would prove unwieldy. For this reason I cannot accept smaller coin. No bronze wrens or copper robins; such currency is too much for me to shoulder easily."

Silence. As if his whisper had sucked the breath right from the room. The chandler's baby hiccupped.

"Paid on completion, you say." Ulia Gol pondered, stepping back from him. "And by what measurement, pray, do we assess completion? When the last rat drowns in the Drukkamag River?"

Nicolas bowed once more, more gracefully than ever before. "Whatever terms you set, Madame Mayor, I will abide by them."

Ulia Gol grinned. Oh, she had a handsome, roguish grin. I think I peed a little in Nicolas's palm. "It cost our town less to build Brotquen Cathedral—and that was three hundred years of inflation ago. Why don't you take *that* instead, my sweet-lipped swindler?"

"Alas, ma'am!" Nicolas shook his red-and-black head in sorrow. "While I am certain that yours is a fine cathedral, I make my living on my feet. I take for payment only what I can trundle away with me. As I stated, it must be gold or silver. Perhaps in a small leather chest or sack that I might lift upon my shoulder?"

He tapped the Mayor's shoulder with his silver pipe, drawing a lazy sigil there. Curse or caress, who could say? Ulia Gol shivered, euphoria once again briefly blanking out her cunning.

"One thousand bright canaries," she laughed at him, "singing in a single chest! Should not they be in a cage instead, my mercenary minstrel?"

Nicolas twinkled a wink her way. "Nay," said he, husking low his voice for her ears (and mine) alone. His next sentence fair glittered with the full formality of the Faerie court. Had I any choice when hearing it, I'd've bolted right then and there and never come out from my hole till my whiskers turned grey.

"But perhaps," he continued, "*thou* shouldst be, thou pink-plumed eyas. A cage equipped with manacles of silver and gilded bullwhips and all manner of bejeweled barbs and abuses for such a wicked lady-hawk as thee."

Pleased with the impudent promise in his eyes, and pink as her candy-colored wig, Ulia Gol spun around. The tassel on her black satin cap hopped like a cottontail in a clover patch. She addressed the hall.

"The Pied Piper has come to drive our rats away. He is charging," she threw the room a grin as extravagant as confetti, "an unconscionable fee to do so. But, my friends, our coffers will manage. What cost peace? What cost health? What cost the lives of our children? Yes, we shall have to tighten our belts this winter. What of that?" Her voice crescendoed. Her arms spread wide. "Citizens, if we do not accept his assistance now, who knows if we will even live to see the winter?"

A wall of muttering rose up against the tide of her questions. Some dissent. Some uneasy agreement. Ulia Gol took another reluctant step away from Nicolas and waded into the crowd. She worked it, touching hands, stroking baby curls, enhancing her influence as she gazed deeply into deeply worried eyes and murmured spells and assurances. Shortly, and without any overt effort, she appeared behind the podium like she'd grown there.

"Friends," she addressed them throbbingly, "already the rats are nibbling at our stores, our infants, the foundations of our houses. Recall how rats carry plague. Do you want Amandale to face the danger that leveled Doornwold fifteen years ago? We shall put it to the vote! I ask you to consider this—extreme, yes, but remember, we only need pay *if* it's effective!—solution. All in favor of the Pied Piper, say aye!"

The roar the crowd returned was deafening. The overtones were especially harsh, that particular brassy hysteria of a mob miles past the point of reasoning with. I wished I had my earplugs back. Ulia Gol did not bother to invite debate from naysayers. Their protestations were drowned out, anyway. But I could see Hans over there making note of those who shook their heads or frowned. My guess was that they'd be receiving visitors later. Probably in the dead of night.

From her place on the stage, Ulia Gol beamed upon her townspeople. But like magnet to metal, her gaze clicked back to Nicolas. She studied him with flagrant lust, and he returned her scrutiny with the scorching intensity the raven has for the hawk. He stood so still that even I, whom he held in his hand, could not feel him breathing.

"Master Piper!"

"Madame Mayor?"

"When will you begin?"

"Tomorrow at dawn." This time, Nicolas directed his diffident smile to the room at large. "I need my sleep tonight. It is quite a long song, the one that calls the rats to the waterside and makes the thought of drowning there seem so beautiful."

"Rest is all well and good, Master Piper. But first you must dine with me."

"Your pardon, Madame Mayor, but I must fast before such work as I will do tomorrow."

Her fists clenched on the edges of the podium. She leaned in. "Then a drink, perhaps. The mayoral mansion is well stocked."

Nicolas bowed. "Ma'am, I must abstain."

I wouldn't say that the look Ulia Gol gave him was a pout, exactly. More like, if Nicolas's face had been within range of her teeth, she'd have torn it off. He had toyed with her, keyed her to the pitch of his choosing, and now he would not play her like a pipe—nor let *her* play *his*. Pipe, I mean. Ahem.

His short bow and quick exit thwarted any scheme she might have improvised to keep him there. Outside in the cooling darkness, cradling me close to his chest, Nicolas turned sharply into the nearest alleyway.

Stumbling on a pile of refuse, he set me down atop it, and promptly projectile-vomited all over the wall.

I'd never seen that much chunk come out of an undrunk person. Fleshing myself back to man-shape, I clasped my hands behind me and watched him. I had to curb my urge to applaud.

"Wow, Nicolas! Is that nerves, or did you eat a bad sausage for dinner?" I whistled. "I thought you couldn't talk to women, you Foxface, you! But you were downright debonair. If the Mayor'd been a rat girl, her ears would've been vibrating like a tuning fork!"

Wiping his mouth on his hand, Nicolas croaked, "She is not a woman. She is a monster. I spoke to her as I speak to other monsters I have known. It is poison to speak so, Maurice—but death to do aught else. But, oh, it hurts, Maurice. It hurts to breathe the same air she breathes. It hurts to watch her courtiers—"

"Constituents," I corrected, wondering whose face he'd seen imposed upon Ulia Gol's. If I were a betting rat, I'd say the answer rhymed with "Airy Fleen."

"So corrupted . . . Necrotic! As rotten as that poor rat-bitten babe shall be in a few days. They—these thinking people, people like you or me"—I decided not to challenge this—"they *all* agreed to the genocide. They agreed to make the orchestra of murdered swans, to abuse the god in the juniper tree. They traded their souls to a monster, and for what? Free music? Worse, worse—they set their children to serve her. Their babies, Maurice! Gone bad like the rest of them. Maurice, had I the tinder, I would burn Amandale to the ground!"

Nicolas was sobbing again. I sighed. Poor man. Or whatever he was.

I set my hand upon his tousled head. His hair was slick with sweat. "Aw, Nicolas. Aw, now. Don't worry. We'll get 'em. There's worse ways to punish people than setting fire to their houses. Hellfowl, we did it one way today, and by nightfall tomorrow, we'll have done another! So smile! Everything's going steamingly!"

Twin ponds of tears brimmed, spilled, blinked up at me.

"Don't you mean swimmingly?" Nicolas gasped, sighing down his sobs.

"I will soon, you don't quit your bawling. Hey, Nico, come on!" I clucked my tongue. "Dry up, will ya? You're not supposed to drown me till dawn!"

I could always make Nicolas laugh.

In a career so checkered that two old men could've played board games on it, I've come near death four times. Count 'em, four. Now if we're talking about coming within a cat-calling or even a spitting distance from death, I'd say the number's more like "gazillions of times," but I don't number 'em as "near"-death experiences till I'm counting the coronal sutures on the Reaper of Rodents's long-toothed skull.

The first time I almost died, it was my fault. It all had to do with being thirteen and drunk on despair and voluntarily wandering into a rat-baiting arena because life isn't worth living if a Swan Princess won't be your girlfriend. Embarrassing.

The second time was due to a frisky rat lass named Molly. She, uh, used a little too much teeth in the, you know, act. Bled a lot. Worth it, though.

Third? Peanut butter.

Fourth . . . one of the elder Cobblersawl boys and his brand new birthday knife.

But I have never been so near death as that day Nicolas drowned me in the Drukkamag River.

He'd begged me not to hear him. That morning, just before dawn, he'd said, "Maurice, Maurice. Will you not stop up your ears and go to the Maze Wood and wait this day out?"

"No, Nicolas," said I, affronted. "What, and give a bunch of poor fixed rats the glory of dying for Dora Rose? This is *my* end. My story. I've waited my whole life for a chance like this. My Folk will write a drama of this day, and the title of that play shall be *Maurice the Incomparable!*"

Nicolas ducked the grand sweep of my hand. "You cannot really mean to drown, Maurice. You'll never know how the end of your drama plays out. What if we need you again, and you are dead and useless? What if . . . what if *she* needs you?"

I clapped his back. "She never did before, Nicolas my friend. That's why I love the girl. Oh, and after I die today, do something for me, would you? You tell Dora Rose that she really missed out on the whole cross-species experimentation thing. You just tell her that. I want her to regret me the rest of her life. I want the last verse of her swan song to be my name. *Maurice the Incomparable!*"

Nicolas ducked again, looking dubious and promising nothing. But I knew he would try. That's what friends did, and he was the best.

You may wonder—if you're not Folk, that is—how I could so cavalierly condemn thousands of my lesser cousins, not to mention my own august person, of whom I have a high (you might even say "the highest") regard— to a watery grave. Who died and made me arbiter of a whole pestilential population's fate? How could I stand there, stroking my whiskers, and volunteer all those lives (and mine) to meet our soggy end at the Pied Piper's playing?

I could sum it up in one word.

Drama.

I speak for all rats when I speak for myself. We're alike in this. We'll do just about anything for drama. Or comedy, I guess; we're not particular. We're not above chewing the scenery for posterity. We must make our territorial mark (as it were) on the arts. The Swan Folk have their ballet. We rats, we have theatre. We pride ourselves on our productions. All the cities, high and low, that span this wide, wide world are our stage.

"No point putting it off," I told Nicolas, preparing to fur down. "Who's to say that if you don't drown me today, a huge storm won't come along and cause floods enough to drown me tomorrow? If *that* happens, I'll have died for nothing! Can any death be more boring?"

Nicolas frowned. "The weather augur under the Hill can predict the skies up to a month in exchange for one sip of your tears. She might be able to tell you if there will be rain . . . "

I cut him off. "What I'm saying is, you have to seize your death by the tail. Know it. Name it. My death," I said, "is you."

His laugh ghosted far above me as I disappeared into my other self.

"Hurricane Nicolas," he said. "The storm with no center."

Comes a song too high and sweet for dull human ears. Comes a song like the sound of a young kit tickled all to giggles. Like the sharp, lustful chirps of a doe in heat. Comes a song for rats to hear, and rats alone. A song that turns the wind to silver, a wind that brings along the tantalizing smell of cream.

Excuse me, make that "lots of cream."

A river of cream. A river that is so rich and thick and pure you could swim in it. You bet your little rat babies there's cream aplenty. Cream for you. Cream for your cousins, for your aunts and uncles, too. There's even cream for that ex-best buddy of yours who stole your first girlfriend along with the hunk of stinky cheese you'd saved up for your birthday.

Comes a song that sings of a river of cream. Cream enough for all.

Once I get there, ooh, baby, you betcha . . . I'm gonna find that saucy little doe who's chirping so shamelessly. I'm gonna find her, and then I'm gonna frisk the ever-living frolic out of her, nipping and mounting and slipping and licking the cream from her fur. Oh, yeah. Let's all go down to that river.

Now. Let's go now. I wanna swim.

Funny thing, drowning. By the time I realized I didn't want it anymore, there was nothing I could do. I was well past the flailing stage, just tumbling along head over tail, somewhere in the sea-hungry currents of the Drukkamag. The only compass I could go by indicated one direction.

Deathward.

Rats are known swimmers. We can tread water for days, hold our breath for a quarter of an hour, dive deeply, survive in open sea. Why? Because our instinct for survival is unparalleled in the animal kingdom, that's why.

Once Nicolas's song started, I'd no *desire* to survive anymore. Until I did. I never said rats were consistent. We're entitled to an irregularity of opinion, just like mortals. Even waterlogged and tossed against Death's very cheese grater, we're allowed to change our minds.

And so, I did the only thing I had mind enough left to do. I fleshed back to man-shape.

The vigor of the transformation brought me, briefly, to the surface. I mouthed a lungful of air before the current sucked me back down into the river.

This is it, I thought. *Damn it, damn it, da—*

And then I slammed into a barrier both porous and implacable. Water rushed through it, yet I did not. I clung to it, finger and claw, and almost wept (which would have been entirely redundant at that point) when a great hook plunged at me from out of the blue, snagged me under the armpit, and hauled.

Air. Dazzle. Dry land.

I was deposited onto the stony slime of a riverbank. Someone hastily threw a blanket over my collapse. It smelled of sick dog and woodsmoke, but it was warm and dry. I think I heard my name, but I couldn't answer, sprawled and gasping, moving from blackout to dazzle and back again while voices filtered through my waterlogged ears.

Children's voices. Excited. Grim.

I considered opening my eyes. Got as far as blurred slittedness before my head started pounding.

We were under some sort of bridge. Nearby, nestled among boulders, a large fire burned. Over this there hung an enormous cauldron, redolent of boiling potatoes. A girl with a white rag tied over her eyes stirred it constantly. Miss Possum, or I missed my guess.

A bowl of her potato mash steamed near my elbow. I almost rolled over and dove face-first into it, but common sense kicked in. Didn't much fancy drowning on dry land so soon after my Drukkamag experience, so I lapped at the mash with more care, watching everything. Not far from Possum squatted Master Froggit, carefully separating a pile of dead rats from living as quickly as they came to him from the figure on the bridge. The dead he set aside on an enormous canvas. The living he consigned to blind Possum's care. She dried them and tried to feed them. There weren't many.

My slowly returning faculty for observation told me that our bold young recruits had strung a net across a narrowish neck of the Drukkamag, beneath one of the oldest footbridges of Amandale. They weighted the net with rocks. When the rats began to fetch up against it, Greenpea, seated on the edge of the bridge, leg stumps jutting out before her, fished them out again. She wielded the long pole that had hooked me out of the current.

For the first time since, oh, since I was about thirteen, I think, I started sobbing. Too much hanging out with Nicolas, I guess. Not eating properly. Overextending myself. That sort of thing. Prolonged close contact with Dora Rose had always had this effect on me.

I applied myself to my potatoes.

Once sated, making a toga of my dog blanket, I limped up to the bridge and gazed at the girl with the hooked pole.

"Mistress Greenpea."

"Hey." She glanced sidelong at me as I sat next to her. "Maurice the Incomparable, right?"

"Right-o." I warmed with pleasure. "Hand that thing over, will ya? My arms feel like noodles, but I reckon they can put in a shift for the glory of my species."

She grunted and handed her pole to me. "I don't see any more live ones. Not since you."

"Well, cheer up!" I adjured her. "We'll rise again. We're the hardiest thing since cockroaches, you know. Besides you humans, I mean. Roaches. Blech! An acquired taste, but they'll do for lean times. We used to dare each other to bite 'em in half when we were kits."

Greenpea, good girl, gagged only a bit, and didn't spew. I flopped a couple of corpses over to Froggit's canvas. "So. This whole net thing your idea, Miss Greenpea?"

She replied in a flat, unimpressed recitation, "Dora Rose said you'd try to drown yourself with the other rats. Said it would be *just like you*, and that we must save you if we could, because no way was she letting you stain her memory with your martyrdom."

I chuckled. "Said that, did she?"

"Something like that." Greenpea shrugged. Or maybe she was just rolling her stiff shoulders. "Before we . . . we hung her on that tree, I promised we'd do what we could for you. She seemed more comfortable, after." She wouldn't meet my eyes. "And then, when I saw all the other rats in the river, I tried to save them, too. Why should you be so special? But, then . . . So long as the Pied Piper played, even though he's still all the way back in Amandale, the rats I rescued wouldn't stay rescued. No sooner did we fish them out of the Drukkamag but they jumped back in again."

"Listen, kid." I returned her hard glare with a hard-eyed look of my own. "That was always the plan. You agreed to it. We all did."

The net bulged beneath us. Greenpea didn't back down, but the bridge of her nose scrunched beneath her spectacles. Behind thick lenses, those big grey eyes of hers widened in an effort not to cry. How old was she, anyway? Eleven? Twelve? One of the older girls in Ulia Gol's child army. Near Ocelot's age, I thought. Old enough at any rate to dry her tears by fury's fire. Which she did.

"It's horrible," Greenpea growled. "I hate that they had to die."

"Horrible, yeah," I agreed. "So's your legs. And Possum's eyes. And Froggit's tongue. And twenty dead swans. We're dealing with ogres here, not unicorns. Not the nicest monsters ever, ogres. Although, when you come right down to it, unicorns are nasty brutes. Total perverts. But anyway, don't fret, Miss Greenpea. We're gonna triumph, have no doubt. And even if we don't"—I started laughing, and it felt good, good, good to be alive—"even if we don't, it'll make a great tragedy, won't it? I love a play where all the characters die at the end."

The Pied Piper stood on the steps of Brotquen Cathedral, facing the Mayor of Amandale, who paraded herself a few steps above him. Hans and his handpicked horde of henchman waited nearby at the ready. Displayed at their feet was Froggit's macabre canvas of corpses. Most of the rats we'd simply let tumble free toward the sea when we cut the net, but we kept a few hundred back for a fly-flecked show-and-tell.

Nicolas's face was grey and drawn. His shoulders drooped. New lines had appeared on his forehead apparently overnight, and his mouth bowed like a willow branch. The pipe he no longer played glowed against his ragged chest like a solid piece of moonlight.

"As you see," he announced, "the rats of Amandale are drowned."

"Mmn," said Ulia Gol.

Most of the town—myself and my three comrades included—had gathered below the cathedral on Kirkja Street to gawk at the inconceivability of a thousand bright canaries stacked in a small leather chest right there in the open. The coins cast a golden glitter in that last lingering caress of sunset, and reflected onto the reverent faces of Amandale's children, who wore flowers in their hair and garlands 'round their necks. All of Amandale had been feasting and carousing since the rats began their death march at dawn that morning. Many of the older citizens now bore the flushed, aggressive sneers of the pot-valiant. In the yellow light of all that dying sun and leaping gold, they, too, looked new-minted, harder and glintier than they'd been before.

Nicolas did not notice them. His gaze never left Ulia Gol's shrewd face. She blocked his path to the gold. Hand over heart, he tried again.

"From the oldest albino to the nakedest newborn, Madame Mayor, the rats are drowned one and all. I have come for my payment."

But she did not move. "Your payment," she purred, "for what?"

Nicolas inhaled deeply. "I played my pipe, and I made them dance, and they danced themselves to drowning."

"Master Piper . . . " Ulia Gol oozed closer to him. I could see Nicolas stiffen in an effort not to back away.

I must say, the Mayor of Amandale had really gussied herself up for this occasion. Her pink wig was caught up in a sort of birdcage, all sorts of bells and beads hanging off it. The bone-paneled brocade of her crimson dress was stiff enough to stand up by itself, and I imagined it'd require three professional grave robbers with shovels to exhume her from her maquillage. She smelled overpoweringly of rotten pears and sour grapes. Did I say so before? At the risk of repeating myself, then: a magnificent woman, Ulia Gol.

"I watched you all day, Master Piper," she told Nicolas. "I strained my ears and listened closely. You put your pipe to your lips, all right, my pretty perjurer, and fabricated a haggard verisimilitude, but never a note did I hear you play."

"No," Nicolas agreed. "You would not have. I did not play for you, Ulia Gol."

"Prove it."

He pointed at the soggy canvas. "*There* is my proof."

Ulia Gol shrugged. Her stiff lace collar barely moved. "I see dead rats, certainly. But they might have come from anywhere, drowned in any number of ways. The Drukkamag River runs clean and clear, and Amandale is much as it ever was. Yes, there were rats. Now there are none." She opened her palms. "Who knows why? Perhaps they left us of their own accord."

Most of the crowd rustled in agreement. Sure, you could tell a few wanted to mutter in protest, but pressed tight their lips instead. Fresh black bruises adorned the faces of many of these. What were the odds that Ulia Gol's main detractors had been made an example of since last night's town meeting in Orchestra Hall? Not long, I'd say. Not long at all.

Ulia Gol swelled with the approval of her smitten constituents. Their adoration engorged her. Magic coursed through her. There was no mistaking what she was if you knew to look out for it. She stank like an ogre and grinned like a giant, and all that was missing was a beanstalk and a bone grinder and a basket for her bread. She loomed ever larger, swamping Nicolas in her shadow.

"Master Piper—if a Master indeed you are—you cannot prove that your alleged playing had aught to do with the rats' disappearance. Perhaps they decamped due to instinct. Migration. After all, their onset was as sudden as their egress. Perhaps you knew this. Did you really come to Amandale to aid us, or were you merely here by happenstance? Seeing our dismay and our disarray, did you seek to take advantage of us, to ply your false trade, and cheat honest citizens of their hard-earned coin?"

The Mayor of Amandale was closer to the truth than she realized—ha! But that didn't worry me. Ulia Gol, after all, wasn't interested in truth. The only thing currently absorbing her was her intent to cheat the man who'd refused her bed the night before. It never occurred to her that the plague of rats was a misdirection of Amandale's attention during the theft of the bone orchestra. Okay, and part of its punishment for the murdered swans.

"Look at the color of his face," Greenpea whispered. "Is the piper all right?"

"Well . . . er." I squirmed. "It's Nicolas, right? He's never all the way all right."

But seeing his sick pallor, I wasn't sure Nicolas remembered that all this was part of a bigger plan. He looked near to swooning. Not good. We needed him for this next bit.

"Please," he whispered. "Please . . . just pay me and I'll be on my way."

"I am sorry, Master Piper." Ulia Gol laughed at him, her loud and lovely laugh. "But I cannot pay you all this gold for an enterprise you cannot prove you didn't engineer. In fact, you should consider yourself lucky if you leave Amandale in one piece."

The crowd around us tittered and growled. The children drew closer together, far less easy with the atmosphere of ballooning tension than were their parents. It was the adults whose eyes narrowed, whose flushed faces had empurpled and perspired until they looked all but smaller models of their Mayor. Nicolas took a step nearer Ulia Gol, though what it cost him, I do not know. He was a smallish man, and had to look up to her. Nicolas only sometimes seemed tall because of his slender build.

"Please," he begged her again. "Do not break your word. Have I not done as I promised?"

I leaned in for a closer look, brushing off Possum's anxious hand when it plucked my elbow.

"What's he doing?"

"Your guess is as good as mine, kid."

How Nicolas planned to act if Ulia Gol suddenly discovered within her scrumdiddlyumptious breast a thimble's worth of honor, compassion, or just plain sense, I do not know.

But she wouldn't. She was what she was, and behaved accordingly.

If she could but smell the furious sorrow on him, as I could . . . scent that destroying wind, the storm that had no center, the magic in his pipe that would dance us all to the grave, then perhaps even Ulia Gol might have flung herself to her knees and solicited his forgiveness. Did she think his music only worked on rats? That, because he trembled at her triumph and turned, in that uncertain twilight, an exquisite shade of green, he would not play a song Amandale would remember for a hundred years?

"Please," the Pied Piper repeated.

Something in Ulia Gol's face flickered.

I wondered if, after all, the Mayor would choose to part with her gold, and Nicolas to spare her. Never mind that it would leave Dora Rose pinioned to a juniper tree, the swans only partly avenged, and all my stylish stratagems and near-drowning in vain. Oh, he . . . naw, he . . . Surely Nicolas—even he!—wouldn't be so, so criminally virtuous!

Voice breaking and black eyes brimming, he appealed to her for a third and final time.

"Please."

The flickering stilled. I almost laughed in relief.

"It's gonna be fine," I told my comrades. "Watch closely. Be ready."

"Henceforth," purred the Mayor, "I banish you, Master Piper, from the town of Amandale. If ever you set foot inside my walls again, I will personally hang you from the bell tower of Brotquen Cathedral. There you will rot, until nothing but your bones and that silver pipe you play are left."

Ow. Harsh. *Fabulous.*

Nicolas nodded heavily, as if a final anvil had descended upon his brow. Then.

To my great delight, to my pinkest tickly pleasure, his posture subtly shifted. Yes, altered and unbent, the sadness swept from him like a magician's tablecloth right from beneath the cutlery. Nicolas was totally bare now, with only the glitter of glass and knives left to him.

He sprang upright. And grinned. At the sharp gleam of that grin, even I shivered.

"Here we go," I breathed.

Beside me, Greenpea leaned forward in her wheelchair, grey eyes blazing. "Yes, yes, yes!" she whispered. "Get this over with, piper. Finish it."

Solemnly, Froggit took Possum's hand in his and squeezed. She lifted her chin, face pale behind her ragged blindfold, and asked, "Is it now, Mister Maurice?"

"Soon. Very soon," I replied, hardly able to keep from dancing. Lo, I'd had enough dancing for a lifetime, thanks. Still, I couldn't help but wriggle a bit.

"Citizens of Amandale," announced the Pied Piper, "although it causes me pangs of illimitable dolor to leave you thus, I must, as a law-abiding alien to your environs, make my exit gracefully. But to thank you for your hospitality and to delight your beautiful children, I propose to play you one last song."

"Time to put that cotton in your ears," I warned my recruits. Froggit and Possum obeyed. I don't think Greenpea even heard me; she was that focused on the motley figure poised on the steps of Brotquen Cathedral.

My caution turned out to be unnecessary. Nicolas was, indeed, a Master Piper. He could play tunes within tunes. Tunes piled on tunes, and tunes buried under them. His music came from the Hill, from Her, the Faerie Queen, and there was no song Nicolas could not play when he flung himself open to the sound.

First he played a strand of notes that froze the adults where they stood. Second, a lower, darker line strong enough to paralyze the ogre in her place. Then he played three distinct trills that sounded like names—Froggit, Possum, Greenpea—exempting them from his final spell. Greenpea licked her lips and looked almost disappointed.

Last came the spell song. The one we'd worked so hard for these three days. A song to lure twenty little Swan Hunters into the trap a Swan Princess had set. A song to bring the children back to Dora Rose.

I don't think, in my furry shape, I'd've given the tune more than passing heed. But I was full-fleshed right now, with all the parts of a man. The man I was had been a child once, sometimes still behaved like one, and the tune Nicolas played was tailor-made for children. It made the tips of my toes tingle and my heels feel spry. Well within control, thank the Captured God.

You know who couldn't control it, though?

Ocelot, the Gravedigger's daughter. Ilse Cobblersawl, her brothers Frank, Theodore and James, her sweet sister Anabel, and the nine-year-old twins Hilde and Gretel. Pearl, the chandler's eldest daughter, who let her sister Ruby slip from her arms, to join hands with Maven Chain, the goldsmith's girl. Charles the Chimneysweep. Kevin the Gooseboy. Those twelve and eight more whose names I did not know.

Heads haloed in circles of silver fire that cast a ghostly glow about them, these twenty children shoved parents, grandparents, uncles, aunts, siblings, cousins, teachers, employers, out of the way. Those too small to keep pace were swept up and carried by their fellow hunters. Still playing, Nicolas sprinted down the steps of the cathedral and sprang right into that froth of silver-lit children.

All of them danced. Then the tune changed, and they ran instead.

Light-footed, as though they wore wings on their feet, they fled down Kirkja Street and onto Maskmakers Boulevard. This, I knew, ended in a cul-de-sac abutting a town park, which sported in its farthest shrubbery a rusted gate leading into the Maze Wood.

"Step lively, soldiers," I barked to my three recruits. "Don't wanna get caught staring when the thrall fades from this mob. Gonna get ugly. Lots of snot and tears and torches. Regardless, we should hie ourselves on over to the Heart Glade. Wouldn't want to miss the climax now, would we?"

Froggit shook his head and Possum looked doubtful, but Greenpea was already muscling her chair toward the corner of Kirkja and Maskmakers. We made haste to follow.

Dora Rose, here we come.

I'd seen Dora Rose as a swan, and I'd seen her as a woman, but I'd never seen her both at once. Or so nakedly.

I confess, I averted my eyes. No, I know, I know. You think I should've taken my chance. Looked my fill. Saved up the sweet sight of her to savor all those lonely nights in my not-so-distant future. (Because, let's be honest here, my love life's gonna be next to nonexistent from this point on. Most of the nice fixed does I know are bloating gently in the Drukkamag, and any Folk doe who scampered off to save herself from the Pied Piper is not going to be speaking to me. Who could blame her, really?) But, see, it wasn't like that. It was never like that, with Dora Rose.

Sure, I *curse* by the Captured God. But Dora Rose is my religion.

It was as much as I could bear just to glance once and see her arms outstretched, elongated, mutated, jointed into demented angles that human bones are not intended for, pure white primary feathers bursting from her fingernails, tertials and secondaries fanning out from the soft torn flesh of her underarms. Her long neck was a column of white, like a feathered python, and her face, though mostly human, had become masklike, eyes and nose and mouth black as bitumen, hardening into the shining point of a beak.

That's all I saw, I swear.

After that I was kneeling on the ground and hiding my face, like Nicolas under his covers. In that darkness, I became aware of the music in the Heart Glade. Gave me a reason to look up again.

What does a full bone orchestra look like? First the woodwinds: piccolo, flute, oboe, clarinet, bassoon. Then the brass: horn, trumpet, cornet, tenor trombone, bass trombone, tuba (that last must've been Dasher—he was the biggest cob on the lake). Percussion: timpani, snare, cymbals (those cygnets, I'd bet). And the strings. Violin. Viola. Violoncello. Double bass. And the harp. One white harp, with shining black strings.

Elinore, Dora Rose's twin sister.

All of them, set in a circle around the juniper tree, glowed in the moonlight. They played softly by themselves, undisturbed, as if singing lullabies to the tree and she who hung upon it.

I'd heard the tune before. It was the same phrase of music the tiny firebird had sung, which later the tree itself repeated in its seismic voice. Beneath the full sweep of the strings and hollow drumbeats and bells of bone, I seemed to hear that tremulous boy soprano sobbing out his verse with the dreary repetition of the dead.

Only then—okay, so maybe I took another quick glance—did I see the red tracks that stained the pale down around Dora Rose's eyes. By this I knew she had been weeping all this while.

She, who never wept. Not once. Not in front of me.

I'd thought swans didn't cry. Not like rats and broken pipers and little children. Not like the rest of us. Stupid to be jealous of a bunch of bones. That *they* merited her red, red tears, when nothing else in the world could or would. Least of all, yours truly, Maurice the Incomparable.

Me and my three comrades loitered in the darkness outside that grisly bone circle. Greenpea, confined to her wheelchair; Possum, sitting quietly near her feet; a tired Froggit sprawled beside her, his head in her lap. Possibly, he'd fallen into a restive sleep. They'd had a tough few days, those kids.

We'd come to the Heart Glade by a shortcut I knew, but it wasn't long till we heard a disturbance in one of the maze's many corridors. In the distance, Nicolas's piping caught the melody of the bone orchestra and countered it, climbing an octave higher and embroidering the somber fabric of the melody with sharp silver notes. The twenty children he'd enchanted joined in, singing:

"Day and night Stepsister weeps
Her grief like blood runs red, runs deep
Kywitt! Kywitt! Kywitt! I cry
What a beautiful bird am I!"

In a rowdiness of music making, they spilled into the Heart Glade. Ocelot was yipping, "Kywitt! Kywitt! Kywitt!" at the tops of her lungs, while Ilse and Maven flapped their arms like wings and made honking noises. A flurry of chirps and whistles and shrieks of laughter from the other children followed in cacophony. Nicolas danced into the glade after them, his pipe wreathed in silver flames. Hopping nimbly over a small bone cymbal in the moss, he faced the Heart Glade, faced the children, and his tune changed again.

And the children leapt the bones.

Once inside the circle, the twenty of them linked wrists and danced rings around the juniper tree, as they used to do in the beginning, when the first of the Swan Folk were hunted and changed. As they whirled, a fissure opened in the juniper's trunk. Red-gold fire flickered within. Like a welcoming hearth. Like a threshold to a chamber of magma.

The children, spurred by Nicolas's piping, began to jump in.

They couldn't reach the fissure fast enough. Ocelot, by dint of shoving the littler ones out of her way, was first to disappear into the bloody light. And when she screamed, the harp that had been Elinore burst into silver-and-red flame, and disappeared. The first silver bloom erupted from the branches of the juniper tree.

Dora Rose shuddered where she hung.

A second child leapt through the crack. Ilse Cobblersawl. The bone trumpet vanished. A second silver bloom appeared. Then little Pearl the Chandler's daughter shouldered her way into the tree. Her agonized wail cut off as a bone cymbal popped into nothingness. Another silver bud flowered open.

When all twenty instruments had vanished, when all twenty Swan Hunters had poured themselves into the tree, when the trunk of the tree knit its own bark back over the gaping wound of its molten heart, then twenty silver blooms opened widely on their branches. The blooms gave birth to small white bees that busied themselves in swirling pollinations. Petals fell, leaving silver fruit where the flowers had been. The branches bent to the ground under the colossal weight of that fruit and heaved Dora Rose from their tree. Into the moss she tumbled, like so much kindling, a heap of ragged feathers, shattered flesh, pale hair.

Nicolas stopped piping. He wiped his mouth as if it had gone numb. He looked over at Froggit, who'd been screaming wordlessly ever since waking to the sight of his siblings feeding themselves to the tree. Nicolas held Froggit in his dense black gaze, the enormity of his sadness and regret etching his face ancient.

For myself, I couldn't care less about any of them.

I rushed to Dora Rose and shook her. Nothing happened. No response. Reaching out, I tackled Nicolas at the knees, yanking him to the ground and pinning him down.

"Is she dead, Nicolas?" I seized the lapels of his motley coat and shook. "Nicolas, did you kill her?"

"I?" he asked, staring at me in that dreadfully gentle way of his. "Perhaps. It sounds like something I might do. This world is so dangerous and cruel, and I am what it makes me. But I think you'll find she breathes."

He was correct, although how he could see so slight a motion as her breath by that weird fruity light, I couldn't say. I, for one, couldn't see a damn thing. But when I got near enough, I could smell the life of her. Not yet reduced to so much swan meat. Not to be salted and parboiled, seasoned with ginger, larded up and baked with butter yet. Not yet.

Oh, no, my girl. Though filthy and broken, you remain my Dora Rose.

"Come on, Ladybird. Come on. Wake up. Wake up now." I jostled her. I chafed her ragged wrists. I even slapped her face. Lightly. Well, not so hard as I might've.

"Maybe she's under a spell," Possum's scratchy voice suggested. "She told us it might happen. She's a princess, she says. She has to play her part."

"Oh, yeah?" I might have known my present agony was due to Dora Rose's inflexible adherence to tradition. Stupid swan girl. I could wring her white neck, except I loved her so. "What are we supposed to do about it, eh?"

I glanced over my shoulder in time to see the blind girl shrug. She did not move from the shadows of the Heart Glade into the juniper's feral light. Froggit at her feet sobbed like he would never stop.

Greenpea rolled her wheelchair closer to us.

"She said that Nicolas would know what to do."

I looked down again at Nicolas, who blinked at me. "Well?"

"Oh. *That*. Well." His face went like a red rose on fire. "You know, Maurice."

I'd had it. Time to show my teeth. "What, Nicolas?" I hissed. "Spit it out, wouldja? We're working within a three-day time frame here, okay? If today turns into tomorrow, she'll be gone. And what'll all this be for? So say it. How do we wake her?"

"True love's k-kiss," Nicolas answered, blushing more deeply and unable to meet my gaze. "It's pretty standard when one is dealing with, with . . . royalty."

"Oh." I sat back on my heels. A mean roil of jealousy and bile rose up inside me, but my next words, I'm proud to say, came out flat and even. Who said I couldn't control my basest urges? "Okay then, Nico, hop to it. But no tongue, mind, or I'll have it for my next meal."

Nicolas scooted away from me, scraping up moss in his haste. "Maurice, you cannot mean it." He ran nervous brown fingers through his hair.

"Nicolas," said I, "I've never been more serious. No tongue—or you'll be sleeping with one eye open and a sizeable club under your pillow the rest of your days."

"No, no!" He held up his hands, blocking me and Dora Rose from his view. "That's not what I meant at all. I only meant—I can't."

"You . . . what?"

"I can't k-ki . . . Do that. What you're saying." Nicolas shook his head back and forth like a child confronted with a syrupy spoonful of ipecac. His hair stood on end. His skin was sweaty and ashen. "Not on your life. Or mine. Or—or hers. Never." He paused. "Sorry."

I sprang to my feet. Wobbled. Sat down promptly. *Limbs, don't fail me now.* Grabbing him by the hem of his muddy trousers, I yanked him back toward me and pounced again, my hands much nearer his throat this time. "Nicolas, by the Captured God, if you don't kiss her right this instant, I'll . . . "

"He *can't*, Maurice," Greenpea said unexpectedly. She fisted my collar and pulled me off him, wheeling backward in her chair until she could deposit me, still flailing, at Dora Rose's side. That girl had an arm on her—even after fishing drowned rats out of the Drukkamag all day. Her parents were both smiths: she, their only child. "He can't even say the word without choking. You want someone to kiss her, you do it yourself. Leave him alone."

Nicolas turned his head and stared up at her, glowing at this unexpected reprieve. If he could have bled light onto his rescuer, I don't think Greenpea'd ever get the stains out.

"We've not been introduced, Miss . . . ? You are Master Froggit's cousin, I believe."

"Greenpea Margissett."

"Nicolas of the Hill." His mouth quirked. "Nicolas of Nowhere."

She frowned fiercely at him. She looked just like a schoolmarm I once knew, who laid a clever trail of crumbs right up to a rattrap that almost proved my undoing. She's how I ended up in that pickle jar, come to think of it. Unnerving to see that same severe expression on so young a face.

"Nicolas," she said, very sternly, "I am *not* happy about the rats."

All that wonderful light snuffed right out of his face. Nicolas groaned. "Neither am I." He slapped a hand hard against his chest, driving the pipe against his breastbone. "I am not happy." Slap. "I will never be happy again." Slap.

With that, he crumpled on the ground next to Froggit and Dora Rose and began to retch, tearing at his hair by the fistful. Me and Greenpea watched him a while. Froggit, meanwhile, crawled over to the juniper tree and hunkered down by the roots to cry more quietly. Nothing from Possum, lost behind us in the darkness.

Presently, I muttered to Greenpea, "We'll get nothing more out of him till he's cried out. It's like reasoning with a waterspout."

Greenpea studied the Pied Piper, her brow creased. "He's cracked."

"Got it in one."

"But you used him anyway?"

I bared my teeth at her, the little know-it-all. Show her I could chew through anything—metal spokes, bandaged leg stumps, leather coat, bone.

"Yeah. I used you, too, don't forget. And your friends. Oh, and about half a million rats. And all those children we murdered here tonight. I used the Mayor herself against herself and made a puppet of the puppet master. I'll tell you something else, little Rebel Greenpea—I'd do it again and worse to wake this Swan Princess now."

Resting her head on the back of her chair, Greenpea whispered, "It won't." I couldn't tell if it was smugness or sorrow that smelled so tart and sweet on her, like wild strawberries. "Only one thing can."

"But it's not—" I drew a breath. "*Seemly.*"

Greenpea's clear grey gaze ranged over the Heart Glade. She rubbed her eyes beneath her spectacles. "None of this is."

In the end, I couldn't bring myself to . . .

Not her lips, at least. That, Dora Rose'd never forgive, no matter what excuse I stammered out. No, I chose to kiss the sole of her foot. It was blackened like her mask, and webbed and beginning to curl under. If she later decided to squash me with that selfsame foot, I'd feel it was only my due. I'd let her squash me—happily. If only she'd wake.

Beneath my lips, the cold webbing warmed. The hard toes flexed, pinkened, fleshed back to mortal feet. I bowed my head to the ground and only dared to breathe again when I felt her stir. I glanced up to see Dora Rose wholly a woman again, Greenpea putting the Pied Piper's motley cloak over her nakedness and helping her sit up. Nicolas scrambled to hide behind the fortress of Greenpea's wheelchair as soon as Dora Rose was upright.

Then Dora Rose looked at me.

And I guess I'll remember that look, that burning, haughty, tender look, until my dying day.

She removed her sole from the palm of my hand and slowly stood up, never breaking eye contact.

"You're wrapped in a dog blanket, Maurice."

I leaned on my left elbow and grinned. "Hellfowl, Dora Rose, you should've seen my outfit when they fished me outta the Drukkamag. Wasn't wrapped in much but water, if I recall."

She turned a shoulder to me, and bent her glance on Greenpea. It brimmed with the sort of gratitude I'd worked my tail to the bone these last three days to earn, but for whatever reason, I didn't seem to mind Dora Rose lavishing it elsewhere. Probably still aquiver from our previous eye contact.

"You did so well, my friend." She stooped to kiss Greenpea's forehead. "You three were braver than princes. Braver than queens. When I hung on the juniper tree, I told the ghost inside it of your hurts—and of your help. It promised you a sure reward. But first . . . first I must hatch my brothers and sisters from their deaths."

Dora Rose moved through the tree's shadow in a beam of her own light. She lifted an exhausted Froggit from the ground and returned him to his cousin. He huddled in Greenpea's lap, face buried in her shoulder. Possum crept toward them with uncertain steps, feeling for the chair. Finding it, she sat down near one of its great wheels, one hand on Froggit's knee, the other grasping fast to Greenpea's fingers. She was not a big girl like Greenpea. Not much older than Froggit, really.

They all patted one another's shoulders and stroked one another's hair, ceasing to pay attention to the rest of us. There was Nicolas, huddled on the ground not far from them in his fetal curl. At least he'd stopped crying. In his exhaustion, he watched the children. Something like hunger marked his face, something like envy creased it, but also a sort of lonely satisfaction in their fellowship. He made no move to infringe, only hugged his own elbows and rested his head on the moss. His face was a tragedy even I could not bear to watch.

Where was my favorite Swan Princess? Ah.

Dora Rose had plucked the first fruit from the juniper tree. I went over to help. Heaving a particularly large one off its branch (it came to me with a sharp crack, but careful inspection revealed nothing broken), I asked, "Now what would a big silver watermelon like this taste like, I wonder?"

"It's not a watermelon, Maurice." Dora Rose set another shining thing carefully on the ground. The silver fruit made a noise like a hand sweeping harp strings. "It's an egg."

"I like eggs."

"Maurice, if you dare!"

"Aw, come on, Ladybird. As if I would." She stared pointedly at my chin until I wiped the saliva away. "Hey, it's a glandular reflex. I've not been eating as much as I should. Surprised I'm not in shock."

As Dora Rose made no attempt even at pretending to acknowledge this, I went on plucking the great glowing eggs from the juniper tree. Soon we had a nice, big clutch piled pyramid-style on the moss.

Let me tell you, the only thing more tedious than a swan ballet is a swan hatching. You see one fuzzy grey head peeping out from a hole in a shell, you've seen 'em all. It takes hours. And then there's the grooming and the feeding and the nuzzling and the nesting, and oh, the interminable domesticity. Swan chicks aren't even cute like rat kits, which are the littlest wee things you did ever see and make the funniest noises besides. Swan chicks are just sort of pipsqueaking fluff balls.

But Dora Rose's silver-shelled clutch weren't your average eggs.

For one thing, when they burst open—which they did within minutes of being harvested—they all went at once, as if lightning smote them. Up from the shards they flew, twenty swans in total, of varying aspects and sexes.

But all a bit, well, weird.

When they finally came back down to the ground, in a landing that wanted nothing in grace or symmetry, I noticed what was off about them.

They had no smell. Or if they did, it wasn't a smell that matched my notion of "swan" or even of "bird." Not of any variety. Second, as the disjointed moonlight shone through the tree branches to bounce off their feathers, I saw that though the creatures were the right shape for swans, that flew like swans and waddled like swans, there was something innately frightening about them. Impenetrable. As if a god had breathed life into stone statues, and that was what they were: stone. Not creatures of flesh and feather at all.

It hit me then. These swans were not, in fact, of flesh and feather. Or even of stone. They were covered in hard white scales. Their coats weren't down at all, but interlocking bone.

Even as I thought this, they fleshed to human shape. Ivory they were, these newborn Swan Folk. Skin, hair, and eyes of that weirdly near-white hue, their pallor broken only by bitterly black mouths: lips and teeth and tongues all black together. Each wore a short gown of bone scales that clattered when they walked. Their all-ivory gazes fastened, unblinkingly, on Dora Rose.

She reached out to one of them, crying, "Elinore!"

But the swan girl who stepped curiously forward at the sound of her voice made Dora Rose gasp. True, she was like Elinore—but she was also like Ocelot, the gravedigger's daughter. She wore a silver circlet on her brow. Dora Rose averted her face and loosed a shuddering breath. But she did not weep. When she looked at the girl again, her face was calm, kindly, cold.

"Do you have a name?"

Elinore-Ocelot just stared. Tentatively, she moved closer to Dora Rose. Just as tentatively, knelt before her. Setting her head against Dora Rose's thigh, she butted lightly. Dora Rose put a hand upon the girl's ivory hair. Nineteen other swanlings rushed to their knees and pressed in, hoping for a touch of her hand.

I couldn't help myself. I collapsed, laughing.

"Maurice!" Dora Rose snapped. "Stop cackling at once!"

"Oh!" I howled. "And you a new mama twenty times over! Betcha the juniper tree didn't whisper *that* about your fate in all the time you hung. You'd've lit outta the Heart Glade so fast . . . Oh, my heart! Oh, Dora Rose! Queen Mother and all . . . "

Dora Rose's eyes burned to do horrible things to me. How I wished she would! At the moment though, a bunch of mutely ardent cygnets besieged her on all sides, and she had no time for me. Captured God knew they'd start demanding food soon, like all babies. Wiping my eyes, I advised Dora Rose to take her bevy of bony swanlets back to Lake Serenus and teach them to bob for stonewort before they mistook strands of her hair for widgeon grass.

Tee hee.

Shooting one final glare my way, Dora Rose said, "You. I'll deal with you later."

"Promise?"

"I . . . " She hesitated. Scowled. Then reached her long silver fingers to grab my nose and tweak it. Hard. Hard enough to ring bells in my ears and make tears spurt from my eyes. The honk and tug at the end were especially malevolent. I grinned all over my face, and my heart percussed with bliss. Gesture like that was good as a pinkie swear in Rat Folk parlance—and didn't she know it, my own dear Dora Rose!

Out of deference, I "made her a leg"—as a Swan Prince might say. But my version of that courtly obeisance was a crooked, shabby, insolent thing: the only kind of bow a rat could rightly make to a swan.

"So long then, Ladybird."

Dora Rose hesitated, then said, "Not so long as last time—my Incomparable Maurice."

Blushing ever so palely and frostily (I mean, it was practically an invitation, right?), she downed herself for flight. A beautiful buffeting ruckus arose from her wings as she rocketed right out of the Heart Glade. Twenty bone swans followed her, changing from human to bird more quickly than my eye could take in. White wind. Silver wings. Night sky. Moonlight fractured as they flew toward Lake Serenus.

Heaving a sigh, I looked around. Nicolas and the three children were all staring up at the tree.

"Now what? Did we forget something?"

The juniper tree's uppermost branches trembled. Something glimmered high above, in the dense green of those needles. The trembling became a great shaking, and like meteors, three streaks of silver light fell to the moss and smoked thinly on the ground. I whistled.

"Three more melons! Can't believe we missed those."

"You didn't," Nicolas replied, in that whisper of his that could break hearts. "Those are for the children. Their reward."

"I could use a nice, juicy reward about now."

He smiled distractedly at me. "You must come to my house for supper, Maurice. I have a jar of plum preserves that you may eat. And a sack of sugared almonds, although they might now be stale."

How freely does the drool run after a day like mine!

"Nicolas!" I moaned. "If you don't have food on your person, you have to stop talking about it. It's torture."

"I was only trying to be hospitable, Maurice. Here you go, Master Froggit. This one's singing your song."

I couldn't hear anything. Me, who has better hearing than anyone I know! But Nicolas went over, anyway, and handed the first of the silver eggs to Froggit. It was big enough that Froggit had to sit down to hold it in his lap. He shuddered and squirmed, but his swollen eyes, thank the Captured God, didn't fill up and spill over again.

To Possum, Nicolas handed a second egg. This one was small enough to fit in her palms. She smoothed her hands over the silver shell. Lifting it to her face, she sniffed delicately.

Into Greenpea's hands, Nicolas placed the last egg. It was curiously flat and long. She frowned down at it, perplexed and a bit fearful, but did not cast it from her. Each of the shells shivered to splinters before Nicolas could step all the way back from Greenpea's chair.

Possum was the first to speak. "I don't understand," she said, fingering her gift.

"Hey, neat!" I said, bending down for a look. "Goggles! Hey, but don't see why you need 'em, Miss Possum. Not having, you know, eyes anymore. Can't possibly wanna shield them from sunlight, or saltwater, or whatever. For another, even if you did, these things are opaque as a prude's lingerie. A god couldn't see through them."

"That is because they are made of bone, Maurice," Nicolas said. "Try them on, Miss Possum. You will see."

Her lips flattened at what she took to be his inadvertent slip of the tongue. But she undid the bandage covering her eyes and guided the white goggles there. She raised her head to look at me. An unaccountable dread seized me at the expression on her face.

"Oh!" Possum gasped and snatched the goggles from her head, back-handing them off her lap like they were about to grow millipede legs and scuttle up her sleeve. "I saw—I saw—!"

Greenpea grabbed her hand. "They gave you back your eyes? But isn't that . . . ?"

"I saw him," Possum sobbed, pointing in my direction. "I saw him tomorrow. And the next day. And the day he dies. His grave. It overlooks a big blue lake. I saw . . . "

Nicolas crouched to inspect the goggles, poking at them with a slender finger. "The juniper didn't give you the gift of sight, Miss Possum—but of foresight. How frightening for you. But very beautiful, and very rare, too. You are to be congratulated. I think."

A sharp, staccato sound tapped out an inquiry. Froggit was exploring his own gift: a small bone drum, with a shining white hide stretched over it. I wondered if the skin had come from one of his siblings.

Best not to muse about such things aloud, of course. Might upset the boy.

Froggit banged on the hide with a drumstick I was pretty sure was also made of bone.

What does the drum do? asked the banging. *Is there a trick in it?*

"Froggit!" Possum cried out, laughing a little. "You're talking!"

A short, startled tap in response. *I am?*

"Huh," I muttered. "Close enough for Folk music, anyway."

Flushed with her own dawning excitement, Greenpea brought the bone fiddle in her lap to rest under her chin. She took a bone bow strung with long black hair and set it to the silver strings.

The fiddle wailed like a slaughtered rabbit.

She looked at her legs. They didn't move. She tried the bow again.

Cats brawling. Tortured dogs. That time in the rat-baiting arena I almost died. I put my hands to my ears. "Nicolas! Please! Make her stop."

"Hush, Maurice. We all sound like that when we first start to play." Nicolas squatted before Greenpea's chair to meet her eyes. She kept on sawing doggedly at the strings, her face set with harrowing determination, until at last the Pied Piper put his hand on hers. The diabolical noise stopped.

"Miss Greenpea. Believe me, it will take months, maybe years, of practice before you'll be able to play that fiddle efficiently. Longer before you play it well. But perhaps we can start lessons tomorrow, when we're all better rested and fed."

"But," she asked, clutching it close, "what does it *do?*"

"Do?" Nicolas inquired. "In this world, nothing. It's just a fiddle."

Greenpea's stern lips trembled. She looked mad enough to break the fiddle over his head.

"Possum can see. Froggit can talk. I thought this would make me walk again. I thought . . . "

"No." He touched the neck of the bone fiddle thoughtfully. "I could pipe Maurice's broken bones together, but I cannot pipe the rats of Amandale back to life. What's gone is gone. Your legs. Froggit's tongue. Possum's eyes. They are gone."

Huge tears rolled down her face. She did not speak.

He continued, "Fiddle music, my dear Miss Greenpea, compels a body, willy-nilly, to movement. More so than the pipe, I think—and I do not say that lightly, Master Piper that I am. Your fiddle may not make you walk again. But once you learn to play, the two of you together will make the world dance."

"Will we?" Greenpea spat bitterly. "Why should the world dance and not I?"

Bowing his head, Nicolas dropped to one knee, and set a hand on each of her armrests. When he spoke again, his voice was low. I had to strain all my best eavesdropping capabilities to listen in.

"Listen. In the Realms Under the Hill, my silver pipe is the merest pennywhistle. It has no power of compulsion or genius. I am nothing but a tin sparrow when I play for the Faerie Queen; it amuses Her to hear me chirp and peep. Yet you saw what I did with my music today, up here in the Realms Above. Now . . . "

His breath blew out in wonder. "Now," the Pied Piper told her, "if ever you found yourself in Her court, with all the Lords and Ladies of Faerie arrayed against you, fierce in their wisdom, hideous in their beauty, and pitiless, pitiless as starlight—and you played them a tune on this bone fiddle of yours, why . . . "

Nicolas smiled. It was as feral a grin as the one he'd worn on the steps of Brotquen Cathedral, right before he enchanted the entire town of Amandale. "Why, Miss Greenpea, I reckon you could dance the Immortal Queen Herself to death, and She powerless to stop you."

"Oh," Greenpea sighed. She caressed the white fiddle, the silver strings. "Oh."

"But." Nicolas sprang up and dusted off his patched knees. "You have to learn how to play it first. I doubt a few paltry scrapes would do more than irritate Her. And then She'd break you, make no doubt. Ulia Gol at her worst is a saint standing next to Her Most Gracious Majesty."

Taking up his cloak from the spot where Dora Rose had dropped it, Nicolas swirled it over his shoulders. He stared straight ahead, his face bleak and his eyes blank, as though we were no longer standing there.

"I am very tired now," he said, "and very sad. I want to go home and sleep until I forget if I have lived these last three days or merely dreamed them. I have had stranger and more fell dreams than this. Or perhaps"— he shuddered—"perhaps I was awake *then*, and this—*this* is the dream I dreamed to escape my memories. In which case, there is no succor for me, not awake or asleep, and I can only hope for that ultimate oblivion, and to hasten it with whatever implements I have on hand. If you have no further need of me, I will bid you adieu."

Alarmed at this turn, I scrambled to tug his coattails. "Hey, Nico! Hey, Nicolas, wait a minute, twinkle toes. Nicolas, you bastard, you promised me almonds!"

"Did I?" He looked up brightly, and blasted me with his smile, and it was like a storm wrack had blown from his face. "I did, Maurice! How could I have forgotten? Come along, then, with my sincerest apologies. Allow me to feed you, Maurice. How I love to feed my friends when they are hungry!"

Greenpea wheeled her chair about to block his way. "Teach me," she demanded.

He blinked at her as if he had never seen her face before. "Your pardon?"

She held out her bone fiddle. "If what you say is true, this gift is not just about music; it's about magic, too. And unless I'm wrong, Amandale won't have much to do with either in years to come."

I snorted in agreement.

"Teach me." Greenpea pointed with bow and fiddle to her two friends. "Them too. Teach all of us. We need you."

Please, Froggit tapped out on his bone drum. *We can't go home.*

"Of course you can!" Nicolas assured him, stricken. "They'll welcome you, Master Froggit. They probably think you are dead. How beautiful they shall find it that you are not! Think—the number of Cobblersawls has been halved at least; you shall be twice as precious . . . "

Possum shook her head. "They'll see only the ones they lost."

Once more she slipped the goggles on. Whatever she foresaw as she peered through the bone lenses at Nicolas, she did not flinch. But I watched him closely, the impossible radiance that rose up in him, brighter than his silver pipe, brighter than his broken edges, and he listened to Possum's prophecy in rapturous terror, and with hope. I'd never seen the Pied Piper look anything like hopeful before, in all the years I'd known him.

"We *are* coming with you," Possum prophesied. No one gainsaid her. No one even tried. "We are going to your cottage. You *will* teach us how to play music. We will learn many songs from you, and . . . and make up even *more*! When the first snow falls, we four shall venture into the Hill. And under it. Deep and wide, word will spread of a band of strange musicians: Nicolas and the Oracles. Lords and Ladies and Dragons and Sirens, they will *all* invite us to their courts and caves and coves to play for them. Froggit on the drums. Greenpea on her fiddle. You on your pipe. And I?"

Greenpea began to laugh. The sound was rusty, but true. "You'll sing, of course, Possum! You have the truest voice. Ulia Gol was so mad when you wouldn't sing up the bones for her!"

"Yes," Possum whispered, "I will sing true songs in the Realm of Lies, and all who hear me *will listen*."

All right. Enough of this yammering. My guts were cramping.

"Great!" I exclaimed. "You guys'll be great. Musicians get all the girls anyway. Or, you know"—I nodded at Greenpea and Possum—"the dreamy-eyed, long-haired laddies. Or whatever. The other way around. However you want it. Always wanted to learn guitar myself. I'd look pretty striking with a guitar, don't you think? I could go to the lake and play for Dora Rose. She'd like that about as much as a slap on the . . . Anyway, it's a thought."

"Maurice." Nicolas clapped his hand to my shoulder. "You are hungry. You always babble when you are hungry. Come. Eat my food and drink my

Faerie ale, and I shall spread blankets enough on the floor for all of us." He beamed around at the three children, at me, and I swear his face was like a bonfire.

"My friends," he said. "My friends. How merry we shall be."

Later that night, when they were all cuddled up and sleeping the sleep of the semi-innocent, or at least the iniquitously fatigued, I crept out of that cottage in the lee of the Hill and snuck back to the Heart Glade.

Call it a hunch. Call it ants in my antsy pants. I don't know. Something was going on, and I had to see it. So what? So I get curious sometimes.

Wouldn't you know it? I made it through the Maze Wood only to find I was right yet again! They weren't kidding when they called me Maurice the Incomparable. (And by "they," I mean "me," of course.) Sometimes I know things. My whiskers twitch, or maybe my palms itch, and I just *know*.

What hung from the juniper tree in that grey light before full dawn wasn't nearly as pretty as a Swan Princess or as holy and mysterious as a clutch of silver watermelon eggs.

Nope. This time the ornaments swinging from the branches were much plainer and more brutal. The juniper tree itself, decked out in its new accessories, looked darker and squatter than I'd ever beheld it, and by the gratified jangling in its blackly green needles, seemed very pleased with itself.

Ever see an ogre after a mob of bereaved parents gets through with her?

Didn't think so. But I have.

Certain human responses can trump even an ogre's fell enchantments. Watching twenty kids disappear right out from under your helpless gaze all because your mayor was a cheapskate might induce a few of them. Hanging was the least of what they did to her. The only way I knew her was by the tattered crimson of her gown.

Mortals. Mortals and their infernal ingenuity. I shook my head in admiration.

And was that . . . ?

Yes, it was! Indeed, it was! My old friend, Henchmen Hans himself. Loyal to the end, swinging from a rope of his own near the mayoral gallows branch. And wearing his second best suit, too, bless him. Though torn and more than a little stained, his second best was a far sight better than what I presently wore. Needed something a bit more flamboyant than a dog blanket, didn't I, if I was going to visit Lake Serenus in the morning? Bring a swan girl a fresh bag of caramels. Help her babysit. You know. Like you do.

Waste not, want not—isn't that what the wharf boys say? A Rat Folk philosophy if I ever heard one. So, yeah, I'd be stripping my good old pal

Hans right down to his bare essentials, or I'm not my mother's son. And then I'd strip him of more than that.

See, I'd had to share the Pied Piper's fine repast with three starving mortal children earlier that night. It's not that they didn't deserve their victuals as much as, say, I (although, really, who did?), and it's not like Nicolas didn't press me to eat seconds and thirds. But I still hadn't gotten nearly as much as my ravenous little rat's heart desired.

The juniper tree whispered.

It might have said anything.

But I'm pretty sure I heard, "Help yourself, Maurice."

JOHNNY REV

Rachel Pollack

That was your black double. You aren't who you think you are.
—Flannery O'Connor, "Everything That Rises Must Converge"

PROLOGUE

In his early years as a Traveler, Jack Shade, Rebel Jack, as people would later call him, studied with the legendary teacher known as Anatolie. He didn't really know her fame at the time, only that she was the one whose name he'd been given by the lion-tamer who'd first shown Carny Jack a glimpse of the Real World in the mouth of a lion.

In the years Jack studied with Anatolie, she annoyed him as much as inspired him, not least because at something like five hundred pounds she did not get around much, and Jack sometimes thought he was more errand boy than apprentice. One day he went to see her in her fifth-floor walk-up on Bayard Street in Chinatown, and as usual had stopped in at the Lucky Star restaurant to pick up the order she'd called down when she knew he was coming. Most of the time Jack didn't really mind bringing her food, but that day he decided he'd had enough. It was time to tell her some hard truth. "Why don't you get a ground-floor apartment?" he said as he arranged the food on a tray big enough to go across her belly. "Or at least one of those lofts with an old freight elevator."

"And why is that, Jack?" she asked softly, as her ancient bone chopsticks began to ferry *har kow* to her wide, flat face.

Jack should have recognized that tone and backed off but he was feeling reckless. Years later, a dealer in the Ibis Casino would tell him, "You were always Johnny Danger back then. Or maybe just Jack Crazy."

"So you can actually leave the house now and then," he told her. "Get out in the street. Experience picking up your own food."

"Oh, Jack," she said, "you still think things are as they appear?" As she moved on to shredded pork and puffed tofu in ginger sauce, she said, in that same bland voice, "Perhaps you should go. You don't seem in the mood for a lesson."

"Great," Jack said. "All this way just to drag your food upstairs."

"Oh, by the way," she said as he was about to leave, "pay attention on the way home. You wouldn't want to miss anything." Jack made a noise and slammed the door.

He was so annoyed he didn't notice anything strange until he was on Canal Street, heading for the No. 6 Subway, and a large woman in a bright red parka bumped into him. She was moving so fast, with heavy shopping bags in each hand like pendulum weights, she almost knocked Jack down. "Hey!" he yelled, and was about to add something very New York when he noticed the woman's gait and the set of her shoulders. "Anatolie?" he said, but not loud enough for her to hear him as she moved through the crowds of shoppers, tourists, and hucksters.

It can't be, he told himself. Even if she could get herself up and dressed and downstairs without his help, how would she have had the time to catch up with him? Distracted, he found himself going past a knock-off shop, the kind of place with oversize, over-bling watches and fall-apart luggage out front, but fake Prada hidden in the back for the right sort of customer. A skinny Chinese man with greasy hair was pretending to flirt with a trio of white teenage girls from the suburbs in hopes they might buy his phony Pandora bracelets. Jack paid no attention until the man called out, "Rolex watch, Jack. Look just like real."

Jack spun around, and in place of the Chinese hustler stood Anatolie, so large she filled the doorway. She held up the watch. "Good quality, Jack. No tell difference."

Jack wasn't sure he could breathe. He turned to the three girls to ask if they too saw the large black woman, only to discover that their skin had darkened and their over-gelled bleached hair had snaked into long dreadlocks. All three nodded and smiled at him.

Jack tried to escape into the crowd but it was no good. The old Chinese ladies with their net shopping bags filled with bok choy and tofu, the guys behind the fried-noodle stands, the homeless man pretending he had someplace to go, the art students with plastic bags from Pearl Paint—they were all *her*.

He did his best not to look at anyone, at least not close enough to see them change, as he rushed back to Bayard Street. For just a second he considered picking up a bribe at Lucky Star, but was pretty sure he couldn't take it if cheerful, loud Mrs. Shen became a five-hundred-pound black woman with dreads that wound around her waist like that Norse serpent that holds together the world. So instead he just ran upstairs, burst into her apartment where of course she was still lying on her oversized, reinforced bed, empty takeout cartons all around her, and he begged her, "Make it stop. Please. I get it, I'm sorry, I'll never say you can't leave your apartment again. Please. You can't be everyone."

She laced her hands across her belly. "Are you sure about that, Jack? Maybe there's just one person in the world, and we're all Duplicates." Jack stared at her, confused. Finally she smiled, and said, "You can go now. It's safe."

He hesitated a moment, then left. All the way home everyone remained themselves, but even so, he stood a long time outside his door before he went inside. For what if his wife Layla's olive skin had turned dark brown, or eleven-year-old Eugenia had put on four hundred pounds?

Now

Jack Shade was walking down Lafayette Street, heading toward Canal, when the Momentary Storm hit. He was on his way to buy a stone frog from Mr. Suke (not his real name) as a present for Carolien Hounstra, Jack's colleague in the New York Travelers' Aid Society. Generous Jack, people called him, though usually not without a half-smile and a lifted eyebrow.

Carolien collected frogs, had many shelves of them in her West Side apartment. Some were netsuke, others jade or malachite or onyx, and a few were so old it was hard to tell what they were. There was a story people liked to tell about Carolien's hobby, that an ancestor had been turned into a stone frog by some malevolent Traveler, or maybe a vindictive Power, and Carolien hoped to find him and turn him back. Others claimed it wasn't an ancestor but an older, or younger, brother, and the enactment had retroactively aged the carving to make it harder to find him. Still others claimed it was Carolien herself who'd stoned her brother—or maybe a lover who'd jilted her—and had done too good a job, so that when remorse set in she couldn't locate him. This last group consisted mostly of people whose advances Carolien had rejected. "The Dutch Ice Queen," some called her, a term that always made Jack laugh or shake his head.

Jack doubted the truth of all these stories. It wasn't that he believed Carolien would not try to rescue a relative. He'd seen how she'd dropped her work at NYTAS and everything else, including Jack, when her teenage cousin from Rotterdam had come to New York for a couple of weeks. No, it was just that people liked to make up stories about her. Six feet tall, one hundred eighty-five pounds, and very Dutch, with long blond hair, large breasts, and a tendency to say or do whatever she wanted, she was a natural target. She didn't appear to notice, but Jack thought that might be an act.

If Jack doubted that Carolien had a relative who'd been turned into a frog, he strongly suspected that Mr. Suke was in fact a frog who'd been turned into a man. He just wasn't sure if the frog Suke had been alive or carved. Jack was wondering if he should outright ask him, and whether that might violate some code of privacy, when he felt something brush against his leg. He smiled, and looked down to see Ray, his reddish-gold spirit fox, moving his tail to get Jack's attention. No one could see Ray but Jack, so when he spoke he kept his voice low. "What is it, buddy? What do you want me to see?"

Ray lifted his head to point his snout downtown, and Jack followed the line of sight to the helix-shaped tower of the new World Trade Center. As Jack watched, a dark cloud rolled over it, until all you could see was grey sky. *Oh shit*, Jack thought, *not again*. But then he heard someone to his left say, "Jesus, look at that," and someone else say, "You can't even see it," and Jack let out a breath. Not an omen, then, or at least not just for his eyes only.

It would take a few minutes before he realized how wrong he was.

As Jack and everyone else watched, the dark cloud poured toward them. Soon it began to rain, hard slashing drops that sent umbrellas and coat collars up, and a few people scrambling into doorways. Jack just stood there, squinting at the rain as if the drops might form a pattern. He looked down and Ray was still at his side, body rigid, tail straight out, telling Jack there was something in the rain. Something about Ray . . . his tail was wet! How could—

A border storm! Half in this world, half in the Other. *Shit*, Jack thought. He didn't like border crossings, no one did. You could meet your mirror, your Traveler From The Other Side, and then things would get really tangled. Some people said that that was how Peter Midnight, all those years ago, had lost Manhattan to the Man in the Black Cravat.

Hold steady, Jack told himself. Even if it was a border crossing it was just a shower. And then the hail started. Not huge, about the size of a shooter marble, it came down heavy, and on wild swirls of wind, so that anyone who'd braved the rain now ran inside shops or doorways. Except Jack. Even Ray had vanished, but Jack knew he couldn't leave, there was something he was supposed to see.

The hail began to move around itself, separating, coming together, forming shapes, columns—a man. Vague at first, not as defined as, say, the Face on Mars (set up by some prank Traveler to embarrass NASA) but still clear. Tall, strong-looking yet somehow graceful, with the long, tapered fingers that marked a Traveler. Jack squinted at him, the posture, the shape of the head. "No," he whispered. Light appeared in the face. Whether from a flash of lightning, or the sun coming through a gap in the storm, it lit up the right jawline from the ear almost to the mouth, showing a surface smooth as melted gold. Down Jack's jawline, his scar throbbed.

"Oh fuck," Jack said, then loud, shouting, "You're dead! I killed you, goddamnit. I *killed* you!"

It took a couple of seconds for Jack to realize that the hail had stopped, and the sun now lit up the street and people had ventured back into the open, only to stare nervously at this man who'd just screamed about killing someone. Some already had their phones out, to call 911 or to take a picture. Either one was as bad as the other. Quickly, Jack glammed himself so that no one would remember him and any pictures they took would be blurred. Then he turned and headed uptown. Carolien's frog would have to wait.

Jack and Irene Yao were playing mahjong in Jack's office in the Hotel de Rêve Noire. The office was really just a two-room suite several floors down from the larger suite where Jack had lived for the past nine years. Irene owned the hotel, but she and Jack had long ago become friends. Elegant as always, the fiftyish woman had let loose her long grey-black hair to flow gently down the back of her maroon linen dress. Jack himself wore a pale yellow shirt, collar unbuttoned, dark brown pleated pants, and a thin red silk tie draped around his neck.

They played with a three-hundred-year-old set of ivory tiles backed with bamboo. Jack couldn't remember exactly when they'd started playing together, but it was always just the two of them, and never for money. Jack was a high-stakes poker player, and even though mahjong was closer to gin rummy, he didn't want to trigger his professional skills by letting the game get serious. At the same time, he kept wondering if Irene was setting him up somehow. The tiles had been in her family a long time.

Two soft knocks came at the door. Startled, Jack looked up from his hand to see that Irene was gone, her empty chair slightly away from the table. Another knock, just one this time, and Jack stared at the back of the door, eyes narrowed. He knew that sound, knew what it meant. He glanced once more at the empty chair, then stood up and went to open the door. Sure enough, Mrs. Yao stood there, dressed the same but with her hair up, and yes, she was holding the small silver tray with Jack's card on it. "Mr. Shade," she said. It was only "Mrs. Yao" and "Mr. Shade" when Jack was working.

Jack looked down at the card. "John Shade, Traveler," it read, and the name of the hotel, and the black horse's head from the Staunton chess knight. Only, someone, the client, Jack assumed, had scratched a jagged line through the embossed head. Like a scar.

Jack didn't need any work at this point. A few months back he'd taken a case to find a missing woman who'd turned out to be the Queen of Eyes, holder of all the world's oracular power. Jack hadn't asked for a fee when the case ended, but a few weeks later his client, the Queen's daughter, had shown up with a check for 100K. Jack was pretty sure the money had come from *La Societé de Matin*, the international order of gangster magicians— his finding the Queen had helped them avoid a faction war—but that was okay. He'd earned it. So he didn't need to work, and didn't want to, but a curse Jack had foolishly put on himself years earlier gave him no choice. If someone showed up with Jack's business card Jack could not refuse the case. Travelers called this compulsory obligation a "Guest," after an old Irish term, *geass*.

Jack sighed. "Thank you, Mrs. Yao," he said, and took the card from the tray. It was cold.

When he looked up, Mrs. Yao was crying. Jack had never asked her how much she knew, but he suspected it was more than she let on. "It's all right," he said. "It's just a case."

She dabbed at her eyes with a fingertip. "I'm sorry," she said, then, "He's downstairs. In your office."

"What—?" Jack looked around, saw he was in the living room of his suite. Hadn't they been—weren't they—something was wrong. For a second, Ray appeared, fur bristling, then vanished, as if—as if someone was blocking him. But Ray belonged to Jack, who could interfere with that?

And then Jack was in his office, sitting at the mahogany table that served as his desk, and across from him sat a man who was hard to see. He looked around Jack's height and weight, six feet and a hundred seventy-five pounds, and was dressed in an open-necked black shirt, black jeans, scuffed cowboy boots, and a long, unbuttoned black leather coat. His face was hard to make out, sometimes blurred, at other moments deeply shadowed. Except—down his jawline, from his ear to his mouth, ran a jagged line of golden light. Only when Jack unconsciously touched his own face did he realize that the light followed the path of his scar.

Jesus, Jack thought. *I'm dreaming*. This was all a goddamn dream. He almost laughed. People could attack you in dreams, but it was easy enough to fend them off.

"I have a case for you," the man said, his voice a harsh whisper.

Jack leaned back in his chair. "Go ahead," he said.

"I have an enemy. Someone who wants to destroy me."

"Do you know why?"

The hidden face flashed brightly, then a moment later faded back into darkness. "It doesn't matter," the man said. "You've got to make him stop."

"How do I do that?"

"You'll find a way. That's what you do, isn't it? I'm hiring you to beat him. I want to win."

Jack said, "I can't just kill him."

"Why not? He tried to kill me, didn't he?"

"You haven't told me who he is," Jack said. "What's his name?"

The man shook his head. "No, no, no, that's the wrong question."

Jack felt his voice dry up, as harsh now as the man's rasping whisper. "What's the right question?"

"*My* name," the man said. Now he leaned forward, as if to bring his face into the light. "You're supposed to ask who *I* am. Isn't that right, Johnny? Isn't that the first step?"

Jack came awake in his bed with a shout. Despite everything, his Traveler training told him it was 4:17 in the morning. The narrow steel posts at the corners of his bed glowed slightly, as if heated. He lay there, unable to move or breathe. *It was him!* The Dupe. Jack Fake. Hidden Johnny. The Man Without A Scar. And now it turned out that the Dupe—the fucking Duplicate—was also a goddamn *Revenant*. Johnny Rev. The Man Who Didn't Leave.

"Goddamn it," Jack said out loud. What the fuck did he do now? His own Revenant had hired him. Did it make any difference that it was in a dream? Dream Johnny still had Jack's card, didn't he? And the man the Rev wanted Jack to kill? Well shit, that was easy enough to figure out. That could only be Jack himself.

People make Dupes for all sorts of reasons—to assist in some enactment, to take their place in a dangerous operation, to trick an enemy or escape a trap. Jack Shade was probably the only Traveler to duplicate himself to go speak to his mother-in-law.

On the worst day of Jack Shade's life, after the poltergeist that had possessed his daughter Eugenia had killed Jack's wife—after Jack himself had tried to save his daughter and ended up exiling her as the only living resident in the Forest of Souls, that dark woods of the unhappy dead—as Jack squatted next to Layla's body on the blood-drenched kitchen floor, rocking back and forth, howling—the doorbell rang.

Jack could never say for sure what drove him to answer it. Did he think it was the police and he should just give himself up? Did he imagine it was a team from NYTAS, the New York Travelers Aid Society, come to take him away for endangering Traveler anonymity? Or did he somehow hope it was Layla's remnant, come to forgive him, and together they would go to rescue Genie? But when Jack opened the door, barely conscious of the blood running down his face and neck from the knives the geist had flung at him, what he saw was indeed a dead person. Just not his wife.

Elvis Presley stood there, young and dangerous, with that lush Captain Marvel Jr. haircut, dressed in worn jeans and denim jacket and a dark T-shirt, and a pair of very scuffed blue shoes. Elvis looked Jack up and down, then cocked his head, as if to say *Yeah, brother, I've had days like that.* Instead, all he said was "Hey, man, my damn truck's gone and over-heated on me." Jack couldn't help himself, he glanced past Elvis to where a rusty old Chevy pickup, from around 1955, was parked at the curb. It sure looked real enough, as oily steam came off the filthy hood. Elvis said, "Ain't nothin' I can do but let it cool down some. So I figured maybe I could go see if there was a friendly face around." He grinned. "And shit, maybe some beer and peanut butter."

Not sure he could speak, Jack just nodded and stepped aside for Elvis to enter the house.

Almost from the moment of his death, Elvis Presley had been a member of the most exclusive group of Friends and Helpers this poor suffering world has ever known, the Dead Quartet. Except for its leader, the Quartet's personnel changed with the times. The current lineup consisted of Joan of Arc, permanent anchor and chief, plus Nelson Mandela, Princess Di, and Elvis.

Anytime someone new joined, he or she wiped people's memories clean of the person they replaced, but that didn't stop people who knew from speculating. Carolien Hounstra had made it a kind of hobby to try to track down any traces of previous members. She was pretty sure that Joan had originally taken over from the Quartet's founder, the Virgin Mary. Mary had gotten sick of it and agreed to Joan's demand for a permanent slot. Di, Carolien said, had replaced Eleanor Roosevelt. She was less sure about Mandela, thinking Che Guevara or Gandhi. And Elvis, she suspected, had taken over from either James Dean or maybe Billie Holiday.

What the Quartet did was pretty simple. They helped people. People lonely, desperate, all out of money, friends, or hope. They were said to specialize: Joan to warriors, queer people, and the young whom everyone had deserted; Di came to the sick and abandoned; Madiba to people in the low ebb of a long struggle; and Elvis to ordinary folks with weights that were too damn heavy, and no one to help carry the load. Jack Shade was not exactly ordinary, but he sure as hell qualified otherwise. In fact, since Elvis mostly showed up at gas stations and 7-Elevens, his appearance at Jack's door made it clear how much Jack needed him.

Jack said, "Come on," and headed for the kitchen with Elvis behind him, as if all that mattered was peanut butter and beer.

When Elvis saw the body he shook his head. "Jesus, man," he said. "You really are in trouble. You off your old lady?" Jack stared at him. "Hey," Elvis said, "wouldn't be the first time. People fight, they get carried away."

"Bullshit," Jack said. "You know what happened here."

Elvis looked at him a long time, then said, "Yeah, I guess I do. Thing is, man, not everybody can see like I can. Anyone who heard anything, anyone who just come up to the door, they're going to see shit they won't understand. You got to take care of this, man."

Jack found himself shaking so hard he had to grab hold of the kitchen table. When he saw that his hands were covered in blood his first thought was that he better not stain Layla's antique oak table, she'd be really pissed off. And then he wondered, was it his blood or hers? He remembered then, he'd been down on the floor, holding her, even as a stone door had opened in the air and a kind of wind had pulled his daughter into the Forest of Souls. He looked at Elvis. "What am I going to do?" he said.

Elvis nodded. "Okay. First thing you gotta do is cast one of them things around the house. What d'you call 'em?"

It took Jack a moment, then he said, "Oh, right. A glamour."

"Yeah. Funny word for it, huh?"

"It's old," Jack muttered. He closed his eyes to concentrate. A glam wouldn't solve anything but it would keep outsiders—non-Travelers, or "nons" as some people called them—from noticing anything.

It was a simple enough action, but it took Jack three tries to get it right. When he did, however, he discovered he felt a little stronger. No cops were going to rush in and take Layla's body away from him. He looked at Elvis. "Thanks," he said.

Elvis shrugged. "Sure. But you know, Jack—" Despite everything, a smile flickered across Jack's face, for he was pretty sure he hadn't told Elvis his name "—this ain't an answer. You're going to have to call those guys in." Jack looked at him. "What do you call them, COLE?"

Jack sighed. "Yeah, I know." The Committee of Linear Explanation existed to clean up messes that the outside world couldn't know about. Without them, Jack could be arrested for killing his wife. And probably his daughter. God knows what the cops would think he'd done with Genie's body. He squeezed shut his eyes a moment, made a face and shook his head, like a child trying to banish everything. But that's what COLE would do, make it as if it had never happened, cast some alternate reality sheet over everything, so that as far as the outside world was concerned, Layla and Genie had just—what, gone on a trip? Left him? Died in some fucking tragic accident? "Shit," Jack said.

Elvis said, "I'll tell you a secret, man. I always loved his singing."

"What?"

"Nat King Cole. He could do that kind of velvety cat voice, but every word was clear as a bell. I always wished I could sing like that. Y'know, they called me 'King,' but he really was. I mean, he was colored and all, but the best goddamn singer I ever heard." Then he smiled sheepishly and waved a hand. "Shit," he said. "No offense, man."

Jack shrugged. "None taken." He stared down at his hands, at Layla's blood.

Elvis put an arm around Jack's shoulders. "Tell you what, man. It's gonna take a while for my truck to cool down. What do you say we grab a couple of cold ones and you tell me about your wife and kid. COLE can fuckin' wait, right?"

So Jack Shade and Elvis Presley sat down at Layla's oak table, knives and cleavers scattered on the floor, with Layla's body at their feet and Genie gone where probably even Elvis and the whole Quartet couldn't find her. And Jack talked about how he and Layla first met, before he was even a Traveler, how he was a carny magician back then, making a few extra bucks doing tricks at a wedding where Layla Nazeer was one of the bridesmaids. They'd gone out for a while, and Jack was smitten, but then he'd lost track of her in the upheaval when he saw the stars and galaxies in a lion's mouth, and his life changed forever.

Jack found Layla again when his teacher, Anatolie, sent him on a training mission to de-possess a law firm. Jack always suspected that Anatolie knew that Layla was working there as a paralegal, but when he asked Anatolie, she accused him of "distraction," the great danger to apprentice Travelers.

When he told Elvis that, Jack had to stop a moment. Not just apprentices, he thought. *Distraction* was what had killed his wife. If he'd been paying fucking attention to the geist that was taking over their daughter, shit, if he'd listened to his wife's fears instead of telling her that poltergeists were harmless—

Jack threw his bottle against the wall. It didn't break. He was shaking now, staring at his wife's body.

Elvis said, "S'okay, man. There's more in the fridge, right?" He brought Jack a fresh bottle. Jack stared at it for what felt like a long time, then took a swallow and began to talk about what it was like when Genie was born.

They went on until dawn, and then Elvis stood up, rolled his head on his neck, as if to loosen his ghostly muscles, and said, "Well, I guess my damn truck's probably okay now. Maybe it's time you called COLE."

"Wait!" Jack said.

"C'mon, man. You can't just stay here in a glammed house. You've got to let her go."

Jack said "What do I do about her mother?" Elvis stared at him.

Nadia Nazeer had never liked Jack Shade. It wasn't an ethnic thing, or at least not overmuch. As Layla had said to him once, if he were an Arab but still himself, her mother probably would have felt the same about him. Maybe if they could have told her who Jack really was, what he did, Nadia might have felt less disappointed in her daughter's choice. Maybe not. Once, after a tense weekend at her mother's house, Layla had done an impression of how her mother might react to the idea of a Traveler. "Sorcery?" she'd said, in Nadia's cultured, scornful voice. "Seriously, darling? Does he go around trapping wayward djinn in old whiskey bottles?"

Jack had said, "Actually, Coke bottles work much better. So long as it's not New Coke," and the two of them had laughed so loud someone at a stoplight turned to stare at them.

Nadia never liked Jack. It wasn't just that she considered him a selfish, lowlife gambler who needed to grow up and get a real job—for after all, what could they tell her except that Jack made his living playing poker? As much as she could barely tolerate her son-in-law, Nadia's real problem was her daughter. A successful businesswoman who'd started out selling cheap jewelry, she'd wanted her daughter to "become something," and considered Jack, and even Eugenia, as Layla's retreat from the world.

All this, Jack poured out to Elvis, and more, things he'd never told anyone, not even Layla herself, like the day Nadia had summoned him to her grand office overlooking Lower Manhattan and tried to get him to leave her daughter. The whole time she was going on about "authentic love" and "sacrifice," Jack kept thinking of things he could do to make her stop. Seal her mouth, of course, but less drastically he could summon a Momentary Storm to drown her out with thunder. Or maybe animate the intricate little metal animals she kept on her desk, and send her screaming from the room. But he'd done none of those things, just sat there through the whole speech, even agreed to "give it your full consideration," because after all, she was his wife's mother, and what would Layla say if her mother reported to her some very strange things that had happened when she was talking to Jack?

"You know," Elvis said, somewhere around the sixth or seventh beer, "your pals in COLE could take care of it."

Jack shook his head. "I can't do that. Let them fuck with her mind, her memories? Even if I make up some lie—I mean, I have to, right, I can hardly tell her the truth—at least it will come from me, face to face. Not some fucking Traveler bureaucracy."

Elvis took a swallow of beer. "If you say so, man."

• • •

Only, when the time came, Jack couldn't do it. He kept bracing himself, swearing he would do it the very next day, before the funeral, after the funeral, and yet he just couldn't face her. Finally, he just decided to make a Duplicate.

There were two kinds of Dupes, "momentary" and "permanent." Momentary Dupes were little more than illusions, like a glamour. They faded as soon as their task was done. For something as complicated as talking to a mother-in-law, you needed the real thing, a replicant that actually existed in the world. Still, the process was stressful but not that difficult, a bit like making a golem, except with more exacting standards, since a golem didn't have to look or sound like anyone in particular. And where a golem could be made of pretty much anything—synagogue dirt, originally, but now garbage, junk mail, recycled cardboard, even plastic (but no Styrofoam), a Dupe needed "donations." Bits of skin from the palms (you had to be careful not to draw blood), clippings from the fourth toe of the non-dominant foot, blood from the little finger of your dominant hand, hair clippings, dirt washed off the body at dawn, sexual fluids taken at midnight, small amounts of urine and feces.

Along with all these physical traces, you had to include some favorite article of clothing or jewelry, money that had been in your pocket or wallet for at least forty-eight hours, and what the manual called "a life token," a photo from a special trip, a ticket stub, an old baseball cap, whatever you'd saved just because it was more than itself. There was a famous story of a woman from an abusive family who'd destroyed all the remnants of her childhood, only to become a Traveler and have to sneak into her parents' house to find something they'd kept that she could use to make a Duplicate. Finally, you were supposed to write fragments of memory, fear, and desire on bits of paper and then cut them up to sprinkle over the mix.

Jack did the operation on the roof of the hotel an hour before dawn, careful to glam the stairway so that any insomniac who'd taken it in his head to look at the city would change his mind and go back to bed. Carefully, he undressed and folded his clothes according to exact instructions, then placed them on a small metal table in the northwest corner of the roof. The Act of Assembly, as the operation was called, was not difficult but had to be done correctly.

It was late August. The night had been cool, and now a sharp breeze tingled Jack's skin as he set down his donations then drew a circle with blue chalk around the small pile and himself. He sat facing due east, his bits of self stacked in front of him. For a moment, he looked at the first glimpses of purple in the night sky, then sighed, and shut his eyes.

Step by step, Jack "closed the gates." Legs and arms crossed, he pressed his lips together, curled his tongue back against the roof of his mouth, stilled his ear drums, narrowed his nostrils, squeezed shut his sphincters. After several minutes like this, a figure began to take shape in the world behind Jack's eyes. The Unknown Traveler, this visitor was called, and even though you could never see him or her, you somehow always knew s/he had your face.

Wholly in the inner world, without actually moving his lips or tongue, Jack said, "I thank you for your Presence. I, Jack Shade, have assembled these donations and fragments of my true self, inner and outer, that they may serve my needs, without selfishness or blame, with all honor to the Founders of our practice, the First Travelers, who opened the way and laid down the paths." There was a time when Jack might have wanted to roll his eyes at the language required for things like this. But not that day.

The Unknown faded, and something else began to take shape, little more than a shimmer of dull light. Now was the time to get to work. The raw form would assemble itself through the power of the donations, but it was up to him to shape it, to get it right. Jack had spent the past four hours staring at himself in the full-length mirror in his bedroom, noticing the tilt of his shoulders, the bends of his fingers, the length and roughness of his ropy hair, the turn of his nose, the left ear a bit larger than the right, the way his left big toe curled slightly inward, the dents in his rib-cage from old fights, the crease in his hips, the knife scar from his battle at the Bronx Gate of Paradise.

On the rooftop, he assembled his Duplicate step by step, detail by detail, getting everything exactly right—until the very end, when it came time to recreate the freshly formed scar that ran down Jack's jawline. He started it, could see it taking shape, almost there. And then suddenly he dismissed it, so that when he abruptly opened his eyes the figure that stood before him was his old self, Johnny Handsome, as Layla had once called him.

It didn't appear to make any difference. Jack spoke the Standard Formula to Activate a Duplicate, "I have assembled you and you will do my will," and the Dupe answered correctly, "You have assembled me and I will do your will."

Now, sitting alone in his bedroom, an hour after the dream had woken him, a glass of Johnnie Walker Blue in his hand, Jack wondered why the hell he'd done that, leave off the damn scar. To make it easier to talk to Nadia was the simple answer. COLE's cover story had indeed been a tragic car accident, and to keep things simple, Jack was supposed to have been far away when it happened, so how would he explain a scar? But he could have glammed the Dupe so that Nadia wouldn't notice. COLE had already set Nadia and everyone else at the funeral not to notice Jack's face, or wonder why Genie's coffin was sealed before anyone could ask to see the supposedly mangled body.

So was it just vanity? The desire to see himself as unspoiled one last time? Jack grimaced, took a sip of whiskey. He didn't like introspection, considered it an indulgence. "*Schatje,*" Carolien had told him recently, using the Dutch word for *sweetheart,* "no one will ever confuse you with Hamlet." Now, however, he had no choice. If he was going to get out of this mess he had to know exactly how he'd gotten into it. Did he just not want to see what he'd become?

Looking at a copy of yourself is hard enough in normal circumstances, not at all like looking in a mirror. When we look in a mirror we automatically compose ourselves, turn or tilt our heads the best way, smile or open our eyes. Looking at a Dupe is like seeing yourself on video, only worse.

He got up and went to the window. The antenna on the Empire State Building flared red for a few seconds then returned to anonymous metal. No, not vanity. Because he remembered how after it was all over—or so he thought—he'd gone back to the house, to his and Layla's bedroom, where she'd kept her old-fashioned framed photographs on top of the dresser, and he remembered how he'd picked up a vacation picture of the three of them, back when Genie was seven, all of them laughing as they posed with some guy in a Batman suit. It wasn't vanity to make the Dupe like he used to be. It was nostalgia. Looking at Handsome Johnny, Jack could pretend, for just a moment, that none of it had ever happened. That it was all a dream.

And at the time it had seemed like no harm had been done. He'd taken care of Nadia, given her an outlet for her anger and grief, and then he'd gotten rid of the Dupe—or so he thought—and everything was good. Only—

The working to destroy a Dupe is called the Act of Dissolution. It's complicated but fairly straightforward, easier than the Assembly, for the Dupe is just a copy, with no will of its own, and cannot help but cooperate in the operation to collapse it into a kind of dust that will simply blow away. Unless the practitioner makes a mistake.

If you don't do it exactly right, if you leave even a shred of the construction untouched by the working, there's a chance the Dupe can reconstitute itself. Coalesce, people called it. Once it re-formed on its own, it became a Revenant, a very different creature entirely, with a will to survive all its own. Revs sometimes tried to take over the lives of dead people, not realizing how disturbing that would be. More commonly, they attacked their originals, showed up at their homes, or work, and claimed they were the real thing.

In rare cases, they killed the originals to make it easier. "Shit," Jack said out loud. As far as he knew, no Rev had ever hired the original to kill himself.

He took another sip of Scotch, vaguely aware he was hardly tasting one of the world's most expensive whiskeys. Down in the street, people rushed back and forth with that purposeful New York stride that never changed, day or night. They all looked the same. Maybe they were all Duplicates, Jack thought.

Jack made a noise, rolled his head around to loosen his neck muscles. He'd been up all night, partly to try to figure it all out, and partly to avoid any more dreams.

Why in a dream? If his Dupe had reassembled and wanted to attack its maker, why not just go at the body, Jack-in-the-world? Maybe the Rev wasn't strong enough. He might still be forming, and a dream body was the best he could manage. In that case, the answer was simple. No more dreams. Never go to sleep. Jack laughed and drank some Scotch.

There was another reason the Dupe might be using dreams, and it was one Jack didn't really want to think about. Two months before, Jack had broken up with a woman named Elaynora Horne. He and El had dated for nine months or so, after meeting outside a Traveler safe house in Red Hook, New York. It wasn't a nasty break up. No broken plates, no yelling, no spells directed at anyone's genitals. Just a generic two adults—this isn't working out—no hard feelings—standard issue. It made things a little complicated that Jack was a Traveler. It made them a little more so that Elaynora Horne was a Dream Hunter.

Elaynora's father was a dispossessed sun god. The tribe that had worshipped him had died out, their lands taken over by outsiders who'd brought in their own gods and astronomical spirits. The lost tribe must have spoken a weird language because Dad's true name was so filled with impossible noises that Jack just called him "Papa Click and Whistle." He had a human name, however, Alexander Horne. It was a professional name, really. Unlike some of his ilk, he did not just ascend to some higher realm to sulk for a few thousand years. And because the tribe who'd worshipped him had believed that dreams came from the sun (true, as far as it went, but they had to pass through the moon to reach us), Mr. Horne now ran a dream agency.

Dream hunters were an odd group. Some of their work was as simple as leading people to solve a problem or be inspired while they slept. Sometimes they helped Travelers get to places they couldn't reach awake. Or they acted as bodyguards against Nightworld mercenaries. Or took on mercenary work themselves. El insisted that she and her father never did that kind of job. "Why should we, Jack? We have a long waiting list."

Maybe El would not stoop to battle-for-hire, but what if she had a personal reason? Jack sighed. There was no way around it, he had to know.

He went over to the hotel desk and opened his laptop to log on to Jinn-Net. When the familiar flashes of fire and wisps of vapor appeared, he clicked on an app titled Teraph.wiz. Soon a child's head appeared, milky face crowned ostentatiously with golden curls. It looked amazed, and frightened, as if it had just turned a corner and seen an angel, or worse. Except it couldn't have turned any corners, for there was just a head. No blood appeared—why be gruesome?—but vague tendrils hung down from the neck.

Originally, long before computer graphics, a *teraph* was an actual severed head. The action was so old no one knew its origins, but if you knew the spell—and had the stomach for it—you could find some kid at the cusp of puberty, behead it, and keep the poor head alive as an oracle. In 1434 the Travelers, and the Powers, and the Renaissance version of COLE had banned the practice. Jack knew of only one modern attempt to create a genuine teraph. In 1927, a sorcerer from *La Societé de Matin* kidnapped a twelve-year-old girl in Lyon. Though the *Societé* are an order of gangsters, they tracked down the renegade before he could really harm the girl—the spell takes nine days—sent her home glammed up to forget everything, then stuck the magician's own head on a pike outside the Lyon Gate of Paradise.

So no, there were no actual teraphim. But that didn't prevent computer simulations. Jack stared at the revolving image. Like its inspiration in the human world, the AI version of a teraph existed half in this world (or at least the online version) and half in the NL, the Non-Linear. Even though it was just a face on a screen, you had to catch its eye, which meant hitting control/enter the instant it looked at you. It took Jack three tries but finally the head stopped spinning.

Jack thought he saw the mouth turn up slightly as a high adolescent voice said, "Jack Shade. Time has passed since you saw us last." Like all oracles, physical or virtual, the teraph spoke in the "divinatory we." And was given to bad poetry.

"Yes," Jack said. "I rejoice to see you, and beg the blessing of your wise sight."

"Very well. You may speak your question."

Jack took a breath. "Is Elaynora Horne helping my Duplicate to attack me?"

The eyes rolled back, and a clicking sound came from the animated mouth. Jack waited for the inevitably vague answer, but when the face focused on him again it said simply, "No. New grass grows clean."

"Thank you!" Jack said. The eyes closed and the head began to spin, the signal that Jack's audience had ended. He turned off his computer. Okay, he thought. Whatever the hell was going on, El wasn't behind it.

Suddenly Jack was exhausted. He hadn't gone to bed until 2:30, and of course had woken up at 4:17. He squinted out at the sky. The sun had not made it over the buildings yet, but it was definitely morning. If you were under attack by dreams, mornings were a lot safer time to sleep than at night. Jack had no idea why. Maybe dreams were photosensitive and couldn't find their targets during the day. Or maybe they followed strict union rules and clocked out at dawn. Jack didn't care, he just hoped that with daylight, and the protection he'd put around his bed, he could sleep safely for a couple of hours.

Like most Travelers, Jack had aligned his bed on a strict polar axis, with the head at north. Four thin silver poles bolted to the floor at the corners created invisible walls around the bed. Now Jack had made those walls real by running copper netting from pole to pole. Dream net, it was called, and looked like mosquito netting, but with an even finer mesh. Some people said dream net was the origin of those New Age toys called "dream-catchers," but instead of trying to grab hold of a spiritual dream (whatever that might be), dream net was meant to block hostile or dangerous dreams from getting to you.

Jack tossed off the hotel robe he'd been wearing since he woke up, then went to the closet to remove his carbon blade knife from its hidden sheath in his boot. A knife resting on your solar plexus, with the blade pointed up toward the heart, gave you added protection. He moved aside the netting on the west wall and laid himself down. Hands loosely on his knife, Jack closed his eyes.

—Ray was walking before him, moving with quick urgent steps, looking back now and then to make sure Jack was following him, letting out short yips, as if to say, "Come on, come on." Jack knew he was dreaming, but also it was safe, for Ray was there, and in his aspect, his red fur giving off flashes of light. Ray was a Fox of the Morning, a solar emanation, and had been with Jack for years, ever since Jack had found himself under attack by demonic chickens.

They were walking through one of the desolated neighborhoods on the outer fringes of the city, with boarded-up windows, urine stench, and doorways and any empty spaces strewn with needles, condoms, and what appeared to be fragments of bodies. Jack didn't look too close. "Hey, homey," a voice slurred, "you wan' some?" Jack couldn't tell if it was a man or a woman and figured maybe that was the idea. He just watched Ray.

The yipping noises speeded up until Ray suddenly stopped, right in the middle of the street, body all stiff as he stared at the courtyard of one of those gulag-like "projects" the city had put up back in the fifties and sixties with such good intentions.

It took Jack a moment to notice the old man picking up small objects, examining them, then throwing some away and stuffing the others in a large canvas bag. You had to look hard to keep track of him, for sometimes he became all shadows, then at other moments vanished in bursts of light. Half turning his head to the left and squinting, Jack managed to get a better view of the man. He wore an oversize dark green coat that might have come from some Soviet Army Surplus store out in the 'stans. It made it hard to see his shape, let alone his face. Jack started to move closer but Ray blocked him, yelping. "Just watch," Ray seemed to be saying.

So Jack stood on the other side of the street and leaned forward, trying to make out what he was seeing. The man picked up everything—crumpled newspapers, condoms, bone fragments, bits of clothing, bandages, a broken knife. Most things he threw away as soon as he touched them, but every now and then he found something he wanted—Jack had no idea why—and stuffed it into his bag. When he did that, he would wave his right hand over his find before putting it with the others. It was a large hand, thick with muscle. Jack could see some kind of marking at the base of the first finger, what people used to call the Apollo finger.

"What is he?" Jack whispered to Ray. "Traveler? Some kind of Scavenger elemental?" These days, Jack knew, there were elementals of everything, from garbage to obsolete video games to spy satellites. But why was Ray showing him this?

Enough sneaking around, Jack thought. "Hey!" he called out. "What are you looking for? Maybe I can help."

Startled, the man half turned without standing up. Jack caught sight of a grin, all sharp white teeth, and then a flare of light blinded him.

He came awake in his bed, gasping. "Goddamn it," he said when he'd caught his breath. He sat up, pressed his left thumb and forefinger against his closed eyes for a second, then made a face at the dream netting. "Lot of good you are," he said.

In the shower Jack turned up the hot water as far as he could bear it, and used lots of olive oil soap to make sure he got rid of any dream residue that might have passed through the net. The soap, made especially for Travelers from the two-thousand-year-old groves below Mount Parnassus in Greece, usually could be trusted to remove anything dangerous clinging to the skin. Jack was not so confident in this case.

As he dried himself off under the bright arc lamp in the bathroom, he noticed his skin in the full-length mirror attached to the door. Jack didn't spend a great deal of time looking at himself. He knew he liked his slightly off-kilter face with all its small scars—he was never sure about the big one—his ropy hair that always looked like he cut it himself (actually it was cut by a hairdresser named Pablo, whose husband Jack had once rescued from a Red Dog pack)—his loose muscles, his long hands with their tapered fingers. He liked himself enough not to need reminders. But now something caught his eye, and he examined his skin, front and back.

There were marks on him, small sparkling dots of silver. Very few, and very small, unnoticeable except under the bright array of the arc lamp. He touched them. No pain. Hard to tell because they were minute, but they felt smoother than his skin. He scratched at one. It didn't come off, and he wondered what would happen if he tried to cut it away. Probably a bad idea.

The one thing he knew for sure was that he didn't like it. The marks signaled the start of *silvercation*, by which a Traveler eventually lost control of his body. If it went too far it could become irreversible, even if the cause—usually an enemy—was removed. Jack examined himself again. He found only four very small marks. Two or three, maybe four days, he guessed, before it became really dangerous. At least he hoped.

He walked over to his closet, where he made a face at the rack of clothes. When he was on a case, Jack dressed all in black—black shirt, black jeans, black boots. Otherwise, especially when he played poker, it was loose clothes and color. But was he working now?

He pulled on narrow black pants, primarily so he could wear his boots with the hidden knife sheath, and then a pale blue shirt untucked over the pants. He was half out the door when he turned around and returned to the closet, where he took down a long cardboard box from the back of the shelf. He examined the various things inside it, then selected a black spray can and a ragged red cloth with a frayed edge. He put them inside a black messenger bag and slung it across his chest.

Down in the hotel lobby, Jack saw Irene talking to Oscar, the night concierge. Jack hesitated a second. Should he warn her? Tell her to watch out for someone who appeared just like him, except without the scar? He noticed her looking at him oddly and feared the silver had spread faster than he'd thought. But then he realized it was the odd mix of clothes, black for work, color for time on his own.

She smiled, said, "Good morning, Jack. You're up early. Or are you just coming home?"

He smiled back. "Nothing so exciting. I've got to go see someone, kind of an early-bird type."

She gave a delicate shrug. "Enjoy the morning. Perhaps it will become a habit." Jack was about to leave when Irene said, "Oh, Jack, I almost forgot. I dreamed about you last night."

Jack managed to force a grin. "Really? What was I doing? Nothing too shocking, I hope."

She did not smile back. "I'm not sure, actually. It was all a bit difficult to see, somehow. You said you wanted to show me something. You looked excited. Then we were walking down some long, dark corridor until we came to a stone door. It was a bit odd, really, it did not appear to be part of a wall. But you opened it, and I saw some dim shapes, and then there was a flash of light that hurt my eyes . . . and that was it. I woke up."

The door to the Forest of Souls. Was the Rev threatening to send Irene Yao to the Land of the Dead? Take away everyone Jack loved?

He said, "Sorry, doesn't ring any bells. Or open any doors." Then, as an afterthought, he said, "You know, I have this odd netting that I found once when I was traveling somewhere. Some sort of folklore thing. Anyway, it's supposed to protect you from bad dreams. Let me know if you want me to rig it up around your bed." Who knows, he thought, maybe it would work better for a Non-Traveler.

Jack expected her to smile, and say something like, "How could a dream of my favorite resident be bad?" but instead she nodded, and said, "Thank you, Jack. I may give it a try."

"Great," Jack said. "Let me know." He wanted to run up to her rooms and rig up the dream net right now, in case she went for a mid-morning nap. But Anatolie always told him that when you deal with Non-Travelers you have to let them take the lead.

Outside, the sun had risen all the way and was shining thinly through strands of clouds. Jack was chilly without a jacket but knew it would warm up quickly. He walked over to 34th Street and raised his arm. Almost immediately, a taxi cut across three lanes of angry commuters to pull up in front of him. The ability to summon taxis on command was one of the minor perks of being a Traveler in New York.

Jack leaned back in the seat. "Broadway," he said, "between Eighty-eighth and Eighty-ninth, east side of the street."

The driver stared at Jack in the rearview mirror a moment before heading into traffic. He didn't say anything, but every half-minute or so he glanced in the mirror. It wasn't until Jack saw the grin on the driver's face that he realized he had to get out of the car, *right now.* He took hold of the door handle, prepared to roll into the street.

Too late. "Hey," the driver said, "I think I dreamed about you last night." And then Jack was asleep.

—He was walking into the bling lobby of the Palace Hotel, behind St. Patrick's Cathedral. He was wearing a smoky brown silk suit and the oxblood wing-tip shoes he'd once taken off an investment banker who needed to follow his wife into the Shadow Valley where you can only go barefoot. Poker clothes.

His friend Annette was in town, from Vegas or Macau, and she'd set up a private game here in the Palace. Jack was excited as he walked up the wide marble staircase in the lobby. Then he stopped, confused. Something was wrong but he couldn't figure out . . . was that Elaynora, over by the wall, reading the *Times*? What was she . . .

And then he was in the elevator, and he didn't remember pressing a floor, but he must have, because it was rising. It stopped at Eleven, and when the door hissed open he headed down the hallway, as if he knew where he was going. "Move forward or get out," Anatolie told him once. "Never hesitate." And sure enough, when he got to 1121 he knew it was the room. Maybe Annette had mentioned it.

He knocked, and Mr. Dickens, Jack's favorite dealer, opened the door. Jack smiled, but before he could say anything, the dealer told him, "I'm sorry, sir, but this is a private gathering." He moved to close the door.

"Charlie," Jack said, "it's me."

The white-haired old man, dressed in a bespoke black suit and crisp white shirt buttoned to the neck but without a tie, only said, "I'm sorry, sir, but this is a closed event."

Jack wouldn't let him push the door shut. "This is crazy," he said. "Annette called me." He looked over the dealer's shoulder to where seven people were sitting around a conference table. All of them wore black, three of the men in Chassidic robes, two in business suits, and a sixth man in a black shirt and black jeans. The sixth man sat across from Annette, who wore a black dress with long sleeves and a low neckline. They appeared to be involved in a large pot, judging from the stack of chips in the middle.

"Annette!" Jack called out. "I got your phone call. Tell Charlie to let me in."

Annette glanced curiously at him for a moment before turning her attention back to the game. "Raise," she said, and pushed in nearly as many chips as were already in the pot.

"Call," the man in the black shirt and jeans said, and suddenly Jack realized it was *him*. The Rev.

"Annette!" Jack said. "That's not me. He's a Dupe. I'm over here." Now he could see that the Rev was wearing black boots along with the black shirt and jeans. Work clothes. *That's not right*, Jack thought, *you keep work and poker separate.*

Annette glanced again at the door, squinting, as if trying to figure something out. But then the Dupe said, "I called you," and her attention flipped back to the hand. As if Jack wasn't there, as if he'd never been there.

She turned over a seven, eight of hearts. "Flush," she said.

The Rev grinned. "Sorry, babe," he said, and turned over the jack, three of hearts. Higher flush. Laughing, he scooped up the chips. "It just gets worse and worse, doesn't it?"

No, Jack thought, you don't do that. When you win, you don't gloat. He would never do that. Not now, anyway. Maybe when he was younger. Before the disaster, before the geist took control of his daughter and killed his wife. Suddenly, Jack realized—the Rev wasn't just Johnny Handsome, the Man Without a Scar. He was Johnny Empty, the Man Without Pain.

Let him win, Jack thought, but it was almost like someone else speaking in his head, a message.

"No," he said out loud, "I can't do that." For if Johnny Empty won, who would rescue Genie from the Forest Of Souls?

Jack woke up to find the taxi double-parked on Broadway. "Twelve seventy-five," the driver said. He sounded annoyed. Tell a guy a weird story and the guy just falls asleep! Jack knew that by the end of the driver's shift the dream passenger falling asleep would become the punchline.

The taxi pulled away and Jack stood outside Kimm's Imports and Delicacies. Marty Kimm sold a mix of Asian groceries—dried mushrooms, packs of noodles, sauces—along with lackluster porcelain bowls, beginner Go sets, notebooks with children waving flags on the cover, cotton shoes, and toys so old-fashioned the neighborhood kids didn't even roll their eyes, they just stared in disbelief. People wondered how "nice Mr. Kimm" could survive in such a competitive high-rent street. It was only a matter of time, they told each other, before another Pret-a-Manger took over and sent "poor Mr. Kimm" to some Korean assisted-living home.

For Mr. Kimm was old, the kind of old that makes you want to guess his age, like guessing the number of jelly beans in a jar. Short and thin, with silver hair cut short, and a constant smile on his face, as if everyone he met was a cute child, he always wore an ironed white shirt, and creased khaki pants. Jack had no idea how old Marty Kimm was. He might have been older than the world.

Jack knew one thing, though. Kimm's Imports was not in any danger of closing. For while it was a genuine store—Jack and Carolien sometimes cooked dinners using only ingredients and utensils from Mr. Kimm—its reason for being there had nothing to do with noodles and chopsticks. Marty Kimm was a gatekeeper.

Every city has a range of gates, New York just has a few more of them than most. Along with the six Gates of Paradise (two in Staten Island, one each in the other boroughs), and most importantly, the Gate to the Forest of Souls in a garage on Fifty-sixth Street, there were several minor gates, such as the Gate of Flowers in the Bronx, or the Gate of New Skin in a basement in Brooklyn. Marty Kimm was in charge of a Gate of Knowing. On the other side was a Living Archive, and if Jack could get through and consult her he would learn more about Dupes than in weeks of research. Most importantly, he would learn what *he* needed to know, though it might be his job to figure out why.

Mr. Kimm was playing with a child's abacus when Jack came into the shop. He looked up, nodded once, then said, "Hello, Jack. I trust you are having a good day?"

Jack said, "I'm having the kind of day where I need to find out things."

"Ah, of course. Do you have a gift?"

All gatekeepers required some sort of offering. For Barney, keeper of the Forest Gate on Fifty-sixth Street, it was a stolen truffle. For Mr. Kimm it was a limerick, and it had to both say something and be "humble."

Jack recited:

There once was a Traveler, Jack
Who everyone thought was a hack
He lost his old key
To travel for free
And now he can't find his way back

"Very nice," said Mr. Kimm, and clapped his hands once, the way you might for a four-year-old who's done a somersault. He nodded toward the back of the store. "She's waiting for you. Perhaps she will have your key."

Jack looked and saw a bead curtain over a doorway at the far wall. Was it there before? *Yes, of course*, his cortex said. His amygdala wasn't so sure. He glanced back at Mr. Kimm, who was once more playing with the abacus. The markers were just painted wood but they gleamed like bright marbles. For a moment, Jack thought they were entire worlds, and a dizziness came over him so that he nearly fell. But he looked again and saw they were just bits of wood.

He stepped through the curtain into a wide, bare room with a polished checkerboard floor. The walls were covered with mirrored panels, set off from each other by thin gold columns. It might have been an eighteenth-century ballroom, except instead of perfume there was a sharp smell, and instead of the minuet there was a staccato of wings. When Jack looked at the back of the room he saw a woman covered by brown owls.

She appeared to be lying on a couch, though it was hard to tell because all he could really see was her face, round and kind, her unwrinkled skin a milky white. The owls, some with horns, others smooth, hid the rest of her. In front of her stood an old-fashioned black steamer trunk, the kind parents used to send with their kids to summer camp.

A Traveler with a strong need to learn about something had several options. The big city Travelers Aid Societies had old-fashioned libraries, complete with frail, ancient books bound in human skin, or even scrolls that might crumble if you tried to unroll them. More isolated Travelers, or just more modern, turned to the Cloud Archives maintained by Jinn-Net. Of course, this particular cloud was not something you could reach via Google. But when even that wasn't enough, when you needed to *know*, right *now*, there was the Mother of Owls, and her treasure box of whispers.

"Hello, Jack," she said, her voice dry and precise and very old. "Mr. Kimm approves of you. I believe he likes you."

"I need help," Jack said. "I need to know."

"Of course. And the subject of your need?"

"Dupes. Duplicates."

"Ah. A tricky subject. So easy to get lost, for the road keeps turning back on itself. One's bird crumbs eaten by one's own mirror." The owls fluttered, lifted up and came back down.

Jack kept his eyes on their mistress. "Can you help me?" he said.

"Perhaps. And what of the other thing?"

"Other?"

"The Duplicate is only half of the quandary. Isn't that true, Jack?"

He found it hard to hold her gaze. "Yes," he said finally. "It's all taking place in dreams." He didn't want to tell her the rest of it, how his Dupe had come back as a Rev, and the Rev had invoked Jack's Guest.

But maybe it wasn't necessary. Mother Owl smiled and said very softly,

"There once was a Jack who was proud
And believed he stood out in the crowd
Until an old dream
Held him down in a stream
And no one could hear him out loud."

Jack nodded, not sure he could speak. The old woman said, "You may open the box."

Jack stepped forward. Owls fluttered all around him, their teeth and razor-sharp claws showing, but he paid no attention. He took a breath and lifted the lid of the trunk.

There were stories of what happened when you released what was in the box. Carolien had done it, of course, for Carolien loved *knowing* more than anything else. She'd told Jack that a bright yellow *kabouter* in balloon pants and a party hat had leaped out and bitten her tongue, then spoke into her blood so rapidly she remembered nothing until suddenly she began to write it all down, filling up a three-hundred-page journal over four days. Others talked of voluptuous women who surrounded you, singing. None of this happened to Jack. Instead, whispers swirled all around him like smoke until he became so dizzy he had to hold on to the lid to keep from falling over. He could hear fragments of words and nothing else, and he worried it was all useless, he would learn nothing he could use against the Rev. Finally, he slammed down the lid and lay on the floor gasping while the ceiling spun above him. "Shit," he said. And then he grinned, for suddenly he realized he *knew* things.

He knew that four hundred years ago, Peter Midnight wrote "the strangest book in the Hidden Library," titled *The Book of Duplicates: A Natural History of Replication*, and to do it, Midnight had to travel back in time to the earliest days of the world. Travelers move through time constantly but usually return an instant before they left, so that they forget whatever they saw or did. Midnight broke the barrier by duplicating himself, transferring the block to the Dupe, and destroying it. And he still might not have known he had done it, except that he woke up in bed with a dead body next to him, and when he turned it over it was himself, with a rolled-up scroll in its mouth.

Jack learned that Dupes once filled the world. Originally there was only one person, amorphous and crude, spit out by the Creator, who'd gotten something stuck in Her teeth. This Original pestered its maker so much that He copied it and said, "There. Now talk to each other and leave me alone." But the two just stared resentfully at each other, each claiming to be the Original, the other a Dupe. To prove the point, one of them made a fresh copy and said, "You see? That's how I made *you*." But the other only laughed and made his own Dupe, saying, "*This* is how it's done. You're just a copy, and a bad one. Look how much better this new one is." As they argued, the two new Dupes stared at each other. Then each of them made a Duplicate.

Some time later, the Creator stirred Herself from the place where She'd hidden from the world. To His horror, He discovered the world was full of Duplicates! They covered the mountains and valleys, they sat in the trees, they walked or swam in the waters. Furious, the Creator urinated across the world, sweeping the infestation away in the flood. At the last second She rescued the last two Dupes, held them in Her hand until the flood subsided, then made one a man, the other a woman. "There," He said. "Now if you want to make more you'll have to do it the hard way. But at least you'll enjoy it more." When She set them back on dry land She hid the secret of Replication so Dupes would no longer clog the Earth.

But the power wasn't lost, for as all Travelers know, *nothing* is ever lost. Hidden, blocked, but always there. No one knows who discovered it. Some say Peter Midnight, but of course, he wrote the book, and Travelers are notorious braggarts. Others—and this was a claim made in the fifteenth century—others say it was a Traveler named John Shade, who went back to The Very Beginning on a mission to rescue his daughter from The Green Dark Woods. No one knows if he succeeded, but he brought back the Great Secret, though he had to surrender it along the way, some thousands of years back. *No*, Jack thought, *that can't be right*. But he had to let the question go, for more and more knowledge came rushing through him.

He learned of a Traveler whose Dupe cut him up and baked him in a pie, or else swallowed him whole.

And another, who thought she'd dissolved her Duplicate, done all the steps, only to discover that when she looked in the mirror she could never see herself, only the Dupe, and when she tried to speak it wasn't her voice but the Duplicate's.

He learned of a Traveler whose Revenant begged to remain. "I won't challenge you," the Rev said. "I'll stay in the shadows. I swear by my maker." But they both knew that could never happen, for it was the nature of a Revenant to try to take over. And it was the nature of a Traveler to cling to the world. Finally, one killed the other, but then the survivor made love to the corpse and brought her back. For this, too, is the nature of a Traveler, to accept no limits, and to search for whatever seems lost.

He learned that certain Travelers have the power to Duplicate themselves in other people, take them over, at least for a time, and he remembered that day Anatolie had become an old woman on the street, a Chinese huckster, a trio of teenage girls.

He learned that the baby Moses who was found in a basket among the bulrushes of the Nile was a Dupe, and that the original was raised as a Traveler in the desert, waiting for the day when the Dupe would show up and the true Moses could cut his throat and set him on fire to ignite the Burning Bush.

He learned that long ago there lived a Traveler named Loud Sue. The name was a joke, for Sue was one of those obnoxious people who *say* that nothing worth saying can actually be said. One day, Loud Sue left home (maybe to avoid speaking) and traveled to an orchard where a pair of Shadow Dogs attacked her. To escape, she climbed a tree with ten branches, and on the third branch from the top found a bird's nest where she could lie down safely and fall asleep. She dreamed that she was not Loud Sue at all, but her Duplicate, Young Sue.

She woke up surrounded by chicks, their mouths open as they waited for their mother to feed them. When she heard a great flapping of wings she clambered down through the branches, back to the Earth. But as she moved, she wondered—was she Loud Sue, who had fallen asleep and dreamed she was Young, or was she Young Sue, even now dreaming she was Loud?

Avoid orchards, the Travelers say. And if you absolutely must enter one, never ever fall asleep.

He learned that sometimes the Dupe takes over—*I want to win*, the Rev had told Jack—for there was once a great Traveler who left the world and allowed her Duplicate to take her place.

He learned that some claim the universe itself is a copy, an unfinished Duplicate of a lost world, which is why so much of existence is *dark*—dark matter, dark energy, dark desire.

He learned that sometimes you can attack a Revenant by making more and more Duplicates, and for a moment he thought he had the answer, only to have the whispers tell him that a strong Rev can absorb the new copies into itself and become more and more powerful, until finally, when the original has exhausted himself, the Rev will eat him, and it will be as if he never existed.

The final revelation came not as a whisper but a vision. He saw a woman, barefoot in a loose white dress, standing at an old wooden table. She was dark-skinned, but with long straight hair. She had her back turned to Jack, bent over the table, writing with a long thin pen on small strips of paper. When she finished each one she folded it and inserted it under a fingernail. Finally she stood up, and Jack thought she would turn and face him, but instead, she stood in front of an old full-length mirror, with her fingers at shoulder level, spread like the ribs of a fan. Under her nails the letters flickered and glowed. "Nothing is lost," the woman whispered.

—and then Jack was on all fours, on a damp concrete floor, an empty steam trunk open in front of him. For an instant he heard the flapping of wings, but when he looked there was no one there, no owls, no old woman, just rows of storage shelves, mostly empty. Jack stood up, shook himself, looked around one more time, then stepped through a dull bead curtain, back into Mr. Kimm's variety store.

The old man moved some counters on his abacus. Without looking up, he asked "Did you find what you need, Jack?"

"Not sure," Jack said. "Maybe too much."

"Ah. Too much, too little, all the same, yes?" His accent had gotten thicker. It was his way of saying good-bye.

"Thank you," Jack said.

"Always here for you, Jack. Always here."

• • •

Outside, the day had brightened, and a look at the sky told Jack it was just after 2:00. He glanced at his watch. 11:44. He wondered, not the first time, why Travelers bothered to wear watches at all. What day was it? He walked to a newsstand on the corner and glanced at the *Post*. Above the blaring headline, the date assured him he'd only lost a couple of hours.

He was about to hail a cab when he noticed the people on the street corner acting strangely. They were looking at their hands, turning them over, staring at the palms, the fingers. They didn't appear upset, just confused. That would change, Jack knew, and quickly. Sure enough, a man and woman, the man in front of a store selling "designer pet food," the woman crossing Broadway from the traffic island, became suddenly agitated. They looked all up and down their arms and legs and midsections, whatever they could see of themselves, and began slapping their bodies, as if to swipe away insects.

The woman stopped in the middle of the street, and stayed there when the light changed, oblivious to the horns and shouts and curses of the drivers swerving around her. The man was breathing heavily, raking his arms with his nails. This was phase two, Jack thought, the sense of attack. Invasion. As he took the spray can and the frayed cloth from his messenger bag he could guess what was next. What the Rev might do.

Sure enough, people began to stare at each other. They pointed and poked, saying things like "Why do you look like me?" and, "Why are you imitating me? *Why is everyone imitating me?*" In fact, they looked nothing at all like each other. They were young and old, male and female, different races, it made no difference. No matter who they looked at, all they could see was themselves.

Jack opened the fringed cloth until it lay in folds all about his feet. Then he shook the can and began to spray the material. He knew that for the best effect he should empty the whole can but there wasn't time, especially since he had to cover his nose and mouth to avoid inhaling. The spray wouldn't harm him but it would dull his senses until his Traveler metabolism shook it off. The formula in the can carried some fancy modern name, but like most Travelers Jack preferred the traditional—Spell-Breaker. If used in time it could nullify a casting, and without permanent damage to the victim. Not in time—the symptoms varied, but for these people, Jack suspected, a permanent state in which everyone looked like their double. They would spend the rest of their lives in isolation, sedated through a hospital ventilation system before a nurse or orderly could bring them food.

Don't think, Jack told himself. Thinking was distraction. Never get distracted, Anatolie had taught him. Jack dropped the cloth and grabbed hold of the smooth side. Then he flipped it open in the air.

A "spread cloth," as it was called, existed partly in this world, and partly in the "World of Extension." Inert, it looked about the size of a king-size sheet and folded down to a square foot. "Awakened," it could stretch so far it appeared to fade into the sky. Jack didn't need anything that radical, he just wanted the tendrils to be able to touch all those frenzied people filling up the street corner. Soon the filaments were snaking and twisting, making crackling noises as they searched for people to heal. They went into an ear, a mouth, an eye, and the people gasped, or sighed, as the ghost snakes entered their brains.

Jack waited until he was sure the tendrils had reached everyone. Then he snapped his wrists back. The snakes withdrew, the cloth began to shrink, and soon it was small enough, inert enough, for Jack to fold it again and put it back in his bag.

The people in the street stared at each other, then at their own arms and legs. Some touched themselves, their faces or chests, even their groins. Then they looked around, horrified or just furtive, suddenly aware they'd embarrassed themselves on the public street. Some said things like, "Oh my god, I'm so sorry, I don't know what—God, I'm sorry." Others moved away as fast as possible. A few looked breathlessly at the person next to them, and if they got the right look back, held hands and walked quickly away.

And beyond the crowd, hard to see in suddenly bright sunlight, a man in black stood, holding up a small rectangular object like a sacred relic. It was him, of course, and what he held was the marker, the Guest. Jack's card.

The Rev said something. Impossible to hear in the noise and traffic, but all Travelers are lip readers. Jack wasn't that good at it, but this one was easy. *I want to win*, the Dupe said. Then he turned and strolled away.

For a second, Jack considered running after him, but if he caught him what would Jack do? So he just stood there and pretended to himself he was making himself useful by checking there were no casualties.

From behind him he heard a woman, cold and stiff, like an old-fashioned pre-Siri computer voice. "John Shade," she said.

Oh fuck, Jack thought. *The last goddamn thing* . . . He sighed and turned around.

There were two of them, a man and a woman. They often did that, as if satisfying some government directive for gender equity. They were dressed in old-fashioned suits, the way the Supreme Court requires lawyers to appear, dull grey for the man, knee-length black skirt and low-heeled pumps for the woman. Grey and black were a pun, of course. The colors of *coal*.

For a second, Jack thought they might be the same two who'd come to the house that long night, after Elvis told him he had to call them. But no, efficiency just always looked the same.

The man's voice came out breathy, little more than a whisper. "This has to stop," he said.

"Yeah, well, I'm not exactly having a great time," Jack said.

"That's no concern of ours," the woman said. "What does concern us is that this feud of yours has begun to involve non-Travelers. That is not acceptable."

Jack glanced around, saw that no one was looking at them. Glamours. COLE was good at that. "It's not my feud," he said. "If you can tell me how to make the Rev go away, I'll be glad to do it."

Jack was surprised to see a half-smile twist the woman's mouth. "Dissolve it," she said.

"I did. Apparently, it didn't take." *No*, he thought, *I did it right*. He brushed the thought aside, for obviously he didn't.

"There are more advanced methods," the woman said.

"It's complicated."

The man said, "Your Guest."

Jesus, Jack thought, *do you people know everything?*

Her tone slightly less techno, the woman said, "We understand your dilemma. Unfortunately, it makes no difference. Preventing the outer population from discovering reality is our sole concern." She smiled, almost regretfully, but Jack got the message. They would do whatever it took to stop the bleed. *Exile*, Jack thought. He and the Dupe removed from the world. No passage back. Like his daughter.

"I'll take care of it," he said.

The man turned and walked away, but the woman hesitated. Sympathy seemed to cut through the mask for a moment, and Jack had the wild idea she would make the telephone gesture with her hand next to her ear and mouth, "Call me." But then she walked off.

Jack stood in the street a moment, head tilted to the left, as if trying to hear a whisper. There was something, some glimmer, in what had just happened. *I did it right*. But clearly he hadn't, there was the Dupe. Finally, he let it go and hailed a cab.

Before he got in, he sprayed Spell-Breaker over the car. He could see the driver make a face and reach for the gear shift, but managed to get inside before the taxi could pull away. *Trust me*, Jack wanted to say, *this is for you as much as for me*. But that never worked, so he just said, "Forty-eighth Street between Ninth and Tenth."

No one was sure just how Carolien Hounstra could afford a six-room apartment in the newly chic Hell's Kitchen. Certainly not from her work at NYTAS, where she was everything from door watch to record keeper, two jobs that were a lot more complicated than they sounded. Nor did she freelance, like Jack. Family money, some said. Found a djinni in a lamp, others claimed. Jack's favorite story was that Carolien was unearthed in a coffin filled with pirate gold, in a crypt beneath Amsterdam's Moses and Aaron Church. She'd been asleep, the story went, until a nun kissed her awake. *Smart nun*, Jack thought.

The ride passed without any dream attacks, and Jack gave the driver a ten dollar tip. Before he could ring the bell for 6E, the buzzer sounded, and Carolien's voice came through the scratchy intercom. "Jack! Come up."

Carolien was standing in the doorway when Jack stepped out of the tiny elevator. She wore light green linen pants and a loose, dark green shirt that came down almost to her knees, but was unbuttoned enough to reveal the wondrous swell of her breasts. Her long, golden hair was braided in a triple pattern that made Jack think of the caduceus. She smiled like the sun breaking through the clouds. There were people who said that the dreary climate of Northwest Europe was a direct result of Carolien Hounstra moving to New York. The smile faded and the blue eyes narrowed as she looked him over. "So," she said. "Trouble. Come in."

Carolien's apartment was decorated in a variety of styles. The living room was fifties "modern," with kidney-shaped glass tables and uncomfortable chairs. Her kitchen was so full of gadgets Jack suspected it could cook a five-course meal all by itself. Her bedroom featured elaborately carved dressers, an ebony bed—on a north-south axis, of course—and a large gold-framed mirror that could probably identify who was the fairest in the land. The hallway that connected all this would appear to any deliveryman (who was not staring at Carolien) as unadorned walls painted a pale yellow. Jack saw alcoves, some filled with clouds and hidden faces, others with faraway scenes, such as people in animal costumes dancing and laughing.

Without a word, Carolien led him to a closed wooden door at the end of the hallway. A wave of her hand and the door opened without her touching it. Jack followed her into what he called "the Reign of Frogs." Shelves of all sorts—polished wood, metal slats, stainless steel—covered every wall. And every shelf was covered with frogs. Most were stone, jade and malachite, but there were lots of wood and netsuke as well. The majority were squatting, but some appeared caught in mid-leap. With a jab of guilt, Jack remembered his abandoned errand to Canal Sreet. *When this is over*, he thought, but then found himself wondering, if the Rev took over, would he go get Carolien a frog?

The only carving not on a shelf was the largest, a big-bellied jade frog wearing a gold crown. About three feet high, "King Frog," as Jack called him, squatted on the floor in front of a shelf of stone subjects. Jack once asked Carolien, "Why don't you kiss him and turn him back into a handsome prince?"

Carolien shrugged. "Maybe he wouldn't like that. Or maybe I would become a frog."

Now they sat facing each other in the middle of a polished black floor. Jack said, "Thank you for seeing me."

She made a Dutch noise. "Am I a dentist now? Why wouldn't I see you?"

"Sorry. It's been a rough couple of days." He reached out and touched her cheek. Whenever he touched her, he was amazed that skin could feel so soft and strong at the same time. *Thank God for Dutch cheese*, he thought.

Gently, Carolien removed his hand. "Tell me what is happening," she said.

Jack took a breath. "I had a visit from COLE today."

"Ah. Were you naughty?"

"Not me. At least, not exactly." He paused, then said, "I'm in trouble, Carolien."

"Tell me."

Jack laid it all out for her, holding back only his errand before the Momentary Storm. She listened without moving, then suddenly leaned forward and kissed him. Surprised, Jack almost backed away before he held her face and kissed her back. *Jesus*, he thought, *maybe this is what I need*. To hell with dreams and Revenants. A wild thought surfaced that when they got naked they would discover his cock had gone all shiny, and he'd have to make up some line, "Once you've tried silver, there's no . . . " But he couldn't think of a rhyme and he gave his attention to kissing the top of Carolien's breasts, moving down—

And then suddenly it wasn't him. He could not have described how he knew, but it was like seeing yourself/not yourself in a dream. The goddamn Rev had his lips on Carolien's right nipple, his hand between her legs. With all his concentration, like some novice Traveler trying to psychically lift a fucking pencil, Jack managed to push the body, the Dupe's body, *his* body, away from Carolien.

And then he was back again, gasping for breath.

"So," Carolien said. "That bad, yes?"

"Jesus," Jack said to her, "that was a test?"

"Yes, of course. How else do we know?"

Jack shook his head. Usually he appreciated Carolien's Dutch frankness. "We are a small country," she'd say, "we have no room for embarrassment." But sometimes . . .

Carolien said, "Your scar is back. Good."

"It wasn't there?"

"For a moment, no."

"So it really was him. How did he do that?"

She sighed. "He operates in dreams, Jack. Dreams are like ooze. They can slide, and cover things. But you know this." Jack didn't answer. "Oh, Jack," Carolien said, "it's not me you need. It's *her*."

"Fuck," Jack said. But of course she was right. When you're hunted by a dream, where else do you go but a goddamn Dream Hunter?

Jack Shade's relationship/affair/fling/experiment/beneficial friendship with Elaynora Horne lasted a little over nine months. El's father may have been an ex-Sun god, but her mother was the Queen of Eyes, and Jack had met El through working that case. They didn't talk about Mom much. The Queen had never publicly acknowledged her, El being the product of a youthful indiscretion, which is to say the young queen-to-be trying to run away from her life. El was much closer to her father. She worked in his dream agency, after all, but it was more than that. You could say she idolized him, if that term wasn't so heavy with meaning in this particular instance.

The first time they made love, on a snowy December night, El had told Jack it had to be at her place, an elegant two-story apartment on the Upper East Side. That was okay with Jack, he wasn't wild about bringing girlfriends to his hotel room. In El's bedroom, he was a bit surprised to see black wooden shutters attached to all the windows, and more so when she systematically closed them all. *Privacy issues*, Jack thought, and then forgot about it as he began to kiss her lips, then her face, her neck, her breasts, and then her thighs as their clothes came off.

They made it to the high bed that looked half as big as a basketball court—no compass alignments, Jack noticed—and El was arching her back, and gasping, when suddenly she pulled away and held up her hand. "Wait," she whispered, "I need you to wear something."

Jack almost laughed and said, "It doesn't look like you need any help at all," but he'd been around long enough to know you didn't question or make light of these things. There'd been a woman in Denver who'd tied streamers on his wrists and ankles and scrotum, another in Paris who put makeup on him and called him "Jacquie," and a Japanese diplomat in Brooklyn who'd had him wear a Barack Obama mask. And once in Boston a woman had spent hours inscribing Jack's chest and thighs with words in some long-lost alphabet. "Messages home," she'd called them.

So he just nodded, waiting for whatever strange thing she would give him, and almost made a noise in surprise when all she did was hand him a pair of dark wraparound sunglasses. But he just put them on and went back to kissing her, though it was a bit strange because he could hardly see. We may think we close our eyes during sex but we actually depend on them much more than we realize.

Jack had once made love to a blind woman, who'd seduced him by telling him that she could see when having sex. What she didn't say was that he would become blind. At first he'd gotten angry and started to push her away, but she clung to him, saying, "Please, Jack, let me have this. Your sight will come back, I promise." So Jack had discovered what it was like to make love entirely by feel. After, he lay in bed while his partner got up, and for a moment he panicked when sight did not come flooding back. But soon flashes came and went, and then glimpses. He saw her standing in front of a full-length mirror, staring and touching, urgently connecting finger knowledge to shapes she would try to memorize. Jack didn't get up until his sight had fully returned. Then he walked over to where she still stood before the mirror, her blank eyes weeping. "I'm sorry," he said, and tried to hold her, but she pushed him away.

"Go," she said. "Please."

"We could do it again. If not now—"

"No! It only works once. Then—then I have to find someone else." Jack had gathered up his clothes and gotten dressed in the hallway before he let himself out.

Now, as he made love wearing glasses so dark he could barely see his partner's outline, he remembered that other time, and closed his eyes to better feel his way around El's body. He began to get hints of why the glasses—and the shutters—as El began to vibrate toward orgasm. Faint flashes filled the air, then died out. Jack could feel them even with his eyes closed, and when he opened them it looked like parts of the room were flaring up, then disappearing.

El began to shudder, and grunt, and the flashes came faster. And then she cried out, and Jack, who'd been using his fascination with the lights to hold himself back, let go so he would come with her. In the midst of that perfect moment, a blast of fiery light flooded the room.

Jack made some kind of noise but held on, unwilling to cut short the experience. When the moment came to separate he fell back on the bed, only to cry out and sit up when he realized how hot—how sunburned—his back was. Gingerly he touched his chest, winced, for it was worse. Made sense, since he'd been facing her. He pointed to the glasses. "Is it safe?" When she said yes, he took them off to look down at the worst sunburn he'd had since he was five and ran away from his parents so he could build the world's biggest sand castle.

"I'm sorry, Jack," El said, but he could see her fighting a grin. "I guess I should have warned you."

"You think?" Jack said, and then they were both laughing.

"It'll wear off," she said, and kissed him. "The sunburn, I mean."

So sex with Elaynora was, well, complicated, though they worked out ways to manage it. Unfortunately, other problems began to surface. Jack got a sense that she considered the work of a Traveler undignified, if not downright low-class. At first she sounded fascinated, wanted to know everything. Then she began to make comments about the tricks Travelers liked to play on each other, such as sending someone through the wrong Gate, so he ended up in Pigworld rather than among the Messengers of Light, or some of Jack's clients. She began to talk of the valuable work the Dream Hunters did, the scientific breakthroughs they inspired ("It's not just the benzene molecule, Jack"), the important clientele, the need to police the dream borders and catch illegal aliens before they could take root. "Dream Hunters matter," she would say. "What we do is important."

It all came to a head about eight months into their time together, the day Elaynora took Jack to meet her father. She looked flustered, excited, which made Jack nervous. Was he supposed to ask Papa Click and Whistle for his daughter's hand? El didn't seem the type, far too modern. But what did Jack know? He asked her if they were going to meet Alexander Horne at home or at work. She laughed, a little too loudly. "At work, Jack. Believe me, you don't want to see where my father lives."

The Horne Research Group occupied a suite on the eighteenth floor of an innocuous office building on Forty-fifth Street, between Lexington and Park. Jack noticed that the floor-to-ceiling windows in the reception area looked out on the Chrysler building, and if you glanced up you could see the gargoyles looming above you. A Korean woman in her twenties sat behind a long empty desk. At least, she seemed like a woman. Standing before her while El said they were there to see "Mr. Horne," Jack caught the faintest aroma of Other about her. Maybe she was a dream.

Alexander Horne came out to welcome them and lead them into his office—the corner, of course. He presented himself as a large man, a couple of inches taller than Jack. Probably that would have been the case no matter how tall Jack was. Probably he appeared two inches taller to everyone. He had a barrel chest and large, strong hands with prominent veins and muscles. His face was wide, with a high forehead, a prominent nose, and a long, thin mouth. His thick silver hair was swept back. He wore a conservative grey suit with a maroon tie.

"Jack!" the ex-deity said. "It's great to meet you. Elaynora can't stop talking about you."

She laughed. "Hardly. Make one vaguely complimentary comment . . . "

They sat down at a circular table made of bone or ivory. A moment later, the receptionist—"Wondrous Jessica," Horne called her—came in with coffee on a polished silver tray.

For the next half hour Alexander Horne questioned Jack about his work as a Traveler. He pretended it was chatting, but Jack could recognize an interrogation, and found himself becoming more and more annoyed. And yet, it still amazed him when Horne said, "So El tells me you might be ready for something new."

"What?" Jack said. He looked at El, who glared at her father, then told Jack, "I didn't say that. Really. That's not what I said."

"Oh?" said Jack. "Then what exactly *did* you say?"

"Just that—that the life of a Traveler is uncertain. And as long as you have that Guest, your life isn't really your own. Anyone at all could hire you. But maybe if you did some other kind of work the Guest wouldn't apply anymore."

Jack stared at her. "You told him about that?"

Horne chuckled. "Don't be angry at her, Jack. Believe me, I've tried and it doesn't work." He sipped his coffee. "I understand. The last thing a guy wants is for his girlfriend to interfere in his career. But do me a favor, Jack. Just think about it, okay? What we do here is challenging and exciting. And it helps people. I know Travelers do that as well, but we get under the surface of things. We don't just fight reality, we shape it."

He paused, put on a serious face. "And something else, Jack. What my daughter said about your—spiritual obligation. The Guest, as you call it. And this comes from me, not Elaynora. We can do more than set this thing aside. If you decide to work with us, we can nullify it."

"What? What the Hell are you talking about?"

"The dream world is a threshold, Jack. It's the only place where true change can occur." He sighed, held up a hand. "Look, let's table this discussion for now. You're angry, I understand that. I've ambushed you here, I apologize. Why don't you take a few days to think about it. No pressure. Just know that this is not an empty promise."

Jack stood. El started to get up as well but Jack turned and walked out before she could say anything.

For the next few days Jack went over Papa Click's offer again and again. He avoided sleep and protected himself with dream net when he had to close his eyes for fear Alexander—or Elaynora—Horne would try to influence his decision. Freedom, he told himself. No more slavery to anyone who showed up with his goddamn card. He thought of creeps like William Barlow, who almost got Jack killed. Or his fear that someday some gangster from *Le Societé de Matin* would show up with Jack's card and hire him to do something truly vile.

Jack had actually tried to break the Guest on his own once. It was early, his third case since making the disastrous promise. A prim middle-aged woman named Amelia Otis placed Jack's card on the table and said, "I suspect my husband—Mr. Chandler Otis—of demonic copulation. I want you to find out if it's true."

"Do you know what sort of demon?" Jack asked.

"Incubus."

Jack had to stop himself from smiling. "I think you mean succubus."

"No," Mrs. Otis said, and cast her eyes down. "Incubus," she repeated more softly.

Jesus, Jack had thought, *it's not the demon part that bothers her, it's the gay!*

After the client left, Jack wondered, was this his life now? Hostage to every sleaze who showed up with his business card? He decided he would unswear his oath. He would say three times, "I, John Shade, absolve and abjure all vows and obligations surrounding my card." As he said it, he would cut the card Otis had given him.

The first time he tried it his hand slipped and he sliced his thumb. The second time, his voice became a whisper and he felt like he'd been stabbed in the stomach. The third time, his throat seized up and his whole body seemed to break into little pieces. He managed to throw away the scissors and fall on the floor.

When he got up again he discovered the card was unharmed, as bright and fresh as if it had just come from the printer.

A couple of times Jack simply tried to ignore a client, and became so sick he ended up in the ER. Only taking some small action to begin the case broke his symptoms. So the one thing he knew was that he couldn't break the Guest on his own. Then why didn't he leap at Horne's offer?

He told himself that he didn't like coercion. Or that he liked being a Traveler. But there was something else, he could feel it. Finally, he went up on the hotel roof just before moonrise, and did a simple enactment to ask the moon to show him the thing he was missing. He expected the light to fall on something, but it was the moon itself that gave him the answer. Just for an instant, as it came into view above the low buildings across the East River, the face in the moon was Eugenia Shade. The image collapsed back into the usual vague form, but for that second it was Jack's daughter, as clear as the picture on the corner of his desk.

He understood now. The Guest came from the worst moment of his life, it was part of his terrible mistake—but it was also his last link to his daughter. He couldn't just throw it away.

Jack showed up at the Horne Research Agency at nine the next morning. Walking past Jessica's protests, he went straight to Horne's office. "I'm not interested," he said, and left before Horne could say anything.

Things were never the same with El after that. She tried to apologize but

Jack told her it wasn't necessary, he knew she meant well, but it wasn't going to happen and he didn't want to talk about it, it was okay. Jack knew that was a shit thing to do to her, but he didn't care. For a while they pretended they could just go back to how things had been, but they got together less and less often, and for shorter times.

One night, as they were about to make love, and El went about closing the shutters, Jack had the sense she was simply going through the motions. Just as he felt her approach orgasm, he took off the dark glasses. Brightness indeed filled the room, but just for a moment, and barely enough to scatter a few dots across his field of vision. When they separated, El smiled with supposed satisfaction until she saw the discarded glasses. "Hell," she said, and lay on her back staring at the ceiling. Jack got dressed and left, and that was the last he'd seen of her.

And now—now he was supposed to go ask for her help. He glanced at Carolien.

"Oh no, *schatje*," she said. "This is one you're going to have to do without me."

Jack made a face. "Maybe she won't be home."

Carolien looked over at King Frog. The eyes glowed red for a second, then returned to dull stone. "Sorry," she said. "She's home. Better hurry." Then her voice got serious. "This is real, Jack. The Revenant is not going to stop. And he came with your card. You need all the help you can get."

Jack nodded. He could hear that voice again, the angry parody of himself. *I want to beat him. I want to win.*

Elaynora met Jack at the door to her apartment. She was wearing a white linen pantsuit with wide legs and an asymmetrical jacket, the left side longer than the right. Her hair was shorter, layered and blow-dried to look like she'd just stepped out from a swim under a waterfall. Jack glanced at the windows, saw the shutters were open, and hoped she hadn't noticed him checking.

"Jack," she said, with what sounded like real concern, "what's going on?" For a second, he wondered again if he could trust her. The oracle had said so, but then her mother was the Queen of Eyes, maybe she had rigged the answer. *New grass grows clean.* No, Jack decided. It wasn't just the Teraph app. Carolien and her frogs would have caught something if El was dangerous.

He said, "Let's sit down, okay? It's kind of a long story."

"Of course." She led him into the living room, where they sat down at opposite ends of her off-white couch. When Jack had told her everything she said, "So all this is because you didn't dissolve it properly?"

Jack found himself shaking his head. "That's the thing. I keep thinking I did."

El frowned. "Maybe that's why it came to you in dreams. Perhaps you did it right in the physical world, but some fragments remained in your skeletal dream frame."

Jack guessed that was Dream Hunter tech talk. He thought a moment, said, "So part of the Dupe remained hidden in my dreams and that's where it reassembled itself?"

"Yes. And since your card, like everything of significance in your life, has its counterpart in the dream frame, the Revenant was able to get hold of it and present it to you."

"Jesus. And now it's starting to break through into the physical." He hadn't told her about kissing Carolien, but the scene on Broadway was enough. El nodded, her lips tight. Jack said "Can you help me? Show me what to do so I can block it? Maybe if I can get the Dupe out of my *frame*, the card, and the job—you know, killing myself—will go with it."

She sighed. "I don't know, Jack. I'm good, but I suspect this is beyond me."

"Fuck," Jack said. He knew what was coming next.

El looked down, then forced herself to meet his eyes. "Jack—I'm afraid we're going to have to ask my father."

The Horne Research Agency was closed for the weekend but its owner opened the office for them. He was dressed casually, an old-fashioned red and black checked flannel shirt, khaki pants, and plain black sneakers. Despite everything, Jack almost smiled at the thought of Papa Click and Whistle jogging in Central Park. Down in the street it was a dreary, cloudy day, but Jack had assumed the office would be bright and sunny. Instead, everything looked dull, lifeless, and very old. A day off is a day off, Jack figured.

He said, "Thank you for seeing me. I know the last time we talked—"

Horne waved a fleshy hand. For an instant, Jack thought he'd seen that before, the hand, the gesture. But the moment passed as Horne said, "Forget it, Jack. I made you an offer and you weren't interested. What's past is past." He turned to his daughter. "Now tell me the problem."

She looked at Jack, who nodded, then she told her father what she and Jack had figured out.

Horne sat down on the edge of his desk. "This is serious," he said.

Jesus, Jack wanted to say, *you think so, Sun boy?* He kept silent.

"As I understand the situation," Horne said, "there are really two problems here." As if running a meeting, he held up his left hand with the first two fingers extended. There were deep indentations at the base of the first finger, like tattoos dug deep into the flesh. He said, "First, obviously, is the Duplicate itself. The Revenant, as you term it. Jack, if there were no other complications, do you think you could successfully repel it?"

"I'm not sure," Jack said. "It's in the dream world, or half in it, and I don't have a lot of experience there. That's why I need your help." *Something's wrong*, he thought.

"Ah, but now we encounter the other problem. Are you even allowed to overcome it? Doesn't your curse, your Guest, as you call it, require you to do its bidding?"

Jack sucked in a breath. "Yes. That's the other reason I need your help."

Horne's eyes narrowed. "What do you mean?"

"You told me once that you knew a way to remove the curse. I know I turned you down, but that—"

Horne slapped his desk, and a gust of wind stopped Jack's voice in his throat. "What?" Horne said. "That was then, this is now?"

El stepped toward him. "Please, Daddy," she said, "he needs our help."

Horne stared at her a moment, frowning. Then he sighed and shook his head. "It was never that simple. If you had joined us, if you had come to work as a Dream Hunter—"

If you'd married my daughter, Jack thought.

"—then over time, gradually, we could have worked you free. But even in the best of conditions it would have been a slow process. No one, neither you nor I, can simply wave a hand and make it go away." As if to demonstrate how hopeless it was, he moved his left hand in the air. To Jack it appeared in slow motion, the tattooed finger like a painting in the air.

And suddenly Jack remembered where he'd seen that before. The dream. The one Ray had shown him. The old man in the projects—picking up odd bits and pieces—waving his hand over them—the indentations at the base of the finger—

Horne said, "I just don't know what we can do, Jack. It's very possible that you simply cannot beat him, that he's going to win."

I want to beat him, the Rev said. *I want to win.*

Softly, Jack said, "Sonofabitch." Then louder, "It was *you*!" And louder still, "You bastard! It was you!"

Horne's eyes caught fire, then immediately went back to normal as he turned to his daughter. "El?" he said. "What is he talking about?"

"Jack?" Elaynora said. Jack could hear the tremble in her voice, the fear of someone who understands but doesn't want to.

He kept his eyes on Horne. "I didn't do it wrong. Not in the awake world or the fucking dream world. The pieces didn't just drift back together again.

You went looking for them. You gathered up the shards, re-joined them, like a broken vase. You gave it my card, and then you told it what to say."

Horne glared at Jack, and once again light like fire came from his eyes, but Jack was ready, his own eyes narrowed to the thinnest slits. His face grew hot, but he could still see. Now Horne looked back at his daughter, his face and voice softer, pleading. "Elaynora," he said, "I'm your father. I've taken care of you all your life. Are you going to believe him over me?"

Without taking her eyes off her father, Elaynora held out her hand toward Jack. "Give me your coins," she said. It took Jack a second to realize what she was doing, then he reached into his pocket and pulled out all his change. Three quarters, a nickel, and four dimes. $1.20. Jack hoped that was an auspicious amount.

El shook the coins in her hand, tossed them on the desktop. She looked, made a noise, did it again, then once more. For a second, she just stared at them, then turned on her father, her fists up as if she wanted to hit him. "You goddamn sonofabitch!" she yelled. "How could you do that? What's *wrong* with you?"

Horne just stared at her, confused. Finally, as if desperate, he looked at Jack. "What did she do?"

Despite everything, Jack had to hold down a smirk. What he wanted to say was, *Asshole*, but instead he said, "What do you think? She asked her mother."

Horne didn't get it. "What?" he said.

Now El threw up her hands. "She's the Queen of Eyes, Daddy! Holder of all the oracular power in the goddamn world. Did you think you could *hide* anything from her?"

His voice suddenly small, Horne said, "I didn't know you could—"

"What? Talk to her? Of course I can. She's my mother! I could have used playing cards, matchsticks—coins are just the easiest." Suddenly, her anger all gone, she said, "Why, Daddy? Why did you do that?"

Horne stood up. Jack braced himself for another flare, but nothing happened. At least not inside. Out in the street, what was an overcast day suddenly brightened. Horne said, "He deserved it! He refused an offer other men would crawl for. I was going to make him my apprentice. Have you any idea how special, how rare, that is? But no, none of that was good enough for him." He paused, then said, "And on top of all that, he cast *you* away."

"*What?*" El said.

Horne went on, "And all because he thinks he's so damn important. Friends with the Queen of Eyes. Student of Anatolie the Younger. Even the murderers in *La Societé de Matin* love him. Well, it was time someone taught him a lesson."

Outside, the sky had gotten still brighter, bursts of light bouncing off the buildings. Jack was sure that if he went to the window and looked down he would see people running indoors. He kept his eyes on Elaynora and her father.

El said, "*He cast me away?* Jesus, Daddy, I'm not some spurned maiden. We broke up. That's it. And he didn't want to work for you? So what? You think he's one of your tribesmen who used to worship you? You think you had a right to *smite* him? Grow the fuck up!"

Outside, the Chrysler Building gargoyles looked to have caught fire. Jack touched El's shoulder. "What?" she snapped, still glaring at her father.

"Look out the window," Jack said.

She turned to him for a moment, then to the glass. "Oh my god," she said. She stepped to her father, began to hit his shoulders, his chest. "Stop it!" she yelled. "You'll kill everyone!"

Suddenly, all the fight drained out of Alexander Horne. He sat down hard on his desk, his head bowed. Outside, it looked for a second as if night had fallen, but it was just the ordinary day returning. "I'm sorry," Horne muttered. He looked up, his face in pain. "Really, sweetheart. I don't—I don't know what came over me."

El crossed her arms, refusing to let him in. "You're going to have to fix this," she said. "Break down that—that *thing* you assembled and scatter the pieces."

"But that's just it," Horne said. "I can't. It's too late."

"What?"

"It's nearly out of the dream world. I can't contain it."

"Then kill it."

"That's not possible. Not until—not until it becomes completely physical. And that means . . . " He stopped, but Jack knew what came next. The Rev taking over. Horne turned to Jack. "I'm sorry," he said. "Please believe me. If I could—he's going to win, Jack. I don't know how to stop him."

Jack's mouth opened, but nothing came out. Instead, he heard the dupe. *I want to beat him,* Johnny had said. *I want to win.* Jack had assumed that meant he would have to allow his own death since he had no choice but to do what the client asked. But nothing was actually said about Jack dying. He looked now from Horne to Elaynora.

"Jesus," Jack said. "I know what to do."

Jack Shade—*Original Jack, accept no substitutes*—stood naked in front of the mirror in his room at the Rêve Noire. This was the second time in two days he'd done this. It reminded him of Layla examining herself on her thirtieth birthday, turning, frowning, pinching, pulling. This was different.

Jack wasn't assessing, he was memorizing. Every part of himself, every fold of skin, every kink of muscle, the palms and backs of his hands, the turns and knots of his hair—even more than when he'd made the Dupe, he had to get it all clear.

The back was the worst, of course. Jack had bought some cheap mirrors at one of those Walgreen's drugstores that could pass for a small town and set them up to reflect his back to his front, but it was still tricky. An old Traveler motto: Where you've come from is always more dangerous than where you're going. You can *see* where you're going.

The silver had spread—a big shiny patch on his upper right thigh, another over his left kidney. He couldn't let himself worry about it. He just had to take it in as more details and make sure he got them right.

Next to him stood the room's mahogany table. He'd moved it from the wall and stacked it with very thin sheets of rice paper and a Subtle Pen. The Pen looked like a thin metal stylus with a very sharp point. In fact, it was a border-crossing device, using ink from the Other Side. Subtle Pens were very rare—Jack had borrowed this one from Carolien—and used mostly for the kind of contracts that could never be broken. The quality Jack needed was simpler, however—the ability to write very, very small, in words that couldn't fade or be erased. Everything Jack saw he wrote, and still it all took up less than two sheets of paper.

Once he'd gotten down everything he could see, Jack used his black knife to cut out every written segment. When he'd finished, the table looked littered with the discarded carapaces of minute insects. Jack placed his palms on the table. A breeze stirred the fragments. They swirled an inch or two above the table, and then, slowly, they drifted over to Jack's hands—and slid under his fingernails.

The sensation caught him by surprise, very soft yet somehow a jolt. Jack gasped, held up his hands at eye level. He couldn't really see the pieces of paper, only a faint shimmer, yet there was a kind of heaviness. Not weight, really, more like a shift in his center of gravity, as if—as if he was doubled. *Just what I need*, he thought, then reminded himself that in fact it was exactly what he needed.

Painstaking as it was, the physical part was easy. The memories, however . . . Someone once said that to set down all your experiences would take longer than it did to live them. But neither could you consciously decide on the important ones. You had to allow them to come to you. So Jack closed his eyes, let out a breath, and invited his life to parade before him.

There were things he would have expected—the lion's mouth, his first meeting with Anatolie, the first time Ray came to him, finding the Queen of Eyes. And of course Layla and Eugenia. So many moments. Precious, angry, stupid, frightened, triumphant.

And then there were the things long forgotten. Stealing a pack of gum when he was seven and being terrified a cop would kill him. Wandering into some gang street where a group of older boys, in colors he'd never seen, taunted him, only to suddenly run away for no reason Jack could figure out. His thirteenth birthday, after his parents had bought their own home in a safe area. Jack had slipped out at night, just to walk around, and one by one, all the dogs in the neighborhood began to follow him. A fight with Layla so ridiculous that neither of them could stay angry. Genie's third grade report card, when she got straight A's except for a B- in PE that made Jack love her all the more.

When he'd let everything come to him that wanted to, he wrote it all down, cut the strips, and then these too took their hiding places under his fingernails.

He was ready, he told himself. Now he just had to wait until the meet time. So why did he feel like he'd missed something? He stared in the mirror. What the hell was it?

He felt woozy, his eyes heavy. *Oh, you gotta be kidding*, he thought. He'd cast dream net over the whole damn room, emptied a fresh can of Spell-Breaker covering every surface. Then his eyes returned to the mirror and he saw Ray, walking toward him as if out of the glass, and he realized it was all right. There was someone behind Ray, a child. Jack squinted, trying to focus, before he realized it would better if he sat down and closed his eyes.

It was Genie, of course. Not as he'd last seen her, fourteen years old and sprayed with her mother's blood, but younger, sweeter, in jeans and a Girl Power T-shirt. Dream Jack made a noise. The photo. This was Genie from that day at the theme park. In fact, it was the actual moment the picture was taken, with that spray of hair lifted by a gust of wind. "Daddy," she said. "You can't go away."

"I'm not—"

"Don't let him get rid of you, Daddy. *Please.* You have to come save me. I want to go home."

Jack looked around. They were in the hotel room, only now there were trees all around, thin and gnarled and leafless.

"Sweetie," Jack said, "it's going to be fine. But even if I screw up, which won't happen, you'll still be okay. Because he'll still be me. So *he'll* come save you. I promise."

"No!" she yelled, and her fists came up in front of her like a shield. "He's *not* you, Daddy. He's nothing like you. *He doesn't have the scar.*"

Jack came awake so suddenly he nearly fell backward. Of course she was right. Jack had made the Dupe—the original copy—as if the disaster had never happened, and that didn't change when Horne put him back together again. He wouldn't care about Genie, not like Jack did.

He walked over and picked up the picture from that faraway day. He looked at it for what felt like a very long time, then brought it to the table, where he removed it from the frame. Now he went to his nightstand and took out a vial of contact dust. He scattered some on a fresh sheet of paper, then pressed the photo onto it. When he picked it up, the image was gone from the photo, while on the rice paper Layla, and Genie, and he himself stared up joyously. He took out his knife and began to cut the picture into pieces small enough to fit under his fingernails.

Once Alexander Horne realized he was caught, and more, that his relationship with his daughter depended on him trying to undo the damage he'd done, he switched completely and just wanted to help. Jack believed him. You probably didn't last long as a former god if you couldn't adapt. He still didn't trust him, of course, but there were ways Jack could use him. Two things, actually, one simple, the other more tricky. And neither of them involved telling Horne, or even El, exactly what he was trying to do.

The simple task involved taking over a New York City street in the evening. For the street, Jack chose the block on Lafayette where the Momentary Storm had opened the border and allowed the Rev to make his first appearance. He got a certain satisfaction at seeing Horne wince when Jack told him the location. The Big Kids hated it when some short-lived human saw through their tricks.

The standard way to take over a city street, day or night, was to fake a movie. So many films were made in Manhattan that people hardly stopped to look anymore, just rolled their eyes in annoyance at the roped-off area and the detour. Jack could have glammed the fake permit and the police barriers himself, but as a businessman, Horne was more connected to the city's power structures. Besides, it gave him a stake in what they were doing.

Jack stepped over the barrier on Lafayette at 9:30. He smiled at the small tech crew hovering around the lights and camera. The equipment was real—NYTAS kept a supply of such things—but the people running it were phantoms. Digital golems, Carolien liked to call them. Jack's smile broadened when he saw the name Carolien had given their supposed film-in-progress: *The Frog Prince of Manhattan.*

For the frogs were there, or at least fifty or so, lined up, some on benches, outside of a retro-eighties coffee shop, a "pointy-shoe boutique" (Carolien's term), and a hipster pet store, with King Frog in the front. Jack nodded to him. Hard to tell, but he thought he saw a light flicker in the king's eyes.

Standing in the middle of the street, Jack looked around. Everything seemed in place. By his request, Carolien had set up the frogs and left. El wanted to come but Jack told her it would work best if no one else was there. They weren't far away, he knew, and that was all right. If it worked he'd be happy to see them. And if not—well, maybe they could try to contain the Rev. Or rather, Jack Shade, version 2.0.

He was just about to get started when two actual people, a man and a woman, stepped over the rope and came toward him, right past the phantom film crew. He had a moment of alarm until he recognized their stern grey and black suits. The man spoke first, in that flat Voice of Authority. "John Shade. Whatever you are doing had better not involve outsiders."

"Of course not," Jack said. "That's the point of the barrier. The one you just ignored?"

The woman said "COLE knows what it's doing." Despite her flat tone and blank expression, Jack caught that hint of interest. Not his concern, he thought.

The man said, "You know that it doesn't matter to us which version survives."

"Yeah," Jack said. "I get that."

"So long as nothing leaks."

Jack said, "Just seal the barrier after you leave and everything will be fine."

When the pair of them had stepped over the ropes and back to the world, they paused for a second to glance up and down the street, and then they left. At the corner, the woman looked back at Jack, nodded slightly, then followed her partner.

Jack stood in the street, facing the World Trade Center, just as when the whole thing had started. He was dressed all in black, partly because this was work—the Rev was still his client—and partly because he knew that's how Johnny would be dressed. The only unusual thing he had on was a small leather pouch hung from a long cord around his neck.

He took a deep breath. "Ray," he said. His fox appeared, tail curled up, face tilted toward Jack. He said, "Tell Horne I'm ready." Ray's tail jerked, and then he vanished.

This was the tricky part. Horne's second task was to bring the Rev. Papa Click was the one who'd created the damn thing, so Johnny would believe him when he said Jack was down and now was the time to strike. But could Jack trust him? He hadn't told Horne what he was going to do, but Horne could still warn the Rev to watch out. Jack didn't think he would. El was watching through her mother, and this was Horne's only chance to get both of them off his back. Jack shook his head. A pussy-whipped god.

There was a kind of crack in the air, something you couldn't really see or hear, and then *he* was there. Dressed all in black, head slightly cocked to the side, a grin at the corner of his mouth. *Jesus*, Jack thought, *do I look like that?* Maybe the Rev was thinking the same thing.

Somewhere behind Jack, a man said, "Holy shit! Did you see that? That guy—"

Another man said, "Dude, it's nothing. Just special effects. You know, CGI."

"CGI?" his friend said. "This is the fucking street, man. That guy came out of nowhere."

"Forget it," the other said. Jack knew that in a second or two they would do exactly that. The barrier didn't stop people seeing things, it just stopped them remembering.

Jack moved a couple of steps closer. It felt like pushing against something—the dream interface, Jack realized. The Rev was still not entirely here. Jack stopped now. Let him make the next move.

The Rev began to circle him, slowly, in long loops. That shimmer continued, and a couple of times Jack realized it was he himself who was flickering. He thought for a moment of something Anatolie suggested once, that there was only ever one person and all the rest of us were Dupes. *Not this time*, he thought. *One of us has to go and one of us has to stay.* It was that simple.

Johnny jerked his head toward the frogs. "Brought an audience, huh? Or maybe Carolien just wanted to have her friends watch me beat you. They were watching when I kissed her. You remember that, right? We're going back to that pretty soon." Jack didn't move.

The Rev gestured toward the pouch around Jack's neck. When he pointed his finger, it was like a stab of light that quickly vanished. "What the hell is that?" he said.

"Dragon seeds."

The Rev looked shocked for a moment, then laughed. "Oh, man," he said, "you that desperate? You're gonna sow a race of warriors to try and beat me? Come on, that never works."

Every Traveler knew the ancient Greek story of Kadmos of Thebes, who created an army by planting the teeth of a dragon. They knew what the story was actually about, and why it was a really, really bad idea.

"Not exactly," Jack said. He lifted the pouch off his neck and emptied the contents into his left hand: six dark brown seeds, smooth and round. Jack was pretty sure the Rev would focus on what Jack was doing, and not on the fact that now they looked completely alike. Except, of course, for Jack's scar.

Jack threw three of the seeds to Johnny's left, the others to his right. Instantly, Duplicate Jack Shades sprang up. They were simple, more like sketches than a finished product, but they were there.

The Rev laughed, clapped his hands. "Wonderful," he said. "Just like our old carny days. Not an army of warriors—a platoon of fake Jack Shades." He looked at them all. "Come on," he said to them. "I'm your brother."

Jack had thought he might have to fake nervousness at this point, but the Rev wasn't even looking at him. The six low-level Dupes ran at Johnny as if to attack him, until the Rev opened his arms wide then clapped his hands. There was a flash, and suddenly the Dupes were gone. For a few seconds, small lights, like fireflies, danced around the Rev's body. "Best you got, Jack? You know what they say—what doesn't kill me . . . "

"Nietzsche?" Jack said. "You do a lot of reading in the dream world?"

The Rev laughed. "I was thinking G. Gordon Liddy."

He's drunk, Jack thought. Drunk on the energy Jack had just fed him. *We're almost there, and he's not thinking.* Because if he did think about it, the Rev would realize that Jack *couldn't* attack him. Not with cheesy Dupes or anything else. Jack had no choice but to let the Rev win.

So he had to keep him off guard, rile him up. He said, "How can you take my place? You're not me. You're not even a real Duplicate. You're just a badly made copy."

"Bullshit!" the Rev said. "I'm you because you made me. Only I'm better than you. I'm you before you fucked yourself up. That's why I'm taking over. To save you. To redeem you."

"Face it, Johnny. You're nothing but broken-up pieces. You were never meant to exist, except a down-on-his-luck sun god managed to dig through the garbage and find enough junk to slap you together."

"Fuck you! He saved me. From your hatred. You tore me to pieces but he found me and brought me back. He filled me with holy light."

"There," Jack said. "You see? That's him talking. I would never say shit like that."

The Rev let out a cry of rage, then charged at Jack. He hit him in the face, the stomach. Jack made a show of fighting back, because the Rev would expect it, and it would feed the Rev's desire to win, but it was just an act, for what could he do, he still had the Guest.

And it was all so strange. The blows were real, his face and body could feel every one of them, and at the same time they seemed far away, something Jack was watching. Like a dream.

And then all his observations, all his analysis, ended, along with any pretense of fighting. He was on the ground now, broken, his lungs on fire, blood all over his face. The Rev reached down and yanked him to his feet.

He held Jack's face next to his, said, "See, Jack? You thought you could beat me. But you're the one who's done. Finished!"

"Bullshit," Jack managed to whisper. "I'm still here. And you're still a fake."

"Not for long." The Rev pulled Jack's limp body against his, wrapped one leg around Jack to hold him in place, and then he opened Jack's mouth and placed his own mouth tightly against it.

It wasn't a kiss, no matter what it looked like. It was more like an extraction. Jack could feel himself pulled inside out, everything that was Jack Shade sucked out of him. Strangely, the last thing he remembered was a man's voice, an onlooker. "Christ," the voice said, "I'm all for marriage equality and shit, but this is *freaky*." In a second or two, what the man had seen, what he'd said, would all be gone. Forgotten, as if they never existed.

Like Jack Shade. Sucked away, pulled into his enemy, nothing left of him. Like a forgotten dream.

Jonathan Marcus Shade, the *new* Jack, former Duplicate, former Revenant, the Man Who Came Back, the Man Who Took Over, stood in the middle of Lafayette Street. "I did it," he said. He turned around, looked at the golems pretending to film it all, looked at the ropes and the stragglers on the other side who would never have the faintest idea of the incredible thing that had just happened here. "I did it!" he said again, "I beat him. I won."

"Horne!" he called out, and looked for his Dream Hunter benefactor. "Are you here? Did you see?" No response. He looked for Carolien too, but all he saw were rows of frogs lined up like spectators. Maybe that's why she'd brought them, so they could watch and report back to her. He imagined how he'd show up at her place later, how she'd greet him with champagne. Or Dutch beer and cheese. He laughed. Maybe he should go see Irene Yao first. Have a cup of tea from that fifteen-hundred-year-old teapot. And then—then he would go to his room. *His* room. *Jack Shade's* room. He laughed. "I won!" he shouted.

He looked down at the street. Just as he thought, there was nothing left of that other one, the so-called original. Not even a bloodstain. In the end, once he came out of the dream world, there could only be one of them. He was never just a Dupe. From the very beginning he was better, Jack Shade without all that suffering.

He was here. He'd made it all the way through. He began to touch himself just to feel that solidness. His sides, his arms, his legs. He reached up and touched his forehead, his eyes, his hair. And then he froze. For his right hand had come up against a gnarled, twisted line of hard skin. A scar.

"No," he said again. "That's wrong. I don't—I'm Handsome Johnny. I can't—" He jerked his hands away from his face, held them in front of him, palms out, fingers spread wide. *It must be a mistake*, he thought. *A residual memory.* In a moment he would check again and it would all be fine, the scar gone, banished like its owner.

Something—something was happening to his hands. They were shaking, tremors he couldn't control, couldn't even lower them. And light filled them. No, not the hands, the fingernails. New Jack stared at them, confused, and suddenly scared. And as he did so, the light lifted off his fingers and into the air, moving like a swirling cloud. No. It was paper! Hundreds of cut-up bits of rice paper glowed and danced around each other in the air. It was right then that Johnny Rev, the Man Who Thought He'd Come Back, realized exactly what Jack Shade had done to him.

He lunged for the papers, the Cloud of Knowing, but it was too late. The papers coalesced into a stream that flew through the air to travel in a great swirling arc—right into the mouth of King Frog. For a moment there was a low grinding noise, and then a multicolored flash of light shot back across the street at the Traveler who just a moment ago had been staring at his hands.

It hit him in the forehead, enough of a jolt to unbalance him, so that he fell backward. He managed to turn in the air and land on his hands and knees. Somewhere behind him, a man who would soon forget he'd even been there yelled, "Cool!" and a woman, his date apparently, whispered loudly, "Shh! You'll ruin the shot." She too would forget, though at the end of the evening, when her friend would try to kiss her, she would turn away, annoyed with him for no reason she could figure out.

Shade was still on his knees, catching his breath, when a woman who never forgets anything came and crouched alongside him. "Jack?" she said. "It is you, yes?"

"Yeah," Jack said. "I'm back."

"Ah, thank god," Carolien said, and when they stood up she kissed him.

When they'd separated, Jack asked, "Was that a test?" Carolien nodded happily, and Jack laughed.

It was Alexander Horne who'd given Jack the clue, when he inadvertently reminded Jack of the Rev's actual words. Not kill Jack, just beat him. If the Rev could somehow win, only for a moment, that would satisfy the Guest. The other clue was the fact that Johnny was not an actual Duplicate, he was a dream of a Duplicate. He could enter the hard world the tough way, step by step—or, take over Jack's body. If Jack could vacate it for a while the temptation would be too much to resist. Johnny would leave the dream world by entering Jack's body and believe it was his own.

The question was, of course, how Jack could return. His final vision in the Court of Owls had shown him how you could transfer your memories, your physical knowledge, your loves and everything that mattered onto scraps of paper hidden under your fingernails. King Frog was the final trigger that would bring him back to his body.

Carolien put her arm around his shoulder to steady him. "Come home with me," she said. "The golems will take care of everything."

He moved away from her and stood up straighter to look around. There, just at the edge of the ropes, stood Elaynora Horne. Jack went over to her. "Are we good?" he said.

"I'm the one who should ask you that. It was my father that did this."

"Screw your father. You and me—are we good?"

She took a deep breath, let it out. "Yes."

Jack nodded, then kissed her lightly on the lips. "Thank you," he said. Then he limped over to where Carolien already had a taxi waiting just beyond the ropes.

Tomorrow, he thought. Tomorrow he'd finally go get her that frog.

EPILOGUE

Jack Shade, Original Jack, stood a long time before the scuffed brown door on Bayard Street. There was something invisible about the doors to the upstairs apartment on this busy street of stores and restaurants. Invisible and all the same, each one a copy of all the others.

Did she know he was there? Probably. If she cared to monitor the street. If she cared to monitor him. Or maybe it wasn't caring, just keeping track. *Pay attention*, she used to tell him. *Don't get distracted*.

He turned away from the narrow apartment door and stepped through the open doorway of the Lucky Star Restaurant. It all looked the same— the worn linoleum floor, the old wooden chairs, the white bowls of *sambal* next to the aluminum napkin dispensers. And at the far end, standing behind the wooden order counter with its stack of paper menus, stood Mrs. Shen, her hair a little greyer, her fingers a little more gnarled, but otherwise unchanged.

There were only two occupied tables in this middle of the afternoon, one where two young neighborhood guys were silently eating a large plate of *guy laan* in oyster sauce, the other with a middle-aged white woman who'd pushed aside the remains of some noodle dish and was writing in a large green notebook.

Mrs. Shen looked up, about to recite some innocuous formula, then her mouth fell open and a second later she clapped her hands. "Jack!" she said. "What a nice surprise."

"Hi, Mrs. Shen," Jack said. "It's nice to see you."

"Are you back?" she asked. "More study?"

He smiled. "Just a visit, I'm afraid."

"Oh, a shame. We've missed you, Jack."

"Me too." He paused, then said, "She like anything special these days?"

"Seaweed and jellyfish salad in sesame garlic dressing."

"Sounds good. Give me a double order, okay?"

"Of course."

When Jack stepped outside again, the door to the upstairs apartments stood open. He smiled and began to walk up the five flights of stairs. At the top, her apartment door was open as well. Jack suspected it was the only door in Manhattan without multiple locks. Without any locks, actually.

"Hello, Jack," she said as he walked in. She looked exactly the same as when he'd last seen her, stretched out on her reinforced bed, hands resting on the rope of dreads that crossed her belly.

"Hello," he said. "I brought you some seaweed and jellyfish."

"Thank you. Please put it on the chair, if you don't mind." Jack nodded, and set the brown bag on the plain wooden chair next to her bed.

Silence a moment, then Jack said, "I was talking to Alexander Horne recently." A smile flickered across her face, so quickly no one but Jack would have noticed it. He said, "He mentioned you. Called you Anatolie the Younger." No reaction. Jack took a breath. He said, "Are you a Duplicate?"

"Yes."

Jack's eyes closed a moment, then he said, "Were you always my teacher?"

"Yes."

"Did I ever meet the origi—Anatolie the Elder?"

"No."

"Is she alive?"

"Yes."

"Where is she?"

"Not here."

Jack was pretty sure he knew what "here" meant. He said, "Is she ever coming back?"

"I don't know."

There was a long pause, then Jack nodded and said, "Thank you." When Anatolie didn't answer, he went back down the stairs.

═══◆═══

ABOUT THE AUTHORS

Aliette de Bodard lives and works in Paris, where she has a day job as a System Engineer. She studied Computer Science and Applied Mathematics, but moonlights as a writer of speculative fiction. She is the author of the critically acclaimed Obsidian and Blood trilogy of Aztec noir fantasies, as well as numerous short stories, which garnered her two Nebula Awards, a Locus Award, and a British Science Fiction Association Award. Her novel *The House of Shattered Wings* (Roc/Gollancz, 2015 British Science Fiction Association Award) is set in a turn-of-the-century Paris devastated by a magical war. Its sequel, *The House of Binding Thorns*, will be published in April 2017.

C. S. E. Cooney (csecooney.com/@csecooney) is the author of *Bone Swans: Stories* (Mythic Delirium, 2015). Her novella *The Two Paupers*, the second installment of her Dark Breakers series, appears in Rich Horton's *The Year's Best Science Fiction and Fantasy: 2016* (Prime). She is an audiobook narrator for Tantor Media, the singer/songwriter Brimstone Rhine, and the Rhysling Award-winning author of the poem "The Sea King's Second Bride." Her short fiction can be found in *Black Gate*, *Strange Horizons*, *Apex*, *GigaNotoSaurus*, *Clockwork Phoenix 3* and *5*, *The Mammoth Book of Steampunk*, and elsewhere.

Ken Liu (kenliu.name) is an author and translator of speculative fiction, as well as a lawyer and programmer. A winner of the Nebula, Hugo, and World Fantasy Awards, he has been published in *The Magazine of Fantasy & Science Fiction*, *Asimov's*, *Analog*, *Clarkesworld*, *Lightspeed*, and *Strange Horizons*, among other places. He also translated the Hugo-winning novel, *The Three-Body Problem*, by Liu Cixin, which is the first translated novel to win that award. Ken's debut novel, *The Grace of Kings*, the first in a silkpunk epic fantasy series, was published by Saga Press in April 2015. Saga also published a collection of his short stories, *The Paper Menagerie and Other Stories*, in March 2016. He lives with his family near Boston, Massachusetts.

Usman T. Malik is a Pakistani writer of strange stories. His work has won the Bram Stoker Award, been nominated for the Nebula, and has been reprinted in several Year's Best anthologies. He resides in two worlds.

Nnedi Okorafor's books include *Lagoon* (a British Science Fiction Association Award finalist for Best Novel), *Who Fears Death* (a World Fantasy Award winner for Best Novel), *Kabu Kabu* (a *Publishers Weekly* Best Book for Fall 2013), *Akata Witch* (an Amazon.com Best Book of the Year), *Zahrah the Windseeker* (winner of the Wole Soyinka Prize for African Literature), and *The Shadow Speaker* (a CBS Parallax Award winner). Her latest works include her novel *The Book of Phoenix*, her novella *Binti*, winner of the Science Fiction and Fantasy Writers of America's Nebula Award for Best Novella, and her children's book *Chicken in the Kitchen*. Okorafor is an associate professor at the University at Buffalo, New York (SUNY). Learn more at Nnedi.com.

Having worked in journalism, numismatics, and the law, **K. J. Parker** now writes for a precarious living. K. J. Parker also writes under the name Tom Holt. As Parker, he has published fifteen novels and seventeen works of shorter fiction, some of which is collected in *Academic Exercises* (2014, Subterranean Press). He has more than three dozen novels as Tom Holt.

Rachel Pollack was born in Brooklyn, New York, and holds an honors degree in English from New York University, a Masters in English from Claremont Graduate School, and has taught English at New York State University. Considered one of the World's foremost authorities on the modern interpretation of the Tarot, she's published twelve books on the subject including *78 Degrees of Wisdom* (Thorsons, 1998), considered a modern classic and the Bible of Tarot reading. As a fiction writer, Pollack has been bestowed many honors and awards, among them the famed Arthur C. Clarke Award for Science Fiction (for novel *Unquenchable Fire*) and the World Fantasy Award (for novel *Godmother Night*). "Johnny Rev" is her third novella featuring Jack Shade.

Kristine Kathryn Rusch writes in every genre she reads, which happens to be most of them. She writes paranormal romances as Kristine Grayson, award-winning noir mysteries as Kris Nelscott, and a few other books under other names. As Kristine Kathryn Rusch, she writes whatever she pleases. Mostly, though, she's known for her science fiction and fantasy. Nominated for every award in sf (and many in the other genres as well), she's also won a lot of awards, including several readers choice awards from various magazines, a World Fantasy Award, and two Hugo awards (one for editing, and one for her short fiction). Her short work has been in over twenty year's best collections, including three in 2016. Her novels have hit bestseller lists worldwide. Recently, she published the eight-volume Anniversary Day

Saga, set in her Retrieval Artist universe, as well as the Interim Fates trilogy as Kristine Grayson. She's series editor for Fiction River, with her husband Dean Wesley Smith, and she edits some of the volumes. In September, her retrospective anthology about women in science fiction, *Women of Futures Past: Classic Stories*, will be published by Baen Books. "Inhuman Garbage" is part of her Anniversary Day Saga.

Born in New York and educated on the East Coast, **Carter Scholz** set foot in Berkeley in the 1970s—and never looked back. The author of the novel *Radiance* and over three dozen works of shorter fiction, he is also a computer programmer and consultant. Scholz is a musician and composer of experimental music. He plays keyboards with the post-bop jazz quartet, The Inside Men, and has (among other things) also played Javanese gamelan.

Bao Shu is a Chinese science fiction and fantasy writer, after graduating from Peking University, he obtained a Master's degree in philosophy from KU Leuven, Belgium. Working as a freelance writer in China, he has published four novels and over thirty novellas, novelettes, and short stories since 2010. His best-known works include *Three Body X: Aeon of Contemplation* (an authorized sequel to Liu Cixin's Three Body trilogy), *Ruins of Time* (winner of the 2014 Chinese Nebula Award for Best Novel), and the novella included here, "What Has Passed Shall in Kinder Light Appear." He now lives in Xi'an.

<hr />

ABOUT THE EDITOR

Paula Guran is senior editor for Prime Books. In addition to the Year's Best Science Fiction and Fantasy Novellas series and Dark Fantasy and Horror series, she has edited and continues to edit a growing number of other anthologies as well as more than fifty novels and single-author collections. She is the recipient of two Bram Stoker Award and an IHG Award, and has been nominated for the World Fantasy Award twice. Mother of four, mother-in-law of two, grandmother to three, she lives in Akron, Ohio.

Acknowledgements

Thanks to Jonathan Strahan and the rest of the *Locus* Recommendation Committee. Special thanks to Nana Amuah, an innocent bystander who was of great help this year.

"The Citadel of Weeping Pearls," © 2015 Aliette de Bodard (*Asimov's*, Oct/Nov 2015).

"The Bone Swans of Amandale," © 2015 C. S. E. Cooney (*Bone Swans*, Mythic Delirium Books).

"Binti" © 2015 Nnedi Okorafor (*Binti*, Tor.com).

"The Last Witness" © 2015 K. J. Parker (*The Last Witness*, Tor.com)

"Johnny Rev" © 2015 Rachel Pollack (*The Magazine of Fantasy & Science Fiction*, Jul/Aug 2015).

"Inhuman Garbage" © 2015 Kristine Kathryn Rusch (*Asimov's*, Mar 2015)

Gypsy © 2015 Carter Scholz (*Gypsy*, PM Press / *The Magazine of Fantasy & Science Fiction*, Nov/Dec 2015).

"The Pauper Prince and the Eucalyptus Jinn" © 2015 Usman T. Malik (*The Pauper Prince and the Eucalyptus Jinn*, Tor.com).

"What Has Passed Shall in Kinder Light Appear" © 2015 Bao Shu, translation Ken Liu (First English: © 2015 (*The Magazine of Fantasy & Science Fiction*, Mar/Apr 2015).

Appendix: Some Notable Speculative Fiction Novellas 1843-1980

A Christmas Carol by Charles Dickens (1843)

"Carmilla" by J. Sheridan Le Fanu (1871-72)

Flatland: A Romance of Many Dimensions by Edward Abbott Abbott (1884)

Strange Case of Dr Jekyll and Mr Hyde by Robert Louis Stevenson (1886)

The Time Machine (1895) and *The War of the Worlds* (1897) by H. G. Wells

The Turn of the Screw by Henry James (1898)

"Heart of Darkness" by Joseph Conrad (1899)

The Metamorphosis (*Die Verwandlung*) by Franz Kafka (1915)

The Shadow Over Innsmouth by H. P. Lovecraft (1936)

"Who Goes There?" by John W. Campbell (as Don A. Stuart) (1938)

"Nightfall" (1941) and "A Sound of Thunder" by Isaac Asimov (1952)

Animal Farm by George Orwell (1945)

"Against the Fall of Night" by Arthur C. Clarke (1948)

The Lion, The Witch, and the Wardrobe by C. S. Lewis (1950)

The Man Who Sold the Moon by Robert Heinlein (1951)

"A Case of Conscience" by James Blish (1958)

A Clockwork Orange by Anthony Burgess (1962)

"Behold the Man" by Michael Moorcock (1966)

"Empire Star" (1966) and "The Star Pit" (1967) by Samuel R. Delany

"Riders of the Purple Wage" by Philip José Farmer (1967)

"Weyr Search" (1967) and "Dragonrider" by Anne McCaffrey (1967-68)

Ubik by Philip K. Dick (1969)

"Ill Met in Lankhmar" and "Ship of Shadows" by Fritz Leiber (1970)

"The Word for World Is Forest" by Ursula K. Le Guin (1972)

"The Fifth Head of Cerberus" by Gene Wolfe (1972)

"The Deathbird" by Harlan Ellison (1973)

"A Song for Lya" by George R. R. Martin (1974)

"The Girl Who Was Plugged In" (1974) and "Houston, Houston, Do You Read?" (1976) by James Tiptree, Jr.

"Home Is the Hangman" by Robert Zelazny (1975)

"Stardance" by Spider and Jeanne Robinson (1977)

"The Persistence of Vision" by John Varley (1978)

"Enemy Mine" by Barry B. Longyear (1979)

"The Unicorn Tapestry" by Suzy McKee Charnas (1980)